RASCALS' HEAVEN

BOOKS BY F. VAN WYCK MASON

Rascals' Heaven

The Young Titan	Golden Admiral
Manila Galleon	Cutlass Empire
The Sea 'Venture	Proud New Flags
Our Valiant Few	Three Harbours
Silver Leopard	Stars on the Sea
Blue Hurricane	Rivers of Glory
Captain Nemesis	Eagle in the Sky

The Adventures of Hugh North
as Captain, Major, and Colonel

RASCALS' HEAVEN

by

F. Van Wyck Mason

1964

DOUBLEDAY & COMPANY, INC., GARDEN CITY, NEW YORK

With the exception of actual historical personages, the characters
are entirely the product of the author's imagination and have no
relation to any person in real life.

This Book Is for
Samuel and Frances Nickerson
In Appreciation of Their Loyal and Generous Friendship
over Many Years

TABLE OF CONTENTS

BOOK II *The Debatable Ground*

BOOK III *Savannah*

FOREWORD

It seems incredible that the fascinating and extremely colorful origins of the only planned Colony of the Thirteen Original States have been so largely ignored. Hundreds, if not thousands, of books have been written concerning the early days of New England, Pennsylvania, Virginia, and New York and yet, as nearly as I can ascertain, not a single major writer of dramatic history—I don't like the term "historical fiction" because it is a contradiction of meanings—has employed Colonial Georgia as a background.

In writing this book, I have attempted, primarily, to shatter an old and, unfortunately, persistent fallacy—that the unfortunates brought to North America by James Edward Oglethorpe were felons, hardened criminals, and persons of low moral caliber; this illusion gave issue to a spate of reports that this was a Heaven for Rascals, a Convicts' Paradise, a Promised Land for the Thief, the Cheat, the Embezzler, the Whoremaster, and the Murderer. Nothing could be further from the truth, as the reader—if he has fortitude and an unbiased attitude—may discover if, and when, he finishes this volume.

James Edward Oglethorpe, in my considered opinion, should rank high among the great founding fathers of America. He was that *rara avis* in the eighteenth century, at once a pioneer humanitarian, a great diplomat, and an enthusiastic but subtly practical imperialist. Like few others in this category, Oglethorpe never stooped to trickery, to a callous disregard for human life, to self-aggrandizement, or to keeping an eye on the main chance.

The spelling of Indian names, tribes and speech in those days, even as now, were strictly phonetic, so I have selected those forms which seemed easiest for the reader. The Indian manner of speech is difficult to reproduce in English. Its constructions and phraseology vary from tribe to tribe, but always their language was flowery, graphic, and grandiose.

Also, I have standardized the use of the Scottish "Mac"—a prefix to the clan name—which appears as "M'," "Mc," or as "Mac," interchangeably. I trust that my readers will forgive this possible offense to family tradition.

As has been my practice for some time, I have studied, as carefully as possible, available contemporary accounts of the period under consideration and have attempted to select the most plausible and unbiased of these publications as the basis for facts. The names of the original settlers with the exception of those listed below—are genuine. However, their characteristics and appearance and eventual conduct and fate necessarily are the products of my imagination.

The only wholly fictional characters are Thad Burton, Laure Rivard, Brother Barnaby, the officers of the *Mystick*, and Winsome Brooks. It is a well-known fact that no one will ever know how many white children were orphaned and then kidnaped by the Indians. Thad Burton and Laure Rivard are only representative. The village of Chaugee Landing is imaginary but is typical of such early settlements in Georgia.

The Sakwari nation is also an invention, but, nevertheless, typical of any number of minor tribes which flourished briefly, only to disappear almost without a trace.

In case the reader is sufficiently intrigued about events subsequent to the end of this tale I have—rather against my inclination—included a brief addendum.

When it comes to the matter of acknowledgments I must, first of all, thank my wife-secretary, Jeanne Hand Mason, for her devoted—if sometimes perplexing—assistance in preparing this story. My thanks again are extended to Mr. Robert H. Haynes of the Widener Library at a small college called Harvard, which I believe is situated in Cambridge, Massachusetts, and to Miss Margaret Franklin, who did much tedious preliminary research for me in the British Museum and in the Colonial Records Office in London.

F. Van Wyck Mason

"Hampton Head"
Southampton
Bermuda

PROLOGUE

The merchant brig *Mystick*, two hundred tons of unimaginative design, lay to her berth near the end of Boston's Long Wharf with stubby twin masts thrusting sturdily at a pale blue sky checkered by small, high clouds. Because the weather was unseasonably warm on this, the twenty-first day of December 1732, myriad gulls shrieked over the harbor's icy gray waters in a generally futile search for refuse or squabbled or basked, quiescent, on lime-whitened roofs and dock pilings.

On the *Mystick's* tiny quarter-deck Captain Elijah Starbuck stood in conversation with his mate, Seth Coffin, and the brig's shipping agent, Marcus Beebe, a genial, bear-like, ruddy-faced individual.

Pinched-looking features framed in ragged, gray-brown whiskers, Captain Starbuck kept a weather eye on the Long Wharf's land end. He remained hopeful, against odds to be sure, that a vehicle of some sort might appear, come bumping out over splintery and manure-dappled planking laden with the few boxes, barrels, or bales necessary to round out his cargo.

Since it was late afternoon not much activity was visible except aboard such vessels as the *Mystick*, which were just about ready to depart and were only delaying until the ebb should set in.

A sheaf of invoices and bills of lading stirred restlessly between Mr. Beebe's mittened fingers and he shivered—he'd a bad head cold—when a strong puff of wind struck out of the northwest. Nevertheless, the shipping agent grinned because a gull, flapping by, let go and effectively splattered that slab of slate which, propped on an easel, stood by the landward end of the *Mystick's* gangway. On it had been chalked information that Captain Starbuck's brig would sail this same day for Port Royal, Jamaica, via New York and Charles Town in South Carolina.

"Come not another piece of freight, Eli, ye've no cause for complaint," drawled the agent, cramming duplicate manifests and clearance papers into the pocket of a shapeless blue-and-white Dutch blanket overcoat. "Yessiree. I figger you stand to turn a very pretty penny on this cargo I've found you." Mr. Beebe blew a big nose between his fingers. "—provided, of course, some picaroon or Spanish *guardacosta* don't raise yer tops'ls."

Mr. Beebe's round, dark brown eyes traveled speculatively over the six old nine-pound guns which were mounted, evenly spaced, along either beam.

"Mr. Coffin, ye reckon such puny popguns would prove sufficient, come an enemy alongside?"

The mate, a lean, leathery fellow with sparse, sand-colored chin whiskers, turned and deliberately squirted tobacco juice over the rail. "Shouldn't wonder. Maybe I c'n learn the new hands how to serve 'em."

"Teach 'em quick, mister; drill the hell out o' 'em," grunted Captain Starbuck, then shifted his gaze shoreward; a pair of furry pack horses were clumping out onto the dock bearing canvas-covered loads.

The *Mystick's* master looked hopeful, then frowned when the pack animals' drover halted them, steaming gently, before a schooner probably destined to conduct illicit but highly profitable trading with certain officials up in that great French fortress of Louisburg which, on Cape Breton Island, guarded access to the Gulf of St. Lawrence.

Mr. Beebe, on glancing over the rail, perceived that wavelets had ceased to lap higher on barnacled-whitened pilings and observed, "Pretty nigh-on slack water."

Mr. Beebe started to offer a hand in farewell but checked himself. "Oh, by the bye, when ye touch Charles Town ye might nose about and learn what there's worth knowin' concernin' a new settlement I hear tell that's to be planted somewheres to the south o' the Carolinas."

"Naow, do tell!" drawled the mate. "Is it to be a hull new province?"

"Likely so. Heard say that there's a Georgia Company been chartered in London and some English nob name of Oglethorpe, I think, is fetching out a shipload of felons to make a beginning."

"Whereabouts?"

"Dunno. Most likely 'twill be somewhere 'twixt Charles Town and the Spanish in Florida."

Under a worn rabbitskin cap Captain Starbuck shook his shaggy gray head. "Sounds plumb crazy to try to start a colony in a hostile country dependent on a parcel of jailbirds. Them Spanishers and their Injun allies play rough and dirty. Ain't no doubt about that."

This time Mr. Beebe produced a voluminous pocket kerchief and loudly blew his rubicund nose. "Well, Cap'n, I ain't the one to argue over that. After my brother's vessel got took by a *guardacosta* he spent the better part of three years in the dungeons of the castle in St. Augustine. Tortured him some, too."

"Don't doubt it in the least," grunted the *Mystick's* master. "Mark my words, Marcus, this Oglethorpe feller won't stand the chance of a snowflake in hell if it's only criminals he'll have to count on for defense."

The mate's lantern jaw worked on a quid. "Aye. There's bound to be a heap of desperate, treacherous characters amongst this nob's following."

"When does this Oglethorpe feller plan to bring over his jail scrapings?"

"Round the first o' the year," the shipping agent averred, but he didn't sound too sure.

"To Charles Town?"

"Yep. It's the only real port in that part o' the Carolinas."

Mr. Beebe rubbed at his still-streaming nose, then cocked a speculative eye at the "sailing day" flag a-flutter in the *Mystick's* rigging. "As I said, Cap'n, might prove profitable to look in on this new settlement provided they find a reasonable port; may as well move in on the ground floor."

When, at the Long Wharf's shore end, a female figure appeared, the occupants of the *Mystick's* quarter-deck watched a rather tall girl clad in brown advance diffidently past the double row of weather-beaten merchantmen. Presently she halted to address a bandy-legged fellow who, in her wake, was trundling a cowhide-covered clothes coffer along on a wheelbarrow. Then she moved on, checking her progress to scan that slate which indicated each vessel's destination.

As the long-limbed and otherwise pleasantly proportioned figure advanced Elijah Starbuck reckoned this female must be around twenty years of age. Apparently she was so uncommonly good-looking that, as she stalked past, idlers and men at work on deck guffawed or put their heads together obviously exchanging salacious observations.

When she was two vessels distant Mr. Beebe emitted a curious, short laugh. "Say, I know who that is. Do you?"

"Can't say's I do," Starbuck admitted.

Coffin's leathery lips pursed themselves into a soundless whistle. "B'God, no matter who she is, she's prettier 'n Sam Nickerson's speckled pup."

"Who in tarnation is she?" Starbuck queried in rising interest.

"Her name's Brooks," the agent informed in a curious, flat tone. "Winsome Brooks. Her pa, Sylvanus, was a doctor up on Beacon Hill. Good one, too."

"Was?"

"Yes. Died last week. Lies up yonder now." Mr. Beebe's mittened hand indicated a snow-covered cemetery sprawling lumpily over one side of Copp's Hill.

Commented Seth Coffin more to himself than to his companions, "Say, ain't the way she walks kind of—well, stately?"

Soon Captain Starbuck was able to decide that the girl had a pale, shield-shaped face, bold, wide-winged brows, a wide dark red mouth, and large eyes. What he could see of her hair, which wasn't much because of her cloak's hood, looked wavy and of a very dark brown.

Captain Starbuck rubbed at his chin whiskers, queried softly, "Now I wonder why those fellers should be gawpin' at her so hard?"

"On account she's been, we-e-ll—er—kind of talked about lately."

"Talked about? What for?"

"We-e-ell." Mr. Beebe's gaze wavered, wandering out over Boston Harbor toward a scattering of small, wooded islands lying to the north and east. "The talk is—that there's been sight more love 'twixt her and her pa than there ought to be 'twixt a father and his daughter."

The agent's shoulders, massive under his Dutch blanket coat, lifted. "Maybe it's so; maybe it 'tain't. Anyhow, this Brooks girl's been keepin' house for her pa ever since her ma took sick and died o' lung fever nigh on six years ago."

The tall young woman now had progressed to the next vessel seaward, a coasting schooner, and must have had difficulty in making out the vessel's destination for she bent low over the slate and by so doing raised the back of a full, dark brown skirt sufficiently to disclose trim, slim ankles. At the same time her hood was flipped back by the offshore breeze, which was beginning to pick up now that the tide was ready to turn, and revealed a heavy mane of deep brown hair that had been skinned back and tied into a bun which was beginning to loosen.

Continued the shipping agent in a lowered voice, "Now I'm no scandal-monger and I'd not have listened to a word of gossip but for somethin' I *saw* her do at her pa's funeral."

Without removing small, red-rimmed gray eyes from that figure all too effectively concealed beneath a heavy traveling cloak and a black woolen shawl, Captain Starbuck queried, "What'd she do?"

Mr. Beebe made a deprecatory clucking noise. "Well, believe it or not, I watched her, with my own eyes, bend and kiss her father's corpse on its lips!"

Seth Coffin combed whiskers fringing his chin with gnarled fingers. "Then 'tis small wonder she's clearin' out o' Boston. Though fer my part, I don't hold that that kiss necessarily was a lewd one. I've seen people do some mighty queer things when they're bowed down by a powerful grief. Minds me of a feller back on Nantucket who howled like a moon-struck dog when his wife's casket"—never by any chance did Seth ever refer to a "coffin"—"was being lowered into the grave. Howled every night over her grave till the see-lectmen put a stop to it."

"Mebbe yer right, Mr. Coffin," the agent agreed somberly. "Hope so. I don't like to think ill of folks just for the sake of it." Again he mopped his swollen, juicy nose. "All the same, 'tis mighty hard fer some folks to rid themselves o' the suspicion that there was some sort of hanky-panky between the doc and his daughter—she being so handsome and full-blooded and never paying heed to any suitor who came a-courtin'. Not even the rich ones."

They watched the Brooks girl raise a delicately pointed face to survey the *Mystick's* quarter-deck. Then, while the barrowman set down his clumsy vehicle and flicked sweat from his brow, she studied the destination slate with care. At length she cupped hands mittened in bright red and called in a clear, carrying voice, "Is one of you captain of this boat?"

Just why Elijah Starbuck felt moved to touch the brim of his cap before he replied he couldn't have explained, but suddenly he felt anxious that this pale-featured young female should take passage with him. "Why, mistress, reckon that'll be me." What if what Mr. Beebe had said about Mistress Brooks were true? Well, Eli Starbuck wasn't exactly young any more; in fact, some people in Newburyport claimed he'd "a real fatherly look" about him.

Placing one foot on the gangplank, the young woman called up, "Can you carry me to Jamaica?"

Experiencing a sudden inner warmth, the *Mystick's* master replied so heartily that both Beebe and Coffin stared. "Sure can, ma'am, and yer passage will cost you but thirty pounds."

The girl's hopeful expression faded. "Oh dear, I—well, I just haven't got that much."

"What can you pay—er, ma'am?"

"I've only twenty-three pounds, ten shillings and tuppence to my name —and, and a little gold chain."

He pointed to her cowhide trunk. "What you got in that?"

"Only old clothes, sir. They're not worth much. Really they're not."

Starbuck summoned a shallow grin. "For you, missy, I'll make the fare twenty pounds, so you can come aboard, but be spry about it—the ebb's begun to run."

BOOK I

The Settlement 1732–33

Chapter 1

WAR PARTY

A bald eagle planed in enormous, leisurely loops above Chattooga Range, which forms the southernmost side of the Blue Ridge mountains and runs parallel to the rounded, forest-shrouded slopes of the Great Smokies lying to the west. Because of incomparable vision the great bird noticed immediately an unusual movement a mile or so below. Without visible motion of his wings, the eagle shifted course and commenced a gradual descent, gaze concentrated upon a steep-sided, heavily wooded valley down which a creek plunged in lacy, silvery haste creating occasionally frothy, swirling pools.

In most respects this hurrying stream was similar to other creeks which, following parallel courses, tumbled in the same direction to merge their waters with growing rivers which, after meandering through the western Carolinas in stately beauty, finally drowned their identities in the Atlantic.

That which attracted the bald eagle's attention was a short file of men who, traveling at a space-eating dogtrot, were following a well-used game trail pounded hard and easily recognizable by the hoofs of countless generations of deer, elk, and woods buffalo.

Inevitably, this run pursued the line of least resistance along mountainsides, down and across ravines, losing itself to sight amid heavily forested areas, only to reappear detouring ponds and bogs and cutting boldly across numerous upland meadows and savannahs.

Although it was still early autumn, hardwoods in these highlands, here and there, already had become tinted by several hard frosts; like a vast patchwork quilt showed the vivid crimson of swamp oaks and scarlet sumach, the yellow of hickories and birches, the orange-red leaves of persimmons from which ripened fruit dangled as a well-nigh irresistible attraction for birds, bears, and possums.

A tawny-backed, white-bellied panther, known to those few white traders who had dared to penetrate these wild highlands as a "painter" or mountain lion, sunning himself on a rock ledge, observed the party's approach and took immediate interest because he knew by experience that, sooner or later, these men would kill game, the remains of which would furnish him with a gratuitous repast.

The best view of this swaying, jolting line of dark-faced runners, however, was enjoyed by a buck deer who, neck grown oily and swollen because this was the rutting season, stood amid the security of a dense laurel thicket. His great limpid eyes watched the raiders emerge, one by one, from the forest and avoid a tangle of fallen timber. Absolutely motionless, the buck watched the leading runner appear out of a clump of ilex bushes —he'd heard the impact of moccasins a long while back, all unaware that, only a few yards behind him, an Indian who had been on his trail all morning also had frozen into immobility.

The buck saw a tall, broad-faced Indian trot into sight with head thrown back and lean, bronzed legs thrusting easily.

Watched by a pair of stupidly fearless ruffed grouse perched in a cedar, Beaver Teeth, the lone Catawba hunter, shrank even flatter to the ground. Small jet eyes glittering bright as those of a water moccasin, he tried to count the number of feet impacting softly along the game trail. How many? For the moment he forgot all about the fine, fat *itchu*—buck—he'd been following so patiently.

Lips thinned, Beaver Teeth, with his forefinger, scratched a groove in the earth every time a nearly naked runner trotted by.

He wasn't pleased with what he saw. This was bad. Very bad indeed. At first sight he knew that these strangers were Northern Indians—Tuscarora Iroquois most likely. He could recognize them by their greater height, paler skin, and the careful, unfamiliar way they'd dressed their raven hair into coarse crests that bristled above otherwise shaven scalps. Beyond a doubt this was a war party because they were stripped to deerskin kilts, leggings, and moccasins. Besides, they were wearing very few ornaments and carried hardly any "possibles" at all.

Among the runners Beaver Teeth indentified an occasional Seneca Iroquois, who were as dreaded in these regions as the ferocious, man-eating Mohawk Iroquois, who fought and raided far to the north and east.

The Catawba's lips flattened gradually over snaggleteeth. No. This wasn't one of those far-ranging hunting parties which, about this time of year, were sent out from various villages and towns to kill game which would help to tide their band over the lean winter months. These warriors were traveling fast and light. Their often-scarred faces were painted for war—scarlet interrupted by a single broad band of black running horizontally across their cheeks and over the bridges of their noses. The Senecas went without the roached crest affected by their Tuscarora kinsmen; instead, they wore strings of bright beads or small iridescent shells, or strips of fox fur worked into circular-based scalp locks which sprouted from the crowns of their pates.

In rising consternation Beaver Teeth became aware that a majority of these invaders—running so deep inside Catawba territory—were carrying new-looking English-made muskets and pistols. In addition they were armed with scalping knives and tomahawks so carefully honed that, with a powerful swipe, one could easily lop off a man's arm or even his head. Only a few warriors were carrying spears or cased bows and arrows in addition to their firearms. One after another sixteen tawny figures flashed by the hidden hunter and the motionless deer.

He who brought up the war party's rear at once commanded Beaver Teeth's attention: first, because this warrior's complexion was very, very light; second, because he appeared much too young to be wearing painted on his chest a large black bird which identified him as a "Raven" or "Experienced Warrior." By half a head he looked to be the tallest of the speeding war party. Against his broad chest slatted an English officer's gorget of gilded silver.

At first glance Beaver Teeth couldn't decide whether or not this big hostile was a half-breed, but the pinkish hue of skin visible beneath his tan and a coating of bear's grease argued that this was a purebred white man. The Catawba lay near enough the trail to note that this huge warrior's scalp must have been dyed black with hickory husks some time ago, because his crest was showing light brown near its roots.

Remaining motionless as a hiding rabbit, the ugly little Catawba stayed where he was for a good while after the last raider had flashed out of sight down that age-old warpath running erratically all the way from the shores of the Great Lakes down to the Gulf of Mexico—called "Mehico" by the Creeks.

Then, with only the brittle splashes of a mountain rivulet breaking the stillness, Beaver Teeth arose cautiously because itchu, the buck deer, remained frozen into immobility. Slowly he nocked a broad-headed hunting arrow to his bow's string, drew, and, causing a loud twang-g!, dispatched the shaft into the buck's sleek, gray-brown side. Although shot through the heart, the buck, nonetheless, made a series of convulsive bounds before collapsing across a mossy log.

Beaver Teeth, foreseeing an exhausting ordeal, took sufficient time, before beginning his long, long run, to cut out the animal's steaming heart, liver, and tongue; such tender tidbits could be devoured raw, obviated the necessity of stopping to kindle even a tiny cook fire—which wasn't a good idea anyway now that an Iroquois raiding party was in the vicinity. The stringy little Catawba then decided he must eat something right away if he were to reach the palisade enclosing the village of Tosneoc in time to raise an alarm. Besides, he hadn't devoured a mouthful since the night before.

Once the yellow-red sun disappeared beyond the rounded, green-mantled summits of the Great Smokies, Utakwate, the Tuscarora Outacity —or "Long Warrior"—commanding the war party, slowed the column's pace and began to look about for a likely place to bivouac. Presently, he found one in the heart of a fragrant-smelling red cedar and juniper thicket situated at a safe distance from the warpath. Only out of policy did he cast an inquiring glance at Kawea, a one-eyed and middle-aged but still powerful Seneca Raven who was one of three who'd come along.

Once Kawea had jerked a nod the war party prepared to bivouac. Its members exhibited few signs of fatigue for all that, since dawn, they'd . covered well over fifty miles of rugged mountain terrain without once pausing for food. After reconnoitering the vicinity with critical attention, warriors carrying case bows slung them to handy boughs while those with firearms propped them against nearby trees.

Squatted in a rough circle on the sweet-smelling ground under the cedars, they commenced to talk in undertones while casting loose draw-strings securing leather pouches of food—greasy, rank-smelling pemmican and smoked fish for the most part. Using claw-nailed fingers, they crammed their mouths full, briefly champed on cracked nuts and parched corn, and then went to quench their thirst. At a nearby rivulet they lapped like dogs; only the pale-skinned warrior drank by conveying water to his lips with his hand.

They resisted a strong temptation to range about in the deepening twilight and kill a few turkeys or some ruffed grouse, which would have been easy; hereabouts such game was as plentiful as it was unwary. But this move wasn't even to be considered so deep in the hunting country of such inveterate enemies as the hardy and warlike Catawbas—eastern-most of all Siouan tribes.

Presently Utakwate, or the Bear's Cub, clicked his tongue. First he beckoned to Kawea, the one-eyed Seneca Raven whose looks scarcely had been improved by a deep trench across his forehead dug long ago by a Huron tomahawk. Next he signaled the tall, pale-skinned warrior and got to his feet, a dim and deadly outline in the gathering gloom. "Kawea, Sakwari-cra, my brothers. Will there be much more running before we reach Tosneoc?"

The scarred Seneca thoughtfully fingered a necklace of panther claws, shrugged. "So many winters have passed since this one has been here that Kawea cannot be sure."

Utakwate narrowed eyes at the young Tuscarora. "What says Sakwari-cra? Did he not raid this way two winters ago?"

Although Sakwari-cra had an answer ready he pretended to deliberate; a man's opinion became important if he delayed, didn't answer too quickly. Squatted on his heels, he scratched an aimless design on the ground before he said in deep and calculated tones, "Utakwate, a half-sun on the trail should bring us to that village of the dog-delivered Catawbas known as Tosneoc."

The Long Warrior's deeply pock-marked features relaxed. "That is well. We will fall upon Tosneoc at first light."

Sakwari-cra, whose name, translated meant "He-Who-Trails-a-Spear," started to get up but the war party's chief, who was wearing a stuffed tanager thrust through the dreadfully distended lobe of one ear and a skinned indigo bunting jammed into the other, signed for the young Raven to remain as he was.

"In what manner does Sakwari-cra think it best to strike Tosneoc?"

Sakwari-cra—he might have been twenty-three—merged wide, straight brows in concentration, stared at the ground, then up into the Bear's Cub's ugly visage. "Three trails lead into that village. The first, the one we now follow, is the most likely to be watched; the second trace leads southwest from Tosneoc toward the lands of the Chickasaws and the Choctaws. Another runs to Keowee and toward the rising sun."

"—also toward Fort Moore and the trading post nearby," added a broad-shouldered Slave Catcher called Tino, who must have been wealthy for he wore three strands of *pe-ak*, fine, dark brown wampum, slung to his muscular neck.

"Where is this English fort?"

"On a height above a great river called 'Savan-nah' by the outlaw Yamacraws," said Sakwari-cra, who'd painted a white circle of pipe clay around one eye and a ring of scarlet about the other. Through these peered the white man's wide-set, rather small blue-gray eyes.

A series of faint grumbling noises to the westward warned that, somewhere among the Smokies, a thunderstorm was brewing. Utakwate paid no attention to it, but, in guttural undertones, continued to explain his plan for the surprise of Tosneoc.

Through the deepening darkness he glanced at the Seneca when, with a sudden movement, Kawea used clawlike fingers to scratch vigorously under his greasy leather kilt; no warrior ever trimmed his nails for to do so would be to deprive him of ten useful and dangerous weapons. Most of the raiders bore ghastly claw marks caused by human fingernails; Kawea had lost his eye in such a fashion.

"Kawea," directed Utakwate, "you and Tino take five Tuscaroras, circle north of Tosneoc and come in along that trace which leads to the east. Sakwari-cra will lead six men and strike from the south. Everyone else will come with me and deliver the main attack from the north—thus the Catawba dogs will be trapped between us and we will cut them, as to-bacco, into little pieces."

Tino grunted assent. Sakwari-cra nodded, although deeply disappointed that the Bear's Cub should have assigned him the least dangerous post while reserving for himself the all-important attack on the village's main gate.

Among the tops of giant oaks and pines a cold wind commenced to sough and cause uneasy, rushing noises. The night sky darkened rapidly and whole galaxies of stars became lost to sight. Soon vivid flashes of lightning began to gleam among mountains to the westward.

Since none of the Iroquois had burdened themselves with even a section of blanket, the warriors huddled close together for warmth, like roosting quail, and prepared to sleep in a sitting position upon a carpet of sweet-smelling mold. Only Sakwari-cra, his gorget dully agleam, found refuge from the approaching storm in a cavity created by the uplifted roots of a great pine overturned by some long-forgotten tempest.

The white Tuscarora's intelligence displayed itself in the fact that only he, of the entire war party, took any precaution to keep his powder dry; he shoved the buffalo horn containing his supply of powder as deep as possible inside the miniature cavern he occupied. Next, he lashed a square piece of greased leather about the lock of a battered Penhallow musket. This was his most cherished possession, having been fashioned a good while ago near a place called "Boston," which great town was said to lie many sleeps north and east of the North Star—or so claimed the Mohawk from whom he'd won it at *chenko*, a favorite gambling game played by hurling stones at a rolling disk.

He also took precautions to protect a little bag of darts winged with cattail down and tipped with porcupine quills dipped in poison. These were expelled from a short blowgun fashioned out of a cane stalk or a hollow reed. Freshly smeared with venom, such darts were so effective that, in a few instants, any form of small game could be shocked into brief and fatal convulsions. These particular darts should prove uncom-monly effective, the Tuscarora hoped because, just before the war party had quitted Seegee, he'd provoked a captive rattlesnake into several times burying its fangs in a piece of rotting deer's liver.

Again Sakwari-cra pondered why, for some reason lost in antiquity, the use of a blowgun on humans or on big game had been forbidden by the *aliktchas*, or wizards. To the young Raven such a prohibition made no sense at all; a bigger blowgun would be silent and, at short range, should prove deadlier than either a musket or a bow.

Recently he'd decided that, wizards or no wizards, he'd experiment with heavier darts and the fashioning of a long tube with a larger bore. Why did he dare thus to think independently? After he'd pondered the question a while he concluded that, even after fourteen years of captivity, he still could recall a forgotten someone's saying that the white man's God was more powerful than any wizard or Indian high god such as Yo-he-wa, otherwise called Sotolycaté. Maybe this explained why he was able quietly to discount the taboos of *aliktchas* and conjurers.

With a hissing roar the wind now began to tear at invisible treetops and lash the forest's undergrowth into frantic gyrations. Twigs, small branches, and leaves in ever-increasing numbers commenced to rain down upon the cowering war party. Heart-stilling crashes of thunder rolled nearer and nearer, reverberated over the ravine, and, even more ominously, the staccato crackle made by lightning bolts became almost incessant. The bivouac alternately became revealed by blinding, unearthly, violet-hued radiances and then plunged into a Stygian gloom, terrifying, almost unbearable by contrast. Threshing trees reeled and bowed low; some crashed to the ground, causing a grinding roar.

Still no rain fell. The raiders, however, could hear its drumming in irregular rolls as, inexorably, it closed in on them. Every second the chill increased until the men's teeth began to click and clatter like wizards' rattles.

By the lightning Sakwari-cra watched his companions—tough, old Utakwate included—covertly begin to stroke potent amulets and charms. Presently a bolt of lightning ripped through a dead oak, caused a pulse jolting *crack!* and set it afire. The pungent smell of ozone filled the bivouac just before a tall nearby pine tree's top broke off and felled smaller trees which barely missed the raiders. Then rain fell in such smothering, deafening torrents it seemed that a waterfall suddenly had begun to deluge the valley. The lightning-fired dead tree steamed briefly, then went dark, its flames extinguished by the tearing, screaming wind and rain which atomized, penetrated a man's eyelids, ears, and nose.

In all directions trees, in rapid succession, began to topple over, creating utter confusion; without pause, bits of bark, twigs, even large branches pelted the cowering Iroquois. The rivulet's modest sounds altered, grew louder, more ominous; in a few minutes, it became transformed into a roaring torrent deadly in its thrust.

For sure, decided the white Tuscarora, huddled and shivering in his muddy little den under the fallen pine's roots, He-Who-Sits-Above must be almighty displeased. Skin pebbling under icy rain which had begun to course down his back, Utakwate wondered in which rite the sacrifice might have been stinted. Had some ritual been overlooked last month during the celebration of *puskita*—the great annual corn dance? Most of the awed raiders were deciding that this evidence of Yo-he-wa's wrath must be interpreted as a warning of some impending disaster. Would this raid prove a failure? Perhaps they were destined to leave their scalps salted and stretched on hoops among the cabins of Tosneoc? Too bad there was no wizard along to advise what could be done to propitiate the outraged Power.

The raiders' numbed terror increased. Yes. Disaster must lie in store; for a tempest of such fearful violence to persist for so long was unprecedented.

Stiff, cramped, and chilled to his marrow, Sakwari-cra struggled to control the wild chatter of his teeth by conjecturing on where wild creatures might find shelter from such a storm. Were they as terrified as he? Then, sternly, he reproved himself; a Tuscarora Raven had no business even to think fleetingly along such lines.

At length the level of icy water rising in Sakwari-cra's refuge submerged and numbed his legs and private parts. He knew he'd have to leave, so, clutching his musket, powder horn, and war bag he blundered out into the chaotic, wind-filled dark to be lashed by successive sheets of rain and flying invisible objects.

He ended by squatting with knees drawn up and back pressed against the bole of a big beech tree, listening to boughs crash down all about him. Amid the lightlessness he sought to foresee how this great storm might affect the projected assault on Tosneoc.

Chapter 2

SURPRISE AT TOSNEOC

So numerous were delays caused by traversing a seemingly endless series of natural abatis created by branches and roots of fallen trees and the crossing of temporary cascades obstructing the warpath that it was not until after midday—instead of first light as planned—that the sixteen raiders, hungry, hollow-eyed, and vicious through lack of sleep, crawled, with great care to remain unseen, to the crest of a wooded and rock-crowned ridge. There they paused and with narrowed eyes studied the Catawba village, still dripping within its encircling palisade.

Sakwari-cra, his greasy hide criss-crossed with scratches, presented no longer a gaudy, martially painted figure. His single, red-tipped bald eagle's feather now drooped between his shoulder blades like the tail of a whipped puppy. Little remained of the garish red and white rings about his deep-set, gray-blue eyes. The designs on his shoulders and chest were either smeared or erased. Worst of all, black dye tinting his topknot had faded, leaving his heavy hair only slightly darker than its natural tawny brown.

Beside him and just below the skyline lay Kawea, the ugly, claw-scarred Seneca; a pace or two in their rear shivered four Tuscaroras occupied in reloading and repriming their firearms.

Shaded by a stand of towering short-leaf pines, Tosneoc lay near the center of a small grassy plain, secure behind its palisade of raw, pointed logs which had been canted outward. Fanning out from the town in all directions lay cultivated fields of various sizes, but, because the harvest had been in for some time, they now appeared desolate. A few lean brown-black pigs were grouting halfheartedly for overlooked sweet potatoes among slate-blue puddles left by the storm. In a farther field the raiders noted a small herd of hobbled horses grazing. Awkwardly, the animals reared and splattered about searching for food under the bored eyes of a couple of tall striplings. With satisfaction Sakwari-cra observed that these youths were armed only with whips of peeled willow.

By circling a little to their left the Iroquois made an interesting dis-covery; near the opposite side of the palisade stood half-a-dozen pack horses loaded with deerskins and ready to travel. Independently, Sakwari-cra and Kawea guessed that what seemed to be a disturbing lack of activity among the cabins was due to the Catawbas' final settling of accounts with some wandering trader and his party. Only a few women and children were to be seen although the sun was shining high and bright above the age-worn and forest-softened summits of the Chattooga Range.

Thin blue fumes mounted from the smoke holes of only a few of the shapeless, mud-chinked Catawba cabins and wigwams scattered hit-or-miss within the palisade below. This was puzzling because, under normal con-ditions, the inhabitants of such a village would have been busy drying out possessions and otherwise repairing the storm's damage.

A little later, Utakwate and Sakwari-cra grasped the reason for this in-activity when, out of a long, narrow structure occupying the settlement's center, strode a pair of long-haired and black-bearded figures in dirt-glazed buckskins. They swung quickly over to where the pack horses were waiting. Chattering and giggling, Catawba men, many of them more than a little drunk, followed the traders out of the long, slab-roofed common house and watched the white men mount thin but rangy-looking saddle horses. They called good-natured obscenities after their visitors when, with a loud cracking of whips, they herded their pack animals off along that trace which led into Cherokee territory.

The Bear's Cub, Sakwari-cra, and the other Iroquois leaders, not being sure of the traders' nationality, were too smart to attack the departing white men. They'd no desire at present to risk provoking Robert Johnson, His Britannic Majesty's governor over South Carolina, for this great chief was well known to be adamant about exacting costly, even bloody, reprisals whenever properly licensed English traders were interfered with.

Nor would the notoriously crafty and short-tempered Chevalier d'Artaguette, commanding not too distant Fort Toulouse in the Choctaw country, take a kindlier view of harm befalling his *voyageurs*.

From a thicket a bluejay screamed a series of derisive farewells while the plodding calvacade became lost to sight in that same hemlock grove in which Tino's party lay flattened and motionless.

As the last hoofbeats faded in the forest, Catawba children, women, and slaves drifted out into the open and listlessly set about performing their usual chores.

Still gabbling, the men started back to the common house, from which senseless screechings and quavering caterwauls continued to rise. Obviously these warriors were too full of trade liquor to move about.

"*Wagh!* This is good," grunted the one-eyed Seneca when perhaps two dozen half-naked brown figures reeled out into the bright, early October day.

Dappled by sunlight, the raiders lay with only their jet eyes in motion, impatient for the signal from Utakwate. So still did Sakwari-cra's detachment lie that a covey of bobwhite quail resumed feeding among a patch of dry weeds not five yards away and a flock of tawny wild doves, perched on a dead locust, remained where they were until three piercing blasts were sounded on the Bear Cub's war whistle, cleverly fashioned from a horned owl's hollow wing bone. Almost simultaneously all three groups of Iroquois burst from their hiding places and, screeching, "*Ooh nah! Ooh na!*" raced down the slopes converging on Tosneoc.

With the imminence of bloodshed, Sakwari-cra felt his neck thickening while a curious, thin, golden-red radiance began to shimmer before his eyes.

Like starving wolves the lean, dark-skinned raiders poured through Tosneoc's wide-open gate before the drunken and utterly surprised Catawba warriors could even guess what was about to happen.

Sakwari-cra, who had won considerable fame among the Tuscaroras as the sturdiest and fleetest runner among a people renowned for swiftness of foot, was the first to be barked and snapped at by curs prowling the muddy, trampled area within Tosneoc's palisade. Experienced in such matters, the young Raven led two other strong runners toward a largish cabin which lay farthest from the gate. He knew that raiders arriving behind him could and would attend to habitations just inside the gate.

When a half-naked, drunken Catawba came lurching out into the sunlight carrying only a casse-tête—a stone-headed war club—Sakwari-cra didn't waste the charge in his musket; he dispatched the stupid fellow with a single sweeping blow of his tomahawk, then, without pausing to lift the scalp, left his companions to handle the rest of the big cabin's inhabitants and ran over to a circular wigwam of red cedar bark in time to split the skull of a Catawba who appeared from its entrance crawling on hands and knees. He took time to spit on the fallen warrior for having proved so ignoble a victim—small honor would be gained through taking such a fool's hair.

The din swelled into an inchoate tumult of ululating war whoops, breathless shouts, and screams of mortal terror. Up into the pine tops beat the clamor of excited dogs, mingled with the howls of terrified children. Women uttered shrill, futile squalls as they rushed, fluttering about without apparent purpose; some of the older squaws were cut down by the dark and deadly Iroquois.

Sakwari-cra felt rewarded that he'd thought to reserve his musket's charge when a huge, disheveled brave rushed out of the common house, screeching like a hurt cougar. He was stark naked and brandishing an enormous *makwa*—a club studded with razor-sharp flint points. In his wake appeared three Catawbas waving cocked and ready pistols.

Coolly, the white Tuscarora halted and, steadying himself, shot from the hip. His charge of buckshot not only blew the club-bearing giant almost in half but also slew one of the pistol bearers.

All the same he might have been in trouble had not Tino shot the other, granting Sakwari-cra opportunity to hurl his blood-dimmed tomahawk at the fourth.

The Tuscaroras and Senecas quickly shot or cut down all visible enemies, then commenced a systematic and merciless search of the wigwams and cabins.

Panting a little, the white Tuscarora beckoned a pair of warriors who, so far, had succeeded in taking only a scalp or two, and waved them toward a well-built cabin located near the palisade's west wall.

Sakwari-cra took care to stand out of the probable line of fire from the door and used his reloaded Penhallow's muzzle to shove it open. Either there were no bars for the door or the occupants had neglected to put them in place, for it creaked open a few inches. As was usually the rule with Indian-built cabins this structure had no windows; the only light illuminating it was admitted by the doorway or beat down through a black-rimmed smoke hole let into the roof's apex.

"Come out, you with the bodies of men and the hearts of girls!"

taunted Sakwari-cra as two of his Tuscaroras ran up, blood-splashed and
with eyes as bright and glittering as a coiled snake's. "Or will you die
where the dark will hide your shame?"

Peering into the rancid-smelling cabin, the Tuscaroras made out a trio
of shadowy, half-crouched male figures; one was in the act of shouldering
an old-fashioned, bell-mouthed musketoon. Sakwari-cra shot him down
amid a flash of fire and a swirl of gray, rotten-smelling smoke. The
Catawba, reeling, also fired, but only blew a jagged hole through the slab
roof. One of the Tuscaroras sprang forward and shot blindly into the murk
from the doorway. He must have hit someone, because an agonized yell
resulted.

Ears singing from the reports, Sakwari-cra crouched and peered through
throat-rasping smoke fumes. He heard someone flopping about on the
floor. Despite all efforts his powder-stung eyes disclosed nothing; nevertheless, he guessed that his shot had hurt a second man or that some
warrior was lying there, falling-down drunk.

The tall young Raven cast his bedraggled companions a warning glance,
then leaned his empty musket against the cabin wall. He would have
reloaded, but he knew it would prove useless in the cabin's confined
space. Once more he gripped the handle of the tomahawk he still carried
suspended from his wrist by a thong.

Groping inward, he stumbled over an inert body, then, crouched low,
he waddled forward through bitter-smelling smoke, ready to leap in any
direction.

From amid the pungent gray fumes a Tuscarora coughed, "Beware, O
Raven! One man remains!"

Sakwari-cra froze, taut, listening, but heard only wheezing gasps from
his right. Before he could find the wounded Catawba one of his companions anticipated him by cutting the dying warrior's throat. At the same
moment a sixth sense warned that someone was about to leap at him
from behind. Eyes smarting and half blinded, he spun about, bracing to
meet the other's spring; it proved to have been misdirected, for the impact landed high and to the left of his body, but as a result Sakwari-cra's
war hatchet missed its swing and he was forced to grapple. As his arms
clamped about the other he became aware of two facts: first, that a blade
had grazed his ribs sufficiently deep to start blood trickling rapidly down
his side, and second, that the body he was crushing against him was
muscular but soft in places which precluded the possibility that this assailant was a youth. Snarling, he dragged his captive over to the door, left
his companions to finish off and scalp the wounded enemies.

His assailant proved to be a tall young woman who writhed and glared
at him while baring white but slightly uneven teeth in a furious grimace.
Large gray-green eyes blazed in futile defiance; they reminded him of a

vixen he'd once seen cornered by bear dogs. Panting, Sakwari-cra scowled at this lithe young female who, he suddenly realized, seemed to be a pure-blooded white!

As was the custom among Southern Indians, his prisoner was nude above the waist except for a necklace of fresh-water mussel shells; her only garment appeared to be a deerskin kilt secured about her waist by a belt of woven thongs.

Subconsciously Sakwari-cra noticed that this furiously struggling creature's bountiful hair was of a hue he'd never before beheld. It was the color of a well-polished copper pot set in the sun, and worn, according to Catawba custom, in a tight roll secured over the nape of her neck.

When this frantic and surprisingly strong young squaw persisted in screeching and trying to claw him, the Raven, irritated by such effrontery on the part of a mere female, ended by savagely driving a knee into the pit of her stomach.

When the girl gasped and doubled up he released her; she fell, eyes rolling, to jerk and writhe convulsively upon a pile of dirty rush matting. Sakwari-cra stood over her grinning, then kicked her a few times before turning aside to join his dark-faced companions in scalping the four Catawbas, who lay draining rivulets of bright arterial blood onto the cabin's floor of hard-packed earth.

Since, unlike an Indian, he wasn't greedy, Sakwari-cra allowed his fellows to scalp the other Catawbas and contented himself by taking his *coup* from the man he'd shot first of all. Kneeling and at the same time keeping an eye on the still-breathless squaw, he deftly inserted his knife's point above his late enemy's left ear. He freed the hair by completing a circular slash back to the original incision, then by gripping the Catawba's braided, oily scalp lock, he ripped it free an instant before the red-haired squaw sprang weakly at him, shrilling imprecations in Muskogean —the basic language of Southeastern Indians.

"*Likwi howe!* Stupid she-animal!" Blood was dripping from his cut side onto her tawny skin as he cuffed her flat, then, planting a knee on her back, secured her wrists behind her. This accomplished, he gripped the captive by her copper-hued tresses and hauled her, still defiant but silent, to her feet.

In guttural Creek the white Tuscarora growled, "Too bad can't torture a squaw—you make good show I bet!" Then summoning a ferocious grin beneath his storm-streaked paint, he added, "No. Perhaps is better you are a squaw."

Leading his prize to the door, he directed a shrewd kick on her rear which sent her staggering outside, then stood with silver gorget jouncing to his mirthless laughter. Amid derisive hoots from the Iroquois she slipped on the mud and fell, but as quickly as she could the redheaded captive sat up, muddied breasts heaving, and treated her huge captor to a look of murderous fervent hatred; but he only grunted, wiped bloodied hands on his deerskin kilt, and returned inside the wigwam to complete the business at hand.

For a while whoops of triumph rang within the palisade of Tosneoc while old men and children were dragged out of hiding. If these proved too young, too old, or sickly-looking to travel well, the raiders methodically used casse-têtes before taking scalps to be flourished and boasted over in the council house at Seegee.

Then young, strong, and hearty-looking Catawbas were tied, cruelly tight, the squaws destined to a life of slavery, the males to a slow and terrible death before some distant torture stake.

Chapter 3

BEAVER TEETH

That great storm which had plagued and delayed the Iroquois ended Beaver Teeth's plan to circle northward far enough to avoid any possible contact with the raiders and also to ensure his reaching Tosneoc in time. As it was, the Catawba hunter had had to spend the night crouched under an overhanging ledge, helpless to move while the tempest raged on and on.

Filled with superstitious dread, Beaver Teeth watched and listened to countless trees crash earthward, forming vast, tangled, dripping windfalls. Worse still, the terrain he had to traverse now became barred by mountain brooks converted into wildly leaping, frothing torrents—formidable barriers not easily to be traversed.

Beaver Teeth, despite his best efforts, didn't reach the valley in which Tosneoc lay until midafternoon. At once the bandy-legged little hunter realized that he'd arrived much too late. From the midst of the hazel thicket in which he lay he watched pillars of gray-blue smoke rise from nearly a score of burning dwellings high into the brilliant autumn sunshine.

Expressionless, the hidden watcher observed those same Iroquois he'd encountered on the Great War Trail collect their loot; he did this with equanimity because, although a Catawba of the Panther Clan, the sapling and cedar-bark wigwam in which he lived by himself lay in a secluded valley half a day's trot to the eastward.

Outside the palisade a few captured horses, too heavily laden with plunder, switched and stamped at deer flies.

The hunter's hollow eyes noted that the Iroquois had been merciless, as usual. A dozen-and-a-half prisoners, only six of them male, stood with arms bound behind them and linked neck to neck with rawhide nooses which quickly would strangle anyone attempting to break away.

To Beaver Teeth it came as no surprise that among the captive squaws was Taqua—the Fire Flower—the red-haired maiden whom he'd longed to possess ever since the mico, as was the custom, had designated her to warm his couch after a particularly successful raid.

Among the flaming dwellings he counted many mutilated corpses—mostly those of children and old people. Already the sky was speckled with soaring kites, black vultures, and brown-black turkey buzzards.

Even while Beaver Teeth studied the scene of disaster a few carrion birds found courage to plane downward to settle upon the gray limbs of a lightning-struck sycamore and began to crane scabby, reptilian necks in anticipation.

Outside the palisade slunk hungry dogs, still wary of disputing the carrion birds' banquet.

Beaver Teeth remained where he was only long enough to make sure that the Iroquois really were preparing to quit Tosneoc. Only Tuscaroras would move out so promptly; Choctaws, Chickasaws, or even Creeks would linger, more thoroughly to enjoy their success.

When he was satisfied that the enemy indeed was ready to move on, the Catawba's next concern was to make out whether the enemy intended to return home or was going to make another raid somewhere else. Once the Bear's Cub's party moved out herding prisoners and pack horses toward the west, Beaver Teeth judged that they were headed for home—if, of course, this wasn't a ruse to fool some undetected survivor. With the sun glinting dully upon those enormous yellow front teeth which had lent him his cognomen the hunter wriggled backward through the underbrush until he could safely stand erect. He then prepared to make faster than he ever had for Estolee, a sizable Catawba town lying one sleep's travel to the northeast.

In the hollow of the trunk of an isolated and therefore easily recognizable gum tree he concealed his hunting gear, then bolted the remains of the buck's liver.

Provided the going didn't prove too difficult after the great storm and if the warriors of Estolee weren't off on a hunting expedition, it might be possible to ambush the Iroquois on their retreat—if, indeed, the Man Eaters really intended a return to their own country.

Chapter 4

BIVOUAC

The sun had swung below the tops of the forest's taller trees before Utakwate's war party regained the Great War Trail, driving pack horses of loot and sullen, despairing prisoners. Of the latter only the males were forced to march with arms secured. All the squaws and half-grown children had been burdened and now trudged along bent under heavy, carelessly arranged bundles of plunder.

On a small black stallion the Bear's Cub rode at the straggling column's head. Like the rest of the war party he had suffered only minor scratches and cuts during the assault and had paused only long enough before quitting Tosneoc to streak his craggy features with paint and to adorn himself with necklaces of *pe-ak*, several silver bracelets, and to secure a great panache of egret feathers to his crest. The rest of the Iroquois traveled on foot both because low-sweeping branches rendered riding a tedious business—a rider continually had to bend or twist to avoid such— and besides, the rest of the captured horses were more profitably employed in transporting the spoils of Tosneoc.

On reaching the Great War Trail, Utakwate rearranged the column, ordered it to proceed single file. Captives were placed near the column's center with the six male prisoners in the lead. Well guarded by Tino's men and secured neck to neck, the defeated warriors swayed along hampered by awkward bunches of pelts slung about their shoulders.

Even yet some of the Catawbas reeked of that raw rum which had contributed to their undoing. The traders, it turned out, had been a pair of Frenchmen named Eugée and Gallian who did business along the Catawba-Atali Creek borders. In a bit of macabre whimsey the men prisoners also were forced to carry slung to their belts clumps of raw, redly dripping scalps.

Since the column now numbered over thirty and the trail was rough and ran uphill it soon became extended over nearly a quarter of a mile. Bringing up the rear and guarding the pack horses were Sakwari-cra, his Tuscaroras, and the war-wise Seneca, Kawea. Continually they swung their heads and studied both sides of the trace before climbing a long slope covered with dense growths of hickory, ash, beech, and red oak.

The female prisoners and older children, who counted an even dozen, stumped along immediately before the line of pack horses.

Because he stood easily a head higher than his tallest companion the white Tuscarora could keep a watchful eye on his personal prisoner, that savage, red-haired young squaw called Taqua, or the Fire Flower. She tramped sturdily along with head bent so low beneath her pack that her loosed flaming hair almost concealed her features. Although she now appeared tamed and spiritless he noted that her feet were being surely planted and that even when she slipped on some mossy stone she promptly regained balance.

Grimly amused, he watched how her head turned whenever underbrush grew thickly and close to the trail. Beneath his freshened war paint, Sakwari-cra even grinned. Granted half a chance, this long-legged, gracefully moving creature would dash off fast as a doe startled while grazing in a meadow. Undoubtedly, she was trying to establish landmarks useful if she managed to escape.

An unfamiliar but not unpleasant sensation began to warm Sakwari-cra when he realized that yonder supple, lusciously fashioned young squaw was his to do with as he pleased, for after he'd tied her up he'd loudly announced that the Fire Flower was his captive and was not to be molested by anyone. He began to look forward to sundown and the necessary halt to bivouac for the night.

Considerably taller than her black-haired female companions in misery, Taqua found no difficulty in keeping up the column's steady dogtrot, even when the Great War Trail wound upward still more sharply toward a magnificent, lacy waterfall swollen and roaring with the tempest's after-effects.

Not far above this cascade Utakwate ordered the column to bivouac at the base of a high, spruce-crowned cliff dominating a ridge from which the War Trail was visible for a considerable distance in both directions. While the horses were being off-loaded, fed, and watered and the Catawba men's legs bound for the night, Sakwari-cra beckoned the red-haired girl and gruffly ordered her to prepare his food and fashion a couch.

He sat on a log and watched her work while dipping into a pair of buffalo-horn tips further to repair his face paint. Tomorrow morning, if Taqua proved docile and clever, maybe he'd allow her to apply fresh designs to his cheeks and forehead; if not, he'd take a stick to her. For a long time he'd felt worse about going around with smeared or tastelessly applied paint than he did over going hungry.

All at once she appeared and with head submissively bent inquired in Muskogean, "How many sleeping skins does my lord want on his couch?"

The Raven's gray-blue eyes narrowed in suspicion of such unexpected subservience. "One below. Two above."

"No more?" Her voice sounded rich and pleasingly low-pitched.

"You will keep me warm."

A slow flush crept out, spread over Taqua's greasy, olive-tinted cheeks and, for the first time, her faintly slanted eyes revealed a sprinkling of tiny gold flecks in their gray-green irises. It wasn't that the girl was upset at being told that she must occupy her captor's bed—since time immemorial that had been the fate of captive females—it was that this would be only the third occasion on which she'd been required to sleep with a man since a Catawba war party, one misty dawn, had pounced on that Alibamu village in which she'd been held since she'd been a very small girl.

As Taqua set about breaking off pine tips to fashion her new master's couch she thought back again, but still the only thing she could recall before her captivity among the Alibamus was the sound of a woman's anguished voice crying, "Remember! Always you must remain Laure Rivard!" No matter how hard, over the years, she'd tried to regain some other memory from her early childhood she'd failed. She was sure that "Always you must remain Laure Rivard!" was exactly what the woman had gasped.

It was odd, reflected Taqua, that, for the life of her, she wasn't able to recall in what language that never-to-be-forgotten admonition had been voiced. For a long time now she thought only in Muskogean or Siouan— the Catawbas being a tribe long separated from their brethren who live beyond the Father of Waters. She felt sure, however, that language could not have been English. When, infrequently, traders from Carolina had appeared to trade among the Alibamus she'd understood never a word of their language—which was not the case when French traders rode into the village.

Perhaps a further clue lay in the fact that whenever *voyageurs* from Biloxi and the mouths of the Mississippi appeared the Alibamus had attempted to keep her hidden, with the result that she'd never talked directly with a white man until this hateful Tuscarora Raven had taken her prisoner.

While kindling a small cookfire Laure Rivard granted hardly a thought to her late Catawba foster father and his brother, both slain by this Tuscarora, for all that they had been reasonably kind and had beaten her only after they'd got drunk or quaffed too deep of *foskey*, the mystical "black drink" which was consumed only on occasions of great solemnity.

From above a little iron cook pot Taqua stole a glance at this light-skinned Tuscarora and for the first time decided that, for sure, he was wholly white. So now he was about to take over her fate—to what end?

Laure wasn't particularly resentful; a squaw must expect such things to happen—that was the way of life as she'd always known it.

Hurriedly, she dropped her gaze lest he catch her studying him and get angry or extra wary. Provided this renegade wearing an English officer's gorget slept heavily enough could his skinning knife be eased out of its sheath? If she could use it to good effect she guessed she could outrun the swiftest of the raiders and make her way to Erachi, where her late foster father's sister was reported to dwell. For a long time she had been able to outrun all the girls and most of the youths in Tosneoc.

A stick whizzed past her head, then Sakwari-cra snarled, "Hurry! Sakwari-cra is hungry! Arrange the sleepskins beneath the beech tree."

Taqua ducked and stirred the pot in which a pullet that had had its neck wrung after the attack was beginning to simmer. She still didn't know what to make of this Iroquois with the wide-set, steely gray-blue eyes and thin-lipped, wide mouth.

Like herself, Sakwari-cra must have lived among Indians for most of his life; one had only to notice his lack of expression, his never-ending watchfulness and fluid movements. As nearly as she could tell, this Raven's bearing and actions were entirely those of a red man. Perhaps this was well; were she smart enough she ought to be able to avoid trouble by anticipating his moods and intentions.

Briefly deserting the fire, Taqua passed a rude picket line stretched between tree trunks and noted that the pack horses tethered to it had been so well secured she knew there'd be no hope of casting one loose under the cover of darkness. Keeping one eye on the rest of the camp, Taqua hunted around until she came upon a bundle of buckskins from which she selected three especially thick and supple hides. All up and down the ridge squaws and children hurriedly were seeking bedding. Older women, their bare dugs swaying like pendulous bags of brown leather, were cooking and smoke drifted off under the trees in acrid strata. So? Utakwate must feel his party sufficiently strong to defy attack.

Lips compressed, the girl on silent, moccasined feet made her way back to the beech tree which her captor had selected for his sleeping place. Quickly she arranged the deerskins, then hurried back to fetch the cook pot and its pleasant-smelling contents.

Her hatred of the white Tuscarora increased when, completely ignoring her, he delved into the steaming mess and fished out a chicken wing. Squatting on his heels, he crunched small bones and spat out the larger ones, then used his concave silver gorget to scoop up broth upon which he blew noisily before swilling it. Her empty stomach growling, Taqua scowled at the ground. If only this warrior weren't so supremely contemptuous of her existence! Probably he was still angry over her attempt to knife him. Yes. That was it. Every now and then his fingers tested that shallow, red- and yellow-encrusted wound she'd inflicted along his splen-didly muscled rib cage. Only when the bird's neck, gizzard, and feet re-mained did he belch and point. "Eat. Tomorrow comes a long march."

To Taqua's astonishment when, before long, they crawled between the erotic-smelling deerskins her towering captor made not the least effort to explore her person. Instead, he used a bone skewer to pin his topknot out of the way, then made sure that his *islafka*—skinning and scalping knife—was lashed to his wrist in such a fashion that she couldn't hope to free it without awakening him. She foresaw that whatever sexual gratifica-tion he desired was going to be postponed when he pulled her half-naked body across his knees and lashed her thorn-raked and mosquito-bitten ankles so securely together that the thongs bit deep into her skin. Finally he fastened the bonds with a curious knot that seemed to defy undoing. Then, clasping her to his bare, muscle-corded chest, Sakwari-cra stretched out on his back, but although he expected to fall asleep at once, he didn't. Not even when Taqua's warm and supple figure relaxed and she ceased to tremble.

For a long while they lay motionless under the beech, listening to the snuffle and stamp of horses, to the muffled snores and groans of various sleepers, and later to the monotonous sobbing of a pretty young squaw who'd been savagely raped by a number of Iroquois. Far away, a panther screeched and then, still farther off, a wolf began to howl. Nearer at hand mice rustled delicately among fallen leaves.

When sleep still would not come Sakwari-cra abruptly queried in a passable Creek, "Woman, do you remember your white name?"

Hesitantly, Taqua replied in Alibamu—another dialect of the Mus-kogean tongue, which served as a trade language among the southeastern tribes. To have answered in Siouan would have been to invite a cuffing. "Once I was told that my white name is Laure Rivard."

"Who made you a slave and when?"

"Only the wind knows," Taqua murmured, fighting down irritation that this tall young fellow wasn't going to grant her a chance at his knife. Trembling at her boldness, she continued, "My master, what were you called before you became a Tuscarora?"

"I had survived nine winters as Thad Burt-on."

"Burt-on?"

"Yes. Thad Burt-on."

"Then you must have been English born—a *Yengee*."

"You also?" He turned his head on the deerskin until by starlight he could glimpse her profile—straight thin nose, fullish lips, and strong, well-rounded chin.

"No. Perhaps I was born *Ispani* or *Francani*—but not *Yengee*."

They fell silent when a warrior guarding the warpath to the south barked like a fox in order to let Utakwate know that he was alert. A look-out posted to the north answered by imitating a screech owl's querulous ululation.

On the top of a nearby mountain the wolf howled again and presently was answered from a different direction. Their cries made the night seem immeasurably lonely and vast.

Chapter 5

LONG RUN I

The Bear's Cub's party, having been on the move since daylight, had become considerably strung out because this stretch of the Great War Trail mounted a steep and narrow ravine clothed on both sides with bright-leaved huckleberry bushes, supplejack, ilex, laurel, and wild grape tangles.

Around midmorning an indistinct roaring sound became noticeable. Gradually it swelled and grew into such an awesome tumult that everyone on the trail stopped to look upward although they had witnessed many such migrations of passenger pigeons. The vanguard of these swift-flying legions appeared above the Smokies like an aerial tidal wave a mile and more in width. As the birds flew nearer their flight formation became transformed into a gigantic, boiling, dark cloud which, again and again, changed direction; sometimes flocks would diverge from the main body, uncoiling like the tentacles of a gargantuan octopus.

Pretty soon the more experienced among Utakwate's followers sensed that the main flight was going to pass several miles to the westward, but, nevertheless, a tremendous flock of pigeons passed right over the war party. This flight was so dense that the entire landscape became plunged into an eerie false twilight. The sibilant whistlings of myriad wings and the birds' shrill, scolding cries became ear-piercing, drowned out any attempt at conversation.

Although a vast, incredible mass of passenger pigeons must have been flying easily two miles above the valley secondary flights sped by sufficiently low for their purple-blue backs, bronzed necks, rose-fawn bellies to be distinguished. Having a two-foot wingspread and an over-all length of about seventeen inches, these migrants with their bodies tapering to fine points at beak and tail were marvelously designed for swift and graceful flight.

When, to a whirring of wings, one huge flock swooped over the treetops and roared on down the valley the pack horses snorted and fought at their halters.

The incessant *pat-pat* of falling droppings sounded like a hard shower of rain, and soon the ground became white-speckled as by the fall of early snow. Now and again sick or exhausted birds would crash earthward to lie in broken brilliance. Under normal conditions the travelers would have halted and fanned out to collect as many fallen birds as they could use, but Utakwate ordered that only those pigeons which could be picked up without checking the column's progress were to be taken. A pity, thought Tino. There wasn't any danger of pursuit by this time, so why not stop and pick up these fine fat birds which, salted down or tried out for their fat, would be useful for a long time?

Gradually the main current of passenger pigeons swerved westward and disappeared beyond the Smokies. Soon the only evidence of their passage was a faraway droning sound, dung, loose feathers, and exhausted birds.

Inexplicably, the Iroquois *outacity* was beginning to sense an uneasiness which, through long experience, he was unwilling to discount. After all, his war party still traveled deep in hostile territory.

Scarred, lean body yielding awkwardly to his mount's stride—the forest-dwelling northern tribes would never learn to ride well—Utakwate's restless jet eyes continued to probe the terrain ahead. All the same he allowed his imagination to run along pleasing lines. When the Great Council of all the Tuscaroras next assembled, why shouldn't the Bear's Cub's name be put forward to be next Chief War Man—an honor he'd coveted for a considerable time?

Utakwate stopped thinking about the future when, not five yards ahead of him, a Catawba, hideous in yellow and green war paint, suddenly rose out of a dense clump of rhododendrons and sent three buckshot crashing into the *outacity's* naked brown chest.

Even before Utakwate's body thudded onto the trail, to be trampled by his terrified horse, war whoops rang from both sides of the ravine. Puffs of gray-white smoke suddenly bloomed among the trees and underbrush as muskets and blunderbusses banged in a ragged, confusing volley.

When Thad Burton, commanding the rear guard, heard the first muskets fired he knew instantly that the war party was being ambushed by a sizable force, also that that initial shot must have been fired prematurely, before the tail end of the Iroquois column was well in range.

In a ringing voice Sakwari-cra shouted over the Catawbas' ear-piercing war whoops and high-pitched screams from women prisoners for Kawea and others of the rear guard to fall back and rally to him. However, several Iroquois got shot down before they could take a step. In the con-

fined space of the ravine gunshots reverberated and the yelling of the
combatants combined to create an unnerving, disconcerting tumult.

All Thad could do was fire his old Penhallow point-blank at the belly
of a tall Catawba who, leveling a spear and wearing a wildcat mask, came
rushing toward him. Snatching his tomahawk from its sling, he charged
through choking billows of smoke toward a knot of warriors attacking
the men who'd been guarding the women prisoners.

He heard an arrow hiss past his ear, then saw a Tuscarora clutch
spasmodically at his chest and reel sidewise with the feathers of the shaft
protruding from between his fingers. While slashing at his nearest enemy
he, from the corner of his eye, glimpsed Taqua dropping her bundle to
crouch like a hiding quail among some huckleberry bushes. She didn't
seem in the least frightened, only looked coolly about as if seeking an
avenue of escape. Yells, howls, and screams swelled into a hideous cacophony.

The gunfire died out almost as suddenly as it had commenced; swirls
of eye-stinging smoke settled low over the warpath. Only when he'd all
but lopped off the arm of his present antagonist did the white Tuscarora
find opportunity to glance about and try to estimate the situation. A wild
fight taking place around the Catawba male prisoners, a melee in which
the flash and shimmer of knives seemed incessant. Since, momentarily,
the attack on the rear guard had faltered Sakwari-cra prepared to lead his
handful of surviving Tuscaroras in a charge up the ravine but, as quickly,
he abandoned the idea; there were too many furious, screeching Catawbas
in action up ahead and all too many Tuscaroras and Senecas had been
mowed down by that murderous first volley.

While he wavered in unfamiliar indecision the nearest Catawbas rallied
and came on, brandishing weapons and screaming threats. Two more
Tuscaroras were killed and another wounded by arrows and spears.

A Seneca in the act of reloading his smoking musket at Sakwari-cra's
left side collapsed, kicking futilely at the frost-browned ferns with a tomahawk sunk deep alongside the roached crest rising from his naked skull.
When another Tuscarora fell, Thad, save for one man, was alone on his
feet. Racing to Taqua, he jerked her erect, pointed down the backward
trail, snarling, "Run! Run hard!"

The renegade's ferocious expression took instant effect, for the girl
raced off down the trail, long, bare legs flashing and flickering past the
undergrowth. Meanwhile, her captor and Kawea, the one-eyed Seneca
started pounding along after her.

From behind sounded a snarling clamor like that made by wolves while
pulling down a weak deer or buffalo.

Although he hated the necessity, Thad, without missing a stride, cast
away his precious but heavy Penhallow, next his powder horn, and finally

his war bag, an essential for survival in hostile territory. Since by now he knew that, for sure, he was about to run as he'd never run before, he even rid himself of his war hatchet.

Yes. He, the girl, and Kawea were in for a long, hard race if they expected to keep their hair. He knew that, because certain young Catawbas also were abandoning firearms and other equipment.

After a quarter hour Thad felt that he had to risk a glance over his shoulder and saw that about a dozen dark-faced Catawbas were pounding along in pursuit. Already they had become somewhat strung out since some had persisted in carrying guns.

At the end of half an hour Sakwari-cra felt encouraged. His breathing remained steady and deep, his leg muscles limber, ready for real testing. Amid the forest's cool shade he scarcely was sweating at all. In endless succession tree trunks, some bright with moss, some leprose with decaying bark, flashed by. Apparently Taqua was quite as untroubled since she was running, flaming red hair streaming loose, with effortless grace. She kept about twenty yards ahead of him and ten in front of Kawea—which was about where he wanted her should she attempt to break away.

After another ten minutes he began to experience doubts whether Kawea could keep this burning pace much longer. The Seneca must be nearing thirty—middle age for an Indian—and further was handicapped by comparatively short legs.

A mile later the Seneca had slowed so perceptibly that Thad had either to push by him or allow the pursuers to come dangerously close. When, on a wide and level stretch of the trail, he overtook the Seneca, Kawea's breath sounded labored and short. Thereafter, the one-eyed warrior dropped steadily farther behind although he, too, had cast aside all weapons except his skinning knife.

Next time Thad took a backward glance he realized that Kawea's scarred brown features had grown bright with sweat and that his head had begun to sway from side to side. His tobacco-stained, yellow-brown teeth were revealed in the contorted grimace of extreme effort.

Bitterly, Sakwari-cra regretted not having more carefully noted this section of the Great War Trail. Had he done so he'd have been able to regulate the fugitives' pace to take advantage of changes in footing and terrain. He kept his gaze riveted on the ground about fifteen yards ahead. Loose stones, fallen logs, creek crossings all had to be anticipated and avoided without loss of speed. To his growing astonishment the captive girl seemed to be having no difficulty at all either in maintaining this grueling pace or in accurately selecting her footing.

The next time he chanced a backward glance he felt encouraged; Kawea seemed to have caught his second wind. Better still, the number of immediate pursuers had diminished to seven long-limbed and powerful young warriors unencumbered by firearms, but these were bounding along with ominous ease, their splendid copper-hued bodies agleam with sweat. No telling how many more Catawbas were racing along the warpath farther back and out of sight.

Chapter 6

LONG RUN II

To watch Taqua continue to travel at such speed over treacherous, varied, and utterly unpredictable footing was a wonderful thing. The Indian simile "speedy as a barren doe" came alive before Thad Burton's eyes. The young, red-haired squaw's progress was epic, more worthy of a celebrated warrior rather than of a miserable female. At the end of an hour he decided that, provided she didn't slip on a loose or mossy stone or trip over a root, the girl who called herself Laure Rivard seemed able to keep running for a long time yet.

Kawea, however, was weakening. He now lagged all of fifty yards behind his companions and must be nearing the end of his strength if the increasingly heavy and unrhythmic impact made by his moccasins was any indication. Next time the fugitives encountered a small clearing Thad looked back for the first time in a long while and saw that the Seneca was running flat-footed; flecks of froth burst now and then from his mouth. That he was breathing in brief convulsive gasps meant the end of his running—and his life—were near at hand. When the warpath suddenly took a steep downward course it enabled the Seneca for a while to increase his lead. But, proportionately the downgrade helped his pursuers so that they gained until the foremost Catawba began to pound along less than twenty yards behind Kawea's swaying figure.

At that moment Thad sighted a game trail forking westward off the warpath. He called for Taqua to follow it because, for some time, he'd debated the wisdom of continuing to fly along the Great War Trail. What if they encountered another party of Catawbas advancing from the direction of Tosneoc? Sakwari-cra soon regretted his decision when he realized that progress along this game trail was going to prove much rougher going and would mean a quick end for Kawea.

Taqua turned off the warpath and ran upward through a hickory grove, bending and swaying to avoid low branches, but hardly slowing her space-eating stride. Thad forgot everything else to concentrate on setting down his muddied moccasins; a slip or fall at this juncture would mean disaster because the game trail was becoming strewn with boulders sheathed in slippery, emerald-green moss. When the upward slope angle increased he was surprised suddenly to find himself running only a few feet behind Laure Rivard's brown, sweating shoulders.

For fear that she might be weakening, he gasped, "Faster, snail-footed squaw!"

The taunt took effect; Taqua spurted until again her flying red hair and bobbing shoulders showed several yards ahead.

While making a wide jump across a brook he heard Kawea halt, panting wildly. "Farewell, Brother—"

At the cost of a possible misstep the white Tuscarora looked over a sweat-spangled shoulder. In the trail's middle the one-eyed Seneca had faced about and was bracing on quivering legs. Kawea unsheathed his scalping knife and, in a pitiable travesty of the blood-chilling Iroquois war whoop, wheezed, "Oo-nah!" and started uncertainly back to meet the leading Catawba—a tall, narrow-chested fellow distinguished by yellow and blue streaks across his cheeks. He was running with tomahawk unslung and ready. Perhaps disconcerted by the Seneca's unexpected turnabout, the pursuer too quickly hurled his tomahawk. At the same instant Kawea bent so the weapon flashed over him. The one-eyed warrior then reeled forward to meet the other's rush and, grunting, drove his knife up to its hilt in the Catawba's belly only a second before a second pursuer buried a tomahawk in his skull.

When Thad looked back again a birch branch skinned the bridge of his nose, but he saw what was happening and wasn't reassured; the Catawbas didn't even break stride when they detoured the fallen men and followed the red-haired squaw and the big Tuscarora along this game trail which was winding into the bold but pleasant foothills of the Great Smoky Mountains.

The track at length led across a lush, green-brown meadow created by some long-collapsed beaver dam, and so permitted Sakwari-cra to make sure how many warriors remained in pursuit. They numbered five. No. A sixth runner flashed into sight at the forest's edge.

Aware that at last his breathing was growing quick and shallow, Sakwari-cra paid even closer attention to the game trail, which, gradually, was growing more indistinct. What if this track came to a dead end or petered out amid a fan of deceptive openings? Suppose this amazing girl suddenly were confronted by an impossible windfall? For him at least, this would mean a fighting death, for if he could help it he didn't intend to be taken prisoner.

Never had he witnessed such a run as the one Taqua was making; the strength, thrust, and sureness remaining in those flashing, mud-splashed legs was wonderful to behold.

While speeding at a steady, space-consuming trot across a small clearing edged by birches the girl began to hitch up the brief kilt of deerskin above her hips, then twisted it around her middle in order to remove even that trifling constriction. Now she ran with small, reddish-pink buttocks working rhythmically and quite nude below the waist save for a hammock-like contrivance supported snugly between her legs by means of a narrow belt. Such protection was generally worn by grown squaws to shield their genitals from dust, thorns, nettles, seeds and other irritants.

For a while the runners were forced because of the trail's increasing rise to slacken their pace, then, to the young Raven's alarm, he felt a "stitch" begin to develop in his side. Soon the pain grew so severe that he began to grind his teeth in agony, but he managed to maintain the pace set by his lithe-limbed companion. He had begun to lag when, as abruptly as it had struck, the cramp dissipated. But would it return? No telling.

Not only did the trail lead upward among rocky, rounded foothills, but also the going became treacherous because of trees felled during the great storm. A dead but still strong branch suddenly ripped the silver gorget from his neck—an evil omen for sure. Ever more frequently the panting fugitives were forced to detour or to hurdle some trunk; time and again they had to duck or bend almost double to avoid leafy obstacles. It came as some encouragement that such hazards must be just as hampering to the Catawbas; branches lashed and stung their nearly naked bodies and wild grape honeysuckle vines also snatched at the pursuers' ankles and on occasion threw them off-stride.

If only the ground would fall away! But it didn't. It continued to rise. After bursting through a series of thickets Thad's breath came in a series of hot, tearing gusts which dried his mouth and seared his throat. Taqua must be experiencing the same sensations, for imperceptibly her gait slackened—small wonder. They must have been running at nearly top speed for over two hours.

Barely in time, the game trail for a short interval ran downhill, then debouched on a bush- and thicket-dotted meadow which afforded Thad time to catch a second wind. Reassured for the moment, he shook his head to clear trickles of sweat from his eyes. He needed to see clearly because he sensed that the Catawbas were about to initiate a maneuver with which the Raven was quite familiar. Any minute now one of the enemy, leaving his companions to maintain a slower but relentless pace, would sprint and so exact a burst of speed from the fugitives.

Once the first sprinter began to tire, one of his companions then would put on a similar burst of speed, thus forcing the quarry to keep running at top speed until he in turn would be replaced.

The third Catawba proved faster than either of his predecessors and succeeded in closing in on Thad's broad, red-brown back to a distance of about twenty yards. This was close, but still not near enough to permit hurling his tomahawk. Through experience Sakwari-cra knew that an enemy must come within forty feet to ensure a reasonably accurate throw. *Wagh!* This third sprinter continued to come up, up. The *thud-thud* made by his feet became clearly audible.

"Faster!" gasped Thad, now pounding along not six feet behind the red-haired squaw.

He saw Taqua jerk a nod although it seemed impossible that she could still be able to move her moccasins so fast.

Over the next three miles or more the third pursuer kept up his pressure, which reduced Thad to snatching shallow gulps of air. His lungs felt ready to explode and his vision began to play tricks. The girl must be suffering too; now her coppery head had begun to sway slightly from side to side.

All at once the third Indian gave up and reeled aside to cling, gasping, to a tree while his successor, a thin, pale-skinned warrior with red and ocher patches enclosing his eyes, spurted to pass him and force the pace.

By the time the runners had covered another two miles Sakwari-cra discovered that this spindle-legged warrior was even speedier than any of his fellows; serious trouble was at hand. Thad realized that when he called for a spurt Taqua, for the first time, could not respond; not that she wasn't still setting a burning pace, but her shoulder blades shone scarlet with effort, were streaming sweat and streaked with welts raised by whipping branches. How her much tenderer face and breasts were suffering was past imagination.

Her footfalls were growing heavier, less certain. For another thing, her high-twisted kilt began slipping and she had no time to hitch it up again.

The leading Catawba was now a tall, almost emaciated fellow wearing a pair of yellow-dyed heron feathers laced into his topknot; like demented canaries these fluttered to his every stride.

Sakwari-cra's leg tendons began to feel like white-hot wires and when his vision became further distorted he knew that he wasn't going to break down this scrawny Catawba; before long he'd have to stop and do what he could in order to stay alive. Only two other enemies remained in sight, but these were nearly a hundred yards behind. Earlier sprinters, after catching their wind, of course would resume the chase, but for present considerations they were out of it.

As in an agonized dream Thad listened a little longer to the soft thud-thudding of Taqua's feet upon the ground; they went *splat!-splat!* whenever she crossed a boggy place.

"Faster!" he choked. The Catawba's footfalls now suggested he was pulling up into tomahawk-throwing range. His present pursuer must be about to make his supreme effort.

This time Taqua's long legs couldn't respond, began to waver and showed other unmistakable, fatal signs of failing. She stumbled slightly now and then and lost ground until Thad was running less than a yard in her rear.

Relentlessly, the Catawba closed in until he must be running within easy tomahawk cast. Why didn't he halt and throw? The possibility occurred that the thin warrior might be planning to come up to leap upon the white Tuscarora's broad back and, riding him to earth, cut his throat—which would be redound to his credit when he came to boast of his victory.

Without warning, Sakwari-cra dropped onto all fours and blocked his pursuer so effectively that the Catawba went spinning, breechclout-over-topknot and got his breath knocked out. In a flash Thad was back on his feet, had snatched up his enemy's tomahawk and had struck hard; unfortunately the blade glanced off the Catawba's skull and crashed onto a stone; the force of his blow snapped the hatchet's shaft. Without pausing to lament, Thad turned and sped dizzily through the sunset-reddened forest after his companion.

He had to risk a backward glance before settling down to run again and saw a Catawba crouched over the fallen warrior, who must have been their fastest man, for his successor made no effort to recommence the chase, only began to pound the ground with empty fists in futile rage that he and his fellows hadn't been able to run down this incredible pair they'd been chasing for almost five hours.

Chapter 7

OLD CAMPSITE

Although Sakwari-cra, now in the lead, gradually relaxed, he and the wildly disheveled and nearly nude girl kept on for a while; experienced, he felt positive that the Catawbas weren't going to give up their pursuit. They'd never hear the end of it if they permitted themselves to be outdistanced by a mere squaw and a white Iroquois. Thad Burton had heard about long runs which had continued for days; famous chases, which had led the participants over hundreds of miles of wilderness.

Gradually recovering their wind, the fugitive couple spent the late afternoon trotting steadily up some valley's eastern slope. At length the Raven thought it safe to halt long enough to wet their parched throats with water gulped from a brook. Taqua went further; after unconcernedly removing her kilt she waded into an icy pool and briefly immersed her entire body. Emerging, in wary silence, she wrung water from her flaming hair, then used quivering fingers to comb it free of twigs and leaves.

An emotion something deplorably akin to admiration seized Sakwari-cra; Taqua voiced never a complaint for all that her face, breasts, and stomach, arms and legs were oozing blood from lacerations inflicted by catclaws, blackberry thorns, and whipping branches.

It pleased him, too, that she'd proved smart enough not to linger in the pool's icy water or to drink too much.

"Taqua swift runner," he grunted in Creek while bending to remove a twig from one of his badly worn moccasins.

"Tuscarora Raven runs better," she muttered, casting him an enigmatic glance from faintly slanting, gray-green eyes. "Clever to kill Catawba like that."

He acknowledged the compliments by a condescending grunt, then stepped back onto the trail and started westward. The more distance put between them and their pursuers the better. Only when thick shadows cast by great pines and hardwoods turned long and blue-black did Thad admit the necessity of finding a resting place before darkness fell, especially because a sickly, yellow-gray sunset argued that this fine autumnal weather was about to end.

At length the white Tuscarora noted a few broken, long-dead twigs on a hemlock and recognized the barest hint of a game path that branched off to the right and disappeared into a dense tangle of rocks, laurels, hemlocks, and spruces.

He took care to run by this place to where a newly fallen tree offered a good turnoff, and ran along it until he could part a clump of yellow birches. Then, with his eyes, he signaled her to follow close.

Taqua nodded and when he started to circle back to the game path she followed skillfully, putting down her feet exactly where his had fallen and exercised great care not to bruise moss, dislodge bark, break twigs, or press any of the coarse mountain grasses.

Thad advanced, small, gray-blue eyes probing every thicket. He was relieved to note fresh buffalo droppings strewn along this barely recognizable path so wasn't alarmed at a crackling of branches just before he glimpsed three big, brown-black shapes moving unhurriedly up this rock-studded gully which was bisected by a cheerfully noisy brook.

Making hardly a sound, the two climbed until, directly above them, loomed a low but sheer wall of grayish rock. Fervently Sakwari-cra hoped

that more buffaloes might mount this path after he and Taqua had
traveled it. He wasn't foolish enough to imagine that in a good light
some extra-sharp-eyed Catawba wouldn't spot the point where they'd
quitted the game trail.

Continuing to climb, he considered their resources. This was easy. All
they'd retained were comparatively whole skins, the scant garments in
which they stood and, most important, their hair.

The sum of his weapons consisted of an *islafka*—his skinning and, occasionally, scalping knife. If only he hadn't smashed the skinny Catawba's
tomahawk handle! Well, he had, and that was that.

When, without warning, Thad halted and froze into immobility, Taqua
did the same. She saw what had stopped him. A ray of sunset revealed a
small, dark outline amid a clump of ilex. Breathless, she watched him ease
his knife out of its gap-fringed sheath. Once the point came clear, Thad
threw with a short overhand snap. Among the ilex bushes ensued spasmodic flopping and threshing sounds and a few bronze-brown feathers
floated out from among the dark and shiny leaves.

Softly, Sakwari-cra cried, "Fetch!"

Taqua slipped past him, reached into the thicket and pulled out a hen
turkey. It was still struggling, but in vain since it had been struck at the
base of its neck. She wanted to compliment the Raven on his exceptional
throw, but didn't dare. When she handed it over Thad made a slit between one leg tendon and the bone; he then forced the other foot
through this aperture, thus rendered the prize easy to carry. Of course it
was risky to lug this bleeding bird up the gully, but he figured he'd no
choice; it was growing very dark and so far he'd not noticed anything like
a place safe enough to risk building a fire.

Already a good many stars had appeared when, at the base of the rock
wall, he recognized the camping place of some long-departed hunter. A
ring of blackened stone and a couple of charred wooden spits lay beneath
a slab of overhanging rock—also the remains of a spruce-tip bed. The
boughs composing it had lost resilience and needles years ago. Nevertheless, with a few fresh tips added, a tolerably comfortable couch might be
fashioned.

Even if they'd not been so near exhaustion it was typical of their
Indian upbringing that, there being no necessity for conversation, neither
would have spoken; they merely set about making preparations for the
night. While Thad commenced to pluck the turkey under the smoke-black-
ened overhang, Taqua ranged about in search of firewood, at the same
time breaking off pine tips whenever they were handy.

She had begun to scoop sodden ashes from the old fireplace when she
straightened abruptly. "*Wagh!* Look!" She couldn't help sounding excited—and was promptly ashamed of so unseemly an outbreak—as she

held out the blunted and evidently discarded flint from a musket's lock.

To her astonishment her captor nodded and even smiled faintly. "Yours are sharp eyes. That is good." Then, as further evidence of his pleasure, he added while ripping out entrails that steamed pungently in the increasing chill, "This is a young bird. It is fat, too." Then, solemn once more, "Go fetch tinder from that dead cedar."

While his companion hurried to comply he placed dead twigs over a handful of moss, then whittled a number of "Indian prayer sticks" by shaving dead pine sticks until they became encircled by ruffs of fine slivers which should ignite quickly. Next he braced his heavy-bladed knife's point upon a log and ground the old flint along its spine until tiny, gold-red sparks commenced to rain down onto the tinder and moss. This, of course, was woman's work, but he was hungry and far too wary to entrust this, his only weapon, to the still-unpredictable young squaw.

Soon little flames commenced to waver and dance under the overhanging slab. These Taqua, boneweary, patiently encouraged with dry twigs and the "prayer sticks," which were calculated to raise a minimum of smoke; there oughtn't to be much danger of the Catawbas' smelling it, since they were encamped high above the game trail and the wind was beginning to blow strongly out of the southeast.

While Thad was skewering the turkey on a green sassafras stick which he supported upon a forked branch and then anchored the thick end with stones, Taqua placed the turkey's heart, gizzard, and liver on a clean strip of bark. Once the bird had begun to roast and to drip into the flames the two, half-numbed by fatigue, broke more bedding from nearby evergreens. Working in near darkness and along a steep hillside proved to be hard work, but it kept them from stiffening up in the increasing cold.

After what seemed like an eternal interval had passed Sakwari-cra could hold back no longer and hacked off the spitted bird's scorched and only half-cooked legs. Largely unclad, shaggy, and as wild-looking as any cave dwellers, the two crouched before the fire tearing at the meat in fearful eagerness.

Some of their grinding fatigue began to disappear once the legs and thighs had been gnawed down to the bone. Belching softly, Thad then sliced off slabs of breast meat and divided them with the greasy-faced girl.

To allow the fire to die down proved difficult; its heat was as a healing balm upon their scarred and all-but-unprotected bodies, but Sakwari-cra placed no more wood on the winking, paling coals.

How far behind were the pursuers? No way of learning until daylight. Moodily, Thad settled back against a fallen tree and for the first time really studied his captive who, at the moment, was preparing a compress of damp moss to bind feet that in several places showed oozing, bloody bruises.

That Taqua, perforce, remained bare-breasted in this cold mountain air apparently did not appear to bother her, for, in seeming unconcern, she was employing a moss swab to wipe away dried blood from a savage scratch scoring a neat and bud-like nipple.

Despite what seemed to be a naturally pallid complexion, long years of exposure to wind, smoke, countless applications of bear's oil, and torrid sunlight had tinted her skin a golden brown. In fact, by the fitful firelight, she appeared as dark as a light-complexioned Creek squaw.

Arms folded over chest, Sakwari-cra came to the conclusion that, in many ways, this girl, save for longer, slimmer legs and narrower hips, greatly resembled a high-born Creek, a nation renowned for the shapeliness of its women, for all her red hair. A piece of branch burned through and in the brief flare he noticed something of considerable significance; above the junction of her high, well-rounded bosoms a small blue turtle had been tattooed.

"Taqua lucky." He tapped a tattoo on his upper arm. "Sakwari-cra also a Turtle."

Although she'd long ago noticed the emblem, she dutifully inclined her head. She *was* lucky in this matter! Members of the same clan, no matter to which tribe they belonged, were bound to show one another at least a small measure of consideration.

Laure looked so worn and weary that, when the wind picked up and blew colder still, he changed his mind and put another stick on the fire.

"How many winters has Taqua dwelt among the dog-delivered Catawbas?"

"Four winters," the girl replied, staring at the white-rose coals pulsing before them. "After Taqua was captured from the Alibamu." The girl's cruelly raked shoulders rose in a slight shrug. "How many winters Taqua spent among them she cannot tell."

When, not much farther up the mountain, some timber wolves raised savage, long-drawn howls, their heads swung sharply to face the sound.

"Not far away," Thad commented, frowning because he guessed that with only a knife for protection, he'd better keep the fire going.

"Those *yahas* could never have caught us today," he added unexpectedly. "Taqua speeds like flung lance."

Pleased because this stalwart Raven had deigned to mention her running for a second time, Taqua cast him a fleeting glance and made bold to inquire, "When did Sakwari-cra become Iroquois?"

"He had lived among the whites eight—maybe nine—winters when a big Tuscarora war party led by Mico Hancock fell upon my father's house and others built by *Kish-kish tarakshi*—'Tied Arse'—named Baron

Graffenried." For some reason Thad began to speak in uncertain, oddly inflected English; of course, she couldn't understand a thing he said. "My father's house was on a river called Trent in Carolina." He switched back into Creek. "On that day ten times ten white scalps were lifted; many prisoners were taken—Sakwari-cra was among them. He was adopted into the Turtle Clan. He has dwelt in Seegee Town ever since he survived *busquenawing*, the puberty rites, and became a 'bow-man' or green warrior."

To escape the wind, Laure went over to sit on the spruce-tip couch, then fell to combing her matted, copper-hued hair with her fingers. After dislodging all manner of leaves, twigs, and bits of bark she set about plaiting it into coarse double braids. "Where did Sakwari-cra learn to speak Creek? Do not the Tuscaroras speak Iroquois?"

"His foster mother was a Creek captive. She said Muskogean—the mother language—is used among many tribes. It is favored by great orators."

For a while the two stopped talking, listened to wolves complain—there were a lot of them and growing bolder. When Thad threw sticks on the fire to make it flare up, several pairs of green-gold eyes could be glimpsed through the underbrush. Then they rubbed their aching feet with turkey fat, but, for all that, splotches of blood still continued to seep through the torn and nearly worn-out soles of their moccasins. Um. How long would this footgear last when the chase was resumed come daylight? Sakwari-cra decided it was wiser not to speculate on that.

Since the white Tuscarora didn't want to talk any more lest he lose dignity, he stretched on the couch and squirmed his hard buttocks among the sweet-smelling spruce tips, then beckoned Taqua to lie beside him away from the fire. While in a sitting position she covered them both with spruce boughs, then sank back into instant slumber.

After a bit Thad forced himself to sit up and only doze; he didn't intend to fall asleep and risk not waking in time to set in motion a bold plan he'd evolved.

Chapter 8

QUOBAH

About an hour before dawn Sakwari-cra stretched stiff, dreadfully sore limbs and forced himself to resume full consciousness. Save for a few coals in the fireplace the night was pitch-dark because clouds had obscured the sky and there was no starlight. All the same the young Raven knew that, because of the cold, Taqua was lying all huddled up. She appeared to be sleeping the sleep of the dead, which wasn't the case, for when, in quitting the couch, his foot dislodged a pebble and caused a small *click!* Laure instantly sat up, peering in all directions. This pleased him. Exhausted or not, she could sleep lightly.

"Sakwari-cra leaves me?" This was more an observation than a question.

Yawning, he ordered, "Taqua will stay here. If anyone comes near hide until Sakwari-cra returns."

It was typically Indian that Taqua should not ask what he intended, where he was going, or how long he would be absent.

He took up the hen turkey's heart and popped it into his mouth, then, chewing slowly, circled silently away from the old campsite until he found, and began to descend, that path they had climbed the previous evening.

Guided more by instinct than by sight, he felt his way downhill until he recognized the game trail; thereupon he started running noiselessly eastward, the direction from which he and Laure had come.

Just before dawn and about five miles from where he'd regained the trail, he pulled up and stood sniffing. Was there? Yes. A smell of wood smoke faintly was tincturing the windless air. Pretty soon he located the Catawba bivouac. Noiseless as a hunting weasel, Thad slipped through tangles of wild grape, myrtle, and underbrush. Contempt boiled within him; although in no danger from wild animals these Catawbas had kept their fire burning and appeared to have posted no sentry even though they were encamped but a short distance off the trail. Such carelessness was insulting when they were hunting a Raven of the Iroquois!

Before long he was able to tell, first, that the enemy numbered no more than three; second, every one of them was asleep and lying down, not sitting up like experienced warriors.

Making not the least noise, Sakwari-cra approached the nearest Catawba and used his *islafka* to sever that thong which secured a tomahawk to the sleeper's wrist. For an instant he hefted the weapon to ascertain its balance. Light filtering weakly through lofty treetops enabled him to make sure of his aim before he sank his blade deep, but not too deep, into the Catawba's head. Instantly he wrenched the tomahawk free and in swift succession killed the two other men. Hardly fifteen seconds had elapsed between his first blow and the last.

Wishing that he dare burst into a triumphant paean, Thad stood with knees bent and legs apart, prepared to spring in case some warrior might have elected to sleep a little apart from his fellows—as he himself often did. Reassured, he contemptuously spat on the bloodied figure of his latest victim, who still writhed feebly; next, he voided his bladder over the other two Catawbas in supreme scorn for such incompetent warriors.

Alert to catch some untoward sound, Sakwari-cra fumbled in the nearest war bag until he found a deer's bladder half-full of *quotash*—a greasy mess of squirrel or turkey meat mixed with corn, beans, and squash—then crammed his mouth full. Chewing, he knelt and took the dead men's scalps, which he stuffed still hotly dripping, into another war bag. Next, Sakwari-cra with minute care examined the condition of the two muskets carried by his victims. Both weapons were ancient and seemed barely fit to be fired, but all the same it was fine to have them.

In a stained and evil-smelling loincloth of scarlet wool he stowed the other men's breechclouts together with their moccasins. Although they all seemed considerably too small Taqua might find a pair to fit her or maybe she could recut and sew some of the others to fit his big feet. Flints and bullets he poured into a single pouch, but he divided the captured gunpowder between two buffalo-horn containers.

Finally he added to his pack a pair of brief buckskin capes; for all that neither was thick or warm they'd afford at least some protection against the weather, which had been growing colder every hour.

Less than twenty minutes had elapsed before Thad Burton guided the carry straps of a hastily contrived pack over his dyed topknot, then cradled the old muskets in the crook of his arm. What with the powder horns and the war bags he found himself burdened with a considerable load.

Before returning to the main trace the white Tuscarora paused. Should he linger long enough to slice off the dead men's genitals? Thus mutilated, their spirits must slink, forever disgraced, about Yo-he-wa's Hunting Grounds.

He was sorely tempted, but a white man's common sense warned against such a waste of time. How could he be sure that a second party of pursuers wasn't within striking distance?

Frequently obscured by low, dark clouds, the sun was lifting above the trees when Sakwari-cra pulled up, scowling, at that point where the path branched off the trail and led up to where Taqua should be waiting at their bivouac. His habitual alertness became intensified, for, very recently, someone had taken the upward path and it hadn't been his red-haired companion; the barely perceptible impressions were those of huge and very broad, bare feet.

Taking care, as before, to quit the main trace without a sign, Thad Burton silently got rid of his burdens save for the better of the two muskets and a Catawba war ax. Noiseless, lithe, and powerful as a ranging panther, he started climbing on a course parallel to the path; the unknown might be lying in wait somewhere along it.

Once he glimpsed the top of that smoke-stained ledge above their bivouac he advanced with such caution that he stirred never a leaf until he could obtain an unobstructed view of the old campsite.

To his surprise he felt a sharp anxiety that Laure should be nowhere in sight. Then, on rounding a lichen-speckled boulder, he sighted a huge, dark figure bent over the spruce couch. It was so outlandishly painted that at first Sakwari-cra took the stranger for a shaman or wizard from some unknown tribe. Then he realized that this crinkle-haired giant's skin uniformly was the color of fresh oak charcoal! He was carrying some uncommonly long arrows in a crude, cedar-bark quiver slung to one shoulder and was holding a broad-headed war arrow ready-notched to the string of a curiously shaped bow, which Thad respected a deal less than the war hatchet this sable-skinned fellow carried jammed into a belt of spotted wildcat skin.

Weird, yellow-and-white designs were painted all over the black man's muscular torso and he wore a length of dirty red cloth twisted, turban-like, about his bullet-shaped head. The battered skins of scarlet tanagers had been pushed through slits in the distended lobes of his ears. For all that Thad had seen many Negroes because many tribes adopted or took into easy servitude slaves escaped from Spanish or English owners, this one looked very different; the other Negroes had had brown-black skins, while this giant's shone blue-black. The young Raven at first glance perceived that this stranger was in poor condition; his ribs stuck out like slats and, under the pipe-clay paint, his cheekbones protruded in sharp ridges to either side of a short, high-bridged nose. His breechclout of bearskin and knee-high leggings looked so ragged and worn that they appeared ready to fall off.

For a split second Thad debated shooting the intruder out-of-hand, but decided against it. A head bearing such short and tightly curly hair wouldn't yield a scalp anyone could be proud of. More important, it still was risky to fire a gun. *Wagh!* If the Creeks, Cherokees, and Chickasaws kept Negro slaves, why shouldn't he capture this big, blue-black fellow and make him carry the Catawbas' gear, thus freeing himself to act instantly in any emergency?

Abruptly he called in Creek, "Drop the bow! Don't move!"

The Negro giant in straightening dropped his weapon, then turned slowly about. In his small, yellowish eyes Thad thought to recognize both defiance and pleading.

With topknot swaying gently and musket held level with the other's shrunken belly, Sakwari-cra advanced toward the couch, but halted far enough away to render futile a sudden lunge made by this outlandish apparition. The Negro, however, made not the least movement, only glowered at his captor.

For a brief interval the two equally tall but otherwise disparate figures surveyed one another. It was then that Thad noticed short ridges of scar tissue arranged in rough chevrons running across the other's cheeks and forehead.

Chancing that this might be some English settler's runaway slave, Sakwari-cra demanded, "Who are you?"

To Thad's astonishment the other replied in guttural but recognizable English, "Me Quobah."

"You escaped slave?"

The Negro's round head went back proudly and a mouthful of teeth filed into dog-like fangs flashed in the sunlight, "Yes. But Quobah, Ashanti prince, never stay slave."

Chapter 9

THE ASHANTI I

It didn't take Sakwari-cra long to perceive that he'd miscalculated; beyond a doubt, this tall, blue-black-skinned fellow had meant it when he'd said he would never submit to re-enslavement. So, he'd either have to kill Quobah straight away or accept him, not only as a follower, but also as a fellow warrior.

Musket still leveled, Sakwari-cra, unlike a real Indian, abandoned his first impulse to slay the insolent captive and took the long view. He was being hunted and deep in hostile territory—where he was he'd not the least idea. Saving for Taqua, who couldn't do much in a fight—even if she wanted to—he was alone. He shot a glance at Quobah, still awaiting his fate with a curious air of dignity and resignation, and set him down as a fighter and a tough customer by anybody's standards. He might make good use of that extra gun hidden down by the game trail.

Laure Rivard, prone on the overhanging ledge, peeped through a crevice and watched Sakwari-cra make the peace sign by raising his right hand skyward with palm turned outward.

In his strangely inflected English Thad Burton was saying, "If Sakwari-cra not kill, you obey, call him chief and fight beside him?"

For a moment the Negro stared in incredulous astonishment, then stepped forward, the scar ridges striping his forehead agleam in the morning sun. Placing hands on knees, he bowed parallel to the ground, looked up, and in smiling again revealed that double row of strong white teeth which had been filed into needle-sharp points.

Sakwari-cra blinked his surprise, then, recovering, pointed downhill. Silently, the two men disappeared among the trees together.

In mingled anger and uneasiness, Taqua watched them depart. Why hadn't the white Tuscarora even bothered to call out or to try to find out what had become of her? Was she so worthless, so unattractive that he should thus ignore her? Why, she might have been killed by the black savage or torn to pieces by a bear for all he cared.

Wagh! She had it! He despised her for her red hair! For years Alibamus and Catawbas had mocked her about that fiery mane, had claimed it was unlucky. All at once, and for the first time in years, her eyes stung and filled at this injustice. Could she help it that her hair was of such ugly color? After the way she'd run yesterday she'd thought Sakwari-cra was going to ignore this dreadful defect. Or was it for some other reason that he'd slept sitting up instead of requiring her to keep him warm in the usual fashion. After all, wasn't she now his property?

A puzzled expression appeared on her scratched and grease-smeared features when she arose and began to rub lacerated bosoms chilled by contact with the rock. Sadly and without making a sound, Taqua made her way down to the deserted bivouac. Brushing off a swarm of ants, Laure, still sniffling, began to tear shreds of meat from the turkey's carcass.

All the same, she wondered why Sakwari-cra hadn't killed that hideous, wild-looking, black giant right away. Ugh! Those sharp-filed teeth of his filled her with an indefinable dread because they probably meant that he must be a cannibal, like the ferocious, tattooed Mohawks up north.

When the sun was an hour older Taqua concluded that Sakwari-cra must have found her so displeasing that he'd apparently abandoned her to go off with an ugly, black-skinned savage. Right then she made up her mind that if he didn't come back pretty soon she'd circle back to the game trail and begin to trot eastward; with luck she might encounter some Catawbas. Perhaps they could be persuaded to return her to Tos-neoc—or what might remain of it. It wasn't that she really wanted to go back, but where else was there to go?

Just then a twig snapped somewhere down in the gully. In a flash she darted into a clump of rhododendrons where she concealed herself as effectively as a frightened fawn. Oblique, gray-green eyes narrowed, she watched her captor and his gaunt companion reappear and stand scanning the campsite's surroundings.

Would the big, young Raven call out? Why did it suddenly seem all-important that he should? Following an interminable pause Thad barked twice like a dog fox, paused, then called softly, "Taqua! Come here."

Without reply—in hostile territory conversation was kept to a minimum unless there was rain or a strong wind blowing—she stood up, gaze humbly lowered as became a squaw in the presence of a warrior.

It didn't take Taqua long to guess what Sakwari-cra had done after he'd deserted her before daybreak. He'd retraced their course of the day before until he'd surprised and slain a party of their pursuers. There could be no other explanation for those muskets carried by Quobah and himself, for the splashes of blood on his leggings, those tomahawks, war bags and that bulging pack.

With a lordly manner he pulled three fresh scalps out of a war bag and held them up, grinning like a boy exhibiting his first rabbit.

"*Wagh!* Alone Sakwari-cra did this!" Laure's admiration was genuine. "He is indeed a very great warrior!"

To her surprise Sakwari-cra abruptly abandoned his lofty bearing and tossed her a breechcloth of blue flannel. "For Taqua."

When, in affected carelessness, he tossed the *coups* onto the ground, Taqua, without being told, carried the scalps over to the brook, where she cleansed them of plasma and clotted blood before drying them with a handful of moss. Happily, she then arranged the smelly but warm blue material about her shoulders like a cape, which succeeded in protecting most of her back and breasts. To pin the cloth in place, she snapped off some cruel black spikes off a hawthorn.

Meanwhile, the gaunt Negro stood to one side obviously not knowing what to make of this pretty young white Indian whose hair was the color of the sun setting over the Gulf of Guinea. She must be a concubine such as he'd kept by the dozen in his princely *boma* near Kumassee on what the English called the "Gold Coast." He'd lived among Europeans long enough to feel sure that, whatever she was, she wasn't this Tuscarora's wife; as no sane warrior, black or red, would wed a female with such narrow hips—a sure indication that she'd be no good at bearing children.

Once the Catawba war bags had been emptied onto the ground Taqua was pleased when Sakwari-cra indicated that she might select moccasins which came the closest to fitting her normally long and narrow, but now seriously swollen, feet; her own were about worn through. There could be, however, no replacing Thad's ruined footgear without much recutting and stitching.

While hurriedly arranging her pack, Laure found herself stealing glances at this impressive black giant so completely dissimilar to those ebony-hued slaves owned by the Creeks who had earlier escaped from English plantations near the Bitter Water.

For instance, this towering savage's metallic-looking skin was not decorated by tattooing, but with strange patterns of cicatrices. For another thing, the gums supporting his dog-like teeth were bluish not pink.

Once the captured goods had been divided into self-sufficient loads, in case someone became separated from his companions, the three slipped on their packs and were preparing to move on when Sakwari-cra stalked over to Taqua and looked steadily into her eyes a long moment before passing over a knife and a hatchet.

Standing straight, slim, and warm under her contrived cape, the red-haired girl impassively accepted the weapons, betrayed nothing of her surprise and hidden happiness.

At a steady dogtrot Thad then led off along a series of indistinct game trails which, in these parts, meandered in a generally northeasterly direction through dense hardwood forests. He didn't pause until the sun had climbed as high as it was going to.

Chapter 10

THE ASHANTI II

Thad Burton halted for the second time when the runners became confronted by a mountain stream which tumbled in a hissing, boiling fury down a ravine hemmed in by magnificent larches, pines, and spruces.

After drinking, the white Tuscarora, with powder horn and gun held high above his head, waded waist-deep out into the icy, frothing current, then waved for his companions to follow. To their astonishment the Raven, instead of wading across, turned left and led them, slipping and scrambling, along the stream's course, which at this point ran in a south-easterly direction.

After an hour's laborious travel Sakwari-cra returned to dry ground on the edge of a small meadow. Dripping, he studied the terrain and was pleased to note several old windfalls nearby—an easy source of good firewood.

Because he'd twice slipped and gone completely under, Quobah shook himself like a dog, then lifted his thin, straight nose to sniff the breeze.

"Sar," he announced in English, which he spoke better than Creek or Spanish, "I smell cold wind coming."

Although it was only midafternoon and they could have traveled several miles more, Thad felt so confident of having shaken off pursuit that he nodded, "We stop here. Tonight much cold."

Without further conversation preparations were made to camp for the night—perhaps longer. When Thad and Laure began gathering materials with which to build a lean-to Quobah without explanation slipped into the forest. After a while the African returned grinning broadly and lugging over his shoulder a big, autumn-fat raccoon transfixed by a reed-shafted arrow of unusual length and fletching. He explained that he'd surprised the creature fishing at a little pool; then, with quick deftness, he skinned his prize.

About an hour before sunset the expected cold wind began to blow and since the meadow was set amid an almost perfect ring of high ridges Sakwari-cra allowed the kindling of a fire. Thad fumbled in his pack and pulled out another captured breechclout, which he draped about his shoulders; Quobah was given one too, but his cloth was wet and gave off tendrils of ill-smelling steam. Soon the surrounding pines began to sigh and complain in their lofty tops. It came as no surprise that, this high in the mountains, small, dry snowflakes presently began to sift through the branches and cause brief, minute hissing noises in the fire.

To supplement their meal, Taqua had found some red-brown chestnuts, discovered while collecting firewood, and just before dark Thad succeeded in scaring some sizable brook trout into a shallow pool and expertly scooped them onto dry ground.

Speckled by futile, delicate snowflakes, Thad and Quobah left Laure to unjoint the raccoon and clean the trout while they rendered the lean-to as tight and windproof as they could. Before the men had done, snow was whirling down in blinding, ever-denser squalls.

Once the fish and then the raccoon's meat—which much resembled chicken—had been consumed, chestnuts were pushed into the ashes to heat and split their husks. Replete, the three then squatted on their heels about the fire, outwardly content and relaxed, but not wholly trusting anyone.

Thad was thinking: How similar to an Indian are Quobah's movements and even his thoughts. He makes no more noise in the forest than an

Iroquois; he's just as proud and watchful and he takes even better care of his gun.

While a frigid wind hissed among unseen branches and snowflakes whirled across the firelight outside the lean-to, Thad sought the red stone pipe and bladder of tobacco he'd found in a Catawba war bag. After drawing a few puffs of the pungent, rank-smelling smoke he passed the pipe to Quobah, huddled under his shawling of breechcloth. Taqua watched the African's lips part in a wide grin.

"Thank 'ee, sar," said he, and, after he had thrice drawn on it, he returned the pipe. Then, in quiet dignity, he replenished the leaping, wind-twisted flames until it was almost comfortably warm in the lean-to.

In silence the oddly assorted trio for a while crouched under their thin coverings, staring at lovely patterns created by smoke and sparks in being whisked away by the whirling snow. Suddenly, Sakwari-cra sat up and, throwing back his head, began, in the time-honored fashion of a victorious warrior, to boast about his slaughter of the sleeping Catawbas.

"A prowling panther could not have reconnoitered the enemy camp with greater craftiness and skill. How stealthily I closed in and pounced. My blows were so swiftly and truly delivered that not one of the stupid Catawbas had time to wake up. My tomahawk I drove deep, but not too deep, into their heads so as not to spoil the scalps. Although they were three warriors, strong and full of life, they died under my blows as easily as little girls."

His voice swelled into a shout that momentarily drowned the storm's rising wails. "While they yet struggled Sakwari-cra took their hair and sprinkled them with their own blood. Then I defiled their foolish corpses. Attend me! This was a great deed for I was one against three and my only weapon was my *islafka*! For generations to come my name will be heard about council fires."

Sakwari-cra jumped up and ran out into the snow to fetch the trophies already stretched by Taqua over willow hoops. After dancing around the fire and brandishing the scalps on high he planted the frames where the smoke blew thickest that they might start curing.

When, finally, he reseated himself, Laure, softly oblique eyes lowered, predicted, "Soon the great Raven, Sakwari-cra, will become the Long Warrior among his people." To which Quobah agreed by nodding gravely.

While the fire leaped and sizzled in fighting with the snow the giant Negro felt called upon also to furnish entertainment. He brushed a powdering of snow from his turban before he said, "In Kumassee so great a feat would have won Sakwari-cra many cowrie shells, gold dust, and elephant's teeth. To his hut would have been brought many well-oiled maidens, young, sleek and ready for love."

Quobah's massive chin rose and the flames picked out the scar chevrons seaming his lean cheeks. "Osai Tutu, my father, Supreme King of the Ashanti people, would have heaped great honors on Sakwari-cra."

Inordinately pleased, Thad stalked through the all-permeating snow over to the woodpile to throw another stick onto the fire. Then curiosity prevailed over the Raven's dignity. "Kumassee is a town—big like Co-weta?"

"Much more big," solemnly assured the Ashanti. "It is chief town on what Danes and Portuguese call the Gold Coast—between the Ivory and Slave Coasts. Quobah great soldier too. Once wore necklace of ears and man-parts cut off Fulah and Fanti soldiers. Quobah not count ears from children, women or old men."

In curt appreciation, Thad nodded. "Where is this fine necklace?"

The triple chevron of cicatrices on Quobah's forehead became merged in a ferocious scowl. "Lost when great army of treacherous, jackal-descended Denkaras attack Kumassee in time of peace. Slew the King, my father, and many others." He glowered at his great knobby hands. "Quobah captured after hard fight." A grayish forefinger touched a long scar coiling across his left arm. "Kill everything, even goats and dogs. Spare only big children, women and men who were young and strong."

Unexpectedly, Taqua invited, "Then?"

The frown on the African's scarred features deepened and his lips flat-tened. By the firelight his eyes glowed like an animal's. "For many days Denkaras drive Quobah and his peoples, all under slave yokes, through jungle to a place on the sea called Khristiansborg."

The girl shivered and, drawing the flannel loincloth tighter about her shoulders, edged closer to the flames. Her breath showed briefly as a golden mist before it was whipped away. "What are 'slave yokes'?"

The Ashanti didn't look at her when he said, "A heavy forked branch bolted across back of captive's neck. At last *koffle* reach great Danish castle on a river." He pursed bluish lips and spat into coals where his spittle hissed and bubbled briefly.

The wind in tearing over the high forest, made a noise like the thunder of distant breakers and created back-eddies which blew a steady current of fine ice crystals into the lean-to and forced its occupants to huddle closer together.

Over the cheerful sparkle and staccato crackling of hickory sticks Quobah continued, "Three moons Quobah and his men lay chained in Danishman's barracoon. Slaves taken from many peoples—Dagombas, Mandingos, Yorubas and such miserable lice—were brought in and sold quick. But nobody buy an Ashanti."

Thad sucked hard at his reloaded pipe. "Why?"

Under his faded red turban Quobah's massive head lifted in a prideful motion. "Slave traders feared buy Ashantis; like Senegals they all fighting

men who not make good field hands. One day the factor ask price so low
an Englishman buy and we go on ship, double-shackled."

Quobah broke off when Sakwari-cra, without expression, suddenly
pulled Taqua onto his lap, then slipped hard hands under her cape to
cup and warm her chilled breasts.

"—many die from spotted fever before slaver come to Port Antonio on
island called 'Jamaica.'" Quobah's round, yellow and black eyes widened
and again he scowled. "Quobah bought by clever planter."

"Clever?" queried the white Tuscarora, whose snow-powdered crest
nodded now and then under the frigid blast. The girl now had slipped
both arms about him and had allowed her head to sink onto his shoulder.
Gradually, the tenseness of her slim but solid frame began to lessen.

"Yes. Because Mastuh Wilkes knew well-fed, well-kept slaves work
harder; he not beat they much. Mastuh, too, knew men from warrior
tribes no good for common labor," Quobah said proudly, then sniffed,
"They not like stinking Ebos and Yorubas."

Layers of powdery snow began to slide off the evergreens; the ground
received it soundlessly. Flakes mingling with wisps of smoke swayed and
swirled about the fire like ethereal ballet dancers executing endless
pirouettes.

"In Jamaica Quobah learn speak English; catch fish for Mastuh Wilkes.
He happy. In sail canoe he almost like free man except he must wear
iron slave collar." He held up a hand with three fingers extended, "So
many rainy seasons Quobah hunt on water, then one day *Ispani* boat
catch him, take him to Havana to be sold again. But Quobah make new
mastuh so much trouble he sold Quobah to mastuh's brother in Spanish
port, San Augustín. There Quobah hunted deerskins until," he held up
both hands, fingers spraddled, "many moons ago he run away, take off
iron collar, join Yuchi tribe."

"That is how Quobah learn Creek tongue," softly murmured Taqua,
conscious of the strong, slow beat of Thad's heart against her side. He
must have sensed her reaction, for he pressed her even tighter to him and
appreciated, for the first time, what a warm and hard yet soft body she
had.

"Why you leave Yuchis?" persisted Taqua.

Without shifting his gaze from the snow-sparkled flames the gaunt
African continued, "One day Quobah's squaw warn that Yuchi wizard
was planning to betray him to San Augustín for reward." Employing a
splinter, the Ashanti prince interrupted himself long enough to dislodge
a shred of raccoon flesh from between pointed, ivory-hued teeth. "Quobah
wait for good time to slay wizard and escape." His voice dropped to a
growl, "Quobah *never* slave again! For half a moon Quobah run toward

setting sun." The black giant grinned under his improvised shawl. "Then he find Sakwari-cra's trail where he left game path. That is all."

While talking, the Ashanti, at the same time, had attempted to make a better estimate of his companions. But he didn't succeed too well beyond establishing that both were pure whites, not half-breeds as he'd thought to begin with. Only the color of their hair, the undertint of their skins, and their European eyes distinguished them from true Indians; their manner, their speech, the way they moved, and their ceaseless vigilance all were typically Indian.

On one point Quobah felt certain: this tall young Raven, no matter what his origin, was a born leader of warriors and, if he lived for a while, he undoubtedly would become a great general. No doubt remained in Quobah's mind that Sakwari-cra was not only fearless, but also shrewd, farsighted, and war-wise for so young a man. Silently, he reasoned that, for the present at least, this white Tuscarora might be a good man with whom to ally himself.

Although a squaw, and a captive one at that, Taqua, also, was possessed of an indefinable strength of character. For the life of him, the big African couldn't decide whether this red-haired female, for all her meekness, wasn't playing a waiting game and biding her time to get rid of her captor one way or another. If she succeeded, he intended taking her over.

After tossing an armload of branches on the fire, Quobah, being the first to stand guard, went over to crouch on his heels at one end of the lean-to while his companions, locked in close embrace, curled up on the bough bed and seemed to fall asleep right away; at least they didn't stir.

Chapter 11

GOGGLE-EYES' VILLAGE

During the next five days the three wanderers worked cautiously down from the Great Smokies into heavily wooded foothills studding a wide valley limited on its east side by the Chattooga Range. Sometimes Sakwari-cra, freshly painted—he had come across some colors in the Catawba war bags—silently led along game paths which paralleled streams that gradually broadened and plunged less precipitously toward densely forested lowlands. Sometimes they were able to make good time by using an Indian trail which appeared to trend southeast.

On several occasions snow fell in a halfhearted way among the foothills, but this soon melted, much to the travelers' satisfaction; it wasn't safe to leave behind easily visible footsteps. As the altitude continued to diminish the air grew warmer, so rain or sleet fell instead of snow.

In ever-increasing numbers herds of woods buffalo, deer, and elk were sighted grazing on broad, brown meadows or in natural clearings in the woods.

On the sixth day of their descent Thad Burton, Laure Rivard, and Quobah Tutu encountered the first of many desolate Indian fields; some evidently had been deserted long ago—others had been abandoned more recently.

Around such admirable feeding places Quobah's reed arrows brought down all the meat they needed; several days earlier, Sakwari-cra had decided that it would be unsafe to use firearms for all that, by now, they must be well south of the Catawbas' hunting grounds and probably were traversing land held by such minor Creek tribes as the Abecas, Tallapoosas, and Coosaws—none of whom were reported to be numerous or especially warlike. As far as Sakwari-cra knew, the Lower or Atali Creeks and the Tuscaroras were now at peace, so there shouldn't be trouble, but one never could be sure. It was fine, in a measure, to relax the ceaseless vigilance.

In this gentler terrain Taqua found occasion to admire strange trees and plants, unfamiliar and often delightfully bright-hued birds. Gradually, Laure commenced to regain weight and to pay more attention to her appearance now that those terrible scratches she'd suffered during the great run had dropped their scabs and had begun to pale out.

Once more she took to twisting her hair into a bun secured by a turkey bone sliver and a length of rather inferior white wampum instead of allowing it slat against her shoulders in a coarse pigtail. She repaired rents in her kilt and recut the loincloth into a proper cape which, while it protected her shoulders and back, did little to shelter her breasts and abdomen.

One gray day the travelers came to a place where a number of Indian trails converged at the head of a little valley. While a few of these trails seemed to have been used recently, most suggested that they hadn't been traveled for a long time; a fact which was both disquieting and puzzling.

At the junction of the trails the men paused long enough to add a few stones to a rough cairn marking the spot where some celebrated warrior had fallen in battle. It wouldn't have done to risk angering the departed hero's spirit. Oddly enough, the African didn't hesitate over making the tribute; it was, he said, a custom observed in his land, also.

Suddenly raising an arm, Quobah halted and sniffed loudly, like a good hunting dog, testing the wind. "Smoke from that way."

He pointed across a frosty meadow toward a rocky ridge crested with majestic hardwoods. Once they were able to peer over its rim they saw a small, palisaded village lying beside a swift-running river. What immediately puzzled the travelers was that smoke was rising from only four out of the dozen-and-a-half dwellings below. Down there only few signs of activity were noticeable; a trio of small, brown-skinned boys listlessly herding lean pigs and half-a-dozen scrawny horses.

No cows were in evidence, which didn't surprise the onlookers; few Indian tribes knew or wanted to keep "the white man's buffalo," which required too much feed and care. With interest, Sakwari-cra noted that a broad trace leading to the village's half-opened gate showed little sign of use except for the flock of chickens scratching busily before it.

Taqua caught her breath, muttered, "The spotted sickness must have struck here."

Her companions grunted assent when they noticed that, at no great distance outside the palisade, a good many whitening skulls and other human bones lay among winter-killed weeds. All had been ruthlessly scattered by buzzards, bears, wolves, and foxes.

Thad thought, The sickness behind that sagging palisade must have been severe; for no other reason would Creeks dispose of their dead in so undignified a fashion. All Muskogean tribes were meticulous about burying their dead to the accompaniment of solemn rites, in a sitting position under the floor of that cabin which had been inhabited by the deceased. Such a dwelling never was torn down; the bereaved family merely built and moved to a new one.

After studying the village for a long while and observing only a few people, Sakwari-cra decided that it would be safe to descend. Taqua now carried Quobah's bow and arrows, with which she had become fairly proficient. All the same, the travelers crawled soundlessly through tangles of vines, underbrush, and dead weeds until they gained the edge of a sandy gray field in which a scattering of withered cornstalks drooped like the pennons of a defeated army. A few crows foraging among them promptly spied the skirmishers and flapped off toward the woods, raising a raucous alarm.

A few yards short of the half-open main gate Sakwari-cra halted and raised the *tchuku*, that long-drawn peace cry, common to all Muskogean tribes, which differed sharply from the *tiwa*, or scalp yell. The only immediate response came from a pack of fierce mongrels such as the Creeks employed in running elk and deer. Although these yelped valiantly and bared their fangs, they were dispersed by a few well-directed kicks and flung stones. Above their yipping arose shrill woman cries and the sound of slamming doors. Never a man's voice was heard.

Following a pause, the wanderers made bold to advance and peer inside the palisade. Aside from the usual council house they saw only a few puncheon-built cabins and some round lodges covered with wide strips of cedar bark. Among these, scrawny, brown-black pigs continued to root unconcerned.

Finally, an old man swayed to the doorway of one of the larger huts and raised a skinny arm, blue with faded tattooing, to make the peace sign. Peering over his bent shoulders shone the eyes of two squaws, who held guns ready to be passed to this ancient.

Sakwari-cra and Quobah halted with muskets leveled; Taqua, arrow on string, stood to one side. Narrowly, the Tuscarora Raven scanned the nearest habitations, which appeared to be deserted, but about that he couldn't be too certain.

Finally, Sakwari-cra called out, "Old man, we come in peace."

"Then be welcome to Guaxule," the old man called in a thin, cracked voice.

Taqua peered in all directions when various doors were unbarred to disclose apprehensive brown faces, most of them small.

"How many do you number?" slyly demanded the ancient.

Thad lied, "We number many more, but they remain in the woods."

Quobah's turbaned head swung toward the gate. "Take care, Sakwari-cra. Young men may be hunting, soon come back."

The old man, supporting himself on a spear, hobbled out on bowed legs. "Turkey Head will lead you to our mico, Steyamaschee."

At once it became obvious that the disease which had stricken Guaxule indeed must have been the smallpox or spotted fever; red-brown scabs typical of that malady were visible on many faces and bodies.

At the council house's entrance Sakwari-cra and the African paused, peered suspiciously into its dim interior. They saw that, despite the epidemic, it was as clean as so important a building usually was kept. It seemed deserted save for a single figure seated, cross-legged, on a black buffalo's hide. Under a mantle of otter skins Steyamaschee suggested a certain dignity despite deeply wrinkled face, gray-streaked hair, and shriveled chest. Thad Burton at once noticed this aged chief's large, glittering, and extraordinarily protuberant black eyes. In silence the intruders watched Turkey Head, the old man who had greeted them, go to squat among the shadows behind his mico.

The two tall but otherwise dissimilar newcomers waited with their shadows dimly slanting across the council house's earthen floor, for someone to break the silence.

At length the ancient mico spoke and with great dignity. "Greetings, Raven. You wear Tuscarora ornaments, yet you say you come in peace?"

Thad thought fast and, although he wasn't sure about it, replied, "There is peace now between the Six Nations and both the Upper and Lower Creeks. Who are you?"

"Strangers," cried Turkey Head, "you stand in the presence of Steyamaschee, mico of the Abecas of Guaxule, who are kin to the Lower Creeks. The *Englasi* traders call him Goggle-Eyes." His voice swelled until it sounded like that of a much younger man. "Once Steyamaschee was ruler of four towns greater than this; he could command ten-times-ten warriors when the war pipe was lit by the Grand Council and the red sticks were sent out."

Haughtily, Sakwari-cra drew himself to full height then advanced toward the mico's dais, pretty sure by now that, to all intents, this village lay defenseless. Taking care that the Catawba scalps dangling from his belt were not being ignored, he cried in a great voice that carried to the farthest dwellings in Guaxule, "Greetings from He-Who-Trails-a-Spear, who is a famous Raven among the Tuscarora, who belongs to the noble Turtle Clan!"

Arrogantly, Thad tapped the three skeins of blue-black hair. "He counts twice five more *tiwas*."

Goggle-Eyes blinked, peered at this haughty young warrior, then spoke. "Since you say there is no war between my people and yours you are welcome to stay among us and eat of our food—what there is of it. My people have sorely been stricken."

Time to be polite, thought Thad, and unbent. "We shall find honor in doing so, O mighty Mico."

"That is well, especially if you and your great Black-faced One will agree to hunt with us this winter." Sakwari-cra could tell that the role of suppliant was unfamiliar and distasteful to Goggle-Eyes as he confessed, "Only two young men in Guaxule remain fit to hunt."

Was it truly so? Again, a strong suspicion occurred that this was a ruse designed to detain him until a party of Abeca hunters should return and surprise him and his companions.

Thad turned to Turkey Head. "Before Sakwari-cra agrees to this he will look about Guaxule."

He in the shadows said in a weary voice, "Look where you will, my Brothers, and if you see more than two strong men take this." He reached up and tapped his sparse, gray scalp lock.

"Think well, Sakwari-cra, my brother," Quobah advised in English. "Perhaps we take spotted sickness if we stay."

At the Negro's unexpected English both Abeca elders looked amazed.

"That depends," Thad answered in the same language, "on how long ago the sickness has left this place."

It was the white Tuscarora's turn to be astonished when old Goggle-Eyes said in guttural English, "The last of my people died two moons ago." His protuberant eyes fixed themselves on the white man's face, disguised by a design done in yellow and blue paint. "Sakwari-cra has suffered it?"

Thad nodded. "Many seasons ago."

Long since he'd noticed pockmarks among the scars on Quobah's jet features; about Taqua he didn't know. He stalked out to the gate where the young woman stood lookout.

"You have had the spotted sickness?"

"Perhaps. There was once spotted fever in Tosneoc."

"Taqua would be afraid to linger in Guaxule now that the sickness has passed?"

Laure Rivard's slanted gray-green eyes swung up to meet his gray-blue ones. "One has heard that, sometimes, the spotted sickness returns after many moons."

Flushing, the girl fiddled with Quobah's bowstring, stared fixedly across the wasted cornfields, then said in a low tone, "Taqua is not afraid if Sakwari-cra stays."

It soon became evident that Guaxule's survivors were most anxious for these wanderers to winter with them. No wonder: they numbered only four grown men, two of whom were away hunting. There also were five youths, the oldest being about fourteen, twelve squaws, and fourteen children and babies, all of whom had taken the pox in a light form.

Up until now the community had been dependent upon an inadequate supply of game brought in by two young warriors: Spotted Tail and Buffalo Calf.

When a careful search of Guaxule disclosed that no other fighting men remained, Sakwari-cra told Goggle-Eyes that they would stay. With winter closing in it was hard to see how he and his companions could hope to improve their prospects by not remaining in Guaxule.

Chapter 12

LONG, HARD WINTER

Thad Burton's decision to winter in Guaxule proved to be a wise one; from the day of his party's arrival the weather steadily grew colder, for the ravaged village lay high among the Chattooga foothills. Sleet fell in place of rain; it snowed and often for Taqua's enjoyment created indescribably lovely and crystalline vistas. The Little Chattooga River began to cast out from its shores fragile fringes of ice; frost coated little backwaters, but, because of its swift current, the stream never froze wholly over, even in the bitterest weather.

The depth of the frost this year was quite unprecedented, according to Turkey Head and Kadapaw, an evil-visaged conjurer who one stormy day had come stumbling into Guaxule, lost and starving. He claimed to be the sole survivor of a plague-stricken village lying on the other side of the Chattoogas.

Once Sakwari-cra became assured that Goggle-Eyes entertained no idea of treachery he and Quobah hunted hard and brought in plenty of game. One and all, the Abecas were delighted by the number of deer, elk, and wood buffalo carcasses fetched in, slung, limp and gutted, across pack horses.

Thad guarded the secret of his successful hunting with care; he never allowed the two Abeca hunters, Spotted Tail and Buffalo Calf, to go along when he and Quobah disappeared into the woods.

Although Goggle-Eyes' remaining warriors attempted in various ways to penetrate the mystery, they got nowhere because, inevitably, Sakwari-cra sensed that he was being trailed, so went nowhere near a little cave in which he stored his stalking head and skin—an invaluable hunting aid apparently unknown hereabouts. This device consisted of the crudely stuffed head and neck of an antlered buck to which the body's skin remained attached.

By leaning on the forelegs, stiffened with sticks, and walking bent well forward with the hide distended over hickory hoops trailing behind him, the white Tuscarora counterfeited the movements of a browsing deer so accurately that usually was able to come close enough to his quarry to drop it with a well-placed arrow. Powder was far too precious to be used short of dire necessity—besides, too much shooting surely would move game out of the vicinity.

So proficient did Sakwari-cra and the African become at this form of hunting that soon considerable piles of erotic-smelling deerskins began to accumulate in their cabins.

For the white Tuscarora life had become agreeable beyond all precedent after he had taken Taqua to live in the snuggest of the death-emptied dwellings. Both were confident that smallpox had departed from Guaxule —until the next visitation.

Quobah, who had filled out considerably since his arrival in Guaxule, shifted for himself until Goggle-Eyes sent a strong, rather ugly and generally silent young widow named Hapeyah to cook and care for him in any fashion he wanted. The oddly assorted couple appeared to be entirely content with such an arrangement and, without visible emotion, set up housekeeping.

This way of life prevailed long after the mountaintops became permanently snow-covered and the last V's of honking Canada geese had honked by to complete their migration on the warm waters of the gulf named "Mehico."

For all that this winter became unusually severe the inhabitants of Goggle-Eyes' village found nothing to complain about since so few mouths remained to be fed and the plentiful supply of meat brought in by the hunters was supplemented by partridge, quail, rabbits, and other small game trapped or snared by the old men and boys.

During long gray weeks which were interspersed with occasional bright and sunny days, no notable event took place in Guaxule save that a middle-aged, thirty-year-old widow gave birth, but, because she'd suffered from the spotted fever, the infant was born dead—a dire omen. The Abecas became even more deeply depressed when the widow died too. Although no one, with exception of Kadapaw, the wizard, referred to these losses, it was evident that the villagers remained convinced that this by no means marked the sum of the evil events in store for them.

By contrast an atmosphere approaching happiness prevailed within the smoky, slab-roofed cabin Thad Burton shared with Laure Rivard. For both of them it was a new experience thus to share life with just one other; it was enjoyable to be able to make love in private and not in a crowded lodge.

Once, when replete with a meal of roast partridge and bear's paws, Thad remarked that Taqua had grown sleek and pretty as a turkey hen. Her waist-long hair now shone like well-polished copper and lately she'd taken to dressing her tresses in various new ways. This, of course, set the Abeca squaws to making disparaging comments. When they did so she only stuck out her tongue, shrugged, and went on tanning deerskins.

Nowadays Laure went about wearing a lynx-skin shirt, a long kilt, and a beaver jacket fashioned out of skins presented by Sakwari-cra.

While her master was away hunting she would cut and sew for him knee-high moccasins, elaborately decorated fringed hunting shirts, and thigh-high leggings of soft, pale buckskin. Also she fashioned for her man a loose cape of rabbit fur to which she affixed a hood with a drawstring which might easily be lifted into position and tightened whenever it sleeted or snowed. No one in Guaxule had ever seen the like of it.

Finally, Laure surprised herself by trying to make up little songs while working. She never thought of complaining when a contrary wind drove acrid, eye-stinging fumes back down the smoke hole in the roof and started tears streaming down her heated cheeks. Why complain? This was to be expected. Nevertheless, she welcomed an excuse to go outdoors to fetch firewood, to pluck a grouse, or tramp the woods in search of that soft, dry moss with which she refreshed her body hammock. When at certain times she was forced to do this more frequently she wondered why her periods lasted so much longer than those of her brown-skinned sisters.

Although neither she nor Thad realized it, their white ancestry gradually was manifesting itself in the ever-increasing duration of their conversation. On occasion they discussed subjects which no warrior, let alone a Raven, would ever have condescended to mention to a mere female.

She felt fairly sure that Sakwari-cra no longer felt contempt for his concubine; in fact, he grinned, now and then, and once he'd even laughed out loud.

To Laure Rivard's surprise she now found herself anticipating, rather than dreading, the moment when darkness would envelop the smoky little cabin and she would go to bank hardwood coals with ashes for the night. Sometimes she quivered with eagerness while turning back their light, but warm, sleeping robes of buffalo calfskins. Expressionless, his stiff crest nodding gently, Thad would look on from among the shadows while she, with no trace of false modesty, stripped naked before sliding into their deep and comfortable spruce-tip couch.

Soon he would remove garments smelling of sweat and bear's grease. Then his huge, hard figure would cause the spruce branches to crackle just before his arms closed about her. They never kissed—Indians hadn't yet learned that pleasure—but, tenderly, she would press her cheek against the soft, golden curls matting his chest, while waiting to learn whether he wished to claim her more intimately.

Never, among the few honored guests which the Mico of Tosneoc had ordered her to sleep with, had she ever approached such ecstatic transports as when Sakwari-cra entered her. Later, when bathed in perspiration and with the robes sticking to their skins, Laure would remind herself of how very lucky she was to be favored of this great runner, this mighty warrior and cunning hunter. It also pleased her that, more and more, old Goggle-Eyes preferred Sakwari-cra's advice to that of his nephews, Spotted Tail and Buffalo Calf.

However, it seemed that the longer she lived with the white Tuscarora the less she understood him or his way of thinking. How different he was from the other great warriors she had observed. Whereas a Catawba brave at a feast gobbled and drank as much as he could hold, Sakwari-cra was comparatively abstemious and so didn't fall down drunk or snore in gorged slumber. Always listened attentively when famous chiefs spoke of battles, ambushes, and raids or described examples of shrewd strategy.

When diplomatic or trade relations with white men were discussed he listened in rapt attention. She also had come to understand that Thad was enormously ambitious and perhaps dangerously self-confident.

She turned onto her side and, by the flickering flames, stared at his profile as if she'd never before beheld it. Deliberately, her long-lashed eyes slowly traveled over his high, broad forehead, straight, well-shaped nose, rather thin lips, and strong, angular jaw.

What did he think about when he sat, as he often did, staring into the sunset or using a stick to trace meaningless designs on the ground before him?

And what about Quobah, that fierce, capable, and generally silent lieutenant of Thad's who seemed such a perfect compliment to Sakwari-cra? Was he, too, developing plans?

One thing was sure, she must never let Sakwari-cra suspect that she was wondering such things. To Thad's rhythmic breathing, she also fell asleep.

Quobah, in his inarticulate fashion, found almost as much happiness in living with Hapeyah, otherwise "Bright Feather." Badly disfigured, widowed by smallpox, the ugly little woman worked extra hard to make up for her misfortunes. She was proud to share this sable warrior's cabin, to cook, to skin the game he brought in, and gladly ministered to his other needs. *Wagh!* No Creek was better built to keep a squaw content than the "Black Panther"—as the Abecas had named him.

One late winter morning while killing turkeys in an alder thicket, Sakwari-cra and Quobah, at the same instant, froze into immobility. From the valley below them had come the faint *clink!-clink!* of metal striking metal.

At once the pair commenced to drift soundlessly down leafless hardwood slopes toward a clump of dark green laurels sprouting from a mound of lichen-gray boulders. Thus concealed, they should be able to get a clear view of that age-old trader's trace coming in from the east.

Once Sakwari-cra had scraped aside enough forest mold to enable him to put his ear to the bare earth he listened awhile, then his gray-blue eyes flickered upward. "Run, Quobah, and tell Goggle-Eyes to close the gate. Armed men on horses are coming. Send boys to bring in Spotted Tail and Buffalo Calf."

Soundless as a hunting owl, the African wriggled backward until he came to the turkeys they'd killed, and paused only long enough to catch up the beautiful bronze-black birds and to sling them over his shoulder before he raced off toward Guaxule.

Thad remained pressed flat to the ground; only his eyes showed between a narrow gap between two boulders. Yes. Undoubtedly a good many horses were drawing near; there could be no mistaking the sucking *squelch!-squelch!* caused by hoofs along one of those mucky runlets which so often followed the course of a forest trail.

The watcher hadn't long to wait before a mounted Indian appeared. Judging by the tall, coarse black crest running from the nape of his neck forward across his shaven head, he undoubtedly was a Creek. The Indian rode bareback, his chunky, dark-skinned body responding rhythmically to the pony's pace; his dark eyes ceaselessly probed the terrain in all directions.

Presently two more Creeks, wearing dirty, blue-and-white Dutch blanket coats, walked into sight. Sakwari-cra grinned like a winter wolf; both were shouldering fairly new English-made muskets!

Next to round a clump of rhododendrons was another horseman; this time it was a lean, narrow-shouldered white man wearing a bushy light brown beard stained by tobacco juice. Pushed back on his head was a shapeless hat of bedraggled red fox fur, the white-tipped tail of which swayed over his leather-covered back.

Like the Creek warrior riding point, he was balancing a short-barreled, brass-bound musket across his pommel, ready for immediate use. Restlessly, his eyes studied his surroundings. He had "Indian trader" written all over him. A thin blanket roll was strapped across his saddle's cantle, riding above two muddied and bulging buckskin saddlebags. To the trader's pommel a brace of heavy horse pistols were slung European-style.

Thad quickly estimated that this sinewy, tawny-bearded trader wouldn't stand very tall but, all the same, he looked almighty tough and capable of instant decision and action.

At the white man's heel trudged a dismounted, thin-shanked Creek who gripped the lead rope of a pack horse into the tail of which was knotted the halter of a second animal; a third beast similarly was attached to the tail of the second. Next in the pack train splashed a bandy-legged

Negro wearing a brown coat of stroud cloth and a greasy, gray felt hat with a broken brim. He, too, was leading a short string of shaggy pack animals.

The next rider to round the rhododendron thicket immediately held Thad Burton's attention. At first he took this rider for a white woman because her skin shone such a rich, golden-white, but when he glimpsed her thin, aquiline nose, high cheekbones, jet-black hair and eyes he decided that she must be a half-breed—probably a Creek of noble descent if that lithe figure, held so erect and easy in the saddle, indicated anything at all.

When her tall black horse splashed nearer the hidden watcher he became aware that this long-legged female was wearing a man's fringed buckskin breeches, handsome red gauntlets, and a cape of oiled leather. He estimated that she must have survived about thirty winters.

She passed close enough for him to see that her eyes were large and alert. A thrown-back hood disclosed hair neatly plaited into a thick bun that gleamed blue-black above the nape of her neck. Several strands of what looked to be very fine *pe-ak* secured this chignon. Sakwari-cra also had time to note that this striking figure's mouth was wide, straight, and with narrow lips the color of ripe sumach berries; her brows were gently arched but a trifle heavy.

In the crook of her arm rested a light, silver-mounted carbine, the stock of which had been lavishly decorated with inlays of pearl shell and ivory.

Immediately in her wake strode two straight-backed Indians who looked more like Cherokees than Creeks. They were guarding three muddy-legged and heavily burdened Indian slaves.

Bringing up the rear was a pair of light-skinned Cherokees who kept on turning fierce, tattooed faces over their shoulders.

When he'd made sure that this column included no more than fourteen people and definitely was not a war party, Sakwari-cra breathed easier. Beyond a doubt here was a Carolina trader traveling unusually early in the year to anticipate his competitors and so secure the cream of this winter's fur and skin crop.

But what was that aristocratic and important-appearing half-breed woman doing here?

Chapter 13

THE MUSGROVES I

The frenzied barking of Guaxule's dogs warned of Sakwari-cra's approach long before the slow-moving pack train could be expected to arrive. To the Tuscarora Raven's astonishment the palisade's gate was standing open and he discovered Goggle-Eyes and Turkey Head, freshly painted for peace and placidly smoking outside the council house. Potbellied, owl-eyed children were playing as usual among the cabins; women were chopping firewood, cleaning game, or pounding dried corn and acorns into flour.

Why hadn't Quobah roused the village? Could he possibly not have arrived? No. There he was seated on his cabin's threshold!

It soon turned out that the Ashanti had decided to double back before setting out for Guaxule to scan the strangers personally. In a rage, Thad cursed the Negro's insubordination, then strode over to the Council House.

Goggle-Eyes explained without emotion, "From what Black Panther says this Englishman who travels with a pale-faced squaw is my friend called Tsul the Fox—John Musgrove among his own people."

"And who is this squaw?"

The old man's popping eyes batted twice. "His wife, Mary Musgrove. On her mother's side she is Princess Coosa-pona-keesa of the Bear Clan. She is daughter to a sister of Old Brims, who, until he died, was great emperor over all Creeks. Only ten and five winters ago he went to dwell in the Land-above-the Sky."

"Old Brims?" Thad repeated. "His name is heard even by the Iroquois."

Turkey Head nodded, a clump of green mallard feathers on his topknot fluttering. "Old Brims was the most famous great warrior among many generations."

"Who was father of Princess Coosa-pona-keesa?"

Meditatively, Goggle-Eyes scratched at the innumerable fleabites scarring his withered arms. "Not even the *aliktchas*—the wizards—are sure. But most *Englasi* traders think he may have been John Griffith from South Carolina."

Using a crooked finger, Thad eased his quiver's sling. "Tsul's squaw rides like man."

"Yes. For a squaw, Coosa-pona-keesa is very wise," Turkey Head informed him. "Her tongue uses English, Creek, Cherokee and Yamasee."

"English?"

"When Coosa-pona-keesa was as short corn she dwelt many seasons among the *Englasi*—or so it is said."

Later, Sakwari-cra was to learn that John Musgrove was also a member of the South Carolina Assembly, where he was much respected for his intimate knowledge of Indian affairs. As a trader, he was well and favorably known for his shrewd but invariably fair trading.

After pausing long enough at his cabin to redo his topknot and allow Taqua to daub yellow and green peace paint on his face he brusquely told her to start preparing food for important guests.

Taking care to make loud talk, Sakwari-cra and his big black companion rode slowly along that trail which paralleled the upper reaches of the Chauga River. They counted on intercepting Musgrove's pack train about two miles east of Guaxule.

Ever wary, Thad Burton took the precaution of reining in on the pine-crowned summit of a ridge where he and the African could be sighted from a considerable distance.

Once Musgrove's leading scout sighted the white and the black warriors he turned and cantered back to the main body. Soon John Musgrove trotted forward and leisurely raised his right hand with palm outturned.

As the trader-politician rode up Thad noted that John Musgrove—the first white man he'd ever seen close-to—was wearing a handsome deep-fringed hunting shirt of bleached buckskin bearing on its breasts and shoulders designs done in beading and red- and yellow-dyed porcupine quills.

The trader's eyes were of a peculiarly piercing blue and always seemed to be exploring the horizon—like those of a sailor—even when, in fact, he was regarding some nearby object. He'd a long, sharp nose and a tawny-red beard, and bristling mustachios of the same hue. Small wonder he was called Tsul the Fox! He might, Thad judged, have seen some forty seasons wax and wane and stood around five and a half feet tall.

When Musgrove reined to a halt Quobah and his companion noted that a bluish powder burn had erased half of his right eyebrow; also that he'd lost the middle finger on his left hand.

From beneath John Musgrove's fox-tailed hat burst a shock of coarse reddish-brown hair which looked as if it had been hacked short just a while ago.

In fluent Creek, he greeted, "*Tchuku-ofan laïkas Guaxule?* May I rest my people in Guaxule?"

Meanwhile, his curiously searching eyes busied themselves with this oddly assorted pair who had ridden out to intercept him.

Why, the trader was wondering, would this powerful young white, obviously a renegade, be wearing a Tuscarora's topknot and ornaments when the nearest Iroquois town lay all of a fortnight's hard riding to the north? What was this giant doing in Steyamaschee's country?

One thing was sure: this figure towering on the big, bony bay horse must have lived among Indians for a very long while. Hum. Since he wore a Turtle Clan totem tattooed on his right forearm he couldn't be a nonentity; besides, there was an innate air of distinction about this young white savage.

Without seeming to, the trader's gaze shifted to the equally gigantic Negro. Although John Musgrove had seen hundreds of blacks in and about the Carolinas, he couldn't recall ever having seen the like of this ferocious figure with the sharp-filed teeth. He noted, also, that this blue-black man's nose was neither broad nor flat, like the typical African's, but was narrow, high-bridged, and somewhat hooked. On Musgrove he created an indelible impression as he sat a horse so small that his huge feet just cleared the ground. The sun picked out in detail the highly polished brass mountings of an ancient French musket and caused his scarlet turban to glow like fire.

Meanwhile, the pack train came up, but halted on the trail at a distance of fifty yards.

After returning the peace sign, Sakwari-cra demanded haughtily, "*Is-tanat*—who are you?"

"I am John Musgrove, known among his Creek friends as Tsul—the Fox." A faint grin gleamed in the depths of his reddish beard. "As my brothers, Steyamaschee and Turkey Head, know very well, Tsul is licensed by *Englasi* commissioners at Charles Town to trade here."

Thad kicked his horse forward, then announced in halting English, "Sakwari-cra brings greeting from Mico Steyamaschee, invites Tsul to camp near Guaxule."

Musgrove pointed to the Ashanti. "Thanks. Who's this?"

"He is my friend," stated Thad.

Quobah suddenly grinned, said in English, "A pleasure, sar, this meeting a honor. I, Quobah Tutu, Prince of Kumassee."

The chunky figure in bleached buckskins stared, then turned in his saddle and called over his shoulder, "Come up, Mary. Both these fellers speak English." He didn't feel called upon to add that neither of them spoke the language very well.

Once the pack train got underway again it reassured Thad to watch the guards uncock their guns and rest them across their pommels. He perceived, also, that the Cherokees among these escorts seemed noticeably taller, finer-featured, and lighter-skinned than their Creek companions.

At a slow singlefoot Mary Musgrove rode up calling in a rich, low voice, "Well, John, seems you owe me a stone marten's pelt. I *told* you one of them was a blackamoor!"

Under his nodding, six-inch topknot Thad's painted features hardened. How foolish and, worse than that, careless he'd been to flatter himself that he and Quobah had gone unnoticed!

She who had been Princess Coosa-pona-keesa rode near, a faint smile curving her wide, dark red lips. Then Thad became aware that Mrs. Musgrove's eyes weren't really black, but of a dark smoky-blue.

After her husband had presented Sakwari-cra, she demanded in rather singsong English, "Tell me, He-Who-Trails-a-Spear, how have they wintered in Steyamaschee's village?"

While the horses clumped along the trading trace Thad spoke in Creek—he didn't want to expose his poor knowledge of English. "They have not gone hungry, O Coosa-pona-keesa, because, during the Green Corn Moon, the spotted sickness killed many Abecas. There remain few mouths to be filled."

In keeping with Indian usage, neither of the Musgroves attempted to learn why a Tuscarora Raven and an Ashanti prince should have elected to winter in Guaxule; no more did Sakwari-cra volunteer an explanation; he merely wheeled his horse and led the way along the Little Chattooga, now full and frothing with the runoff of snows melting in the higher mountains.

By the time the sun disappeared amid a welter of yellow-and-gold clouds the Musgroves and their followers had made themselves at home near the palisade, where they might be safe from those who, yearning to plunder a pack train, might be following it westward.

Wisely, perhaps, the visitors prepared to pitch tents rather than occupy any of the empty cabins, for all that the smallpox had shown no signs of returning—much to Taqua's deep, if unspoken, relief. The horses, after Musgrove's Indian slaves had rubbed them down, were hobbled and turned out, under guard, to graze on the first blades of new grass showing in the brown fields.

To the Abecas it was fine again to witness so much activity; too long had their palisade echoed hollowly to a single set of footsteps, to a solitary child's cry, or to the lonesome sound made by someone chopping wood in the distance.

Laure Rivard experienced a shy but special pleasure when straight-backed Mary Musgrove stopped at her cabin. Gracefully, the aristocratic half-breed settled onto a stump to which Sakwari-cra had nailed a board for a back—for all that he still preferred to squat on his heels. To begin with, the caller remarked upon how wonderfully neat and clean this cabin was kept. Taqua flushed with embarrassed delight.

"How are you called?" the princess invited in Muskogean, because by now she'd ascertained that Sakwari-cra's concubine understood only a few words of English and could speak less.

Laure straightened, passed a slender, work-roughened hand over a forehead dampened by the cook fire's heat. Simply, she explained, "My Catawba foster parents named me 'Taqua.' "

Mary Musgrove smiled faintly. "Ah, the Fire Flower. What a very pretty name. Tell me, Taqua, have you ever worn European clothes?"

Laure stirred her squirrel and quail stew with unnecessary vigor, discreetly lowered her gaze. "No, Coosa-pona-keesa. Taqua has never even seen any, but she would not like being covered all the way at all times. If she needs to run she does not want her legs tied like that."

Mary Musgrove leaned forward resting elbows on knees. She frowned a little on recalling a rumor she'd heard, not so long ago, concerning some prodigious running done by two enemies of the Catawbas. Even they had had to admit that this feat of endurance was something shining, something to be remembered and told about.

So this red-haired young woman was she who had outrun the fleetest warriors among the Catawbas—she and her master, this extraordinary renegade who called himself Sakwari-cra—"He-Who-Trails-a-Spear."

Mary Musgrove returned to the present. "I understand. Sometimes I, too, wish to let my skin breathe all over, as in my childhood." She sighed softly. "Unfortunately, my husband's people believe it immodest, even shameful, to go about even half covered."

Laure looked up in frank curiosity; the fire created flaming tints in her loosely plaited braids. "Taqua does not understand. Surely it is good to feel the sun and the rain beat upon one's skin? Cloth holds old sweat, which smells bad."

Gravely, the trader's wife observed. "Many of the white people's ways I cannot understand even yet." Mary now spoke, not as to a European, but as to one of her mother's people.

With the weather growing warmer Taqua again had taken to going about bare to the waist, unconsciously statuesque and as magnificently proportioned as the Greek goddess Artemis.

Briefly, Mary Musgrove's liquid dark eyes held the red-haired girl's faintly oblique ones of gray-green. "What was—is your European name?"

"I once was told it is 'Laure Rivard.' "

"By whom?" Looking startled, Mary Musgrove delved into her amazing memory until she recalled the name of one Jacques Rivard, a Frenchman who once had traded among the Talahasses and Alibamus.

"A woman. Taqua does not remember her name."

Mary Musgrove pointed to the totem tattooed between Laure's round, upstanding breasts. "You are a Turtle." She added with a touch of condescension, "Were you of the Bear Clan I might—" She started to say "help you" but decided against it. Instead, she pointed to the cast-iron pot simmering on its lug pole. "We are lucky that one no longer has to cook with hot stones dropped into a bark pot."

The girl nodded shyly, it being the first time within memory that she'd ever found herself alone with any woman other than a full-blooded squaw.

"My husband, Tsul, and I heard from a wandering hunter in Amercario of the great run you made with Sakwari-cra. Even the Catawbas hold you in respect."

Taqua shrugged. "It was Sakwari-cra who killed the pursuers and saved us in the end."

Mary crossed over to inspect Sakwari-cra's hunting gear, hung with un-Indian-like orderliness from a row of pegs driven between logs. "And what are you cooking?"

"Partridges and squirrels. They are fat this year, but would taste better if I had real salt." She shrugged smooth, honey-hued shoulders. "It was used up half-a-moon ago."

"Tomorrow you shall have all you need," promised the stately half-Creek, standing pillar-straight above the cook place's ring of blackened stones. "Before John Griffith, my father, took me to Pon Pon in Carolina. I was a papoose then. There never was enough salt in Coweta."

As she arose from her squatting position Taqua was surprised to hear herself asking, "Was it in Pon Pon that Coosa-pona-keesa learned to speak so well with the *Englasi* tongue?"

"Yes. I dwelled among the *Englasi* about ten seasons before I was summoned back to Coweta, the chief town belonging to the emperor. Old Brims was my mother's brother," she added casually. Selecting a handful of black walnuts from a hickory splint basket, Mary fell to cracking them between powerful, pale brown hands. "How did you fare among the dark-skinned Catawbas?"

Laure exposed small and irregular teeth, which she kept uncommonly white through scrubbing them daily with the end of a chewed elder twig. "Well enough. Perhaps this was so because Taqua could remember no other life. Yes. She was happy enough until just after her *husquen-awing*—puberty rites—had been celebrated."

John Musgrove's wife understood and nodded almost imperceptibly; following such rites a nubile girl was expected, when directed by the mico, to lend her body to distinguished visitors and, on rare occasions, to a warrior who had accomplished some feat of valor.

Taqua knew she had been lucky in this respect because old Kadapaw, the Catawba *outacity*, secretly had been fascinated by her red hair and so had not told her to sleep with many guests, although this was considered an honor for an unmarried girl.

This custom, as Mary Musgrove was well aware, had also a practical significance; were a maiden unlucky enough to be barren the fact soon became known and then prospective husbands shied away.

Taqua had grieved that, evidently, she must belong to this class of unfortunate females. Never once had she missed repairing in due time to that cabin in which the village's menstruating women were sequestered.

While stirring water into dried fungus flour to make some tuckahoe bread, Laure Rivard thought it a fine thing that Sakwari-cra hadn't yet learned of her seeming inability to become pregnant; in return she was especially obedient and passionately co-operative under the buffalo robes. Perhaps, if, in time, she could bear him a child, then he just might decide to go through those simple marriage rites which would transform her from a captive concubine into Sakwari-cra's acknowledged First Squaw. Besides, had she not accomplished the long run with him?

With her first glance into the cabin's freshly whitewashed interior, Coosa-pona-keesa of course had understood the nature of the relationship with the white Tuscarora. While not a bit shocked, nevertheless, Mary Musgrove had been puzzled only because these young people both were full whites; their living together like this seemed a bit shameful.

Watching Taqua lay out cherrywood bowls, Mary wondered what would happen if these two ever tried to live among their own people. Through her own experience, she guessed that the odds against their finding happiness would be heavy, very heavy; they'd lived far too long among red men.

Mary said pleasantly as she started for the door, "If roasted meat is to be served before the council house tonight, please don't cook my husband's portion too much. Unlike an Indian, he doesn't abhor a little blood in his meat."

The feast offered by Steyamaschee was as bounteous as the season could produce: quotash pudding, boiled buffalo tongues, turkey, roasted venison chunks, squirrel and quail stew, and tuckahoe bread sweetened with willow sugar.

While licking his fingers free of quotash, Sakwari-cra attempted to conceal his resentment that John Musgrove allowed his wife to eat with the men instead of sending her to a separate place, there to squat and feed with the Abeca women and children. John Musgrove's sullen, copper-skinned slaves, of course, crouched in still another spot where they fought the village dogs for such scraps and half-gnawed bones as might be tossed in their direction.

Chapter 14

JOHN AND MARY MUSGROVE II

To Thad Burton it was significant that, while he'd been expected to cut meat with the mico, his brother, and the two Musgroves, Buffalo Calf and Spotted Tail had been sent to eat with Quobah and the restless-eyed pack-train guards.

Sakwari-cra was glad that the conversation was conducted in the Atali, or Lower Creek, dialect of Muskogean; he wouldn't have to risk misunderstanding as he did when English was spoken. During the course of the long-drawn-out repast he gathered that Musgrove of the mangled hand had set out something over a week earlier from his factory established in Estoto, an unimportant Yamacraw village which, the trader explained, lay on the Savannah River, not far from the sea. It was into this great stream that the Chauga rushing so noisily by Guaxule, eventually emptied.

Said Musgrove, emitting polite belches in tribute to Goggle-Eyes's hospitality, "This food is fine. I was hungry because for ten days we have followed the trail from Amercario and did not stop to cook much."

"Amercario?" Sakwari-cra asked. "Where is Amercario?"

"That is the capital of Tomo-chichi, mico thlucco of the Yamacraw people."

At the mention of Tomo-chichi both the mico and Turkey Head scowled and spat contemptuously into the fire.

Goggle-Eyes grunted, "*Hólwaki!* Why has this outlaw not yet met the dog's death he deserves?"

Thad cast an inquiring glance at Mary Musgrove, who, squatting on her heels, delicately was gnawing on a partridge's leg. Wiping grease from her lips with the back of her hand, she explained in English, "Many seasons ago Tomo-chichi offended Old Brims—even yet, nobody knows how—so he was forever banished from the Creek Nation. Taking friends and relatives and their slaves with him, he descended the Savannah until, near its mouth, he built a village on a bluff."

A series of yelps attested that the slaves again were driving off the village dogs.

"Since Tomo-chichi's people were few and he was a very wise man he set about collecting people from broken tribes."

Mary glanced at her bushy-bearded mate, who then took up the tale. "He established an outlaw tribe which are called the Yamacraws. They're mostly Creeks, but for all that, they're not recognized by the Great Creek Council at Coweta."

After a pipe equipped with three reed stems attached to a large, red-clay bowl had been lit, the men comfortably extended themselves on buffalo robes, belching and rumbling in their bellies.

Thad listened very attentively while John Musgrove continued talking. Among other matters he learned that an unlicensed trader named Sam Browne, by his cheating transactions, had caused so much resentment among the Alibamus that he'd been stripped of his goods and expelled from their territory. However, the rascal on reaching Charles Town some-how had succeeded in bribing his way to a pardon and the issuance of a new trading permit. Even now he was reported to be preparing an expedi-tion among the Elaté, or Over-the-Mountains Creeks.

"If he values his hair, Browne better not come this way," Musgrove remarked, combing food particles from his beard. "Damn him fer a cheat-ing bastard! His sort makes trouble fer us all."

The trader eased thongs securing the neck of his handsome hunting shirt. "Mary, suppose you tell 'em why Cunnel Bull's so keen about butterin' up Tomo-chichi—and the hull Creek Nation fer that matter."

Gravely, the half-breed considered the two Abecas, whose wrinkled faces were deeply etched by the dancing flames. "Know, O our brothers, that the *Englasi* of Charles Town have grown so fat from the skin trade that they fear lest the *Ispani*—the Spaniards—will come from St. Augustine with their Yamasee allies and kill, burn and lay waste the whole colony."

A gray burst of rank-smelling smoke burst from Musgrove's mouth. "*Wagh!* Coosa-pona-keesa talks a straight tongue. Because of this, the *Englasi* of Carolina wish to establish some strong villages between them and the *Ispani*. Sotolycaté's curse on those treacherous Papists!" Mus-grove's voice had grown loud; those crouched around other eating fires peered apprehensively over their shoulders.

Turkey Head, rubbing his wrinkled belly, nodded vigorously. "That is wise."

Goggle-Eyes roused, his protruding eyes suddenly young-looking and alert. "What land do the *Englasi* wish to buy?"

John Musgrove hesitated, then chose his words with care. "It is said they want a strip of land along the Savannah River up to where the tide ceases to rise and fall; that, and some little islands at the river's mouth where forts can be built."

With shriveled, talon-like fingers, Turkey Head commenced to repack the pipe. "Who will be the *uker*, the peace chief of these new *Englasi?*"

Musgrove, using calloused fingers, plucked up a glowing coal and held it over his pipe's bowl. Between puffs he said, "In Charles Town they say this *uker* will be a mico thlucco named James Oglethorpe—a very rich *Englasi*."

By the light of the dying fire Goggle-Eyes blinked like a sleepy cat and squirmed deeper into his otter-skin mantle. Said he in his thin, old man's voice, "This mico thlucco will need much wisdom and help. He should know that the *Ispani* will not be his only enemy."

Thad raised an interrogative eyebrow and Mary Musgrove interpolated smoothly enough, "Steyamaschee means that the *Francani*—the French— and their Choctaw allies are equally to be feared."

"Yep," her husband resumed, "not long ago Jean-Baptiste le Moyne, their governor, sent reinforcements to his garrison at Fort Toulouse— that's deep in the Alibamu country. When spring comes the *Francani* figger to send a lot of traders and *voyageurs* among the Cherokees and Over-Mountain Creeks. Remember this, young feller; the *Francani* control all the trade which follows the Mississippi Valley from the Great Lakes clear down to the Gulf."

Presently Musgrove's wife arose, formally thanked her hosts, then disappeared among the dwellings.

Once his wife had departed, the trader cast Goggle-Eyes a quizzical look. "Have your people taken many deerskins since the Rutting Moon?"

The mico arose stiffly, gathered his fur mantle about wizened shoulders until he suggested an old turtle peering out of its shell. "In the storehouse are many Number One skins. Sakwari-cra has more."

"*Wagh!*" Musgrove grinned, tapped the ashes from his pipe against the haft of a tomahawk slung to his waist belt. "In the morning we shall make trade talk, O my brothers."

"It is well. Tsul, my brother, go, sleep in peace."

Lying with fingers laced behind his head, Sakwari-cra for a while listened to the even breathing of Taqua as, quite naked, she lay pressed beside him, delightfully soft, warm, and fragrant-smelling, too. Even though the Chauga remained icy she would bathe every day and then used oil of sweet grass tinctured with fern on her hair and under her fluffy armpits.

When the river got too cold Taqua would build a fire and heat many stones to be placed in the village's little bathhouse; when the rocks got hot enough, she would pour water onto them until steam obscured the edifice and a bather could sit and sweat to his satisfaction.

Ostensibly, she made such preparations for her man's benefit, but Sakwari-cra knew that the moment he emerged and went about his business she would dart in to huddle in the cleansing steam.

The white Tuscarora found it disconcerting that nowadays he found himself devoting more and more thought to his concubine for, after the first few weeks, he'd become satisfied that Taqua really was trustworthy.

Moreover, she seemed in every way eager to please and was clever in bed. He guessed he'd never forget how the young squaw could run; he still could picture her bounding, sure-footed and unfaltering, over mile after mile of treacherous track and trail.

Who was Laure Rivard really? Her name was French, or so Mary Musgrove had suggested at the feast.

As he lay listening to mice scurrying and rustling among a bundle of rough-cured deerskins he tried to find flaws in her character. If there were one, it lay in a certain persistent curiosity about matters belonging to a man's province.

Of course she wanted him to marry her, but he didn't intend to; things went well enough as they were. Why, at this time, burden himself with a family? He'd too many grand schemes slowly taking shape. *Family?* Why hadn't Taqua become pregnant by him or by any of the warriors she avowedly had slept with? For more than four months now, they'd coupled often enough.

The realization that Laure must be barren came to him both as a disappointment and a relief. *Wagh!* He who planned someday to become a modern Emperor Brims shouldn't take a barren woman to wife. Without sons to succeed him, what point would there be in creating a new nation?

His ruminations ended when Taqua stirred and a warm arm groped to settle about his neck; then a fragrant lock of hair tickled his chin as, quite sound asleep, she nudged her head into the hollow of his shoulder. Her movements gratified him; not one of the tawny-skinned young squaws bedded after a successful raid had made the slightest advance—they'd only been stupidly submissive.

Once the girl's breasts began rising and falling rhythmically against him, Sakwari-cra turned to the realization that tomorrow, for the first time, he was going to barter for furs and deerskins on his own account! Heretofore, he'd turned over such valuables to Smells-like-a-Bear—his Tuscarora foster father. Just before falling asleep he decided he'd better hold back his stock and observe how the Abecas went about dealing with John Musgrove.

In his hut Quobah Tutu also remained awake, peering into the pungent darkness. Beside him Hapeyah, his plain and slightly bowlegged squaw, lay snoring softly on his left; an Ashanti warrior always kept his right arm free to wield a weapon.

Thinking in Ashanti, the African wondered what had become of the kingdom he someday intended to reclaim. Had slavers struck at other Ashanti places like Obutu, Krobo, and Jukwa? What had become of his men who'd been sold with him in Jamaica?

Yes. Prince Quobah Tutu could feel pleased with himself. Wasn't he again free and his own master? Hadn't he formed an alliance with the ambitious and brainy Sakwari-cra? Hapeyah stirred in her sleep, reminding him that he, also, had as dutiful and industrious a woman as any he could have hoped to find among his own race. Best of all, when this winter ended he was likely to enjoy all the warfare he wanted.

Meantime, he pondered what sort of price he was going to get for his share of the furs and deerskins taken by him and the white Tuscarora.

Ignoring a succession of fleabites, the Ashanti tried to peer into the future, but found it hard going. He did decide that it would be wise to fall in with Sakwari-cra's immediate plans; there was a man who could outthink the craftiest Indians! When Prince Quobah Tutu went home he didn't intend to return alone and unattended; he'd bring along an imposing retinue of Africans freed from slavery.

Although Quobah hadn't yet heard of it, the Spanish already had established near St. Augustine an all-black community of freed slaves called Negrito. They had even allowed these Negroes to build a fort and had provided a few old cannon to protect it. Of course, self-interest alone had motivated the Spaniards' tolerance of this semi-independent community in their midst. Besides, contrary to popular belief, they were much gentler with their black slaves than the English and French or, worst of all, the Dutch.

Through bitter experience, the Spanish rulers in Florida had learned that purebred blacks made the best laborers who could be counted upon to fight for their masters in the event of an Indian war.

Chapter 15

TRADE TALK

The sun barely had lifted above the pine tops to dapple those gray-brown meadows on which the trader's hobbled pack horses were browsing without much success when, under John Musgrove's direction, slaves and train guards began to unlash specified packs.

The Cherokee guards, Thad Burton noted, were far more heavily tattooed than were their Creek companions; they stood taller and were more powerfully built.

Abeca squaws now fetched bundles of stiff and pungent deerskins which were graded as large, medium, or small and then stacked in separate piles.

In the meantime, Mary Musgrove superintended the laying out, on bare ground just inside the palisade, goods to be offered for barter. There were the usual ax and hatchet heads, cast-iron cook pots, hand mirrors to aid in applying face paint, yard goods in brilliant red or yellow cotton, and plenty of Stroudwater cloth—a coarse but very warm material which could be used for either clothing or bedding. Also for offer were matchcoats, woolen caps, and bright-colored ribboned garters which warriors liked to tie about their arms when they danced.

Spread out on horse blankets were other essential trade goods such as brick salt, cone sugar, bullet molds, bar lead, flints, and gunpowder of varying degrees of fineness—from F to 4F. In addition to this tempting display, Musgrove offered for sale a few brassbound English muskets and a pair of Highlander pistols made by Alexander Campbell of Doun. There were also Sheffield knives with extra heavy blades, buckles, buttons, and a dazzling collection of beads and bangles, bracelets and necklaces. Most appealing—and expensive—of all these offerings were some burning-glass lenses. With such, a fire could be quickly kindled on a sunny day.

Although Goggle-Eyes and Turkey Head, familiar with Musgrove's methods, had ceased to expect a gourd dipper of watered rum before the trading began, it was still a disappointment. Most packmen did offer a drink calculated to dull an Indian's sense of value. Neither did this South Carolinian insist on offering liquor in exchange for furs and deerskins.

Mary Musgrove had seated herself on a bale with small, booted feet pressed primly together to support a weather-beaten account book upon her buckskin-covered knees. She noticed Sakwari-cra's puzzlement, then in Creek explained, "There are only a few packmen even half as fair and decent as my husband. Rascals like Sam Browne and Ben Drake would have got you all roaring drunk last night and today would charge you double for what you swallowed."

"Sakwari-cra would not have got drunk," Thad Burton stated seriously. "Firewater does not mix up his head like those of his red friends."

The sleek half-breed's dark red lips curved into a smile. "Then you are indeed fortunate. You have bartered before?"

The young white man's stiff, freshly dyed black crest swayed jauntily over his shaven skull when he bent to untie one of several bundles of deerskins brought by Taqua. "The Tuscaroras never allowed Sakwari-cra to watch their barter with *Englasi* traders. Besides, all pelts he brought in belonged to his foster father; he never had anything to sell."

"Then you must know that Tsul, like most *Englasi* traders, buys skins according to size and weight." She indicated a heap of tawny hides. "There is the Number One Grade pile; it contains only the largest pelts, which

weigh at least two pounds each one." Coosa-pona-keesa fixed fine, dark
eyes on the well-painted white Tuscarora. "Attend what I say now. Medium or Number Two Grade must weigh between one and a quarter to
two pounds. Lighter or smaller skins are considered Number Threes.
And remember this, too: two mediums or three small skins count as a
single Number One."

Narrowly watched by Quobah, who was crouching beside his personal
stock of stiff and pungent deerskins, John Musgrove's men got out a
folding tripod and suspended a steel weighing yard which had a hook
at one of its ends. When a hide was hung to this hook, Musgrove slipped
one of several iron rings back and forth until the yard was balanced.
Then he'd call out the weight, which Mary entered in her account book.

The two old chiefs and their hunters together with a few half-grown
boys squatted in a loose circle about the tripod, their jet eyes missing
nothing of what was going on.

So expert was the South Carolinian that hardly an hour was required
to weigh as many of Guaxule's hides as John Musgrove intended to buy.
Invariably, he rejected skins too poorly cured or blemished by overlarge
holes, tears or spoiled through careless skinning.

Once Mary had read off the sum of each man's credit, the Abecas
closed in, inquiring the price of articles they needed or, more often,
what had attracted their curiosity. Goggle-Eyes saw to it that his toothless
old squaw purchased a generous quantity of brick salt because the mico
long was heartily sick of such substitutes as burnt water weed and hickory
ash.

In exchange for thirty-seven First and Second Grade deerskins and a
miscellany of wildcat, fox, wolf, and coon pelts, Thad bought a dozen
first-quality French gunflints at one buck each; six gills of 3F priming
powder at three bucks the gill; six flasks of ordinary gunpowder and four
bars of lead along with a bullet mold which looked as if it might cast a
ball that would fit the gun he'd captured from the Catawbas.

Fervently, Sakwari-cra wished he'd enough credit to permit the purchase of a new lightweight musketoon made by Jordan of Birmingham
and adorned with shiny brass mountings and butt plate—but he hadn't
nearly enough. He'd about finished his buying when he noticed Taqua
standing in the background with the other squaws. She was fixedly staring
at a bolt of scarlet- and yellow-striped calico, so, quite casually, he bought
six yards of the stuff, then topped off his purchases with a brace of Stroudwater blankets and an iron kettle. It was big, but shouldn't prove too
heavy for Taqua to carry on the march. Devoid of expression, he dumped
these last items onto the ground before her.

Old Brims's niece noted, said in an undertone, "John, that redheaded girl hasn't the least notion of how pretty she is. Give her a mirror and a green necklace out of my share."

"Damn' if you ain't forever a bag of surprises," Musgrove grunted. He went over to Laure, held out the gifts, "Here, miss, these are with my missus' compliments," he said, grinning from the depths of his explosive red-brown beard, and, turning, gave orders that now that business was over the long-hoped-for rum-and-water was to be issued.

While the first gourds were being circulated John Musgrove concluded an agreement with old Steyamaschee that the latter should care for the newly bought skins until called for.

"I'm on me way out," explained the trader. "Headed for Cherokee country."

Because she was still peering into her mirror and fingering that wonderful string of glittering glass beads, the midday meal wasn't ready; Thad felt forced to cuff Taqua a bit. She didn't mind. Although the strands of *pe-ak* she habitually wore in her hair were worth many times more than her tawdry new necklace, Laure was wild about it; and to think that Coosa-pona-keesa had given it to her!

Once Sakwari-cra had departed to see the Musgroves off on their long trip to the west, Taqua hung up the mirror and stared in frank curiosity on features she'd heretofore beheld only imperfectly reflected by still water. For the first time she became aware that tiny golden particles gleamed amid her slanted and rather small gray-green eyes; also that dimples showed at each corner of her mouth.

All in all, Laure Rivard felt happier than ever before in her life.

Chapter 16

LES VOYAGEURS

About a week after the Musgrove's pack train had departed along the trace which led into the vast hunting grounds of the proud and warlike Cherokees, another set of traders appeared before the rotting palisade at Guaxule.

Spotted Tail, hunting deer across the Chauga, heard horses following that trail which eventually led to Fort Toulouse, deep in Alibamu territory.

On reaching the council house the young Abeca breathlessly informed

Goggle-Eyes that a long string of pack horses, headed by a Frenchman and an ugly mulatto, were headed for Guaxule. From his hiding place Spotted Tail had counted no less than sixteen pack animals and at least as many heavily burdened Indians slaves guarded by Choctaws all armed with muskets.

Goggle-Eyes reacted promptly. The palisade's gate was closed; boys were sent running to call in the white Tuscarora and his Ashanti companion, who were found dressing out a woods buffalo. By the time they appeared, Taqua and other squaws had closed loopholes in the palisade. Under Turkey Head's direction every serviceable firearm was loaded and children filled earthenware pots with water to put out fire arrows.

Sakwari-cra and Goggle-Eyes mounted a crude ladder leading to a shooting platform, built inside the palisade, which commanded the gate. The old mico appeared so frail it seemed doubtful that he could shoulder the antique Spanish wheel-lock that Buffalo Calf passed up to him. Turkey Head, Buffalo Calf, Spotted Tail, Quobah, and Taqua, who had learned to use a musket, were posted at strategic loopholes. But, for all that, everyone knew that such precautions must prove futile. If this party out of the southwest proved as numerous as Spotted Tail had reported and if they intended to sack Guaxule not much could be done to prevent them.

When only three strangers rode out from the forest Sakwari-cra took it for a good omen; had these people been bent on mischief they'd have invisibly encircled the village before raising the *tiwa*—the scalping cry.

Astride stubby little horses the three emissaries came jogging across still-stark fields repeatedly making the peace sign. Their foremost man was a swarthy, thick-bodied European wearing a dirty dark green uniform jacket and fringed Indian leggings over blue- and black-striped cotton trousers. A battered tricorne hat bound in tarnished gold braid rode upon the leader's shoulder-length black hair.

Two dark-complexioned and flat-headed Choctaws, hideous with paint and tattooing, pulled up to the European's right and left.

Teeth glinted briefly under an enormous mustache when the white man called out in resonant Creek, "Greetings to the great Steyamaschee, mico of Guaxule!"

Goggle-Eyes, visibly relieved, hesitated, then stood up on the firing platform to return the peace sign. In an undertone he explained to Thad, "That is Lasti-Tiwa, the Black Head. Among the *Francani* his name is Antoine Joyeuse. Lasti-Tiwa has been here before."

In his cracked old voice the mico then called down, "Be welcome, O Lasti-Tiwa! But take care. The spotted sickness has visited Guaxule," continued the crafty old man. "You will do well to make camp among the fields."

"That is straight talk," commented Antoine Joyeuse, then issued orders which sent his Choctaws trotting back into the forest with muskets balanced across their pommels.

Once the Choctaws had disappeared Goggle-Eyes ordered the gate opened and cautiously invited M. Joyeuse to enter.

Once inside, the Frenchman covertly studied his surroundings and judged, from the very few people in sight, that Steyamaschee hadn't been lying about the smallpox having visited his village.

Peering through her loophole, Taqua watched a crowd of dark figures emerge from the woods and start to make camp amid a grove of bare-limbed black walnuts. She attempted to count the distant figures, but could only estimate that there were about twenty-five strangers out yonder.

She heard an angry growl escape Quobah as into Antoine Joyeuse's camping place plodded a string of Indian slaves loaded under such heavy burdens that these unfortunates walked bent almost double. Even at this distance it was evident that they must be in desperately poor condition; they set their feet down heavily, with no trace of springiness. What particularly enraged the African was the fact that these slaves were tied, neck-to-neck, in a long line just as, on the Gold Coast, the Denkaras had secured him and his companions, but in place of a wooden slave yoke each captive's neck was imprisoned in a broad iron collar to which a ring had been forged.

Under a rush of bitter memories Quobah began to grind pointed teeth and to growl under his breath. Infuriated, he commenced to shake, found it difficult not to rush out and, cost what it might, attempt to free those poor creatures. From glowering eyes Quobah Tutu watched the Frenchman's slaves stack burdens while cringing under their Choctaw guards' free use of sticks and quirts.

Hardly had the distant beasts of burden been off-loaded and the pack horses hobbled when Antoine Joyeuse, grinning broadly, came swinging back to the gate. Accompanying him this time was the muscular, broad-shouldered mulatto. Yonder, the white Tuscarora decided, was a man to be wary of; his freckled, light brown features were finely formed and his manner alert. When the mulatto passed through the gate, Thad saw that he was disfigured by a half-healed scar running across his right cheek; also that he was missing the top of the ear on that side.

This mulatto was Guillaume Potier, a trader well known among the Illini, whose country, Sakwari-cra vaguely recalled, was thought to lie somewhere to the north and west.

Joyeuse, sleek sable hair agleam in the sunset, swung up to the council house and, offering two gourds of unwatered brandy, invited Goggle-Eyes, Turkey Head, and the rest to partake. The Abecas, of course, accepted readily enough; when had an Indian refused a free drink? *Francani* brandy, as everyone knew, was much smoother than the raw Jamaica rum offered by *Englasi* traders.

Taqua grew anxious when Thad grabbed a gourd, tilted back his head, and gulped the largest possible mouthful. She really should not have worried. Sakwari-cra wouldn't suck the last drop from the gourds and then begin to giggle, like the Abecas; Sakwari-cra's unmixed white blood would leave him relatively unaffected. He wouldn't get knee-walking, falling-down drunk or attempt to swallow live coals as she'd seen happen more than once in Tosneoc.

Abruptly, Quobah refused to drink any more, so he was able to support Sakwari-cra when the white Tuscarora successfully hinted that Joyeuse and Potier might offer some other sort of entertainment in their camp.

Thad paused long enough at his cabin to slip a freshly sharpened skin-ning knife into his belt and to warn Taqua that she and Quobah's woman must bar the gate the moment they left. She was not to open it for anyone other than Quobah or himself.

On gaining the trader's camp near the forest's edge, they looked about for the Frenchmen's hobbled horses and found them guarded by a pair of Choctaws, at the moment kindling a watch fire.

Other guards were lashing crude wooden shackles about the ankles of Joyeuse's Indian slaves after securing their hands behind them. Almost naked in the chilly night, these shivering wretches were forced to lie on the damp and sandy ground without covering of any description.

After more brandy had been circulated Sakwari-cra pretended to lose his dignified manner and when a flat-headed Choctaw—his head had been deliberately deformed in infancy through the pressure of a board bound across its forehead—produced a tom-tom and began to dance, he sprang up and, with ornaments aglitter, leaped high into the air. Brandish-ing his knife at the sky, he pranced around and around the campfire, at the same time, raising a screeching Iroquois war chant. Joyeuse and his mulatto partner were impressed; they'd heard a lot about the warlike qualities of the Six Nations. Neither seemed to suspect that this huge Tuscarora was nowhere near as drunk as he was acting.

On the other hand, it was ludicrous to observe how quickly the liquor took hold of such guards as Joyeuse allowed to drink a little. They reeled about, posturing and giggling like women.

Thad, when at last he dropped, panting, onto a bale of trade bales, noticed that Quobah's scarred visage had assumed a ferocious expression; only his glowing, yellowish eyes betrayed his position among the shadows.

Then he noted another interesting fact: Guillaume Potier, the only other person present with African blood in his veins, all along had seemed to ignore the lordly Ashanti's presence, but when he did glance in Quo-bah's direction, it was in open malevolence.

At length the mulatto, who, using a couple of sticks, had been tapping out rhythms upon an empty brandy keg, got up and swayed over to the fettered slaves. Cursing loudly, he kicked them awake, ordered them to stand.

In weary resignation, the captives obeyed and a round dozen of them stood up, weaving, hampered by the clumsy wooden stocks lashed about their ankles. Thickly, Potier ordered them to sing and when they hesitated he savagely laid about him with a set of rawhide bridle reins until the luckless creatures raised a high-pitched, wailing song.

That the Frenchman and his freckled, buff-hued partner owned two very different types of slaves Sakwari-cra had noted long since. Six of these unfortunates were Chickasaws recognizable by their light skins and hawklike features. Hard-bitten fighters when in condition—which, at present, they certainly weren't—they looked gaunt as mummies. As tirelessly as the Iroquois, the Chickasaws, for generations, had fought the French and their Indian allies. The hatred in these proud prisoners' eyes was deadly.

On the other hand, a half-dozen Natchez slaves, swarthy, short-legged, and otherwise ugly, appeared utterly cowed and devoid of spirit.

When a Chickasaw failed to sing loudly enough to suit his Choctaw guards, one caught up a spear and used it to jab the offender's back or buttocks.

Only after the singing, drumming, and dancing had gone on for a long while did Sakwari-cra and his impassive Negro companion finally make excuses and return to Guaxule, completely informed as to the armament, strength, and composition of the Frenchmen's pack train.

The sun had risen before the visitors roused and, by way of fostering poor judgment, sent gourd bottles of watered brandy into Goggle-Eyes' village. Thad, however, intercepted and spilled these offerings before the Abecas could get at them and get so drunk they couldn't hope to transact business in a rational fashion.

About midmorning, Antoine Joyeuse, teeth flashing in a friendly fashion, sauntered up to the gate and demanded admittance, but Sakwari-cra temporized with the explanation that Goggle-Eyes, Turkey Head, and the rest were still too hung-over to appear before midday. To the white Tuscarora's surprise, Joyeuse only shrugged good-naturedly, said, "Alors. Tout à l'heure, à midi."

When, finally, trading began, Antoine Joyeuse and Guillaume Potier grew angry over the disappointing quantity and quality of the pelts and skins being offered. Why, they demanded, had not the visitors been told, straight off, that other traders already had visited Guaxule and had carried off the cream of the winter's hunting? It particularly enraged the mulatto that he and his partner should have wasted so much time and brandy to end by having to haggle over miserable skins rejected by John Musgrove.

Smothering his resentment, Antoine Joyeuse, for a trifling sum, then bought the culls in the French style, by purchasing them by number and total weight, rather than by graded sizes.

Leaving his mulatto partner sourly to conclude the deal, Joyeuse began to explore the village under the pretense of bestowing a few trifling presents on the youngest and prettiest squaws. To Thad's uneasiness, the Frenchman quite casually peered into this wigwam and that cabin, all the while chattering in friendly fashion, until he was able to confirm a suspicion that John Musgrove had left his purchases under Goggle-Eyes' protection. Musgrove, outward bound along his trading route, scarcely would have burdened himself at the outset of his journey when, quite easily, he could retrieve these purchases on his way back to Charles Town.

Mais oui! The Abecas' best skins almost certainly were still in Guaxule. This suspicion was satisfied when he spied, in a shadowy corner of the council house, a pile of packs neatly corded and ready for transportation.

Sakwari-cra noted how Joyeuse, grinning under his enormous mustachios, sought his partner and, after a bit, returned to their camp in high good humor.

Repairing to his cabin, the white Tuscarora found Taqua serving sagamite—a coarse corn pudding mush—to a Choctaw train guard who evidently was of superior rank. Something in her unusually friendly manner with a stranger warned him to co-operate by offering the guard a drink of strong corn beer.

Soon the Choctaw began to boast, saying that the commander at Fort Toulouse had heard about plans for a new English colony to be established south of the Carolinas. The guard smirked over this Tuscarora's bland disinterest in this significant bit of news, for, down in Biloxi, Governor Jean-Baptiste le Moyne had got very excited and bellicose, the establishment of yet another English colony upon the Guale Coast being the last thing that worthy desired. If it came to choosing between the *Englasi* and the *Ispani*, the Governor would not hesitate over his decision; while he could contain and check the *Ispani*, the *Englasi* were another matter.

Why, even at this moment, the Sieur le Moyne was preparing to dispatch missions to micos controlling tribes of dubious allegiance to the *Englasi*. These, declared the Choctaw while spearing a chunk of cold venison on the point of his knife, included the Yuchis, Cherokees, Coosaws, Tallapoosas, and certain subtribes belonging to the Creek Confederacy. The *Francani* felt that they could count on the loyalty of the Choctaws, Moviles, Biloxis, and the fierce Illini who roamed near the

Great Father of Waters. These emissaries were to encourage a sudden, overwhelming, and merciless assault calculated to obliterate the projected colony before it could take root.

While chickens scratched in the sunlight beyond the cabin's door, the flat-headed train guard sat on his heels, champed noisily, and guzzled as much beer as Sakwari-cra would give him. Soon he became sufficiently mellowed to confide that Governor le Moyne had sent an especially qualified representative to interview Cussaw, King of all the Cherokees, and to presuade him, at the right time, to send out runners bearing red-painted sticks which would cause the *caw-waw-noo-dee*, the dreaded Cherokee war cry, to resound against the *Englasi*.

Smiling winsomely at this foul-smelling warrior, Taqua observed that only a Choctaw *outacity* as clever as himself could foresee whether this messenger was likely to succeed in weaning the Cherokees away from the *Englasi*.

"*Wagh!*" grunted Thad without apparent guile. "It is sure that he will fail. Cussaw and the Carolinians have kept peace over many seasons."

"He will *not* fail!" growled the Choctaw. "He is no ordinary ambassador. He is a priest among the Jesuits, an *Alémani*, who calls himself Pierre Albert. M'sieur Joyeuse says his real name is Christian Priber. He has lived among our people many, many seasons and understands our ways and speech.

"This wizard called Priber is very wise," continued the heavily tattooed train guard, slipping his knife back into a well-worn sheath and noisily sucking bits of deer meat from between snaggleteeth. "His tongue is skilled in many forms of Muskogean and speaks also as the *Alémani*, *Francani*, *Ispani*, and *Englasi*."

"Sakwari-cra hopes Priber will meet with success." Thad Burton offered a pipe loaded and ready for smoking. "The Six Nations hate the *Englasi*—" He didn't add that they hated the French far worse.

"Who can tell?" remarked the Choctaw, expelling a great cloud of rank smoke. "Priber has only just arrived among the Cherokees."

Grimly, he added, "If Cussaw listens to him the Carolinians will be cut like tobacco into many, little pieces."

Chapter 17

THE SLAVES

Not long after sunset drumming sounded among fires marking the Frenchmen's bivouac on the forest's edge. Thad Burton stiffened when he heard someone scratch softly at his cabin's door. When he opened it he wasn't surprised to make out Quobah standing among shadows cast by a pale half-moon.

Once Taqua had pulled a buffalo bed robe up over her smooth brown breasts, Sakwari-cra beckoned in the visitor. The night, he noted at the same time, was so very still that he caught the sound of a dog scratching fleas outside a nearby cabin.

On enormous moccasins the Negro entered silently. The cicatrice patterns decorating his cheeks and forehead appeared especially prominent.

Thad considered the Ashanti a long moment, then hazarded, "You have come to ask me to help you free the *Francani* slaves?"

"That is so, O my brother," admitted Quobah, fingering the haft of an extra-long-handled tomahawk which somewhat resembled the war ax he'd so effectively wielded in Africa. Slowly, he added, "No man should be made to wear a collar of iron and linked by his neck with another."

"You are right in that, my brother," agreed the white Tuscarora with a readiness which surprised Taqua no less than Quobah. "We will go to the *Francani's* camp."

Truth was that, for an entirely different reason, Thad already had decided on such a move.

"However, only the Chickasaws are to be freed. Though thin, they are well made and seem able to travel fast and far, but the Natchez look spiritless and being short-legged would slow us so much that the *Francani* and their Choctaws would soon overtake us."

Albeit unwillingly, the Ashanti inclined a head turbaned in brilliant scarlet cloth purchased from the Musgroves. Quobah crossed to the door, opened it a crack, and peered out. Everything seemed quiet except for the screeches of a panther hunting among the foothills. "We strike tonight?"

Without making reply, Sakwari-cra began to select weapons. Then he explained, "It long has been in my mind to gather a band of strong captives and fighting men from broken tribes. From these I will create a following of my own." His voice deepened. "I will enlist none save the craftiest and bravest who will help me conquer so many weak tribes that I will become a great war chief and rule like the Emperor Brims!"

Taqua's expression lit. *Wagh!* She had not been mistaken about this man's ambitions.

"To begin with," Thad continued, gray-blue eyes intent and bright, "I will ally my Sakwaris with micos who are strong but not powerful enough to defeat their enemies singlehanded."

Among the shadows sounded Quobah's guttural voice. "What of black runaways and freed men of my people? Will you enlist them?"

Thad paused while buckling on his war belt, then treated Quobah to a steady look. "Such will be welcome among my people as long as they prove strong, fearless and obedient to my will.

"Collect food for the trail and plenty of it," Thad directed, easing his war bag's sling over his nodding dyed crest. "We do not stay here."

Taqua, meanwhile, had been pulling on her few garments and now hurriedly plaited her hair into tight twin braids. "No blankets?"

"No—nor any clothing."

Taqua's oblique eyes appeared huge in the half-light. "What of your peace ornaments, my dress-ups?" It was clear that she wasn't cheerfully going to desert such possessions.

Despite his preoccupation, Thad patted her cheek. "Soon we must run perhaps as hard as we did last year. Pack only food, weapons, the new cook kettle and spare moccasins; have everything ready when I come back."

Quobah had run to awaken Hapeyah, the Abeca squaw who'd been attending to his needs. Curtly, the sable giant offered her the choice of coming along or remaining in Guaxule.

"Will come," Hapeyah announced, then added simply, "Tomorrow, after you have stolen their slaves the *Francani* and his Choctaws will be very angry. Perhaps they will fall upon Guaxule and slay all in it."

"No," grunted Quobah, cramming into his war bag a small, hideously ugly idol he'd carved out of black cherrywood. "They will only carry off those skins Goggle-Eyes keeps for John Musgrove."

Her eyes peered at him, owl-like, out of the gloom. "Why?"

"These *Francani*, too, are only at the beginning of their travels among the Lower Creeks. They would not dare go among them if they slay Steyamaschee and his people—who also are Creeks."

Soon Thad and Quobah were trotting soundlessly among dwellings occupied by Abecas noisily sleeping off the effects of the Frenchmen's liquor. Long since they had learned where every useful weapon in

Guaxule was located, so it wasn't very long before they'd selected three sound muskets, plenty of powder, tomahawks and a few pouches of bullets. When they arrived at Sakwari-cra's cabin Taqua hurriedly was dividing food and other supplies into well-balanced packs.

Once Thad and his companion had reconnoitered the Frenchmen's camp they discovered that most of Joyeuse and Potier's Choctaw guards lay sprawled in drunken slumber, their dark, flat faces turned unseeing toward the magnificent, moonlit sky. The Frenchman and his mulatto partner lay huddled, snoring regularly, near the bivouac's center.

A Choctaw, who, presumably, was standing guard, sat beneath a tree with chin sagging on chest and skinny legs splayed loosely apart. He slept so soundly it seemed safe for Thad and Quobah to crawl, silent as hunting martens, among the Chickasaw slaves. These, with characteristic hauteur, had gone to sleep somewhat apart from their companions in misery, the Natchez.

Razor-edged scalping knife clamped between teeth, Sakwari-cra squirmed up to the nearest Chickasaw, who was lying almost as collapsed-looking as a dead man. With emaciated limbs only faintly revealed by the moonlight he lay with mouth sagged open and eyes sunk deep into his skull.

Because he was Indian, the Chickasaw made no noise or motion when he felt Thad's hand on his shoulder; only his eyes flickered open. At a glance he appeared to take in the situation. Deftly, Sakwari-cra sliced through rawhides securing the slave's wrists, then freed him of his clumsy wooden stocks.

So swiftly did he and Quobah work that they freed all six Chickasaws in a matter of moments. The Natchez slaves, laying only a few feet away, continued their exhausted slumber undisturbed.

Once the hollow-cheeked Chickasaws had flitted, owl-silent, after their liberators into the woods, the white Tuscarora led them in a wide circle to the far side of Guaxule, which they entered by simply uprooting a certain log in the palisade.

Quobah, bringing up the rear, suddenly and without explanation, turned about and vanished in the direction of Joyeuse's bivouac.

To the Ashanti's immense relief, no alarm had been raised and the guards continued to snore. Scarred features intent, Quobah cut the nearest Natchez free, then pointed across the river. Without hesitation the slave lost himself among the shadows. The next Natchez Quobah set free didn't wait for his companions either; he fled all alone—a dark, squat figure running clumsily but silently. Soon the last of the Frenchmen's slaves had begun wading out into the fast-running Chauga.

None of these Natchez had evinced the least sign of gratitude, Quobah noted, but without surprise. No more had any of the Chickasaws.

Thad Burton's burst of rage over Quobah's insubordinate and quite unexpected maneuver faded when he judged the Ashanti's motive, which was to force upon the traders a choice of trails to be followed in pursuit of their property.

While awaiting the African's return, Sakwari-cra instructed the freed captives to help themselves to such food as was not to be carried along. They needed no urging, only stuffed their mouths in dreadful eagerness. Meanwhile, Thad distributed the weapons collected earlier that night.

"Which among you is senior?"

A broad-shouldered, one-eyed fellow stepped forward, jaws working. "I, the Raven Chula. Shatara is only Slave Catcher."

Once Quobah reappeared the column of eight men and two squaws quitted Guaxule and at a rapid trot set off along a game path which led in a northeasterly direction into the Chattooga mountains. Thad had chosen this course for the good reason that it coiled sharply away from the intended route of Joyeuse's pack train—always provided the Frenchman hadn't been lying.

After a half hour's hard running, the white Tuscarora glanced over his shoulder and was pleased by what he saw by the setting moon's light. All six Chickasaws were running strongly—or seemed to be—and were handling their weapons with ease. Three were carrying muskets, the rest bows; each had been equipped with a knife and a tomahawk. Nearly naked and barefooted, they suggested the vengeful shades of warriors long departed to the Happy Hunting Grounds of Yo-he-wa.

Taqua, as before, was running easily, although on this occasion she was hampered by a bow and arrows, a pack, and the cradled weight of a heavy horse pistol Thad had taught her to use. From her other hand swung the precious new cook pot.

In silence the party jogged on and on, ever upward through the chill, pine-scented forest where, here and there, grotesque shadows lurked like enemies in ambush. Now and then a skunk or a porcupine might lumber off the trail; sometimes an owl hooted among the treetops.

After a while Thad called a halt on becoming aware that the Chickasaws, despite stoic pretenses, were showing signs of complete exhaustion. What seemed to bother these people the most was the fact that they had neither the time nor the materials with which to paint their faces! Furthermore, Hapeyah, whose legs were both short and bowed, was commencing to lag although the Ashanti had relieved her of her pack a good while back.

Although Sakwari-cra was careful to hold the pace to the ex-slaves' capability, he succeeded in leading the little column high among the Chattooga foothills. Just before dawn he ordered his companions to pause long enough to gulp a few handfuls of pemmican. Soon they resumed their flight toward the sunrise, roughly paralleling the Chauga River's course.

At length the trail led across a wide and level meadow limited on its far side by a bold, rocky ridge. At once Thad realized that now was the time to find out whether he was being pursued. Were Joyeuse's people closing in, they could be seen from the ridge in ample time to prepare a possibly successful ambush; after all the fugitives carried five reasonably reliable muskets, bows, and spears in addition to Taqua's pistol.

When, after crossing the meadow, Thad ordered another halt, the one-eyed Chickasaw, called Chula, knelt to press an ear against the earth. All except Quobah and the squaws followed suit and agreed that a large body of men was hurrying up from behind.

It was then that Thad Burton more fully appreciated Quobah's decision to free the Natchez, for not all the Frenchmen's force came trotting out of the woods on the meadow's far side. Guillaume Potier, wearing a gay, bright yellow shirt, was leading only eleven well-armed Choctaws. Undoubtedly, Joyeuse must be leading the rest in pursuit of the wretched Natchez.

Sakwari-cra's lips tightened and his expression grew hard. "Taqua! Take Hapeyah, run well up yonder ravine and hide. Leave no tracks." Then his gaze met hers and the ghost of a smile appeared. "If they kill us there is no point in losing such a fine red scalp."

She protested. "I know how to use this pistol—and the bow, too."

He scowled ferociously. "Go at once!"

By the time the mulatto and his followers got about halfway across the meadow Thad and three of the starveling Chickasaws had concealed themselves amid a mound of laurel-crowned boulders to one side of the trail while Quobah and the rest had hidden behind a pile of storm-felled timber.

The enemy were running as easily as foxhounds following a strong, fresh scent. Some men kept their eyes on the trail, others turned painted heads, peered this way and that. It was discouraging to realize that every last one of Potier's men carried a firearm of some description. The freckled, brown-skinned leader loped along, holding his short-barreled musket parallel to the ground.

Sakwari-cra glanced at the Chickasaw called Chula and felt pleased over the businesslike manner in which he and his lanky Slave Catcher were checking musket flints and priming—a precaution unusual for an Indian.

Behind the blown-down trees on the trail's opposite side crouched Quobah, scarlet turban and blue-black skin dappled by bright flecks of sunlight. The other Chickasaws lay beside him, hastily winding their dull

and greasy hair into shapeless knots. Already they'd warmed their bowstrings and had stuck arrows into the ground ready for quick use.

Gradually, the white Tuscarora's pulse rate accelerated; he began to
grin when the enemy drew nearer and slowed down as they commenced
to breast the slope leading up toward the ambush.

It now could be seen that Guillaume Potier, easily the biggest of the
pursuers, was lugging a French gun—a mighty handsome affair, brassbound
and decorated with designs done in mother-of-pearl. Since the mulatto
had stripped himself to the waist, great, chocolate-hued freckles marking
his wiry shoulders became clearly visible.

Unfamiliar with his new followers' readiness to follow orders, Sakwari-
cra prayed that none would get rattled and shoot before he gave the
word, for this promised, at best, to be a chancy affair; the pursuers carried
twelve guns against his party's five, and weary, semistarved men
couldn't be expected to shoot extra well. Only if the enemy were allowed
to come really close was there any chance of success.

Chula flattened and, as so many Indians did in anticipation of battle,
began to grind his teeth.

Some sixth sense must have warned Potier some thirty yards short of
the ambush, for suddenly he slowed his pace and waited for his men to
close up.

The fact that none of those flat-headed and dark-complexioned Choctaws was sweating hard or even panting was disconcerting. Obviously, all
were in fine condition as they trotted up the slope, setting their moccasins
down lightly and with care.

When Potier, whose crinkly black hair now was noticeable because he'd
lost his headgear, gained the crest of the ridge, Thad calmly drew a bead
on the mulatto's sweat-shiny chest. An instant before his forefinger tightened over the trigger's cool surface he drew a deep breath and then
squalled the ever-terrifying Iroquois war cry of "*Oo-nah! Oo-nah!* Kill!
Kill!"

Sakwari-cra was hardly aware of his weapon's kick before he dropped
it; he'd be granted no time to reload. Smothered by choking powder
fumes, he grabbed up the tomahawk he'd sunk, handy-like, into a branch,
and waited to see what should be done next.

Wham! Boom! Wham! Other muskets obscured the early spring sunshine with further billows of woolly, rotten-smelling smoke. From beyond
the fumes arose yells, strident screams, and dull thumps caused by bodies
falling heavily. Then sounded the singing *twang* of bowstrings at work.

When Sakwari-cra again was able to see the trail he saw that Guillaume
Potier had fallen onto hands and knees near the trail's center and was
coughing up torrents of bright scarlet blood; with each spasm his back
would arch like that of a frightened cat. Three Choctaws lay sprawled,

quivering convulsively amid the underbrush. A fourth was limping away, desperately, hopelessly, on a badly damaged leg. Two more were staggering off with a pair of arrows protruding at grotesque angles from their sides.

The surviving Choctaws, in a panic, had thrown away unfired weapons in order to sprint, unhampered, back across that broad, sunlit meadow. They'd no desire to be overtaken by the Chickasaws they'd so long tormented and humiliated—an even more unforgivable offense.

Thad was about to leap down and lift Potier's short and curly scalp, but he pulled up and permitted Chula to claim the trophy, being shrewd enough to understand how far such a gesture would go toward restoring the Raven's self-respect.

Quobah, meanwhile, cut down the leg-wounded Choctaw. Two Chickasaws ran down and killed the men who'd had arrows sticking out of them. No effort was made to chase the other survivors; everyone was aware they'd no chance of coming up with them—the ex-slaves were in too poor condition.

Once the scalps had been lifted and hung, dripping redly, to various belts, the defeated party's arms were collected and distributed. Sakwari-cra took for himself Potier's handsomely decorated *fusil*, which was newer and lighter than the Catawba musket he'd been lugging all these weeks.

When the squaws appeared to gaze dispassionately upon the bodies sprawled limply upon the trail Thad ordered them to build a fire. Later, after they had eaten, the white Tuscarora and his warriors would take their rest and make a brag about their prowess and cleverness.

Chapter 18

DOWNSTREAM

Following four days of hard travel, Thad Burton's band had bivouacked —a brief and very simple process—on the banks of the Chauga, which continued to fall steadily toward the south and east.

As Taqua rubbed bear's grease onto her long and narrow feet she looked about, felt strangely pleased with what she saw. Yonder stood Sakwari-cra—handsome and more impressive than ever in his freshly applied paint—in conference with Quobah and the Chickasaw Raven called Chula. The last two were listening with turbaned or crested heads inclined; now and then they nodded gravely.

Since the slaying of Potier and his Choctaws matters with Thad's band had progressed from good to better. Thanks to a measure of rest and plenty of food the tough and wiry Chickasaws swiftly had recovered their strength—and pride—especially after they'd been able to dress their hair, shave naked portions of their scalps, and, above all, to restore ceremonial paint to their lean and hawklike visages.

Taqua went over to help short-legged Hapeyah work her arms through her pack's carry straps, then, easily, she shouldered her own burden and cased bow. Last of all she picked up her cherished kettle.

It was indicative of rising morale that now brass butt plates, ferrules, and musket-barrel mountings all glowed in the sunrise.

The young red-haired squaw was proud that only she knew what course Sakwari-cra was intending to follow, but wild horses couldn't have dragged from her a single word on the subject.

Quobah showed his filed teeth in a grin as he strode over to take his place at the short column's rear. To Taqua's vast surprise, none of the new warriors seemed in the least inclined to question the giant African's status as second-in-command. It was certain that they inordinately admired his powerful physique and skill in war. Possibly there might also be a touch of superstition in connection with their acceptance of his superiority? Although they'd had plenty to do with Negroes and had even kept some as slaves, they'd never met up with one even faintly resembling this ferocious, blue-black African prince.

In the late morning they sighted the smoke of a village which proved to be called Chowan. It was of about the same size as Guaxule and, like most Lower Creek settlements, lay on either the northern or the eastern bank of a river or stream.

The Chauga had considerably broadened since its escape from the mountains; therefore its course ran slower and wound in noisy little meanders among steep hills and magnificent forests.

Sloffkaw, the heavily tattooed mico of Chowan, proved taciturn, suspicious, and, at first, anything but cordial to this oddly assorted band who, continually making the peace sign, strode up to his palisade and boldly demanded admittance. Because Sloffkaw could field no less than thirty strong young warriors and so had no reason to fear this handful of strangers, he grudgingly returned the peace sign and ordered opened a gate strongly constructed of pointed logs.

Gradually this mico of the Atali, or Lower Creeks, unbent, but couldn't seem to remove his gaze from Quobah, a fact which piqued Thad Burton no little. The atmosphere grew friendlier still when it became known that

both Sakwari-cra and Quobah, last winter, had been adopted into the
Abeca tribe by old Goggle-Eyes, the once-renowned War Chief.

At length, thanks to the presentation of ornaments stripped from Potier's
people, Sloffkaw's surliness evaporated so completely that he ordered his
women and slaves to put up for the Sakwaris—as Thad had begun to call
his band—a trio of bark wigwams. These were soon thrown together
on a pleasant little meadow beside the river where it would be easy
to fish and to bathe. To Thad and Laure it seemed fine to be near a
healthy, well-populated village again; to hear squaws bickering, children
squalling at play, and dogs barking. Besides, Sloffkaw's horse herd was
something to admire.

After their arrival in Chowan, the again proud and haughty Chickasaws
filled out even more and spent long hours playing rough, warlike games.
They began to devise even more ferocious paint designs for their rugged
bronze-hued features.

One day, about a week after the Sakwaris' arrival in Sloffkaw's town,
a party which had been hunting in the vicinity of Goggle-Eyes' village
told how they had found Steyamaschee and Turkey Head consumed with
helpless rage. It appeared that, although Antoine Joyeuse hadn't killed
anyone, he'd thoroughly looted Guaxule and had carried off the skins
belonging to John Musgrove as compensation for the loss of Guillaume
Potier, five Choctaw guards, and the bulk of his slave train. As near as
Quobah could learn through patient questioning of the hunters, only
two Natchez had been recaptured.

Laure Rivard took quiet pride in observing that this report enhanced
Thad Burton's prestige no little among the inhabitants of Chowan.

One fine but chilly spring evening the white Tuscarora lounged in his
wigwam absently watching Taqua wince and grimace as, one by one, she
pulled out her pubic hairs with the aid of clamshell tweezers. That this
process was painful Thad was well aware, having depilated himself earlier
in the day; one had to do this every so often lest curls offer a refuge to
nits, lice, or body crabs.

It was something of a shock to realize that, never before, had he felt
nearly so pleased with life. At the same time intuition warned that such
dangerous sensations might preclude disaster. Yet, as he sprawled on the
bough couch, he couldn't help reflecting that, no matter how one looked
at it, it was a good thing to own an obedient, intelligent, and industrious
squaw of his own race.

Best of all was the news Taqua recently had imparted—she wasn't
barren, after all! A bit shyly, she'd admitted that twice in succession she'd
not had to observe her monthly withdrawal period.

At length Laure sighed, put away the clamshells, and, once more smooth as polished flint, tied on her hammock and kilt then, unconcernedly, set about stitching a new hunting shirt for Thad.

Ignoring swarms of flies buzzing about the wigwam's pleasantly warm interior, Thad locked fingers behind head and, unseeingly, studied the five-foot blowgun he was drilling out of a cane stalk. When he found time he intended to experiment with heavier darts—darts that could kill a man. Um. How was he going to feel about Taqua's having a baby? How long would her neat figure remain swollen and ungainly? He'd never paid much attention to such purely female considerations. Was it because he was an all-white that he needed a woman far oftener than did his red-skinned fellow warriors, who seldom were downright lecherous in speech or in deed?

Would an infant prove much of a nuisance and make a lot of noise? How would it be to have a child with red rather than jet-black hair? Maybe he wouldn't mind having a pale, all-white papoose running around his lodge. Even in his childhood he'd felt an instinctive mistrust of half-breeds.

Thad Burton's gaze wandered out over the sunset-reddened Chauga and watched big trout jump and swirl at a new hatch of stone flies. Then he shifted gaze to Quobah and Hapeyah, who, working in concert, were stretching a fresh deerskin over a willow branch frame constructed, African fashion, by the Ashanti. Although they worked in silence, the giant Negro and the squat brown woman, nevertheless, seemed to have achieved harmony—if not happiness.

Just to make sure Laure hadn't begun to swell too noticeably, he made her stand up by grunting, "Fetch my pipe, then find Chula and Shatara. Send them to me."

Wearing a faint smile on features pleasingly freckled once more now that the sun was regaining its warmth, Taqua fetched his favorite red-stone pipe and silently loaded it from a bladder pouch she'd recently decorated with the Turtle totem executed in blue- and vermilion-dyed porcupine quills. Thad's gaze shifted from the turtle on his forearm to the smaller tattoo glowing, bright blue between Laure Rivard's perceptibly increasing breasts. It was a good thing that, since clan membership was inherited only through the mother, the baby, whatever its sex, also would be a Turtle, which was one of the more aristocratic clans.

The sun was close to setting before Taqua at last found the two Chickasaws participating in a rough game of stick-and-ball being played on a small, level savannah. Not even to answer their young mico's summons would either of the two sweating, bleeding, and breathless Chickasaws quit playing—their side was behind.

Taqua understood, and sat watching the ever-shifting, hurly-burly, and erratic flight of a feather-stuffed leather ball. Finally, the Chickasaws ran up with heads, arms, and shoulders lumpy and striped with dark red weals raised by hard-swung bats, and expressed willingness to depart.

Silently, they seated themselves cross-legged before Sakwari-cra—mico thlucco, or long warrior, of the new Sakwari tribe, as the wanderers called themselves, despite the unspoken contempt of Sloffkaw and his Creeks.

After Quobah had put in an appearance, Thad delayed long enough to render his words impressive, then said, "Today, I have had big words with the Mico Sloffkaw. Tomorrow, the Mico Sloffkaw will send a runner to Coweta to ask the Great Creek Council to admit my people"—Thad was sufficiently pretentious to say "people" proudly, as if his followers numbered in the hundreds instead of just eight men and two women —"as a tribe allied with the Creek Nation."

"*Wagh!* That is good," Chula and Shatara grunted in unison.

After a sedate delay, Chula spoke for his fellow tribesmen. "This is good, O Sakwari-cra. The Chickasaws are cousins of the Creeks and, for many seasons, have lived in peace."

Sakwari-cra's dyed crest inclined. "Chula speaks with a straight tongue." Craftily, he then played on their obligation to him. "What chanced that Sakwari-cra should find Chickasaw warriors slaves in a *Francani* pack train?"

Chula's small jet eyes flashed briefly, like the priming charge of a musket fired at night, then sought the ground beneath his knees. "It is right that our mico should know the truth," he growled, but for a long moment the Raven continued to rock in silence on his heels.

"At the beginning of the Rutting Moon when the first *fusul*—wild geese—start toward the land of Mehico a war party of the Seneca, without first sending out red sticks or war hoops, raided deep into our lands. They were many, but we surprised these men from the north as they retreated.

"We killed many and took away their ornaments, although they fought as the Iroquois always fight, fiercely. We set free their prisoners, then started for our homes by following a trail which, for a short distance, ran across land belonging to the dog-conceived Choctaws."

The Chickasaw Raven broke off to watch a large-mouth black bass lurch out of the water and snap up a bullfrog which had been croaking monotonously upon a muddy snag.

"Since for three hunting seasons a truce had been kept between the Squirrel King—our Grand Mingo—and Coosaw, the Choctaw mico, we suspected no trouble and met with none until we were surprised and overwhelmed on the trail to Tuscawilla by a great band of French and Choctaws."

While Taqua and Hapeyah began to set out wooden bowls of food,

Outacity Shatara, a magnificent fellow just entering middle age, took up the account. "Although surprised by such treachery, we defended ourselves so well that some *Francani* and many Choctaws died before most of us were killed and lost our hair. We who were left were driven into Fort Toulouse, together with our Seneca captives."

An angry undertone arose from the other Chickasaws as Shatara continued in a low, stifled voice, "To complete our dishonor, O Sakwari-cra, the Choctaws stripped me and my brothers naked as young birds in a nest and made us dance. For that, many *Francani* and Choctaw scalps will dry before our lodges."

Proudly, the Chickasaw's narrow, crested head tilted backward. "Because they feared us, they used us worse than the other slaves and fed us only a little. Often, they beat us for no cause."

A young runner appeared early one morning from downstream bringing news which prompted Sloffkaw to send at once for his Ravens, senior warriors, and, belatedly, for Sakwari-cra.

Adorned by a crown of redbird and blue-jay wings, Sloffkaw folded lavishly braceleted arms across his chest. "Brothers, attend! It is reported that Tomo-chichi, mico thlucco of the outlawed Yamacraws, has agreed to sell lands belonging to the Creek Nation!"

"Sell to what peoples, O Sloffkaw?" demanded an aged Slave Catcher.

"To *Englasi* chiefs who came down from Char-les Town."

"How dare Tomo-chichi even to think of such an outrage?" demanded a Raven wearing a badger's black and white mask for a headdress. "Such a sale is not lawful!"

Everyone present was aware of this; title to land occupied by any tribe belonging to the Creek Confederacy—even an outlawed one—could not become valid until such a sale had been approved by a convention of the Great Creek Council at Coweta.

Anxious to have recognized his claim to the rank of mico, Thad asked, "Who are these *Englasi* chiefs?"

The runner was pushed into the inner circle to give his answer. "Colonel Bull, Captain MacPherson and Rangers from Char-les Town; all are known to us."

The messenger, a spindle-legged youth with slightly crossed eyes, then stated that Tomo-chichi, who was reputed to be very wise, had believed Colonel Bull to be talking straight when he'd said that the *Englasi*, who want to build a new town, had promised to occupy no territory other than that which had lawfully been bought and paid for. The *Englasi* long man and Tomo-chichi had exchanged valuable gifts before the *Englasi* had sailed back to Char-les Town.

Although he couldn't possibly have explained why, Thad Burton strained to miss not a word that was said. What was it to him that certain *Englasi* were mad enough to plan a settlement on the lower Savannah, where not only the French but also the Spaniards and their ferocious, *Englasi*-hating Yamasee allies easily could massacre them? Then, abruptly, he recalled what that Choctaw guard of Joyeuse's had said about Christian Priber being sent among the Cherokees. This Colonel Bull must be a great fool to doom so many of his own people to capture or certain death.

Surely the *Englasi* should be warned against such an obvious folly. Who would do so? Certainly not Sloffkaw, or any other Creek mico for that matter. Why should they? Weren't the tribes being pushed gradually farther inland every year? He should think of none but himself. Why, *why*, WHY? Was it only because his parents had been foolish enough to let themselves get scalped? What has the white man ever done for him? Hum! Would the *Englasi* furnish him with arms and the sinews of war to help create his new nation? Never!

While the runner swilled eagerly at a bowl of watery Indian beer, the white Tuscarora continued to ponder whether Colonel Bull could have heard that the *Francani* in Biloxi already were taking steps to annihilate the proposed settlement.

While Sloffkaw and his elaborately painted elder warriors argued hotly over Tomo-chichi's forwardness, all-but forgotten recollections commenced to stir in Thad's memory; recollections which included terrible shrieks and screams, of the deafening banging of firearms, of the smell of scorched flesh.

To his own surprise, Thad found himself on his feet, rudely interrupting the runner's peroration. "Where lies the village of Tomo-chichi?"

The runner gulped the last of his beer, then wiped his mouth on a sweaty forearm. "You will find the outlaw mico and his band encamped near Amercario, which lies on the Savannah River a day's paddle up from the Bitter Water."

When the assembly broke up it was with a general sense of outrage over the Yamacraw mico's intended sale of land. Quietly, Sakwari-cra returned to his encampment, collected his people, and announced that, within an hour, the band must be packed for the trail and ready to move out.

None of the Sakwaris showed surprise; it was commonplace for Indians to make even so significant a decision as this on a moment's notice.

Since, without warning, the weather turned bitterly cold again, Sakwari-cra hurried his band along a faint trail that followed the Chauga's north bank until finally that stream merged with a slower-flowing broad mountain river which Thad reckoned eventually must empty into the

Savannah. Invariably, the young mico ordered camp made at a spot where various kinds of fish and game promised to be plentiful.

Thanks to a huge oak which, felled during last autumn's great storm, had created a natural bridge, the band found little trouble in getting across the Keowee, which, after running in a roughly parallel direction for a while, eventually became the Savannah. But when the Sakwaris reached steep-banked Cuffy Town Creek, Thad was forced to lead his followers upstream for several miles before a succession of huge rocks, fallen from a soaring cliff, afforded a precarious crossing.

When, a few days later, the confluence of Turkey Creek with the Savannah was reached, Sakwari-cra decreed a two-day halt. He felt confident that he still was in time to warn Colonel Bull of the dangers confronting the proposed settlement; besides, the squaws needed time to rest and to cut and sew new moccasins replacing footgear worn out through this long, hard journey toward the Bitter Water.

To replenish their food supply proved no problem at all; at this lower and warmer altitude the travelers came upon great herds of deer and woods buffalo, as well as innumerable flocks of turkey, partridge, and bobwhite quail.

Again Sotolycaté, or Yo-he-wa—He-Who-Sits-Above—smiled, for, at that point where the Three Runs empties into the Savannah, the Sakwari band was fortunate in discovering a log canoe hidden in the depths of a wild-grapevine tangle. Here, the Chickasaws again proved their worth; they were expert canoemen, a skill at which neither Thad nor Quobah was adept, so once crude paddles had been carved the Sakwaris and their belongings soon were ferried across the savagely swirling current, which boiled fearsomely over rocks and huge, slimy snags.

Perhaps needlessly, Sakwari-cra decided to play safe and make a wide detour around Fort Moore, a log stronghold which the General Assembly of South Carolina had caused to be constructed some ten years earlier. One could never be sure what might happen if a weak body of men were to venture too close to a military outpost, besides one never knew whether another of those savage little frontier wars might have erupted. In such an event, the hard-bitten Carolina Rangers garrisoning Fort Moore would pot strange Indians as quickly as rabbits.

The fort was reported to stand upon a height near that point where Scotia Creek mingled its icy gray waters with the Savannah's hurrying, light brown current. The site of Fort Moore, Thad perceived, had been well chosen; it dominated the main trace traversing that region.

Although such a detour involved a long, slow, and difficult struggle through pathless forests, none of the band questioned their young mico's decision.

From a party of deer-hunting Yuchi Creeks, encountered a day's travel below Fort Moore, the white Tuscarora heard that Tomo-chichi's village at Amercario now was called Yamacraw Town and was supposed to lie about two days' hard paddling or six days' walking downriver.

For a time it appeared that the Sakwaris were going to be hard put to find a way of getting across the Savannah into Tomo-chichi's hunting grounds and, for the first time, Thad Burton began to worry whether he could reach Yamacraw Town in time to warn the *Englasi*.

For three cold and rainy days the band had huddled under hastily improvised shelters when a Carolinian trader by the name of John Spencer halted a sizable pack train at the river's edge. Grizzled and gap-toothed, Spencer carried a musket balanced across his pommel and stared incredulously upon the big white Tuscarora and his handsome redheaded squaw.

"Funny thing," Spencer drawled once he'd learned that Thad spoke a little English, "I got me a feelin' I seen that gal o' yourn—or someone who's her spit and image." Leathery brow wrinkled, he scratched thoughtfully under a worn badger-skin cap. "Yep. I c'ld vow I have."

"Where?" demanded Laure in Muskogean.

"Sorry, ma'am, I can't rightly rec'lect where 'twas—or even when."

Thad exhibited no interest. He was much more concerned whether this trader could be persuaded to ferry the band over to the Savannah's southern bank in one of those wonderful folding boats which his Yuchi train guards had commenced to assemble.

These craft consisted of well-oiled buffalo skins sewn together and cleverly cut to stretch over stout, portable wooden frames. While such craft looked hopelessly awkward to manage, they, nevertheless, turned out to be practical and able to carry a considerable cargo.

"Yep. Designed the durned things meself," Spencer allowed, still staring in unabated curiosity on this deeply tanned young white man wearing Tuscarora ornaments and displaying a Turtle Clan totem on his arm. For all his ragged gray hair and beard, Spencer's red-rimmed blue eyes hungrily sought Taqua's swelling breasts, plainly visible through the opening of a loose leather shirt.

Whether Laure Rivard's auburn beauty or Thad's offer of a pair of prime otter skins carried persuasion, the trader ended by consenting to set the band across the river once he'd completed the transfer of his goods and his horses had been safely swum across.

After subtle Indian circumlocutions, Sakwari-cra began to speculate on whether the *Englasi* really intended to build a settlement on the lower Savannah.

The Carolinian scratched at a dirty, balding scalp, then sprayed tobacco juice upon a clump of winter-killed ferns. "Yep. Reckon them crazy fools *are* plannin' to build a village somewheres near Tomo-chichi's old hangout at Amercario." Spencer broke off to curse sulphurously at one of his assistants, who carelessly had deposited a bale of duffel goods on soggy ground. "Iffen they do, there'll be a heap of fresh scalps tanning round this neck o' the woods come summertime."

Thad's clear gray-blue eyes widened. "Why is that?"

"I heard tell up in Charles Town that the big chief o' this mob's a loony English nob by the name o' Oglethorpe who won't have a dozen real fightin' men 'mongst the nigh on three hundred souls they say he plans to fetch along."

"Why not?"

Again Spencer divested himself of tobacco juice. "'Cause the heft of this feller's followers are *ex-convicts!* Now I ask ye, are felons, jailbirds and the like, which the Crown is anxious to get shut of, likely to make good settlers? Like hell they will!" Spencer fixed Thad with faded blue eyes. "You heard anythin', upcountry, 'bout the Frenchies makin' war talk 'mongst the Cherokees and Upper Creeks?"

Sakwari-cra's tall black crest and new silver earrings swayed to a sedate nod. "In Guaxule, a Choctaw said a Black Robe named Priber even now stirs up Squirrel King's people."

"Hum. Choctaws is slippery folk who use a forked tongue, but, be that so, then Mr. Oglethorpe's hangdogs ain't going to last longer'n a snowflake on a hot knife blade."

Keeping an eye on his train guards who already had started to knock apart the collapsible boats, the Carolinian queried, "Say, Mico, could we make a deal? I could use three-four o'yer Chickasaws fer train guards account of I'm headin' into the Debatable Territory. Can you spare me some?"

Sakwari-cra shook his head.

"Reckon ye're right. What're ye aimin' to do?"

Thad's broad brown shoulders lifted. "When I reach Yamacraw Town I will make talk with Tomo-chichi. It may be that I will make him my ally."

Spencer grinned at this young fellow's arrogance. "Now that ain't a bad idee. Heard tell the Yamacraws is whittled down to round fifty families."

Thad made a mental note of this. "Why is Tomo-chichi a Creek outlaw?"

Ragged fringes asway, John Spencer swung up onto his mount. "Dunno. He's been a outlaw a right long time, but, somehow, he's always been able to paddle his own canoe. Only trouble is, Tomo-chichi's growin' old—nearin' ninety, so they say."

Chapter 19

TOMO-CHICHI

To send Chula into Yamacraw Town as a herald seemed a smart move. As a rule the Chickasaws and the Creeks, being blood cousins, got on fairly well—far better than did the Creeks with the neighboring Catawbas or Yamasees. Thad figured that this little attempt at pomp might lend the Sakwaris at least a semblance of prestige.

At first, Sakwari-cra had thought to dispatch Quobah, who certainly presented an unusual and a warlike figure. However, he decided against sending the African; from time immemorial his race had been associated in the Indian mind with inferiority and slavery, so he could not expect to be received with due respect.

To fulfill this mission, he selected Chula, who hurriedly applied fresh blue and yellow paint and, cold as it was, donned a breechclout of that thin, bright red and yellow calico Sakwari-cra had purchased from John Musgrove. Otherwise, he was wearing fluffy red foxtails bound below his knees. His fellow Chickasaws then lent the prospective herald their handsomest ornaments and helped him to shave his skull and then dress his scalp lock into a lofty blue-black topknot secured with strips of silvery otter fur.

Chula had been in Yamacraw Town less than half an hour when he reappeared running with his characteristic, long and springy stride to report that the mico thlucco, Tomo-chichi, seemed hospitably disposed. In fact, he would be pleased to enter into conversation with Sakwari-cra.

Observing Indian custom, Thad Burton delayed his appearance in Yamacraw Town until afternoon, by which time Tomo-chichi should have been afforded ample opportunity to prepare whatever type of a reception that wily old man intended to offer.

Tomo-chichi received his towering young visitor before his personal dwelling, for, having just recently moved from the heights of Amercario, he hadn't yet had time to complete the usual Creek council house. Only its framing stood in the center of the town, which, as usual, was enclosed by a stout palisade.

The Sakwari emissaries, who included Sakwari-cra, Chula, Shatara, as well as Quobah, found the deeply wrinkled Yamacraw chieftain seated cross-legged on a rare and enormously valuable albino buffalo's hide.

To Thad it came as a profound relief that Tomo-chichi and his senior warriors held the visitors in sufficient respect to have painted designs of yellow and green checks on their faces. Squatting in a brilliant semicircle behind the mico thlucco were easily twenty warriors. These Thad found out later included Toonahowie, Tomo-chichi's nephew, the Yamacraw's Beloved Man—or peace chief—and a handsome Raven named Kawea— like the Seneca who had run so well.

A long and penetrating silence, broken only by the yapping of dogs, ensued when the Sakwaris halted before Tomo-chichi. Solemnly, Sakwari-cra, appearing mighty tall under a shimmering, emerald-green headdress of parrot wings, raised a hand to make the peace sign.

Taqua had also decorated the self-styled mico's face, neck, and even his shoulders with ornate designs done in red, blue, and yellow paint. To the assembled Yamacraws the powerful play of muscles under Thad's tawny skin was impressive. The assemblage also appeared impressed by the arrogant manner in which this huge red-white man threw back his head while chanting his name, his clan, and then boasted of the great deeds he had done, including the Great Run and its bloody aftermath.

Tomo-chichi, as the trader John Spencer had said, was indeed aged, but the expression of his deeply furrowed features, which were the color of freshly cured tobacco leaves, remained shrewd and alert. The Yamacraw mico was wearing a headdress of delicately nodding egret plumes, also a crescent-shaped breastplate of gleaming nacre over a European red flannel shirt, the tails of which flapped incongruously above a turquoise-blue loincloth and yellow-and-blue buckskin leggings. Small gold coins had been let, one above the other, into the rims of Tomo-chichi's ears—three to a side.

As a testimonial to his long friendship with the *Englasi* the aged mico wore a big silver medallion bearing the heavy Hanoverian profile of King George I, slung to a thin silver necklace. Wide silver bracelets decorated with turquoise had slipped so low on the ancient's stringy arms that they clicked over his wrists.

The old mico returned the peace sign, then, still without speaking, shifted his gaze to Quobah, whose skin, freshly oiled with bear's fat, shone like polished ebony beneath a collar of panther claws collected during the winter's hunting.

The Ashanti prince, as usual, was wearing a turban, this time of scarlet-and yellow-striped cloth and, in honor of the occasion, he'd also donned an elaborate breastplate of cleverly jointed bird bones done in the African manner. In addition to his musket, the giant Negro carried a pair of assegais he'd forged in Sloffkaw's village. These spears with their broad, leaf-shaped iron heads in no way resembled weapons of local manufacture.

At long last, Tomo-chichi, his crinkled features devoid of expression, spoke in dry, high-pitched tones. "Sakwari-cra and your band"—Thad stiffened because the old man had said "band" instead of "people"— "are welcome to build dwellings near us, to hunt on our land and to make war with us when the red sticks are sent out."

To regain face, Thad decided on a bold stand, cried loftily, "So shall it be, O Mico Thlucco, but in battle, I alone shall command my warriors; they will take orders from me alone. Otherwise, you shall count them among your fighting men so long as this alliance endures. I speak with a straight heart." He stared unblinkingly into the old man's cunning little eyes.

Ever a master diplomatist, Tomo-chichi was in no hurry to confirm this overbold young fellow's claim to the rank of mico, so he said slowly, "The Mico Sakwari-cra surely knows that before such an alliance is agreed upon the matter must be debated in council."

The Mico Sakwari-cra! The title sounded fine, fine as a mouse's whisker. *Wagh!* It meant much thus to be acknowledged by an independent chieftain as powerful and as widely respected as Tomo-chichi; compared with him, Sloffkaw was but a surly nonentity.

At the same time Thad commenced to wonder just why the ancient should have conceded this dignity so readily. Did he stand so much in need of reinforcements? And if so, why? Had the Yamacraw a war in mind? Possibly he might have tricked the *Englasi* in the matter of selling land and was preparing to attack the projected settlement first of anyone, and so grow rich with plunder?

Tomo-chichi crooked a gnarled forefinger at a young Bowman who brought outdoors an already lighted pipe adorned with a fan of snowy swan feathers which swayed gracefully from its stem.

Thad sank onto his heels before the venerable mico thlucco and accepted the peace pipe. Then, not knowing what else to do, he followed the Tuscarora custom of blowing a puff of rank-smelling smoke toward the sources of the Four Great Winds.

To impress upon everyone that Quobah, although a Negro, wasn't in any sense a slave, Thad quickly transferred the pipe to the Ashanti, who, after baring doglike teeth in a ferocious grin, clapped bluish lips over the brass mouthpiece and drew such a long, deep puff that it all but burned out the tobacco remaining in the bowl. Quobah exhaled a puff of smoke as large as that made by a signaling cannon and sent it billowing through the still, sunlit air.

Once the pipe had been replenished and circulated, Tomo-chichi indicated a clump of trees beneath which a bevy of squaws were at work preparing tender young dog and plenty of buffalo ribs for roasting over a wide bed of coals. The serving of so prized a dish as young dog lent strength to Sakwari-cra's hunch that, whatever his plans, Tomo-chichi regarded him and his seven warriors as a reinforcement of considerable importance.

Impassive of manner, Thad decided quietly to take measure of Toonahowie, peace chief of these Yamacraws. If anything happened to the old man it seemed likely that this brawny, intelligent-appearing nephew would become the next mico thlucco.

Tomo-chichi's feast of welcome continued until dusk, then, gorged and belching loudly, most of the Yamacraws sought their huts, but quite a few remained to hear what news might have been brought by a messenger who'd come paddling upstream. He had to report that a number of canoes, one of which had contained Coosa-pona-keesa, John Musgrove's wife, had been sighted paddling up from the sea; beyond a doubt they were making for Yamacraw Town.

Coosa-pona-keesa? Thad tried to dispel his torpor and think clearly. He must try to understand why Mary Musgrove should be coming to Yamacraw Town at this particular time.

As for Taqua, her softly freckled features flushed with pleasure over the prospect of meeting Mary once again. Right from the start, Hapeyah, in her taciturn way, always had been friendly and helpful, yet Laure never had felt for the ugly, bowlegged little squaw that curious affection she felt for the stately half-breed princess.

The fact that Mary Musgrove was the late Emperor Brims's niece was attested by the fact that, despite the huge meal he'd just consumed, Tomo-chichi roused, ordered fresh food prepared, and sent heralds running to cry the news not only within the palisade but also among wigwams, huts, and cabins scattered, hit or miss, throughout the surrounding forest.

Standing somewhat aloof, Sakwari-cra watched Indians of all ages, chattering excitedly. Dark was fast closing in, so two bonfires were kindled at the canoe place on the river's south bank.

Once the visitors' lead canoes loomed around a bend overgrown with massive water oaks, hand drums commenced to throb and reverberate across the inky water. Then a party of wizards, outlandishly caparisoned, pranced over the sand down to the water's edge, shaking rattles and blowing ear-piercing notes on whistles made of turkey wing bones. Yelping cries of joy arose when Mary Musgrove stepped ashore.

Gravely, Coosa-pona-keesa addressed the wrinkled old mico as "my venerable father" and at the same time she quite concealed her puzzlement over the nature of the other celebration which her arrival had terminated. She came as near to expressing surprise as the Indian side of her temperament permitted on glimpsing that giant African she'd last seen in Goggle-Eyes' village. Her curiosity mounted when she saw the equally tall white

Tuscarora standing somewhat apart, expressionless. Mary permitted a half-smile to appear on her clearly outlined dark red lips, then requested Tomo-chichi to invite Sakwari-cra and Quobah to come closer—which evoked an astonished murmur from the Yamacraws.

When the white Tuscarora stepped forward with chin held high, he called out, "Greetings, O Coosa-pona-keesa! Always the sun, the moon and the stars shine brighter in your presence!"

"Greetings, Sakwari-cra! Greetings, Quobah!" replied John Musgrove's wife in English. "Tsul and I have heard of your great coup against the people of Antoine Joyeuse." Her smile faded. "While that feat cost us the loss of all those skins we left in Goggle-Eyes' village, we are not angry with you."

Her gaze swung to the muscular Chickasaw gathering behind Thad. "For you to free slaves from the French for fighting the enemies of King George was a praiseworthy deed. Georgia will need every hand that can be raised in its defense."

Thad Burton blinked, queried, "What—Georgia?"

Mary reverted to Muskogean. "By that name the new *Englasi* colony will be known. It is so named in honor of their king, who is the second George."

Toonahowie spoke up. "Then the *Englasi* are determined to build a village on *this* side of the river?"

"So my husband, Tsul, has heard in Charles Town." As Mary's gaze swung back to Tomo-chichi her manner became markedly grave. "Tell me. Is it true that you, my father, have made talk with Colonel Bull over the selling of land?"

The Yamacraw chieftain's eyes glittered briefly among the ravine-like wrinkles, then, in monumental dignity, he arose and one could tell that in his prime he must have stood over six feet tall.

"Coosa-pona-keesa speaks about that which concerns her not." Coldly, he turned aside. "Food waits before my lodge." Tomo-chichi stalked away followed by Toonahowie and others of the Yamacraw Council.

Mary Musgrove's white blood caused her to make a wry face before she turned to the chief paddler and issued orders that her people should bivouac above the canoe place high enough to avoid the risk of being flooded out should the river rise suddenly, as it often did at this season. She glanced briefly back at the landing, where, under shadowy stalactites of Spanish moss, her escorts already had begun to unload their gear.

On her way to Tomo-chichi's dwelling she was greeted affectionately by so many Yamacraws that Thad figured that, for a long while, Mary Musgrove must have been on intimate terms with the outlawed Mico Thlucco and his people.

Countless stars shone through tufted pine tops when a young Creek approached the grove in which the Sakwaris were encamped. "Coosa-pona-keesa would make talk with the Mico Sakwari-cra," he announced, then merged again with the shadows.

Once Thad had sunk onto his heels before a fire burning in front of Tomo-chichi's guest lodge, Mary Musgrove offered him a burl bowl of what turned out to be English beer—the first he'd ever tasted. He found it wonderfully full-bodied and potent. Deliberately, Mary spoke. "I am pleased to find you again, Thad Burton. I see also that your woman is growing a great belly."

Seated upon a stump before the fire, Mary now spoke in Muskogean. "What is your feeling toward Taqua, now that you have become a mico?"

"If she bears a son, perhaps I will free her and marry her. She is a Turtle too, and a strong woman."

Mary Musgrove laughed softly, musically. "Why wait? After all, are not you and Laure Rivard both full-blooded whites?"

"So what of that?" growled the white Tuscarora.

"Why, among the Englasi 'tis customary for couples who—well, live together to get married. Their wizards—they call them 'ministers'—insist upon this and banish all who refuse to wed their women."

Across acrid tendrils of wood smoke Thad stared at Musgrove's wife in almost comic disbelief. "This makes no sense. What if such a squaw later grows disobedient and quarrelsome?"

"Attend my words, Sakwari-cra. If such a wife is allowed to become lazy, shrill and disobedient, it is the man's own fault. Another thing, Englasi do not allow their women to go about bare-breasted—at least not in public! That to them means a lack of modesty." She laughed softly. "Oh yes. All whites admire modesty. If you ever dwell among them you must remember these things I have told you."

Thoughtfully, Thad dug at a flea nipping shrewdly under his loin-cloth. "Sakwari-cra does not wish ever to dwell among the Englasi—or any other white men! The little he has seen of such, he does not understand. Besides, were he to live among them he would not rank as a mico. They would call him a stupid savage who cannot understand well their language or their speech on paper. No, Coosa-pona-keesa, I will stay with my people and make them grow great."

In the uncertain firelight, Mary nodded slowly, feeling sorry for this puzzled young man. "You are right. The Englasi would not accept you as the mico of a powerful tribe. The Sakwaris are too few."

Furious at her logic, he flushed and sprang up, gray-blue eyes flashing. This, after he had traveled so far to warn Colonel Bull! "Sakwari-cra does not care what the Englasi think! He does not love them as he loves his red brothers." Shaking with anger, he raised his voice. "He cannot think as they think, nor does he choose to live as they live!"

Mary Musgrove smoothed her skirt of fringed, well-bleached doeskin, said softly, "Perhaps someday you will, Thad Burton."

He glowered down at this handsome woman sitting so unconcernedly before the dying fire. "No! And that is true, as the sun will rise tomorrow. He will not live like an *Englasi!*"

"That tomorrow the sun will rise above the sea indeed is certain," Mary agreed, then lifted her eyes to consider the multitude of stars glowing above Yamacraw Town. "Nevertheless, whether you like it or not, you are *all* white—not part, like me," she added with a touch of bitterness. Almost sadly, the trader's wife looked him full in his painted face. "Soon, some of your people will need help as, even now, they ask for mine."

Thad began to calm down. "Coosa-pona-keesa speaks of a village the *Englasi* mean to build near here?"

"Yes. Without help from some who understand my mother's people's ways these strangers will survive no longer than a pea blossom under a strong frost."

For the life of him, Thad Burton couldn't have explained why suddenly he squatted again and described in detail what Joyeuse's Choctaw guard had told him concerning the Jesuit, Christian Priber, and his troublemaking among the Cherokees. "Perhaps the *Englasi* should know of this?"

"Of a certainty," Mary said, smiling. "But why does Sakwari-cra worry over a parcel of helpless palefaces? Surely the fate of these miserable *Englasi* can be of no concern to the mighty Mico of the Sakwaris."

Next morning, before dawn, Thad Burton woke Laure Rivard and, to her amazement, told her to conceal her bust under a hunting shirt, then to pack for the trail. Next, he sent Shatara and Chula to purchase two canoes in good condition and ordered the rest of his band to get ready to move out on short notice.

BOOK II

The Debatable Ground

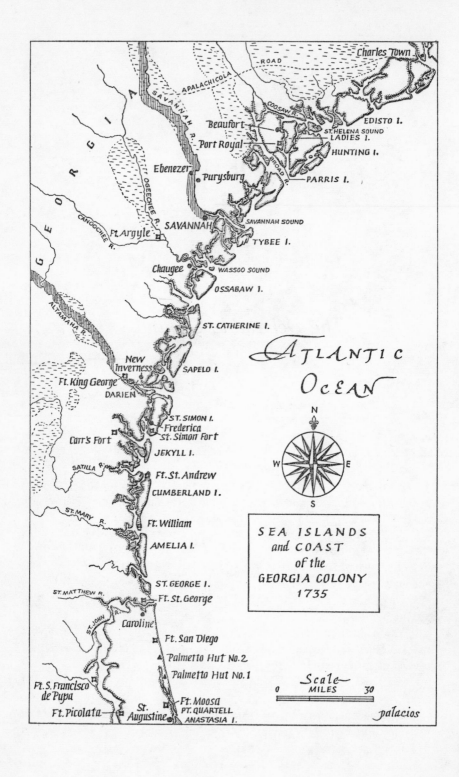

SEA ISLANDS
and COAST
of the
GEORGIA COLONY
1735

Chapter 1

CHARLES TOWN BAR

Bowling along under a stiff breeze from the northwest the brig *Mystick*, out of Boston for Jamaica, shortened canvas, then wore onto a starboard tack in preparation of grappling with the treacherous currents forever foaming over Charles Town Bar.

To Captain Elijah Starbuck—plunged into a villainous mood on this cold and gloomy morning—it seemed that this incommunicative, blunt-featured King's pilot who was conning his vessel out of Charles Town seemed uncertain about how best to approach that wide band of boiling white water which marked the bar's position.

On deck Seth Coffin, the *Mystick's* mate, considered his captain's glowering countenance with dour amusement, then ordered the watch on deck to brace the brig's stubby yards farther to port.

B'God, mused the mate, 'twill take a month o' Sundays for Lije to get over getting so neatly cozened—and by a female to boot! For all that a flirt of spray, cold as Christian charity, had struck him full in the whiskers and had begun to trickle icily down under his oilskins, Coffin began to chuckle, then, as the depth of Elijah Starbuck's humiliation struck him, he laughed right out loud.

The gray-bearded mate's thoughts ran back to a certain pleasant evening off the New Jersey coast when, through the cabin's transom, he'd been startled to overhear the Brooks girl saying in a cold fury.

"Take heed, Captain! Don't you ever talk or act like this again! Not ever!"

The captain had growled, "Aboard my ship I talk and act like it pleases me, and you can lay to that, Sissie!" Surprisingly, his tone then had softened, had become almost pleading. "Ah-h be nice, won't ye? Can't ye understand? Your sort would set a stone saint on fire!"

Seth had tried to peer through the transom, but to his disappointment had found that the pair below were standing out of his range of vision.

"That's as may be, but this is not my fault. I've never once encouraged your attentions, so please don't carry on like this." For the first time a trace of desperation had crept into Winsome Brooks's voice. "I-I'll not listen any longer to your d-disgusting proposals so please t-take your hands off me; *please*, Captain!"

Captain Starbuck had fairly snarled, "No, b'God! Ye'd *better* favor me an' yer not a complete ijit."

" 'Better!' Why?"

"An ye don't, I'll spread the news."

"What news?"

"Why, what everybody in Boston says—that you and yer pa had unlawful knowledge of one another!"

"Oh-h—" The girl's cry had reminded Seth of the noise made by a rabbit he'd once snared by a leg. Even now, as he watched the foaming bar loom nearer, Coffin could recall very distinctly the anguish in Mistress Brooks's voice. "But that's a foul lie!" she'd shrilled. " 'Twas only a filthy falsehood invented by a pack of nasty-minded old maids and neighborhood gossips. Surely, I loved my father, I-I adored him, but I-I loved him only as a daughter should!"

"So say *you*, Sissie," the *Mystick's* master had sneered, "so that's as may be. But I know what I heard tell in Boston, and that, b'God, is what I'll repeat and you don't favor me better."

"*You'd not!*"

"I will!" Then Elijah Starbuck had adopted a wheedling tone. "For God's sake, girl, try to understand! I ain't slept sound since we cleared Sandy Hook. Be good and I'll do all in my power to please ye. Now if ye'll only stretch out on that locker."

At that moment the brig had come about with such a creak-and-rattle of yards and loud slatting of canvas that the next thing the mate had heard was the smooth-faced Brooks wench saying in a level, lifeless tone, "Very well, I will make a bargain with you. Promise to treat me with respect during the rest of this voyage and swear forever to hold your tongue concerning those awful lies and I'll promise to marry you when we reach Jamaica."

That the Old Man should have proved so ready to fall in with the girl's offer had surprised Seth Coffin considerably. As a rule Lije wasn't one to make up his mind in such a hurry, least of all about such a delicate matter as marriage. B'God! The old goat must really be hot for the wench.

Hum! Another thing. Were she completely innocent, why should she seem to be in such mortal terror of having the rumor spread? Hum. The old saw decreed that "Where there's smoke, there's bound to be fire."

The mate had decided that Winsome Brooks had charmed Elijah Starbuck clean out of his wits for sure when he'd said, "Fair enough, Mistress Brooks, but God help ye an ye don't keep the bargain. I'll see ye jailed if it's the last thing I do on this earth. Not that I believe you'd cheat me. In a dozen ports they'll tell you Elijah Starbuck's seldom mistook in his jedgments."

The King's pilot's bawled orders to the helmsman snapped Seth Coffin's attention back to present considerations.

The *Mystick*, bearing down on the bar's wild water, had begun to rear and plunge like a spirited colt at the end of a breaking longe.

Seth Coffin's jaws worked faster on a "chaw" that made his cheek bulge like a nut-hunting squirrel's. A glance at the quarter-deck told him that the Old Man was rigidly clutching the taffrail. He was wearing a greasy felt cap jammed low over his ears and, like "Irish pennants," his gray chin whiskers were whipping in the breeze.

Again the mate grinned when the skipper shook his fist in the direction of Charles Town, looking small and insignificant on the tip of a peninsula formed by the confluence of the Cooper and Ashley rivers. Seth Coffin sobered a trifle when, on regaining the quarter-deck, he noted the terrible expression contorting Elijah Starbuck's sallow features. The mate couldn't help thinking, God help Winsome Brooks the day Elijah Starbuck comes even with her!

Imagine that demure Boston puss having so slyly eluded the deck watch to slip ashore two nights ago. Maybe she'd been justified in breaking her promise. After all, she had been forced into the bargain. What would become of that tempting yet strangely self-possessed young woman? Nothing easy, so much was certain-sure. When she'd jumped ship she'd taken nothing with her; only the duds she was wearing. The rest of her scant possessions had been left aboard the *Mystick*.

Again, the brig's violent plunges demanded Coffin's attention; she was about to enter those heaving, pyramid-shaped waves edging the bar. About then the mate, who'd been keeping a wary eye on the brig's straining top hamper, became aware that another vessel was bearing down on the bar but from the opposite direction. Although she looked smallish, she was frigate-rigged and was beating in from the Atlantic. By her lines Coffin took her to be English and was correct in this, for, presently, he made out a bright new Royal Jack snapping from her wildly swaying maintop.

He had no time to study the stranger any longer, for, with a squattering rush, the brig entered a welter of white-headed cross-currents churning above that ever-treacherous sand bar. With salt-smelling spindrift growing stronger in their nostrils, the seamen on deck grabbed for the nearest stay or shroud. In sickening arcs the brig's stubby topmasts commenced to rake the gray-blue sky. In noisy protest the *Mystick's* shivering and swaying yards screeched across parrels while, from every direction, sheets of icy spray burst over the bulwarks. Because the wind blew from astern the brig's travail was brief; she re-entered deep water and resumed her normal motion.

As a matter of course the King's pilot steered as close to the inbound vessel as he dared. In this remote land news from Home was as precious as jewels and fine gold.

Moodily, Elijah Starbuck watched the frigate beat nearer, automatically took note of her condition. That yonder sailed no ordinary merchantman he could tell with half an eye; too many heads were lining her rails. In fact, the frigate appeared to be jammed with passengers. Thought the *Mystick's* captain, Her paint's so faded and her rigging's so gray and seaworn she must be completing a stormy transatlantic crossing. Yep. She's an immigrant ship, b'God, else I'm sure mistook in my—Starbuck winced. A pox on that sly wench! Oh, how shamefully, how thoroughly she'd cozened him!

How rejoiced those seasick wretches yonder must be over sighting even so forlorn a prospect of the low, sandy coast of what now was known as the "Colony of South Carolina," since the original charter had lapsed in 1729. Nowadays, the original Colony of Carolina had been divided and rechartered as His Majesty's Colonies of North and South Carolina. Since this division had occurred barely five years earlier, most people forgot to make the distinction.

Nearer struggled the stranger, heeled far over to port. "Look alive! Dip the Colors!" yelled Starbuck. When the inbound vessel drew nearer he estimated that this seaworn frigate was only a little larger than his own brig—say of about two hundred fifty tons burthen.

Then the *Mystick's* master noticed something unusual. On the inbound vessel's poop deck were gathered a number of brilliantly garbed figures— obviously high-ranking officers of some sort.

Once the stranger had threshed within hailing distance the New Englander caught up his speaking trumpet and bellowed, "What ship is that?"

Faintly, because the wind was against him, someone shouted back, "Frigate *Anne*, Cap'n John Thomas—seven weeks out—Gravesend— Madeira for Charles Town. Who—you?"

"Brig *Mystick*, Cap'n Starbuck, out o' Boston and Noo York bound for Port Antonio, Jamaica!"

The pilot, through cupped hands suddenly shouted, "Ahoy, there! Be we at war wi' France?"

"Not when we sailed." The other speaker could now be heard more distinctly.

Starbuck elbowed aside the pilot. "What about Spain?" He needed reassurance on that point; wasn't he heading for the Caribbean?

Over the hissing of waves under the *Mystick's* counter came a wind-distorted reply. "Not yet—but soon, heard so in London. Best be wary if ye're headed south."

As if he wasn't going to be cautious! What Starbuck had heard about Spanish prisons wasn't in the least inviting.

When the other ship sailed by not fifty yards abeam the crowd of people aboard her began to wave and yell like so many idiots.

"Who've ye aboard?"

"Actin' Governor o' Georgia—some o' his people!"

Starbuck knitted shaggy brows, glanced inquiringly at the pilot. "Now where in tarnation is Georgia?"

With his weight steadying the brig's whipstaff the flat-faced pilot grunted. "Why, 'tis the name they've given a new colony they're figgerin' on plantin' on the Savannah River."

The *Mystick's* master looked thoughtful as, for the first time, he altogether forgot the treachery of Winsome Brooks. "But don't the Spanishers claim that land?"

"That's c'rect," grunted the pilot. "The Dons won't never stand for English settlers south o' the Savannah—too close to St. Augustine. Them poor devils yonder wunt last long'rn a snowball in hell."

Chapter 2

THE FRIENDLESS ONE

On the morning of January 13, 1733, a skinny little Negro boy, clad only in an old sack with neck and armholes cut into it, approached a haystack on the edge of town in which, frightened, cold, and hungry, Winsome Brooks had been concealing herself for two interminable nights and a day.

Picking hay from her hair, Winsome emerged only after casting a searching look about.

"The black brig is gone?"

"Yassum. She fo' suah done gone off down de ha'bor."

"Did she anchor?"

Grinning, the boy rolled his eyes. "No'm. She done cross de ba' an' go away."

A warming flood swept through her with the realization that the *Mystick* at last had put to sea. Or had she, really?

Desperately, she needed to move about and eat some real food, though the good Lord alone knew how she'd ever get to pay for it. As it was, since deserting the brig she'd only drunk from a spring that rose in a nearby spinney and had eaten a little cold corn pudding which, for a ha'penny, fetched by this little colored boy who, while hunting rabbits, had stumbled on her hiding place. Fortunately, the child had not seemed in the least excited over his discovery.

While the pudding had proved nourishing past expectation, thanks to the few bits of pork it contained, it hadn't gone far toward settling the demands of her famished young body.

"You actually *saw* the black brig sail?"

"No'm, but dey all say she sho' lib fo' de sea," the boy assured her. "Sway to God, missis, 'at's Gawd's own truf."

Once the lad had wandered away crossing a wide gray field toward his owner's cabin, Winsome thought as hard as she ever had in her life. Had Captain Starbuck, burning with rage and disappointment, repeated that ghastly gossip concerning her? She could only cling to a frail hope that, perhaps, the *Mystick's* master had held his tongue, hoping, until the very last minute, her penniless state would force her to return aboard. True, he'd evidently delayed his brig's sailing by a whole day although such a layover must have cost him a pretty penny.

Trying to forget, Winsome strove to ignore the rumbling of her empty stomach and decide upon a sensible course of action. One precaution was obvious: she must take another name, at least long enough to make sure that Elijah Starbuck hadn't slandered her reputation. She knew nothing, of course, about Carolinian standards of morality; why, they might even be harsher than those of New England.

What pseudonym should she adopt? Winsome considered various possibilities and, as usual to most beginners, selected the alias of "Winifred Crooks," which she reckoned sounded enough like "Winsome Brooks" to save her explanations were someone to use her real name.

Supine on the rough and sour-smelling hay, she hitched up her skirt, permitted the morning sun to warm long, straight legs uglily concealed by darned and shapeless black woolen stockings. Soon she began to perspire, which immediately she regretted because, nowadays, she reeked of stale sweat and female body odors—which was understandable for, since the brig had cleared from New York, she'd never once enjoyed a whole bath.

A black and white hen and a trio of half-grown chicks drew so near that they gazed at her from clear, sherry-colored eyes, unafraid because they'd encountered her before and she hadn't scared them. They continued to scratch and hunt for insects in the loose hay ringing the stack.

Despite the nipping of hunger pangs, Winsome forced herself to lie where she was a little longer. There'd be no point venturing prematurely into town to discover that Elijah Starbuck's brig had returned to port!

To while away the time, Winsome sat up and used fingers to comb her oily but still wavy dark brown hair into some sort of order. While the results were nothing to brag over she did succeed in braiding and twisting it into a crude chignon, which she secured with a length of thread yanked from a badly soiled underpetticoat.

Not until after midday did the fugitive seek the spring, where, employing fine sand scooped from its bottom, she scrubbed her face, neck, and hands until they tingled, and then attempted to conceal her hair's deplorable state under a rumpled kerchief.

Before quitting the spring she took stock of her appearance by using the water as reflecting glass. Sobering, she noted that her narrow hazel eyes had retreated into their sockets enough to expose a rather fetching pale blue tinge on their upper lids. It was disappointing, however, to notice that those tiny, bright green specks which usually were present in her irises seemed to have vanished—temporarily at least.

One thing was sure, Captain Starbuck's lecherous antics had cost her considerable weight. Recollections of that awful voyage down from New York still made her aching stomach squirm. The cruel, unfair part of it was that she'd said or done absolutely nothing calculated to invite so persistent a persecution.

On leaving Boston she'd been so abominably seasick that she'd seen only a little of Captain Starbuck—or anyone else for that matter. Therefore, she'd not had any warning of what lay in Starbuck's mind until, on the night of New Year's Day, 1733, the salty old rascal suddenly had entered her cabin without even so much as a single knock.

Resembling a scrawny ghost in a nightshirt which flapped about his ankles, Starbuck had kissed her before she knew what he was about and, babbling endearments, had attempted to strip back the bedclothes of her bunk. How utterly repulsive he'd been with his ragged gray whiskers, dirty, old-smelling body, and indescribably foul breath.

For all his eagerness, the captain reluctantly had yielded to her furious protests, had allowed that he just might have been rushing matters a trifle.

A couple of nights later he'd caught her sitting alone on the cabin's transom and enjoying the moonlit sea off Cape May. To discover how quick that bony old fellow was had been a frightening experience. All in an instant, he'd slipped a hand garter-high under her petticoats before she'd even suspected what he was about, but then she'd fetched him a clout which surely must have caused his few remaining teeth to rattle. Recovering, he'd grabbed her arm and had twisted it unmercifully until she'd moaned and had had to quit struggling.

The man at the *Mystick's* wheel must have known what was going on but had had no intention of interrupting his captain's idea of sport.

"Don't be so damn' hoity-toity!" Starbuck had panted, grinding bearded lips against her face. "Yer pa weren't ever half the man *I* am, so don't be a ninny, sweeting. Admit ye've always hankered fer older men. Come on, I'll be generous wi' ye, Winnie, 'fore God I will. You'll see. I'll buy ye a mort o' pretty presents after we dock in Jamaica."

If, at that moment, Winsome could have slain the *Mystick's* captain, she gladly would have. How dared this odious old villain compare himself with Pa? Dear, gentle Pa, who'd only needed a little tangible affection after Ma had been laid to rest.

She had managed to break free only by landing a shrewd kick on Starbuck's shin and then had bounded down the companionway to the main deck, where the fortuitous arrival of Mr. Coffin had put an end to the episode.

But even then the old man hadn't been willing to give up. Almost meekly, he'd apologized the next morning and had admitted that what he'd heard in Boston most likely was but a scandalous rumor without foundation of any sort. Yessiree, any sane person could tell with half an eye that Winsome Brooks was as pure as the driven snow, nothing else but.

While the brig had plowed southward Starbuck's manner had remained ingratiating, almost servile. For example he'd always lift his ratty old cap on drawing near to wish her "good morning" whenever she risked a daylight appearance on deck.

At night she'd barricaded herself in her tiny cabin staring fearfully into the darkness whenever footsteps sounded on the companion ladder.

The evening the brig had sighted the low gray-white outline of Cape Hatteras he'd been humble, had invited her into the cabin so politely that she'd accepted.

"Please, Mistress Brooks, hear me out and forgive the trouble I've given ye. Plain fact is, I respect ye mightily and I want you like I've never wanted a mortal woman before. So just name yer terms and I'll marry ye —like I've said I would."

By then Winsome Brooks had figured she'd best use her wits and quickly, too. On a ship at sea her captain was at once law, judge, and jury. As he'd implied, there had been nothing to prevent his preferring any kind of charge when they touched in Charles Town and having her imprisoned. So she'd given her promise to wed him in Jamaica.

Winsome lingered beside the spring, leaning against a gum tree and attempting to read the future while she watched a lone buzzard wheel in apparently aimless circles about the pallid sky. She only half-heard a bell sound noon from some distant church spire. So, if the little black boy had been telling the truth, the *Mystick* by this time must have crossed Charles Town Bar and be scudding along to Jamaica.

She arose again, thankful that the sturdy low shoes she'd selected for her escape had proved to be comfortable; her full-skirted gown of rumpled Lincoln green serge was warm and so modest of cut that it shouldn't attract anyone's attention.

Drawing a deep breath and subconsciously squaring sloping but well-formed shoulders, the girl set foot to a cowpath which appeared to lead in the general direction of Charles Town. Was it an omen that, just as she set out, the sun should slide behind a cloud bank and a chilly wind should commence to blow out of the northwest?

Chapter 3

FOREIGN SHORE

From the *Anne's* tiny, swaying quarter-deck, James Edward Oglethorpe, Esq., M.P., thoughtfully read the name "Mystick of New Bedford" on the stern of a small brig that bore away downwind. Then the tall Englishman's attention, like that of his immediate companions, Captain John Thomas, commanding the frigate, Chaplain Henry Herbert, and Mr. Peter Gordon, the projected colony's chief magistrate designate, became centered on the *Anne's* sudden frantic plunges, twists, and crazy lurchings which flung unwary immigrants onto the deck and caused the rest to hold hard to the nearest support.

The *Anne's* pilot was able—he'd delayed until the little frigate might ride a flood tide—so her ordeal among the bar's furious currents and boiling sands proved brief and she soon entered the Outer Harbor's steady waters.

The King's pilot wiped spume from weather-beaten features, then, grinning, queried, "Wal, how d'ye like that, Yer Excellency?"

"A difficult maneuver handsomely executed," Oglethorpe assured in a rich and resonant voice.

"Ain't no man understands this bar better nor I, sir."

The acting governor's wide-set and unusually large and clear brown eyes swung to consider the town beginning to show as a low, dark line across the great harbor's tea-colored water. Dense clouds of waterfowl continually rose, flew about, and then settled again.

The Reverend Herbert glanced at this courtly gentleman who had toiled so long and so diligently to offer this company of unfortunates a new chance in life.

While surveying James Oglethorpe, Esq., the chaplain noted that the coarse-grained skin of his unusually long nose and face was flaming with sunburn. His chin might have been a bit heavy but was strong and well rounded, his heavy dark brows formed pleasant but firm arcs. Standing just short of six feet, the Georgia Company's "accompanying trustee" at thirty-six looked to be—and was—in the very prime of life.

James Oglethorpe, Member of Parliament (for Haslemere), guessed that he was soon to be accorded a welcoming ceremony of some sort, so had donned a full-bottomed brown wig, a long-skirted bright blue velvet coat, yellow satin knee breeches, and scarlet silk stockings. On his long and narrow head the acting governor had set a black tricorne edged with crisp white ostrich plumes which kept undulating in the wind. In honor of the impending ceremony he further had buckled on a jeweled walking sword which he was entitled to wear both as a gentleman and as a former officer of the Regular Establishment.

Settlers, crowding the vessel's deck, kept peering up at their leader, this being the first time they'd seen him wearing other than sober, simple garments of gray, black, or brown.

Now that the *Anne* was plowing steadily across Charles Town's huge harbor her forecastle and waist became densely packed with immigrants who leaned out over the bulwarks the better to crane necks and study this low-lying and drab-hued land in which most of them were expected to live out their lives.

Ex-poachers among the would-be settlers exclaimed over huge, smoke-like clouds of ducks, geese, coots, and majestic white swans which kept rising and milling about, only to settle once more, quite unfrightened. Soon appeared a number of small, sandy islands, then brown marshy headlands dotted with dwarf palmettos and wind-contorted scrub pines.

"Cor!" chuckled a broad-faced youth. "Now will ye luke at all them swans! Do they belong to the King over here?"

"Naw," grunted a passing seaman. "Ain't no game laws in America."

"Then there's no need to risk swinging for killing milord's game!"

A big, beetle-browed fellow jumped up onto the bowsprit and, clinging to a stay, yelled back to the quarter-deck, "Gor' bless ye, Guvnor, ye've bought us out o' jail and fetched us safe and sound to the Promised Land!"

This was true for, of the one hundred eighteen souls who had slunk aboard the *Anne* at Gravesend only two sickly infants had died during the seven storm-tossed weeks required for the frigate to make her westing.

When a great shout had died away James Oglethorpe gravely lifted his hat, bowed acknowledgment, then called out, " 'Tis the company, not me, you should thank, my friends; always remember that when dark and fearful days come, as come they must, for all of us."

Never before during the colonization of English North America had a company of penniless and friendless emigrants been granted treatment so decent. From the start they'd been furnished with fairly good food, rough but warm clothing, and, on special occasions, treated to a noggin of Alderman Parson's Best Beer.

Carefully concealing a sense of elation, Oglethorpe considered, quite without intending to, those of his colonists who during the voyage had captured his attention.

Pressed against the forecastle stood surly John Stonehewer and his tiny wife. The Stonehewer woman seemed to be explaining the ever-shifting swarms of waterfowl to Tim and Tom, their eight-year-old twins. James Oglethorpe recalled his first encounter with the cantankerous cloth weaver.

It seemed hardly possible that less than three months had elapsed since that day when, in Fleet Prison, John Stonehewer had been led in chained, scowling and defiant. Upon inquiry, Oglethorpe, representing the Parliamentary committee appointed to inquire into "the State of Gaols in this Kingdom," had ascertained that the weaver had been committed by creditors who, having advanced sums to further Stonehewer's improvements on Sir Thomas Lombe's silk-weaving machine, had called in their loans all at the same time.

Even now, the accompanying trustee could recall how very straight Stonehewer had stood despite his rags and heavy chains. How would yonder immigrant fare here? Probably well, were he able to overcome his furious resentment against an unjust Society. Hum. Stonehewer, a born leader of men, *could* become a troublemaker. Well, time would tell.

Oglethorpe's gaze shifted to a tall, well-set-up young fellow who called himself Archibald Glen. According to the account given to the committee, he'd formerly served as an officer, albeit a lowly cornet in The Blues of the Royal Horse Guards. This lean young fellow frankly admitted having gone into debt through the heedless purchase of expensive uniforms and equipment.

"Then, like a great fool," he'd admitted, "I gambled to recoup and lost so much you find me, gentlemen, an honored inmate of Marshalsea Prison." He'd laughed harshly. "Well, gentlemen, I believe I've learned my lesson and am most eager to resume a military career an you will redeem me."

Young Glen had created so favorable an impression during the voyage across the Atlantic that Oglethorpe's secretary, John West, already held among his papers a brevet lieutenant's commission. Only the acting governor's signature was required to restore Archibald Glen to the service of His Britannic Majesty, King George II.

In Secretary West's traveling desk also reposed a commission bearing the name of Petre Ballou, a grizzled Swiss who was, so he claimed, a veteran soldier of fortune. Spouting oaths in German, French, and Italian, he'd sworn, but could produce not a single written credential, that he was a trained civil and military engineer. Were Ballou's story true, he had, over the years, served as a senior mercenary officer in the employ of the King of Sweden, the Czarina of Russia, and the Margrave of Brandenburg, not to mention the King of the Two Sicilies.

Whatever the truth of this curious individual's services, he almost certainly had been present at the siege of Belgrade when, back in 1717, Oglethorpe himself had served as a very junior aide-de-camp to the redoubtable Prince Eugene: Petre Ballou's description of the terrain and of the Turkish defenses coincided remarkably well with the acting governor's own recollections.

While the *Anne* heeled to a puff of wind beating down the Ashley River, James Oglethorpe tried once more to decide whether this crusty soldier of fortune could be trusted. Fervently, he hoped so. Defense of the new settlement must be the first and most urgent consideration. What with powerful Spanish forces close by in Florida and possibly hostile Indians dwelling on all sides, the new colony's future promised to be parlous.

Thus far, he'd not been able to identify among these emancipated debtors a dozen men with even rudimentary military experience. Definitely, the majority had been peaceable tradesmen.

He still was considering the short, thick-bodied Swiss when the old soldier of fortune was joined by a younger man who also claimed a certain degree of military experience.

Briefly, Oglethorpe fumbled for the fellow's name, then recalled that this pleasant, glib, and plausible young man had given his name in Warden Acton's office as "John Savey." His manner at the time had been coolly aloof and he'd worn his tatters as if they'd been court dress. Among other things Savey had told the investigating committee was that he'd served in the Duke of Cornwall's Regiment of Foot; also that he'd been a bank accountant as well as a lawyer's clerk.

Even in adversity Savey had managed to retain such charm of manner and speech that, after only a few moments' deliberation, James Oglethorpe and his fellow committeeman, James Vernon, had agreed that the Georgia Company should discharge John Savey's indebtedness and convey him to America "on the Charity."

The little frigate wore onto the larboard tack and in so doing disturbed a huge raft of canvasbacks and redhead ducks. As he watched them whirling skyward, a small smile curved Oglethorpe's rather pursy lips when he recalled how dramatically Savey had flung himself onto his knees, weeping and vowing that the Georgia Company never would find cause to repent their interest in his case.

Standing nearly as tall as Oglethorpe himself, John Savey enjoyed a classic Greek profile, finely formed features, and brilliant, expressive dark eyes which in a way compensated for a sallow complexion and rather scant dark brown hair.

Wary of some unseen shoal, the pilot abruptly ordered the frigate put about; blocks rattled, yards creaked and whined as they were braced about, then the *Anne's* canvas slatted briefly before filling again, caused a series of reports loud as the explosions of so many signaling cannon.

Gradually, the *Anne's* bowsprit swung until it aimed toward the Cooper River's mouth, which formed one side of White Point, that peninsula upon which Charles Town had been established. Along this point's other side flowed the tea-colored Ashley, less broad and impressive than its sister stream.

From the foot of the quarter-deck ladder a girl's voice called, "A good morrow to Your Excellency! May our lives in Georgia always prove as pleasant as our arrival!"

An audible sniff sounded from the Reverend Herbert's direction, but Captain Thomas grinned. He always did when pretty little pink-and-white Mistress Bayless cast him a slow, perhaps unintentionally warm smile.

Smiling, James Oglethorpe waved and called down to the main deck, "Aye, mistress, all of us should give thanks to God."

Mistress Bayless fluttered and boldly blew the accompanying trustee a kiss.

The Reverend Herbert noticed and frowned. "Mark my words, nothing good will come of so brazen a baggage!"

"Ah-h, Rev'nd, she meant naught by that," chuckled Captain Thomas. "She's scarce more than a child."

The Bayless girl's face was heart-shaped and framed in heavy chestnut ringlets. Standing easily five and a half feet tall in her clumsy shoes, she nevertheless was delicately formed—almost to the point of fragility. As a further attraction she'd mastered the trick of opening large and heavily lashed violet eyes in a slow, trustful fashion.

Before returning his attention to the port, now showing up in greater detail, the acting governor tried to recall out of which prison Helen Bayless had been redeemed; he'd an idea it had been Westminster Jail but he couldn't be sure because Lord Percival, another selection-committee member, had handled her case.

All he could recall was that, reportedly, Mistress Bayless had been cast into the debtor's prison for cutting herself a gown from a bolt of her employer's goods. Unfortunately, lacking a mere two pounds, she hadn't been able to repay Mrs. Hartley, her employer, who had sworn out a warrant. All the same, Mrs. Hartley, for some reason, had prepared a notarized letter attesting Helen's otherwise exemplary character, not to mention her proficiency as a seamstress and pattern cutter. The prisoner also had exhibited to the interviewing member a number of other testimonials describing her sterling qualities; oddly enough, all had been penned by gentlemen. Lord Percival had thought it a pity that so clever a young female should have allowed vanity to outweigh practical considerations.

James Oglethorpe readily identified other faces among the crowd staring shoreward while swaying in unison to the frigate's motion as she bore down upon shipping anchored off Charles Town. Briefly, he wondered how many of these ex-debtors, most of them embittered and discouraged, would benefit the projected colony? Their number included cabinet-makers, wheelwrights, smiths, farmers, potash manufacturers, silk weavers, vine growers, breeders of livestock, and other respectable trades or professions.

Only God knew.

Chapter 4

CHARLES TOWN

Winsome Brooks repeated to herself, "I am Winifred Crooks, sometimes called Winnie Crooks." Winifred Crooks. Winifred Crooks. Winifred Crooks. Making her way past a row of unpainted clapboard houses bordering the waterfront, she was startled by a dull booming of cannon in the still, cold air. From the regular spacing of the reports she guessed that those distant guns were only salutes. She'd often heard such fired by the castle guarding Boston Harbor.

Here, as at home, dogs, pigs, and chickens continued, undisturbed, to forage for bits of swill along the muddy, hole-filled street. Unobtrusively, she hoped, Winsome mingled with an increasing throng of inhabitants uniformly moving toward White Point. Wandering along the unpaved streets, she prayed silently that no one who had seen her aboard the *Mystick* remained in this small, sprawling seaport which reeked of rotting fish and other garbage.

She was passed by a party of swift striding, leather-featured men clad in green and brown hunting shirts. Soon she learned to recognize them for Rangers—as this part of the local militia was termed. These lanky fellows didn't look at all smart, didn't in the least resemble the scarlet-and-black-uniformed members of the Ancient and Honorable Artillery Company of Boston.

Only a few Rangers affected bits and pieces of what might, by a stretch of the imagination, be called a uniform; for the most part they wore greasy-looking fringed hunting shirts and leggings or well-worn and out-moded European civilian garb.

On nearing the waterfront she noticed perhaps twenty-five or thirty vessels of all rigs and tonnages. Some lay berthed at crude, jerry-built docks; others swung to moorings or were anchored farther out in the harbor. Presently, Winsome discovered the cause for this activity.

A number of brightly uniformed figures were collecting at the far end of a very long wharf. Above them waved a cluster of flags and banners, the designs of which meant nothing to her.

"'Tis the governor's Committee of Welcome," she overheard a woman say.

"Welcome? Who fer?"

"Why, the Georgia Company's vessel, ye ninny. That's her right now coming to anchor."

Winsome shoved through the crowd and finally obtained a view of the new arrival. Painted brown and black, she looked mighty insignificant, although new Royal Jacks were fluttering in her rigging and a white and red pendant easily fifty feet long was curling lazily from her fore-topmast. Gray-white puffs of woolly smoke burst from the strange vessel's forecastle and, a heartbeat later, sounded the first dull *boom!* of her guns saluting the port.

Under a cloud of shrieking gulls, the *Anne's* captain dropped his best bower anchor about a quarter of a mile offshore, whereupon the little frigate at once became surrounded by a swarm of bumboats, fishing skiffs, pirogue, and log canoes. These last were paddled by curious Indians and Negroes.

Winsome pushed as close to the water's edge as she dared, then, for a better view, climbed onto an empty hogshead in time to watch the strange frigate—she'd lived in a seaport long enough to recognize al-most any rig plying the North Atlantic—hoist out her longboat. Once it lay alongside, a quartet of men in gay costumes clambered down the frigate's ladder. Her crew shoved off and began to pull rather raggedly toward a landing float moored to the seaward end of the long wharf.

Looking about her, Dr. Brooks's daughter noticed that upper windows in nearby homes and warehouses situated along Bay Street had been opened. Bright-colored lengths of cloth, shawls, capes, even yellow or scarlet petticoats were hung out. Up on flagstaffs above batteries designed to defend White Point climbed flags of all description.

A pimply, gangling youth clambered onto Winsome's perch on the hogshead and all but shoved her off of it. She cut short an angry reproof when he grinned, said, "Sorry, ma'am. Didn't go for to jostle yer. Mind if I steady yer wi' my arm?"

To have objected might have attracted attention, so Winsome nodded. "Perhaps you'd better. I don't want to fall." She treated him to a cool stare. Quickly she decided the boy was merely eager and not being forward or disrespectful. He was fairly jigging in his excitement.

"Say, ma'am, ain't this *somethin'*? Look at all these great folk. Never seen so many together since Mr. Johnson, our noo guvnor, took oath."

She scarcely heard him add, "My name's Joe Philbrick, but folks mostly call me Joey."

Curiosity overcoming caution, Winsome ventured, "There seem to be a great many people aboard the ship out there. Where does she come from?"

"England," the youth stated with another wriggle of excitement. "Hear say she's bringing out a parcel of people to settle a colony that's to be started somewheres down the Guale Coast."

"Wherever is the Guale Coast?"

Pleased to appear knowledgeable, the young fellow exposed a row of enormous yellowish teeth in a wide grin.

"Why, ma'am, the Guale country is that stretch of our coast which runs south from here right down to St. Augustine."

"St. Augustine? Where's that?"

"'Bout eighty miles south of where we're standin' right this minute. It's the Papist capital down in Florida; it's a big, fortified town."

With detached interest the tall girl from Boston watched the *Anne's* longboat splash shoreward.

"Who is the leader of these—these new settlers?"

The shock-haired youth almost upset them in an effort to survey his companion better. "Why, Paw allows 'tis a English bigwig named Oglethorpe or sumpin' like that."

"Then he's a nobleman?"

"Naw. But he's a Member of Parliament, so they say, and a big man about London town."

"Why does everyone seem so—so, well, pleased to see these immigrants?" inquired the hazel-eyed girl, relieved that the crowd's attention was diverted from her presence. In such a raw little seaport every stranger, sooner or later, was bound to get noticed and commented upon.

The youth batted whitish eyelashes, then craned his thin neck to see over the crowd now milling about the landward end of the King's Wharf. A rank of soldiers was having trouble to keep the mob from swarming out toward the float on which stood the receiving dignitaries.

"Why, ma'am, reckon must be on account of we'll welcome English settlements 'twixt us and the Spanishers and their"—Joey Philbrick hesitated over using a bad word but decided to go ahead just to make this pretty young female realize that he was getting to be a man and knew a thing or two about cussing—"their damn murderin' Yamasees. Guess you ain't heard 'bout the awful massacre of 1715? Would ye believe it? Them bloody Spanishers and their Injuns killed or carried off nigh on to two hundred of us."

All but unbalanced from her perch by the jostling crowd, Winsome was forced to steady herself by clutching young Philbrick's encircling arm. Hurriedly, she said, "No, I've not heard of it. You see, I—I've but recently arrived here."

"Well, I've heered 'bout it ever since I was borned. Fact. Them dirty Papists sent in spies and hostile Injuns who turned the planters' slaves 'gainst their masters. Like I said, they slew near two hundred traders, soldiers and people living in the outsettlements. Fact. 'Sides that, they carried off a whole great passel of our nigras to St. Augustine. Paw says the Papist Guvnor down there set 'em more or less free and settled 'em on land nearby his big fort.

"Say." He stared in frank curiosity. "Say, what's yer name, ma'am?"

Her heart surged but Winsome managed an easy smile. "Why, 'tis Winifred, Winifred Crooks. If you want, you can call me Winnie. Tell me, Joey, what sort of people have they fetched over to build these settlements you speak of?"

"Dunno. Reckon they're mostly English—like us."

Just then Winsome recalled a remark dropped by Mr. Coffin during the voyage down from New York. It had been to the effect that a lot of ex-convicts were being sent out to establish a new colony south of the Carolinas. In renewed interest she considered the frigate whose crew now were laying out on the yards to furl her canvas. Perhaps among those liberated criminals out there must be some who, like her, had suffered unreasonably at the hands of Society?

Abruptly, Winsome abandoned her line of thought because someone had grabbed her by the wrist and jerked her off the hogshead. Her heart almost stopped; she reckoned the watch must already have recognized her, for it was a man in uniform who eased her to the ground.

"How dare you!" she faltered. "I—I've done nothing wrong."

"Who's claiming you have?" Her captor grinned but still held her tightly by the wrist. "Now just come along with me, ma'am, and I'm going to find you a better view of the goings-on."

Although immeasurably relieved she nonetheless glared at her captor a moment—just to put him in his place. He proved to be a towering, yellow-bearded and very broad-shouldered young man who had the most coldly piercing and clear blue eyes she thought she'd ever beheld. The cheekbones of his long and deeply tanned features were prominent and tinged with red.

On a thick shock of sandy hair he was wearing a black leather skullcap sporting a faded cockade of green silk edged with a red squirrel's tail. Otherwise, this young fellow, who looked to be in his late twenties, was clad in a green-dyed uniform jacket set off with brass buttons which afforded an odd contrast to fringed Indian leggings worn over European breeches of gray duroy.

Under one arm the stranger was carrying a short brass-barreled musketoon, and slung to his broad belt was a huge knife protected by a fringed sheath of red-dyed leather.

Before she could decide what course to follow he observed pleasantly, "You've no need to fear me, ma'am, for I'm your humble, obedient servant, Captain Wallace Challenger, of the South Carolina Rangers." While raising his brimless leather cap—a trifle mockingly, she thought— he at the same time treated her to a curt head bow.

"And how are you called, ma'am?"

She hesitated, then stammered, "Why, s-sir, I-I'm Mistress Winifred C-Crooks."

The Ranger's penetrating blue eyes shone briefly. "Ah, so you're maiden? This must be my lucky day."

"That, sir, remains to be seen," Winsome countered primly.

"So it does," he grinned. "Well, then, Mistress Crooks, will you come along?" His speech was slow, almost drawling, and was tinctured by what seemed to be a very faint Scottish accent.

"Thank you, sir"—she drew herself up as a well-reared young lady should when approached by a stranger—"but I find I am very well right here."

"You'll do better wi' me. Come." The Ranger captain laughed quietly and, gripping her by the elbow, plowed through the crowd with the ease of a bull passing through an alder thicket. Several men started to curse him but when they recognized the tall, sandy-bearded figure their scowls vanished.

"Why, heyo, Wallace!"

"When d'ye git back to town?"

"Lift any hair this trip?" And so on.

When they neared a cordon of militiamen a raffish fellow saluted Captain Challenger with his espantoon, then stepped back to allow the pair to proceed out onto the King's Wharf.

An officer in a similar green tunic called out, "B'God, if it ain't old Hawk-Eye in the flesh! Where did ye snare such a pretty bird?"

"Under a tobacco leaf."

Next a big-bosomed wench tittered when in passing the Ranger dexterously pinched her bottom. "So Wally's back. Come and see me when you tire of your new friend."

Miserably embarrassed, Winsome felt all manner of people staring at her. Why, oh why, should this mischance have had to happen?

Moving with a long, loose-kneed stride, Wallace Challenger literally hauled his prize through the crowd toward a second cordon, this time composed of whiskery, leather-jacketed Rangers. These, greeting the captain with coarse familiarity and his furiously blushing companion with lewd appreciation, let them by.

Presently, Captain Challenger pointed to a pile of sweet-smelling pine planks awaiting export. "Climb up, lass, and you'll ha'e a view as from the royal box."

Wretchedly aware that now everyone would notice her, Winsome obeyed; to have refused would only have served to attract more attention.

Seated on the longboat's stern locker, Acting Governor James Edward Oglethorpe rearranged the set of his snowy, lace-edged stock and at the same time considered the waiting group of colonial officials. For the most part, they were either untidily or roughly turned out.

Then a log-and-earth battery off to the right began to fire salutes which, at irregular intervals, drowned out the crowd's wild cheering. It struck Oglethorpe that everyone appeared genuinely pleased to see him arrive. Men shouted, women were waving kerchiefs, and children, screaming excitement, jumpd up and down so that a couple of youngsters fell into the water and had to be pulled out. Ever astute to public reactions, Oglethorpe couldn't help wonder what emotions were prompting this wild enthusiasm.

While the Anne's longboat nosed in toward the float Oglethorpe inquired of the Reverend Herbert, "You recognize any of the gentlemen yonder?"

"Only Robert Johnson, the royal governor, Your Excellency; we met in the Colonial Office some years ago. He's the stout, red-faced gentlemen in the gold-laced green coat. Just now he's lifting his hat in your direction."

Dirty water separating boat from wharf narrowed rapidly but afforded

Oglethorpe time to form a quick impression of this brown-faced governor whose squarish head and blocky body suggested nothing so much as a series of superimposed rectangles; even his stumpy legs, encased in yellow silk stockings, suggested parallelogram. Clad in a long-skirted coat of bottle-green velvet, Governor Johnson suggested a woodchuck preposterously wearing an old-style Ramillies wig.

To the governor's right and standing at least a head taller was a man the acting governor, in his inexperience, at first mistook for a half-breed Indian. He had a swarthy complexion, thin curving nose—it showed a deep nick in its center—and restless jet eyes that perfected the illusion. All this tall officer in the red and black uniform needed were a few feathers laced into lank, shoulder-length jet-black hair.

Within a few minutes the accompanying trustee was to discover that this unique figure was none other than Deputy Governor Colonel William Bull, who commanded the Armed Forces of South Carolina.

Beside these two stood a gaunt individual clad in a quasi uniform of food-spotted Lincoln green, leather breeches, dusty jack boots and a narrow-brimmed black hat which sported a small device done in brass and secured to its front.

Later, Oglethorpe would learn that this was Captain Jacob Matthews, a redoubtable frontier fighter, who still used a broad Lancashire accent for all he'd lived many a year in America.

More cheers started to arise but were punctuated by coughs and curses caused by those dense clouds of burned gunpowder which came rolling across from the saluting battery.

Once the longboat had drawn alongside the float and its crew had tossed oars to the perpendicular, an enormously fat individual wearing a mayor's chain of office lifted his hat and came waddling forward. Under his weight water commenced to creep over the float's planking.

James Edward Oglethorpe, Esq., experienced a unique sense of exultation as, for the first time, he set foot on the New World. How long had he planned, importuned, struggled, and contrived for this moment! For many wearisome and often discouraging years.

Huzzahs from aboard the *Anne* rang louder when a squad of Rangers, halfway down the wharf, fired a ragged *feu-de-joie* as the governor and his deputy doffed hats and, grinning widely, offered hard, sun-darkened hands.

"Welcome to Carolina, sir. Be thrice welcome!" boomed Governor Johnson. "I trust your passage proved agreeable?"

From her perch on the lumber pile Winsome Brooks overheard little of what was being said, but, to judge by their expressions as the officials came tramping shoreward, everyone appeared to be in a most happy mood.

Just before the party drew near, Captain Challenger scrambled down in time solemnly to present his musketoon. There was something so distinguished and yet so simple about Oglethorpe's bearing that Winsome couldn't help calling out, "May the Lord prosper your noble enterprise, sir!"

Oglethorpe looked up and saw her perched on the lumber pile. Smiling gravely, he lifted his plumed tricorne in her direction and above the din cried, "I thank you, ma'am, from the bottom of my heart."

While the officials went by Winsome decided that she'd never before beheld a stronger, more serenely commanding countenance, for all Mr. Oglethorpe's close-set dark eyes and long, narrow nose. His manner seemed self-confident without appearing arrogant. What chiefly intrigued Dr. Brooks's handsome daughter was the presence of certain unmistakably humorous lines at the corners of his full-lipped mouth.

To everyone's surprise, Negroes, congregating along the water's edge, raised a singsong chant of welcome. Captain Challenger guessed that this was because, from some unfathomable source, they'd heard that Negro slavery was to be forbidden in the projected new colony.

Grinning, mouthing, and rolling their eyes, they accompanied their chant by twanging on instruments fashioned of strings of dried gut stretched over half-gourds. Captain Challenger explained that such were called "ban-johs."

As if to render this reception even more auspicious, the sun brightened enough to cast a radiance over this untidy little port, growing without plan or foresight, between the two great rivers.

Once the official party had gained the shore, Captain Challenger drawled, "Now I'll venture that yonder goes a good and maybe a great man. Don't know why I think so, but I do." The Ranger flushed under his tan as if ashamed of such a sentiment. Quizzically, he then glanced at the rumpled figure standing beside him.

"He seems a—a person of force," Winsome agreed uncertainly.

"Aye. He'll have to be if he and his followers are to long survive on the Guale Coast."

The crowd fell in behind the official procession as it quitted the wharf and, driving off foraging pigs, dogs, and chickens, started up muddy and deeply rutted King Street toward Charles Town's new brick State House, which loomed at the junction of Broad and Church streets. Across from it stood the Watch House.

Winsome Brooks's sense of elation gave way to a griping hunger pang and renewed realization of her destitute and friendless condition.

As she and Challenger wandered toward the center of Charles Town she noticed at the end of a side street a gallows from which were dangling four attenuated figures; rags covering these grisly, blackened remains stirred faintly in the breeze. "Wha'—who are those?"

"Pirates, ma'am," Challenger explained carelessly. "Executed only last week. Should be more. Of late such picaroons have become a plague along our coast for the first time since Stede Bonnet got his neck stretched back in '18."

Challenger halted and, facing her, said with a slow, crooked smile, "Well, Mistress Crooks, now that the show's over I suppose I'd better be seeing you home."

Undecided as to what course to follow, Winsome dropped her gaze. "Why—why, thank you, sir." Brightly, she explained, "I'll not go home so quickly. I wish to wander about and further observe the festivities."

The Ranger quirked a thick, sandy-colored brow and seemed to consider her more carefully. "Well, suit yerself, mistress." His slightly red-rimmed eyes narrowed. "By the bye, just where are you lodging?"

Winsome felt as if a race tide were closing in. This necessity of having to invent, to prevaricate, was something utterly unfamiliar. She was no good at lying—and knew it. "Why, sir, I—I—only this morning I decided to—to change my lodgings and I've not yet decided where I shall move."

While speaking Winsome looked about and was surprised to notice Joey Philbrick, the pimply youth who'd climbed onto the hogshead beside her, loitering before a shopwindow across the street and watching her with ill-disguised interest. Why?

"So? Well, now, in that case, Mistress Crooks, perhaps you'd best try the Carteret Arms. It ain't expensive and, for a seaport ordinary, 'tis fairly clean. I know. I live there."

Unexpectedly, he patted Winsome's shoulder, then straightened his belt. "I must now report for duty at the Watch House."

In turning away he checked. "Mistress Crooks"—to her dismay he seemed to dwell upon her pseudonym—"since ye're a stranger in town I advise you to leave word at the Carteret where you decide to take up lodgings."

Take up lodgings? Winsome almost laughed out loud. In her soiled "show" petticoat's pocket now reposed a single pine-tree shilling—and that was of uncertain value so far from Boston.

"I certainly shall," she promised without the least intention of so doing.

Challenger adjusted the ammunition bandoleer that slanted across his tunic's green front and set to swaying the row of powder charges which, done up in greased paper, dangled from it as so many fat and leather-covered tassels. He twirled his small yellow-blond mustache and winked one of those penetrating bright-blue eyes. "If worse comes to worst and you don't come across quarters to yer taste, I'll be pleased to provide shelter for you at the Carteret Arms."

Winsome's chin rose and, peering steadily into this tall young fellow's brown features, she said with an icy clarity, "Thank you, Captain Challenger, I doubt very much that I'll avail myself of your offer."

He grinned in the depths of his curly yellow beard. "As to that, m'dear, we shall presently see. Good day." He touched his leather skullcap and set off down King Street with an easy, bent-kneed stride which suddenly reminded Winsome of those lean and restless Indian traders and backwoodsmen who, in the early spring and late fall, came to Boston to replenish their supplies.

For a while the girl with the luminous hazel eyes lingered on the splintery board sidewalk across from the State House, trying to decide what she should do next. Now and then she became aware of peddlars offering cooked crab cakes, fried chicken, and a variety of strange fruits. Also on offer were yams, coconuts, and flat, yellowish cakes made of coarse-ground maize meal called "pones."

Almost all of the not unmusically chanting vendors were either small boys or Negro women who wandered about with loaded pipes or cigars in their mouths. Without exception, these hawkers carried their trays or baskets skillfully balanced on brilliant turbans tied into a wide variety of designs.

Gentlemen on fine horses trotted past the bewildered girl. She reckoned they must be on their way to a reception at the State House. Two-wheeled carts rumbled along, headed for the waterfront.

After a while hunger pangs forced Winsome diffidently to approach a small, very black boy balancing a wicker tray of pones on his fuzzy round head.

"How—how much are they?"

"Fo' a penny, missis, you c'n hab two, or five fo' tuppence."

"I'll take tuppence worth."

The boy's eyes whitened when she held out her silver pine-tree shilling, but he fairly snatched it from her. In return he gave her five fat pones and some big copper coins which might have been French, Spanish, or Portuguese. If he was cheating her, she had no way of knowing it.

On deciding that nothing of interest was to take place near the State House she sauntered inland along Meeting Street toward St. Philip's Church, a new and handsome edifice. To eat slowly proved difficult, but, in order to get full benefit from the pones, Winsome forced herself to chew every crumb into minute bits.

All at once, she noticed, with alarm, that Joey Philbrick undoubtedly was dogging her, but she quickly relaxed. This pimply youth remained so shy and distant that she soon began to smile. Twice, Joey seemed to pluck up sufficient courage to come up and address her, but both times he lost spirit and contented himself by trailing her.

Presently the girl from New England entered a foul-smelling square

which seemed chiefly used for the buying and selling of cattle, but along
its perimeter stood small stalls exposing all manner of merchandise for
sale. Thanks no doubt to an influx of visitors come to welcome James
Oglethorpe's expedition, most merchants were conducting an uncommonly brisk business.

With longing eyes Winsome was peering into a grimy window when
she heard behind her a voice say, "Reckon she's the one, all right."

Winsome's heart seemed to congeal when, in the poorly glazed window's reflection, she saw two men standing close behind her and both
were wearing rectangular brass plates strapped about their left sleeves
which identified them as constables of the peace!

The taller constable, a swarthy, brown-bearded fellow, inquired civilly
enough, "Yer name, please, ma'am?"

While the earth seemed to tremble under her feet, Winsome gulped,
then quavered, "Why, 'tis W-Winifred Crooks. If you please, gentlemen,
why do you question me? I've done nothing wrong."

"Mebbe so," grunted the second constable, distinguished by a large
and hairy wart riding a twisted nose. "Whereabouts d'ye dwell?"

"Why, why, at—at an inn near the waterfront."

"Which inn?"

"I—I can't remember."

"Ah, come on, missy, up wi' the truth straight off and it'll maybe go
better with ye."

While a crowd commenced to collect, Dr. Brooks's daughter prayed
that some miraculous force might whirl her away over the rooftops.

"Wot did ye say's yer name?"

Her lips were so fear-stiffened that Winsome could barely breathe. "I
—I'm W-Winifred Crooks."

"Winifred Crooks? Why, damn me if that ain't mighty close to Winsome Brooks." The short officer sniggered. "Why will silly fools fleein'
the law always choose a false name so near to their real one?"

The bearded constable grabbed Winsome's arm. "Well, Jemmy,
seems like we've found that Yankee captain's strayed lamb. Description
fits to a T."

"Come now," invited the shorter constable. "You *are* Winsome Brooks
from Boston?"

Unwisely Winsome let her temper flare. "Suppose I am? Under what
charge d-dare you arrest me? I tell you I've done nothing wrong."

The swarthy constable stepped forward. "Mebbe, mebbe not—that's
up to the magistrate to decide. Now, missy, will ye come peaceable or
must I use this?" He tapped a length of greasy cord dangling from his
belt.

"Oh no! No! But please, gentlemen, I swear I've done no wrong!"

"Nothing wrong in jumpin' a indenture bond?"

"How could I jump a bond when I've never given one?"

"So say you, but, not a week ago, a Boston sea captain made deposition to the magistrate as how a young female who was bound for five years' domestic service in Jamaica skipped his vessel."

The short officer's hard fingers clamped down hard when, yielding to panic, she tried to break away. "Oh no, ye don't!" growled the constable while the crowd of onlookers grew denser; 'twasn't every day one saw so personable a young female get taken up by the watch.

"Hi! What's up?"

"Pickpocket's been caught!"

"Naw, she looks more like a bawd. She's purty enough."

"Listen! I just heard she's a bond servant trying to get away."

"More likely she's a escapted debtor!"

Somehow, Winsome lashed her native intelligence back into obedience. Proudly, she lifted her disheveled head and, staring levelly about, called in a clear, carrying voice, "I'll not deny that my name is Winsome Brooks —but please, good people, believe me when I do most heartily deny that I ever signed a bond of indenture with Captain Starbuck or with anybody else. Instead, I *paid* that rogue for my passage to Jamaica in full—twenty pounds, Massachusetts currency."

While the crowd closed in and street dogs yapped excitement, the shorter officer shook his head. "If, as ye say, ye'd paid yer way, then how come ye jumped Starbuck's vessel? No, my girl, ye'll have to come up wi' a likelier yarn."

"But he—he made lewd advances."

"What kind of advances?" rasped the tall constable. "Come. Out with it!"

Hopeful that, despite his anger, Starbuck might not have mentioned the libel which had driven her from home, Winsome mumbled, "Because, sir, he believed himself a fiery young gallant instead of an evil old man in his second childhood."

"A likely yarn!" The bearded constable took her by the wrist. "Come along, missy."

Chapter 5

STATE BANQUET

Acting Governor James Edward Oglethorpe, Esq., consumed with impatience to set his sick and seaworn colonists ashore, found it difficult to remain affable while sitting out a seemingly interminable banquet proffered by the Governor and Assembly of South Carolina.

So consummate a politician had he become that no one suspected his uneasiness while listening to a series of long but also generally informative addresses, from which he derived a number of constructive conclusions. Among these was the conviction that his hosts were prepared to go a long way toward ensuring the immediate and permanent success of the Georgia Company's venture.

For instance, to protect his colonists from possible "annoyance through straggling Indians" the Assembly already had ordered one Captain James MacPherson and a party of Rangers to accompany Oglethorpe's people to their destination, wherever that might be. Moreover, they were to remain as guards until the ex-debtors were able to conduct their own defense against raids by masterless Indians or depredations from escaped Negro slaves, of which there appeared to be a considerable number lurking along the Guale Coast. Oglethorpe's concern deepened when it appeared that several such attacks had taken place during the past few months.

Governor Johnson's lumpy features, grown still more fiery with the wine and rich viands, capped the Carolinians' offers of assistance. "Aye, straightaway, we'll lend Your Excellency the *Hawk*, a fast new scout boat; 'tis reported she's uncommon manageable and of extra-shallow draft so, without loss of time, ye'll be free to explore your grant and select a site for yer principal town."

He pulled off his wig and with a yellow bandanna mopped a shiny, hairless scalp. "Colonel Bull, here, will assist you; he knows the Savannah country better than anyone else. Once ye've determined upon a situation the Assembly is prepared to devote to your use five well-manned plantation boats. These should prove sufficient to convey your people and their belongings to their new home."

Oglethorpe arose and surveyed the sun-darkened faces surrounding him.

Many were almost ugly, some appeared to be common-looking, but there was no suggestion of weakness in any of them.

"Gentlemen, these are indeed handsome and most welcome offers of assistance. I pray that God will reward such humanity, particularly your offer of soldiers to protect us during our days of weakness, for I must confess to you that I am deeply concerned over the almost complete dearth of fighting men among my followers."

Colonel Bull smothered a belch. "You once were an officer of the King were you not, sir?"

Oglethorpe inclined his head and his wig's long and carefully trained curls swayed forward. "I served for a time as a staff officer with Prince Eugene when he fought the Turks. However, I resigned my commission when I stood for Parliament."

"What was yer constituency, sir?" demanded the chubby little Mayor of Charles Town.

"Haslemere, sir. Which I still have the honor to represent."

Governor Johnson gulped from a handsome goblet of gilded silver, then wiped his mouth on the back of his hand. "To help you form a trained band I'll send you, as quick as may be, a couple of Ranger officers. They'll instruct yer men in the Indian mode of warfare." He turned to Colonel Bull. "Who'd you suggest?"

"Wallace Challenger," came the prompt reply. "Maybe Sergeant Felton should go along too."

"Their help will be most acceptable," Oglethorpe stated while re-settling his lace stock. "I vow, gentlemen, I'm most sensible of this solicitude for our success."

Johnson held up a hirsute hand, grinned broadly. "You ain't heard all of what we've planned for you. Once your people have put up some shelters you will be sent a hundred black cattle plus five breeding bulls —all donated by Mr. Whitaker over there." He indicated a sallow, horse-faced individual. "You will also receive, through public subscription, twenty sows, five boars and twenty tons of rice."

Before resuming, Governor Johnson took another pull at his goblet. "You'll no doubt be pleased to learn that certain plantation owners among us are prepared to lend you some blacksmiths, carpenters, housebuilders and gangs of blacks trained in felling and shaping of timber suitable to your purpose."

He paused to beckon a passing waiter and help himself to a handful of sweets. "I trust, Yer Excellency, that you'll not take it amiss an I suggest that you leave in our care any of your felons you think may prove troublesome or who might run away once they get ashore." With a touch of pride he added, "We have recently completed a strong and commodious jailhouse."

At the word "felon" Oglethorpe's long features contracted, but quickly
resumed their pleasant expression. "Gentlemen, please! I had thought
that the trustees of the Georgia Company already had conveyed by letter
the fact that there is not a true felon—in the common sense of the word—
aboard the *Anne*. Nor will any such be shipped out in the future."

A stoutish, gray-bearded officer in a red tunic showing dark sweat stains
at its underarms frowned. "I fear I don't understand you, sir. We were
given to understand that the people accompanying you recently have been
inmates of various jails. Why aren't they to be considered jailbirds?"

James Oglethorpe's brows merged, then parted, leaving a small V between them. "They are, but, as I've said before, only in a broad sense.
My followers all were imprisoned for only one reason—debts. Most of
these debts were incurred through irresponsibility, mischance, bad judgment or through the enmity of competitors or even the connivance of
selfish relatives."

The guest of honor deliberately fanned at a halo of flies which came
pouring in through the open windows. "Gentlemen, I cannot impress
upon you too deeply that we of the Parliamentary Prison Reform Committee have thoroughly investigated the character of each and every person we have transported to these shores. All are deemed to be funda-
mentally honest, industrious, and desirous of making a fresh start
in life. Not a man is leaving his wife or children behind." James Oglethorpe's voice carried evenly through the Governor's Mansion's dingy little banquet hall.

"Please believe that we have selected only persons following trades or
professions calculated to be of use in the wilderness. Among these immigrants are masons, coopers, carpenters, ironworkers, weavers, farmers—and
even a pair of medical doctors. One, Dr. Cox, volunteered his service
gratis and has paid for his passage."

He smiled fleetingly. "Of course, it cannot be guaranteed that we shall
not suffer disappointment in some of these ex-debtors. Had their characters
been altogether flawless they would not have become inmates of His Majesty's prisons."

A short and rather elderly officer who'd been introduced as Colonel
Vanderdussen, reared back in his chair and at the same time picked at a
beaklike nose. "Now I ain't had time to read all that printed matter yer
board sent over, sir, so I'm wondering what's meant by the mention of
the 'Margravate of Azilia?'"

Before making reply, Oglethorpe took a sip of some rich but rather
sharp red wine he couldn't identify. "Why, sir, Azilia—or 'Place of Refuge'—was the name given to an idealistic society conceived in 1717 by an
humanitarian named Sir Robert Montgomery.

"He caused plans to be drawn up for what he conceived to be the perfect community. Provision was made for wide, parallel streets and spacious squares with wide intervals between houses to avoid the danger of a conflagration. All public buildings were to be strategically situated. Further, the plan for Azilia called for outworks, palisades, bastions and other defenses."

Unhurriedly, he in the blue velvet coat replaced his goblet on the littered table. "Alas, Sir Robert's political acumen proved not to be on a par with his gift for town planning; his bill to establish the Margravate of Azilia therefore perished in a Parliamentary Committee. As someone observed, 'his scheme died amid a magnificent burst of rhetoric.' Sir Robert proved unable even to obtain confirmation of the royal charter granting him that land which His Majesty had promised would be his."

"Where lay this grant?" queried Colonel Bull, revolving a glass between stubby and none too cleanly fingers.

The accompanying trustee's reply was crisp. "Azilia was to include all the territory lying between the Savannah River on the north and the Altamaha River on the south. Westward, the grant included all land as far as the Pacific Ocean lying between a parallelogram based on the headwaters of these two streams." Oglethorpe permitted himself a wry smile. "Rather a sizable bit of real estate."

The militia colonel undid his waistcoat buttons and began to laugh. "In that case, Your Excellency, Azilia would have included a territory vaster than the whole of Europe!"

Oglethorpe lifted his full-bottomed peruke to let some air in under it. He detested wigs and wore them as seldom as possible. "Yes, Colonel, I'm well aware that such boundaries are fantastic yet"—his light manner vanished—"they are identical with those the Crown has granted to the Georgia Company!"

Instantly, the company sobered; many were red-faced with anger and others looked glum with the fear that this still-unborn colony might someday tower like a giant beside South Carolina, which had come out on the short end of the territorial division with North Carolina.

"No!"

"Well, I'll be damned!"

As quickly as he could, Oglethorpe attempted reassurance. "Please, gentlemen, believe that I—that the company never asked for such a territory. Little as I know of this country, I am aware that we shall indeed be fortunate if, for a long while, we can hope to settle and defend more than a few hundred square miles."

Governor Johnson agreed, albeit with some acidity. Alas, that the welcoming spirit seemed to have departed—temporarily, at least.

Charles Town's fat little mayor fingered his gilded silver chain of office. "There's another point those great fools in London have overlooked. Aside

from the Dons, our French friends in Louisiana will be more than interested to learn of your grant because they claim all land west of the
Mississippi, and a deal more to the southwest of us. We call it the 'Debatable Land.' Moreover, they've already established forts and trading
posts there—too many for our liking."

"I wonder," speculated the guest of honor while barefooted Negro servants circulated bottles and earthenware demijohns, "whether any of you
gentlemen would be good enough, for my benefit, to recapitulate the
history of this Debatable Land?"

Governor Johnson glanced at Colonel Bull. "Billy, reckon you're the
one best suited to answer that."

The Colonel grimaced. "Well, Yer Excellency, I expect you're already
aware that England and Spain have been disputing possession of the
Guale Coast for over two hundred years."

Oglethorpe nodded. "So I have heard. I believe our claim is based upon
the explorations of Captain Sebastian Cabot, who claimed this territory
for Kings Henry VII and Henry VIII, by right of discovery. Am I correct?"

"Entirely so, sir," Johnson agreed. "Cabot's claim is further sustained
by the fact that, over a hundred years ago, Admiral Sir Francis Drake
laid siege to and captured St. Augustine. On that occasion he reasserted
the Crown's claim."

While the Negro servants commenced to carry out the broken food
now chilling on the sideboard, most of the guests listened with absorbed
attention.

It was nick-nosed and leather-faced Colonel Bull who continued the
account. "His Majesty Charles II later granted the Guale Coast to Lord
Carteret and other lords proprietor."

At this careful restatement of more-than-uncertain rights various plantation owners nodded, cried, "Hear! Hear!"

"That's correct," boomed Robert Johnson. "After Charles Town was
founded back in 1672 or thereabouts, our outposts gradually were advanced southward down to the St. John River." He turned to look steadily
at the guest of honor. "This fact is most important, sir, because our possession of this stretch of the Guale Coast was confirmed by the Spanish
Crown in the Treaty of Utrecht of 1713! Am't I not correct, Billy?"

Colonel Bull momentarily steepled forefingers above his dented beak
of a nose, obviously probed his memory. "Aye, Robert. That passage was
included in the treaty because in 1702 the Dons, without warning, attacked
both our settlers and tribes friendly to our interests."

The speaker's voice hardened. "Spanish troops savagely destroyed our
outposts first on the St. John, then along the Satilla and finally upon the
Altamaha River which, as Your Excellency may not yet know, flows only
a few dozen miles down the coast from this very spot."

Oglethorpe became conscious of many eyes attempting to gauge his reactions.

"During the bloody Yamasee War of 1715, which was solely provoked by the Governor of Florida"—Bull's voice sank to a harsh undertone— "above three hundred British subjects lost their lives. And as many more were carried off into captivity or robbed of all they possessed. Those, indeed, were fearful days."

It was then that old Colonel Vanderdussen explained, "We were too spent to accomplish very much against the Dons until Governor Nichol-son sent Colonel Barnwell to reconstruct Fort King George on the Al-tamaha back in 1721. This fort, with another near Beaufort, was our sole defense south of Charles Town until 1727, when, during the rule of Governor Craven, we drove the Papists and their Yamasee devils all the way back to St. Augustine and the St. John River."

Vanderdussen shrugged and spread his hands. "We were on the verge of winning a decisive victory when we ran out of supplies and ammunition and so were forced to retreat and abandon Fort St. George on the St. John. Today, therefore, the Guale Coast remains unprotected, unsafe for Englishmen below Beaufort."

A large-framed, black-browed planter fetched a deep sigh, then sent tobacco fumes rolling about the smoky dining hall. "May I warn Your Excellency to be most wary and ever suspicious. No man can have neighbors more treacherous than the Spaniards and their Yamasee allies. All smiles and flattery, a Spanish officer will swear by all the saints that he'll respect this or that boundary and attack the next day, if it suits his purpose."

Subdued curses and an angry undertone circulated the banquet board.

At length Colonel Bull said heavily, " 'Tis well, Yer Excellency, that ye should know from the start how inhumanly cruel these Spanishers can be. On many well-attested occasions they've been known to crucify, boil or skin alive hostile Indians, Englishmen and sometimes even Frenchmen. 'Tis for this reason that we of the Assembly had decided that I and some Rangers should go along when you search for a place to settle your people. Is it true you intend establishin' your colony somewhere upon the Savannah River?" He added, smiling, "Hereabouts, we call such a move 'seatin' a river.'"

"That is true, Colonel." Oglethorpe made a slight bow. "My fellow trustees and I have been reliably informed that the climate along the Savannah's banks is generally salubrious."

Grunted dark-faced Captain MacPherson, "Aye, sir, 'tis a likely region, except in summer, when ye'll find it hotter nor the hinges o' hell itself and fair swarming wi' all manner o' reptiles, mosquitoes and flies, but then that's true of any place south of New Berne."

Colonel Bull selected black walnuts from a battered silver bowl and began to crack them between muscular hands. "I was down that way last month, chasin' runaway slaves, when I came upon a spot which I've a notion may satisfy your needs."

Oglethorpe's lively brown eyes lighted. "Pray tell me more about it."

"Why, sir, 'tis a broad plateau which lies on a high bluff that rises on the south bank near sixteen miles upstream from Tybee Island and the sea. Just north lies Amercario, a village belonging to the Yamacraw tribe. Nearby is a truck house run by a licensed trader named Musgrove and his wife, who is a half-breed but smart as a whip."

"Are these—these Yamacraws likely to prove friendly?"

Bull exposed gapped and irregular yellow teeth in a taut grin. "Well, sir, let's say old Tomo-chichi's people right now ain't exactly unfriendly, but who can be sure how long they'll stay that way? Always remember, Yer Excellency, the Creeks gen'rally are fickle about their allegiances and the Yamacraws are Creeks, even if they're a banished tribe."

Governor Johnson, who was beginning to look sleepy, made an effort to rouse himself. "Needless to say, if you disapprove the site Billy's mentioned, ye're free to select any place ye fancy *south* of the Savannah, which, as you know, forms the boundary between South Carolina and— and— What is your colony to be called? Georgia, isn't it?"

"Yes. In honor of His Majesty the present King." Oglethorpe used a serviette to brush crumbs from his lap as he arose. "And now, gentlemen, since I must set my followers ashore as soon as may be, you'll appreciate that I am anxious to commence a survey without loss of time." He raised a brow at Colonel Bull. "How soon will it be possible for us to set out?"

"When you please, sir; tomorrow, if you say the word."

Again, it became inescapable that, for reasons which just had become evident, the Assembly of South Carolina were pinning great and far from unselfish hopes on the success of the new colony.

Governor Johnson, rising at long last, remarked, "When we were advised that Yer Excellency actually had set sail for America, we made provision to receive and refresh your settlers at the port of Beaufort, which lies a scant forty miles down the coast."

In a voice suddenly thickened by emotion, Oglethorpe said, "Gentlemen, I scarce know what to say about your uncommon kindness save that 'tis most unusual in this selfish and unfriendly world." He then offered the governor a graceful court bow. "And now, if Your Excellency will excuse me, I will straightaway return aboard the *Anne* to make your generosity known to my followers."

Chapter 6

THE WATCH HOUSE

If, since her father's funeral, Winsome Brooks imagined that she had attained the nadir of despair, she now knew that she'd been mistaken. Here she was, locked into a small and noisome cell with two disreputable-appearing females. One of her fellow prisoners was a coarsely handsome but foulmouthed wench who was so hugely pregnant that she seemed about ready to give birth at any moment. The other was a scrawny and sallow-faced Creole prostitute who must be suffering from the *lues venerea* in its secondary and most virulent form. As a doctor's daughter, Winsome could recognize her symptoms at first glance.

She guessed she'd never understand how she had endured, with a whole mind, her first night of imprisonment. Adding to her misery was the unwashed state of her clothing, which attracted to her person a multitude of lice and voracious fleas which soon sprinkled itching lumps over her sour-smelling body.

Since a heavy oaken door had slammed behind her, the noon before, all she'd had to eat had been a wooden bowl of lukewarm corn-meal mush and a slab of stringy, cold salt pork which, lacking eating utensils, she'd been forced to cram into her mouth with her fingers.

Nil desperandum—never despair—had been one of Dr. Brooks's favorite mottoes. He'd often employed it while instructing his lively, hazel-eyed daughter in the Latin tongue; right now, Winsome found the slogan hollow and utterly inapplicable.

Soon it became evident that Polly, the pregnant girl—who readily had confessed to being a runaway bound servant—was rather feeble-minded; when she wasn't recounting, in disgusting detail, apparently countless sexual adventures, she giggled incessantly or repeated nonsensical jingles to herself.

The Creole, Adeline, claimed to be French and averred that she came from Biloxi. A truly pitiful figure, she possessed the saddest imaginable liquid black eyes and pinched, olive-hued features.

To her cellmates' confidences Winsome responded guardedly whenever a reply seemed inescapable. Crouched on a clumsy wooden stool, she sat staring at the straw-littered floor and wondered that she'd ever

become capable of hating any human being as much as she now hated
Elijah Starbuck. It wasn't right that any man should be able to cause such
intense, soul-crushing misery, especially when she'd not given him even
the shadow of an excuse.

Why, O Lord, have You permitted him to vilify my good name? Why
has he been allowed to threaten me, insult me, and finally to cheat me
out of my passage money? O Lord, You know this isn't right!

Sometimes, during that first awful night, Winsome was able to shake
off her despair and rally an innate courage. She *would* survive, despite
Elijah Starbuck and other evil-minded souls, and live again as a respectable person.

Because her skin revolted on contact with the foul-smelling truss of
straw on which she was supposed to rest, she forced herself to try sleeping in a sitting position. What was the old saw Pa was given to saying
when striving to save some patient's life—"It's darkest before dawn."

Unable to sleep, she attempted to foresee the future and decide upon
an attitude which might help to ensure a decent existence. Only good
health, intelligence, and determination remained at her disposal.
Stranded in this strange port, she'd hardly a penny, no influence, in
fact no standing whatever.

What most bothered the brooding young woman was the realization
that she'd no notion of how soon she might be brought to trial or of
what kind of justice she might encounter. Should the magistrate prove
venal, as too many were in English courts, Winsome realized that, being
destitute and friendless, she wasn't likely to get off scot-free, no matter
how innocent she might be.

Tears stung her eyelids, then slid, hot and salty, over her thin cheeks.
Even this far south of Boston it was dank and unbelievably chilly in this
cell.

If only Pa were here to comfort and advise. Dear Pa with his wise gray
eyes, soothing voice, and gentle hands. "Oh Papa, dearest Papa, help
me," she whispered. "What *am* I to do? Oh, why did the Lord have to
call you and leave me alone to meet this challenge to my good name?"

Challenge? *Challenge?* Challenger! She jumped up and, stepping over
the women sleeping uneasily on the floor, sought the cell's single triple-
barred window and peered out as if she fully expected to see Captain
Challenger waiting in the moonlight. Of course he wasn't.

Following her refusal to share his lodgings had he any reason to remember the untidy wench he'd picked up yesterday on the waterfront?
Unreasonably disappointed, despite her innate common sense, she returned to her stool. All the same, when daylight came, she would see
what might be accomplished toward getting word to him at the Carteret
Arms. Even if he heard from her, what could he do—why anything? She

was all but a stranger and one who'd rebuffed his offer of a possibly innocent friendship.

Of course the turnkey would expect a bribe to carry a message for her and right now she'd only three broad copper coins to her name! Nevertheless, she knew she *must* communicate with the yellow-bearded Ranger, even if it meant allowing the turnkey fellow to pat her bottom or maybe even to kiss her.

The Creole began to struggle in the grip of a nightmare, alternately moaned like a sick animal or babbled in garbled French.

Toward dawn it grew so cold that Winsome's teeth began to chatter. Shivering, she settled back against the brick wall and finally sank into a restless sleep which endured until the turnkey came to bang on the cell's door.

Rousing, Winsome hurried over to a small window let into the oak door where an iron "Judas shutter" slid aside, exposing the jailer's blear-eyed and unlovely countenance. He peered inside, then unlocked the door with one of many keys he carried dangling from a brass hoop.

He set a wooden tray on the floor grunting, "Here's yer vittles. Eat 'em quick, you lazy bawds. I'll soon be back."

To Winsome's dismay the turnkey proved to be in a foul humor, probably because he was wearing a kerchief knotted about a jaw swollen by what must be a raging toothache. Nevertheless, she forced a tremulous smile as she picked up one of three small wooden bowls filled with steaming porridge.

"Please, sir, would you be kind enough to bear a message from me to a—a friend?"

"To be sure I will, an you pay me well enough."

"My friend will reward you," Winsome assured him with forced cheerfulness.

"Maybe he will, more likely he won't. Come now, how much can *you* pay?"

"Why—why, as to that, sir, I fear I—I've only three copper pennies in my possession."

"Bah! Fer that I'd not piss across the hall!" Muttering, he backed out, relocked the door, and tramped off down the cell-lined corridor.

Dr. Brooks's only child managed to fight back bitter tears only because she was his daughter.

Watched in wondering silence by her fellow prisoners, she forced herself to half-drink, half-eat the not unpalatable porridge and found herself wishing that she'd been given a larger portion. Lord! In all her twenty-one years she'd never been half so hungry. In an effort further to fill her stomach, Winsome drank deep from a battered earthenware water pitcher crudely mended with lead. Next she dabbed water on hot and sandy-feeling eyes.

"Don't waste that, ye muckin' fool!" snapped Polly, snatching away the pitcher. "We'll see no more till nightfall."

Adeline said nothing, only dipped listlessly into her porridge and ate only half of it. Polly gobbled the rest.

Now that there was no chance of communicating with Captain Challenger, what could be done to extricate herself from this dreadful place?

The sun arose, reluctantly, it seemed, and commenced to dispel the bone-piercing chill; street cries arose and the sound of vehicles and hoofs in motion began to beat through the bars.

Think as she would, Winsome had found no solution to her problem when, toward midmorning, there came a trampling of feet and the sound of voices down the corridor.

Almost at once the principal keeper of the Watch House yelled, "Now, hear me, all you rogues. Tidy yerselves up, quick-like, and if His Excellency quizzes ye, if ye don't smile and vow ye're treated fair and decent, I promise ye'll rue it."

"Lawks!" giggled the pregnant runaway. "I'll lie the best I can if"— she slapped her enormous abdomen—"I don't drop me brat at this bigwig's feet."

The Creole said nothing, only glowered at the floor, but she did make a halfhearted effort to retie soiled black velvet laces securing her bodice. As for Winsome, she hastily twisted her dark brown hair into a fairly neat bun.

A key clucked in the cell's ponderous lock then the principal keeper appeared a step ahead of two men. One of them Winsome Brooks instantly recognized as James Oglethorpe, on this occasion clad in sober brown serge. His erect figure was so tall that he had to bend his head to enter the cell. He was wearing a sedate yet entirely pleasant expression. Then, to Winsome's incredulous surprise, Captain Wallace Challenger appeared!

"Like I said, Yer Excellency," the principal keeper was reminding him, "I does the best I can for me prisoners with wot moneys I'm granted— which ain't half enough, considerin' these lawless times."

Oglethorpe cut him short. "You need say no more, my man. I've heard the same in England from half a hundred prison warders."

His close-set brown eyes darted so quickly about the cell that they reminded Winsome of swallows she'd seen flitting around Grandpa's hay barn.

Oglethorpe gave a civil "Good morning, ma'am" to the girl Polly, who, giggling, ducked her head but, because of her great belly, her effort to curtsy proved a ludicrous failure.

The visitor then nodded kindly at the Creole, who managed a wan smile, muttering, "*Bon jour, votre Excellence, et merci.*"

When James Oglethorpe's gaze swung in her direction, Winsome Brooks drew herself to full height, lifted her chin, and looked him full in the face. "Sir, I understand that you are not only a just man but a humanitarian as well. Therefore, I appeal to you as an unfortunate, conspired-against person who, as surely as God reigns in heaven, has committed no crime."

"Eh?" In the act of turning away the Acting Governor of Georgia checked himself. He'd heard hundreds of such avowals voiced quite as convincingly. In deliberate dispassion, he considered this hazel-eyed young woman with the pointed chin and winged brows.

"Your name, ma'am?"

Winsome hesitated, then told the truth. "I am Winsome Brooks, sir, daughter to the late Dr. Brooks, a physician in Boston in the Colony of Massachusetts Bay." Words flooded from her. "You must believe me, sir! Please credit that I've been most infamously put upon by the master of a ship on which I paid in full for a passage to Jamaica."

"In that case, why are you here?" Oglethorpe queried sharply.

Winsome's lips quivered. "Your Excellency, Captain Starbuck of the *Mystick* so persistently forced unwelcome attentions upon me I felt forced to quit his vessel."

Time seemed to hesitate. If Starbuck had spread the slander, it must come out now. She almost fainted when Captain Challenger stepped forward.

Piteously, she tried to catch the Ranger's blazing blue eyes. As from afar off, she heard Challenger saying, "Your Excellency, I can attest for the truth of this person's statement."

Oglethorpe's surprise was evident. "Can you, indeed?"

"Aye, sir, I've met this young lady before. I am positive she's telling you the truth. As you can see for yourself, sir, this is no common wench; she is too gently spoken."

Oglethorpe treated the bronzed and yellow-bearded Ranger to a penetrating look. "Young sir, exactly how long have you known this female?"

The ruddy line of Wallace Challenger's craggy cheekbones reddened still further. "Why—why, sir, to be truthful, only since yesterday."

"Hum. And in so short a time you feel qualified to attest her good character? Remarkable!"

Winsome's heart seemed to shrivel, so definite was the change in Oglethorpe's manner as he turned to the principal keeper. "On what charge was this young female imprisoned?"

"Yer Excellency, 'twas by virtue of a warrant sworn out by the very man the prisoner has named—one Elijah Starbuck, who is master of a vessel out of Boston. He charged that Winsome Brooks, here—who, by the way, only just now has admitted her true name—did unlawfully violate an indenture bond to serve him or his assignees as a servant over a period of five years."

Winsome's uncleanly cheeks went scarlet and her voice sounded taut as an overstrained cable. "Believe me, Your Excellency, as God reigns above us, I signed no article of indenture! As I've said, I paid Captain Starbuck for my passage in Boston." Frantic, when doubt appeared in Oglethorpe's expression, she added, "I'll gladly take Bible oath to that."

Again the visitor in the Quaker-brown frock coat began to turn away. "Whatever the facts, mistress, you have my sympathy."

"Only sympathy?" Winsome wailed. "Then, indeed, I have been cruelly deceived about you, sir! How often have I not heard that you are a true philanthropist and benefactor of the unfortunate."

Challenger saw the line of Oglethorpe's long jaw harden, but he kept on for the cell's door.

Eyes streaming, Winsome called after him, "*Vae pauperibus sine amicis!*"

As sharply as if brought up at the end of a rope, James Oglethorpe, Esq., halted and turned about. "'Woe to the poor without friends?' Do you indeed speak Latin? How is that?"

The girl glared through tears of outrage. "Because, O False Judge of Mankind, I have been instructed in that language by my father."

Oglethorpe's straight, rather heavy brows climbed. "Ah, say you so? Tell me. Do you also possess knowledge of the healing art?"

"More than a little. I can select, grind and compound herbs and drugs according to a physician's instruction. I can clyster, bleed and cup an the need arise. I can make pledgets and bandage and apply such in the latest, most approved manner."

Oglethorpe nodded as if to himself. "Were I to take you 'on the Charity' as we put it, would you sign an agreement to remain in Georgia of your own free will, until legally released?"

Winsome started to cry in earnest, but managed to control herself. "Yes, sir! I'll undertake to serve Your Excellency and your people faithfully and well."

A slow smile crossed Oglethorpe's full-lipped mouth, but he spoke curtly. "Very well. I will take a chance on you. Once you have signed a covenant with the Georgia Company you will be provided with shelter, food and clothing. Further, you will enjoy a small stipend until such time as you shall marry or become able to support yourself. Is this satisfactory?"

"Oh-h, y-yes, sir."

Challenger barely suppressed a grin when this enigmatic female at last burst into tears.

Imperturbable as ever, Oglethorpe addressed the jailer. "My secretary, Mr. West, forthwith will post security for this young woman's person, it being expressly understood that should Captain Starbuck return to Charles Town and enter suit for the alleged breach of bond committed by Mistress Brooks, she will at once be returned to your jurisdiction. Captain Challenger, kindly escort Mistress Brooks outside."

The bound girl, Polly, waddled forward whimpering, with hands outstretched in supplication. "Wot about me, Yer Ludship? I be freeborn English too!"

"Freeborn she may have been," the jailer hastily intervened, "but, 'tis a fact, sir, Polly's always being taken up for whoring. Worse still, she's twice been convicted of breaking her indenture."

"Ah! The Devil gripe yer guts!" snarled Polly. "Ye were ever a rackpenny scoundrel who seldom paid me my due!"

As for the Creole, she said nothing, only gazed dully on the visitors from hopeless, lackluster eyes.

Winsome followed Captain Challenger's broad green back into the principal keeper's office and suddenly felt so giddy from relief and consuming hunger that only with difficulty was she able to comprehend what James Oglethorpe, Esq., was saying.

"Young woman, within an hour's time you must present yourself on the King's Wharf prepared to go aboard the *Anne*. In order to accomplish this—" His hand slid into a side pocket of the long Quaker-brown coat and reappeared holding a dozen-odd silver shillings. "Here is scarcely a princely sum, ma'am, but I trust it will suffice for the purchase of, er— intimate necessaries. Aboard ship, you will be furnished with clothing designed for the rude life in store for us all."

On dusty, brass-spurred jack boots, dark-faced Colonel Bull tramped in, saying, "Yer Excellence, Captain MacPherson and the Rangers who are to go with you are ready to stand inspection."

When Oglethorpe's tall, quietly impressive figure had disappeared Challenger grinned. "Damme if you weren't smart to think of using that Latin tag. It saved the day for you."

Winsome took the Ranger captain's scarred brown hand between hers. "It wouldn't have if you hadn't spoken in my behalf."

Golden lights shone briefly in the depths of his short beard. "No need to, lass. Come along." And he patted her lightly on her bottom whereat she colored furiously but only tucked a stray lock of hair back into place.

"I—I would like in some way to prove the depth of my gratitude."

The broad-shouldered figure in buckskins summoned a raffish grin.

"Don't worry, I'll let you know when opportunity offers; since now you must be ready for the immigrant vessel in a short while, there ain't much we can do about it right now, so my pretty little *hoktudshi*—"

"'*Hoktudshi?*' What's that—"

"Why, it means 'sweetheart' in Muskogee." He laughed softly, "And maybe something else, too. Anyhow, if ye'll tell me what you need most I reckon I can steer you to places where ye stand to get the best value for yer money."

As they were nearing the market place Winsome queried a little dazedly, "I wonder what prompted His Excellency to visit the Watch House jail this morning?"

He grinned down at her. "Why, reckon maybe 'twas because I suggested it. You see, I heard that you'd been taken up and thrown into the pokey."

"Who told you so?"

"Joey Philbrick, that lad with the sog spots all over his face. He saw us standing together on the King's Wharf when His Excellency came ashore."

After taking her arm, Challenger led off saying, "I then looked up Mr. West, His Excellency's secretary, because 'tis well-known Mr. Oglethorpe is deeply interested in prisons and prison reform."

After the purchase of some sugar buns Winsome let herself be guided, eating hungrily all the while, to a draper-mercer's shop. She didn't fail to note that Captain Challenger seemed to be well and favorably known by its pretty and full-figured proprietress. "La, if it isn't Wallie! Where've ye been keeping yerself?" she demanded, bridling.

"Out in back country, m'dear," he replied easily. "Now, Peggy, will you wait on my friend, Miss Brooks? Since her ship is due to sail within the hour will ye show her any female garments you have that're already made up?"

"Why, yes, Wall—er, Cap'n," the proprietress, flushing, ran frankly curious eyes over the Ranger's bedraggled companion. "I've a cotton blouse and two petticoats fashioned for Missus Marceau St. Julien but it's now two months and she ain't called for 'em. I judge they'll about fit you. Then I've also on hand two pair of black thread stockings from England what turned out too small to fit Missus Rhett."

Winsome said, "Then I'll have them provided they're not too dear."

Chuckling, Challenger pinched the proprietress' florid cheek. "I'm sure they won't be too dear, now will they, Ducks?"

For a reason which Winsome could surmise easily enough, they weren't expensive. In fact, these garments went so cheap that, Laus Deo!, she was able also to buy a warm woolen scarf, some kerchiefs, a few hair ribbons, a gray camlet short gown, and an apron of striped calico. Finally, providing for the future creation of certain critically needed undergarments,

Challenger's hazel-eyed protégée purchased some lengths of India muslin, needles, and thread. When she had done buying she retained only a few pennies of James Oglethorpe's donation.

A glance at the clock in St. Philip's graceful octagonal steeple warned that, very shortly, Winsome must present herself on the King's Wharf. Although she desperately wanted to bathe in the public bathhouse, she forced herself to accompany the tawny-haired Ranger officer to the Carteret Arms and there sip a glass of rum punch.

Finally, Challenger wiped his short yellow mustache and beckoned the potboy. "Alas, m'dear, I must be about my duties and you off to the King's Wharf." Quite unabashed by the amused stares of the taproom's other patrons, he put arms about her and bussed her hard upon the mouth.

As they were emerging into pale, wintry sunlight his mood changed. Said he soberly, "M'dear, just before I quit the guardroom, word arrived that two settler families have been massacred close by Fort Moore."

Winsome's eyes rounded themselves. "How—how terrible! Where is Fort Moore?"

"On the upper Savannah."

"But—but I've always heard that only in New England do the Indians attack settlers!"

"Then you've heard wrong. When it comes to cruelty, deviltry and treachery our Southern savages yield nothing to the Iroquois, Abenakis, Hurons and the like."

"Who killed all those poor people?"

"Spanish-led Yamasees and mustees, I reckon." He added with calm but somehow chilling ferocity, "An we come up with those hellions we'll surely skin 'em alive or maybe slow-roast 'em.

"Well, *hoktudshi*, I must be off. God keep you safe till I come to claim my reward."

With a finger tip Challenger touched his brimless leather skullcap and, with well-worn fringed leggings asway, swung off down the street.

Chapter 7

DR. TAILFER'S ASSISTANT

Acting Governor Oglethorpe, watching Mr. West check assorted freight being loaded into the *Anne's* longboat, noticed from the corner of his eye the approach of a slender but sturdy young female. "Ah, Miss Brooks, this is quite a transformation! I scarce recognized you."

She managed a hurried curtsy, stammered, "I trust I—I haven't k-kept your Excellency w-waiting?"

"No," said he shortly, "but you might have been left behind had you delayed any longer. Come, the rest of the supplies will come out on a wherry."

Oglethorpe handed her into the heavily laden longboat as if she'd been a lady of high degree instead of a luckless ex-prisoner who, only a short while ago, had been released on bail. The realization she *hadn't* been acquitted, that she remained under indictment, was infinitely disconcerting to Winsome. What if Elijah Starbuck returned to Charles Town? She would be forced, out of loyalty to her word, to surrender and stand trial. The very possibility of a return to the Watch House jail nauseated her.

Crouched on freight stacked in the longboat's waist, Winsome watched the oarsmen's shoulders and backs swing in response to the coxswain's rasping chant, then seized this opportunity covertly to study her benefactor as he sat on the longboat's stern locker deep in conversation with swarthy and thick-necked Colonel William Bull.

Because the tide was about ready to turn and only a mild wind was blowing the *Anne* rode placidly to her anchor amid a loose ring of garbage and other debris. Sailors tarring her rigging hailed the deck to report that the longboat was drawing near. At once immigrants appeared in increasing numbers to peer over the battered bulwarks; a few waved.

A Jacob's ladder equipped with narrow wooden treads soon was lowered from the lowest point in the *Anne's* waist to sway between the muzzles of two cannon which had been run out in order to admit air into the foul-smelling 'tween decks.

Once the longboat had rounded-to alongside and Oglethorpe, Colonel Bull, and Mr. West had clambered up to a shrilling of the boatswain's pipe, the coxswain yelled, "Hey, you! The woman passenger! Climb aboard and get a move on! We ain't got all day."

Although alarmed at the prospect of having to ascend that flimsy, unstable ladder, Winsome hurriedly picked her way over clusters of wild-eyed chickens lying bound and panting on the bottom gratings, then squeezed past a pair of bawling, wild-eyed brown-and-white calves.

As Winsome gripped the ladder and prepared to mount, a spate of bawdy speculations broke out as to what her undergarments might consist of. Having once been a confirmed tomboy, she ascended easily until, about halfway, a vagrant puff of wind billowed her skirt and single petticoat waist-high. Normally, she would have been wearing three or four underskirts, the weight of which would have kept her limbs decently concealed—neither pantalettes nor underdrawers had yet been devised. Seamen peering upward from the longboat whooped delightedly and, for the benefit of their fellows on deck, made lascivious comment on the exposé.

Since of necessity both Winsome's hands were occupied by the act of climbing she couldn't do a thing to restrain her wildly fluttering petticoat and skirt. After what seemed an eternity she was helped, scarlet-faced and furious, over the rail and eased onto the deck amid a guffawing of men and the tittering of women.

"La! Wish my bottom was so pink and pretty!" called one woman. "I'd get me a noo mate in a quick hurry."

"Aye. Her arse is smoother nor a little kitty's."

"Ecod! *Ain't* she the dainty dish?"

"Dainty or not, the wench must be shameless to be wearin' but a single petticut."

For a moment Winsome remained peering defiantly about. Never before in her limited experience had she beheld a deck so fearfully crowded; every available foot was cluttered by people, rigging, spare spars, or cargo of varying description.

Dr. Brooks's daughter hesitated, clutched her bundle of purchases, and grew steadily more outraged until a petty officer drew near and, for a wonder, respectfully knuckled his forehead.

"Ye're Mistress Brooks? Best follow me." Whereupon he conducted her down a steep companionway into a dimly lit hold which reeked of bilges and of humanity too long unwashed. Some ex-debtors sat leaning against the side quietly whittling, knitting, sewing, or mending. Children squabbled or ran about playing with boundless energy. Other immigrants puffed or snored in the 'tween deck's gloom on crude cots or occupied canvas hammocks slung to the deck beams overhead.

"Where's 'e bloody physicker?" the guide kept on asking, but no one seemed to know.

Eventually, Winsome's escort shoved open the door to a small, almost lightless cuddy.

"Ha! There ye are, Dr. Tailfer!"

"Aye, can't you see I'm occupied? What's amiss? Not another broken limb!"

"No, sir, but His Excellency sent you this here female who claims she's skilled as an apoth'cary. He wants ye should report whether she's truthful."

Frowning, the gray-bearded practitioner glanced over a shoulder while kneeling beside a thin, dark-haired young woman sprawled on a heap of old sailcloth. She was breathing with painful deliberation. Winsome heard her muttering something unintelligible. "Very well, we'll soon find out. God send she's what she claims; I need even a poor apothecary's assistance."

When Dr. Patrick Tailfer straightened, grunting softly, she realized that he was fat, of average height, and had red-rimmed gray eyes which peered brightly from under enormously shaggy brows; further, he lacked both of his front teeth.

He treated the bedraggled girl to a penetrating look. "Now, mistress, let's have no nonsense. You recognize the nature of herbs, simples and drugs? Can you compound medicines and decoct formulae?"

Over the thump and rumble of stores being landed and trundled about on the deck above she said, "Indeed, sir, until his death my father was an eminent physician in Boston."

"Boston in England?"

"No, sir, in the Colony of Massachusetts Bay."

"Humph! Seems I've a crude and probably ignorant provincial on me hands!" He stifled a groan. "Ah well, any help in a crisis is better than none, I suppose."

"'Crude provincial,' sir?" Winsome drew herself up to her full five feet five inches, eyes blazing. "You, sir, are being unnecessarily rude even for an Englishman!"

While forcing a draught of medicine between the patient's lips Dr. Tailfer looked up, at once amused and puzzled. "Why damn me for being English? You're English yourself, aren't you?"

"No. I'm *not* English-English; I'm New England-English."

"Dear me, how vehement we are! However, Dr. Cox is still ill and I've no one to help me so you'll have to do—an you are able to." He pointed to a traveling medicine chest. "Somewhere in there you'll find jalap and ipecacuanha. Now I want mixed a draught, half and half, in a wineglass of canary wine with a pinch of smellage seed if you come across it."

A new voice interpolated, "There's smellage hereabouts, ma'am, seeds and other kinds."

Only then did Winsome perceive that a young man so short that he suggested a midget had been crouched, all this while, amid deep shadows beyond the bed of sailcloth.

"That'll be enough o' yer Irish wit, Hendy O'Brien," the doctor said, not unkindly.

A flat, heavily freckled face appeared out of the gloom and tiny pale blue eyes blinked nervously. "Sorry, sor, but I'm *that* worried over Bettie."

A considerable search was required before Winsome located the required drugs, but she offered a silent prayer of thanks on discovering that Dr. Tailfer's ipecacuanha bark already had been pulverized, especially because the small brass mortar and pestle in the medicine chest couldn't have been cleansed in a very long time. Quietly, she mixed the draught as directed and held out the wineglass.

Again Dr. Tailfer straightened to a crackling of joints growing stiff with age. "Now then, O'Brien, you'll encourage your wife to swallow all the water she can take and mind you, give her fresh stuff that's just been fetched aboard. Her fever should diminish once she's drunk this decoction."

"God bless you, Doctor; poor Bettie's been sort of out o' her wits since sunup."

Dr. Tailfer yawned and caught up his medicine case. " 'Tis no wonder; takes a woman—even as young and healthy as your wife—time to recover from a miscarriage, especially one so advanced in pregnancy.

"And now I must continue my rounds," Tailfer explained in a tired voice. " 'Bide here, Mistress Brooks, awhile, and see what effect this draught has. Here, you'd best administer it yourself. Hendy's no doubt gentle and clever with horses, but he's too apt to forget that his wife's not a mare! That done, you'll return on deck and wait for me amidships. I expect the ship will soon be getting under weigh. His Excellency's afire to get moving southwards."

Since the little port of Beaufort lay scarcely forty miles to the southeast and the weather seemed inclined to remain fair, Captain Thomas had decided to spare his crew the exhausting task of hoisting the *Anne's* small boats in board. Therefore they were towed in line astern, crewed only by livestock which, according to their species, grunted, mooed, or blatted out their terror.

Once Dr. Tailfer had completed his rounds, he placed a hand lightly on his assistant's shoulder. "You, young woman, are knowledgeable past my fondest hopes. We'll get on. Now you'd better go stow your stuff; you'll probably do well to bed down with the O'Briens for, after all, 'tis to be only a short voyage. Besides, you can keep your eye on Bettie. You've a sight more sense than that jockey she wed in a careless moment."

She found Elizabeth O'Brien's diminutive husband clumsily offering his wife a drink of water. The young Irishman looked infinitely relieved when Winsome set down her bundle and announced her intention of sharing their gloomy compartment.

For the first time since that awful, blizzardy day when Pa had departed to join Ma in heaven, Winsome Brooks began to feel sure of herself.

At the recollection of Pa, lying so white and still in his coffin, her eyes started to fill. Savagely, she controlled herself and almost snapped, "Isn't there a basin somewhere? Mrs. O'Brien could stand having her face bathed. Look how hot and sweaty it is."

"Aye, mum." Hendy O'Brien returned with a wooden basin in which a gray rag floated soggily, like a drowned catbird.

Deftly, Winsome then wiped off an accumulation of sweat and grime from the patient's smooth, delicately formed, and pointed features. Had her chin not been quite so narrow and a trifle receding Bettie O'Brien, what with gracefully sloping shoulders, high, full bosoms, and plentiful dark brown hair, at present coiled in a damp braid about a high forehead, might have been considered a real beauty.

Experience warned Winsome to dilute Dr. Tailfer's powerful prescription with plenty of Canary wine. She was tilting an earthenware cup to the girl's fever-cracked lips when a woman entered the cubicle and crossed to bend above the pile of sailcloth.

Over the rushing of seas alongside and whining protests from the *Anne's* fabric, the visitor queried in a rich, slightly husky voice, "And how does your wife fare now, Hendy O'Brien?"

"Why, Mistress Bayless, somewhat better. Leastways, the sawbones has seen her and this young leddy is tending to me sweet darlin'."

"How good of you," murmured the Bayless girl. "You've just come aboard, haven't you, mistress—"

"Brooks," Winsome supplied while easing the patient's head onto a lawn petticoat she'd folded to serve as a pillow. She thought to hear a faint mew, glanced upward, and realized that the visitor was pressing a small black and white kitten to her bosom.

"This is Helen Bayless," O'Brien explained. "She's been helpin' tend Bettie."

Winsome stood up, but because the light was so poor she could make out little of the newcomer's appearance beyond that she was tall above the average and well built. "How do you do?"

The other girl laughed softly. "Well enough, considering we've been at sea near three months. I'll go wait outside."

When the Bayless girl had withdrawn, the diminutive Irishman turned to Winsome, burst out, "God bless yer heart, mum. I—I mean well, but I'm so igorant 'tis wonderful ye're here. 'Tain't that I'm mistrustin' the good doctor, mind you, but he's sore overworked since Dr. Cox got struck down by 'e bloody flux."

O'Brien cocked his sandy head to one side and reminded Winsome of a bantam rooster she'd owned when a little girl. "D'ye know? I've a feeling that ye're not only knowledgeable, but also extra-fine-bred—like Rosa-o'-lea, a filly I once rode to win at Newmarket. Billy Jason, her regular jock, got himself thrown so he claimed she was tricky and mean but Rosa-o'-lea proved sweet and with the heart o' a lioness. 'Tis many the fine purse she's won for her owner and Hendy O'Brien."

Winsome couldn't repress a chuckle. "So, Mr. O'Brien, you deem me sweet—and fast?"

The little man grimaced. "Faith and ain't it like Bettie says, I'm always puttin' me big toe where me tongue should be. No, ma'am, that was *not* my meaning—far from it!"

Winsome considered the harassed little man with sudden uncertainty. Jockeys, in fact all horse dealers in the Bay Colony, were considered to be nefarious characters: tricky, coarse-mannered, and loose-living.

The deeply flushed and still delirious girl stirred restlessly, began to babble.

"Och, me poor darlin'. Would I could take yer sufferin' on meself." Hendy slipped an arm beneath her shoulders and crooned, sweetly enough, a child's lullaby. Winsome, meantime, briskly flapped the washrag to cool it. Once she had folded it across Bettie's brow she began to quiet, the girl's mumbling grew clearer.

"You may be my father, sir, and vow that you love me—yet—all the same, you're—treacherous—" Teeth locked, the O'Brien girl writhed and her small fists beat feebly against her coverings. "No! No! I'll not forsake —Hendy's Irish, but no Papist—" Hendy glanced up, nodded, pale blue eyes filling. "Please, Father! You'd never do so evil a thing!"

Bettie suddenly managed to sit up, but the expression in her large, sherry-hued eyes was vacant. "You can't—mustn't; I love Hendy— 'Tisn't right—not honest. He never bought— Oh, Hendy, sweetheart, what will become of us if you're thrown—debtor's prison?"

"There, there, me darlin', please lie easy," pleaded the small man, forcing her back. "Things will soon go fine with us. Remember, Mr. Oglethorpe has settled our debt and has brought us, free, to America."

The sick girl commenced a fitful sobbing. "Oh-h—can't bear being imprisoned. Oh, oh, Hendy! Your Worship! I swear my husband would *never* have ordered so costly a harness—no need for such. Plead innocent—"

Through the malodorous gloom young O'Brien peered at Winsome, anguish written broad across his flat red face. "Of course we're innocent, my love. Yer father lied out o' hateful pride."

"That you, Hendy?" Mumble, mumble. "Where's my babe—"

"The babe is well, so rest easy, me love."

Winsome arose, announced almost brusquely, "Sorry, but I really must go find Dr. Tailfer. Soon's I can, I'll try to find your wife a bit of fresh fruit."

The ex-jockey suddenly grabbed her hand and, kneeling, fervently kissed it. "Then ye'll come back, honor bright?"

"I will," promised the girl from Boston. "Meanwhile, take heart, Mr. O'Brien. Your wife is better, gaining strength already. Hear how softly and regularly she breathes."

Helen Bayless waited outside the compartment, her curvaceous figure yielding slowly to the frigate's motion. She still was attempting to forget a certain physical anxiety by fondling her black and white kitten. "You've a rare fine way with the sick," she told Winsome in lazy-sounding tones. "'Tis a crying shame you've not been aboard since Gravesend. Poor Bettie's been in need of real care."

Smiling, Winsome considered the Bayless girl and enviously noted that she enjoyed what was known as a British "peaches-and-cream complexion" and also large and melting sherry-brown eyes. An unkind person might have described them as "bovine." What with full red lips and ample bosom Mistress Bayless suggested, in all its simplicity, the word "ripe."

Winsome decided that this young woman kept herself neat to admiration—for all she was clad in the plain garb of females who were emigrating "on the Charity"; square-toed black shoes, brown serge skirt and jacket, coarse white linen blouse, and a small, winged white cap that could be tied on under the chin.

"In case Hendy hasn't told you, I'm Helen Bayless, spinster from Bury St. Edmunds, where I was born and brought up. Stop it, you naughty—"

The kitten had extended a fuzzy paw to dab tentatively at a strand of naturally wavy dark brown hair.

"What a sweet thing!" Winsome ventured, tickling the smoky-eyed little creature's chin. "What's her name?" She became aware that other occupants of the 'tween decks were watching in something like disapproval.

Helen Bayless laughed softly in her throat. "She's a him. His full name is Ipswich Nicholas St. Edmund Bayless, a weighty name for so tiny a creature to carry, isn't it?"

"I'm sure Ipswich will grow up to carry his name with a flourish." For Winsome it was incredible relief to laugh wholeheartedly again but, then, her training reasserted itself. "How long ago did Mrs. O'Brien miscarry?"

The Bayless girl pursed full and shiny lips. "Let's see; why, 'twas about four days ago. The poor soul all but perished. 'Tis a great wonder the fever she'd taken in prison didn't cause her to abort long before it did."

"Prison?"

Helen Bayless's liquid and sherry-hued blue eyes wavered, sought the long unswept deck. "To be sure. Mr. Oglethorpe and other trustees of the Georgia Company bought her and her husband out of a debtor's prison—like the most of us."

Winsome failed so conspicuously to conceal her curiosity that Helen treated her to a lazy smile. "Come on deck and I'll relate what's known about 'em."

Chapter 8

"A COMMON TALE"

In the shelter of the *Anne's* lee bulwarks the two young women remained on guard lest they got drenched by capricious flirts of spray because, for a second time, the frigate was preparing to cross Charles Town Bar. Lacking a cap like Helen's, Winsome could do little to restrain the wild whipping of her hair, but she secured it as best she might under one of her new kerchiefs.

"'Tis hard to credit," began the young woman from Bury St. Edmunds, "that any civilized human could so abuse a legitimate child the way Sir Hector Trusdale did his daughter."

"My father was very different," Winsome confided over the shrill strumming made by the wind among the main shrouds.

"Bettie's father was, and is, of the landed gentry. He owns a huge estate in East Anglia called Scopwick Manor," Helen explained while she restrained another of her kitten's sudden, frantic attempts to escape.

With that stretch of tormented water rapidly drawing near, Winsome remained silent. Moreover, a strong breeze out of the southwest was heeling the *Anne* over so far that the few passengers who had remained on deck were forced to clutch for handholds. All manner of loose gear and unsecured freight commenced to rattle and slide about.

Deck officers began to bawl orders, concerned over the boats in tow, which were becoming so smothered by flying spray that they were almost lost to sight.

Winsome was reminded of the subject under discussion when Helen Bayless said, "Seems poor Bettie was Sir Hector's only child and the apple of his eye. He'd planned for a fine, advantageous marriage for her with a neighboring nobleman when she cast her eye on Hendy O'Brien, who

Sir Hector had imported from the North of Ireland to train and ride his race horses."

"I gather Mr. O'Brien is not a Roman Catholic."

Helen shook her head. "Lord love you, dear, no! He couldn't be."

"Why not?"

"Under our charter persons of any conviction—even Jews, Greeks or Mahometans—are to be welcomed into the new colony and may own land—but not Catholics."

"But why?"

The Bayless girl stuffed Ipswich Nicholas tighter into the bight of her shawl, both to keep the kitten warm and to control its persistent efforts to escape while the frigate plunged and rolled in crossing the bar.

When the *Anne* re-entered deep water Helen resumed, "'Tis said the trustees fear for the loyalty of such; they believe that Roman Catholics might be persuaded to conspire against the colony with the Papist Spaniards in Florida or the French to the westward."

"Ah, now I understand; in Canada such are a constant threat to us. Lord knows how many of our poor people the French and their Indians have murdered or carried off into captivity. But you were speaking of Bettie O'Brien—"

"So I was. Aren't I the featherbrain? Well, when Sir Hector's daughter eloped with Hendy O'Brien his rage was so terrible it must have driven him to do the dreadful thing he did."

Helen dabbed a wind-whipped curl from her eyes when the *Anne* wore, before bearing away on a southerly course, past a series of desolate, sandy, gray-white islets.

"What did he do?"

"Why, he put spies on the lovers' trail and must have paid 'em well for they quickly came up with the runaways in London. Once he learned where they lived, Bettie's Pa swore out a warrant declaring that Hendy and his bride had run out on a debt of fifty pounds they owed for a set of Spanish harness they'd bought from him. Both Hendy and Bettie swore in court they'd done no such a thing but Sir Hector bribed the magistrate to find 'em guilty, and so they were carted off to Fleet Prison."

A sharp rattling of blocks and a loud slatting of canvas drowned out the narrator's voice when a brief squall pounced on the little vessel. "Finally, the angry old baronet visited his daughter in the jail, pleaded and promised freedom and a lot of costly gifts if only she'd divorce Hendy and return home. When Bettie refused he raged swearing, 'By the Eternal! I'll see to it that you and your bog-trotting lover stay in here till you come to your senses'—ouch!"

Her kitten finally had succeeded in sinking pin-sharp claws into his mistress's arm so shrewdly that she let go, whereupon Ipswich Nicholas raced, flat-out, about the deck until a grinning seaman cornered the little creature amid the deck cargo.

"Oh! You wicked little villain!" More securely than before, Helen swathed her wild-eyed pet into her gray shawl.

Pink-cheeked from exertion, she dabbed spray from her cheeks. "Where was I? Oh yes; for three long months the poor things suffered as only decent souls can suffer in prison—you've no idea of how awful it is—or have you ever been imprisoned?"

"Well, I—well, that is, not really—" Winsome simply could not bring herself to admit that Dr. Brooks's daughter had actually spent a night in jail.

Fortunately, she was spared further evasions because the girl crouched beside her on the windswept deck chattered on. "If you haven't, I can tell you it's the nearest thing to hell there is on earth.

"Well, seems some friend told the Parliamentary Prison Reform Committee about their case so, after hearing their story, Mr. Oglethorpe arranged to pay off the debt on condition they'd agree to immigrate to America."

She got up to glance over the rail. "Oh dear, what a dreadful-looking wilderness! Never a roof or a field or a wall. Can it be all so cold, gray and lonely-looking? Already I'm afeard of it. Are you?"

"Of course not." Winsome spoke sharply. "America's not all like this; far from it."

"How do you know?"

"I was born here, you silly creature, only much farther north. Up there, we have great towns like Boston, Philadelphia and other seaports full of people and fine houses. They say New York's growing apace, but that it'll never catch up to Boston."

Long since, Winsome had made up her mind that yonder low-lying and otherwise uninteresting coast was nowhere near as beautiful as the pine-clad and rocky shores of New England.

Glancing astern, the taller girl noticed that a trim Carolina government scout boat, green-painted and schooner-rigged, also had crossed the bar and was overhauling the *Anne*. The little vessel was heeled far over and sending clouds of lacy spray from under her sharp bows.

The young women leaning over the lee rail overheard a sailor say, "B'Jesus, I sure like to see that bloody scout boat come up so quick."

"Who is she and why's she dogging us?" queried a lantern-jawed passenger.

"She's 'e *Hawk*, a armed scout boat. Glad to have her so handy by."

"Why fer?"

"She's got some colonial soljers aboard which would be fine to have around if we fall in wi' pirates."

"Pirates?" gasped a gaunt immigrant woman. "Why, in Lunnon we was told such have all been hanged or driven off years ago!"

The seaman laughed. "That's guff, pure and simple guff, old woman. In port, I heard 'tweren't but a short time back that those bloody brutes, Lowther and Low, was snappin' up vessels right off Charles Town Bar. Plenty o' such murderin' rascals is still plyin' these waters."

Helen Bayless looked frightened. "Is this really so? Or are the sailors funning us?"

Winsome looked her concern. "No. Of late buccaneers and pirates have been growing bold—even off Boston and the Grand Banks. Last year several ships were taken and their crews murdered."

Then, through teeth clicking with cold, Winsome queried, "Can I go below and maybe draw some warm clothes? I—I've only these thin cotton things."

"No, I doubt if the supply agent will distribute anything till we reach Beaufort." She brightened. "Suppose you hold Ipswich Nicholas while I duck below and fetch my spare cape. It's woolen, so it will keep you warm."

In slow good humor she presently clasped a thick black cape about Winsome's spray-soaked shoulders, asked, "Any sign of Dr. Tailfer?"

"No. I'd go look for him if I knew where to find him, but I don't."

In her droll, deliberate manner Helen drawled, "I suspect you're wondering why I'm aboard this ship and 'on the Charity.'"

Winsome smiled. "Yes. I've been wondering; you're so very soft and gentle and kind."

The full and shiny red lips briefly flattened themselves. "Like the rest, I'm an ex-debtor but very thankful to be aboard this ship! By the bye, my name *is* Helen Bayless, my real name, which isn't true of many of our fellow passengers."

At a sudden tilting of the deck Helen flung out a hand to steady herself, but, hampered by her kitten, might have fallen had not Winsome clasped an arm about the smaller woman's waist. "Thank you! I can't ever seem to get those sea legs everybody talks about. Well, as I was saying, until four months ago I was employed in London as governess to the children of Sir Arthur Ingersoll, a fashionable and well-to-do barrister."

The huge, rather vacuous eyes sought Winsome's as if begging for credence. "When my father, a notary, died three years ago of the pox I, an only child, was left alone and unprotected except for a wee inheritance. Since I'd been well educated at a school for young ladies, it seemed only wise to accept a position as governess-tutor to Sir Arthur's little girls. I'd been with the family almost two years when I met a handsome young attorney—no point in mentioning his name." Helen's round features slowly contracted. "At any rate, this gentleman courted me and appeared so in earnest that I agreed to marry him. Walter was clever, well thought of in his profession and ambitious—much too ambitious—as matters turned out.

"At first I was happy as any affianced girl could be. Then he began to postpone publication of our banns from one week to the next. His explanations were always so plausible that I was quite unsuspicious. At length, even I couldn't understand why we weren't getting married." She smiled sadly. "And then the blow fell."

Affecting only casual interest, Winsome gathered the borrowed cape closer about her for, as the *Anne* drew farther offshore, the wind was growing colder, more damply penetrating. "Blow? Then your intended was already married?"

"No, rogue though he was! Quite by chance, I discovered that my paragon of a lover was courting another female, whose father is not only a celebrated judge but who also enjoys valuable connections with the Court of St. James."

The Bayless girl blushed, emitted a taut laugh. "At long last, Walter swore to set the date and begged me to accompany him to a small hotel on my day off. Not that I was surprised by this because, foolishly, on several occasions I had—well—had permitted him certain prenuptial intimacies." Then she admitted with engaging frankness, "But always we used his chambers."

Briefly, the former governess stared over the heaving gray ocean. "We were still abed in the hotel when a terrible pounding began on the door and in burst a constable of the peace who threatened to bring the most awful charges—for unlawful carnal knowledge among other things. Walter thereupon offered this wretch so great a sum of money that he went away and I thought to have had my fright over nothing until Walter, as he was pulling on his clothes, said casually as you please, 'My darling, if I were you, I'd straightaway pay off Mrs. Hartley, that sempstress who has been making your wedding gown. I'm told that she's getting uneasy over her money because it's so very costly.

"'Really, my dear, a gown of silk! You shouldn't have been so extravagant, even on my account.' And the villain smiled as he said it. 'Here's a copy of her bill.'"

Helen's round and dimpled chin quivered and her eyes grew moist. "Believe me, it had indeed been drawn by a Mrs. Hartley, whom I'd never even heard of! And it was for all of forty pounds! Mistress Brooks, I'll swear before God Himself that I never had ordered this gown or filched the material for it, as she claimed later on. Why should I have, since aside from being a governess, I'm a sempstress and an excellent one, too, if I may say so? Of course I could no more find forty pounds than fly to the stars."

"What followed?" Winsome queried in a muted voice.

"My paragon of a fiancé then pointed out in a nasty, legal way that, in view of what had just happened, I now had the choice of being jailed for a common harlot—hadn't the constable found us in bed? Or of simply going to prison for debt, with my honor unsmirched.

"Later, I learned that the judge's daughter had consented to wed him so Walter took this devilish means of getting rid of me." The great dark blue eyes lifted pathetically to her companion. "You do credit my tale, don't you?"

Dr. Brooks's daughter said bitterly, "Yes, completely. I also have had my reputation traduced. What did you do?"

"I was helpless because the scoundrel already had bribed Mrs. Hartley to swear out a creditor's warrant which he caused to be served even as I was hurrying home from our rendezvous—Walter always was thorough about everything he attempted.

"In less than an hour, I was clapped, terrified and penniless, into Marshalsea Prison. There the warders, doubtless well paid by my former spark, refused leave to send word of my plight to my employer, Sir Arthur." Helen fluttered her hands. "Since I'd not a farthing on my person, I couldn't bribe the warders to grant me even the simplest of necessities. So, for three months, I endured the most sordid and horrible degradations you can imagine, until a party of gentlemen representing the Georgia Company discovered my plight."

"I can only hope," Winsome said, "that the Devil is reserving some especially hot corner of his domain for your betrayer." She drew a deep breath. "Well, let us both hope that we have done with sorrow and abuse."

Flushing, Helen Bayless glanced down at Ipswich Nicholas' small black and white head peering out of the engulfing shawl. "Would that I could. Alas—"

"Alas what?"

"Alas that, in my joy over beginning life anew, I during this voyage once yielded to the pleading of a certain young gentleman standing at present not far away. Ah, me. That moonlight off Madeira was *so* unbelievably beautiful."

Chapter 9

A PORT CALLED BEAUFORT

The wind blew so fair and steady all night that, even before true dawn broke, it was possible for the *Anne's* pilot to make for the dim, low-lying shore of St. Helen's, which was one of several marshy islands disguising Broad River's entrance. In many ways the coast in this vicinity was reminiscent of the approaches to Charles Town.

Gripped by widely varying emotions, the frigate's company roused considerably in advance of the usual hour, for, if all went well, the immigrants soon would feel firm ground under their feet for the first time in nearly three months. Silently, more than one seaworn passenger vowed that, come what might, he'd never again set foot aboard another vessel!

Escorted by the *Hawk*, that saucy Carolina scout boat, the *Anne* tacked around a long and sandy point which, darkened by palmettos, projected southward from what the pilot identified as Hunting Island. On the island itself stood clumps of very tall and slim pines of a variety which, growing no branches near the ground, suggested gigantic parasols.

Both vessels were preparing to stand into the river's mouth when a lookout at the masthead suddenly yelled, "Ahoy the deck! I spy two—no, three sail."

The officer of the deck cupped hand to his mouth and bellowed, "Where away?"

"To 'e sou'-sou'east, sir."

Captain Thomas panted up the quarter-deck ladder with a wrinkled nightshirt half tucked into his pants and grizzled hair still sleep-stuck about his forehead. Snatching a brassbound speaking trumpet from its rack on the binnacle, he shouted to the lookout, balanced astride the fore-top-yard. "What do they look like?"

"Two small schooners and a big sloop, sir."

"How do they sail?"

"Bearing straight down on us, sir."

Since the strange ships probably would not be visible from the scout boat, Captain Thomas ordered a warning gun fired and an alarm signal hoisted.

Promptly, the *Hawk* acknowledged by firing a single gun. The report sounded dull and flat as it reverberated about the estuary. Among the immigrants arose a gabble of excitement; many, to secure a better impression of the situation, clambered up on the rail, only to be restrained by cursing sailors.

The scout boat, meanwhile, ran out her six little cannon and her crew scurried to battle stations.

"Of course, Yer Excellency," Captain Thomas informed the coldly calm accompanying trustee when he appeared on deck, "yonder craft may prove friendly merchantmen inbound from Jamaica or Barbados, but, sir, having brought you this far in safety, I ain't prepared to gamble on that." He turned aside, roaring orders which sent both watches scrambling aloft and out on the yards to set every useful sail.

The *Anne's* master cast a glance at an anxious crowd collected in the waist, then stumped across the quarter-deck to where James Oglethorpe, Esq., stood leveling a pocket telescope. Just then the pilot called anxiously from the steering flat, "Captain, sir, shall I make for an inlet I know of where them people won't dare follow, or shall I keep our present course?"

Oglethorpe turned to Captain Thomas. "It would appear wiser to maintain our course till it becomes certain these fellows mean to attack us."

The three strangers' topsails now had appeared on the horizon as tiny white squares.

Oglethorpe queried at the end of twenty minutes, "What do you make of them?"

The pilot allowed these unidentified vessels were either Spanish *guarda-costas* or buccaneers, which, in his opinion, were one and the same thing. Meanwhile the scout boat, though armed only with six eight-pounders, went scudding valiantly off on an intercepting course.

Oglethorpe suddenly spoke in a curt, impassive tone, "We'll follow the *Hawk*, Captain. For all we're unarmed, yonder rascals don't know that, so, together we may overawe them."

The two British vessels stood out to sea for perhaps a half hour when, to James Oglethorpe's inexpressible relief, the unknown vessels put down their helms and, pointing their bowsprits northward, continued on their course up the coast of South Carolina.

To Winsome Brooks the variety of bird life visible once the frigate had entered Broad River became astonishing. In every direction the sky was streaked by dense, ever-shifting skeins of waterfowl. Closer to the surface flapped irregular lines of brown-gray pelicans, blue or white herons, and glossy black cormorants. Small, comical-looking brown ducks with white patches on their cheeks sped by the ship's sides, suggested overgrown bumblebees.

"Them's boobies," explained a sailor. "They flies dretful fast."

Enormous flocks of ducks kept billowing about the pale January sky like smoke from a great conflagration. On occasion, by their very numbers, they obliterated the shore line and darkened the sky.

Once his ship had weathered Hunting Island Point, Captain Thomas ordered courses clewed up and gallants furled, so, under only topsails and jibs, wonderfully the *Anne's* pilot commenced to thread a course among an amazing complex of shoals, sand bars, and tiny, reed-crowned islets. Finally the frigate was headed up a tributary to the Broads, upon whose shores great live oaks marched down to the shore and dipped hoary beards of Spanish moss in the water.

On higher ground loomed tall, unbroken ranks of dark green long-leafed pines.

The pilot drew near Oglethorpe, touched his narrow-brimmed straw hat. "If Yer Excellency is interested, over there's Parris Island; 'tis fair alive with deer and alligators. Many's the time I've hunted there." He pointed to port. "See that pile of bricks among the trees near the mouth of yonder creek?"

"Yes. It looks like the ruins of an artillery emplacement."

The pilot looked respectfully surprised. "Why, so 'tis. How would you know that, sir?"

Oglethorpe smiled. "Why, simply because that would be a good position to emplace a battery."

"Well, sir, ye're right as rain; a ruined battery is what's over there. The damn' Spaniards took it by surprise back in 1686. That was when they slew or made captives of the garrison and every last settler hereabouts." Frowning, the pilot spat into the river. "'Twere a sorry business, sir. Next, they cruised on up the coast and fell upon Edisto, where they massacred those of Lord Cardross's Highlanders who hadn't been smart, or lucky enough, to give up and leave the place a year earlier."

Um. Still another evidence of Spanish and Indian incursions; the conviction grew in James Oglethorpe's mind that, back in London, a far from an accurate account of conditions along the Guale Coast had been presented to the trustees of the Georgia Company.

His wide mouth tightened with the realization that, if the enemy struck while the new colony was being established, he was likely to lose everything. He'd no fighting men of his own. So thank God for the presence of Captain MacPherson and his handful of South Carolina Rangers!

He was recalled to immediate considerations by the first officer. "Yer Excellency, those islands up ahead are called Cranes and Ladies—Beaufort lies behind 'em, so you'll not spy the port right away. First, you'll see the new fort."

"Thank you, sir." Moodily, Oglethorpe ran an eye over a seemingly impenetrable tangle of vines and moss-draped trees defining the shore line. "Tell me, does Beaufort lie on the mainland itself?"

"No, sir, 'tis situated on Port Royal Island, which is separated from the main by a wide river called the Coosaw."

Now sailing well ahead of her consort, the *Hawk* fired a salute in honor of the still-invisible fort and sent countless thousands of land and water birds spiraling into terror-stricken flight.

Above the end of a low island densely overgrown with water oaks, cedars, and cypresses climbed a cloud of gray-white smoke which was followed by a booming report which was acknowledged by both scout boat and frigate. Once the *Anne* had weathered a wooded point her company sighted a square, red brick fort above which a ragged Royal Jack was fluttering. From it, another cloud of grayish smoke drifted out over the tea-colored waters of a well-protected bay where several small vessels lay at anchor or were tied up to rickety-looking little wharves. At this harbor's far end showed the roofs of a pretty, snug-looking village which lay, sprawled haphazardly under towering pines, well back from the water's edge.

There was small need for the Reverend Doctor Herbert to invite the ex-paupers to fall onto their knees and join him in a prayer of thanksgiving. Winsome Brooks knelt with the rest and, joining palms, raised her eyes skyward in heartfelt gratitude.

A six-oared barge came pulling out, exchanged noisy banter with the scout boat's crew. It was steered by a muscular young man wearing a scarlet infantry tunic, a pipe-clayed sword sling worn over a brown linen hunting shirt, and Indian leggings.

"Reckon yonder comes Lootenant Watts," the pilot announced over a pot of beer. "He's in command here; Ensign Farrington's his second, or was, last time I put in here."

Once the barge had threshed alongside, the officer at her tiller swung his hat in circles, yelling, "Welcome to Carolina! Welcome! Welcome!" He was cheered to the echo by the entire ship's company and, farther off, by knots of townspeople who, in increasing numbers, were flocking down to the water's edge.

Broad-shouldered Lieutenant Watts managed a dress sword with skill while scaling a boarding ladder. He was followed less handily by an older man who lacked his left arm.

After saluting Oglethorpe and Captain Thomas, Watts presented his companion. "This gentleman is Mr. Delabarre. He owns a plantation nearby and has offered small boats and a gang of slaves to help carry your people ashore. Later, they'll aid Your Excellency in seating your river."

"I had scarcely anticipated such generosity, sir." Oglethorpe bowed toward the crippled planter. "Believe me, the company will remain forever in your debt."

Then he turned to the fort's deeply tanned commander. "Mr. Watts, can you possibly find immediate accommodation for one hundred and twenty-five people?"

"Aye, Yer Excellency. When Rob—er, Governor Johnson, heard that you'd soon arrive, his council sent orders that barracks designed to house His Majesty's Independent Company be hurried to completion. There should, therefore, be ample shelter for all your people."

When John Stonehewer planted his big feet on Beaufort's wide and sandy gray beach he bent and patted the earth. "S'help me God, I'll never again willin' quit solid ground again!" Then, with his buxom wife and half-grown twin sons, he knelt and, with deep fervor, again recited the Lord's Prayer.

A throng composed of whites, Negroes, mestizos, and mulattoes—the first that most of the immigrants had ever beheld—had collected about the landing place. Farther back, near the edge of the woods, stood or squatted a number of impassive, copper-hued people with straight jet hair. Their presence disconcerted the newcomers; these, then, must be some of those red Indians about whom they'd heard such terrifying stories. But the redskins didn't look fierce at all, just dully indifferent. For the most part they wore ragged cloaks and kilts, but a few showed traces of paint on their faces and wore bedraggled feathers in their topknots.

Curs raced noisily about and children, grinning broadly, waved broken palmetto and fan-palm branches in biblical greeting. One boy was carrying a pet raccoon about in his arms.

Clearly, this was a day everyone present would long remember as a welcome break in the monotony of existence in this wild and isolated spot.

Soon it became evident that the *Hawk* and the *Anne* had been reported while well off the Guale Coast, for Beaufort's inhabitants already had made considerable preparations for a feast. Near the newly completed brick barracks pits had been dug, fires lit, and heavy iron spits rigged for use.

Sweating but cheerful black slaves in coarse duroy trousers and Osnaburg shirts were chattering unintelligibly while barbecuing turkeys, pigs, and cattle which, already, were giving off mouth-watering odors. On a row of trestle tables nearby reposed many bleeding piles of ducks, swans, and wild geese ready for plucking.

The immigrants gazed in openmouthed curiosity when a band of Indians appeared from among the woods. They drew near carrying the limp carcasses of two gray-white deer which still had arrows sticking out of their sides.

The men were freshly painted with gaudy designs done in red, yellow, and blue. Most of these newcomers were unarmed except for knives and war hatchets, but some carried cased bows and quivers of arrows. About their shoulders these Indians had slung capes of glossy otter skin or the spotted pelts of wildcats. The few women accompanying these hunters went bare-breasted and wore no paint whatever, but had decked themselves out with ornaments of copper, brass beading, and pearl shell.

Once the immigrants had deposited their bundles of immediate necessities before the barracks, they wandered off among the houses. Generally these consisted of but two rooms, simple, unpainted frame structures. Gradually overcoming the shyness inherent in an isolated community, the inhabitants introduced themselves and soon were occupied in trying to answer a flood of questions—some sensible, some downright ridiculous.

Farmers among the colonists-to-be were quick to note that a herd of rather small, rough-coated brown cattle was grazing on a nearby meadow guarded by two youths armed with ancient musketoons. Pigs, gray geese, and chickens roamed at will, apparently unconcerned by this influx of strangers. Lines of washing, flapping under a gentle breeze, lent a homely, infinitely reassuring air to the settlement.

As for Hendy O'Brien, he felt his heart soar like a hunter over a three-bar gate on spying a handsome black stallion pacing restlessly about a stout post-and-rail paddock. His joy increased when he found several sleek brood mares and spindle-legged foals placidly switching flies in a fenced pasture behind the officers' tiny brick quarters. The smile widened on the ex-jockey's flat, freckled features. God's love! Yonder animals all appeared in fine fettle and a few even showed indications of thoroughbred blood.

Chirruping softly, Bettie's husband went over to stroke the nearest colt. Contact with the little animal's satin-smooth muzzle sent a thrill down his spine. Och! Mayhap life in this wild country mightn't prove altogether unpleasant. Then a curious thing happened. A wild, painted Indian drew near, whereupon the mares snorted, stamped their hoofs, and, white-eyed, herded their foals as far away as they could. Hendy decided that this was because Indians, in passing, left behind a rank, musky odor—something like that found about a fox's den.

Winsome entrusted the O'Brien girl to the care of a motherly-looking housewife whose home stood close by the harbor and, with Helen Bayless, wandered about Beaufort, forming swift impressions of this crude but pretty little village. She had, of course, on occasion, paid visits to frontier settlements in Massachusetts; such straggling, log cabin hamlets as Stoughton, Weston and, farthest inland, Deerfield, where, in the winter of 1704, French-led Abenaki Indians had conducted a hideous massacre.

Here, as in the backwoods of New England, almost all the men wore a weapon of some sort; they moved quietly and their eyes seldom were at rest. Here also, children seemed old for their ages and made much less noise than town-raised young ones.

"Seems as if they expect trouble all the time," observed Helen Bayless. "Have you noticed that the cannons mounted in that fort out on the point are placed to protect not only the harbor but the town as well. Oh-h! Ipswich Nicholas, for shame! How could you?" Laughing quietly, Helen shook her finger at her kitten, busily digging his first hole in the soil of the New World.

"My, isn't it wonderful to stand on solid ground again? I believe I'm going to like living here. The trees are so queer-looking and there are birds and flowers everywhere, even though 'tis midwinter at home."

She seemed so happy it was hard for Winsome to credit that, very probably, she was carrying within her the beginnings of a bastard child. Although ever since Helen had confessed her indiscretion Winsome had maintained a quiet lookout, she remained without the least clue as to which of these immigrants had seduced the former governess.

Long before a pallid sun achieved its zenith the *Anne* had been towed in to Beaufort's only real wharf and a start made toward setting ashore most of the ex-paupers' pitiful personal possessions and the bulk of the company's supplies. This proved reasonably easy, for, with unprecedented foresight, the trustees had caused the cargo to be stowed in the proper order; farming and construction tools beneath everything else; then dry goods, then, most accessible of all, staple foods such as hard bread, flour, salted pork and beef, pickled fish, and molasses.

Standing to one side with the expedition's principal officer, Oglethorpe felt encouraged at the willing manner in which his male colonists joined with the ship's crew at unloading and trundling the perishable supplies to shelter of the Independent Company's storehouse, puncheon-built structure of sturdy logs. At the same time it gave him cause for reflection that, despite this seemingly peaceful atmosphere, Colonel Bull, Captain Mac-Pherson, and a few of the Rangers lost no time in mounting horses offered by the inhabitants and riding away to reconnoiter the vicinity. Others quickly departed for the same purpose afoot or in dugout log canoes.

Winsome and her companion needed no second invitation when a frowzy and enormously fat woman waddled up and said, "I declare, missy, you look *that* pale ye better take somethin' to eat and drink. Lawks! Ye're thinner nor any shitepoke, and the feast won't start till sundown. Come along, and no back talk."

Dr. Brooks's daughter felt a sudden warmth flooding her being. How long since anyone, let alone a stranger, had addressed her with such hearty and disinterested kindness? "You're most generous, ma'am, but my friend and I must attend to a sick fellow passenger. Otherwise we'd be most pleased to avail ourselves of your hospitality."

"Land's sakes; bring yer ailin' friend along. Say, it's main fine to hear people talk the same way I did when I was young. You won't believe it, but I was born near Southampton. My folks fetched me out here 'way back in '15. Where's yer friend at?"

"Lying under a tree down by the landing, Mrs.—"

"Call me Maggie Benton," she cackled, "or anythin' but Late-to-Table. What are your names?" When she'd been told, she pointed. "See that there dwelling under them two big cedars? Well, that's where my Tom and I live. I'll go ready a cot fer yer poor friend."

Huge breasts surging unrestrained under a food-spotted Calicut blouse, the Benton woman waddled off toward a house of rough-sawn planks.

By the time Bettie O'Brien had been carried to the Bentons' yard, deathly pale, on a human "chair" formed by her husband and another man of short stature, Maggie Benton already not only had arranged a mattress on a settle under one of the cedars but also had laid out on a crude table board bread, a cold roast mallard, slabs of pork, and, best of all, an iron pot of steaming venison stew.

"Eat hearty," boomed the hostess, perspiring freely while piling wooden plates with food. "This year, praise God, we've aplenty to eat. 'Tain't like last year when a parcel of Yamasees and runaway blacks slew or drove off most of our pigs and cattle. Those villains just loves pork—specially the blacks. Wish my Tom was home; for all he's a Welshman, he'd love to hear the news from England, but he's away on guard duty down to Tybee Island. Picaroon vessels have been hanging offshore there nigh to a fortnight."

"Picaroons?" mumbled Helen through a full mouth. Lord, how wonderful it was to taste something other than ship's food! "Are they a tribe of Indians?"

"No. Picaroons, curse their black and cruel hearts, are common buccaneers, pirates, or corsairs."

The immigrants wobbled about, still on their sea legs, then clustered about the barbecue pits and, encouraged by the Carolinians, gorged themselves until a few grew queasy.

Meantime, James Oglethorpe, Esq., Colonel Bull, and the garrison's two commissioned officers dined under a moss-hung cypress towering just outside of Fort Beaufort.

Successfully, the accompanying trustee pretended to savor a goblet of his hosts' strong but acid Spanish wine. He would have much preferred one of his own French vintages stored deep in the frigate's hold.

Across the starlit harbor, where shallops, sloops, and pirogues lay at

anchor, voices began to raise Old Country ballads and airs. A few immigrants drew aside and began to sing hymns.

Oglethorpe peered through a veil of mosquitoes at Colonel Bull across
the table, then glanced at black-haired and bittern-thin Captain MacPer-
son—at dusk they had returned, reassured, by their reconnaissance. "Gentlemen, if you deem it wise, I propose that, as early as possible tomorrow,
we board the *Hawk*, proceed to the Savannah River's mouth and ascend
said stream as far as you deem it practicable."

Bull elevated a shaggy brow and demanded of the hosts, "Well, boys,
what d'ye say on that score? Yonder country quiet?"

Hurriedly, Lieutenant Watts gulped a mouthful of barbecued beef.
"Yes, sir. Bill, here's, just been up to Amercario."

Ensign Farrington, a beetle-browed young man with a cleft chin and
long, bluish jaws, set down his wine cup. "Well, Cunnel, when I rode
that way only a few days back I saw no war sign anywhere. Only Indians round Amercario were Tomo-chichi's Yamacraws and a wandering
band who call themselves Sakwaris."

Colonel Bull looked surprised. "Sakwaris? Never heard of such a tribe."

"Nor have I, sir. Seems they're only a small party of mongrel warriors
who are camping outside Tomo-chichi's village. They're nothing to take
account of I'd say, sir." The young officer sucked hard on a red-stone pipe,
then expelled a lungful of smoke that went whirling across the table and
briefly discouraged the clouds of whining insects.

"Mongrels, ye say?"

"Yes, sir. I made talk with Toonahowie about 'em. He says they're
mostly stray Chickasaws and some Creeks and Apalachees. They've even
a few Niggers among 'em. Queerest thing of all, sir, is that their mico,
Sakwari-cra, is a Tuscarora but he's also a full white."

Colonel Bull lit a pipe of his own, puffed several times while an owl
raised its quavering cry in darkness behind the fort. "Expect me to credit
that?"

"Don't know about that for sure, because I didn't get to see him, sir,
but Toonahowie says this fellow's English name is Thad Burton. Claims
he got captured as a young boy and was adopted into the Turtle Clan of
the Tuscarora Iroquois."

"Strange," Oglethorpe ventured, "that a real white man would become
an Indian chief. Does that happen often?"

Full to capacity, Lieutenant Watts sighed and eased his sword belt.
"Hardly ever, Your Excellency. Plenty of English, French, and Spanish
children get captured and adopted by the savages, but they seldom get
to rate very high in the tribe."

Always intrigued by human psychology, the tall Englishman inquired,

"And do these—these unfortunates—retain any of the—well, say the natural instincts of their race?"

"No, sir. Mostly they grow up wild as wolves and, on account of they're a sight smarter than most redskins, they cause us plenty of grief. Nothing's trickier than a half-breed or a renegade."

Oglethorpe inclined his head to use his serviette. "I can credit that. Does this fellow called Burton speak any English?"

"Only a little, sir."

"Sufficient to act as a linguister?"

The ensign shrugged. "I rather doubt it, Your Excellency. But don't let it concern you because if John Musgrove's wife, Mary, is around, she'll translate for you and do it excellently well."

"Who might be John Musgrove?"

"He runs a truck house or a trading post on the Savannah River a little upstream from Tomo-chichi's town, near where Amercario used to stand."

"That's the place," announced Colonel Bull, "where Judge Whitaker and I think you might do well to seat your people. He'll be arriving here before daylight. Both Mr. Watts and the ensign here also favor the location since it's known to be healthy and has plenty of pure springs all about."

Ensign Farrington, not a little pleased to become the focus of attention, smothered a belch behind a thorn-scarred hand. "Yes, sir. Can you win Mary Musgrove's favor, you'll have gone a long way toward avoiding trouble with the Yamacraws, who own—or claim to own—the land Colonel Bull has mentioned."

Oglethorpe pretended to savor his wine. "Am I right in thinking neither the Yamacraws nor the Sakwaris are very numerous?"

"Aye, that they're not, sir," Captain MacPherson informed him. "Together, they might field fifty warriors—always provided Sakwari-cra ain't recruited some more drifters for his band."

"Recruited?"

"Aye, sir. As Mr. Watts said a while back, this white mico is so eager to found a powerful new tribe that he's adopting wanderers from broken or leaderless bands or even escaped Indian prisoners—provided they're strong and warlike. I understand he's even accepting runaway Negro slaves. They say his 'long warrior,' or second-in-command, is a giant Negro called Quobah, who has bought a few blacks free from the Indians."

Puzzled furrows creased Oglethorpe's high forehead as, long since, he had set aside his wig and replaced it with a silk scarf bound over close-cropped brown hair. "So this white chieftain has a Negro lieutenant? Hum. They sound like unique characters—to say the least."

"Burton is," agreed the Ranger captain. "Tomo-chichi once told me this young fellow's a natural leader, for all he's yet to see his twenty-fifth year."

"From what Indian race are these Yamacraws descended?"

MacPherson opened wide his mouth, used a dingy forefinger to dislodge a bit of walnut shell. "They're of pure Creek stock, sir-r, but outlaws. All the same, the lands they hold belong to the Creek Nation as a whole. They canna sell a square foot of their hunting grounds wi'out their Great Council's permission so Yer Excellency had better start out by winning Mary Musgrove to your project."

Alert to every implication, Oglethorpe softly queried, "Why does this woman wield so much influence?"

"Because, sir, Coosa-pona-keesa, which is Mary's Creek name, is a niece o' Old Brims, who, till he died a while back, was a very great warrior and emperor of all the Creeks. Therefore, Mary rates as a Creek princess."

Colonel Bull got up, stalked over to pluck a brand from the fire, and used it to light his long-stemmed clay pipe. "Her pa was supposed to have been a Carolina Indian trader named John Griffith. So Mary's half white and long married to John Musgrove, who's a full white. She was brought up at Pon Pon, near Charles Town, so she speaks perfect English."

Colonel Bull knit his massive brows and seemed to regret the necessity of continuing. "I presume Your Excellency ain't forgotten something that was said at that banquet in Charles Town?"

"Pray refresh my memory. So much of importance was mentioned on that occasion."

"Maybe ye'll recall, sir, that, as I've pointed out, this territory which was granted you under charter from the Crown is in defiance of Spanish claims?"

"Yes. I recall that—perfectly."

"Well, that ain't all. Nobody thought, or wanted, to tell you that your charter *also* violates a treaty made between the Yamasee Indians and the Crown Colony of South Carolina."

"No. How, if you please?"

"Why, sir, some years back it was agreed that no English settlements were to be placed between the Savannah and the Altamaha River—which territory I reckon is included in yer charter?"

"It most certainly is." Oglethorpe appeared definitely taken aback. "'Tis a great pity, Colonel, that I was not made aware of this long ago."

"Better to warn you late than not at all, because, sir, the Yamasees are a very powerful, cunning and warlike people. Like the Spaniards, who arm and incite them, they consider all Englishmen their mortal enemies."

The acting governor heaved his muscular frame erect and began to secure his waistcoat's buttons. Next, he buckled on a straight sword which, judging by its scarred and weather-beaten scabbard, must once have seen a deal of campaigning. "Thank you, gentlemen. This information is invaluable. Colonel Bull, I trust you'll not mind if I take a solitary turn along the shore? 'Tis my custom before going to bed."

Lieutenant Watts also arose and secured his sword. "Very well, sir. But please to walk heavily and, if you get challenged, don't move until you're recognized. By the way, sir, tonight's password is 'safely landed.'"

"And the countersign?" demanded the acting governor.

The fort's brawny young commander grinned. "'James Oglethorpe.'"

Chapter 10

STROLL BY STARLIGHT

Wearied by multiple problems, James Oglethorpe, Esq., remained alert only through a concerted effort as he crossed the trampled sand of Beaufort's village square. Even at this late hour a few immigrants and natives remained awake. They loafed, smoked, and talked quietly among the shadowy houses; to a man, they had eaten to satiety at the barbecue. Most of the ex-paupers, however, were resigned to spending the night under the parasol of pines, in sheds, or under drawn-up small boats because the new barracks had proved barely capable of housing the sick, the women, and the younger children.

The accompanying trustee found pleasure in viewing the effect wrought on innumerable pendants of Spanish moss which assumed delicate, rosy-gray hues whenever a fire flared up. Since little or no wind was blowing, strata of acrid wood fumes hung low over Beaufort, blended with billows of smoke raised by brush fires burning brightly on the mainland. Residents had explained that such were kindled by either Indians or colonists with intent to clear land for crops.

The solitary figure paused on occasion to address groups of lounging men, but he soon desisted because they insisted on jumping up, uncovering and sometimes raising a cheer.

Once Oglethorpe had left outlying dwellings behind he was disconcerted over being challenged by sentries crouched, invisible, amid shadowy undergrowth. Hum! Why weren't these men walking their posts in soldierly manner, as guard was kept in Europe? Once again challenged, he heard the unseen picket call out, "Gawd bless ye, sir! Maybe now we c'n go capture St. Augustine 'n drive them murderin' Papists and their Yamasees into the sea and sleep sound o' nights."

Oglethorpe faced the shadowy woods, then called in his deep and penetrating voice, "Thank you, my friend. Perhaps, someday, we will have to do just that thing."

The unseen sentry warned, "Best stick close by the water's edge, sir. We've killed off most of 'em but there are still a few tigers lurking in the woods hereabouts. Ye've no need to fear snakes or alligators; they sleep this time o' year."

At length Oglethorpe made his way out to the tip of a barren sandspit showing ghostly pale in the starlight and discovered that he could see not only lights and fires blinking in Beaufort but also riding lights aboard the *Anne* and the *Hawk* and in the rigging of a huddle of anchored plantation boats, sloops, and small coasting schooners.

With the night wind stirring the ends of his scarf-turban the accompanying trustee let his imagination run free. Hmm. For the twentieth of January it certainly isn't cold here. Seems hard to credit that, thus far at least, I've confounded those long-faced doubters, Sir Robert Sutton and Robert Walpole, but I must not deceive myself. The greater and most hazardous part of our scheme remains to be accomplished. But, damme, it's worth attempting.

Wavelets whispered delicately, drowsily a few inches before his fashionably cut boots of fine cordovan leather while his thoughts flew backward to that occasion when, back in 1729, he'd been appointed chairman of a Parliamentary committee formed "to Inquire into the State of Gaols in this Kingdom" and had, for the first time, ventured into that sordid institution known as Fleet Prison. All too vividly he recalled his revulsion at the sadistic brutality, callous inhumanity, and astounding venality of Warden Thomas Bainbridge. But the fellow had proved to be no better or any worse than William Acton of Marshalsea and other prison governors.

He remembered, also, his efforts, along with Lord Percival, General Wade, James Vernon, and others, to convince Parliament that conditions prevailing in the debtor's prisons constituted "A Stench in the Nostrils of the Almighty and a Disgrace to the Crown of England."

Characteristically, it never occurred to the acting governor that he had won a notable triumph by conveying a petition to the Throne itself which requested not only the remission of debts in certain attested cases, but which promised the ex-paupers free transportation to the New World at the Georgia Company's expense.

He drew a slow, deep breath. Pray God my fellow trustees won't lose faith and fail to send out the next party of emigrants promptly.

To its last line, James Edward Oglethorpe could visualize one particular passage in the company's charter, published on June 9, 1732:

> —*That many of his poor Subjects were, through Misfortunes and want of Employment, reduced to great Necessities, and would be glad to be Settled in any of His Majesty's Provinces in America, where, by Cultivating the Waste and Desolate lands, they might not only gain a Comfortable Subsistence, but also Strengthen His Majesty's Colonies and increase the Trade, Navigation, and Wealth of His Majesty's realms; and that the Province of North America had been frequently Ravaged by Indian Enemies, more Especially that of South Carolina, whose Southern Frontier continued unsettled and lay open to the Neighboring Savages; and to Relieve the Wants of said poor People, and to protect His Majesty's Subjects in South Carolina, a Regular Colony of the said poor People should be Settled and Established on the Southern Frontiers of Carolina.*

Chapter 11

THE PROMISED LAND

A colorless winter sun was burning almost directly overhead when, some sixteen miles upstream from that point where the Savannah River emptied into the Atlantic amid a maze of reedy islands, Colonel William Bull ordered hawk-featured Captain MacPherson and ten soft-treading Rangers to debark on the river's southern bank. A half-mile upstream loomed a very high bluff which towered, rampart-like, above the Savannah's swift-flowing and icy waters.

Commented the acting governor to Judge Benjamin Whitaker, who had boarded the *Hawk* just after daybreak, "This is indeed an impressive stream; it must be nearly a mile across hereabouts."

"Aye, Yer Excellency, 'tis all of that," agreed the Carolinian. Bull's gaze meanwhile was fixed on the dense, moss-and-vine-draped woods lining the riverbank. "'Tis not only wide," continued the judge, "but also navigable, thus far, to ships of up to two hundred tons burthen."

Employing his pocket telescope, Oglethorpe also began to study the surrounding country. "About where is the spot you've in mind as a possible seat for the colony?"

Colonel Bull's blunt brown forefinger swung to the high, reddish bluff. "Yonder's the place, sir, up there lies a wide and fertile plateau with plenty of spring water handy. Last year, whilst I was scoutin' this country to site some military outposts, I examined that there bluff with extra care." Bull rubbed at the two-day bristles darkening his chin. "You mayn't agree, but I deem that bluff top the likeliest situation for a town I've spied south o' the Savannah."

The acting governor smiled. "Also, the town would lie in an ideal position to protect Charles Town from Spanish and Indian raids." For several minutes Oglethorpe's lively, close-set brown eyes probed the eminence in question. Among other things, he noted that magnificent stands of timber not only crowned the bluff but also almost completely covered a long, flat island lying opposite the height indicated by Colonel Bull.

"At first glance I am inclined to favor this site and the fact that the river, thus far, is navigable for large ships, which counts heavily in its favor since it is my intention to establish my settlement accessible to sea trade. In time of need, help could arrive quickly from that direction."

Colonel Bull nodded absently as he watched the cautious advance of Rangers who had fanned out in a line of skirmishers and, moving inland from the river, were advancing into the forest as an all but invisible brown ripple.

A Ranger who'd remained aboard the scout boat suddenly turned to Bull. "Sir, ye noticed a little flash just now?"

"Aye, Talbot. Reckon there must be some savages lurkin' by the bluff's base. Keep an eye on 'em. If you note more sign, fire a warnin' for Cap'n MacPherson and his boys."

Presently the wind died out, leaving the *Hawk* to drift with the current until the scout boat's crew got out sweeps and resumed progress toward the great bluff.

"Yer Excellency," drawled Bull, "were you to construct a strong fort on Tybee Island, it would command this river's mouth and could turn back pirates and any other enemies save a strong Spanish flotilla; a garrison there could delay even so powerful an enemy long enough for you to ready your defenses and summon help."

The colonial, however, said nothing about what might happen to the new settlement should the ever-encroaching French decide to lead powerful Choctaw and Alibamu allies in an attack delivered from the west or southwest.

Earnestly, Colonel Bull tried not to let this courteous, deadly serious gentleman guess how appalled he was over discovering that there weren't

more than a half-dozen ex-officers or former soldiers among his immigrants.

Oglethorpe, who with characteristic modesty had not dwelled upon his
own military training and service in action, turned to Judge Whitaker.
"The first thing I intend, sir, once the town is established, is to protect it
with a ring of fortified outlying hamlets, therefore I will be infinitely
obliged if, when the time comes, you and Colonel Bull will advise me as
to where such defenses should be located."

Bull stuffed shredded tobacco into a leathery cheek. "Glad to. I'll
lend you either Captain MacPherson or Captain Challenger. Both of 'em
know this part o' the frontier like the business end of a rum bottle. Maybe
better.

"Best thing about this here site—which goes by the name Amercario—
is that the land up there is richer than cream and can always be watered
from never-failing springs. Best of all, you'll find an abundance of fine
timber standing ready to hand."

"Hey, Bill!" The gapped and weather-stained fringes along Colonel
Bull's sleeve swayed when he beckoned the scout boat's captain, a gnarled,
lynx-eyed individual answering to the name of Ferguson. He scrambled
between the sweep swingers and up to James Oglethorpe and Bull, standing beside a cannon mounted on a short deck at the bow.

"Willie, can we land below the bluff?"

"Naw, sir, but there's an easy beach a little ways upstream."

"How runs the tide?"

As the scout boat was nosed closer to the steep and wooded bank,
Ferguson grunted, "Not much tide up here; water's so fresh ye can drink
it an ye're thirsty enough." He cast Bull a quizzical glance. "If ye mean
to use Tomo-chichi's landing place, ye'd best get ready. See that?" He
indicated flashes of metal in the woods just beyond the great bluff's base.
Quietly Lieutenant Watts, Judge Whitaker, and a local planter named
Hugh Bryan looked to the priming of their weapons.

"Ready yer arms. Yonder's Yamacraw Town," said the scout boat's
captain. "Which is where Tomo-chichi moved his folks after quitting
Amercario."

Instantly, Oglethorpe demanded, "Why did he leave the place if it is
all that desirable?"

The scout boat's captain spat overboard and grinned. "Dunno, sir, except that the redskins are bone-lazy. Likely enough, they hated climbin'
that high bluff all the time. Now, sir, iffen you peer, careful-like, you'll
note a mess o' pirogues and dugouts drawn up on the beach below
Yamacraw Town."

Oglethorpe pulled out his pocket telescope, screwed up his eyes, and
studied Tomo-chichi's capital. "I see a lot of men yonder and beyond

what looks like a palisade of pointed logs and the roof of a long building inside it."

"That'll be the Yamacraw council lodge."

"What is that big log structure standing outside the palisade?"

"John Musgrove's truck house, sir," Lieutenant Watts answered. "Let's hope, sir, that John and his wife aren't away on a trading trip."

Obeying Captain Ferguson's command, the sweep swingers used their oars just often enough to hold the scout boat a cautious hundred yards offshore until MacPherson's men appeared and stated that the armed Yamacraws clustering about the landing place intended no mischief.

Captain MacPherson finally came down to the river waving a green bough.

"All's well," Bull remarked. "We can go ashore, Yer Excellency."

By the time the *Hawk's* killick—a homemade anchor fashioned of stones imprisoned within a hardwood frame—had splashed overboard and the little craft had rounded to its cable, a throng of Indians of all ages had begun to collect about the canoe place.

It interested Oglethorpe that, despite reassuring signals from Mac-Pherson's men, both of the *Hawk's* swivel guns were manned, and boat-men holding smoldering slow matches were prepared to fire charges of grapeshot at an instant's notice.

"No use taking chances," commented Judge Whitaker, "for all old Tomo-chichi's supposed to be a good friend of ours."

The scout boat's crew picked up their firearms when some thirty hide-ously painted and fully armed warriors began to hover about the water's edge. Others could be seen skulking among misshapen and unpainted canoes.

On viewing, at close range, the first wild Indians he'd ever beheld, James Edward Oglethorpe, Esq., felt his throat muscles constrict and his pulse rate quicken. A new experience—something far removed from the formal parleys conducted between European troops or even with Turkish Janissaries. How should he bear himself? What should he do to avoid giving unintentional offense to these proud and gaudy savages?

Stealing a glance at Colonel Bull, he was relieved to watch him spit out his chew of tobacco before he raised an arm in the peace sign. Then Lieutenant Watts called out in Muskogean, "*Hesake toonsec este omvet ye pun!* May the Gods keep peace among us."

A garishly painted figure wearing a panther's mask and skin cloak stepped forward and, using both hands, raised an ancient musket above his headdress of gray heron plumes. "*Inukua atigin katkis.* Come in peace, white men."

"The bloody naturals seem well disposed," Bull remarked more to him-self than to anyone else, then added, "Thank God."

More painted and befeathered Yamacraws appeared from within the palisade. Some wore cloaks of soiled scarlet cloth or capes of glossy mink skins. For all he'd been feeling self-conscious about it, Oglethorpe now was glad he'd heeded a suggestion on the part of MacPherson and the officers of the Beaufort garrison that he don a semimilitary tunic of brilliant orange laced with silver braid. To further this colorful getup, he'd attached a panache of jade-green ostrich feathers to his tricorne hat.

While the scout boat's dinghy neared the shore Bull explained, "Your Excellency, that wrinkled old man in the long-tailed yellow coat is Tomo-chichi, their mico, or king. I needn't warn you to act haughty but friendly."

Oglethorpe agreed with a barely perceptible nod, then transferred his attention to two figures who stood out among the mass of copper-skinned Yamacraws as sharply as a pair of ravens on a snowy cornfield.

One of these was a towering blue-black African who, instead of adorning his head with fur or feathers, was wearing a close-wound turban of scarlet- and yellow-striped cloth. Beside this Negro stood a warrior who loomed as big, or bigger, than the black man. Despite the weird designs done in black and yellow paint, disguising his features, Oglethorpe at once guessed that this must be Sakwari-cra, otherwise Thad Burton, the white Indian he'd heard about.

The renegade was clad in buckskin leggings dyed dark red and a fancifully embroidered hunting shirt so brief that it barely covered the loincloth concealing his crotch.

As the small boat's bottom grated up a beach of coarse reddish sand Oglethorpe noted that this white mico had a short, straight nose and that his deep-set eyes were of a clear gray-blue. Long silver earrings set with blue stones dangled from small ears lying flat against his skull.

"Is John Musgrove here?" Colonel Bull queried of the warriors standing about. No one said anything until Thad Burton called out in curiously inflected English, "No. He gone to Cherokee."

"Then is Coosa-pona-keesa here?"

Captain MacPherson's wiry figure appeared, roughly forcing a path through the swarm of painted and feral-smelling Yamacraws.

"Yes, sir-r, and I've already sent for her. She's on her way from their truck house."

Without loss of time, the acting governor's party was conducted to the base of a huge water oak under which Tomo-chichi, bent and emaciated by age, was seated, cross-legged, upon his white buffalo robe.

The planter named Bryan came sidling up beside the acting governor and muttered from the side of his mouth, "Take care what you say, sir. Tomo-chichi's smart as an old wolverine and understands English a deal better than he lets on. The old man's not kept his hair all this time through being anybody's fool."

Taqua, peering out of a sassafras thicket along with Hapeyah and other unusually venturesome young squaws, watched the strange white leader in the orange coat advance toward the seated figure in unhurried dignity.

"*Tchimi!*" muttered Taqua. "This man bears himself like a mico thlucco!"

Hapeyah agreed. "Indeed, this tall stranger casts a long shadow."

Pride stirred in Laure Rivard when, after having again made the peace sign, Mico Tomo-chichi arose and, curtly waving aside his nephew, Toonahowie, beckoned Sakwari-cra, standing to one side with Quobah; they both looked mighty proud and fierce.

Due to Mary Musgrove's casual attempts to teach her English, Laure was able to grasp at least the drift of the talk commencing under graceful stalactites of gray-green moss.

She heard the *Englasi* in the orange-colored coat—evidently an important man if one judged by the deference accorded him by his fellow whites—address Sakwari-cra. "Sir, may I inquire your name?"

Thad's yellow-painted chin lifted as he replied so pretentiously that Tomo-chichi frowned, "Sakwari-cra, mico of the Sakwari people."

An invitation to friendship showed in Oglethorpe's lively dark eyes as, smiling, he said, "I mean, sir, what is your English name?"

The tall Tuscarora abandoned some of his arrogance and haltingly replied, "When boy me called Thad Burton."

"Burton, eh? Well, sir, that's a true English name."

"Can be, O Mico Thlucco, but me not *Englasi*. Me Sakwari."

Suddenly Taqua realized that by now Thad had become one of the central figures in this parley; even a knot of hairy sailors gathered beside the tender with musketoons and blunderbusses held ready, but with deceptive negligence, were looking at him.

"Where the devil's Mary?" Bull demanded of MacPherson in an angry undertone.

"Don't know. Said she'd come directly, but you know how women are. Probably she's stopped to pretty herself."

Meanwhile Oglethorpe was saying, "Please be good enough, Mr. Burton, to inform this venerable chieftain that His Majesty, King George II, extends greetings and salutations to his cousin, the great Tomo-chichi, and that later I will present him with gifts from His Majesty."

Colonel Bull considered the accompanying trustee with increasing respect while Thad translated after a fashion. Although the white Tuscarora evidently could understand English reasonably well, he certainly couldn't begin to speak it with any fluency or accuracy.

"Pray inform His Highness," Oglethorpe told the now patently embarrassed young man, "that, as His Majesty's deputy, I wish to consult with him concerning the purchase and cession of some land."

Even under his face paint Thad's flush showed. "Cession? Me not know meaning."

With a touch of impatience, Judge Whitaker snapped, "Young man, what His Excellency means is that he wants to buy some land around here to settle his people on."

Relying partly on sign language, Thad attempted to translate, but he didn't get very far. Under the weight of this responsibility tiny pearls of sweat were beginning to break through his face paint. All the same, he struggled on until there was a stir in the crowd and onlookers stepped aside to clear the way for Mary Musgrove. She drew near, walking straight-backed and serene of countenance.

Colonel Bull, Captain MacPherson, and Lieutenant Watts greeted her with varying degrees of respect.

"Your servant, ma'am." The accompanying trustee whipped off his emerald plumed hat and offered the trader's wife a formal court bow while making a quick estimate of this remarkable female, for, to his surprise, John Musgrove's wife had taken time to dress herself in a not badly cut European gown. Moreover, her glossy blue-black hair was dressed up, English fashion, under a neat straw bonnet.

The curtsy she returned was both fluid and correct. Then, in her rich, slightly husky voice, she said, "I am your humble, obedient servant, sir."

Thad Burton's jaw almost dropped when, with perfect aplomb, this *Englasi* mico thlucco "made a leg" in acknowledgment. Lieutenant Watts couldn't help smiling over the way His Excellency's sword canted stiffly up behind. It reminded him, ridiculously enough, of a dog's tail.

After acknowledging Tomo-chichi's presence with a short but respectful head bow, Mary Musgrove queried briskly, "How, sir, may I be of assistance?"

Oglethorpe explained to such good purpose that presently Tomo-chichi, wrinkled features still devoid of expression, arose from the ceremonial robe and, with monumental dignity, led his visitors and chief followers toward the palisade and into the bark-roofed council house.

When, about an hour later, Oglethorpe, Colonel Bull, Judge Whitaker, and rubicund Mr. Bryan emerged, Captain MacPherson, Lieutenant Watts, and the Rangers who had remained, ready and observant, outside guessed from the relaxed bearing of the English leaders that Mary Musgrove must have secured something like tolerance of the projected settlement.

They were correct; certain important undertakings had been agreed upon. Pending confirmation by the Great Council of the Creek Nation, Tomo-chichi was willing to sell around five thousand acres on the Savannah's southern bank, centered on Amercario. For this the company was prepared to pay a fair price and solemnly swear to respect the Yamacraws' hunting rights over this territory.

Once the white men had filed out of the palisade amid a wild yapping of dogs and the blank, wide-eyed stares of the inhabitants Mary Musgrove asked of Bull, "I presume His Excellency wishes to inspect the suggested townsite without loss of time?"

Escorted by the Long Man, Toonahowie, a handsome light-skinned Yamacraw with restless, sly-seeming eyes, Thad Burton and what seemed like an unnecessarily large band of well-armed warriors, Oglethorpe, and his companions set out for the bluff.

In quitting Yamacraw Town, Oglethorpe, like the trained field officer he was, noticed what was surely a red-haired white girl squatting on the threshold of a large hut pounding corn in an oak-stump mill.

The acting governor briefly wondered who might be this handsome, strongly built girl whose skin was the color of clover honey. When told she was Thad's concubine it interested him that Laure Rivard, even though she had lived so long among savages, would go about naked to the waist in the presence of white men, and without a trace of embarrassment. When his shadow crossed the ground before her Taqua glanced up and peered blankly at him.

Touching his hat, he said casually, "A very good day to you, ma'am," just as if she were some society matron he'd chanced to encounter on Pall Mall.

Oglethorpe inquired of Mary, easily matching his long stride, "Who is that white girl?"

"Her Indian name, sir, is Taqua, meaning Fire Flower—due of course to her red hair."

"She has a white name?"

Mary's delicately aquiline profile inclined as the party commenced to ascend the bluff's northern slope. "Yes, Your Excellency. She told me that, long ago, she once was called Laure Rivard but she has no recollection of who her people were, or where they were from. John and I judge that, most likely, she is French and was, first of all, captured by Chickasaws who long have been the deadliest enemies of the *Francani*."

When the grade increased, the party gradually became strung out and conversations shortened. Judge Whitaker and Mr. Bryan began to pant, but the other colonials' breathing remained as level as Oglethorpe's own.

"Taqua is Thad Burton's woman."

"You mean his wife?"

"Not at all, sir. As I've said, she's only a concubine."

"How did that come about?"

"He captured her last autumn during an Iroquois raid upon the Catawbas."

Mary spoke so casually that Oglethorpe batted his eyes in surprise. "Dear me! Surely, Mistress Musgrove, Burton doesn't intend to go on living in shame with this poor creature? After all, they're both white."

Mary's expressive smoky blue eyes wavered up to a black squirrel scolding explosively from the top of a white oak. "Sir, I know it will be difficult for you to understand, but neither of them consider themselves white."

"Have you and your husband reminded them that, nonetheless, they are not true Indians and never can become so?"

"We have, Your Excellency, but it's no use. They have lived among Indians so long the red man's customs and way of thinking are first nature to them. Believe me, they're quite content to remain as they are."

The accompanying trustee frowned. "Hum, all the same, 'tis a bad example for my settlers. Perhaps contact with their own sort may change their attitude."

"Let us hope so, sir," answered the stately half-breed. "But I doubt it."

Moving in a long single file, the oddly assorted party continued to breast a pine-covered slope after Sakwari-cra, who climbed easily, magnificently muscled shoulders glinting bronze-brown in the sunlight. In the distance a pileated woodpecker commenced to hammer loudly upon a hollow log; high overhead a red-shouldered hawk looked down and whistled a piercing protest.

Once the reconnaissance party had halted atop the bluff under a stand of four lofty longleaf pines growing in almost the exact center of the plateau, Colonel Bull studied Oglethorpe and was relieved to see the pleased expression worn by the accompanying trustee. He mopped his broad, dark brown forehead. "Please to note, sir, those springs I've mentioned. They rise wherever you see underbrush and alders flourishing most."

Mr. Bryan then drew Oglethorpe's attention to encircling woods composed of stately pines that, in ordered rows shot skyward, reminiscent of columns in a Gothic cathedral. Such splendid straight trees, Mr. Bryan commented, were admirably suited for easy conversion into planks and timbers.

Attempting to foresee possible drawbacks and disadvantages to this place, James Oglethorpe ranged tirelessly through underbrush covering the plateau.

One of the Rangers kicked at the ground. "D'ye note, sir, how rich and deep the earth is up here? Once these trees are cut I warrant even a middling-poor farmer could grow tall grain."

Standing on the plateau's rim and looking down on the Savannah,

Sakwari-cra experienced an unfamiliar sense of foreboding. It wasn't as though he was alarmed; he wasn't. He reckoned, if he wanted to, he could take the scalp of about any man present. What, then, was wrong? Were the unfamiliar movements, the loud, deep voices, and confident bearing of the strangers to blame? Or was it that he'd never before seen so many white men together and didn't know what to make of them? For one thing he didn't like the way the Carolinians and this tall *Englasi* Mico Thlucco kept looking at him as if he were some sort of an oddity like a white deer, blackbird, or raccoon.

Thad paid small attention to the sibilant *whoosh!* emitted by a young buck which leaped out of a thicket near the edge of the pine woods and bounded gracefully away with flaring white flag asway. There were plenty of other deer around; everywhere their dainty droppings lay, still fresh and shiny, among winter-killed weeds and grasses. Many huge, bronze-black wild turkeys flushed, as did such members of bobwhite quail it seemed as if a covey always was exploding out of the underbrush. Great flocks of doves fled with erratic, arrow-like speed.

Finally, James Oglethorpe, accompanied only by Mary Musgrove, sought the bluff's edge and remained there in prolonged silence, awed both by the incredible immensity of this land and the realization that, for better or for worse, he was going to plant the colony on this spot, that he now was standing on the northern frontier of a new domain, a social experiment as idealistically conceived as Plato's republic.

Across the river, flowing deep and wide at his feet, lay South Carolina, settled now for over a hundred years and growing richer and more powerful every day. Could he and his defenseless and inexperienced ex-paupers hope to rival such a success? Only God in His infinite wisdom knew the answer.

Already, the grave-faced acting governor had come to appreciate the natural strength of this place; a palisade and a few batteries judiciously emplaced along the bluff's edge, in addition to a fort on Tybee Island, as suggested by Colonel Bull, should protect the new community from any but an overwhelming attack by sea. But a successful defense against an assault made from the land very likely would prove another matter.

"This seems a fine, easily defensible townsite, eh, Mrs. Musgrove? And a surpassingly beautiful one, too."

A slow smile curved the half-breed's dark red lips. "My uncle, the Creek emperor, wished to establish his capital here, but could not because it lay too far away from the heart of his domains."

Colonel Bull came tramping up, employed the cuff of his dingy green tunic to wipe sweat from his nicked nose and broad, weather-beaten features. "Well, Your Excellency, are you minded to look elsewhere?"

"No, Colonel. I have pretty well decided that this is where I will settle my people. This terrain can accommodate a town similar to the Margravate of Azilia." He offered his hand. "Sir, my fellow trustees and I can never sufficiently thank you, Judge Whitaker and the Rangers for your advice and guidance."

Chapter 12

"SEATING THE RIVER" I

Drawing on a short black pipe held with bowl inverted against rain piddling from the branches of towering loblolly pines, John Musgrove wiped moisture from his powder-marked forehead and turned to Captain MacPherson. "I'm thinkin' this weather is no good omen for those rascals who are coming here." Thus far, this memorable day was proving uncommonly cold and wet. Rain squalls, driven by a southerly gale, whitecapped the river and soughed fretfully through the pines. Especially heavy showers were so dense that they suggested smoke while lashing the Savannah's lead-tinted water and at times the South Carolina shore was lost to sight. Drifting, weed-draped trees, snags, and other debris dislodged by the storm continued to drift past the bluff.

MacPherson observed while averting craggy brown features from the rain, "Wi' such a wind behind 'em, yon vessels from Beaufort should heave into sight pretty soon, provided they got started on time."

"If they're not away, prompt-like," observed the Indian trader, "I'm mistook in James Oglethorpe; for he's a real thruster."

The Ranger captain pulled the oiled leather cape of his hunting shirt like a hood over his black, brimless cap. "Say, John, a while back I noticed a white mon in a canoe swimming his horse across the river toward Yamacraw Town. D'ye ken who 'twould be?"

"He's one of yours," Musgrove grunted, restless eyes reverting to a heavily wooded point lying maybe a half mile downstream. "He'd a big dog in his canoe," he added.

"That'll be Wally Challenger."

Musgrove asked, "Tell me, Jamie, is't true you're to make a long scout to the west'ard?"

"Guess so. His Excellency wants me to look around for likely outpost sites." He glanced sidewise, raised a bushy black brow. "Know something?"

The trader grinned, drawled, "Not much. Why?"

"Unless I'm sore mistaken, this fellow Oglethorpe, for a' he's English-bred and wears a civilian title, seems experienced i' military matters."

"What makes you say that, Jamie?"

Like the Indian trader's, MacPherson's hard gray eyes ceaselessly probed the dripping woods, scanned the river in both directions. "First thing Oglethorpe asked about after he'd decided to build here was what's the country like to the west and south of us. Is't high or low, wooded or swampy? How many roads—as if there were any—traces or trails lead into French and Spanish territory and can cavalry or wagons use 'em?"

Brief hissing noises resulted when Musgrove used his mangled hand to empty pipe ashes into a puddle between his moccasins. "So already, he's figurin' on maybe blockin' 'em off?"

"Aye, John, but he can't come even close to doing that, not for a long, long time." The Ranger captain fished out a hunk of chewing tobacco, held it poised before his mouth. "I've already told him so. He'll first have to recruit a big lot of good woods fighters, which, right now, is nigh impossible. Told him, too, he'd better not try calling in any damned, heavy-footed British regulars to do the job."

"What did he say to that?"

"Oh, he laughed, easy-like, and said the Crown wouldn't spare him even a corporal's guard from the Home Establishment."

To a soft rustle in the underbrush MacPherson spun about, hand on war hatchet. As quickly, Musgrove readied a pocket pistol. They relaxed when Captain Wallace Challenger, his soaked buckskins clinging to him like a second skin, emerged from an ilex thicket.

The yellow-haired Ranger strode forward, bearded features red and heated through his having climbed the bluff in a hurry. Beside him, equally drenched, trotted a big, rough-coated, fawn and black mongrel.

Challenger called, "Heyo, boys," but offered no further greeting.

MacPherson bent to pat the lop-eared part mastiff called Claymore. "Greetings, Wally. Spy anything worthy o' note on yer way south?"

Using his fingers, Captain Challenger pinched and tidily blew his nose. "Only a band o' wandering Yuchis."

"How many?" demanded Musgrove.

"Twenty—thirty—counting squaws and papooses."

The truck-house keeper's eyes narrowed. "Then they'd families along?"

"Yep. It was no war party." Windmilling his tail, Claymore meantime bounded over to the Rangers' campfire. Long since, he'd scented several old friends who made much of him in their heavy-handed fashion.

"Those Yuchis were just a huntin' and fishin' party headed for salt water." He pulled off and wrung water from his shoulder cape, then added, "All the same, Jim, I told Ben Gordon and Ned Carmody to keep an eye on 'em; if they start movin' in the wrong direction we'll hear of it in plenty of time."

All three men fell silent to watch a long, low-sided log canoe appear around a wooded point downstream. Its occupants were paddling hard.

"Don't like it when Injuns hurry like that," Challenger drawled. "Wonder what's bitin' 'em?"

At the same time the clouds began to thin, creating patches of light. "Who's in yonder canoe?" MacPherson wanted to know.

John Musgrove spat tobacco juice, wiped bearded lips on the back of his three-fingered hand. "They'll be Toonahowie, Sakwari-cra and Quobah. They went downriver at first light."

"Toonahowie I recognize," Challenger presently remarked, brilliantly blue eyes narrowing. "But say, am I seein' things or ain't the other two paddlers a black and a white man?"

"Yer eyesight's as good as ever," Musgrove said. "Quobah's the biggest, meanest-looking black I ever laid eyes on. He's Sakwari-cra's sub-mico. The white man is Sakwari-cra whose English name is Thad Burton. He bosses a little band of stray Injuns. Like a chew?" He offered a plug of oily-black tobacco scalloped by tooth marks. "I'll be curious to learn what you make of that there renegade."

"Now hold on," Captain MacPherson interjected. "Burton's not exactly a renegade—at least not in my book."

"Why not? Ain't he all white?" Challenger demanded. "White fellow who lives, willin', among the savages ain't anything but a renegade, is he?"

"As a rule ye'd be right," Musgrove said. "But such are rascals who've been raised white and don't like it or else they've done somethin' to make 'em run off. Now, as Mary and me knows for sure, Burton was captured and carried off by Tuscaroras when he was only a little kid. Knowin' no better, he grew up like an Iroquois and was adopted by 'em."

The yellow-haired Ranger nodded, swiftly shed his equipment, and yanked off his sodden shirt to expose muscle ridges rippling about a deeply sunburned torso.

"Hum. Then he must ha' got captured when the Tuscaroras made their great raid along the Trent and the Pamlico rivers and tortured Surveyor General Lawson to death. When was that?"

"Seventeen eleven," Captain MacPherson said. "Remember 'cause I went along with the pursuit till we got ambushed and chased back."

Bearded jaws working, Musgrove mumbled, "Anyway, that Burton feller's Injun name is Sakwari-cra, meaning 'He-Who-Trails-a-Spear.'"

"Whatever he calls himself, he is sure big as a horse," observed the yellow-haired officer, absently rubbing bristles growing in the place where his beard had been.

"Yep. Reckon he could take on and lick about any of Tomo-chichi's braves."

A big man himself, Challenger laughed harshly. "Hum, so this buck fancies himself as a top dog. Well, well."

Jamie MacPherson, dour, dark-complexioned, and Scottish-born, guessed accurately enough at his fellow officer's reactions. After all, Wallace Challenger was of Scottish extraction too, even though he'd been born and reared in Carolina and was reputed to be one of the toughest rough-and-tumble fighters south of Virginia.

"He's a real warrior—smart, too, for his years, but not so smart as he thinks," commented Mary Musgrove's husband. "He's already taken a dozen scalps—and can show 'em."

Challenger's voice sounded muffled because he'd begun to tug his long-skirted hunting shirt back on. "Huh. That's two less than I tally."

As if in a final bit of spite, an icy shower suddenly lashed the scene and set everyone to cursing.

Once the squall had raced on upriver, the wind dropped and the sun commenced timidly to shine just as Sakwari-cra and Toonahowie, wearing limp white buzzard and green crane plumes in their scalp locks, drifted out of the woods.

Toonahowie, impassive as ever, held up a hand and one finger to indicate that he and his companion had sighted six boats sailing upstream.

Musgrove nodded to himself. "They'll be Mr. Woodward's sloop and some plantation boats."

Unexpectedly, Thad Burton asked in deep-toned English, "Plantation boat—same as big pirogue?"

Challenger stiffened a trifle while gazing with curiosity at this painted white man's roached Iroquois crest. Said he, talking rapidly on purpose, "That's right. Such gen'rally run about thirty to forty tons burthen, step two masts, have a small cabin aft and a smaller fos'c'le—if you know what that is." The blond Ranger's hard blue eyes bored steadily, truculently into Thad Burton's unwavering steel-gray ones.

Even better than MacPherson, John Musgrove sensed the significance of this moment; a wrong expression or gesture on the part of either man could lead to trouble of a sort the new settlers could not afford. Fortunately, a Ranger who'd wandered over to the rim of the bluff let out an Indian-like yelp and called out, "Yonder they come!"

Off the wooded point shone a faint glimmer of canvas.

James MacPherson glanced at Challenger. "That's sure enough Mr. Woodward's sloop in the lead—roomy old scow!"

"That's just as well," the Indian trader grunted, and sent a parabola of dark brown juice spattering the underbrush all the way down to the river's edge. "Look! They've packed people into her like cattle."

This was true, Challenger agreed; the blunt-bowed craft's deck was dark with huddled humanity. One and all, they must be drenched to the skin. A dominating figure standing on the boat's tiny poop was easily recognizable as James Oglethorpe, Esq.

By the time the last plantation boat had heaved into sight and had jibed to commence the last of many tacks, the weather really cleared. Buzzards, fish hawks, and bald eagles appeared and, in leisurely fashion, began to plane about the pale wintry sky. In the woods finches, thrushes, towhees, and assorted warblers uttered tentative notes. Bobwhites, scattered by visitors, commenced to whistle their rallying call.

Inhabitants of Yamacraw Town began to turn out when they spied the vessels approaching the bluff's base and steering for that sandy beach north of the height where Toonahowie and Sakwari-cra had beached their canoe.

As became men of dignity, Tomo-chichi and his chief warriors did not turn out with the rest.

By the dozen brawny warriors, youths, and half-dressed squaws were joined by almost the entire population of the Sakwari camp in splashing along the shore to gape in wonderment upon this, the largest concentration of white men's vessels any of them had ever beheld.

On the bow of a clumsy pirogue lent to the expedition by a planter named St. Julian, "Colonel" Petre Ballou assumed an arrogant attitude. A brace of well-polished Swiss-made pistols suspended by rings let into their butts dangled from a baldric of russet leather and over his left hip hung a battered and businesslike campaign sword. Near him stood Lieutenants Archibald Glen and John Savey, newly commissioned by the acting governor. Neither of them could have been half as old as the Swiss soldier of fortune.

"Colonel"—as he insisted on being addressed—Petre Ballou was feeling chagrined and mightily put upon. *Nom de Dieu!* Had he not sworn on his sacred word of honor that he'd once held a colonel's commission in the service of His Majesty Stanislaus I of Poland? Had he not commanded a brigade of engineers at the disaster at Poltava? Why had the acting governor not at once granted him command over the handful of able-bodied ex-paupers who'd volunteered to serve as militiamen?

Probably, Monsieur Oglethorpe, like so many of his military countrymen, was unduly suspicious of foreign mercenaries. Being Swiss and therefore practical, "Colonel" Ballou foresaw that, soon enough, his services would be greatly in demand. In time *le bon gouverneur* certainly must come to credit the fact that a bomb had burst in his tent during the siege of Fredrikssten, and *had* destroyed a chest containing his commissions and decorations.

With an expert's eye the Swiss considered the bluff, then nodded to himself. No troops in the world could hope to scale such a steep slope under fire. Thus seen, looming boldly against the cold blue sky, the bluff put Ballou in mind of Gibraltar. Yes, here was a Gibraltar in miniature.

A few cannon judiciously emplaced up there easily could control use of this river, the island opposite, and even a length of the Carolina shore. How soon would His Excellency come to his senses and invite an expert's opinion on the construction of defenses? Ballou felt confident he'd soon be called upon.

Archibald Glen tugged at a short, sand-colored mustache while he studied the landing place toward which the sloop was nosing. "And so we arrive at journey's end."

"Evidently," grunted Petre Ballou. "But I do not like the presence of all those natives when we are all but defenseless."

Ventured handsome Lieutenant John Savey, "Defensively, the situation seems fine; I daresay neither the Spaniards nor anyone else can attack up such an incline."

"Colonel" Ballou stared down a long and rubicund nose, sneered, "My dear young man, 'tis obvious that, in you, we have a military genius."

Excitement spread among the rain-soaked ex-paupers crouched upon freight and baggage stowed, helter-skelter, in the pirogue's waist.

A frowzy little woman broke into noisy sobs. "I—it just can't be true. After all these weeks and months, we've actually arrived!"

A grim-faced carpenter muttered, "If *this* is the Promised Land, why 'tain't nothing like me and Lucy has pictured it. It's just a ugly wilderness."

In Mr. Hume's plantation boat, next astern, the Hendy O'Briens, Winsome Brooks, and Helen Bayless, although jammed closely together, and shivering in rain-drenched clothing, remained outwardly cheerful. Hendy thought, So this great, empty country, so strange-looking, is to be where Bettie and me are to live out our lives?

Mused Winsome, How different this is from New England, saving only its vastness! Oh dear, what fate awaits me here?

"Did ever you see such a great beautiful river and so many lovely birds all about?" the Bayless girl demanded as if to encourage herself. Meanwhile, she pressed down hard on the lid of a little wicker basket from which her black and white kitten seemed determined to escape. "Did you ever see such fine, tall trees and shrubs?"

O'Brien nodded absently. His little pale blue eyes were occupied with a wide, flat island lying opposite the landing place. B'God! Between clumps of trees showed wide strips of what appeared to be rich meadowland. His heart gave a happy little flip as, in his mind's eye, he pictured herds of fine, strong-boned horses grazing yonder. Aloud he queried,

"Wonder how soon, Bettie, they'll be sending us some horses from Beaufort and Charles Town?"

"Soon enough," answered his wife, smiling. "Surely, they'll need such for hauling."

Hendy's joyous expression faded. "Hauling? Cock's bones! That's oxen's work, me darlin'. 'Tis fine saddle horses that'll be needed here."

He was still privately outraged that among the livestock loaded into Judge Whitaker's big, unpainted plantation boat there hadn't been included even a single horse! No, he didn't enjoy not seeing any horses around.

Bettie O'Brien, looking deceptively healthy because of her new sunburn, smiled. "It's great luck, isn't it, dear, that Winsome and Helen have been assigned to the same ward as us."

"Thank you, Bettie. We can help each other a lot, I reckon." Wishing that her hair wouldn't stick so limp and lank about her face, Winsome turned to brawny John Stonehewer. "Have you heard how many wards there are to be?"

Stonehewer, who'd been studying the riverbank with the intensity of a shipwrecked sailor glimpsing land in the offing, turned his big, dark head and said in a grating voice, "Four, mistress. If I ain't mistook they'll be called Heathcote, Percival, Derby, and Decker after certain of our kindhearted trustees." He jerked his head toward his dark-complexioned wife and equally swarthy twin sons. "We've been assigned to Ward Derby."

"Me, I'm for Ward Decker," announced a spindly little man. "Ain't it a wonder how many small things His Excellency's foreseen?"

James Edward Oglethorpe, Esq., felt his heart lift as he shifted weight to set foot again on soil uncontaminated by the sins and oppressions of the ages. If only some of those men who had labored so hard to win the support of the Chancellor of the Exchequer and the Master of the Rolls could be present! They would include Colonel Onslow, Lord Percival, Sir James Vernon, and many more.

Over the gabbling of sailors and the higher-pitched chattering of the Indians he recalled, all in a fleeting instant, what the Reverend Samuel Wesley, Jr.—who'd promised soon to come out to the new colony—had written:

> Yet Britain cease thy captives' woes to mourn
> To break their chains, see, Oglethorpe was born!

And now, incredibly, the Great Experiment was about to get under way, but the big question remained: Could or would these former prisoners recover their lost self-respect through hard work?

The accompanying trustee waved to a strangely assorted group gathered to receive him. Yonder, cap in hand, stood dark-featured Colonel Bull and leather-faced Captain MacPherson together with a huge, yellow-headed young fellow he vaguely recalled having seen in Charles Town.

Yonder also waited Toonahowie, Tomo-chichi's nephew, seemingly at ease for all that the rain had caused his face paint to run and his turkey feather headdress to droop. Equally big and equally expressionless stood that curious white Indian known as Thad Burton or Sakwari-cra.

A ragged but spontaneous cheer arose from the plantation boats while Oglethorpe strode up the trampled sand and shook hands with William Bull.

For some inexplicable reason Wallace Challenger felt prompted to cup hands and yell up to a ragged rank of Rangers grinning and darkly outlined on the bluff. "Hey, you timber beasts! Three cheers for His Excellency!"

Hastily Oglethorpe called out, "Many thanks, sir; instead let us all raise a cheer for His Gracious Majesty King George."

Many more than three cheers arose both from the plantation boats and along the shore. Although they'd not the least notion of why they were doing so, the Yamacraws suddenly joined in, raised shrill, ear-piercing whoops, screeches, and yips.

Soon the beach became a scene of confusion, what with the ex-paupers. either teetering down a narrow plank or, impatient of delay, jumping out of the boats and, for all the water's merciless chill, wading ashore in trembling eagerness.

Oglethorpe queried of Judge Whitaker, "Sir, how soon d'you think the slaves can rig a tackle to raise the freight up to the heights?"

"'Twon't be long, sir," promised the red-faced South Carolinian. "I've already sent a party up there with blocks and tackles; with luck, some tents and a part of the dunnage ought to be up there before dark."

Chapter 13

"SEATING THE RIVER" II

Such was James Oglethorpe's genius for organization that, before darkness fell on the first of February 1733, several large marquees, one for each ward, and nearly twenty tents had been pitched in an orderly arrangement around a clump of four gigantic pines which, in aloof grandeur, towered near the plateau's center. In fact, shelter of a sort had been provided for everyone who'd come ashore.

Nor were the newcomers quite defenseless. The acting governor had insisted that the handful of South Carolina Rangers be reinforced by men drafted into his still completely unorganized militia. Not that they proved to be of much use, as Captains MacPherson and Challenger soon discovered to their no great surprise. But at least the presence of armed men reassured people, who were ready to panic at the least noise from the dark, who pictured bloodthirsty savages lurking in every patch of underbrush.

They gathered, fearfully, about cook fires throbbing yellow-red before four marquees in which women were preparing rations raised from the riverbank. Around the tents lingered curious groups of Yamacraws.

"Lord's sake, they look just like witches," whimpered a leggy, half-grown girl. "I'm turrible feared, Ma. Do they aim to scalp us?"

"Hush your nonsense!" her mother ordered. "Ain't nowt going to harm us so long as His Excellency's here."

Just before a drum was beaten to announce the hour for retiring, Oglethorpe invited the Reverend Henry Herbert to offer a prayer of thanksgiving that the Lord so surely and safely had guided these new Children of Israel to their Promised Land.

A scowl on his scarred features, Quobah watched a gang of burly Negro laborers lent by various Carolina planters swing double-bitted axes to cut firewood. The sight started his slow mind to moving along unpleasant lines, for all these slaves seemed well-fed and content. The old resentment flared as he made his way back to the cabin he shared with Hapeyah.

Around him loomed the dim outlines of huts belonging to the Sakwari band, which lately had grown to around thirty souls. The new tribe included not only full-blooded Indians and Negroes, but also half-breeds of varied origins. Now that the word was spreading, numbers of wandering Indians and escaped slaves in need of food and shelter begged to join the white Tuscarora and the Ashanti. Not all applicants were accepted; only the strongest and cleverest were permitted to participate in weird initiation rites adapted by Thad Burton from Creek, Iroquois, and Cherokee sources.

The young mico's most pressing problem nowadays was to find women suitable to mate with his braves; Negresses were hard to come by, except in Spanish territory or near Carolinian plantations. So he sought, whenever possible, to buy strong and healthy young women from their Creek owners or from traders dealing in Indian slaves.

By noon of the day following, the bulk of the company's supplies, as well as all of the ex-paupers' meager possessions, had been raised to the plateau by the use of a crane so cleverly designed by crabbed old "Colonel" Petre Ballou that his claim of being an accomplished military engineer seemed to have been substantiated.

With the coming of daylight slave gang axes flashed and thudded all over the plateau, felling long, straight pines. Carpenters among the new colonists vied in expressing their delight on discovering such fine, straight-grained timber right at hand. Best of all, there appeared to be no end to this stately forest hemming in the site of Savannah on three sides.

Among the first structures to be erected was a stout paddock designed to receive livestock which, still out on the river, mooed, grunted, and blatted in manure-splashed plantation boats.

Dozens of medium-sized pine trees destined to form a palisade were cut, trimmed to a sharp point at one end, then piled along the bluff's rim awaiting erection. Since midmorning, Oglethorpe, Colonel Bull, and the grizzled Swiss soldier of fortune had supervised the planting of pegs to indicate where the palisades were to rise.

Colonel Bull, experienced in such crude frontier fortifications, was surprised to find himself generally in agreement with the European-trained Swiss about the position of various salients and gun emplacements. However, it was Oglethorpe who decided that the palisade should be erected a bit farther back from the bluff's edge. Explained he, "We've no way of estimating how rapidly the bluff may erode."

"*Mais oui, Monsieur le Gouverneur,*" rumbled Ballou. "And again, it may prove advisable to dig a *fosse*—what you call it?—a ditch before the walls."

"That may well be," Bull grunted, so Lieutenants Glen and Savey began to move the peg markers inland a good ten feet. The accompanying trustee and his advisers deliberated longest over selecting the best location for a guardhouse and the watchtower which was to rise above it.

There was noisy activity everywhere on the plateau. More marquees and tents were being pitched and such was the efficiency of Oglethorpe's planning that, already, foundation markers for several family dwellings were being driven at designated points.

Meanwhile, under Captain MacPherson, a party of Rangers were ranging the surrounding forest to establish outposts at likely points. Most of these sentry posts were spotted along trails showing considerable use, such as the one leading down to Yamacraw Town.

Throughout that all-too-short winter's day, groups of well-armed Yamacraws were noticed hovering along the edge of the woods; their expressionless jet eyes watched all that went on. Never once did an Indian offer advice—let alone raise a helping hand. Timorous settlers took alarm over this unbroken surveillance; their work suffered by consequence.

Chapter 14

"THE RED HOOPS ARE OUT"

It was only three days after the landing that yellow-haired Captain Challenger and a pair of Rangers rode up to the accompanying trustee in company with a bearded and wildly disheveled white man who, wearing a bloody rag knotted about his head, appeared to be on the brink of complete exhaustion.

"Who is this?" Oglethorpe demanded of John Musgrove in a sharp undertone.

"Why, damme if it ain't Dick Blakeslee, who runs a tradin' post down at Cofitachique in the Yuchi country. Mostly, Dick traffics with 'em and the Lower Creek villages 'twixt here and St. Augustine."

Musgrove swung over to the trader, who, with eyes glazed and half shut, remained slumped on a sweat-whitened horse. "What's up, Dick? Bang your noggin 'gainst a limb?"

The rider batted his eyes, managed a weary grin. "Hell, no. Some cuss'd Creek took a pot shot at me outside o' Apatai."

Wallace Challenger dismounted, walked up to James Oglethorpe, who, sweating and in shirt sleeves, had been working with Petre Ballou on the construction of a gun embrasure. Deliberately, the acting governor put down his hatchet.

The Ranger pulled off his black skullcap, then scraped a coating of muddy sweat from his forehead and failed to salute. Under Oglethorpe's suddenly bleak regard, Challenger stiffened to attention and saluted in casual fashion. "Sir, Your Excellency, that is, I think maybe you'd best listen to Blakeslee, here, for all he's not bringin' news you'll be glad to hear."

The stocky Indian trader then slipped off his mount and swayed so badly he would have fallen had not Musgrove and Challenger reached out to steady him.

"That tall gent yonder's mico thlucco of these new settlers so be respec'ful," Musgrove advised.

Blakeslee managed an uncertain smile and offered a hand spotted with dried blood. "Howdy. Thought mebbe you oughter know about what's been goin' on south o' here."

Oglethorpe promptly shook the trader's hand. "I take it very kind of you to come here, sir." He then turned and called his servant. "Papot! Fetch this gentleman a tot of brandy from my medicine chest."

He with the grimy and blood-streaked face gaped because never before had an English bigwig, especially one fresh from Home, ever talked even half so kind and neighborly. "Shucks, Guvnor, I ain't really that bad off." Then, hastily, he added, "But I'll have that swig all the same."

John Musgrove slipped a supporting arm about Blakeslee's waist. "Come on, friend, spit it out; His Excellency's waitin'."

"Well, sir, I wuz in Tauco which is a Highagee village on the north bank o' the St. John, when a Spanisher comes gallopin' in madder'n a singed bobcat. Cussin' mighty fierce, he told the Highagees that us English is raisin' a permanent town south o' the Savannah and the Spanish governor in St. Augustine is boilin' mad about it, says he."

Blakeslee steadied himself against Musgrove's knotty shoulder and peered about the busy plateau. "By the looks o' things I see that Spanisher weren't lyin'. This Spanisher—reckon he was a army officer of some sort—raised a almighty ruckus among the Highagees, swearin' this here land belongs to Spain and always has. Is that true, sir?"

Oglethorpe sighed. "It is, and it isn't. Depends on whose claim you recognize."

"Well, anyhow, this officer wanted the savages to arrest me so's he could carry me down to St. Augustine for questionin'. Ah!" Eagerly Blakeslee grabbed at a little pewter cup of brandy and drained it at a gulp, then grinned. "Old Bear Paw likely might ha' turned me over if I hadn't allus traded with his people fair 'n' square."

"What did the Highagees do?"

"Well, sir, Bear Paw pretended to keep me prisoner in my truck house till dark; then set me on my best horse and told me to clear out because him and his people weren't no ways pleased about Englishmen settlin' south o' the Savannah."

Grunted Musgrove, "You were lucky, you old whoreson."

"Goddam lucky," Challenger agreed.

"That I wuz. They got pretty hot 'cause, along with the Yuchis and Yamasees, the Highagees think they have a firm bargain with the Carolina Assembly that there'll never be no British forts or settlements built south o' yonder stream."

Gravely, Oglethorpe inquired of Challenger, "Would this explain Tomo-chichi's uneasiness when I first appeared?"

Under a battered broad-brimmed hat Musgrove's head inclined. "Yep. Old rascal's mighty worried, too, over what micos farther south may do when they learn he's granted you even a short lease. An they get properly wrathful, sir, 'twill take a small army to keep 'em from wipin' out this settlement before it's well started."

Oglethorpe thought hard, bitterly resented the fact that no one, either in London or Charles Town, had emphasized the gravity of this nebulous, but apparently binding, agreement. To break faith with the Indians at the very start of this undertaking seemed a poor beginning, especially because he'd declared, on many occasions, that he never would trick or cheat the original landowners.

Briskly, he returned his attention to Blakeslee. "What chanced after you were released by the Highagees?"

That the accompanying trustee possessed an uncanny memory for Indian names, no matter how difficult, wasn't lost upon either Challenger or Musgrove. So many Englishmen couldn't or wouldn't even try to remember such, even after spending years in North America.

"Well, sir, I rode hell-fer-leather along little-used back trails but, for all that, word got up the coast ahead o' me. At Cholee the micos already was in council so I figgered I'd best not tarry there and try to learn what they was fixin' to do. Then just outside Sukehio I come on a runner carryin' a red hoop—"

"Damn!" growled Musgrove. "So the red hoops are out?"

Oglethorpe looked mystified, so the blond Ranger spat tobacco juice and explained. "A red hoop, sir, is a scalp stretched over a hoop of red-painted wood; acts as a summons to a council of war. Go on, Blakeslee."

"Wal, I'd swum the Altamaha after my nag foundered and wuz travelin' shank's mare, when outside of Echy I chanced on Billy Ferguson—you mind Scotch Billy?"

"Sure," Musgrove said. "Go on."

"Wal, when he heard that red hoops were travelin' he lent me yonder crow bait." He pointed to the rough-coated horse he'd been riding. "Billy allowed that war talk hadn't yet reached his tradin' place so ye can figure I was plenty took aback to hear tom-toms thumpin' and the *caw-waw-noo-dee* raised in Estoto, which is a sight nearer to Amercario. Sure hope Jake Matthews is still wearin' his hair."

"Jake will be all right," said Challenger. "He wasn't foaled yesterday."

Mary Musgrove's husband grinned. "Aye. When it comes to handlin' Injuns, Jacob c'n talk his way out o' a stoppered stone jug."

"Pray proceed with your account, Mr. Blakeslee," the accompanying trustee invited. "I judge that time is of the essence now."

"Sure thing, Yer Honor. Wal, I kept on so fast as I could till I reached Chaugee—that's where the old-time Yamasees used to have a big town. I wuz circlin' around it upstream when I come sudden-like on a passel of Atali or Lower Creeks. Mebbe I startled 'em—mebbe they was only out huntin'—but they raised a screech and let fly. One creased my scalp."

He touched the fly-covered and bloody rag over which lank strands of his greasy brown hair spilled like a small and dingy waterfall, swayed, and this time was steadied by Captain Challenger. "Well, Yer Honor, I expect that's about all there is to it. So, if ye'll excuse me, reckon I'd better go and find me some rest and a bait of vittles. I'm hollow clear down to my moccasins."

Once the trader had been helped toward the half-built guardhouse Oglethorpe preceded Musgrove and Challenger into the command tent, then, with engaging simplicity, inquired, "Well, gentlemen, do you believe these Indians are about to rise and attack us?"

While scratching his tawny pate, Challenger deliberated. "I don't reckon so, but ye'd better see what Jamie MacPherson an' Billy Bull have to say. If I'm any judge, the Atali Creeks will first call a big powwow or council of war and figger out what to do about you. Without such a powwow, they can't accomplish much in a big way.

"Because they hate the Spaniards so much, they may decide not to take up the hatchet till they're surer of what you really intend here. They favor us because we offer 'em better trade goods and don't cheat 'em as much as the Dons."

The acting governor's expressive brown eyes sought Musgrove's powder-blued features. "And what, sir, do you think?"

Flattered by Oglethorpe's manner, Musgrove stared at the ground. "I think Wally Challenger's guess is a damn' sight nearer right than wrong, but there's one thing ye might do right away, an ye don't mind."

"And that is?"

"Let me go talk with my Mary; she'll go see Tomo-chichi right away. She'll remind him that you aim to do only the square thing with all Injuns. You mayn't credit this, sir, but that crafty old buzzard in Yama-craw Town sets considerable store on Mary's say-so."

"So I have heard, and thank you, Mr. Musgrove," Oglethorpe said, smiling. "Kindly instruct your wife to promise him and the Lower Creeks any gifts which could assist the old chief in keeping them friendly. One thing more." His voice deepened and his expression grew graver still as he plucked his coat, which he'd hung to a lopped-off branch. "Mrs. Musgrove must make Tomo-chichi believe that I had no knowledge of any formal agreement by which His Majesty's subjects are prohibited from taking up land south of the Savannah River."

"I'll do that, sir." The trader pulled on his disreputable old hat and mounted a thorn-scarred buckskin pony which stood switching flies under a small pine. "By the bye, sir," Musgrove called over his shoulder. "Forgot to tell ye Mary thinks Tomo-chichi'll maybe come to visit yer settlement this afternoon. If he shows up, ye can likely tell by his manner how ye stand. I'd be on hand only I've got to go up to Purysburg."

"Where is Purysburg?" Oglethorpe demanded of Challenger, who was about to mount.

"Yer Excellency, 'tis a little town that lies about six miles upstream on the other side o' the river. It's named after Jean Pierre Pury, a Swiss fellow who founded it a few years back."

"Why have I not heard it mentioned before?"

"Sir, 'tis but a mean place which ain't prospered because the location is unhealthy and its soil is meager and sour."

Before swinging up into his saddle, Captain Challenger cast Oglethorpe a curious glance and in a low voice queried, "Sir, by any chance did John Musgrove tell you that Tomo-chichi sent out runners just before we found Dick Blakeslee?"

James Oglethorpe stroked his long, bluish chin—a mannerism of his when deeply perturbed—as, narrowly, he regarded the Ranger officer's red-brown features. "He said nothing about it, Captain. Can you guess the nature of the message those runners carried?"

"No, sir. I doubt if even the Musgroves could tell you for sure."

"If war *is* intended what steps do you think should be taken?"

"Strong, well-armed pickets—as many of them mounted as possible—should be posted well out on all traces and trails leading toward this settlement. Woodcutters and farmers should be called in, given arms and warned to stand ready."

Challenger's vivid blue eyes seemed to shine brighter still. "Livestock should be driven in and secured and food supplies had better be concentrated in the ward tents. Oh yes, your settlers should be warned to collect their children and stay close to their wards' marquee."

"In your opinion, does Tomo-chichi really intend to pay us a visit, a friendly one—let us hope?"

"I think so, sir. Whilst I was ridin' in I noted some of Tomo's top warriors paintin' and prettyin' themselves up."

"In that case"—Oglethorpe pulled on his plain brown coat—"please dispatch runners to warn Judge Whitaker, the Reverend Herbert and all Ranger and militia officers to turn out handsomely dressed and as soon as possible. And"—this came as a palpable afterthought—"Petre Ballou."

Oglethorpe's deeply sunburned features relaxed. "Oh, one more thing —tell Mr. Savey that I wish the ward cooks to bestir themselves and prepare the best possible food."

"What about liquor, sir? The savages always expect some."

"Thank you, Captain, I will instruct Papot to break out a supply of spirits."

Within the hot, lemon-hued shelter of his field officer's tent, which he'd ordered pitched under the four pines which towered behind that ever-busy crane of Ballou's, Oglethorpe indulged in a weary sigh and tried not too successfully to cope with anxieties raised by Blakeslee's report. Dear God! What if the southern tribes did rise and strike?

He called James Papot, his plump, smooth-faced Maltese body servant. "Lay out my best gold-laced scarlet tunic, the white satin breeches and red silk stockings. Also a dress hat—the one with yellow ostrich trimmings."

"Aye, aye, sir." Papot, having once served as a caterer to the officers of H.B.M.S. *Royal Oak* while she lay in Valletta Harbor, never let anyone forget about his brief and tenuous connection with the Royal Navy. Soft-footed, the servant crossed to a brassbound oak chest and set about unknotting lashings which had secured it all the way out from England.

Meanwhile, the accompanying trustee stripped off his sweat-sodden work clothes and, lost in anxious speculation, sponged his spare but hard-muscled torso at a bucket of spring water.

To his disgust, Oglethorpe discovered that he couldn't relax even when he made a deliberate effort to; Dick Blakeslee's news had been too fraught with ominous possibilities. His always lively imagination visualized swarms of painted savages sweeping among the tents and half-built dwellings, screeching as they bloodied tomahawks, spears, and scalping knives.

And what about Tomo-chichi's real intentions? Almost certainly the mico thlucco would be attended by a sizable number of well-armed Yamacraws.

While continuing to dress he thought ahead: If treachery were in the air, what sort of a defense could be offered? Only a feeble one at best, although Lieutenants Glen and Savey had been instructed to arm that handful of immigrants who appeared to understand the use of firearms. These, decided the harassed acting governor, had better be concealed in a ward tent standing near his headquarters, but could these undisciplined fellows, naturally anxious about their families, be depended upon to keep quiet and obey orders?

Lost in thought, the accompanying trustee watched Papot select a towering peruke which he began to powder with practiced ease.

If only I'd taken time to talk with that amazing white savage. Possibly, if he holds a secret grudge against the Yamacraws, he could have furnished useful intelligence. Well, there's no time now to send for him, so I'd best quit worrying and trust in God.

Oglethorpe was slipping into a tunic of glaring scarlet when in the distance sounded shrill, ear-piercing blasts on bone whistles, a moaning of conch-shell trumpets, a wild clattering of rattles, and the blood-quickening *thud-thud* of what sounded suspiciously like war drums.

Papot hurriedly was arranging the acting governor's jabot of frothy Mechlin lace when Captain Challenger scratched at the tent's fly and called, "Sir! Sir! Mrs. Musgrove's just arrived and begs immediate word with you."

"Kindly show her in." Oglethorpe quickly secured gold buttons securing a long, white satin waistcoat, then slipped on a sword sling elaborately embroidered in petit point.

Mary Musgrove appeared dressed as a high-ranking Creek princess, wearing fringed white buckskins, silver necklaces, bracelets, and rings. On her sleek black hair reposed a circlet of cloth of gold which, bound with rare black wampum, supported a nodding panache of misty white egret plumes.

The half-breed's expressive dark blue eyes were gleaming and her olive-hued forehead spangled by perspiration.

"Excellency!" she panted. "Tomo-chichi, all his *outacitys* and Ravens and above forty warriors are drawing near."

Above forty warriors! Somehow, he managed an easy smile. "My earnest thanks, ma'am. Pray be kind enough to advise me how a representative of His Britannic Majesty should receive a mico thlucco?"

"Summon your chief followers—who should be dressed as brilliantly as possible—and order them to line up, according to rank, before your tent. None of them should look about, or say anything, until you make your appearance."

"Captain Challenger, you've heard Mrs. Musgrove's advice?"

"Yes, sir."

"Then, as quickly as may be, see that her suggestions are put into effect. Now then, ma'am, what other steps should be taken?"

Almost demurely, John Musgrove's wife reached up to straighten her headdress. "Only when Tomo-chichi himself has come to within fifty paces of Your Excellency's tent should you appear and stand in front of your officers—say at a distance of four paces."

"Four paces. I will remember that."

"Then, when the *aliktcha*, or chief wizard, halts his dancing, you should advance exactly six steps toward Tomo-chichi. Above everything, do not speak or appear surprised by anything that may follow. Try to remain expressionless."

While the outlandish din swelled louder, Oglethorpe couldn't help putting the crucial question. "Can you tell me whether Tomo-chichi comes in good faith—or otherwise?"

It deeply disturbed him that the half-breed's expressive and faintly slanting eyes should waver aside an instant before she said, "No, Your Excellency, I cannot tell you that, well as I understand the old man."

From among tents, half-finished houses, and piles of lumber, Winsome Brooks watched a throng of sunburned, dusty, and decidedly uneasy ex-paupers converge on James Oglethorpe's marquee. On the other hand, the children were fascinated by these prancing, howling, outlandishly painted and caparisoned Yamacraws.

The Stonehewer twins, mouths sagging open in delighted wonder, watched antics performed by the chief wizard, who, weirdly accoutered, capered, spun, and leaped along some thirty feet before old Tomo-chichi's emaciated but stately and lance-straight figure.

From her post a pace behind and to the left of James Oglethorpe Mary Musgrove called in a low voice, "That medicine dancer is Outanti, the paramount wizard of the Yamacraw tribe. He is much feared."

It was then that experienced frontiersmen like Colonel Bull and his Rangers noted a significant fact: Sakwari-cra and his two principal warriors, a fierce-looking black man with dog-like teeth and a lean, one-eyed Chickasaw, were advancing somewhat apart—just far enough away to point out that Thad Burton and his people were not to be considered as Tomo-chichi's vassals.

All at once Outanti ceased to advance and began to howl and prance about on the same spot, whereupon the savage music gradually died out and the main body of Yamacraws, tossing plumed heads and brandishing weapons, collected in a wide semicircle behind their mico thlucco.

There were, thought such veterans as Challenger, MacPherson, and Bull, a disturbing number of firearms in evidence.

Oglethorpe heard the half-breed woman hiss, "Now, sir, advance six paces."

Immensely dignified, James Oglethorpe, a tall, glittering, and quietly impressive figure, took the requisite number of steps and halted. He appeared to ignore the chief wizard even when Outanti leaped high into the air, then sank onto his heels. Howling like a moon-struck hound, he then leaped up and sprang at the acting governor, holding out two great fans made of the white vulture's black-tipped tail feathers. These fans were affixed to short yellow rods decorated with jangling brass bells.

Outanti ceased his frantic caperings and began to stamp rhythmically upon the dusty red ground. At the same time he raised a quavering chant so piercingly pitched that Oglethorpe was only just able to catch Mary Musgrove's explanation.

"Outanti recites the great deeds of his tribe's ancestors. Do not move or speak."

Obediently, James Oglethorpe kept his gaze fixed on Tomo-chichi's wizened visage, seeking to read the Yamacraw's intentions. Then Outanti, screeching like an amorous she-lynx, grabbed the fans by their handles and began to hop like a huge, impossible toad around the brilliantly garbed Englishman and used the glistening white-and-black feathers to stroke Oglethorpe's face, shoulders, arms, and even his silver-buckled shoes.

When a great yammering arose from the Yamacraws, the Rangers braced for instant action. Oglethorpe, however, heard Mary Musgrove whisper, "All is well. Peace is intended."

Among the few people who hadn't fixed their attention on the wizard were Colonel Bull and Wallace Challenger. They kept on watching Sakwari-cra and his followers. Challenger thought to read on the white Tuscarora's powerful, painted features a curious blend of suspicion, arrogance, and puzzlement.

What was the young mico thinking?

Challenger was surprised when Sakwari-cra began to stare back at him, treating him to a hard, unwavering look that suggested challenge coupled with frank curiosity.

Their gazes clashed for a long and infinitely meaningful instant before separating.

Over Oglethorpe's scarlet and gold-laced shoulder came Mary's warning. "The mico thlucco will now advance toward you. You must match step for step, moving no faster nor any slower."

So much depended on what might happen during the next few instants that a ripple of little cold shivers descended Oglethorpe's spine as Tomo-chichi drew near with one stringy hand raised above his head.

When at length the two leaders stood separated by only a couple of feet, Tomo-chichi shook hands, Indian fashion, by sliding his knobby right hand up the Englishman's left sleeve until it rested upon his shoulder. Because, on several occasions, he'd watched Colonel Bull and Mac-Pherson greet Indians in this fashion, Oglethorpe merely repeated the gesture by placing his hand on the glossy otter skin covering Tomo-chichi's left shoulder.

During a long instant the two leaders peered fixedly at one another; each somehow aware that a powerful, if unexplicable, bond was being forged.

Chapter 15

"THE LANDSKIP IS VERY AGREEABLE"

The evening of February 10, 1733, being unusually cold and blustery James Edward Oglethorpe, Esq., summoned his secretary. Around thirty years of age, John West didn't resemble the usual concept of a quill driver in that he was straight of back and stockily built. Moreover, he'd a round, ruddy face and there usually was a twinkle in his spaniel-brown eyes. Also, he had a ready laugh which, on many a gloomy occasion, had rendered life more enjoyable for his employer.

Since it would soon grow dark, West hoped that His Excellency wasn't going to be garrulous on paper, which, in Mr. West's opinion, was about the accompanying trustee's only failing—except for a curious penchant toward playing practical jokes that seldom were cruel or in bad taste.

Seating himself at a field desk, Oglethorpe began to riffle through documents in a bulging portfolio. The secretary, while awaiting dictation, looked outside. Hum. For once, not a single vessel lay at anchor below the bluff, not even a plantation boat, but a pair of fishing skiffs were tied up to a rough wharf erected directly below the freight crane. On that long, flat island opposite Savannah a herd of brown Carolina cows could be seen grazing placidly, ignoring prolonged showers of cold rain.

Even though dusk was about to close in, the dull rasping of saws and the *tchunk-tchunk!* of axes continued, occasionally punctuated by the grinding crash of a felled tree.

Oglethorpe at last emitted a weary sigh. "Ah me! I fear the time has come to inform my fellow trustees concerning the state of this venture."

"Aye, sir. 'Tis time indeed." Silently West added, This time, I'm really in for it. Needlessly, his blunt fingers smoothed the sheet of foolscap he held ready. Delicately, he dipped a freshly pointed quill into a leaden ink bottle from which the screw cap had been removed.

"Yes, sir?"

Eyes fixed on the darkening river James Edward Oglethorpe, Esquire, commenced, with exasperating deliberation, to dictate.

From the Camp near Savannah,
February 10th, 1733.

To the Trustees for Establishing the Colony of Georgia in America:

Gentlemen:

I gave you an Account, in my last, of our Arrival at Charles Town. The Governor and Assembly have given us all possible Encouragement. Our People arrived at Beaufort on the 20th of January, where I lodged them in some new Barracks, built for the Soldiers, while I went myself to View the Savannah River.

I fixed upon a Healthy Situation, about ten Miles from the sea. The River here forms a Half-Moon, along the South Side of which the Banks rise about forty feet High, and on the top Flat, which they call a Bluff. The plain high Ground extends into the Country five or six Miles, and along the River side about a Mile.

Ships that draw twelve-foot Water can ride within ten yards of the Bank. Upon the River side in the Centre of this plain I have laid out the Town.

Opposite to it is an Island of very rich Pasturage, which I think should be kept for the Trustees' Cattle.

The River is pretty wide, the Water fresh, and from the Key of the Town you see its whole course to the Sea, with the Island of Tybee, which forms the Mouth of the River; and the other Way, you see the River for about six miles up into the Country.

The Landskip is very Agreeable, the Stream being wide, and bordered with high Woods on both Sides.

Our People still lie mostly in tents; there being only Two clapboard Houses complete, and three sawed Houses framed.

Our Crane, our Battery of Cannon, our Magazine, are finished. This is all we have been able to do, by Reason of the Smallness of our Number, of which many have been Sick, and others unused to Labour, though I thank God they are now pretty Well, and we have not Lost One since our arrival.

Recently Colonel Bull returned to Savannah with four Laborers, and Assisted the Colony, he Himself measuring the Scantling and setting out the Work for the Sawyers, and giving the Proportions of the Houses.

Mr. Whitaker and his Friends sent the Colony one hundred head of Cattle. Mr. St. Julian himself came to Savannah and stayed directing the People in building their Houses and other Work.

Mr. Hume gave a Silver Boat and Spoon for the first Child born in Georgia, which being Born of Mrs. Close, were given accordingly. Mr. Joseph Bryan, himself, with four of his Sawyers Works in the Colony.

The Inhabitants of Edisto sent sixteen sheep. Mr. Hammerton gave a Drum. Mrs. Ann Drayton sent two pair of Sawyers to work in the Colony.

Colonel Bull and Mr. Bryan came to Savannah with twenty more Servants, whose Labor they gave to the Colony. His Excellency Robert Johnson gave seven Horses, valued at £25, Carolina Currency.

Yr. humble, obed't servant,

James Edward Oglethorpe

John West, while warming a stick of sealing wax over a candle flame, made bold to remark, "So encouraging a report I trust will inspire your colleagues in England to speed the departure of the second expedition of emigrants."

"Let us hope so, John. So much, in fact everything, depends upon the prompt arrival of reinforcements and supplies."

BOOK III

Savannah

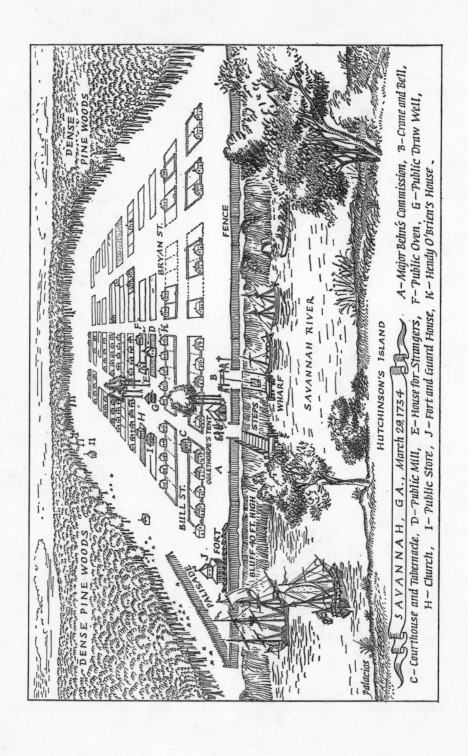

SAVANNAH, GA., March 29, 1734

A—Major Behn's Commission,   B—Crane and Bell,
C—Courthouse and Tabernacle,   D—Public Mill,   E—House for Strangers,   F—Public Oven,   G—Public Draw Well,
H—Church,   I—Public Store,   J—Fort and Guard House,   K—Hendy O'Brien's House.

Chapter 1

MARKET PLACE

As the unshaven and shirt-sleeved town crier appeared, plodding bare-foot, along a sandy lane which someday would become Bull Street, he revolved his wooden rattle until a crowd gathered, eager to hear what he had to say.

"Hear ye! Hear ye! Be it known that the savages who are hired to hunt for us are come into the market place with a supply of fresh deer meat!"

Since the crier had halted only a few houses down the lane on which she lived, Winsome Brooks could hear him clearly, so she stopped grinding cinchona bark in Dr. Tailfer's brass mortar and glanced across the narrow room to where Helen Bayless sat writing out a ration return for Ward Derby.

Ipswich Nicholas, now half-grown and lanky, lay sprawled in lordly indolence across a sheet of foolscap upon which he had deposited numerous tiny blood spots drawn by robust Georgia fleas. At the same time Ipswich rolled over and began a series of playful dabs at the writer's busy quill.

"Well, Helen, shall I go draw our lots or do you want to?"

The Bayless girl straightened, pulled forward the damp fabric of her dress, and, pursing soft lips, blew down its front. Spring now was so advanced that, during the middle of the day, it often grew uncomfortably warm.

By consequence, every day, more loathsome snakes, crocodiles, and alligators concluded their hibernations. To the settlers' alarm reptiles of all sizes began to appear in the swamps and marshes bordering the

Savannah. Worse still, these fearsome creatures took to lying in ambush among reed beds, along creekside trails and traces. After a number of dogs, young pigs, and even a calf or two had disappeared without a trace, the Georgians, as they had begun to call themselves, declared war and killed many such reptiles in traps or with spears and firearms. At first, the roaring of bull alligators had had a terrifying effect, but soon the immigrants grew accustomed to such awesome sounds.

With the further advance of spring many more species of snakes appeared, and although most of these were harmless, some were venomous, so work in the woods and the fields became a question of perpetual vigilance.

Although Rangers and visiting Carolinians attempted to identify the dangerous species, few ex-paupers ever became able to distinguish a bull snake from a rattler or a cottonmouth moccasin from a friendly black snake, which hunted only mice, rats, and other rodents. For them, any snake remained a serpent and a familiar of Old Scratch.

Riding into the raw, half-built town of Savannah after a tour of scouting duty, Captain Wallace Challenger reined in his thorn-scarred black nag before that hut in which Winsome Brooks and Helen Bayless kept house for Drs. Tailfer and Cox—both of whom were bachelors. He saw the two young women standing over a slowly writhing grass snake that just had had its back broken by a stick Winsome still held.

"What for," he drawled, "d'you want to go and kill a poor, harmless critter like that?"

"Why, why, it's a snake! It's loathsome," snapped the New England girl.

"Let me show you how to recognize venomous snakes." Challenger, laughing softly, swung down from his saddle, stirred the dying reptile with a scuffed moccasin. "You're barkin' up the wrong tree; such a critter couldn't harm anything fiercer than a frog."

He reached into a deerskin saddlebag, brought out a small bundle which he untied by jerking a rawhide thong. "Now look and learn, ladies. Mark these diamond patterns well because that's the hide off a rattler. They're the worst and commonest poisonous snake you'll find round here." Next, he selected a short, slim black and red specimen. When he exhibited it, his horse snorted, flinched away. "This here's a coral snake; you won't find too many of 'em this far north, but beware, sure as one strikes you, ye're a gone goose. Not even an Injun can save you—and their squaws know plenty about curin' snakebite."

Winsome glared at this young giant in use-shiny buckskins. "Aren't you ashamed of trying to scare us?"

"No. 'Cause I'm not. Don't shy off, ladies, and look sharp." He selected a handful of skins. "All these are harmless as kittens. This one's a ribbon snake, this bigger one's a chicken snake—which don't kill chickens—and this one with the horny spur on its tail is a bull snake—which don't kill bulls."

His air of humorous condescension was intolerable, Winsome decided. Time Captain Challenger got taken down a peg. But he went right ahead, showed them the shapes and markings of a coach-whip snake and what a glass snake looked like.

"None of them can, or will hurt you," he concluded. "The only serpents to watch out for are moccasins, corals, and rattlers. No use in gettin' scared over nothing 'cause this country's as full of snakes as an egg is of meat."

"A most profound observation, O most sapient sir!" Winsome said with elaborate sarcasm, but, before she could think of a really clever or crushing comment, the Ranger stuffed the skins back into his saddlebag and rode off as unconcerned as you please.

She was recalled to immediate considerations by Helen's saying, "Perhaps you'd better go draw our rations. I—well, my stomach's a bit queasy again. I might throw up all over the market place."

Winsome went indoors to find the market basket, then reappeared wearing a serious expression on her pointed, bronzed features. "Let's hope the savages have fetched in some buffalo meat. I'm *that* weary of venison I could cry. Why is it always so sweet-tasting and soft-grained?"

While tying a kerchief about her wavy dark brown hair she heard Dr. Cox moving about on the upper floor—to which access was gained only by a set of ladder-stairs built outside.

From the heavy way he walked, it would appear that poor Dr. Cox's dropsy wasn't getting any better; she had to admire the stubborn way he completed his daily rounds. Lately, so many settlers had fallen victim to a number of unidentified fevers, infected insect bites, and the common run of accidents that Dr. Tailfer couldn't begin to attend them all.

Other ex-paupers suffered from boils or had got themselves horribly poisoned by unfamiliar creepers and bushes which they soon came to call "poison ivy" and "poison oak." When a young child or a sickly grownup got stung by a venomous snake, there wasn't much that could be done except to suck at the fang holes, pray, and try to reach the Yamacraw village in time; squaws there knew how to apply poultices compounded of herbs which, more often than not, pulled the victim through.

Today, the sun was so hot that, before she left, Winsome donned a shapeless, wide-brimmed hat woven by squaws out of plaited strips of cornhusks. Whereas the girl from Boston didn't begin to suffer from sunburn as badly as immigrants of English origin, she heeded Wallace Challenger's casual warning that, even this early in the year, the effects of the Georgia sun could be deadly.

After shoving Ipswich Nicholas back indoors, Dr. Brooks's daughter made her way to the market house, which, at present, consisted of a roofed structure lacking walls. While plodding along, she felt annoyed that, already, the warm red dust was sifting inside her shoes.

Alert to her surroundings, Winsome looked about, was again astonished to see how rapidly Savannah was growing. So many dwellings were built or going up that, why, by now there must be nearly forty of them—some, even, with two stories. Each dwelling was centered on a plot covering one-eighth of an acre—the standard town lot granted to each settler and his family.

This property formed only part of the basic holding of fifty acres guaranteed by the Georgia Company. Beyond the town limits there were also garden plots for every settler, consisting of seven-eighths of an acre; these already had been surveyed and some actually were being farmed. The remaining forty-nine acres of the company's grant still lay hidden within pine forests. Eventually, this land, too, would be cleared and planted according to the company's master plan.

Young boys, girls, and women, uniformly untidy and mostly barefooted, appeared on the settlement's sandy street lugging rush baskets or bags of knitted thread. Inhabitants of Ward Percival, in which the market house stood, already had congregated and stood about gabbing as they awaited arrivals from Wards Derby, Heathcote and Decker.

Bettie O'Brien, her short, straight nose fiery and peeling, called out, "Greetings, Winsome! High time we got together, but I expect you and Helen have been every bit as busy as Hendy and I." To Winsome it remained remarkable how fully the young Irishman's wife had recovered from the nearly fatal effects of her miscarriage.

"How are things going with Hendy?"

Fanning aside clouds of flies, Bettie smiled. "Fine! Fine! He's happy as a lark fencing off a pasture for horses just come down from Carolina. His first paddock's grown too small." Bettie laughed happily. "What's got my man in a real spin is that, courtesy of Governor Johnson, there are a blooded stallion and two mares in this shipment. Hendy vows we'll have racing come another two years."

"That *should* prove an interesting occasion!" Winsome predicted. "Is your house well built? The roof on ours leaks dreadfully."

"Our home isn't quite finished, but it does well enough, I suppose. Of course, we haven't a stick of furniture beyond a bed and the boxes and barrels we sit on and eat off. Hendy'd have made me some only he's been too busy breaking colts. He's confident that some of 'em will make real racers."

A shifting haze of hot, fine dust thickened, lowered over the market house until this miasma resembled a brick-tinted mist. Winsome noticed that, to one side, stood a group of small, rough-coated, and sleepy-looking horses which must belong to those hunters the acting governor had hired to keep his settlement supplied with fresh meat. At the start these professional hunters had come in nearly every day, but by now they had hunted local game so hard they were forced to range ever farther afield and therefore fetched in meat only twice a week.

On pushing her way through a swarm of buzzing flies into the market house's shade Winsome sighted several piles of unskinned deer and shaggy buffalo quarters stacked on a low platform. To one side of this stood scales suspended from a tripod beside which bearded butchers were sharpening heavy-bladed knives. Phew! How heavily the sickish-sweet odor of warm meat and stale blood hung in this hot and windless atmosphere!

Looking out into the sunshine, Winsome noticed two horses being relieved of dusty brown buffalo quarters by Indians directed by that enigmatic giant called Sakwari-cra.

To her surprise Winsome found herself studying this curious white Indian. Did he *always* wear paint and dress like a savage? Hum. What kind of a figure would this impressive savage cut in European garments? Probably he'd look ridiculous and feel vastly uncomfortable.

Long since, she'd heard that Thad Burton and his heterogeneous band of savages were bringing in more game than Toonahowie and his Yamacraw hunters, who certainly must be far more familiar with these hunting grounds.

Yelling excitedly, children scampered about the market place poking at the game's dust-glazed eyes with pointed sticks. Gaunt and furtive dogs from Yamacraw Town slunk hopefully about, mingled timidly with the gathering throng.

Striding about, as officious and domineering as ever, was the settlement's newly appointed bailiff. Winsome, along with a good many others, deemed Thomas Causton a loudmouthed bully who, whenever his superiors were present, skillfully concealed his incompetence and self-importance behind a hearty and ingratiating manner.

"Now then, stand back, the lot of you!" he shouted. "*Stand back*, I say. Gather yerselves by wards and have yer ration papers handy." Afflicted by a ferocious squint and a huge bulbous nose covered with blackheads and enlarged pores, Tom Causton's appearance created very few pleasant first impressions. "Don't crowd! No point in it. I've ordered no meat to be issued till *all* of these beasts have been divided to my satisfaction."

At length the bailiff scrambled onto the meat platform and ordered the crier to sound his rattle. When a measure of silence resulted he shouted, "Today, Ward Derby has the first choice among piles." Employing his riding whip, he indicated four large, fly-covered mounds of dull red meat. "In each pile there's a chunk of flesh for every household—or ought to be. Of course," he added with a false laugh, "the rations can't *all* be just the same size and weight, so don't bellyache if ye draw short."

Arguing fit to waken the dead, the crowd lined up. Winsome took her time about taking her place. Long ago, she'd learned that it didn't make much difference where she stood in the queue—each applicant was forced to accept the ration issued by a butcher who sat with his back turned and merely speared the handiest piece of meat which was plopped into whatever receptacle was offered.

Gripping her basket, Winsome finally began an advance toward the platform when, to her complete astonishment, Thad Burton strode up carrying a large piece of redly dripping meat. Streaks and splashes of blood marked his sinewy brown arms, also his leggings and moccasins.

The white Tuscarora's features as usual were devoid of expression, but his deep-set eyes were shining. "Tender young buffalo," he grunted. "You take."

Smiling into his broad, high-cheekboned features, Winsome, for the first time, noted the blue turtle totem tattooed onto his upper arm— also the small, crescent-shaped scar marking his left temple. Feeling not a little regretful and absurdly self-righteous, she shook her head. "Thank you very kindly, Mr. Burton, but I can't accept your gift. I really mustn't. It should be included in the common supply."

The gray-blue eyes flashed. "No. This for you. You take!"

"But don't you see? I can't! It wouldn't be fair to the rest."

Under his streaked red and yellow paint, Sakwari-cra scowled, then stamped a moccasined foot. "Take! White men not pay for this."

Winsome's cheeks turned very red under her cornhusk hat. "I wish I might. Please try to understand, Mr. Burton, why I, well, why I just *can't* accept your very generous offer."

"You dare refuse gift of Sakwari-cra?" His crested head went back and, haughtily, he glared down his nose at her.

"I do, but—I'm so sorry, sir. I really am."

"Sure! You be sorry soon!"

In monumental dignity, Burton then turned and tossed the filet he'd so carefully trimmed from the underside of a young buffalo's spine to some shaggy Indian dogs. Immediately, they fell to fighting over it.

Without a backward glance the tall young mico stalked over to a buckskin stallion, vaulted effortlessly astride, and rode away.

Chapter 2

KUMA

Loping away, Thad swore feelingly in Tuscarora. Aren't squaws—especially white squaws—favored children of Chitokaka, worst of all the evil gods? No matter their age, they're all jealous, unreasoning, weak, and talkative—except maybe Taqua. In all fairness, he had to admit to himself that she never had been garrulous. She was as strong as most young men and could outrun the fleetest of them; never would he forget the magnificent way she'd run that time. *Wagh!* Some great warrior's spirit had been wasted on a squaw.

The young mico was feeling both baffled and insulted. How dare the white woman refuse a gift from the great Mico Sakwari-cra, he who could brandish eleven scalps taken in battle? Speaking better English, perhaps he might have made that cool-eyed, straight-backed squaw understand that the offering had been taken from a young buffalo he'd slain expressly to feed himself and Taqua. The unforgivable part of this business was that she, a miserable squaw, had humiliated an Iroquois warrior before a crowd of palefaces.

Through talk overheard in the market place, he knew that Mistress Brooks was reputed to be skilled in the art of healing. The first time he'd really noticed Win-some was when she'd appeared with Dr. Cox to set a Yamacraw lad's broken arm.

The young fellow's jaw tightened on recalling a recent incident: he'd been conferring with the mico thlucco, Ogle-thorpe, about the intentions of certain Yuchi micos when he'd noticed Captain Challenger ride up to the dwelling of Win-some and drop a pair of turkeys onto her doorstep, and recalled that, without hesitation, she'd smiled and had accepted the birds.

Reaching forward, Thad angrily slapped some green-headed horseflies from his mount's neck and created bloody patches on the buckskin's rough hide.

Why should this creature with the clear green-brown eyes accept a gift from Captain Challenger and then refuse his offering? Was it—he hesitated in framing the thought—was it because the Ranger officer dressed, acted, and talked like a white man? His own blood was pure—she must know that; everyone did.

Did she or anybody believe that this big yellow-haired swaggerer was stronger or wiser in war? *Wagh!* If that were the case then someday soon he would remove any doubt on the subject. All the same, he had to admit that the Ranger captain was fearless, shrewd, and a superb woodsman much admired by the rough and independent men under his command.

Using a single rawhide rein, Thad guided the buckskin toward Sakwari village, which now had come to shelter not less than forty warriors—not counting a handful of squaws.

His mount proved too weary to shy when a pair of bobwhite quail burst from under its hoofs like small brown-and-white bombs.

A new possibility occurred; Win-some must be acting so coldly because he kept Taqua—as he had every right to do—for a bedmate!

One evening Coosa-pona-keesa had spoken of bad talk circulating about his keeping a purebred white girl as a concubine.

A flush mounted under his fading red and ocher face paint. How dared such stupid cattle, who, anyway, were only waiting to be massacred, dare to criticize a mico? There was no sense to it. Why couldn't they understand that Taqua was supremely content with her lot, especially since her belly every day was growing rounder.

Thad now began to regret having flung away that filet; cooked by Taqua, it would have proved a choice morsel to satisfy his hunger.

Well, there was at least one good result from this situation; he wouldn't be riding into Savannah much longer. On each hunt it was proving more and more difficult to locate sufficient game to feed these cow-clumsy settlers. Continual hunting and timbering were driving away, not only the deer and buffalo, but also all manner of smaller game.

Nowadays, even turkeys were only to be found a long way off, and delicious-tasting Savannah cranes were fast disappearing from nearby marshes. Ducks and other waterfowl, their nests repeatedly despoiled, were seeking safer regions. Yes. Soon it would be time to move his people to a less populated country.

The question arose: Should he lead the Sakwaris westward, or back up north into a country he knew something about? On the other hand, perhaps it would be wise to lead them south toward the Altamaha River. Chula and Shatara, who had recently hunted in that direction, reported that the local tribes there had been hard hit by last winter's epidemic of spotted sickness.

Wiry, half-naked body responding to the buckskin's gait, Thad trotted down a shallow ravine toward the encampment, to be greeted by the yelping and snarling of many hunting dogs. Stiff and proud, he started to ride across a clearing toward the Sakwaris' bark lodges and crude cabins.

The more he reflected the better he felt about migrating in a southeasterly direction. It stood to reason there'd be many widows and single squaws along the Altamaha; since Indian females invariably greatly outnumbered the males, his bachelor warriors should find plenty of choice.

Powerful legs dangling loosely from the knee, he rode up to his cabin and dismounted. It pleased and reassured him to find Taqua seated on a stump busily working red- and blue-dyed porcupine needles into the breast of the new hunting shirt she'd been making for him.

He was considerably surprised, however, when she stood up, smiled uncertainly, and, embarrassed, tugged at the end of a red-gold braid before she called, "Hello," instead of greeting him, as usual, in Muskogean.

To his surprise he replied in English, "Hello, Laure. Musgrove's squaw must have been here."

Laure Rivard giggled, groped until she found the right words. "Yes. She spend—spent—whole day. Mary say—said—she enjoy—my company."

When she drew near he was further disconcerted to notice how much rounder her belly had grown. Why, the little blue turtle tattooed on her bosom had almost become eclipsed by the new opulence of her breasts.

Following that unfortunate exchange with the white girl called Winsome, he found it distasteful to continue talking English, so he lapsed into Muskogean. "Enough of this. Tomorrow we take the trail and go where there is no need to speak *Englasi*."

Laure's tawny features lit and her uneven teeth flashed whitely. "*Wagh!* That is fine, Sakwari-cra. Quobah grows more restless each day. The men are not happy here. They want to go where rum can be bought and game is easier to kill. Besides, it is not pleasant to see how *Englasi* women look at me, then whisper and go to laugh among themselves."

Sakwari-cra called a passing youth, tossed him the buckskin's rein, and ordered him to rub down the little stallion—a bit of care few redskins would have deemed necessary. Thad wouldn't have, either, if Hendy O'Brien hadn't proved how quickly a tired animal recovered strength through such attention.

Said he, "*Hoktudshi!* It is *not* because the *Englasi* here do not sell or use rum that we move on. Rum is crazy-making. Sakwari-cra does not want his warriors to fall down, or in their madness to kill one another, or for nothing to give away their horses and all that they own."

Taqua nodded, then because of her bulk she squatted somewhat awkwardly over an open hearth built in the cabin's center.

As she crouched there, bronzed arms and haunches agleam, Thad tried to imagine Taqua in European garb. Would she appear as appealing with her flaming hair combed, neatly dressed, and piled upon her head?

Probably not; under flapping skirts and roomy upper garments the fine, clean lines of her body would become hidden. Similarly, what sort of a spectacle would he present in a long-skirted jacket, knee breeches, hose, and a ruffled shirt? Like a hungry chipmunk, curiosity gnawed at his imagination.

Sakwari-cra went over to sniff at their stew pot, which, as in most Indian dwellings, was kept simmering all day, for regular meal hours were unheard of; the time to eat was when one felt hungry.

Thad had begun to gnaw on a partridge leg when, abruptly, he stopped chewing; loud voices were rising where Quobah and his Africans had built their shelters.

Pushing open a plank door, Sakwari-cra peered out and saw that every Negro, mulatto, and mustee in the place had collected and all were gesticulating and talking before Quobah's door. Silently watching them from a distance stood a group of Yamacraws.

Quickly, Thad realized that the center of interest was a stranger, an all-but-naked Negro who was squatting, tiredly, on a stump.

Since it was beneath a mico's dignity to walk over and investigate, Sakwari-cra returned his attention to his food. As he'd foreseen, it wasn't long before the crowd converged on his cabin and Quobah's deep voice called, "Please, Sakwari-cra, you come outside?"

Still chewing and with greasy drops falling from his bristle-covered chin, Thad Burton purposely delayed a bit before going outdoors. Quobah's yellowish eyes were round and gleaming as he shoved forward the gaunt stranger. "O my brother, please listen to this man."

At a glance, Thad identified the visitor as another Ashanti; he had a blue-black complexion, filed teeth, and wore blunt chevrons of scar tissue on cheeks and forehead. He was, however, nowhere as big or as well built as Quobah.

"Kuma has just escape' a barracoon." Quobah's voice quivered with intensity.

"In St. Augustine?"

"No." Quobah pointed northward. "From across river."

Then, in his native language, he ordered the gangling, terribly emaciated fugitive to speak up, which he did in barely recognizable English, mumbling, "Me, Kuma, Ashanti."

"Who was your owner?" Thad queried sharply.

It turned out that, until two days ago, Kuma had been a slave, a field hand on Fair View, a plantation belonging to a Major Smollett situated not far from Estoto.

His uneasiness mounting, Thad noted that Kuma was wearing a heavy iron slave collar complete with a rusty shackle eye, then queried, "Why did you run away?"

For answer Kuma turned around, whereat angry groans arose from the black and half-black Sakwaris. Even Thad, inured to horrible sights, was shocked. The fugitive's back was deeply criss-crossed by rows of swollen purple-red weals which, suppurating, were attracting swarms of blowflies.

Someone on the crowd's edge explained, "Major Smollett from Barbados." Throughout the Carolinas, emigrants from Barbados—of whom there were a good many—were detested for the severe, often savage treatment they accorded their slaves.

Thad directed in an impassive tone. "Quobah, take Kuma to your hut. Feed him, have Hapeyah treat his hurts. When he gets stronger bring him before me."

Chapter 3

CROSS-PURPOSES

When Kuma reached Quobah's hut his knobby gray knees buckled and he fell to the ground in a stupor. Hapeyah, although heavy with child, consulted other squaws and, among other remedies, applied to the sufferer's back thick poultices of lily-flag root. The fugitive did not rouse till night had fallen.

Meanwhile, in a dark corner, Quobah squatted on his hams, African fashion, elbows resting on knees, fondling a hideous juju which he'd adorned with inlays of brass and mussel shell and had equipped with an enormous phallus. In a crooning voice, Quobah prayed to it, invoking guidance and aid.

Next morning, Taqua brought in a report that increased Sakwari-cra's uneasiness; apparently his sable sub-mico had been talking a lot—and in secret. Why in secret? Common sense warned that he must be contemplating some move which he knew wouldn't meet his mico's approval.

Thad had about completed preparations for a near-final meat-hunting expedition but still had found no explanation for his new blood-brother's strange behavior, so he sent for him, principally because he reckoned that this next trip likely would keep him away overnight.

Decision taken, Sakwari-cra waited in rising impatience for Quobah to appear, but not until the afterglow was darkening did the Ashanti's scarlet turban loom through the half-light. "Sakwari-cra sent for Quobah, his brother?"

Thad stared a long minute, then said stiffly, "Why has my brother waited so long to obey his mico's summons?"

"Quobah need to learn everything about place where Kuma was slave."

"Why should Quobah need to know about such things?"

From the doorway, Taqua watched the two in conversation and grew increasingly uneasy; she could see, plain as day, that a clash of some sort impended. She felt badly because this was the first time she'd noticed even a trace of discord between the two giants.

Under the pretense of gathering firewood, she drew near enough to hear Quobah saying hotly, "Kuma only one of many who suffer from the Barbadian's cruelties. Major Smollett's black slaves must be freed! Will Sakwari-cra not lead?"

She heard Thad's breath drawn with an odd little *click!* as it always did when he got really angry. His powerful jaw line hardened, but he checked the outburst Taqua had fully anticipated and thought hard, instead.

Immediately, Thad perceived the folly of such an attempt; even if successful, the foray would provoke all sorts of trouble. Of course, he didn't despise slavery with the same intensity as the African ex-prince; all his life he'd seen slaves of varying sorts about him, so their lot hadn't troubled him. For that matter, he'd personally enslaved not a few people—Taqua among them.

Was not the taking of captives an honorable, as well as a profitable, undertaking? He'd freed Chula and the other Chickasaws only because he'd needed men and they'd belonged to Antoine Joyeuse, who was a Frenchman and therefore the enemy of all Iroquois. Oddly enough, not until now had it occurred to him that Quobah, on that occasion, might have been motivated by another purpose.

Still without speaking, Sakwari-cra sank onto moccasined heels before his cabin's entrance; after momentary hesitation, Quobah followed suit, his fierce, scarred features assuming a purplish hue in the twilight.

"O my brother, tell me. What is it that you would have me do?" Thad queried in so friendly a tone that the turbaned Ashanti's expression relaxed.

Said he, eagerly, "Lead a party of our warriors to a ford which lies beyond the Tied Arse village." Quobah employed the Indian term for those Swiss and German settlers at Purysburg who were given to wearing *lederhosen,* or tight leather breeches supported by galluses. "Kuma say the watch kept by the Tied Arses is so poor that we can cross unnoticed."

"And if you reach this plantation, what then?"

When the Ashanti heard Sakwari-cra say "if *you* reach," not "if *we* reach" he started scowling again, said, "We will slay neither Major Smollett nor any of his people, except out of necessity. We raid only to rescue my countrymen! Will Sakwari-cra lead us?"

Thad stood up, stared into Quobah's round, black-and-yellow eyes. "No! No such raid will take place. To attack an *Englasi* plantation is moon-madness."

"Not if you command us. Sakwari-cra is a wise warrior," Quobah's harsh voice insisted.

Thad's Iroquois crest swayed to the violent shaking of his head. "Such a raid would cause trouble between the Sakwaris and the *Englasi* both in Georgia and in Carolina."

Quobah's always pungent body odor grew more acrid while he growled, "Has my brother forgotten that it is against the law of Mico Thlucco Oglethorpe's people to own black slaves? It is forbidden to the dwellers in Savannah even to hire black laborers."

"That is truth. But this is not so in Carolina and, always, the *Englasi* stand together. If the Carolinians demand it, the Georgians will surely punish anyone who raids across the river. Therefore, I, Sakwari-cra, forbid any raid on *Englasi* property."

Thad then cried in a voice that carried throughout the encampment, "Sakwari-cra will not see his people hunted by anyone, either the *Englasi* or by their Indian allies, who number as the leaves on a tall tree."

A fringe of tarnished silver thread on Quobah's turban glinted when he threw back his head to glower into Thad's impassive features. Then in silence the African arose and retreated through the smoky darkness in lofty arrogance.

From the depths of the couch they shared, Taqua queried softly, "To-morrow, where will you go to hunt?"

"Among the canebrakes along Brim Creek. Toonahowie says they are seldom hunted because they lie too far from Tomo-chichi's town. A fire hunt should bring us plenty of buffalo."

"A fire hunt will call for many men."

"Yes. I will take with me all the Chickasaws and some other good hunters, too." He crawled in beside her, became conscious of the unfamiliar bulge of her belly pressed, smooth and warm, against the small of his back. He sighed, wondered why the contact somehow felt reassuring.

Would Quobah dare to disobey? Impossible. He, Thad Burton, Mico of the Sakwari Tribe, had spoken.

Chapter 4

FIRE HUNT

Determined that this, probably his last hunt for hire, should produce a record supply of meat, Sakwari-cra studied the densely wooded countryside with more than usual attention. Plenty of fresh deer trace and piles of buffalo droppings that were still hot—the hunters weren't reluctant to test by hand for heat—made him confident that a sizable herd must be feeding farther down a narrow peninsula formed by fast-flowing Brim Creek and the Ogeechee River.

With the exception of one-eyed Chula and Huspah, another Chickasaw, Thad posted his men in a loose line across the peninsula's base. Always attentive to detail, Thad guided his buckskin along the line to make sure that every hunter was carrying an adequate supply of arrows as well as charges of powder and buckshot for those few who had firearms.

As a final precaution the white Tuscarora saw to it that the party's horses were collected and securely tethered in a scrub pine grove maybe a quarter-mile behind the line of blockers. To guard them he detailed a pair of Yuchis known to be undependable marksmen; when whiffs of wood smoke reached them horses were apt to panic. If they weren't watched, they'd sometimes pull loose, panic, and likely break their legs.

Meanwhile, Chula and Huspah, a bandy-legged Chickasaw with drooping, fat eyelids, followed a game path winding along the river's edge; all the while they kept a sharp lookout for water moccasins and alligators lurking among the canebrakes. Such were very apt to be around on so warm a spring day; they'd also be hungry and short-tempered after their long hibernation. Several times the riders had to ride their mounts to higher ground because subtle splashings and the sudden agitation of canes and reeds argued that a crocodile or alligator might be nearby.

Once the riders reached that point where Brim Creek flowed into the Ogeechee they looked carefully about, then swung down from their horses, which they promptly hobbled. Chula looked pleased that the wind, at present, was blowing up the peninsula.

The day was so still that the Chickasaws could hear groups of feeding buffaloes snuffling, grunting, and breaking small branches as they moved about. While they waited for a distant blast on the mico's whistle, a pair of huge, black-red-and-white, ivory-billed woodpeckers swooped down to cling and feed on grubs breeding in a dead tree. Myriad warblers trilled saucy songs. Breeding ducks and water hens chuckled and quacked amid the reed beds. It seemed very peaceful, but neither hunter appreciated such serenity.

By the time that the signal sounded, faint as the cry of a lone goose winging high in the sky, the Chickasaws' greasy red-brown hides were beginning to become spangled with excitement.

Already, Chula had selected a thick clump of winter-killed broom grass which, with a handful of sun-dried moss, caught sparks from the flint and steel and almost exploded into flame. Tendrils of smoke shot skyward, then pale, yellow-red tongues of flames fanned out and, with terrifying speed, formed an irregular, crackling rank of fire that spread from one side of the peninsula to the other. An unnatural silence descended upon this scrub-pine wilderness; birds ceased to sing and all manner of creatures paused to estimate the nature and extent of their peril. Thanks to a breeze which sprang up and commenced to blow briskly in from the ocean, the conflagration soon made such a roar that the Chickasaws' hobbled horses stamped, plunged, and whistled in white-eyed terror.

Taller underbrush caught and spewed volcanoes of sparks into the air; spreading flames caused staccato reports, loud as pistol shots. Flames licked upward, but not quite high enough to ignite the lofty underbranches of loblolly, shortleaf, and slash pine. However, it fed greedily on myrtles, scrub palmettoes, magnolias, and swamp azaleas. Like fiery serpents, flames twined themselves about tangles of honeysuckle, wild grape, and supplejack. Now and then, the blaze would touch off a festoon of Spanish moss which, however, burned with reluctance.

"*Wagh!* Much game. Eat plenty, soon," grinned Huspah when in the piny woods sounded a chorus of frightened bawlings and snorts and the crashing of heavy bodies forcing passage through vine tangles and canebrakes along the bottom land. Higher, faster, spread the acrid wall of flame.

On remounting their trembling horses, the two Chickasaws had to fight hard to keep them under control; only through the merciless application of quirts were they able to force them to move back and forth over charred areas still smoldering from the conflagration.

At the same time the drivers yipped and yelled at the tops of their lungs. Flocks of doves, jewel-bright, green-and-yellow Carolina parakeets, quail, turkeys, and even an owl or two whirled out of the smoke and with robins, warblers, and woodpeckers flew frantically away over the water. Louder sounded crashing in the woods ahead of the flames.

Chula's pony almost threw him in avoiding a wildcat which bounded into sight, screeching and with its spotted fur smoldering. The cat, how-

ever, raced for Brim Creek and, plunging in, started swimming for the
far bank. It didn't get far before an alligator swirled into action. The
wildcat vanished as did most of the dozens of rabbits and foxes; muskrats
and raccoons, always fine swimmers, escaped for the most part. Terrible
sounds made by small animals perishing in the flames often penetrated the
roaring of the conflagration.

Once the wall of fire had consumed everything within reach, it rolled
inexorably onward, leaving behind dead or dying creatures, small birds,
and an amazing number of fatally scorched snakes, skinks, lizards, and
less familiar reptiles.

All at once Chula's companion, lean features streaming sweat, grunted
and pointed upward. Already flocks of huge, white-tailed vultures had
begun to circle, lower and lower, impatient for that moment when they
might plane earthward to feast on roasted box turtles, snakes, toads,
frogs, and salamanders. Inevitably, these handsomely feathered scavengers
would gorge themselves until they could scarcely hop about, let alone fly.

The drivers followed the conflagration's progress along the peninsula
until it reached a dark patch of woods where the undergrowth grew scant
for lack of sunlight. Now the flames seldom flared higher than six feet
above the ground, so the Chickasaws were able to see that the Ogeechee's
yellowish current was dotted with the heads of swimming animals: possums, coons, and even a panther and his mate. Probably through their
instinctive fear of alligators, no deer or buffaloes had taken to the water,
instead had fled inland at top speed.

Out of the smoke rocketed covey after covey of quail, several of which
fell suffocated under the horses' hoofs.

Rushing on again through comparatively open country, the fire roared
louder than ever as it swept on to meet a backfire set by Sakwari-cra and
his blockers.

Shortly after the first swirls of acrid smoke came drifting through the
trees, Thad Burton sighted a big buck. Apparently this deer wasn't really
frightened, was advancing with only normal caution. But when the buck
saw the backfire, which was just beginning to crackle, he went *whoosh!*
and his flag went up as he bounded back in the direction from which he
had appeared.

Soon, increasing numbers of deer ran up and halted before the twenty-
yard backfire, which was being checked by the main body of hunters
who used broken-off boughs to restrain flames burning toward them.

Once the backfire was brought under control, these bewildered creatures offered easy targets for Sakwari-cra's men. Dropping their branches,
they began whooping with excitement, caught up their weapons, and
started shooting. At such a range, twenty yards, a load composed of
three buckshot, propelled by an extra heavy charge, seldom failed to knock

over the target. Whenever an animal, driven frantic by the roar of the flames rushing up from behind, started across the strip, the bowmen got busy.

Thad Burton's heart hammered painfully, just as it had during his first fire hunt. He'd shot maybe three deer when he remembered, and yelled through ever-increasing clouds of hot, eye-stinging smoke rolling up the peninsula, "Kill no more deer! Wait for buffalo."

Although to obey was difficult because so many young bucks and wide-eyed does accompanied by spindle-legged, spotted fawns raced by almost close enough to touch, the Sakwaris remained obedient; they'd respect for their mico's sagacity.

Crashing sounds grew louder and Thad felt the ground tremble slightly, then a line of shaggy black-brown heads with short, curving black horns loomed amid the whirling sparks and billowing blue-gray smoke. Eyes rolling in terror, three bearded bulls galloped straight toward the gum tree Sakwari-cra had selected as his stand.

When Thad's musket boomed, the leading bison's front legs crumpled and, bellowing, it rolled over and over upon the backfire's black width. Then its grunting stopped and it fell over onto its side with one set of legs sticking stiffly upward.

For quicker results, the white Tuscarora then put aside his gun, to grab a heavy hunting bow and snatch a broad-headed arrow from the quiver hung to a handy limb.

As more horned and woolly heads burst out of the fumes, bowstrings began to sound in a series of harplike twangs, but a few muskets banged off to the right, so the musty reek of gunpowder continued to blend with the whirling wood smoke.

By the time the main conflagration closed in on the backfire's blackened area, a dozen huge buffaloes lay slumped, humped and ungainly, on the still-smoldering ground, among the slimmer carcasses of fallen deer.

In the woods behind the line of blockers, wounded animals were blundering, limping about, and bawling in pain. Most of these hurt animals, mainly cows or calves, were quickly run down and dispatched with more arrows whose gaudy scarlet feathering showed up sharply against rough brown pelts. Then the hunters ran about, expertly cutting the throats of the fallen game, it being essential to bleed these animals as soon as possible lest their meat spoil.

Meanwhile, the main fire had encountered the already burned-out area, so, finding nothing to feed it, it commenced to die. The stench of fresh blood, scorched flesh, and burning hair grew almost intolerable, an offense even to Indian nostrils.

For a space none of the killers, whose eyes glared whitely out of soot-darkened faces, said anything; they just caught their wind and gazed about, while the heat of their excitement died within them. Then they laughed and patted flat brown stomachs; this hunt had surpassed all expectations.

Thad next sent his less weary bowmen into the woods to kill off the balance of the wounded animals. The rest he ordered to cut out those perishable frontier delicacies, deer and buffalo tongues.

That his Sakwaris had slaughtered three times as much meat as could possibly be packed into Savannah bothered Thad not at all as he used damp moss to wipe blood from his hands and knife handle. Why worry? Didn't limitless herds of buffalo roam farther inland? All the while boasting of their prowess, the blood-splashed hunters selected only choice cuts from young buffalo and deer.

Long since the sky had become crisscrossed by ever-increasing flocks of carrion eaters who, enboldened by the reek of butchered carcasses, planed down to settle on dead trees to crane scaly heads and naked red necks. When the skinners deserted an outlying carcass these swooped down by the dozen and fell to tearing with dreadful efficiency. Soon the ground became covered by hissing, awkwardly hopping scavengers; some buzzards indulged in grotesque tugs-of-war over greenish-red entrails, dragged them back and forth over the charred ground.

Sakwari-cra had finished cutting out an especially fine buffalo's tongue when he became aware of a faint thudding noise. At first he reckoned it was caused by some lightly wounded buffalo circling back in search of its companions, but after he listened more carefully he knew he'd made a mistake. What he'd heard were the hoofs of a horse being ridden at a headlong gallop. Quickly, he guessed that the rider must be following a trail which wound northwest toward Savannah. He wiped reddened hands on his loincloth and ran over to retrieve Guillaume Potier's handsome musket.

His first guess was that this would be a messenger bringing news of a French, Spanish, or Yamasee raid.

"Arm! Arm!" he yelled to the scattered hunters. "Come here!"

The Sakwaris had just concealed themselves behind a windfall when the hoofbeats ceased. The rider had reined in among the startled buzzards and began to call in a strained, high-pitched voice, "Sakwari-cra! Sakwari-cra! Come to me quickly, quickly!"

To Thad's amazement Taqua rode into view with red hair streaming wildly and her face cruelly lashed by branches.

"Stop yelling like a starving bitch!" He spoke angrily because his first impulse was to cuff her for having ridden so hard when big with child. He strode out into the open, ready to haul her off her mount, but something about her expression restrained him.

"Why have you come here like this?"

Streaming sweat, gray-green eyes congested, Taqua for a moment could only gasp, then panted, "Come aside, Sakwari-cra, so no others hear."

"Well?"

"Last night Quobah, the blacks and the mixed bloods went away!"

Thad felt as if someone, unexpectedly, had slapped his face. Incredible; his sub-mico and blood brother should deliberately have disobeyed a direct command!

After helping Laure off a lathered mare he rasped, "In what direction did the black dogs start away?"

Taqua paused to gulp a mouthful of water from a gourd bottle fetched by Chula.

"Upriver. Toonahowie and some riders followed their trail till they crossed the river above the Tied Arse Village."

"Sure?"

"Sure." Laure dabbed at a deep scratch across her chin which had begun to sting because salty sweat was running into it.

Wagh! So at this very moment Quobah was leading his deserters toward Major Smollett's plantation!

Thinking hard, Thad kicked angrily at a clump of weeds, then, wooden-faced, said to the weary, disheveled girl, "You have done well, Taqua. Rest yourself. When Chula and the rest have finished dressing out, you will go back home with them."

"And you?"

"I go and try to stop this evil thing." He pelted over to jerk free his buckskin's rawhide halter shank, then mounted, all the while shouting instructions.

For a short while the bewildered hunters heard the buckskin's hoofs. It reminded Chula of the noise made by a ruffed grouse's wings drumming against a hollow log.

Chapter 5

A MATTER FOR THE RANGERS

When Acting Governor James Oglethorpe heard what Thad Burton had to say he reacted with promptness. He turned to John West, "This would seem a matter for the Rangers. Who is officer of the day?"

"Captain Challenger, I believe, sir. Captain MacPherson sailed for Beaufort this morning."

"Find Captain Challenger and present my compliments. I wish him to report here at once with ten Rangers, well-mounted and provisioned for a three-day absence."

"Aye, Your Excellency," and the secretary went pelting off as if the Devil was breathing fire on his coattails.

Oglethorpe called to a sentry pacing in the hot sunshine before his tent—he had insisted upon remaining under canvas until the last settler had been housed—"Leave your musket and run to the wharf. Tell the sergeant on duty that I wish readied at once a flatboat large enough to ferry Captain Challenger and ten mounted men over to South Carolina."

"Yes, sir!"

Once the militiaman had raced away, raising a series of evenly spaced puffs of dust behind him, James Oglethorpe settled back in his camp chair and, for the first time at close range, scrutinized the white Tuscarora.

"That you should ride so far and so hard to apprise me of Major Smollett's peril altogether astonishes me, Mr. Burton. Somehow, I had come to believe that you care very little for your own race."

Thad Burton drew himself up so abruptly that his high, twig- and leaf-speckled crest brushed the tent's fly. "I not care! I think only of trouble for *my* people!"

A silence followed in which the buckskin's labored breathing could be heard; the stallion was trembling with fatigue and was much too blown to wander off.

Oglethorpe jerked a nod. "Do such sentiments, sir, seem complimentary to your own kind? Apparently not; however, I thank you. In my position, it would prove exceedingly embarrassing to have a plantation in South Carolina attacked by a lawless band from Georgia. Since the prospect displeases you also, what do you think should be done?"

The two oddly assorted leaders surveyed each other until finally Thad Burton said, "O Mico Thlucco of the *Englasi,* let some Rangers ride hard to the plantation. Maybe they come too late. I go too." In a recurrence of rage over Quobah's insubordination, Thad ground his teeth just as would any thoroughly enraged Indian. "Try to find Quobah, turn him back."

From crest to moccasins, Oglethorpe surveyed this sinewy, barbaric figure liberally spattered with dried blood. "Mr. Burton, with pleasure I have observed how faithfully you have fulfilled your undertaking to supply my people with fresh meat. I wish you to consider enlisting in the militia as a scout. I stand prepared to pay you very well."

Deliberately, Thad folded arms across his wide, sweat-spangled chest as he drew himself up in the monumental dignity of a Tuscarora Raven. "Sakwari-cra thanks the *Englasi* mico thlucco, but where Sakwari-cra goes, he commands."

Lord! How pretentious could this small-time chief become? The corners of Oglethorpe's wide mouth twitched in silent amusement.

"I regret, sir, that you find it beneath your dignity to serve in the Georgia militia. D'you know, it's odd but *I* don't feel in the least inferior about obeying orders issued by my lawful superiors.

"However, I wish to express in tangible form my deep appreciation for your having ridden so far to bring me this warning."

Oglethorpe arose, bent over an ironbound chest. When he straightened he held out a pair of lightweight, silver-mounted dueling pistols. "I trust, Mr. Burton—or should I say Sakwari-cra?—that you will accept these trifles, with my compliments."

Thad Burton's deep-set eyes glistened. W*agh!* These graceful little pistols were by far the handsomest he'd ever seen. Of course he yearned for them, but he managed to shake his head. He might have accepted them if only the mico thlucco hadn't kept on calling him "Mr. Burton."

"No. You really must accept these, Sakwari-cra," Oglethorpe urged with a warm smile. "I am sure you will always employ them with honor."

The white Tuscarora hesitated, then suddenly grabbed the proffered butts with a schoolboy's eagerness. "Thank you—very much, O Mico Thlucco."

He cocked both pistols and tested the trigger pull before, in obvious delight, stroking their slim, silver-mounted barrels. Finally, he eased the weapons inside a broad rawhide belt. "Now Sakwari-cra kill plenty men, enemies of me—and you," he added quickly. He wanted better to express his gratitude, but the right words escaped him. All he could find to say was, "Sakwari-cra go now, scout for *Englasi.*"

Smiling, the accompanying trustee then presented his huge guest with a copper powder flask filled with fine priming charges, a bar of lead, a bullet mold to cast balls for these pistols, and a small pouch containing ready-cast bullets, then said, "I believe I hear the Rangers arriving. Please come with me." He stepped out into the sunlight.

Thad's buckskin, which had begun to nibble at a patch of sun-dried grass, raised its blunt head and stared at a party of horsemen who came trotting over from the guardhouse.

In one easy motion Wallace Challenger pulled in a long-legged brown mare and dismounted. Utterly ignoring the white Indian, Challenger halted and offered Oglethorpe such a careless salute that the acting governor frowned and barely nodded an acknowledgment.

"Please come inside, Captain. I will give you your orders."

When the yellow-haired Ranger captain emerged a few moments later, he walked up to Sakwari-cra and said in friendly enough fashion. "Understand ye're to go along with me. Well, ye're welcome." He stuck out a broad, bronzed hand.

Thad looked uncomfortable because he hadn't ever before shaken hands like a white man. All the same, he pumped the Ranger's fist vigorously enough until Challenger suddenly squeezed with the strength of a bear trap. Thad's knuckles crackled, then he returned the pressure so effectively that the Ranger laughed and let go. "That buckskin o' yours looks played out; you'd best use the spare mount we've brought along."

The weather-beaten and generally bearded Rangers grinned as they lolled comfortably sidewise in their saddles. After biting off a chew, one drawled, "Wal! Wal! 'Pears like we're finally goin' to have some doin's with the mysterious squaw man."

"Lay off that!" rasped Challenger. "Mr. Burton is to rank as a commissioned officer on His Excellency's staff. Besides, he rates as a mico among the redskins."

A swarthy sergeant named Sam Felton led a bony, black gelding over to Sakwari-cra. "Ye'd better let out them stirrups as fur as they'll go. Damn' if ye ain't longer-legged nor a Savannay stork."

He with the shaven head and black-dyed crest made no comment, merely jerked loose the rawhide cinch securing his own crude wooden saddle. When he lifted it off he exposed two bright red saddle sores.

"By Jesus, he *is* more Injun than white!" grunted the sergeant. "Look at that critter's back. Hey! What you fixin' to do?"

"Sakwari-cra ride own saddle."

"Like hell you will!" roared Challenger. "I ain't fixin' to have that mount's back ruined."

Oglethorpe appeared under his tent's fly, called, "Let Mr. Burton ride as he pleases, Captain. There is no time to be lost." He looked steadily into the Ranger officer's bright blue eyes. "With regard to Mr. Burton, my instructions are to be followed to the letter, sir."

Wallace Challenger's brown, high-cheekboned features assumed a stubborn expression. "Please, Yer Excellency, *don't* send this—this fellow along. We can find Smollett's place easy enough 'thout him. And please remember, sir, 'tis part of this fellow's own band we're going out against."

Bent to secure his new mount's cinch, Thad went scarlet under the old paint and dirt streaking his face; he always did, when he recognized contempt in a white man's tone.

In the fly's yellow-black shadow Oglethorpe's soldierly figure stiffened. "When I require advice from you, Captain Challenger, I will invite it. Meanwhile, you will obey orders!"

Presently, the Rangers rode down the bluff to the landing place, where a large flatboat lay manned and ready. Six fourteen-foot sweeps edged the craft out from shore and commenced to buck the current while the horses aboard stamped, quivered, and stared about them white-eyed. A pair of silvery-winged ospreys, hovering high above the river, whistled resentment over having their fishing interrupted.

When for two hours the detachment had trotted along a buffalo trail familiar to Wallace Challenger, he ordered a halt, despite Thad Burton's insistence that the detachment push on fast if they hoped to reach Major Smollett's plantation in time to forestall the Ashanti.

"Now you listen to me, ye damn' renegade!" Challenger snapped out of the gloom now closing in on the trail. "If you fancy I'm going to founder good horses and tire the fellers out so they can't shoot straight, yer in error. Misuse yer own horseflesh all you damn' please—Indians have plenty of crow baits to switch to when one gives out—but us Rangers have only *one* horse to carry us God knows how far, so we make much of 'em."

In order to learn, Thad fought down his anger; it was well known that most whites had forgotten more about horse handling than many redskins would ever learn.

" 'Make much'?"

To the white Tuscarora's astonishment Challenger dropped his hostile manner as if flattered by Sakwari-cra's genuine curiosity.

"Well, 'makin' much' means, first off, you always care for yer horse before yerself. For instance"—Challenger spoke slower, realizing that Thad was having trouble in understanding him—"when he's hot and tired he gets walked and rubbed down, so's he cools out easy.

"Only *after* yer nag's well cooled out do you let him drink and eat. Above all, you must always keep yer mount's saddle place clean so galls and sores don't form—like those on yer buckskin."

Thad learned a lot more about horse care during the next few hours. For instance: a horse should be allowed not more than a gulp or two of water when hot and on the move; hoofs should be examined frequently for splits or bruises; nostrils should be sponged out after a dusty ride—and so on.

"Why you loosen cinch—lift up saddle?"

"When us Rangers dismount for a little while, which is about every hour, we ease our mounts' girths and lift the saddlecloths free to let air get under a saddle blanket and let blood flow free under the critter's skin. Prevents galling."

"Why sometimes you get off and lead horse?"

" 'Cause it loosens a fellow's leg muscles; men don't tire so quick if they walk once in a while."

When it became impossible to see the trail any longer, the Rangers stopped to bivouac by the light of a three-quarter moon. Once saddles and blankets had been removed the Rangers fell briskly to rubbing the horses' legs; next they watered their mounts at a brook.

Only then did Challenger's men delve into haversacks and begin to munch greasy, crumbling chunks of corn bread and slabs of cold boiled meat.

Chapter 6

DAWN ATTACK

Amid luminous semidarkness owls quavered, whippoorwills and other night birds uttered often melodious notes. Foxes, wildcats, coons, and other small animals could be heard moving about. Farther away, a family of woods bison snorted and crashed their way through the forest.

For all that Thad Burton's legs and hard, lean buttocks ached from the long ride up to Savannah and then beyond, he remained strangely wakeful, so he tried to figure where Quobah and his men most likely would be at this time. All he could be sure of was that his insubordinate sub-mico's party had been on the move for about twenty-four hours.

While the Rangers lounged under a huge live oak and slapped mosquitoes until they fell asleep with heads pillowed on saddles, Sakwari-cra wondered whether Chula and the rest had packed the meat into Savannah before too much of it spoiled.

More fleetingly, he debated whether Taqua could have suffered any ill effects from her ride. It surely would be annoying were she to miscarry. Of course if she did, now that she had proved to be fertile, it would be easy enough to get her with another baby.

Maybe Laure was deserving of a reward of some sort? For instance, that pretty red petticoat he'd seen in Musgrove's trading house. She might make a pretty good squaw; certainly, she would turn out to be more useful than that puzzling Win-some creature. Well, if Taqua really wanted him to marry her perhaps, when he got back, he'd humor her; on the other hand, she appeared quite happy as she was.

He returned his thoughts to Quobah and decided that, very likely, the Ashanti probably would descend upon Major Smollett's plantation from a northerly direction. If he did, he must have had to make a long and circuitous route to avoid a series of all but impenetrable swamps through which flowed the sluggish Coosaw River.

If he knew Quobah, the African would keep the raiders moving all night so as to reach the vicinity of Smollett's plantation just before dawn. Then, in all probability, he'd pause long enough to send Kuma ahead to spy out the situation. The runaway, familiar with Fair View's layout and routine, could tell Quobah how best to circumvent the slave guards.

Since Thad hadn't been able to learn anything about the placing of Major Smollett's buildings there seemed to be no use in trying to plan any further. The time, he judged by the moon's position, must be well after midnight. Accordingly he went to sleep.

It seemed as if Sakwari-cra had just closed his eyes when he heard Challenger calling softly, "All right, you timber beasts, rise and shine! Feed yer faces. We move out in twenty minutes!"

Wide awake in an instant, Thad pulled a lump of rank-smelling, cold bacon from his war bag and chewed steadily on the greasy, gristly stuff.

In silence, the brief column then continued at a steady jog-trot along an old buffalo path.

Since waking, Thad had reached a decision. He would do his best to persuade Challenger to let him leave the Rangers—who seemed to know the way to Smollett's well enough—and, by dashing across country, attempt to intercept the raiders.

When he judged that dawn was less than an hour away, Thad kicked his horse abreast of Challenger's.

"I go now," he announced softly, eyes faintly aglitter in a patch of moonlight.

"Go where?"

"Ride north—cut Quobah's trail—make him turn back."

Challenger straightened in his saddle. "The hell you preach! You're not going anywhere but with me. I aim to teach those sons-o'-bitches a lesson that'll discourage nigra stealin' for a damn' long time." He peered hard at Thad. "Do I make myself clear, Mr. Burton—or isn't yer English good enough to understand what I'm sayin'?"

Thad fought down his rising anger, shrugged, "Sakwari-cra understands. I do what you say—now."

When the detachment was nearing a fork in the path, Sakwari-cra again urged forward his horse until he was only a stride behind Challenger and hissed, "Not make quick move, Capt'n!"

When Challenger turned slowly in his saddle, he realized that the white Tuscarora was holding one of Oglethorpe's pistols cocked and in line with his kidneys. Wisely, he kept quiet when Sakwari-cra swerved onto the trail's left branch and galloped off into the gloom. He figured that the Rangers wouldn't fire at him for, on a night so still as this, shooting would be heard a long way off.

Since crossing the Savannah, Quobah Tutu had been forced to rely upon Kuma to guide his fourteen dark-skinned raiders. Despite his poor condition, the escaped slave all night long had maintained a slow but steady dogtrot. The Ashanti's skinny, almost calfless legs led them around flower- and mosquito-filled swamps fringed by moss-festooned water oaks and majestic cypresses. Sometimes his course took them through cool glades of loblolly pine, laurel, red oaks, and myrtle. Occasionally, the now strung-out file plodded in grim silence across hot, palmetto- and scrub-pine-covered sand barrens which often appeared to be limitless in extent.

As second-in-command, the ex-prince had designated a half-Alibamu, half-Negro mustee who called himself Santo. Lacking both ears, he had a huge, hooked beak of a nose and was otherwise ugly.

Once the raiders lost considerable time when Kuma followed a wrong fork in the trail which led them several miles away from Major Alexander Smollett's handsome, white-painted plantation house, which dominated a complex of barns, stables, sheds, and slave quarters. The great house lay, Kuma claimed, near the center of a wide pattern of sour-smelling rice fields.

Every once in a while, for his guide's benefit, Quobah would order a halt to permit his followers to drink from a brook and gulp down a few mouthfuls of food brought from the Sakwari encampment. Not that there was any real need of rest for these dark-skinned Sakwaris; one and all, they appeared tireless, but the escaped slave's strength seemed to be giving out. More frequently now Kuma's eyes began to roll in their sockets and he set his big splayfeet down heavily. Toward sunset the fugitive's blue-black skin began to assume an ashen hue. Then, without warning, he pitched flat onto the trail, gasping and moaning feebly.

There was nothing for it but to halt. So, to speed his recovery, the raiders made Kuma as comfortable as possible and Quobah even risked kindling a small fire in order that a chunk of jerked buffalo meat could be boiled into a strengthening broth.

While he lay recuperating, Kuma described some of the Barbadian's punishments. Often, after an offender had been flogged, the major would order capsicum, salt, or red pepper rubbed into a man's or even a woman's back. Lesser culprits would be locked into tiny, airless cells, fed only on salted stockfish. When their throats began to constrict and burn unbearably he'd pretend to relent and order them to be given all the water they wanted—salt water!

Any even halfway comely young Negress would surely be summoned to the great house, there to perform lascivious dances in the nude before the major and his guests; the alternative to an uninteresting performance was a whipping administered on the spot.

Although Fair View had been seated only a short time ago, already there were plenty of light-skinned babies scampering about the "quarters"—which was no wonder because here, as in Jamaica and Barbados, white "bookkeepers"—slave drivers in reality—were offered a bonus for every mulatto they begot, mulattoes fetched fancy prices on the slave block and were in great demand as house servants.

The dark-complexioned Sakwaris listened, squatting on their hams with fingers tight about their few firearms or on the hafts of Indian spears and tomahawks.

The moon had drifted past its zenith before Kuma muttered that he felt able to continue. Even to Quobah, it was remarkable that this scarred starveling could so quickly have recruited his strength. Probably this was due to the fact that he once had been an Ashanti fighting man.

The guide's eyes shone clear again, his step was almost springy as he led off at a faster trot than before. The few ornaments Quobah had given Kuma to build up his self-respect set up a soft *clink-clink* to his stride.

False dawn was tinging the sky a faint leaden-silver color when the raiders splashed across a rocky ford, then paused on the edge of a wide, flat area in which glowed many smoldering stumps, evidence that, before long, this would become another of Major Smollett's rice fields.

"Between here and the great river," Kuma panted in Ashanti, "lies the barracoon in which new field hands are kept. The older ones with families live in a little village beyond the great house." He turned to Quobah's massive outline. *"Kwee!* my prince! Shall Kuma go and find out where slave guards are?"

"Go at once, Kuma, but return with all speed. Dawn is not far off."

Once the fugitive had disappeared into the underbrush, Quobah in a harsh undertone said, "Attend to what I say, and remember to obey. No Englishman is to be slain unless your life surely is at stake. The English have long memories and are merciless when they believe themselves wronged. I know."

By brilliant moonlight, Sakwari-cra's sub-mico studied one ebony face after another and felt reassured by their expressions. All the same, he felt trouble in his stomach. Had he set a wise example by so openly defying Sakwari-cra's authority? Let but a single small exception in the application of tribal discipline appear, then who could predict the end result? He was sufficient of a soldier to appreciate such a danger. Sadly, he wished that Sakwari-cra had been willing to come along.

Sakwari-cra dismounted and by the light of early dawn commenced, at a dogtrot, to lead his horse along a trail on which he'd found a number of fresh footprints. When it grew lighter it didn't take him long to conclude that, for sure, Quobah's raiders had passed this way—and very recently. Muddy water was still seeping into footprints made when they crossed the boggy stretch. One imprint was so enormous that none but Quobah's foot could possibly have created it. At the sight of it Thad's anger surged anew: what motive could have caused the experienced sub-mico, usually so levelheaded, to embark on this worse than absurd at-tempt?

The approach of daylight soon made it possible to determine that the disobedient African had brought with him about a dozen men. Since the trail grew wider at this point he remounted and, after breaking off a switch, lashed his mount into a jolting trot which gave him little time to bend under low-sweeping limbs and to avoid loops of honeysuckle and other creepers.

Every time the rider entered a piny woods or sand barren he switched the Rangers' mount into a lumbering gallop which set the air to whistling past his short silver earrings and chilled the shaved areas on his scalp.

To Thad's disgust it became evident that this ungainly beast must be tiring, for the gelding began to tick sharply while jumping fallen logs, then it stumbled and almost fell. Bitterly, he lamented that the Tuscaroras never had been a "horse tribe," so he'd been forced to learn riding and horse handling as best he might.

Chapter 7

FAIR VIEW PLANTATION

The sky began to redden so rapidly that Quobah Tutu ground filed teeth in an agony of suspense before Kuma reappeared with gaunt and ribby body dripping with mingled sweat and dew, but his sunken eyes seemed bright and alert.

"I bring good news to Quobah, son of Osai Tutu," he wheezed. "No *buckra* yet stands before the barracoon gate."

Quobah demanded sharply, "No guard? Is not one soldier always on duty there?"

"Yes, My Lord. Sometimes two."

Like spurs, anxiety began to rowel Quobah's mind. Why was there no sentry at a customary post? Could this be a ruse or a lucky accident? Should he go on with this attack or pull back and wait for nightfall?

An immediate decision was imperative for, already, songbirds were testing their morning notes and groups of graceful gray-brown Virginia
deer began to browse steadily toward the forest's edge.

"We attack now," he announced, and with a quick gesture straightened
a long white heron's feather drooping from his turban.

As he'd seen Sakwari-cra do a hundred times he checked his musket's
flint and priming, then warned others bearing firearms to do likewise.
The rest merely spat and again ran thumbs along the razor-sharp edges of
spears and war hatchets.

At a jolting trot, the raiders started off along a cart track which was
invisible from the plantation buildings because of banks of earth
raised to dike a new rice field.

Once the buildings came into view the Ashanti's heart began to pound
with the hope that, in a little while, a good many fellow Africans would
be following him toward Georgia and freedom across the Savannah. He
was glad now he'd warned Santo that he must guide the fugitives to
safety should a rear-guard action develop.

Taking a fresh grip on his musket, the black giant, at a dead run, raced
across a wide, mist-veiled field toward a low hurdle fence which stood before the log barracoon's low outline.

Quobah soon remembered and slackened his pace in order to permit
his followers to deploy into a reasonably even line abreast. All were running like hungry wolves after a cow moose—all except Kuma, who again
had collapsed.

All at once, the African giant saw a man run out of a barn toward a
bell mounted on a thick post near the barracoon. Obviously, it must be
used to sound an alarm or to toll the hours for the plantation's daily
routine.

The Ashanti at once put on a burst of speed, hoping to reach the
hurdle fence before that bell could sound. He was gathering himself to
leap over when, from behind the fence, appeared a short row of heads
and gleaming musket barrels. He was only a few yards from the barrier
when screeching yells arose and muskets roared in his face.

Quobah, son of Osai Tutu, felt a heavy ball smack into his left forearm with an impact so powerful that, big as he was, he was spun half
about and forced to drop his musket. Half-dazed, the black giant swayed
and almost fell, but the sound of shrieks and shrill screams rising to
either side made him rally.

A white man's deep voice bellowed, "Somebody shoot that damn' slave
who's crawling off to the left!"

Then Captain Challenger roared, "No! Hold yer fire, boys! Save as
many of these damn' cutthroats for hangin' as ye can!"

The smoke cleared sufficiently to reveal a bald, heavy-bodied *buckra* who must be Major Smollett. Red-faced, he was brandishing a brass-guarded cutlass and bellowing, "Hell's fire, no! Cut 'em down! Then gut 'em and hack off their hands and heads!"

With surprising agility, Smollett then scrambled up onto the fence and, jerking a pistol from his belt, yelled, "Come on! They're running!"

Instantly, Challenger's voice, harsh as the rasp made by iron against a grindstone, rang out, "No! Stand fast, Rangers! May be more of 'em around."

Making thin, shivering noises, ramrods quickly were driven home and powder horns were tilted.

Quobah uttered a wailing cry, then yelled, "Back! Go back! Each for himself!" *Ehu!* This was as bad as that raid on Kumassee, when he'd been taken prisoner for the first time. Bent well over, he bounded across the field in a series of zigzags which carried him toward a tongue of underbrush licking out from the woods.

More muskets banged and, all about him, bullets buzzed and whined. One stung him on the left shoulder, but the African plunged on, clutching his useless arm.

Somehow he found the place where Kuma, Santo, and two others were waiting, eyes white-ringed with terror.

"Scatter! *Buckras* close!" he panted, then dashed on, leaving his turban dangling from a low branch.

Alarmingly soon, tracking dogs began to set up their deep and fear-inspiring clamor. Locking his teeth against almost unbearable pain the huge Ashanti, followed by Kuma and Santo, pelted back along the trail they'd followed earlier. He knew he was leaving a trail of blood, but there wasn't a thing he could do about it. When the pursuers came closer would be the time to peel off this path one at a time. Possibly, the bloodhounds, in their haste, might miss some of these branching trails.

The instant Sakwari-cra, who'd heard shooting in the distance, recognized the belling of hounds, he reined his mount out of sight into a myrtle thicket. Lips tightened into a grim slash, he waited until Quobah pounded into sight with eyes gleaming white as bleached clamshells. Thad fought down his wrath and kicked his mount back onto the trail. Before the African knew he was there, Thad had bent and, heavy as Quobah was, had heaved him, dripping blood, across the bay's withers. Although the gelding staggered under this additional weight, it managed to recover and lurch heavily onward.

Nothing was said until Thad reined aside after following a deer path a short distance. Callously, he shoved Quobah onto the ground, where he sprawled with his wounded arm draining into a patch of emerald-green moss.

Sakwari-cra snarled, "*Konut tchigi i aynum aulidshio!* A skunk should stay under his house! Never come near me!" Then he drummed his heels against his mount's side and guided it into the depths of the brightening forest.

Sakwari-cra reached Savannah at dusk of the same day that Quobah's attack had failed. Tight-jawed, he gave Lieutenant Savey, officer of the day, a curt, lying explanation as to how he'd become separated from Captain Challenger's detachment. Despite the lieutenant's profane orders that he remain and explain further, Thad remounted and rode off to his encampment.

First Taqua and Hapeyah, then Chula, Huspah, and Shatara came out of their huts; all looked deeply anxious, but none spoke.

Ignoring the rest, Thad took his two Chickasaw Ravens aside, growling, "If any disobedient ones return, kill them or drive them away. They are no longer Sakwaris."

This order proved unnecessary; not one of the warriors who'd departed with Quobah ever reappeared.

A day later, Wallace Challenger and his party rode in and reported to James Oglethorpe that five raiders had been killed, four others had been run down, branded, and enslaved for Major Smollett's benefit. Their leader, unfortunately, had managed to escape.

Of the three who'd escaped nothing more was heard until, a few days later, a wandering Yuchi trapper drifted into the Sakwari encampment. Among other bits of news he reported that a giant Negro with a festering, badly shattered arm and a one-eyed mustee had been sighted in the vicinity of Fort Moore. The Yuchi thought they were heading toward French territory.

Just before sunup next day, Captain MacPherson strode up to the acting governor's tent. There was an uneasy expression on his Indian-like features.

"Well, Captain," said James Oglethorpe, "what brings you here so soon after Phoebus has guided his chariot o'er the horizon?"

The Scot looked baffled. " 'Phoebus,' sir-r? Some Indian?"

"Forgive me. 'Tis too early for classical references—even pointless ones. You wished to see me?"

"Aye, sir-r." MacPherson's slash of a mouth flattened. "Last night the Sakwaris pulled out, dog, squaw and papoose."

Oglethorpe hoped his dismay wasn't evident. Here was an unpleasant surprise coming so soon after he'd sensed that Thad Burton might be won back to civilization and of service to the Crown.

"Sorry to hear this. Where is Burton taking his people?"

"No one knows, sir-r. He may have gone to join the Yamasees."

Oglethorpe was startled into saying, "Surely he'd not do that! The Yamasees are our only known Indian enemies!"

"Would he not? Don't doubt it, sir-r. There's no trusting a renegade. Ever!"

Chapter 8

A CORNET OF THE BLUES

One very warm night shortly after Captain Challenger's return from across the Savannah, Winsome Brooks awoke to a series of muffled moans and stifled sobs from Helen Bayless. Evidently her roommate was suffering from another of those vivid nightmares which, lately, had been afflicting her. Propped on an elbow, Winsome listened to the blood-thirsty whining of myriad midges and mosquitoes which bit like the stab of a thousand dull needles and alternated during the day with clouds of stinging flies to render life a misery.

The light of a gibbous moon beating in the sleeping room's glassless window revealed Helen squirming on coarse blankets thrown back because of the night's humid heat. Her roommate's short but slim legs worked convulsively—so did her arms. Her sweat-soaked night rail had worked down from her shoulders enough to expose large, dark-nippled, and increasingly rotund breasts.

In her sleep the girl began to wail, "Have pity, kind sir, I vow—I didn't —wrong. Oh-h-h, what—awful place! Can't abide horrible prison—stink— Please, sir, I'm so very hungry."

Curious, despite herself, Winsome, although plagued by the whining mosquitoes, sat up and continued to listen when the dreamer broke into incoherent mumblings, spoken this time in easier tones. "See the moon is scattering—star-diamonds across—wave tops. Oh, Archie, sweet Archie. Archie, mustn't— Just kiss—there's a pet. No. Of course I—love—but, ah —ah, please, let me be. Watch out. Here comes a sailor—"

Archie? Yes. Irritably, Winsome fanned at the tormenting insects, then, despite the sweltering heat, pulled up her blanket to protect her head and shoulders.

So, as she long had suspected, it had been blue-eyed Lieutenant Archi-bald Glen with the cavalryman's heel-dragging stride and powder-marked cheek who was responsible for that hard swelling which was causing limpid-eyed Helen Bayless daily to ease her apron ties.

Why hadn't that silly girl long since acted sensibly and told her seducer about her condition? Well, one thing was sure, Helen must soon face facts since her pregnancy couldn't be kept secret much longer. But the one time she'd suggested telling Glen, that habitually placid young woman had flared up and vowed she'd never do such a thing. Further, she'd extracted a solemn promise that never, under any conditions, would Winsome discuss her problem with anyone.

Half suffocated under her sour-smelling pillow, Winsome began to get angry, decided: If that pretty, young idiot won't speak up I'll have to contrive some means of apprising this ex-cornet of The Blues of his responsibilities. But how? Wish I hadn't sworn not to speak to anyone. It's really too bad we Brookses never go back on our pledged word.

Winsome broke off musing because of a dry scraping noise just outside the house. The cat, Ipswich Nicholas, who'd been sleeping at Helen's feet, leaped up, back and tail bristled. Who was out there? A skulking settler trying to steal something—of late there'd been a lot of petty thieving. An Indian? Then she heaved a sigh of relief when the dry scrabbling of claws over hard-packed earth told her that another alligator had invaded Savannah's streets in hopes of catching some household animal unawares. Several dogs and a calf had vanished in this fashion. The settlers, justifiably, were terrified of these brutes. Presently, the saurian, evidently a big one, rustled onward, leaving Ipswich to brood darkly on Helen's feet.

Unable to endure such stale air any longer, Winsome tossed away her pillow and, emitting a soft *whoosh!*, pushed aside a strand of hair that was stuck to her sweat-beaded forehead and resigned herself to feeding insects for a while. What *was* to be done? In a few days, Helen's pregnancy must become obvious to even the most imperceptive inhabitant of Savannah—which by now boasted nearly forty one- or two-story dwellings of rough-sawn planks. How, without breaking her word, could she let Archibald Glen know what was amiss?

"A fine night and a-a-all's well!" Through the window came the faint hail of a sentry atop the recently completed watchtower. Forty feet tall, it loomed at the end of the guardhouse and a barracks which now housed bachelor officers of the newly formed militia in addition to the twenty settlers who were called, every twenty-four hours, for guard duty.

Because, for the moment, she could find no answer to her dilemma, Winsome contented herself by listening to other sentinels along Savannah's perimeter report in varying clarity and volume. Many had criticized Oglethorpe's decision to keep twenty able-bodied men always ready for action—this practice seriously reduced the force of laborers, already thinned through accident and disease; long since, the Negro workers lent

by Carolinian planters had departed and none could be had to replace
them. The acting governor, however, had remained inflexible on this
policy of defense despite Tomo-chichi's assurances that the ex-paupers
had nothing to fear either from his Yamacraws or from any band owing
him submission.

This peaceful state of affairs, the shriveled mico thlucco had declared,
would prevail at least until the Great Council of the Creek Confederation
convened in the near future; after that who knew what might happen?
Some people insisted upon calling the Creek Confederation an "empire" for all that, at present, it was headed only by a paramount chief
who was not an emperor like Old Brims.

This Great Council, Colonel Bull, predicted, probably would be held
near the middle of May at Kashita, the confederation's peacetime capital;
in times of war Coweta became the center of the Creek Nation's military
activities.

Now hopelessly wide awake, Winsome recognized the distant grumbling
and coughing of a new guard detail turning out to relieve sentries who'd
been on duty since sundown. Presently, she thought to recognize Archibald Glen's clear, carrying voice issuing commands.

There followed a dull *tramp-tramp* of feet shuffling along. Owls,
which for some time had been hooting, abruptly fell silent, but the roar
of bull alligators fighting amid the marshes bordering the Savannah never
let up.

Without difficulty, Winsome could visualize the relief's route. First, this
sleepy, ill-tempered detachment of armed civilians would straggle past the
southeast spring, which was where women living on this side of the settlement drew water and did their washing. Next, the detail would follow a
winding wooded path which, passing above the laundry point, led on
toward Post Number Two.

Certainly, it was Archibald Glen who spoke: "Pick up those damned
feet, you clods! Won't you ever learn to move without making a racket?"

Then, like a vivid shooting star, an idea flashed across Winsome's
imagination. To learn which militia officer would post the reliefs tomorrow, and at what time, would be easy enough to ascertain from the duty
roster, which always was tacked to the guardhouse door.

It proved simplicity itself for Winsome to learn that Lieutenant Glen
had been ordered to make an inspection tour of the outposts at five the
next afternoon. This, she felt, was fortunate; by that hour the spring
would be deserted, the women having gone home to cook supper.

Artfully, Winsome delayed Helen's and her own departure to the
laundry place until late in the day. "'Twill be cooler then," she pointed
out. "And we won't have to listen to such a lot of malicious gossip."

The two young women, supervised by Ipswich Nicholas, were engaged in beating not only their own undergarments but also smallclothes, belonging to the two doctors, on a flat stone using broad wooden paddles, when at last Winsome heard twigs crackle and the sound of feet on the patrol route.

Ipswich, who had been stalking an imaginary mouse in a clump of ferns, also caught the footsteps, paused to cock pointed, white-tipped ears. Breathless all at once, Winsome judged that whoever was up yonder soon would come within earshot.

Heart sinking for fear she might miscalculate the moment of Glen's passage, Winsome said in a clear, carrying voice, "Say what you will, Helen, I think it's high time you faced up to facts, no matter how unpleasant. This morning I noticed Mrs. Coltbred looking mighty hard at you. Surely, she's guessed that someone, if not Archibald Glen, has got you with child."

The inspecting officer's footsteps weren't loud; all the same, she noticed that, abruptly, they ceased.

Helen, with a terrified expression, raised a dripping forefinger to her lips. "Sh-h-h! Do be quiet. Remember, you promised never to breathe a word about it. Suppose someone overheard you?" The former governess, face aflame, dropped her paddle and cast fearful glances all about.

"Hate me if you will, Helen Bayless, but I'm not going to stand idly by and let you ruin your life. In a few days everybody will notice your swollen belly."

"Quiet! For God's sake, be quiet!" wailed the distracted creature.

But Winsome remained inexorable. "Know what will happen then? You'll be brought before the governor's council, then God only knows what they'll do with you!"

Convinced that he on the patrol path must be listening, the Brooks girl wrung Dr. Cox's shirt with almost savage vigor. "They'll want to know who got you with child, and they'll find out, too."

Great tears formed in the Bayless girl's large, sherry-brown eyes and commenced to slip down her sunburned cheeks.

"Have pity, Winsome!" she whimpered. "How can you torment me so? I—I don't know what to do. Maybe I'd best run off to Purysburg or maybe even to Charles Town."

She felt so sorry for the girl, but Winsome remained relentless, although it was difficult. "And how would you be received in either place? You with no wedding band and a belly big as a washbasin?"

"Well, there's always the river—"

"You stop such wicked, senseless talk! If worse comes to worst"—she lowered her voice and, bending above the flat stone, began to scrub a badly patched petticoat—"I'll try to find you a better way out."

Silently, she added, And I'll do it, too. I've survived a worse situation.

Despite the afternoon's drenching heat, the girl from Boston shivered
on recalling the aftermath of Pa's funeral, Captain Starbuck's advances,
and that night in Charles Town Jail.

"Oh, I—I hope you can. You're a true friend and I—I'm so afraid."

Many minutes after the two had resumed their laundering Winsome
heard the invisible listener's footsteps move on—more softly than before.

That evening Captain Wallace Challenger sat with heavy, sun-bleached
brows joined in concentration. He loathed paper work of any sort but
had been forced to complete an inventory of the armory's contents, when
Lieutenant Archibald Glen tramped into the mess hall-orderly room, sailed
his hat so expertly that it settled upon a peg driven into the log wall.
Next, humming cheerfully, he seated himself behind a board table upon
which reposed a wooden platter of sea biscuits, a few slabs of cold roast
wild pig, and the scant remains of a turkey.

"Thank you, sir, for trading inspections." Glen slipped a long-bladed
knife out of its sheath and impaled a piece of meat. "I'll confess I was
curious to learn what sort of an out-lot the trustees have assigned me."
He fell silent and began to chew while Wallace Challenger laboriously
signed the inventory.

"And what was it like?" the Ranger demanded without looking up.

"Well, sir, while I'm no farmer or forester, it looks good. At least my
forty-nine acres aren't worthless pine barrens like those poor devils have
been allotted." The ex-cornet of The Blues gulped down a huge mouthful
of spring water. "There are several stands of fine big trees on it. Pines.
Don't know what kind but they look stout enough for the Royal Navy."
Glen cut off a turkey wing, went on, "'Nother piece of luck—my ground's
already been burned over and a good while back."

Rawhide bands holding together the captain's hickory chair creaked
under his bulk when he straightened. "Ye intend to farm it? The trustees
expect it, you know."

"I suppose I must, though I loathe laboring with my hands. I'll try to
sell it as soon as I can. After all, I'm a soldier, not a bloody peasant."

Challenger shook his big blond head. "That you'll not be allowed to
do for a long time. If you don't farm yer grant it will revert to the company."

"Now there *is* a rum note!"

"You should have read yer undertaking more properly."

"Expect I should have," answered Glen, then dropped onto a backless
stool and, thrusting out slim, well-shaped legs, used a jack to tug off his
well-patched ankle boots. When one of his toes leaked through a
grimy sock he summoned a wry grin and wiggled it. "Lord! if Lord
Wilton—he was my capt'n in The Blues—ever saw such a sight, I'd have

caught holy hell. Suppose I'd best look for a woman willing to mend for me."

Challenger considered his companion for a long moment and at the same time rubbed yellow bristles sprouting on his jaw. "Aye, yer right. You'd better find for yerself a woman willin' to sew for ye *right away*—and I don't mean just anybody!"

The Ranger's altered tone prompted Glen to peer across the mess-room, smokily illumined by thick slivers of candlewood crammed into crude wooden sconces.

Before the militia officer could comment, Challenger continued, "Before yer—er—misfortune, I believe you were an officer in the Household Cavalry?"

The handsome young fellow began to look uneasy. "Why, yes, sir. I was indeed, but only a cornet. What of that?"

"Being a cornet—if my British-trained friends ain't misinformed me—meant that you were waiting to become a commissioned officer—and accepted as a gentleman." A sardonic smile appeared on the Ranger's leathery lips. "Of course, being only a semisavage colonial, I ain't too sure on that point. Am I right?"

Lieutenant Glen got to his stockinged feet, features flaming. Said he in clipped Hampshire accents, "I fear, Captain Challenger, I don't perceive what you're driving at."

"Be patient and you will. So, if you were a cornet in The Blues it means that you, presumably, were *almost* a gentleman?"

The flush deepened on Glen's high, sharply outlined cheekbones. "Of course. Why, sir, do you ask?"

Looking his homespun-shirted subordinate straight in the eye, the Carolinian said not unpleasantly, "Because, Glen, I've a notion you'll soon be called upon to act like one."

A penetrating stillness prevailed until Archibald Glen, his pale blue eyes narrowing, spoke in a taut voice, "Captain, I begin to find your manner and speech offensive. Perhaps you'd better explain."

In no great hurry, Challenger heaved his dark-green-shirted bulk to its feet, pushed back his chair, and, legging fringes tapping softly, swung over to confront the younger man. "During yer trip over from England, Glen, did you, or didn't you, have er—intimate relations—oh, hell! Did ye tumble a certain young lady?"

The bluish powder stains on Glen's right cheek began to show up sharply as his color receded. "Lady? There were no ladies aboard the *Anne*. Every last female among 'em was traveling 'on the Charity.'"

"I fear my colonial speech confuses you, so I'll be blunt. Did you, or did you not, seduce a young woman by the name of Helen Bayless?"

Young Glen's jaw fell open and his aggressive attitude vanished. "Why

—why—yes, sir." Then he stiffened once more and glared. "And if we did—er—tumble, as you put it, what of that?"

Challenger's expression relaxed. "It means nothin' to me, but I'll venture it's of considerable concern to Mistress Bayless."

By the candlewood's yellow-red smoky glare, Challenger watched the other's eyes waver. Glen looked miserably confused. "What else did Helen tell you?"

"She's told me never a word. What I've learned about her sorry condition was by pure accident. Since you don't seem to be aware of it, young feller"—which was absurd because Wallace couldn't have been his elder by more than two or three years—"she must be near three months in the family way."

The ex-cornet looked genuinely aghast. "Oh, my God! Then Helen is *pregnant?*"

"If you've any doubts, just look at her closely."

"But—but *why* didn't she tell me?"

He raised his eyes, looked the huge Ranger full in the face. "I swear on my honor, sir, although I see her almost daily, Helen's never given me the least hint."

"Well, now you've more than a hint; in fact, ye're faced with a certainty."

Again a silence descended in which night noises became abruptly noticeable.

Archibald Glen drew a slow, uneven breath, then said steadily, "Now I understand, sir, your remarks concerning a cornet of The Blues. I may have been a fool regarding money matters, sir, but I assure you that I am no rogue."

Challenger's heart went out to this unhappy young man. After all, he himself had done plenty of things which were best forgotten. "I take it, then, that you'll do what's right?"

Glen smiled faintly at his superior. "Isn't it fortunate that, other considers aside, I am very fond of Mistress Bayless?"

Challenger thrust out a calloused hand covered with blond hairs, "Best wishes, Mr. Glen."

Banns were published the next day and tacked to a notice board planted before Savannah's half-built courthouse.

A week later, Helen Bayless, bound agonizingly tight around her middle, and Archibald Glen, Gent., were joined in holy matrimony by the Reverend Henry Herbert in the presence of James Edward Oglethorpe, Esq., and the council.

Chapter 9

STRATEGIC SURVEY

Acting Governor Oglethorpe settled back in his chair and, quite with-out appearing to, studied his council's brown, care-lined faces on either side of the document-littered table. While Dr. Tailfer droned on, speaking at too great length concerning a new treatment for snakebite, his gaze traveled from Colonel Bull's nick-nosed, rugged features to "Colonel" Ballou's lean and parchment-hued visage.

Closing invisible "ear lids" upon Tailfer's pedantic voice, the accom-panying trustee again debated this enigmatic character's true history. Was this tough old Swiss only partially a *poseur*, or had he actually participated in all those campaigns he'd mentioned?

Ballou's accounts contained so many obvious truths and yet so many contradictions and elements of braggadocio that he was inclined to place him in a class with Captain John Smith and his egregious *History of My Life*. What a flamboyant character, that fellow Smith! But it was certain that he'd figured largely in the painful beginnings of Jamestown.

What a coincidence that Petre Ballou and Captain John Smith both should claim to have fought—always with distinction—for the Kings of Poland and Hungary. Strange, also, that this Swiss also claimed to have been captured and enslaved by the infidels. Stranger still, Ballou, too, claimed to have escaped through the devotion of a lovesick harem girl.

Nor did the parallel end there; no less than John Smith, the old Swiss was not reticent in claiming well-deserved honors unjustly denied. He could describe in colorful detail his part in the wars waged by mighty, but unheard-of, African kings and emperors.

Yet an exasperating fact remained; plans drawn by the adventurer for the defense of Savannah were sound, if not brilliant.

Oglethorpe's gaze then sought the angular features of Archibald Glen, wearing the fatuous, slightly bemused look of a recent bridegroom. Glen's promising, thought the accompanying trustee, but not overly clever yet.

On Glen's left brooded hawk-nosed and saturnine Captain MacPher-son. At the moment he was scratching an infected mosquito bite on the back of his neck. What a typical, hard-bitten Highlander he was! Right now he suggested an Indian, rather than a Scot, because he'd allowed his lank black hair to grow long enough to hang in braids.

Beyond the senior Ranger captain sat Thomas Causton, Savannah's recently appointed bailiff, a hearty, blatantly ambitious individual who, to Oglethorpe's way of thinking, seemed much too prone to fawn before his superiors.

Finally, Oglethorpe considered Wallace Challenger, lounging comfortably beyond Causton; like MacPherson, he had the indefinable restless, half-wild manner of men reared in the wildernesses of North America.

After smoothing a map crudely drawn at his request by John Musgrove and James MacPherson, the accompanying trustee spoke up. "Gentlemen, I take it that we are agreed upon the policy, nay, the *necessity* of protecting Savannah by establishing a cordon of strategically situated and enforted hamlets."

Colonel Bull's ponderous head inclined, "Reckon so, Yer Excellency. Me, MacPherson, Challenger and Mr. Ballou"—wickedly, the Carolinian emphasized the civilian title and thereby earned an angry glare from the wrinkled Swiss—"are set to go along with you in locating such strong points."

"That is a very handsome offer, sir. Most certainly I shall entertain your suggestions. For instance, Colonel Ballou"—ever tactful, Oglethorpe was at pains to assuage the old mercenary's feelings—"once such sites are selected I will rely upon you, as a distinguished military engineer, to lay out the defenses—such as they may be!"

Oglethorpe's rich and even accents continued, "Since I deem it necessary to take with me both of our Ranger officers—and most of their men —I desire Mr. Causton to remain in command here. Lieutenants Glen and Savey will serve as his subordinates. During my absence, Mr. Causton also will act as chief magistrate.

"Colonel Bull, how many Rangers ought we to take along? And how many Yamacraws?" Once again Oglethorpe had cause, silently, to lament the abrupt departure of Burton and his dependable Sakwaris.

Bull tilted back his head to stare at leaf shadows silhouetted on the sun-drenched canvas above. "Well," he drawled, "I reckon we can make out with, say, ten Rangers and two dozen Yamacraws and I'll want either Toonahowie or Kawea to go along. They know this neck o' the woods down to the last rabbit trot. 'Tis a damn' shame, sir, the Yamacraws have got to bickerin' with the Yuchis again. We just might run into trouble in that direction, sir."

Oglethorpe got to his feet, announcing pleasantly, "Very well. The survey party will set out tomorrow at seven of the morning. Gentlemen, I bid you all a very good day."

Chapter 10

A MULTITUDE OF TROUBLES

Departure of the acting governor and his reconnaissance party to select the sites for outposts was postponed indefinitely because alarming rumors arrived in Savannah. For one thing, it was reported that many Lower Creek micos had been outraged by Tomo-chichi's illegal cession of Creek lands to the Georgia Company. In fact, Oglethorpe realized that, if something were not done, and promptly, to convince these malcontents that the Yamacraw lease was only a temporary measure, hostilities inevitably fatal to the infant colony were certain to break out.

The acting governor, therefore, hurriedly sent out such reliables as John Musgrove, Ned Carmody, and Richard Blakeslee bearing gifts and reassuring statements. They separated to visit Coweta, Estoto, Tauco, Seegee, Chattogee, and other important Atali Creek Towns.

To compound James Oglethorpe's troubles, a sharp-eyed Spanish-speaking mestizo brought in grim news. Lieutenant John Savey, translating, explained that, close under Tybee Island, a pair of Carolinian coasters had been run down, plundered, and burned by a flotilla of Spanish picaroons. Some of the crewmen, said the mestizo, had perished under tortures so horrible that even Indians heard of them with respect. The rest had been carried off to the living death of slavery in Cuba and Florida.

"Nor is that all, sir," reported Savey, lively dark eyes gleaming. "This fellow declares that Capitán General Sanchez, who is the Governor of Florida, has sworn a great oath that never will an English colony be allowed to flourish so near his capital. In short, he is now busy collecting arms and recruiting free Negroes and Indians with the amiable intent, sir"—Savey treated his superior to a taut smile—"of exterminating this place."

"How very interesting. Tell me, Mr. Savey, where did you acquire so perfect a knowledge of Spanish?"

"Why, from my mother, sir, who was born a noblewoman of Cádiz. Eventually, she married my father, who was a major in our garrison at Gibraltar." The interpreter then reverted to translating so smoothly that Oglethorpe was both puzzled and amused.

"This fellow—who claims that he trades with the Dons a lot—says that, in his rage, Morales Sanchez is making conciliatory overtures to the French in Louisiana." Savey looked thoughtful, rubbed a slightly cleft chin. "Shouldn't wonder, sir, but he'll invite the French, as fellow Catholics, to join in an assault upon us *heréticos.*"

As if to pile the Pelion on the Ossa of Oglethorpe's problems, Quobah's raid had provoked a serious rift in the previous warm relations between Georgia and South Carolina. Despite all denials of responsibility from Savannah, Governor Johnson and his assembly insisted that Quobah and other survivors of the raid even now must be enjoying asylum south of the Savannah.

Since it was imperative that this misconception be corrected at once, Oglethorpe decided to make a quick trip to Charles Town by sea, picaroons or no picaroons. He needed to convince the Carolinians that he had had no advance knowledge of the raid, that he deplored it as much as they, and that his ex-paupers were sheltering no survivors.

What an ill time to beg further assistance! Still, he would have to; the supply of European food staples in Savannah was about exhausted. True, a second company ship was expected from England any day, but by now she was so far overdue many feared that she'd either foundered in a storm or been lost to pirates or to the Spaniards.

No sooner had the scout boat, carrying the accompanying trustee and Colonel Bull, disappeared downriver than an indefinable sense of uneasiness pervaded the half-built settlement. Complaints which, heretofore, had only been muttered now were voiced in no uncertain terms. Warnings and threats from Bailiff Tom Causton and beetle-browed Herman Verplank, the recently appointed chief constable, accomplished little or nothing.

Once he turned over command of the garrison to Captain MacPherson, more dour and short-tempered than ever, Challenger set out for the O'Brien home because, following Helen Bayless's marriage, Winsome had moved in with them; as a single girl she couldn't go on sleeping under the same roof with Drs. Cox and Tailfer. Dr. Tailfer, especially, was annoyed over her departure, but then, he seemed always to be in a foul humor nowadays; apparently, Savannah was not turning out to be quite the American paradise he had envisioned.

When Wallace Challenger reached the O'Brien house he found Winsome seated on a log bench by the front door in conversation with Militia Lieutenant John Savey, who had just presented her with a length of dufil cloth. "Don't thank me, ma'am," he'd said. "This is only issue from the common stores. Thought maybe you could find use for it."

A smile spread slowly over Winsome's pointed, pale brown features. This young fellow with the crisp and curly dark brown hair was easily one of the handsomest men she'd ever come across. "I'm that surprised and pleased, Mr. Savey, for I've heard of no other cloth being issued."

"It's the first, Mistress Brooks." This, at best, was only a half-truth; no other dufil had been distributed, or was likely to be. Perhaps unconsciously, John Savey turned, presenting his fine, classic profile to the afterglow. "You may rely upon it that you'll always be provided for whenever there's a company issue."

Winsome debated asking this pleasant officer to stay for supper, but decided against it; not that she disliked or mistrusted John Savey, in fact, she'd come to enjoy this unusual young man's company and his lighthearted descriptions of indiscreet adventures in foreign lands. Right now, he was telling of an escapade at the University of Salamanca.

"In spite of this, you received your degree?"

A twinkle showed in Savey's liquid dark eyes as he shook his head. "Mistress Brooks, I must confess that I was forced to quit that venerable seat of learning—shall we say?—a trifle abruptly."

"May I ask why?"

"Alas, the Reverend Fathers, while investigating a, well, call it a scrape in which I was involved, discovered that I wasn't quite the devout Catholic they'd taken me for. In fact, I wasn't even a communicant of the Church!"

Winsome tried to be tactful, to change the course of conversation. "Then you speak Spanish?"

"Fluently, ma'am." To prove it, he quoted, glibly enough, passages from Cervantes' *Novelas Ejemplares* and laughed within himself because this firm-bodied wench from New England obviously understood nothing of the obscenities he was reciting.

"So you see, ma'am, although I also converse reasonably well in Italian and French, Spanish remains my second tongue. As I said, my mother was—" He checked himself, then continued smoothly, "Let us hope the trustees' second ship arrives soon. Our storehouse is near empty, so, very soon, our people must go on short rations now that your admirer, Sakwari-cra, and his smelly savages have vanished."

Winsome uttered a most unmaidenly sniff, elevated her pointed chin. "Really, Mr. Savey! That renegade was no admirer of mine. Whoever lent you such a notion?"

The lithe young fellow laughed softly. "No one, but many's the time I've observed him watching you as closely as if you'd been a hostile savage. Didn't he often manage to see that the best of the meat he brought in landed in the pile for your ward?"

"I assure you, sir, of that I was entirely unaware." She arose from the log. "However, I am gald the Sakwaris have departed. I hated seeing a white man, especially of English origin, despise civilized ways."

Savey also got to his feet, slapped successive puffs of red dust from clean duroy trousers. He might have glimpsed Wallace Challenger's tow-

ering figure at the far end of Bryan Street. At any rate, he offered a
quick bow, murmuring, "Must be on my way. Should you stand in need
of anything from the storehouse, you have only to notify your humble
servant who now is in charge."

"Thank you for the blanket, Mr. Savey, and now you must excuse me
if I'm to keep the stew from scorching."

Winsome went inside and briskly stirred a chowder of pork, fish, and
sea biscuit. Next, she cast an anxious glance into a Dutch oven in which
a corn-meal cake was browning for supper. It was so near done she
hoped Hendy wasn't going to be late again. He wasn't; the little man
soon appeared, looking hotter and angrier than she'd ever seen him.

"B'God, 'tis an outrage," he sputtered. "A damned infernal outrage!"

Fearfully, Bettie came hurrying down a flight of roughhewn slab steps
leading to the upstairs room. "What's wrong, darling? Did one of your
horses get hurt?"

Violently, Hendy slammed a shapeless cornhusk hat onto the floor,
then kicked it sailing. "Ah-h, the Devil fly away with these canting Jack
Presbyters!"

"What's happened?" Bettie implored, clinging to Hendy's frame. She
hadn't seen him half so angry since that time Papa had had them jailed.

For a long instant Hendy glared, flat red features quivering. "Me and
Chauncey Wardrop was only havin' us a little runnin' race along the back
edge o' the town and— Remember the leggy, golden-bay filly—the one
with the wee white blaze on her forehead that came from Charles Town
last week?"

"What about her?" Winsome demanded.

"Well, Wardrop wagered a shilling that, over a half mile, she could
show her heels to my Arduagashel."

Winsome ceased to smile. "You mean you ran a race *for money!*"

The little Irishman's freckled features dissolved into a wide grin. "Sure
and we did just that thing! Faith, I wish ye'd seen the grand way Ardua
flattened out and left that filly behind by three lengths at the finish."
Hendy's frown reappeared. "Chauncey was payin' me off when out o' the
woods tramps that slab-sided Constable Verplank and one o' his men.
Straight away they arrest us for the mortal sin o' racin' a horse on a wager!"
Hendy again kicked his hat.

Bettie's features crumpled and she began to sniffle. "Arrested! Hendy!
Hendy! Oh, Hendy, how awful! What will—what can they do to you?
You know any form of gaming's against the law!"

"Dunno," came the sullen reply. "But Verplank's summoned me to
stand before the council come its next meetin'. Sure, and a sorry state of
affairs it is when a couple o' honest lads can't make a wee bet 'tween 'em
and run horses to settle it."

He strode over to a water bucket, swallowed a dipperful, then turned small blue eyes looking hard as flint. "Damn it, Bettie, I'm beginnin' to feel this settlement's too damn' pious and bluenosed for us, or any full-blooded fellow."

An abrupt darkening of the entrance announced Challenger's arrival. "I overheard that, friend O'Brien," he chuckled. "And ye've made a considerable point. To my way o' thinkin', religion's fine on Sundays, but only for those who enjoy it. To try to rub everybody's nose in religion and enforce blue laws makes no sense and generally leads to trouble." The Ranger pulled off his black leather skullcap, carelessly ran fingers through his shoulder-long hair. "What about that, Winsome?"

"Well, I'll say this much: I've never noticed that forcing religion on unwilling people gets worth-while results." Then, with a start, she realized that she'd only been repeating what she'd heard Pa say time and again. Dear, wise Pa.

Using a corner of her apron, Bettie dabbed at her eyes. "Captain, won't you stop and take a bite with us? Winsome has cooked up a right tasty dish and we've plenty, I think."

Challenger glanced at Winsome, but she had turned and was busying herself before the fireplace. He felt a small stab of disappointment. Why didn't she back up Bettie O'Brien's invitation? Damn her for a chilly and ungrateful baggage! You'd never believe I saved her bacon that time in Charles Town, and I haven't even suggested repayment. Further, she owes me somethin' for havin' helped her with her clumsy plot to get Helen Bayless married.

What *was* wrong with Winsome Brooks? Something queer, because he was pretty sure she liked him more than a little. By damn! He decided to stay for supper whether or no!

When the meal was over Hendy arose and, with a sidewise glance, announced that he was going down to the mare paddock, where a foal was expected to be dropped, then added, "Some Indians said a tiger's been seen prowlin' nearby."

Hendy disappeared into the hot and breathless night where fireflies spiraled and an occasional whippoorwill complained.

"Now why on earth will you people go on callin' a panther a tiger?" Using his skinning knife, Wallace cut a splinter from a stick and used it, leisurely, to pick his teeth. "There's no such creature as a tiger in all North America, though they do speak of *tigres* down in Mexico, which is a kind of leopard because they're spotted and not striped. I've seen their skins."

He smoked a clay pipe in silence while the women cleaned up the supper dishes. Finally, he drawled, "Winsome, heard say there's to be a ghost dance in Tomo-chichi's village tonight. Toonahowie says it's a very old dance which ain't done much any more. Like to look in?"

Winsome glanced up quickly from the fireplace, which had warmed her pointed features to a rosy-brown. "Why, how very kind of you, Capt—er, Wallace. I'd like to accompany you. I'm sure 'twill prove a most interesting experience."

"I'll be back within the hour; no use going down there till the dancers really get warmed up." He nodded to Bettie, then set off with his characteristic light and loose-kneed stride.

"Mercy sakes!" Bettie burst out. "You talk stiff as a stick. Why can't you act a little warmer? Wallace Challenger's a fine man."

Puzzled, Winsome said, "I wish I knew how to, because, well, I *do* like him—quite a bit. Trouble is I—I guess I feel I can't quite trust him alone."

"Why? He's always polite as pie with you, even if he has the reputation of a petticoat-ruffler."

Winsome's high, smooth forehead furrowed itself. "Oh, that doesn't bother me. It—well, it's just that I fear he's grown hard and cruel from the life he's led, and what I need is tenderness. I fear Wallace will do just as he pleases with me once he gets the chance. Perhaps I'm wrong, but you must admit he's very masterful."

Bettie continued to rinse the hickory troughs they'd dined out of. "Maybe so, Winnie, but always remember that a man's got to be that way if he expects to survive in this fearsome land."

Chapter 11

THE FIRE OF DISCONTENT

The Yamacraw ghost dances proved to be both fascinating and fantastic. Hideous masks and headdresses and other weird paraphernalia created unforgettable figures, especially when seen by the leaping flames of a huge bonfire. Reed flutes, whistles, and gourd rattles punctuated intricate, blood-quickening rhythms beaten out upon variously pitched tom-toms and crude tambourines.

The fact that teams of grotesquely adorned dancers from time to time spelled one another indicated that these rites would continue until daybreak.

Then was danced one of the few figures in which young males and females danced together; the performers writhed about in movements so frankly obscene that Wallace said, "Come along. We've seen enough."

But, to his vast astonishment, Winsome, flushed and with gleaming eyes, shook her head and appeared to be fascinated by this new trend in the dancing. It would have required very little encouragement, she was realizing, to send her running forward to join in the lascivious, posturing, and swaying confusion.

With a bland smile Challenger yielded. By damn! All along he'd been right about her! Under that cool, reserved New England surface ran currents as torrid as any a fellow would expect to find along the waterfront. He began to grin when her hand sought his forearm and began, ever so gently, to tremble while her breathing quickened and deepened. As soon as the erotic dancing ended, Challenger stood up. Winsome meekly accepted his arm and clung to it tightly when they started to climb back up the bluff.

Once they had gained the plateau, the Ranger suddenly halted and pointed to firelight shining faintly through a tangle of honeysuckle.

"Reckon I'll go take a look," he stated quietly. "There's no regular camp over there." Maybe some of Thad Burton's people have come back, he thought, hopeful of catching Quobah; he still felt disappointed over not capturing him at Smollett's.

He was surprised and pleased to note how quietly Dr. Brooks's daughter followed him. Previously, she'd crashed through the woods like a heifer scenting a bear.

Peering cautiously through festoons of vines, Challenger saw that about twenty-five or thirty shaggy-haired and for the most part bearded settlers were seated on the ground about a small fire. Among these ill-dressed fellows Dr. Tailfer's black-clad figure loomed prominently; he recognized big John Stonehewer, James Papot, Thomas Trippe, Hendy O'Brien, and several others of Savannah's better-educated inhabitants.

The moment Wallace and Winsome arrived, unnoticed, within earshot the Ranger signaled a halt. Stonehewer was standing above the fire, long, discontented features dyed scarlet.

He was saying, "I'm no farmer and never have been so I don't know the first thing about planting. I told the company's agents so in London. 'Me,' I said, 'I'm a silk weaver and a member of the Mercers' and Drapers' Guild.' Says they, 'Why, that's fine because the company plans to grow and weave silk in Georgia as soon as can be.' So I told 'em, 'Say the word and I'll build you a fine mechanical loom which I've invented. 'Tis a great improvement over Sir Thomas Lombe's patented contraption.' Said they, 'Fine! Sign here and go along to America!'"

He waved blistered hands in exasperation. "So, in all fairness, why should I be forced to plant my fifty acres? It's not that I'd complain about growing food for my family, nor would I object to planting my land in mulberry trees. Silkworms will need more mulberries—a lot more than grow wild hereabouts."

Angrily, he stuck out his bushy, dark red beard. "This very day that arrogant bastard, Causton, told me I've no choice but to plant my land in grain, straightaway. Now I ask you, friends, is that either fair or sensible?"

"No, by God! It's neither!" cried Dr. Tailfer. "It's like telling me to hoe corn instead of tending the sick."

Invisible among the honeysuckles, the eavesdroppers watched Thomas Trippe, a short, bandy-legged master mason, get to his feet. "Another thing I don't like is this male-tail law," he said, and earned a ripple of subdued laughter. "Not if it means what I think it does."

"What does it mean?" called a voice beyond the fire.

"Means that when a fellow dies he can't will his property to his wife, daughter or any female; in other words, an heir in this enlightened colony has got to be male and nothin' else but."

"That ain't right!" angrily burst out a lean-faced sawyer. "Me and Maria have four youngsters, so far, and they're all of the cloven sex."

Another settler, wearing a patched shirt, jumped up. "If we own this land, as they say we do, then why do we still have to pay quitrent? Why are we forbidden to sell any part of our holding? Suppose one of you smart fellows answer that!"

The onlookers watched a skinny, rather haggard individual pull horny bare feet under him before heaving himself erect. "Reckon it's a move calculated to discourage a shiftless man from trading property for a spell of easy living, after which he'd become a burden on the industrious."

The speaker's sunken eyes wandered about the gathering. "Tell you what: our noble trustees don't want anybody in this settlement ever to own more than fifty acres. Is *that* encouraging industry?"

The sawyer said, "The guvnor says Georgia ain't planned to be like Carolina, where one rich man can own a great plantation whilst his neighbors haven't a pea patch to call their own."

"That may be so," Stonehewer admitted sourly, "but it's against nature. No matter what the laws, no matter where you go, you'll always see a few smart men take over from their fellows."

To Winsome's complete astonishment, Lieutenant Savey stood up behind the holly bush which heretofore had concealed him. "How true! During my military service, I've noted that, about a week after any regiment's payday, maybe a dozen soldiers will have pocketed practically all the money; in another few days it'll have found its way into the hands of around five defenders of Our Gracious Majesty." He laughed lightly. "Odd, isn't it? And it's always the same five men."

"Be that as it may," growled Stonehewer, "I'm not going to try farming, no matter what the council threatens."

A short-necked, walleyed individual named Watson got up. "Boys, how d'you feel about this law says we can't even *hire* a African or a Injun slave—let alone own him? Ain't it downright stupid to expect us whites to labor in the hot sun all day long? Niggers can stand it, but we'll keel over with the sunstroke. That being so, how are we to compete with the Carolina planters who can raise any crop they please on as much land as they can buy and have it worked by slaves?"

His gaze traveled from one firelit face to the next. "Don't tell me the Carolinians ain't always goin' to undersell us, no matter how hard we toil —if we're fools enough to do it."

Winsome glanced sidewise at her companion's shadowy countenance. Challenger saw the gleam of her face, muttered thoughtfully, "Fellow's right, but there's another consideration he's overlooked. The Creeks don't like being forbidden to farm out their slaves in Georgia; they lose a lot of money that way."

Stonehewer made a wide motion and coughed when a swirl of smoke stung his nostrils. "There anything else to be talked over?"

"You bet there is!" yelled a chunky fellow with "farmer" written all over him from sun-bleached hair to dirty bare feet. "Like everybody knows, workin' under this damn' hot sun is main parchin'; while beer's a help, it don't easy a man like a good swig of rum. How about it, Marrauld?"

Men who heretofore had been listening in halfhearted fashion began to pay attention.

After brushing dirt from his breeches, Marrauld heaved himself so stiffly to his feet that he reminded Wallace of an old horse getting up on a frosty morning. "Damn' if the cussed council don't aim to revoke my ale license account of the other day I sold just a mite of watered Jamaica rum along with the beer and wine I vend. Know what they did? As a part penalty they've ordered me to distribute a hundred copies of Dr. Hale's pamphlet, 'Against the Drinking of Distilled Liquors.'

"By what right," he demanded in a suddenly far-carrying voice, "do these bloody trustees deny a freeborn Englishmen the right to drink what he wants so long as he's orderly about it?" Marrauld shook his fist in the direction of Savannah. "Me, I'm getting sick of this place and its crazy laws!"

Winsome watched Dr. Tailfer nod so vigorously that the brim of his rusty old black hat fluttered like a bird's wings. "This prohibition of the sale of spirits is idiotic; a law which *can't* be enforced is the worst kind; everyone knows that rum is being smuggled over from Carolina nearly every day in the week." The physician hooked thumbs into the pockets of a stained scarlet waistcoat and assumed a pedantic manner. "Now, my friends, I'll put you another question: How can traders licensed by this colony hope to compete with the Carolinians in the Indian trade if they aren't allowed to offer barter rum for skins? You already know the answer; our licensed traders will get nowhere because our gentle red brothers just can't do without their firewater."

Among the hot and airless shadows, Challenger whispered, "Your friend the doctor is making good sense. When an Indian craves rum bad enough he'll quit the trading post where there isn't any to be had, and head elsewhere. They'll even do murder to get it. Ben Todhunter got done in that way."

Dr. Tailfer continued, "I imagine His Excellency, being a reasonable man, secretly agrees with us about this prohibition. But, being a man of honor, what can he do? Nothing, without the assent of those purblind bigwigs back home in England."

Dr. Tailfer broke off, then, with fine dramatic timing, remained silent while deliberately surveying the gathering.

At length he resumed, "Friends and neighbors—and occasional patients," he amended with a broad, gap-toothed grin, "it seems clear to me how we feel about these grievances. Point is, how *strongly* do we feel?"

Stonehewer began waving his arms for attention. "Sure! What's to be done about these grievances? Suppose, Doctor, you tell us how much action to take—and when."

Challenger's tall figure emerged so swiftly and soundlessly into the zone of firelight that Winsome hardly was aware that he'd left her. Grinning, the Ranger halted and raised a huge, bronzed hand. The fire's fitful flickering picked out the brass buckle on his belt and the outlines of that war hatchet and skinning knife which seemed a part of him.

Almost insolently, he stared first at Savey, then at Dr. Tailfer, and finally on Stonehewer, before announcing in his big, lazy-sounding voice, "You'd better listen to me because I've just heard what you've had to say. You there! Sit still and don't get yer wind up," he snapped when several men started to edge into the shadows. "Most o' yer complaints are well founded, but now isn't the time to start bickering among yerselves." Winsome saw his broad front teeth flash. "Not while you lie open to attack from any and all directions. My God! *Can't* you dumblocks understand that it wouldn't take much of a war party to lift every last scalp in Savannah and leave the place in ashes?

"Now, if you've the wits of so many bug-tits you'll disperse right now, go home and keep yer traps shut till the time's ripe to speak up."

By the time Winsome and Challenger reached Hendy O'Brien's place
the moon stood so high that the shadows it wrought in Savannah's deserted streets were short and pale. Variously pitched snores raised by bone-
weary men and women beat through nearby windows; despite swarms of
mosquitoes, it was much too hot to keep them closed. From the river
sounded the *splash!* made by a big fish jumping, the monotonous hoarse
grunting of bullfrogs, and the occasional *gra-a-wk* of night herons hunting them.

Owls and whippoorwills raised querulous cries in the woods, which,
day by day, relentlessly were being pushed farther off the plateau.

Moonlight picked out the Boston girl's wide, flaring brows and lively
eyes as she said softly, "I'm so glad you spoke as you did to those dis-
loyal rascals."

He peered down at her, surprised. "Now hold on. Those men are nothin'
of the sort! They've got just grounds for complaint, and the right to
voice 'em."

Unexpectedly, she smiled. "I suppose you're right, but, all the same,
your restraint surprises me."

He laughed softly, deep in his throat. "Are you actually sayin' you've
found something about me to approve of?"

She was astonished to hear herself saying, "On the contrary, from the
beginning I have found much to admire in you."

"Oh hell!" Swift as the strike of a snake, his arms shot out and closed
about her. His bristled chin burned her skin while he ground leathery lips
against her soft ones. Instinctively, she responded, pressed her breasts
against him and dragged at his lips a long instant before beginning to
resist the bone-crushing embrace. Suddenly, she ceased to struggle, but
her body lost none of its inflexibility.

His day-old beard continued to rasp her cheek until she managed to
twist her face aside, gasping, "P-please stop. Please. I'm not strong enough
—to make you."

Challenger's arms fell away; he stepped back and peered at her heated,
moon-silvered features as if he were beholding them for the first time.
"Don't say you didn't enjoy it!"

Winsome's trembling fingers dabbed mechanically at a lock of hair.
Like a warm millrace, a yearning was surging through her as it had not
since Pa's death. Coldly, she demanded, "Do I appear to?"

Although his broad features contracted, he continued to smile like a
friendly mastiff. "You sure do. Why all this fiddle-faddle when you like
to hug and buss as well as the next girl? Whyn't you admit you've a real
fidgety fork?"

"Don't be—be dis-disgusting." Panic-stricken, Winsome began grop-

ing behind her for the door's latch. "I will never admit to something I—
I don't feel."

He stepped closer, towered over her. "I dare you to deny your need of
a man! If you haven't such, what's wrong with yer head—'cause there's
surely nothing wrong with yer body." He spoke more softly, tried another
tack. "Perhaps you've forgot ye're somewhat in my debt?"

Her expression altered to one of embarrassed confusion. "Oh-h no. Of
course not. How could I ever cease to be grateful for what you did for
me in Charles Town? But you misjudge me if you think I—I would—"

"—go for a frolic in the pine barrens? Well, maybe ye don't feel that
way right now, but, sure as shootin', you will, and you'll come willin'."

He took her in his arms and kissed her again, then put his hands on her
hips and drove them slowly down over her thighs. She only sighed and
struggled hardly at all.

"Look, Winnie, by this time you should know I'm none of yer roman-
tical, English-bred gallants. Favor me and I'll try to save yer hair for you
when the Dons and Yamasees come this way and, sure as God made
little apples, they're going to."

Chapter 12

THE ATALI CREEKS

Dusty and hot after a midday inspection of sentry posts, Lieutenant
Archibald Glen hurried toward the small two-room dwelling he shared
with his bride. Smelling of fresh-sawed pine, it stood close by the log
fort, which now mounted a few cannon and was protected by a stout
palisade of crudely pointed logs.

Feeling very much the family man, he swung along, rather marched
like a guardsman, setting his feet down hard and in rhythm. He found
Helen red-faced but stubbornly attempting to cook at the furiously smoking fireplace. Poor girl, she'd kindled much too big a blaze for her purpose and consequently was being roasted. Alas, the former governess
wasn't quick to learn about such practicalities.

Helen sprang up, ran to meet him. Heated features lighting, she clung
to him. "Oh, my poor darling Arch. I feared you'd never come off duty."

Glen stripped off his ammunition bandoleer, then unbuckled his sword
and propped it in a corner. Ipswich Nicholas, black and white tail waving

a graceful welcome, wandered off to sniff the scabbard's scuffed and well-polished leather covering.

"'Twasn't by choice, lovely. What with the governor still absent, Captain MacPherson's all of a fret over having so damn' many savages gathering around this place with the fort still unfinished."

Helen's clear brown eyes widened. "Why, isn't it all right? Haven't these Indians just come to confer among themselves before they talk with His Excellency?"

"That's what they've told MacPherson, but it's clear he doesn't half believe 'em. And it's no wonder, they're a wild and brutal-looking lot. Know something, pet? Their eyes are just like a snake's eyes; cold, black and glittering."

"What sort of Indians arrived this morning?"

"A mico of the Coosaw Creeks called Malatchi and another named Chikilly have brought along a mighty big escort of warriors."

Glen bent to wrench off patched European military boots—as a former cornet of The Blues, he still couldn't bring himself to wear moccasins while on duty. He drained a dipperful of warm water from a wooden bucket. It tasted stale. Helen, of course, should have refilled it at the guardhouse spring during the morning, but he made no complaint. She was trying so hard to make a good housekeeper.

When Ipswich Nicholas flopped before him inviting attention, he scratched the cat's snowy belly before saying, "Sergeant Felton says both of these chiefs are sons of the old emperor, so I presume that makes 'em cousins to Mary Musgrove.

"Felton claims this lot of savages have traveled over three hundred miles to attend this council. Still, they haven't come nearly as far as the Cow Keeper, a mico whose land borders on the Cherokees' country."

Glen wiped his face on a grimy towel, then looked over it with a serious look. "Have you noticed, my pet, how well I've begun to remember Indian —no, Injun names and tribes?"

"Yes, darling. You're wonderfully clever at— Oh-h!" Helen uttered a squeak of dismay when her stew boiled over and, on slim bare feet, ran over to grab up a wooden hook with which to catch the iron pot's handle and swung it off the crane.

Sighing, Glen unbuttoned his sweat-soaked shirt clear down to his belt, then blew over his chest; this was proving to be the hottest day yet. In the distance arose a disquieting din caused by pounding drums, shaking rattles, and shrill, ear-piercing notes drawn from many bone whistles.

"Must be some other mico arriving. Wish to God Mr. Oglethorpe would return." Glen grimaced and glanced through the glassless window, fearful lest a militiaman come pelting down the path in search of him.

Helen cried sharply, "Don't you dare stir from here, Arch Glen, till you've had your food."

She filled a pewter bowl with smoking-hot sturgeon stew, crumbled a ship's biscuit into it, then shoved forward a wooden plate of charred sweet potatoes.

Tenderly, she placed an arm about Glen and kissed him. "I fear you haven't married much of a cook, sweeting, but I'm studying to improve, just as you're trying to learn these beastly Indian languages which, if I may say, sound about as melodious as noises from a pigsty."

The meal was only half consumed when a musket boomed on the watchtower.

"Damn! Here comes a runner."

Still chewing, Glen started to tug on his boots but stopped because the messenger proved to be only a long-legged, freckled youth who panted, "Sir! Sir! 'E governor's wessel's in sight!"

James Oglethorpe, Esq., appeared at the headquarters tent, flushed and breathless from his too rapid ascent of the bluff, but nonetheless he radiated confidence. His principal officers soon discovered the reason for this cheerful manner: he had succeeded in convincing the Carolinians that he and the settlers at Savannah had neither participated in nor had condoned the raid upon Major Smollett's plantation; nor had they sheltered any survivors.

As a result, the assembly in Charles Town had voted their neighbors to the south the generous sum of £1200 sterling. Further, they had promised assistance in the event of a Spanish invasion which was felt to be imminent—there were so many alarming reports coming in.

Oglethorpe at once dispatched Captain MacPherson and a squad of Rangers, burdened with gifts, to inform new arrivals that, as soon as the Atali Creeks had concluded their deliberations, he would be pleased to meet their mico thluccos and micos in Savannah or in Yamacraw Town —whichever place they preferred.

Next, the indefatigable acting governor, accompanied by Wallace Challenger and "Colonel" Ballou, conducted a quick inspection of progress made on the defenses during his absence. He found much to approve of: the principal blockhouse was finished, as were barracks designed to accommodate the town guard; a deep ditch, studded with sharp stakes, now stretched between the palisade and the plateau's rim.

Also completed was a brick flour mill and a public baking oven, both situated on the corners of Whitaker and Bryan streets. Better yet, risers for a second story to the Strangers' House now loomed, starkly yellow, above Savannah's wide and dusty main square, which was becoming a favorite haunt for pigs and poultry.

Clad in European finery, Mary Musgrove sat vainly trying to cool herself with a turkey wing fan in the shade cast by Oglethorpe's tent fly, for it was terribly, humidly hot.

Shortly after noon on the day following Oglethorpe's return, the half-breed princess had hurried up to report that the great powwow of the Atali Creeks at last had come to an end and that, within the hour, a delegation would appear in Savannah. This, she explained, was because Oue-chachumpa, the *tostenuggo-hlako,* or supreme mico of all the Lower Creeks, did not wish to honor the outlawed Yamacraws by announcing the council's findings in Tomo-chichi's town. Or was the real reason that the fierce Atalis, having ascertained the puny strength of the new town's defenses, were plotting to overwhelm the settlement with a minimum loss to themselves?

Presently, Oglethorpe, in dress uniform, emerged from his quarters and seated himself facing Coosa-pona-keesa. "While we await our guests please tell me something about the Creek religion, I fear I have but a very imperfect grasp of its general meaning."

Mary's fine, olive-hued features fell into thoughtful lines and she fanned faster. Perspiration was beginning to darken the azure-blue silk of her European gown under her arms and at the nape of her neck.

Oglethorpe was in worse case, wearing as he was a long-skirted dress coat of scarlet velvet lavishly adorned by arabesques done in gold lace. His jabot of Mechelin lace sparkled like new snow, his knee breeches were of Prussian blue satin, while the silk stockings covering his muscular legs matched the scarlet of his tunic.

A huge peruke, glistening with powder freshly applied by Valet James Papot, stood ready on a block beside him—it was much too hot to be donned until the last unforgiving moment.

"Your Excellency, for a European it is difficult to understand," Mary began in her measured and musical accents. "I will explain this much: they all believe in a Supreme God, Yo-he-wa, sometimes called Sotolycaté, which means He-Who-Sits-Above. Most Muskogean tribes do not worship idols, but worship various spirits by rites which most Englishmen deem to be outlandish and more often obscene.

"Their wizards, shamans and such attempt, by spells and sacrifices, to placate a host of invisible spirits, some kindly, some wicked. Each year, at one of the festivals which are regularly observed—such as planting and harvesting—minstrels sing the praises and describe the deeds of their tribe's most famous warriors, although many of them may have been dead for a long time.

"Among other things we"—she smiled faintly—"the Muskogean, that is, believe that all nations are descended from two brothers—one white, one red; the first being ancestor of all Europeans; the second was the Father of all red men. A primitive belief, is it not, Your Excellency?"

"No more so than the legend of Adam and Eve." Oglethorpe fanned away at ever-present swarms of flies, meantime he wondered if these unpredictable savages were ever going to put in an appearance.

"Now, Mary, please tell me what you can about Ouechachumpa." He pulled out a lace-trimmed handkerchief and mopped his brow.

Pride entered the former princess's manner. "The *tostenuggo-hlako* is a very great warrior indeed. He is famous not only for his leadership in war, but equally for his craftiness. Most of the micos who will come along with Ouechachumpa are also men famous for strength and bravery."

Captain MacPherson appeared on silent, moccasined feet and saluted with something approaching military precision. Had he not served under James Oglethorpe for five months?

"Yer Excellency, following orders, I've had those clods of militiamen smarten themselves up as best they could. They still don't look like much, but they are now drawn up in the main square before the Strangers' House."

Mary Musgrove shot him a penetrating glance. "I presume, Captain, you've readied plenty of dry wood so that if the council fire is kindled it can be done right away?"

MacPherson's dark and leathery features relaxed with a slow smile. "Now, Mary, ye know damn' well I'd scarce overlook so important a matter."

Chapter 13

THE RAZOR'S EDGE

On the advice of Captain MacPherson and John Musgrove—Colonel Bull having remained in Charles Town to attend to his properties—a heavy armchair of elaborately carved and gilded oak had been placed for Oglethorpe's use in the center of a brilliant Oriental rug and shaded by a canvas fly.

James Oglethorpe, miserably uncomfortable and desperately anxious, sat bolt upright upon this improvised viceregal throne with dress sword balanced across his knees. He was feeling a trifle foolish because the tricorne Papot had put out was too small and so perched awkwardly upon his peruke.

Behind him and to his left, the colony's civilian authorities stood in a single rank; they streamed sweat, fidgeted, and appeared uneasy. To the acting governor's right stood Colonel Ballou, Lieutenant Glen, mighty stiff and correct, and Captains MacPherson and Challenger, who, in the honor of the occasion, were armed with claymores and were wearing tartan mantles. The steel basket hilts of their claymores glowed with polish, as did the brass butts of the dags, or Highlander pistols, which they'd jammed into broad waist belts.

"I misfavor the bearin' o' yon micos," MacPherson muttered out of a corner of his mouth as the first Creek leaders strode out over burned brown grass on the square fronting the House of Strangers.

"And I too," whispered Challenger. "If matters go wrong, I aim to kill Ouechachumpa, so don't you shoot at him too. Kill the Cow Keeper; he's almost as tricky."

Instinctively, Glen's and Savey's hands tightened on their officer's fusils—light, small-bore muskets. The men in ranks began to shuffle and spit under the growing tension.

Only Colonel Ballou remained relaxed—at least outwardly. The veteran mercenary kept gnarled, freckled hands crossed over his cavalry saber's tang. *Merde!*, he was deciding. They are many—too many. Why have they been permitted to come here? *Mon Dieu!* This is worse than when the Mamelukes came to treat with the prince before Belgrade.

Quietly viewing the spectators, gathered under those four lofty pines which dominated the main square, was a newcomer to Savannah. Representing as he did a type by no means unusual in this wild country, his presence passed almost unnoticed.

Micah Oxford, trapper and trader, had arrived aboard the same scout boat which had conveyed Oglethorpe back to Savannah. Undistinguishable in his hunting shirt of homespun and thorn-scarred Indian leggings, he loitered on a small rise behind the crowd. From it, he should be able to see what was going to happen—and also be able to slip quickly into the woods if need arose.

In mounting wonder he'd observed the trustfulness of these raw immigrants. Pathetic, careless, and absurd! How could they be so complacent with a swarm of fully armed and arrogant warriors gathered in their settlement? In no respect did the atmosphere here remind him of any powwow he'd attended during his many years of trapping and trading among the Mohawks, Oneidas, and other Iroquois tribes.

He simply couldn't credit his eyesight. Why, most of these yokels were carrying no weapon of any description. Hum. Maybe they were taking their cue from the acting governor. James Oglethorpe, Esq., appeared to be quite at ease as he sat on his gilded chair chatting with members of his staff. Apparently yonder long-featured gentleman hadn't yet learned much about an Indian's capability for treachery.

God above! There must be at least three hundred well-armed warriors converging upon Savannah, more than enough to wipe out the place in short order, and there weren't above forty unsoldierly louts scratching themselves in the ranks of the Georgia Militia! Morosely, Micah Oxford counted less than a dozen Rangers—the only force likely to prove of use if the Creeks suddenly attacked.

Oxford glanced over his shoulder again. Yep. He could be into those woods in less than half a minute.

For all the newcomer was shrewd, his estimate of James Oglethorpe's state of mind was wide of the mark. Far from complacent, the acting governor inwardly was aghast. How very easily a bloody period could be put to the Georgia Company's experiment in philanthropy!

None of his Rangers more accurately understood the futility of any attempt at defense. What most disturbed the accompanying trustee was the fact that neither John Musgrove nor his wife had been able to obtain any indication of the Atali Creeks' intentions. As the former put it, "There just ain't no way o' tellin' which way the bobcat is fixin' to jump."

Fingering the cock of a French *fusil des bois*, Oxford conducted a shrewd study of the brilliantly painted and arrayed Indians who began appearing on the plateau in ever-increasing numbers. A few of them must have noticed the northern cut of his moccasins and the foreign design of the frayed and broken beading decorating them. They also would remember him by his short beard which was shaped into twin points.

To a casual stranger, Micah Oxford would appear to wear a friendly if not genial expression, but a shrewd observer would have observed that his narrow eyes held cruel lights in their stone-gray depths—eyes which must have witnessed a deal of hardship, suffering, and brutality.

Oxford already foresaw that to trade successfully around this neck of the woods wasn't going to prove easy. Although fluent in Abenaki, Huron, Iroquoian, and other Indian languages of the northeast, he couldn't speak or understand even a bit of Muskogee. All at once, he remembered something; on the scout boat a Ranger had allowed that now and then one came across a Tuscarora slave who, of course, was able to speak Iroquoian. Yep. Once he got the hang of things down here, he'd hunt up such a captive.

On this occasion no wizard capered about while Atali warriors flooded into the square, then halted under a shifting haze of dust.

Watched openmouthed by the ex-paupers, Ouechachumpa called together eight hideously daubed micos carrying firearms in addition to tomahawks, feather-tufted spears, and crude but deadly casse-têtes.

Walking stiff-legged, like dogs getting ready to fight, the Creek leaders started for the fly under which the acting governor sat erect on his chair of state, silent and frozen-faced.

A good ten feet in advance of his companions stalked the towering, magnificently barbaric figure of Ouechachumpa, *tostenuggo-hlako* of all the Atali Creeks. Into his scalp lock was braided a fan of beautiful white vulture feathers which, being tipped in black, reminded Oglethorpe of royal ermine. Broad twin bands of brilliant vermilion paint climbed from under Ouechachumpa's chin to his forehead, then streaked over the shaven part of his scalp and plunged to the nape of his neck. Beneath several strands of *pe-ak*—precious black wampum—a breastplate of articulated mother-of-pearl shell glittered upon the chieftain's lean and splendidly mucular chest.

Lieutenant John Savey, in charge of the distribution of gifts, narrowly watched the delegation's approach; among other skills, he fancied himself as a gifted aquarellist, so he noted details of the more striking regalias.

When Ouechachumpa, splendid headdress asway, threw back his head and halted some ten feet short of the gilded chair of state, Oglethorpe arose slowly, lifted his tricorne, and, at the same time, offered a curt bow.

Then, at a signal from their acting governor, the Georgia Militia fired a ragged but satisfactorily thunderous salute into the hot, still air. Scowls appeared on the Rangers' weathered features; now these ex-jailbirds' muskets were empty and couldn't be reloaded without the risk of offending.

Oglethorpe, fighting hard to preserve a serene and unruffled manner, motioned Mary Musgrove forward and made a speech of greeting which she rapidly translated.

"In the name of my king, His Majesty King George II, I am pleased to welcome to this place so many warriors famous throughout the land. Their names and great deeds are on every tongue."

His close-set brown eyes traveled rapidly over the barbaric figures hemming him within a loose semicircle. Only with difficulty was he able to conceal his anxiety when he realized that his firm friend Tomo-chichi seemed not to be present; but, a moment later, he spied the aged mico standing, stony-faced, with his nephew, Toonahowie, among a group of Yamacraw warriors on the square's far side. Behind them had gathered quite a group of settlers; it was as if, instinctively, they were drawing a measure of reassurance through being near known friends.

"In the strongest possible terms," Oglethorpe instructed Mary, "assure the *tostenuggo-hlako* that we have not come to this country with any intent to dispossess, cheat, or abuse those whose land this has always been. Tell him that we desire to live in harmony and friendship with our red brothers and hope to purchase from the Creeks only a very small portion of their vast territories."

Even while speaking, he in the red and gold tunic kept his gaze on Ouechachumpa's stern features, but quite failed to detect any reactions to what was being said.

"We are ready, O Mighty Chief, to pay a fair price for such land and will make rich gifts every year to the sellers."

Ouechachumpa remained silent, expressionless.

In a frightened undertone, Mary Musgrove hissed, "Quick! Invite him to order the council fire lighted."

Oglethorpe sensed that the colony's very existence now was balancing on a razor's edge; this instant was crucial. He drew a deep breath. "Request the *tostenuggo-hlako* to order the fire lighted."

Vermilion-streaked visage contorted into a ferocious scowl, Ouechachumpa fingered the eagle-feather-decorated lance he was carrying and remained silent so long that Micah Oxford, the Rangers, and other frontiersmen among the onlookers began to figure on what they had better do next.

To Winsome Brooks, this unnatural stillness became almost suffocating.

Abruptly, the *tostenuggo-hlako* elevated his spear to arm's length and in a resounding voice cried, "Let the fire burn!"

So, for the present at least, there was to be no massacre! Oglethorpe, icy finger tips playing trills along his spine, breathed, "O Lord my God, I thank Thee for thy mercy toward us."

A Ranger rushed out and pushed a flaming torch under logs uptilted into the form of a miniature wigwam. Once the flames, pale in the blazing sunlight, had taken hold, Ouechachumpa imperiously waved forward eight of his mico thluccos. These brought forward and spread before Oglethorpe's silver-buckled shoes as many magnificent, cream-colored buckskins.

"Those represent the eight principal tribes among the Atali," muttered Mary Musgrove.

This done, Ouechachumpa began an address which Mary translated at great speed. "The *tostenuggo-hlako* says that he knows that these gifts are of little value. They are intended to serve only as an expression of confidence in Your Excellency."

The Creek leader plunged his spear's point into the earth, then raised his hands skyward. "Brothers, attend!"

Seated upon a pile of lumber intended to complete the Strangers' House, John West, Oglethorpe's secretary, could hear the Indian clearly, so he took down Ouechachumpa's speech verbatim:

"Let Sotolycaté—He-Who-Sits-Above—bear witness that I speak from a straight heart. We acknowledge the superiority of the white men to the red; we are persuaded that the Great Spirit who dwells above and around all has sent the English hither for our good; and, therefore, they are welcome to all the land we do not need."

The magnificent savage paused. "We are grateful also for your kindness and hospitality in dealing with our venerable friend Tomo-chichi. He has spoken of your friendliness and your desire to do that which is right. Outlaw though he may be, we honor him for his valor and great wisdom. Let Tomo-chichi come forward."

The old man obeyed and with no less dignity than that displayed by Ouechachumpa. Today, the octogenarian appeared more ancient than ever, perhaps because he was wearing a huge headdress of gray-white osprey feathers which emphasized grayish tints in his deeply wrinkled brown skin; his back, however, was straight as a lance when he strode up to the chair of state.

Toonahowie followed, carrying a large bundle secured with rawhide thongs. This he cast upon the deerskins, then bent and jerked its bindings undone.

Meanwhile, the Yamacraw mico thlucco offered a low obeisance to Olgethorpe. West also recorded what he said in his thin, cracked voice. "When the white men came, I feared that they would drive us away, for we were weak; but they promised not to molest us. We wanted corn and other things, and they have given us supplies; and now, of our small means, we make them presents in return. Here is the hide of a white buffalo adorned with the head and feathers of an eagle. The eagle signifies speed, and the buffalo strength.

"The English are swift as the eagle, and strong as the buffalo. Like the eagle, they flew hither over great waters, and, like the buffalo, nothing can withstand them. But the feathers of the eagle are soft, and signify kindness; and the skin of the buffalo is a covering, and signifies protection. Let these, then, remind them to be kind, and to protect us."

Once Oglethorpe, deeply moved, had expressed his gratification, he invited Ouechachumpa, Tomo-chichi, Toonahowie, and the eight mico thluccos to join him in the awning's shade. When the visitors had seated themselves on the warm ground beneath the fly, Oglethorpe lost no time in presenting a treaty he had drafted before leaving for Charles Town. John West read its terms in slow, measured terms so that Mary Musgrove might exactly interpret the document's provisions.

Lieutenant Glen, a-drip with perspiration, stood so close behind the acting governor's chair that he could see the written terms of alliance, which bound the colonists to regulate the Indian traffic and to enforce its provisions. Also, there was a schedule of reparations for injuries and inequities affecting the natives. Finally, in case of war with a common enemy, the newcomers were committed to defend their red brothers to the limit of their capabilities.

In return, the Creeks undertook, freely and formally, to cede to the Georgia Company (1) all of the territory lying south of the Savannah River as far south as the Ogeechee River, (2) all of the seacoast from the mouth of the Savannah down to the river Altamaha, (3) westward, the white men were to own all the land as far as the tide flowed, (4) also to be ceded were islands lying offshore except those known as St. Catherine's, Sapelo, and Ossabaw.

Once the Indian leaders had painted their totem mark on the documents and James Oglethorpe had signed for the trustees, a squad of grinning militiamen under Lieutenant Savey's direction set out a long row of gifts.

To each mico thlucco was presented a gold-laced red coat, a hat, and a fine cambric shirt. On each mico or war captain was bestowed a new musket, a pound of bullets, a pound of powder, and all the food he could carry. For lesser warriors there were gifts of dufil blankets, flints, brass kettles, and other valued items.

To each of the eight Atali towns were donated a barrel of gunpowder, four kegs of bullets, a length of broadcloth, a bolt of Irish linen, and a cask of those long-stemmed clay pipes which the Indians esteemed so highly.

It's a pity, thought Winsome as, weary and more sunburned than ever, she made her way homeward, that Sakwari-cra had not been on hand to share in King George II's largesse. Certainly, during the settlement's earliest days, he'd done much to earn such a reward. She wondered where that extraordinary character might be at this historic moment. Nobody seemed to know for sure; some reported that he and his band had been hunting and fishing somewhere to the south of the Ogeechee River. But why should she care what became of the renegade and his white concubine? After she had climbed into bed and lay watching the stars, it irritated her that so often she found herself thinking of Sakwari-cra.

Chapter 14

MICAH OXFORD

Although none of the civil officers appointed by Oglethorpe yet had been confirmed in office by the trustees of the Georgia Company, bulb-ous-nosed Thomas Causton, in addition to his duties as bailiff, for the present was acting as commissioner for Indian affairs. Eventually this authority would be shared by a chief commissioner, a secretary, and a treasurer whose duties were to hear complaints, shape the colonial coun-cil's policy in dealing with the savages. The treasurer would be responsible for the keeping of accounts of cash and the security bond paid by men purchasing a license to trade in Georgia.

Fretfully, Tom Causton was cursing the heat while rearranging papers heaped, helter-skelter, upon a plank table-desk, when he realized that someone had entered his office without making a sound and now stood looking down at him. How he hated the incredibly silent way these leathery frontiersmen could move. It was downright disconcerting.

A broken front tooth glinted in the depths of Micah Oxford's forked beard as he offered an engaging smile and said, "Now, sir, I don't know how to go about it, but I'd admire to get me a license to traffic with the savages, iffen I can buy a Tuscarora to speak fer me till I learn the lan-guage they speak round here."

"Could you pay for such a slave?"

"Guess so." Which was true. Micah Oxford could afford to pay plenty for a linguister; his illicit traffic in arms had filled his wallet to bursting just before that piece of extraordinarily bad luck had run him out of upper New York a few buck-jumps ahead of the law.

Silently, Micah Oxford decided that, if he played it smart around here, he ought to do well; anybody should who'd dealt with the Six Nations.

Causton blinked, scratched a nose so scarlet with sunburn it seemed about ready to burst into flame. "Well, sir, I'll confess that I don't know much more about this licensing business than you do, but I expect that you can get a warrant all right—provided His Excellency sees fit to ap-prove you."

Gaze busy with his caller's chilling gray eyes, he selected and held out a printed form. "Now, friend—er, what is your name?"

"Oxford, Micah Oxford." He grinned. "They called me Micah before I got big enough to lick anybody who didn't call me Mike."

Causton nodded. "Well, Mike Oxford, you'd better read and remember these rules. His Excellency gets savage over any kind of disobedience; he's a real Indian-lover."

Causton glanced across the stuffy little office at pinch-faced Recorder of the Council John Grady, who was doubling as temporary secretary for the Indian Commission. "What about bond money?"

Grady looked up with a jerk that freed a drop of sweat from his nose tip. "No bond, no license, mister. Presume you've brought along some money?"

"Guess so." Oxford shifted a wad of tobacco from one whiskered cheek to the other, then reached inside his hunting shirt and pulled out a red-brown weasel-skin purse secured by a drawstring of rawhide. "How much?"

"How much ye got?" countered Grady.

With such expert speed that the others couldn't even guess at the amount of his money, Oxford counted fifteen pounds in silver and gold coins! "That enough?"

"Guess so," Grady grunted. "You'll owe ten shillings more for issuing you a license, *if* you get one."

"Fair enough." Oxford pushed back his cap of mangy lynx fur and scratched at thinning red-brown hair. "Suppose one of ye tell me about what's on this here paper; you see, I don't read so purty good."

Again, Causton stroked his roseate nose. "Well, one thing ye'd better understand right now is that, here in Georgia, the savages have the right to complain against any trader if they believe he's cheating them. If they do this, you'll have to come to Savannah and answer the complaint personally or forfeit your bond."

"The hell you preach!" Micah burst out. "Why, that's crazy! Since when does a complaint lodged by any Indian against a white receive real attention?"

"Crazy or not, that's the way it's going to be in Georgia," Grady stated.

"What other crazy rules are they?"

"You'll not have anything whatsoever to do with tribes hostile to us or to the Atali Creeks. You are also forbidden to have any kind of intercourse with the French or the Spaniards or with their Indian allies; you can get tried for treason and hanged if you get caught at it."

"Never fear," grunted he in the dirty linen hunting shirt. "I've plenty of scores to settle with the goddam Frog Eaters."

Grady queried curiously, "Where did you and the French clash?"

"Upper Noo York. That's where. A party of French-led Hurons caught my partner. They slow-roasted him for three whole days."

An oxcart plodding by in the sunlit street, with axles screeching like a tortured soul, supplied a weirdly appropriate sound.

Narrowly studying the applicant, Tom Causton resumed, "Unless you elect to trade near the Chickasaw nation, you'll have to report here every year to renew your license."

"When would that be?"

"You can appear anytime during the spring."

"Why's it different trading near the Chickasaws?" queried the Northerner, whose slightly nasal accent differed considerably from the slower, soft speech of native-born Carolinians and Virginians.

"It's because the Chickasaw country lies so far away. Deal with them and you'd only have to renew your license every eighteen months." Grady glanced up from the regulations to which he kept referring. "And remember, if you do locate 'mongst the Chickasaws you are prohibited from trading, in passing, with any tribe on your route to or from Savannah. Understand? Traders holding concessions among them will lay you out if you try to."

Despite deep disappointment, the Yorker never altered his pleasant expression and continued to finger his little forked beard. "That's fair enough. Does this license allow me to take along some help—white help, that is?"

"You may employ two white assistants," John Grady informed him, "provided you post bond for their good behavior, but only *you*, the principal licensee, are allowed to do the actual trading."

Oxford inclined his round, balding head. He'd encountered—and got around—uninforceable regulations before. "My God, reckon I better fetch along a lawyer."

Causton began to view this hard-eyed stranger with suspicion; the air of honest simplicity Oxford affected, somehow, seemed at odds with his possession of so much gold and silver. "Go on, Grady."

The recorder obeyed. Said he, "Georgia-licensed traders under a forfeit of fifteen pounds, sterling, are forbidden to employ Negro or other slave labor, nor are they allowed to discharge a white assistant while in Indian country. However, if such a fellow deserts you, no other trader is allowed to hire him."

"Fair enough. Say, what's this paper?"

"A license form. Fill in the name of the town you want to base on and then the territory you want set aside as yours. If I were you, I'd ask for plenty; you can only get turned down."

Causton got a sudden idea and his small eyes narrowed. Were this stranger from New York under obligation for certain favors and private advice, he might become very useful in certain schemes the bailiff had in mind. Said he, "Oh, one last thing, Mike, under a Georgia license, you're specifically forbidden to sell or even give spirituous liquors to the savages."

Micah for the first time began to get angry. "My God! D'ye mean I can't even tote along a kag or two—for—for my own use?"

Causton's heavy, pocked features formed a grimace so brief that Grady could not possibly have noticed. Softly, he said, "We can talk about that —provided you get your license."

At this, Micah Oxford's prospects looked brighter; from away back he'd been able to sniff a fellow rascal almost as soon as he clapped eyes on one. "It'll be worth yer while, friend," he muttered, "an ye mark me a clear trail on such a matter."

Causton blinked, then sang out, "Grady, suppose you go look up the guvnor's secretary; tell Mr. West I'd like for him to fix a time, soon as convenient, when I can talk with His Excellency about Mr. Oxford's petition."

Once the recorder had pulled on a shapeless straw hat and ambled out into the broiling sun, the bailiff reached into a chest and pulled out a bottle of rum.

"Take a swig, friend. Somehow, I've a notion that, after I talk to H.E., you'll get your license all right, so let's drink to it!"

He passed over a misshapen black bottle from which Oxford took a generous pull, then let the fiery Jamaica "spread out" before he queried, "Now, what's in yer mind, friend Causton? I'm all ears."

Causton took a pull, wiped his mouth on the back of his hand, and chuckled, "Not quite all, friend. What happened to the top of your left one?"

Unruffled, the Northerner replied, "Why, a Mohawk squaw thought so much o' me she cut it off for a keepsake and ate it. Some Iroquois, especially Mohawks, are cannibals, y'know. Course I was tied up, so I couldn't nowise get a bit of her tit to remember *her* by.

"Now, what was the advice ye'd in mind, friend?" he prompted over the eternal buzzing of flies.

"Forget about the Chickasaws. From what I hear their country's a sight too far off to give you a quick and profitable turnover on your merchandise. You'd better work somewhere along the Guale Coast. The other night MacPherson—he's the senior Ranger officer around here—let drop that a Carolina trader among the Tallapoops lost his hair not long back."

"Purty careless of him. How come?"

"He sold those red devils some rum, but not enough to satisfy their craving, so they went crazy and killed him—or so MacPherson thinks."

Thoughtfully, Micah wriggled bare toes inside trail-worn moccasins. "Now, how would I go about layin' in a decent supply of rum?"

"Friend, there's plenty of creeks and inlets along the coast to the south which any Carolina pirogue can enter. Now, I know a coaster captain who'd accommodate you—*if* we get along."

Oxford arose and offered a stubby hand. "Suppose, friend Causton— if I was to pay right now—fer a couple o' assistants' licenses, would ye leave the name spaces blank?"

Meanwhile, he slid a few more coins out of his weasel-skin poke and Thomas Causton's eyes began to shine as he counted the money into a drawstring pouch.

Chapter 15

GRAND RECONNAISSANCE

More than once Micah Oxford had kept what remained of his hair through heeding sound advice, so right away he abandoned any notion of going 'way out west to trade among the Chickasaws. He figured he'd take Tom Causton's counsel, hang around Savannah for a few days, listen a lot, and talk small. That way he ought soon to get the feel of things in this unfamiliar land; no point in plunging off into the Georgia wilderness like a bee-stung bear.

The minute he learned that Acting Governor Oglethorpe was preparing to ride away on a long scouting expedition to the south and west to pick the locations for forts and strong outsettlements, Oxford decided to go along—if the authorities would allow it. When he sought out the officer of the day, he and Wallace Challenger took to each other; in fact, right away they got along "like pups in a basket" as Savey put it.

Drawled the yellow-haired captain of Rangers, who was busy stuffing supplies into a stained old war bag, "Ye're more than welcome to come along, mister. I can use anyone who's handy in the woods and understands Injuns."

"Hold on, Cap'n," grinned the Yorker, and stooped to pat Claymore's ugly, scarred head. "I don't aim to lie to you. Right now, I don't know the firstest thing 'bout the savages hereabouts and so far, I c'n only talk to 'em by sign language; all the same, Cap'n, I gen'rally pick up a new Injun lingo purty quick. 'Nough to trade with, anyhow."

Gravely, Challenger inclined his massive head. "Ye won't need to talk so long as ye can track well and smell an ambush in time. You must be handy with a musket else you'd not have survived among the Iroquois."

A bleak smile spread over Oxford's flattish features. "Ever had aught to do with 'em?"

"Not really. Had a brush or two with Tuscaroras in upper Carolina, but I've never tangled with Mohawks, Cayugas, or Oneidas. Hear they're meaner'n panther piss."

"Specially Mohawks. Well, Cap'n, how's about it?"

"Ye're hired. Same pay's any Buckskin private. Four shillings a week and found."

The mastiff plunked himself down and started languidly to scratch fleas for all he knew his effort wouldn't accomplish anything, but he made it out of force of habit.

"When do I show up—and where?"

"At the barracks, 'bout half an hour 'fore sunup tomorrow. Meantime, ye'd better find yerself a strong, fast horse." Challenger heaved himself to his six-feet-two and stuck out a huge hand. "Glad to have you along, Mike. To my mind, His Excellency isn't taking along near sufficient Rangers for the hard scout ahead of us."

"Expectin' trouble?" Oxford's narrow eyes slitted themselves.

"Yep. They're plenty of Atali subtribes who don't think a thing of that treaty the governor signed with Ouechachumpa."

Oxford stared out the fly-filled doorway, then jerked a nod. "Shouldn't wonder but ye're right. Well, Cap'n, reckon I'd better go buy me a hoss."

Claymore whuffled, thumped his tail in a polite, if somnolent, farewell.

Challenger called after Oxford, "Make sure you carry along plenty of powder, a bar of lead and a bullet mold to fit yer weapon."

Walking quietly down a sandy, ovenhot street of this raw, mushrooming town, the Yorker guessed why Oglethorpe was taking along so few fighting men. Except from the river, this settlement lay wide, almost invitingly open to attack. Were a sizable force of hostiles to strike this place a jim-dandy massacre would follow and there'd be plenty of new slaves in the backwoods.

When a sultry-looking sun appeared above a welter of crimson clouds on this, the eleventh day of June 1733, most of the reconnaissance party already had collected upon an uneven parade ground fronting the barracks.

Watched by his massive dog, Challenger ran a thoughtful eye over the gathering.

Straight-backed, but all the same easy in his saddle, James Oglethorpe bestrode a handsome gray stallion which the Carolinians had given him during his recent visit to Charles Town. Privately, Challenger deemed it a mistake to ride so light-colored a horse on an expedition of this sort; such an animal would show up in the woods like a knight in shining armor.

He would have ventured a remark to that effect, only he'd learned, long ago, that a mere colonial wasn't supposed to advise a home-grown English officer.

He himself was riding a broad-chested, Roman-nosed chestnut gelding which he reckoned would stand steady under fire; also, it was trained never to whicker when under saddle.

Captain James MacPherson, sharp-faced as a fox, had slung his saddlebags across a scarred, long-legged buckskin which he led by reins looped over an arm while he inspected the ten Rangers detailed to accompany the governor.

John Musgrove sat easy on his horse, one knee hooked over the pommel, unshaven jaws working rhythmically on his eternal wad of "eatin' tobacco."

In sharp contrast, Colonel Ballou looked as if he had been frozen on his saddle and then nailed into place. All the same, the Swiss could guide his horse by leg pressures alone, a valuable skill since, as Challenger appreciated, this left both the rider's hands free for fighting. Long ago, Hendy O'Brien had recognized him for an expert horseman—in the formal, Continental manner, of course.

Present, too, was a Mr. Vincent Palmer, a Virginian reputed to be not only a fine civil engineer but also a capable cartographer. He'd sailed down from Charles Town with His Excellency with another surveyor by the name of Tobias Brodbelt. The latter had in his employ a pair of Carolina frontiersmen who understood something about the uses of a surveyor's chain, transit, and spirit level.

Brodbelt's little party had departed a day in advance of the main expedition in order that they might have accomplished something by the time they rendezvoused with Oglethorpe near the mouth of the Ogeechee. Brodbelt's mission was to survey and mark the southwestern limits of that territory purchased from Ouechachumpa and the Atali Creeks.

While waiting for something to happen, Micah Oxford passed the time by reviewing recent events. Following his interview with Wallace Challenger, he'd gone down to Yamacraw Town, there to dicker for a wiry black mare which seemed to possess a dash of hot blood somewhere in her breeding. He didn't have too much trouble in concluding the dicker for, quite easily, he'd begun to pick up the rudiments of the Muskogean language. Although it was unrelated to any other tongue he'd ever met up with, he needed only to have some object identified, then he'd repeat the Muskogean name aloud five or six times; after that, he could always remember. Nouns were dead easy: *hlahlo* was a fish; *itchu* was a deer— and so on; but he knew he'd have trouble with verbs and tenses.

Once he'd acquired the mare, he bought a saddle, bridle, and a pair of trade blankets from John Musgrove; next, he sought the bailiff's office.

Tom Causton grinned and nodded pleasantly when the Yorker plunked onto his desk a deerskin bag quill-worked with Mohawk symbols. It clinked cheerfully.

"Friend Tom, I want you to keep this for me in your treasure box till I get back."

"To be sure. Your property will be safe as a church, friend Oxford." He added, casually, "You'll keep your eyes open when you get down the coast?"

"I'll keep studyin' for a likely place to set up business—somewhere along the creeks and rivers, not too far from here nor too far from the sea."

Causton's massive black brows merged. "B'God, you're turning out just as smart as I'd deemed you. What you want is a place *close* to shore—deep enough where a sizable ship could tie up and unload unnoticed."

"I'll do that," Micah promised after accepting the receipt Causton had penned.

Now, as Oxford sat the black mare quietly watching the expedition assemble on the dusty parade ground, he again became impressed by that long-faced English gentleman named Oglethorpe—for all that he wasn't overfond of home-grown British officials.

After counting noses, the fugitive Yorker decided that no more than twenty-five men were going along—and that included himself. All seemed tolerably well mounted and he was glad to note that plenty of strong pack horses were being led up. They looked fit to replace such mounts as might die of snakebite, fall sick, stray away, or break a leg on the trail.

At last, James Oglethorpe rode slowly over to the head of the column. Today he was wearing a Ranger's leather skullcap which shouldn't get knocked off by branches, but also he carried a palmetto-fiber hat which he'd soon don to protect his head from the blasting sun which, every day, seemed to grow fiercer. Otherwise, the accompanying trustee wore a sensible light-gray riding coat, brown breeches, and worn but comfortable knee boots.

He reined in beside that taciturn Scot James MacPherson. "Well, Captain, are we ready to move?"

"Aye, Yer Excellency. We're as ready as e'er we will be."

"Then, if you please, we will march at once."

Over an angular shoulder MacPherson called to his Rangers, "Pr-r-re-pare to mount. Mount!"

As they should with such a long ride in store, the guides, Musgrove and MacPherson, moved their horses into a leisurely walk a few lengths in advance of the acting governor.

At Oglethorpe's heels rode Colonel Ballou and the Virginia engineer, Mr. Palmer. Right away, they began to discuss a standard layout for the new outsettlements. The Virginian made no secret of his amusement over Petre Ballou's rigid military seat, privately wondered how long this tough old man could maintain it once the party entered those endless swamps and tangled forests along the coast.

While the expedition jogged through a series of clearings begun on the perimeter of Savannah it was noticed that, even at this early hour, many settlers already were out plowing, weeding, and otherwise tending crops which had begun to wither under Georgia's torrid sun. Others, more practically employed, were cutting small, straight pines for use as fence rails.

Oglethorpe was pleasantly surprised to note how far outer stump lots were delving into the forest. Next winter, these browning slash pines and jagged stumps would be burned, permitting the fields to be properly plowed.

Poor devils are just wasting time, thought Wallace Challenger, who, with shaggy brown and black Claymore trotting sedately alongside, was bringing up the rear. They'll never bring in a harvest *this* year.

Hendy O'Brien, sullen and resentful over the fine the council had slapped onto him, stopped working on a foaling box and enviously watched the horsemen jog by under a shifting haze of sun-reddened dust. By rights he should have been taken along to look after and, if necessary, doctor those mounts. Not one of these blasted, tall-talking colonials really understood the fine points of caring for a horse. It wasn't right for His Excellency not to allow him at least to show what he knew about curing a sick or lame horse. No, by grabs, it just wasn't fair!

Then and there, Hendy O'Brien resolved to do something about such stupid injustice—and before long. He was growing almighty sick of the noise, heat, and piety prevailing in and about Savannah, Georgia. Sure, there must be some place where a man could breed and train fine, blooded horses and also *race* them free of interference. He lingered, scowling, till the last horseman had vanished along that widening trail which followed the river's course southward.

At the end of the first day's ride, James Oglethorpe had seen enough to decide that at least twelve families might profitably be settled on a site which he intended to call "Hampstead," lying only five miles to the southeast of Savannah.

Another twelve families would be designated to take up land at a spot which would bear the name of "Highgate." This seemed a particularly promising location, since here an abundance of fast-flowing springs rose on a low hill surrounded in all directions by wide and rich bottom lands.

On both sites the inhabitants would be required to construct a number of "enforted houses"—strong, semiblockhouses. These must be erected close together, according to a plan prepared by Colonel Ballou.

Mike Oxford, although he hadn't been consulted, was strongly in favor of such concentration of dwellings. In his time he'd come across too many lonely, burned-out cabins occupied only by the bones of their murdered owners.

Next day Musgrove and MacPherson led the expedition farther downriver until they halted at a place where bubbled a foul-smelling sulphur spring long favored by the natives for its medicinal qualities. At this point, deep water came almost as close inshore as it did at Savannah, lying only a dozen miles upstream.

Oglethorpe instructed Surveyor Palmer to write "Thunderbolt" as the name of the settlement on the map he was drawing, for here stood a huge white oak which had been split almost precisely in two by a bolt of lightning. Strangely enough, this patriarch had declined to die, as did most trees struck in such a fashion. Three families were considered sufficient to start with, but no doubt more would be sent later because, as Colonel Ballou pointed out, this point offered an excellent position to erect a battery which could protect Savannah.

Camp on the second afternoon out was made on a height above the river where random breezes might dispel the humid, bone-melting heat while Oglethorpe awaited the arrival of a scout boat which was due to appear the next morning to transport the acting governor and his principal officers for a reconnaissance on Skidaway and Tybee islands.

Only after pickets had been posted, horses cared for and securely tethered to a short picket line was the men's rough-and-ready supper cooked and greedily devoured.

Challenger and Claymore had just finished their rations when MacPherson appeared wearing his usual sardonic smile. Claymore drifted over to sniff at the Scot's fringed Indian leggings, then gazed mournfully in the direction of a partridge carcass recently tossed by his master into the underbrush; the mastiff knew better than to go nosing about without permission—which was presently accorded.

Employing a blackened fingernail, Jamie MacPherson picked at brownwhite teeth. "Harken weel, Wallace. As ye already know, His Excellency sails downstream tomorrow wi' me and the other officers, so his wish 'tis that ye're to lead the rest o' the party and our pack animals doon to the Ogeechee."

He paused, listened to the screeching yowl of a wildcat hunting muskrats in a nearby canebrake. "Ye ken that canoe place where, in olden times, the savages used to have a fishing village—I mean the one where a hook-shaped sand bar reaches oot into the water?"

"Aye, Jamie, I ken it well." It was curious, Challenger reflected, that in MacPherson's presence he quickly dropped into the use of Scottish words and inflections.

"Ye're to name yer ain lieutenant and leave him and most o' the beasties at that canoe place. Next, ye'll select three gude men and scout across the Ogeechee, which won't be easy. Snakes, alligators, and crocodiles lie about thicker than turds round an auld campsite."

"I'll get across. What then?" Challenger queried over sharp crunching noises from Claymore's direction.

"Ye're to ride doon the south bank and take a look-see at that place the Yuchis call Chaugee Landing and decide whether it's wur-rthy o' inspection by His Excellency. Pairsonally," the senior Ranger officer ventured while slapping mosquitoes peppering his forehead, "I'd no' favor establishing a settlement south o' the Ogeechee so close tae the sea; too easy for picaroons and Papists to get at. However-r, 'tis best ye see what's there and decide for yer ainself. Ye'r no greenhorn.

"Next, yer to locate Surveyor Brodbelt's party. Tell him His Excellency wants him to wor-rk no farther south the noo; he's to drive a wee bit north o' west for a distance of thairty miles, blazing his line as he goes."

He offered a bladder of tobacco from which Challenger filled his pipe. "While ye're aboot it, Wallace, best ye ride for mayhap half a day south o' the Chaugee and sniff out the country. Before we left, I heard unrestful tidings about a wanderin' band reported to be Talas—Yuchis of the Wolf Clan who don't hold wi' Ouechachumpa's treaty. If ye've time, sound oot Hachey, their mico; H.E. says to promise him the moon and a' if he'll r-respect the treaty."

Challenger sank onto moccasined heels and, plucking a blazing twig from his tiny cook fire, lit his redstone pipe. "How many warriors is this Hachey supposed to have with him?"

"Some say one thing, some another-r, so 'tis for ye to find oot—*if* ye've the time. Mind, ye'll report to His Excellency no more than three sunsets from now. Ye'll find us encamped on the Ogeechee's north bank whaur Beaver Dam Creek flows into the main stream."

MacPherson reached out to pat Claymore, who, having thoroughly disposed of the partridge carcass, sighed and flopped down to doze beside the redly blinking coals. "I've a notion His Excellency means tae plant a r-really strong for-rt at yon spot where a few cannon can command the main trade r-routes tae the south—always provided that auld braggart, Ballou, and the Virginia surveyor agree 'tis the fittest place."

Chapter 16

DOWN TO THE CHAUGEE

Riding across a seemingly endless succession of flat, pine- and palmetto-dotted sandy barrens, some burned over, some not, Micah Oxford decided that he'd seldom been even half so hot or thirsty. While keeping a sharp lookout for rattlers, he employed a tufted switch of longleaf pine to protect his horse's neck and head and his own as well from swarms of savagely stinging green-headed deer flies and enormous red-and-gray horse-flies.

Riding last in line of this party of four, he watched the monotonous landscape shift and shimmer under a merciless sun. Claymore, as usual, was plodding along behind Challenger's mount with tongue lolling so far out it resembled a pink necktie. Silently, the New Yorker swore that tonight he'd discard his damnably hot fur cap and weave himself a wide-brimmed hat of palmetto leaves such as his companions affected. Challenger had pinned up one side of his hat and, in jaunty fashion, had secured its brim with a turquoise-headed silver skewer.

All three Rangers rode humped over in their saddles as if cowering under the sun's lashing rays. Their moccasined heels sometimes traced short grooves across the sandy, gray ground. The only time they roused was when their mounts jinked at the sudden *whir-r-r* made by a rattlesnake coiled, half seen, amid yellowish bunch grass or under stunted palmettoes.

The ex-gunrunner thought longingly of the cool, dark fir forests that stretched far southward from the St. Lawrence and the Great Lakes, all carpeted with emerald-hued mosses and laced by swift-running brooks.

Micah debated whether it'd be wise to bite off a chew and so moisten his parched mouth, but he decided not to because, hot as it was, nobody else was chewing. Probably the Rangers weren't aiming to have their trail thus identified; very few southern Indians seemed to chew tobacco.

Queer thing about this huge and apparently uninhabited area; in reality, it was better populated than the northern regions in which he'd grown up. Somehow, these scrub-pine and palmetto barrens made a fellow feel as if he were exploring a deserted continent, except for the fact that, almost always, somewhere on the horizon smoke was climbing.

Late in the morning, Wallace Challenger pulled up his horse on the crest of a high ridge, both to allow the lathering horses a breather and to let him study the terrain ahead. About half a mile ahead loomed clumps of tall, umbrella-shaped pines veiled by a creeping ground fire. Farther south, denser and darker woods appeared, patrolled by soaring buzzards. Challenger knew that, a couple of miles farther on, the pines, water oaks, cypresses, and cedars would begin crowding down to the broad and placid Ogeechee. Beyond them lay rank-smelling mangrove swamps and canebrakes which afforded food and refuge to game, countless birds, alligators, and crocodiles.

Mopping bronzed, sweat-brightened features with a soggy bit of rag, the Ranger captain beckoned forward Sergeant Felton. "As I recall, Sam, this river fairly swarms with gators."

"Yep. Specially round the ford by the old Yamasee fishing village. I figger mebbe we ought to try the next ford above—you know, the one next to that big, old Injun mound." Felton pulled off his shapeless palmetto hat and fanned himself. "Better still, there's the next one upstream, where three water oaks grow on a little islant; river narrows there considerable, too."

"Yes, but because of that the current flows a damn' sight faster; the horses would have to swim just as far." Brow furrowed, Challenger deliberated. "Reckon we better try the mound ford."

It was midafternoon when the four men rode down to the Ogeechee's north bank to water their horses at the base of some long-dead hero's burial hill, which now was covered with mature trees shrouded by long festoons of Spanish moss. A few of these had died and now afforded roosts for kingfishers, white egrets, and fish eagles. At some period, a considerable town must have stood here, for huge piles of oyster and mussel shells gleamed white as a snowbank beyond a wide meadow.

Walking slowly, Challenger led his horse toward the verge of a wide, swampy meadow dotted by alder thickets and pierced by sloughs in which reeds and cattails grew higher than a tall man's head.

Oxford led his mare over to a Ranger called Jim Bartow and said in an undertone, "Somethin' big's movin' round in yonder patch of reeds."

Bartow's whiskered features assumed an exaggerated expression of surprise. "Now do tell! There'll be a lot o' big somethin's there—big gators and mebbe a croc or two. Look. Yonder's one."

The fork-bearded Yorker watched a muddy crocodile, easily fifteen feet long, slide smoothly into the water. It swam by with only its knobby eyes and the tip of its snout showing above the brown, oily-looking surface.

Grinned Mike, "Use to think we had some mighty unpleasant critters up north: wolverines, bears, wolves and Mohawks, but, thank God, we'd never to put up with the like of *that*."

On a mudbank across the river several dozen large brown-and-gray saurians lay basking quite oblivious to the attentions of many beautiful little white heron-like birds. These long-legged fowl wandered among the reptiles halting, now and then, long enough to peck a morsel of food from between some sleeping reptile's dagger-shaped teeth.

"How'd you boys figger on gettin' by them critters?" Oxford queried, steel-colored eyes fixed on the sleeping monsters.

"What would you do?" challenged the Ranger.

"Ain't never been this way before, nor found myself in such a fix—so I give *you* leave to answer my question."

Bartow chuckled, swatted a deer fly on his mount's salt-reeking neck. "You'll see."

Challenger rode upstream, following a well-used game trail. That the Rangers were concerned by this concentration of alligators and crocodiles was obvious; to a man, they knew that just as many more monsters lurked, invisible, among the cattails, reeds, and mangroves.

Commented Bartow, who was beginning to take a liking to this terrier-like Yorker, "Don't ye never git fooled into takin' a chance that them clumsy-lookin' critters can't run fast."

Mike raised a furry brow. "Ye mean they really can make tracks?"

"Sure. Over a short distance a big bull gator can overtake the fastest horse you ever heard tell of. No, Mike, this time I *ain't* funnin'. Just take care."

For all his woods experience, the ex-gunrunner wondered how Challenger aimed to get this party across the Ogeechee all in one piece.

Soon, the riverbank loomed higher and there appeared a series of small meadows on which bushes and grasses grew high and tender—a fine feeding ground for deer and buffaloes.

Felton wiped trickles of sweat from bearded, nut-brown features. "Wallace, I figger ye're fixin' a drive below the ford?"

"You figger right, Son," Challenger drawled, then grinned; Sam Felton must be easily twice his own age. "All right, boys, space out 'bout a hundred yards apart and when I toot, drive slow. Remember, I'll skin alive and rub with salt anyone who whoops or shoots before I whistle. All right. Ready yer weapons."

Bartow predicted. "We're sure to rout out plenty of deer and mebbe a buffler or two. But I hope there ain't too many in there."

"Why?" The Yorker was as ready as ever to learn something useful. Fools might stay mum for fear of being thought ignorant, but not Mike Oxford.

Explained the Carolinian, "Bufflers ain't extry good swimmers, so the brutes won't take to water lest they got no choice—they'd a heap d'ruther charge a horseman—specially a cow with a calf."

After the Rangers had used the "worm" or screwlike tip attached to an end of their ramrods to draw single bullets from their muskets' bores they substituted "buck loads"—a smaller lead ball and three buckshot. Quickly and dexterously, Micah followed their example in reloading.

By the time the party had strung itself out over nearly half a mile of tree- and jungle-grown riverbank they'd seen plenty of gray-brown deer browsing on the meadows. At length, Challenger turned his horse toward the water and shoved a small silver whistle between heat-cracked lips. When he sounded two piercing blasts the other Rangers urged forward their mounts and began to whoop and shout just as if closing in during a raid. Delightedly, Oxford threw back his head and screamed some Mohawk war whoops: "*Oo-nah! Oo-nah!*" Claymore, taking his cue, galloped forward roaring like a bull.

Because he was riding on the far left of the line, Oxford was able to sense what he should do. When the drivers began to yip and wave their hats he did the same; when they drove their fly-stung mounts, withersdeep, out onto the meadow he kept abreast of them. Deer raised heads, stared an instant, then turned and flashed away from this thin but noisy line of horsemen; many more, sleeping or resting in the shade, jumped up.

Mike judged there must be easily three, even four dozen of these graceful creatures swinging their heads while trying to decide in which direction lay their greatest danger. Then a huge buck, whose knobby new horns still were gray and blunt with velvet, took off toward the Ogeechee in a series of tremendous bounds; the rest plunged after him, snowy tails waving like flags of surrender.

Oxford screeched like a lovesick panther and hurried his mount forward to cut off game attempting to escape along the riverbank.

Challenger's brown and black mastiff now was having a fine, large time racing about and raising enough clamor for a whole pack of hunting dogs. He caused such a fearful racket that only a few does with half-grown fawns proved sufficiently determined to discount his noise and dash inland to safety; most of the herd stampeded out over the shallows toward deep water.

Only then did Challenger gallop down to the water's edge, drop his reins, and dismount. Experienced, he waited until the first fleeing deer began swimming; then his musket boomed. Other Rangers opened fire. Struck by bullets or buckshot, five or six fugitives fell or reared up, staggered, and began to thrash spasmodically among the weeds and raise a white welter of spray.

Oxford fired after Bartow and Felton; he could have beaten them both in dropping a pair of young bucks, but he didn't think it wise to show off just yet. As soon as blood began to tinge the Ogeechee's yellowish current, the Yorker noted a sudden activity along both banks of the river. Rousing from snags and sand bars, alligators and crocodiles came slithering out of the reed beds. Stimulated by the smell of blood in the water, they made straight for swimming, dead, or disabled deer. Twice, Micah saw uninjured deer check their swift and even progress then rear high above the surface with hoofs lashing in desperation. All in an instant, they would disappear from sight, smoothly, without any fuss.

In a matter of minutes the river's surface boiled with saurians speeding to join in the slaughter.

The Yorker was recalled to present considerations by a hoarse shout from Bartow. "C'mon, ye Yankee dumblock! Ride! Ride hard!"

Already the bandy-legged Ranger was galloping upstream in the wake of Challenger and Felton. Oxford followed, drumming heels against his mare's ribs until she caught up with the rest.

At the fording point, Wallace reined hard left, whistled for Claymore, then trotted into the water's edge; at the same time he hitched his powder horn and war bag as high as possible onto his shoulders. When his mount splashed out over the shallows, he raised his musket at arm's length above his head. Once his gelding reached deeper water, it seemed to shrink in size until, when it struck out into the current, only its head and its rider's shoulders remained visible. Gripping his bridle's crown-piece, Challenger allowed himself to be towed along and so managed to keep dry his possibles, gun, and ammunition. Claymore followed, swimming strongly, but not nearly so fast as his master's horse.

Derisively, Felton yelled over a shoulder, "C'mon, Yank! Mind ye don't soil yer britches—makes gators awful mad."

Never a scary man, Oxford nevertheless drew a deep and fearful breath when his mare began to splash out from the shore. Suppose some of these hideous monsters hadn't yet reached the scene of slaughter below? His panic faded when he realized how mighty cool and fine the water felt in washing his thighs and buttocks free of sticky sweat; the current soothed his body clear up to its armpits.

Towed along by the mare's powerful action, he began anxiously to search for a landing place, all the while hoping that no redskins were waiting to catch the party disorganized and unable to shoot effectively.

Almost before Micah realized it, the party, dripping and grinning with relief, began to collect on the Ogeechee's south bank. It was so hot nobody even tried to wring out his duds; they preferred to enjoy the evaporating water's cooling effect.

Chapter 17

BUZZARDS IN THE SKY

After breakfast of oysters and fish quickly and easily caught, Micah Oxford queried, "What's this place called?"

Sam Felton spat out a slender bone, then licked his fingers. "Gen'rally 'tis called Chaugee Landing 'cause boats and ships sometimes come in here to water up if they can't last to Charles Town." He tossed a bark plate onto the fire and returned his skinning knife to its sheath. "There's a couple o' fine, big springs back o' yonder rise; clearest water you ever did see." He stooped and rolled up the tattered blanket in which he'd spent the night. "'Nother good thing, the deep water hereabouts runs close inshore."

While the rest twisted their blankets into rolls to be strapped across their cantles, the sergeant drawled, "Now, I ain't no part of a boatman, but them's that is, claim this is a fine place to wood up at. With half a eye, ye c'n see there's plenty o' fine cypress and oak growin' all about and, if ye're partial to farmin', there's supposed to be rich black dirt all round this place. Me, I hate farmin'; that's black men's work."

Wallace Challenger, having fed his dog, looked about and decided that this area offered a promising site for a "strong" settlement"—except that it lay dangerously open to attack from the sea. Back of the camping place showed many wide, flat areas that should afford fine grazing for livestock. Best of all, this site, for the most part, rose high enough above the river to avoid getting flooded, except perhaps when a *huracán* came roaring out of the Caribbean and up the coast.

Yep. Shouldn't prove too difficult to build a cluster of self-supporting "strong houses" on that wooded point behind a big sand bar which narrowed the channel to less than a quarter of a mile across. A cannon or two, judiciously emplaced and well served, should be able to let daylight into any ship that wasn't welcome.

If old Colonel Ballou were to come on here, Challenger felt certain he'd recommend that a battery be constructed on a low height behind the landing where it could command the river's entrance. However, for reasons of his own, he decided, unless asked, to make no mention about Chaugee Landing in his report to the acting governor.

While saddling up, the yellow-haired giant noticed that a hell's mint of wild mulberries was growing all about. Hum. If the Georgia Company ever got its projected silk industy under way, such trees would be worth a lot for silkworm food.

Leaving his followers to unhobble their horses, Challenger mounted, then walked his gelding in a wide semicircle about the landing place. The more he studied this place the better he liked it. A maze of flat, little islands and marshes lay to the eastward, which meant that there ought to be famous wildfowling among them during the spring, autumn, and winter. And as for fishing, well, great piles of bleached shells and bones argued that, around here, it must be fine indeed.

From the summit of a steep, wooded bluff, the Ranger captain discovered that he could glimpse a profusion of flat and generally treeless marshy islands stretching away toward that faint blue streak which was the Atlantic.

He was about to return to camp when he noticed that, a long way off to the south, a considerable flock of buzzards and vultures were wheeling, then dropping out of the still-opalescent morning sky. The cloud of scavengers looked so dense he guessed that they'd been attracted by something more important than a sick or aged deer or buffalo which wandered off to die by itself. Um. Since, in any case, he was leading the party in that direction, he reckoned he'd better take a look-see.

Oxford, who had ridden out onto the sandspit, called, "Say, Cap'n, what's all them vultures so curious about?"

"What d'you think?"

"Maybe there's been a fight or a raid down yonder." Cold gray eyes narrowed, the Yorker continued to watch the carrion birds, which, at this distance, appeared as tiny as flies.

Challenger considered this compact outlander with the ginger-colored, two-pointed beard. "How come you can tell so much from the way these buzzards fly?"

"Dunno, 'cause we've got no buzzards where I hail from, but ravens tell you when somethin's amiss and in pretty much the same way."

Felton and Bartow swung up into scuffed and use-shiny saddles, then rode alongside the Yorker. The former asked, "Well, Mike, what d'you make o' this here Chaugee place?"

Having satisfied himself that deep-looking water did indeed curve close in to the bank, Oxford nodded vaguely. "It's a pretty place, all right. But I don't fancy it 'cause it'd be so easy to raid either from the land or the water. Eh, Jim?"

"Yep. Noticed a pair o' well-used traces less'n a half mile upstream."

"To my mind," said Oxford, "'twould be no drawback to command the trade routes this far south of Savannah. But, if I'd the say, I'd build

the blockhouse farther upstream and"—recalling the alligators—"on the
north bank."

"Fer a Northerner, yer smart," Felton chuckled. "Glad yer along with
us."

Without saying so, Oxford agreed. His trader's eye had perceived additional advantages to this location which had escaped the Rangers; but
then, these timber beasts weren't considering Chaugee from his point of
view; not by a long chalk.

Hundreds of warblers, thrushes, catbirds, and mockers trilled and sang
and, in shaded places, dew still glistened, pearly, on leaves.

Once they had set off, all four men rechecked flints and priming, then
kept their weapons balanced across their pommels—ready for instant use.

When they had left behind the hardwood forest surrounding Chaugée
Landing, the riders trotted southward along a clearly defined trading
trace which, eventually, led them onto increasingly flat and sandy terrain.
On it, slash pines, dwarf and stunted palmettoes grew in abundance,
but when the route swung back toward the seacoast red bays, white
cedars, and live oaks reappeared and the beards of silver-gray Spanish
moss dangling from their branches grew longer.

Presently, the trace reached the edge of a vine-festooned cypress swamp
inhabited by vast numbers of Carolina parakeets, green parrots, herons,
egrets, roseate spoonbills, and summer ducks. Spoor shaped weirdly like
human handprints, warned that alligators must be lurking not far away;
their droppings glistened with freshness. Water moccasins slithered off toward swampy ground.

Claymore now trotted very close to his master; the mastiff knew that
gators fancied nothing so much as a bait of dog meat.

Oxford, riding a horse's length to Sergeant Felton's rear, gasped an
obscenity when, without warning, his horse shied and almost threw him.
A wave of repulsion swept him when he heard a *hiss!* like steam escaping
a gigantic kettle. Criminently! Among a clump of reeds sprouting from
a boggy spot was coiled a monstrous coal-black snake. At least six feet in
length, the reptile reared backward, jaws gaped, its hooked fangs agleam
in a mouth that shone white as new snow. Its baleful, greenish-yellow
eyes were slit by vertical jet pupils.

Revolted, the Yorker jerked his war hatchet free of a beaded sling,
flung it, and decapitated the reptile with such accuracy as to inspire
profane admiration from Jim Bartow, riding next in line.

"Je-e-sus, mister! Ye do hurl a hand ax mighty neat! That there throw
was faster'n greased lightning."

Micah pinched leather-hued lips together lest they quiver. "Wha—what
d'ye name such a varmint?"

"That wuz a cottonmouth moccasin; when it comes to killin' a feller real quick, there ain't no pick 'twixt them and a diamondback."

" 'Diamondback'?" Mike dismounted to retrieve his weapon from amid slowly writhing sable coils.

" 'Nother name for a big, dry-country rattler."

Challenger, who'd missed this byplay, continued to study his surroundings; more buzzards were appearing, now flew almost directly overhead.

Once his party had closed up after crossing a shallow creek where they disturbed a host of gay, blue-black-and-yellow butterflies, Challenger made a warning hand signal. The trace swung right before entering a wide, marshy meadow dominated by a huge oak. It had been dead for so long that only remnants of its larger branches groped, like the bleached fingers of a skeleton, into the air. Whatever was attracting these scavengers must lie somewhere near this savannah's far side.

"Sam," Bartow called back over a shoulder grown dark with sweat, "What's yer bet on what we'll find?"

The sergeant blinked in the incandescent sunlight. "Two buckskins'll get ye one there's likely more'n one dead body yonder."

Bartow's yellow-brown teeth showed briefly when he pulled out a plug of tobacco and tore off a ragged bite. "Ye'd never bet short o' a tight girth, now would ye, Sam?"

Challenger suddenly raised an arm; everyone, including Claymore, halted in his tracks. They heard the dull *thump!* made by still more buzzards settling onto the ground.

In a gentle undertone, Challenger observed, "Whatever's dead hasn't been that way overlong. Leastways, I don't smell anything. Felton, you'll hold the horses; the rest of us will walk up."

The Yorker's gaze flitted about, read the ground, probed for sign, but he saw nothing worthy of note this side of the bleached, dead oak, in which dozens of belatedly arrived buzzards were perching.

Weapons held ready, the three men deployed into line abreast and advanced so soundlessly that they were right among a feeding family of quail before the handsome brown-and-white birds took fright and whirred off into a tangle of honeysuckle, myrtle, and cat briers.

About the same moment all three skirmishers saw what had attracted the scavengers; beyond the dead oak was a heaving, shifting mound of black, brown buzzards and white vultures. They were squabbling, hissing, flopping awkwardly about in three separate groups.

Challenger, Oxford, and Bartow halted and stayed where they were until they made sure of their surroundings. Their expert gaze missed no detail. When Claymore barked, some scavengers arose and climbed, flapping heavily, into the hot and windless air, but, for the most part, the carrion eaters continued to struggle, peck, and fight over their feast.

Challenger clapped hands, yelled, and, waving his arms, ran forward, whereupon the big, naked-headed birds reluctantly teetered over the ground and, flapping broad pinions in order to gain flying speed, took off. There were so many buzzards that Oxford wondered that some didn't collide or get pulled down by the dog. Shadows floated wildly about the clearing; then, all at once, it was devoid of carrion birds. Only then were the skirmishers able to learn what had happened.

Three hideously mangled human bodies lay on the claw-scarred ground. Considering how many buzzards had been at work, they remained relatively intact because, although all had been scalped, they still were clothed. Quickly Micah Oxford observed, but without comment, that in these latitudes the savages didn't take anywhere near as much of a scalp as was lifted up north. Instead of following a victim's hairline all the way around, these Indians had taken a section only six inches in diameter from the crown.

Judging by the vivid color of shreds of flesh adhering to the dead men's heads and hands, Oxford estimated that they must have been surprised and slaughtered just about daybreak.

Obeying signals from Challenger, the mastiff explored the nearby underbush. Satisfied that nothing alive was worthy of attention, he returned, tongue lolling out, and sat down before his master. The Ranger captain then bent over the nearest cadaver, which was that of a short, thick-bodied man who'd been wearing boots of European cut. "Reckon Toby Brodbelt's run his last chain," growled the Ranger captain.

Jim Bartow, inspecting another of the fallen bodies, spat angrily. "Damn my eyes if this mess ain't all they've left of Bill Pierson."

Challenger looked dubious, since the body was almost shapeless. "How can ye tell?"

"Bill lacked the middle finger on his left hand and this thing's short one too. Who'd be this other feller, Wallace? You bin around Charles Town more'n me."

"Hard to say. Could be Jim Phillips; he used to do some surveying."

"Naw, that'd be too big for Jim; more likely 'tis Jake Cox. Someone said he was going off with Brodbelt." He nodded to himself. "Yep. That's who 'tis. Jake was wearin' a Choctaw belt last I seen him—that there's what's left of it."

Only by such means was it possible to identify the murdered surveyors; the buzzards had almost completely stripped the skulls of flesh; those supreme delicacies, the eyeballs, of course had been devoured first of all. Scattered over a wide area centering on the ashes of a campfire lay some broken surveyor's instruments, but a portfolio, bound in oiled and waterproof cowhide, hadn't been touched. Frowning, Wallace Challenger stowed it in his saddlebag.

Heads bent, the scouts circled, examining every inch of ground. It wasn't much use; scrambling, tugging, fighting buzzards had obliterated all but a very few significant clues.

Sergeant Felton rode up leading the other horses, which began to snuffle and stamp at the sickish-sweet stench of blood and the sour reek of torn entrails. Felton dismounted. Face darkening with rage, he swore horribly.

Challenger treated the Yorker to a searching glance. "Oxford, I'd like to hear what you think happened here."

"We-ell, I'd hate to sound too sure"—Micah tugged at his little forked beard—"but it looks to me like these fellers had broken camp and was gettin' ready to saddle up. The hostiles was hid 'mongst yonder myrtles." He pointed, hard gray eyes agleam. "They waited until they was sure there weren't no more to the party."

"How many attackers?"

"Mebbe seven—eight. I think Brodbelt and his boys got cut down by a single volley—hadn't no idee what hit 'em."

"Ye're right," Bartow grunted. "I figger that's about what happened."

"And after that?"

"The hostiles caught two of these fellers' mounts and their pack horse and led 'em off to the south, but a fourth, somehow, broke loose. Ye can see where the critter tore off through the bushes and escaped into the woods with maybe an arrow or two in him to speed him up," Micah said while studying the ground and tugging thoughtfully at his mangled ear. "Them hostiles was only halfway done plunderin' when somethin' scared 'em off."

The gaunt sergeant frowned on a smashed transit. "What d'ye think that somethin' was?"

"Dunno as yet. Yep. They sure got scared off, else they'd have stripped the bodies; a man c'n always use leggin's and moccasins good as these."

Under the broad palmetto hat with its jauntily upturned brim, Challenger nodded, then turned to Bartow. "Jim, you know most about the tribes hereabouts; who's most likely done this?"

The buckskin pushed his hat back on lank, greasy black hair and stared up into the great dead oak, to which a few bold buzzards had returned. "Now, Wallace, that'd be hard to say right off. Might ha' been a party o' Yamasees, but Yamasees would have struck these fellers whilst they still slept. Besides, they'd surely have cut throats after scalping; Yamasees crave the sight o' running blood."

"Which way did they head?"

Oxford, ready now to show off a bit, said quickly, "South, Cap'n. Back the way they come."

"How far are they now?"

"That depends on— Hey, Cap'n, what ails yer dog?"

Claymore had pointed his grizzled rough nose at the sky and was swinging his shaggy head in slow semicircles.

The scouting party readied their weapons, then remained as still as so many snowshoe rabbits "freezing" at approach of danger.

Finally Challenger muttered, "'Tisn't Injuns or Claymore's bristle. Now, what the hell—"

Somewhere, in the hot and breathless woods, a voice, high-pitched and off key, had begun to sing:

> *"In our weakness and distress*
> *Rock of Strength, be thou our stay*
> *In the path of wilderness*
> *Be our true and living way . . ."*

Silent and lithe as panthers, the four whites abandoned their horses in the open, but with bridles linked—just as Felton had brought them up; thus joined, they couldn't travel far. Then the men merged with the woods.

> *"The sun is ruler of the day*
> *The silver moon of night*
> *The stormy hosts adorn the sky*
> *In ordered ranks of light."*

"Take it easy, boys. Reckon I know who that'll be," Bartow said, relaxing his grip on his musket.

Challenger's bright blue eyes slewed about, questioning.

"'Tis a half-crazy galoot who calls himself either Brother Barnaby or the Eternal Wanderer. Folks claim he once was a sure-enough minister, but, somehow, his mind got addled. Now he wanders 'mongst the tribes preaching of Yo-he-wa and no Injun will hurt him 'cause they worship a top-dog god by that name. Besides, he's a *loco* and therefore sacred among all Muscogees. Barnaby's harmless, even if he was eddicated in England."

"All right, Jim, fetch him in," Challenger directed. "Sam, you take a quick look along the trail whilst I figure what's to be done."

Even with half an eye, Oxford could tell that the Ranger captain was a heap more puzzled and upset over these murders than he was letting on.

For one thing, many more than ten or twelve horses had traveled this trace and not too long ago. Again, one of the surveyors' horses had got loose and plunged into the forest almost in a direct line with that point where the singing had risen and then abruptly ceased.

It wasn't long before Jim Bartow reappeared leading an outlandish figure whose bare feet caused no more noise than did the Ranger's moc-casins. Except for the tattered remains of a long-skirted, rusty black cassock which time and again had been mended with deer sinews, Brother Barnaby wore Indian garments and slung over one shoulder was a nearly empty Yuchi war bag bearing Alibamu totems. This wild-eyed fellow's only weapon, if it could be called one, was a long staff which had had a rough wooden crosspiece lashed to it with rawhide.

In his free hand this apparition carried the remains of an incredibly worn and weather-beaten Bible. The most incongruous thing about Brother Barnaby was the fact that he'd painted Latin crosses in white upon his nut-brown and cleanly shaven cheeks! Another white cross shone above the juncture of extremely bushy dark brows.

Once Brother Barnaby entered the clearing beneath the dead oak, he lifted his staff and, rolling back his eyes, he raised another hymn—which came as a surprise to Wallace Challenger because he'd expected the Wan-derer to start reciting a prayer for those pitiable lumps of flesh now al-most lost to sight among clouds of green and blue bottle flies.

> *"Yea, we too groan within ourselves*
> *And their adoption want*
> *For which the Holy Spirit's seal*
> *Did us predestinate."*

The Rangers listened to the Wanderer's cracked, caterwauling voice only a little while before Wallace Challenger lost patience. "That'll do, reverend sir. Hadn't you better offer prayer for the repose of the souls of these poor, murdered men?"

Unexpectedly, a measure of reason seemed to supplant the wild gleam in the Wanderer's intense dark eyes.

"Dear me, sir, I am *indeed* remiss!" he muttered, and drove the pointed end of his improvised cross-staff into the sandy soil. Raising thorn-raked arms skyward, he tilted back his strangely painted head and, in clear, resonant tones, cried, "Brothers, kneel with me and let us pray. But we need not grieve unduly over the death of these fellow sinners. Let us rather find comfort in the thought that they have won surcease from the trammels and pains of this earthly existence, and are now at peace with our Heavenly Father."

The weird figure droned on and on in a rich, resonant, and unmis-takably cultured voice. Sometimes he spoke words of wisdom and great beauty, but more often he intoned sheer gibberish.

At length Challenger, whose knees were beginning to ache from this unfamiliar position, arose. "Reckon that'll be about enough to start these fellers on their way toward salvation. Now, friend, suppose you take this hatchet and go cut some wood for crosses whilst the rest of us dig."

He knew it wouldn't do to leave the murdered men unburied; Indians felt an almighty contempt for anybody who would leave their dead unattended.

All the same, Challenger hated to waste time in digging a grave, since it was a near certainty that bears and wolves soon would dig up the remains unless protected by a pile of rocks. Since no stones were to be found in this vicinity, he foresaw that these dead would have to take their chances about having their eternal rest disturbed.

Perhaps it was the business of planting the crosses that, for a flash, restored Brother Barnaby's reason. In a perfectly rational tone he said, "Forgive me, friends. I fear you have found me on one of my bad days. Pray, who are you?"

Challenger informed him.

"And who are these unhappy men we have buried?"

This time Sergeant Felton supplied the answer, then asked, and not without respect, "Who are ye—really?"

The irregular white crosses painted on the Wanderer's fine features flashed as he drew himself up and announced in impressive dignity, "I was ordained in the Anglican Episcopal Church as the Reverend Edward Nicholson; but that was so long ago, I—oh, dear, I—I fear I really cannot recall. No matter." Then, obviously unaware that he'd already knelt, he fell onto his knees. The others exchanged glances, then followed suit while their horses, trailing reins, began to crop at heat-withered leaves and grasses.

The Reverend Doctor Nicholson just had completed reciting the service for the dead when he jumped up, crying in agitation, "And now you may bring the babe before me. Hasten! We must make sure this new soul is received into the Community of Christ. Where *is* the infant?"

Unexpectedly, Micah Oxford spoke up, "Brother, they've forgot to fetch him. Reckon he's still in the Indian village. You know where to find it?"

Brother Barnaby made a vague gesture over his tattered cassock's shoulder. " 'Tis that way—and not far off."

"You sure?"

"Aye. I have dwelt among them, on occasion, for nigh on three months; they are fine people."

Bartow rasped, "I'll bet! 'Specially round a torture frame."

"Sir, you are in error," Brother Barnaby insisted in clipped, precise English. "These *are* truly good people. I have been instructing them to understand the Word of the Lord."

"In English, Latin, or Muskogean?" Challenger couldn't help gibing.

The Wanderer replied, "In a dream the Lord God appeared and spoke, saying, 'My son, you must instruct these savages in the English tongue, that they may more exactly comprehend the truth of My Word.' And so—I—I—" He in the patched cassock cackled crazily, then wildly began to sing the Muskogean "New Corn Song."

Shocked, Wallace Challenger swung over to confront the eldritch figure. "Stop that! Now give me a straight answer else I'll take this quirt to you. What band lives in the village you spoke of?"

Unimpressed, Brother Barnaby batted blank, very dark brown eyes. "I cannot recall by what name they call themselves. To me it is sufficient that they are ignorant savages lost amid the darkness of abysmal ignorance. They have come down from the hills to fish and to feast on crabs, oysters and clams supplied through God's unmeasurable bounty."

"Did they have anything to do—with this?" Challenger pointed to the mound of raw earth.

The Wanderer giggled, spread gnarled hands tipped with yellow, claw-like nails, then uprooted his cross-staff. "I departed from their village two, maybe three sleeps ago; I cannot say."

"Where've you been, meantime?"

"Wandering about the forest, dear sir. Often, like St. Francis of Assisi, I find a reward in preaching to the birds and beasts."

"Like hell ye have, ye daft mountebank!" snarled Felton. His hand shot out, closed so hard upon the rotting bronze-black cloth covering Brother Barnaby's chest that some seams parted enough to expose pale white skin underneath.

Brother Barnaby stiffened, then rolled his eyes so far back in their sockets that their pupils became invisible. "Please, kind sir, you are tearing my vestments. Besides, I am telling the truth."

Challenger swung over to his horse, curtly saying, "Leave go of him, Sam, and make him take us to the village. I'm right curious."

Chapter 18

NEW CAPITAL I

At a walk, Wallace Challenger followed the Wanderer's ungainly but fast, loping progress through the woods, then turned in the saddle and drawled, "Sam, whilst I follow this loon for a while, I want you and Mike to go back to the trade track and keep on it till you arrive about opposite this village yer crazy friend's talking about. There's been a sight more horses on this trace than the murderers could have used. Keep yer eyes peeled, I don't aim for you to join Brodbelt and Company."

The Yorker bared gapped, yellowish teeth in a brief grin before kicking his mare on after the sergeant; quickly, his leather-clad back became lost to sight among dangling festoons of Spanish moss and drooping lianas. For a space the pair's progress could be traced through the raucous protesting screeches of parrots and Carolina parakeets.

While holding in his gelding to match Brother Barnaby's erratic stride, Wallace Challenger had continually to duck low boughs and loops of vines as tough and dangerous as snares set along a rabbit trot. As for Claymore, he was now content to follow—might be too many snakes ahead or off to the side. Bartow rode far enough behind his leader to allow himself space to wheel and get away should anything go wrong.

Judging by the number of pallid columns of smoke rising above the treetops, yonder, Challenger guessed that no inconsiderable village lay ahead.

He rode up alongside the Wanderer. "Say, Brother, how many lodges are there yonder?"

Some quirk of his madness sealed Brother Barnaby's lips and, in silence, he continued on through the forest, deftly managing the cross-staff he carried over his shoulder like a pike.

The blond giant commenced to sweat from more than the humid, ovenlike heat. If the occupants of this village proved hostile, the chances momentarily were increasing that the Wanderer might, perhaps consciously, be leading him and his lone companion into an ambush.

At the unnatural movement of some fern fronds ahead, he reined in at the base of a thick-trunked red bay tree. In Creek, he called out sharply, "Hi ligo! Inata atassimi. Come out of there, thou cowardly snake!"

Then the Ranger captain suffered a big surprise, for Sakwari-cra's tall figure materialized among the greenery. He was carrying a cocked French fusil in the crook of a massive, silver-banded arm. When Thad Burton made the peace sign, he looked very much as Challenger remembered him except that his roached Tuscarora crest must have been freshly dyed for, in the dappled sunlight, it showed blue-black instead of brown-black.

Challenger was relieved to note that the renegade mico was not painted for war; in fact, he was wearing no paint at all, a fact which emphasized the pallid scar slanting across his left temple.

Grimly, Challenger returned the sign. "Howdy, Burton. Glad to see ye're not painted red and black because the governor and the rest of us ain't but a short space back."

For a few breaths the two big men stared at one another, the Ranger's bright blue eyes fencing, probing Sakwari-cra's gray ones.

At length the white Tuscarora said in correct but oddly accented English, " 'The rest of you?' I would not like to resume our acquaintance by calling the great Captain Challenger a liar, but I must; Mr. Oglethorpe and his followers are no closer than the north bank of the Ogeechee River. I also know just as well that you made camp at Chaugee last night. Tell your companion to take his finger off that trigger!"

"Well, I'll be damned!" Challenger's expression relaxed. "How in hell did you better yer English—you weren't always so glib."

Just then Brother Barnaby stepped out of a tangle of honeysuckle and myrtle with leaves and bits of bark sprinkling his long black hair. Raising the cross-staff, he chanted, "The Lord God's blessings upon thee, my son. I trust Mistress Burton and the child are well?"

Ignoring Challenger and Bartow, Sakwari-cra went over to shake the Wanderer's hand. "They do very well, thank you, Brother." Then he returned his attention to the Rangers. "Since you two can't do harm, you shall come into my capital, Captain."

Challenger felt he was being mocked and didn't like it. "Reckon we better not. You'll have plenty of yer mongrel warriors on hand."

"You will come with me!" harshly insisted the white Tuscarora.

"Then what d'ye aim to do? Murder us, like you did those harmless fellows earlier on?"

Sudden rage contorted Thad's broad, deeply bronzed features. "*Hól-waki!* I and my Sakwaris did not slay the *Englasi* surveyor and his two men."

Challenger snorted, glowered down at the huge man standing by his horse's head. "If ye're telling the truth, *Mister* Burton, then how in hell would you know that Brodbelt was a surveyor? How would you know that he'd two men along? Did a wizard or some rain crow tell you that?"

Thad halted and gripped Challenger's bridle. "Captain, you had better not take me for a fool. Ever since those *Englasi* surveyors crossed the Ogeechee I have known where they were."

Challenger kept peering restlessly in all directions—saw plenty of hidden men. "In that case, why d'ye wait so long to knock 'em off?"

"I would have done nothing to discourage those surveyors unless they tried to cross the Altamaha—and then," Thad added quickly, "act only for their safety."

"I'll bet!" rasped Bartow.

The distorted shadow of a fish hawk flapping toward the Ogeechee River sailed over the treetops, flitted, intact, over open spaces. In the distance could be heard the continuous rumble of breakers rolling up some distant beach. Subconsciously, Challenger decided that they must have come much nearer to the ocean than he'd calculated.

Since no immediate advantage was to be gained by acting suspicious, the Ranger captain said, "All right, Mr. Burton. I'll take yer word on that score. Mind if the rest o' my men ride into your camp?"

He watched the white Tuscarora's gray eyes, expressionless as any Indian's, flicker aside before he nodded. "It will be all right. Two more men can accomplish nothing."

They had proceeded only a short distance when Bartow yelled, "Hi, Wallace! Our loony friend is runnin' off!"

Brother Barnaby had abandoned his cross-staff and, ducking and twisting, was plunging through the underbrush. The Rangers started after him and could easily have caught him had not Sakwari-cra warned sharply, "Let him go! He is harmless. My wife and I are deep in his debt."

Challenger affected surprise. "'Wife'? You mean to say ye've married that red-haired wench you were keepin' outside Yamacraw Town?"

The gigantic figure in loincloth and leggings halted in mid-stride, turned, glowering. "Mind your tongue! Brother Barnaby married us the same day he baptized my son."

Bartow sniggered, "Double-barrel action, eh? So the pup wasn't a bastard for long. I—"

Burton snarled like a cornered bobcat and, in a fluid movement, aimed a light, silver-mounted pistol at the Ranger's leather-covered chest. "You keep still!"

Challenger laughed at the way Bartow gaped before he growled, "Aw right. Keep yer hair on. I was only funnin'."

Thad stared at Bartow a moment, then lifted an owl's wing-bone whistle and sounded it three times. At once eight or ten unpainted but tough-looking warriors emerged from the woods. They looked ready, if not eager, to lift these white men's scalps.

Riding among an untidy collection of palmetto-thatched huts composing Sakwari-cra's "capital," Wallace Challenger recognized quite a few of Thad Burton's followers: for example, the one-eyed Chickasaw called Chula, and Shatara, from the same tribe.

Also visible were several Tallapoops, Yamacraws, and a good many Yuchis. All looked to be poised for action, not at all relaxed or friendly-like. Briefly, Challenger wondered whether the insubordinate African called Quobah had rejoined Burton's band, until he noticed not a single mulatto, mustee, or full Negro among Thad's followers.

The Sakwaris were encamped amid a grove of lofty, red-trunked pines growing upon what, ages ago, had been a dune. The ground hereabouts looked dark but so sandy that rain would drain off at once, leaving no unhealthy mud.

By quick estimate, the Ranger officer decided that at least thirty or forty lean-tos and huts had been raised in the shade of these fragrant-smelling pines. By the riverbank lay a large number of pirogues, canoes, and small rafts.

Upstream from the encampment, a herd of rather good-looking horses switched flies, rolled in the dust or drowsed about a rude corral. The usual bevy of shifty-eyed hunting dogs roused only long enough to bark halfheartedly; it was too hot to get excited, which was just as well, because Claymore began to roar defiance. He got no takers for all he was bristling and fairly itching for a fight.

The farther the Rangers penetrated the encampment the more tribes they saw represented: Alibamus, Abecas—even a Suwanee or two—were to be recognized. But to Challenger's surprise relatively few Yuchis were in evidence, although that once-powerful nation some time ago had broken up into wandering bands.

"Captain, you come with me," Thad enunciated with the unnatural precision of one who only recently has acquired grammatical mastery of a language. "You must be hungry after digging that grave."

Walking with ridiculous pomposity, the mico led the way to a very large lean-to before which Taqua, clad in the clean but badly stained remains of a European calico gown, was nursing a baby. She looked up, smiled, and called out, "You are welcome," but she didn't bother to pull up her blouse or remove the infant's mouth from the breast at which he was tugging and kneading.

Steely glints flickered in the depths of Thad's eyes as he said in his stilted English, "Captain, I expect you will remember my wife?"

The Ranger thought it wise to offer a short bow to this deeply sunburned, young woman with faintly slanted, gray-green eyes. "Your servant, ma'am. I trust I find you and your infant in good health?"

The red-haired girl smiled uncertainly and obviously rehearsed her reply. "As well as I hope you find yourself, Captain."

"This is my son, James." Thad pronounced it "Jeems."

"James? Why James?"

"I think your governor is a great and a wise man."

Bartow grinned sourly, then stared hard at the jet-eyed, half-naked warriors who crowded about, fingering their weapons. In a fix like this it paid off to act arrogant.

It proved difficult for Challenger to credit the change which had taken place in Burton and his wife—if, indeed, a British court would consider her his spouse. The Reverend Edward Nicholson, being mentally unbalanced, very likely no longer held the right to marry anyone.

Chapter 19

NEW CAPITAL II

After easing saddle girths and watering their mounts at the river's edge, the visitors took a careful look about—without appearing to. At first they noticed nothing untoward; fat puppies and fatter red-brown children chased one another among the huts; women and half-grown girls crouched along the riverbank gutting and scaling a large catch of fish which would be split and set out to dry on flat stones.

Veiled in clouds of flies, several squaws were engaged in scraping fresh deerskins stretched on frames; others were weaving rushes into baskets or matting useful for a dozen purposes. Those of the men and older boys who weren't out on the river fishing or emptying traps made of willow withes lolled, smoking or dozing, in the shade.

Not much time passed before a commotion arose on the outskirts of the Sakwari camp and a warrior, a former Alibamu by the look of him, jogged into sight carrying his cocked musket parallel to the ground. He cast a scornful glance at the visitors before reporting to his mico that another Ranger and a trapper had been encountered on that trail which led toward the country of the Tala Yuchis, which lay across the Ogeechee.

Escorted by a party of dismounted warriors, Sergeant Felton and Micah Oxford soon rode into camp, hot and carefully expressionless.

By now Wallace Challenger had estimated the present strength of Sakwari-cra's band at around two hundred souls, of which at least fifty were warriors fit for the warpath.

Although the latest arrivals dismounted without comment, Challenger deduced from their overly casual manner that they'd gathered significant information of some sort, but it would have to keep. Now was no time to exchange intelligences.

Taqua, once more lithe and graceful, supervised the serving of succulent roasted oysters, cold boiled crabs, and broiled fish—a move which surprised the visitors because most Indians ate little or nothing during the middle of the day.

Although retaining outward composure, Thad Burton grew uneasy when a dark gray horse which obviously had belonged to the surveyors, because it was shod, broke away from boys who had been grazing a herd on a lush meadow lying well back from the river, and ran into camp. Shatara quickly caught the runaway and had started to lead it away when Felton slammed down his bark plate and called sharply, "Hold on! I know that there nag. It belonged to Mr. Brodbelt."

Challenger turned to Sakwari-cra and demanded in a flat voice, "Reckon maybe you'd better explain what that mount's doing here, *Mister* Burton."

Before replying, Thad looked deliberately out over the river where some boys were shrilling as they pulled in an extra-large fish. "Soon after we heard shooting to the north early this morning the horse came into my capital by itself."

Face hardening, Challenger lurched to his feet, whereupon the mastiff and his followers did the same. In all directions, previously somnolent Indians jumped up and commenced to converge toward their mico's big hut. "Sam, reckon it's time you tell me what kind of sign you and Oxford read on the main trace."

"There was a hell's mint of fresh hoofprints." Sam Felton's hatchet-shaped face contracted as he continued. "Funny thing. Maybe a dozen kept on toward a ford below here, but most of the horses were turned off the trail and ridden straight in here!"

"The others go cross the river?"

"Dunno. This renegade's bucks surrounded us 'fore we could find out."

Briefly, the tawny giant studied the equally huge white Tuscarora now standing beyond the cooking fire in guttural conversation with Shatara. Challenger almost yielded to an impulse to tangle with Burton and set-tle, once and for all, who was the better man. But he made no hostile move, only raised his voice. "D'ye know what I think, Sam? I reckon Sakwari-cra sent across the river such risky evidence as fresh scalps, cap-tured weapons and horses—course he's slipped on that last."

As intended, Thad Burton overheard. Forgetting his perfect English, he burst out, "That not true! I—I no kill! My people no kill!"

"Then," rasped the Ranger captain, "just how d'ye account for Mr. Brodbelt's horse and a Carolina saddle being in yer village?"

More Sakwaris caught up weapons and, scowling, commenced to close in on the four whites.

"Sakwaris *not* kill surveyors!" roared Thad. "Horse come by self."

Taqua hurried forward, talking rapidly in Creek. To her dismay, she sensed that Sakwari-cra was close to working himself into one of those murderous, blind rages of which only Indians were capable.

"That *echoclucco*—horse strayed in," she shrilled, whereat the baby be-gan to squall and Claymore to growl ominously deep in his throat. She turned to her husband, imploring, "*Tchuku ófan läkäs!* Let peace remain in this house."

Challenger found it difficult to control his temper—and thereby the situation. Grounding his gunstock, he remarked mildly, "Very well. Since you both *say* that neither you nor any of your people took part in the killings, I'll believe you."

The Sakwari mico also fought down his rage and commenced to regain his command of English. "As I said—that horse strayed into this place. I not lie—I am not lying."

Laure Burton, meanwhile, slipped into the palmetto-thatched hut to place Jeems on his bed of dried reeds; the baby gurgled sleepily when she groped beneath him for the second of those dueling pistols which, last winter, the Mico Thlucco Oglethorpe had given Thad.

She heard Sergeant Felton's hoarse voice rasp, "Be you speaking straight, what about them hoofprints we saw come this way?"

With lofty dignity, Thad explained, "When we heard the shooting at daybreak I led a mounted party to find out what was going on, because some Tala Yuchis are camped across the river."

From where she stood, ready to use the pistol she held concealed behind her, Laure recognized a dangerous glow still in her husband's deep-set gray eyes.

"We came too late; those who had killed the surveyors heard our horses and rode away."

"You didn't chase 'em?" sneered Felton. "I wonder why?"

"It was not my affair. My band is still small; I cannot afford, for the sake of three whites, to make enemies of a stronger tribe."

As Thad continued, Challenger nodded and gave the sergeant a warning look. "I have not allied my tribe with the Georgians and so I am not bound to protect them or to fight their enemies."

Oxford, infinitely relieved, spoke up, "See anything of them as did the job?"

When Burton snapped, "No. I did not," Challenger grew certain that Sakwari-cra was lying. He and his men simply could *not* have followed the same trail soon after dawn without encountering the killers at some point—if, indeed, he hadn't directed the whole thing himself. The more he thought the surer he grew that the Sakwaris were responsible for the murders and all this talk about Tala Yuchis was a red herring drawn across the trail of their guilt.

Felton duplicated his commander's thinking. "That renegade's no fool," said he later. "He knows there's a strong expedition not far off, so, like I said, he sent the scalps and most of the captured horses where we can't find them."

Thad Burton must have guessed the white men's disbelief, for he began to scowl again and his roached crest to quiver, as it always did when he got really angry. Taqua stepped a little closer to these two gigantic figures once more confronting each other. Mike Oxford felt mighty curious. Who'd be the first to speak or to make a move? Up north, whoever spoke first would lose prestige.

Sergeant Felton, sensing the dangers of such an impasse, ended it by saying, "Cap'n, this ain't buttering no parsnips. What say we ride back to the guvnor? He'll be wantin' to hear what happened to Brodbelt and his boys and maybe do somethin' about it."

"Maybe he will," Challenger said without removing his eyes from the mico. "Go get your horses, boys."

Before turning stiffly away, Sakwari-cra said, "Think what you will, Captain; I still say that I did not attack the surveyor's party."

"Since this seems a poor time to dispute yer word, Mr. Burton, we'll take our departure."

"You have my leave to go." Thad had started to turn away in stiff dignity, when he checked himself. "Captain, will you convey my fond respects to Mistress Winsome Brooks?"

Winsome Brooks! Challenger almost broke out laughing, but, instead, he affected the lisping accents of fashionable English gentlemen. "La, sir, 'pon my word, 'twill be an honor to obleege you and convey yer—er— fond respects to Mistress Brooks."

Once the scouting party, silent and watchful, had regained the trace they reined left and, at a brisk trot, started northward. For over an hour Challenger halted every quarter-hour to listen and make sure the Sakwaris weren't following.

When they regained the scene of Brodbelt's murder a few carrion birds were hopping, disappointed, among the crosses above the common grave. Gleefully, Claymore gave chase, even caught a white vulture which he killed with a single snap of massive jaws.

Bears and wolves, Mike figured as they rode on, wouldn't start digging at the grave till after nightfall, but then they'd find easy pickings.

That evening, as they sat cooking tasteless rations, Challenger glanced at Oxford's dimly illumined figure. "Mike, I know you've never been in this country before, but you sure do understand Indian ways. Tell me, what really happened to Brodbelt's party?"

Before replying the Yorker batted his hard little eyes several times. "Well, Cap'n, since you ask me, I'd say that the Sakwari sachem—mico, I mean—knocked off Brodbelt and company because he don't want whites to keep moving south and spoil his new hunting grounds. Bein' smart, he claimed the killing was done by parties unknown; he knows we can't prove anything different."

"Now fer a Yankee," drawled Bartow from beyond the tiny mound of glowing coals, "that's damned shrewd reasonin'."

The fork-bearded Yorker started to get mad, but held onto his temper. "Guess you fellers down here don't know that a Yorker *ain't* a Yankee, never was and never will be! Yankees, or 'Yengees'—which is the northern Injuns' way of saying 'English'—come from Connecticut and north, and I claim they're mostly a pack of sharp, mealymouthed sons-o'-bitches."

An amused chuckle arose from the Carolinians.

Oxford belched, then settled back, using his saddle for an armrest while he smoked his pipe. "Yep, they're so mean folks claim a Yankee will try down a mouse for its tallow. Met just such a character in Charles Town whilst I was waiting to go aboard Mr. Oglethorpe's scout boat."

"Where?" demanded the Ranger officer.

"Why, 'twas in the Queen's Head Tavern."

Just to be polite, Felton asked, "What sort of Yankee was he?"

"Ship's captain; smelly, loudmouthed old bastard just in from Jamaica. You wouldn't credit how that man carried on about some bound girl he claimed had skipped his vessel in Charles Town durin' his outward voyage."

Something stirred at the back of Challenger's mind. "Recall the name of his vessel?"

"Yep, only because it had a funny name—*Mystick*, but there weren't nothin' mystical I could see 'bout his stinkin' little tub."

Mystick! Challenger felt his breath stop. "Wha—what did he say about this—this runaway bound girl?"

"The old poop claimed he'd been done in the eye by a wench from Boston; claimed he'd played the good Samaritan by takin' her aboard when she was bein' run out of town."

Yawning, Mike tapped ashes from his pipe against a stick of firewood. "He said folks up in Boston told him that she'd been bundling with her pa and got found out."

Had a flask of gunpowder exploded in the fading fire Wallace Challenger could not have been more startled, but he didn't let on. Instead, he drawled in studied disinterest, "Was the Yankee captain certain-sure about this?"

"He claimed to be."

"What had her goings-on to do with this Yankee?" lantern-jawed Felton queried over the querulous wailing of whippoorwills, the whine of mosquitoes, and subtle noises from among the trees.

"Nothin', 'cept that when she skipped his ship this Starbuck feller—that was his name—swore out a warrant in Charles Town. He said he knew, for sure, his warrant had got served and that she got arrested, but, somehow, she escaped from jail and disappeared."

Challenger placed a stick on the dying fire. "Do the Carolina authorities know where this girl went?"

"Cap'n Starbuck swore that they did, but that they wouldn't say so—which was what made that piss-ant of a Yankee so mad. Anyhow, he ranted about the tavern that he wants the hussy took up and put back in jail fer defraudin' him out o' his passage money. He's even offered all of five pound reward for news of her."

Chapter 20

NEW ARRIVALS

After the acting governor had ridden away on his grand reconnaissance the public's confidence in Savannah and the Georgia Company again deteriorated. Quarrels and grievances came out into the open. There were even several examples of lawlessness verging upon open rebellion, all of which was deplored by the Reverend Samuel Quincey, Chief Bailiff Thomas Causton, and others in authority. However, they appeared so incapable of coping with the situation it became apparent that whenever James Oglethorpe went away the colony's affairs promptly stood at sixes and sevens.

First of all, food, forwarded from Charles Town as a result of the accompanying trustee's visit, proved inadequate and rapidly became exhausted, which was most unfortunate because the settlers' laboriously planted crops either had failed or else weren't ripe enough for consumption.

To make matters worse, contract hunters now were forced to range so far abroad that meat appeared only infrequently in the rat- and fly-plagued Market House.

Even wild turkeys now were hardly ever sighted in even the most distant fields. Sadly, the people recalled those good old days when, only a few months ago, Sakwari-cra and Toonahowie and their hunters kept fetching in slathers of venison and buffalo meat.

Therefore, great joy prevailed when a militiaman on duty in the watchtower fired his musket and called down that a large European ship was coming upstream! Her progress was slow because there wasn't sufficient wind to keep her canvas filled.

For all that powder in the magazine was in short supply, Lieutenants

Glen and Savey decided to fire a salute on recognizing a British Union Flag curling at the stranger's maintop.

The muskets' report, sounding thunderous on such a still, hot day, set everybody capable of movement hurrying to line the bluff's edge. There, waving cloths and green branches, they waited for two hours under the burning sun. Word was spread that, at long last, the Georgia Company's second transport was actually arriving, bringing reinforcements and all manner of supplies from Home.

Once the ship, the *James*, Captain Yoakley, dropped anchor opposite the crane used to hoist heavy objects up the bluff, her master had himself rowed ashore. To the Town Council he reported that he had on board one hundred fifty immigrants of which one quarter had come out at their own expense. The majority, however, like the original settlers, were penniless ex-debtors brought "on the Charity."

Moonfaced Captain Yoakley was pleased to learn that he had won a cash prize through having brought in the first transatlantic vessel to unload in Savannah.

Abruptly, dissension and insubordination vanished. Everyone seemed glad to take a new outlook on life. For the deeply tanned exiles it proved sheer joy to think that yonder weather-beaten vessel had left Old England just a few weeks ago. Dear Old England! Almost everyone tended to recall only the happiest aspects of the years lived there.

"My God, don't they look pale? They're whiter'n skim milk!" Hendy O'Brien remarked to Bettie as they sat on the edge of the bluff. Although her pregnancy had not yet become too obvious, she hadn't been having an easy time. "Look at 'em laugh and dance about the deck. Ah-h, those poor fools! They'd better enjoy themselves before they learn how they're going to live."

John Stonehewer, standing not far away with arms folded, grunted, "Pray God they've some farmers, blacksmiths and carpenters and other useful folk among 'em. We can do without more preachers, lawyers and lily-handed gentry."

The dark-faced weaver-inventor later was pleased to learn that several of the *James's* passengers in some way were connected with the culture and manufacture of silk; artisans like Paul and Nicholas Amatis, who'd come over in the *Anne*. One was Jacques Camuse, a master silk spinner, who had brought along not only his wife, three children, and some apprentices but also a number of machines necessary to the trade.

"Lord God," groaned Hendy, "and for what would we be wantin' with silken finery when 'tis beef and wheat and cabbage we need for us, and proper fodder for the horses?"

It amused the few Carolinians present to observe how heartily the first-comers to Georgia laughed at the wondering way these newly landed folk stared and gawked about, quite forgetting that they, themselves, had done exactly the same thing only six months earlier.

Lieutenant Archibald Glen watched the men coming ashore, mentally selected recruits for the militia. With regret, he noted that there didn't seem to be very many who appeared even halfway qualified to become soldiers.

Lieutenant John Savey, standing beside him, was feeling better satisfied; quite a few well if not richly dressed older people were clambering ashore. They must have paid for their own passages and brought along some money. Also, there were a few pretty young girls.

Hendy lost some of his gloominess when someone told him that the *James* had on board a pedigreed racing stallion and four purebred mares; all had survived the passage well. Whistling, the ex-jockey got himself rowed out to the ship and spent a long and happy while below decks jawing with the horse handlers.

A scattering of punts, sailing skiffs came down from Purysburg to join the swarm of Indian dugout canoes, pirogues, and buffalo-hide coracles which, in increasing numbers, circled about the *James*. Already high-pitched Indian voices were offering for sale all manner of third-quality hides, skins, and furs.

The second contingent sent out by the company barely had identified the plots of land already allotted to them and still were finding their way about when a third company ship appeared. Although smaller than either the *James* or the *Anne*, the *Two Brothers* seemed to be better found. At least she appeared more shipshape when she anchored off the wharf below the bluff.

Along with Helen Bayless Glen and Bettie O'Brien, Winsome Brooks hurried down to the landing place of Tomo-chichi's all-but-deserted village, for, fearing the white man's diseases, that wise old Yamacraw had moved his tribe several miles upriver and re-established his town a short distance from the Savannah. Only a few sick or aged Yamacraws continued to live at the old site.

As the first lot of passengers scrambled into a barge drawn up alongside the *Two Brothers*, Winsome remarked, "What queer-looking clothes some of those people are wearing!"

Certain of the male passengers had on round black hats bound in brownish fur and were clothed in ankle-long, cassock-like black garments. Black, corkscrew curls dangled over these men's gaunt and generally sallow cheeks. For the most part, the women out there looked to be small and plump and wore kerchiefs bound over glossy sable hair knotted under their chins.

Helen's finger tips pressed themselves to her lips. "Why! Why! Those must be Jews! Hebrews!"

"How d'you know they're Jews?" Winsome was perplexed.

"There are many around London. Only these look more foreign, somehow."

Not all the newcomers were so distinctively appareled; a second barge landed a group of olive-skinned Jews finely dressed in well-cut suits or gowns of somber hue. Some even displayed flashes of white lace at throat and wrists; this lot of immigrants had thin, mobile, hawk-like features and intelligent, liquid dark eyes.

Once the second barge had grounded on the beach, a tall, gray-haired man of distinguished appearance stepped ashore to be greeted by Thomas Causton. Politely enough, the chief bailiff doffed his hat and even made a leg. "And whom, sir, do I have the honor to address?"

Said the newcomer, bowing low but not removing a small black tricorne trimmed in sparkling silver lace, "My name, sir, is Nunis. I am Dr. Daniel Nunis, late of Bristol and Lisbon." On his saturnine features appeared a thin smile. "I am the elected leader of our little congregation."

Abruptly, Causton's tone grew less deferential. "You are a doctor? Of what sort?"

"Of medicine, sir, in a modest way." He indicated a delicate little woman in a gray silk gown. "This is my spouse, Sipra, and this is Jacob Olivera, my second-in-command. This lady is his wife, Leah, and those are his children, David, Isaac and Leah the Younger."

Next, this supremely dignified Hebrew, with a graceful wave of a slender hand, indicated a lean, lively eyed younger man. "This, sir, is Benjamin Sheftall and his wife; like the rest of our coreligionists, they have come out from England at their own expense."

The Reverend Samuel Quincey now advanced warily, "And what, my dear sir, are your religious affiliations?"

Slowly Dr. Nunis swung his narrow head to face the chaplain. "Reverend sir, although there are some Levites among us, the most of us are Hebrews of the Sephardic persuasion, whose ancestors were driven out of Spain and Portugal many years ago. Since then, like our ancient forefathers, we have wandered in many lands."

He raised brilliant black eyes to the brass-hued sky and spoke with modest fervor, "Earnestly we do beseech Thee, the Lord God Jehovah, Creator of us all, that here, in this beautiful land, so free, so new and so wide and unspoiled, we will reach the end of our wanderings and homelessness. Let us hope that at last we have attained a new Promised Land."

Reverend Doctor Quincey, visibly touched, murmured, "With God's help, let this be so."

To the astonishment of these alien-appearing new arrivals, the rough-looking first settlers really seemed ready to make them welcome. They helped to carry their baggage ashore with such alacrity that many Israelites were moved to tears.

"They may be a parcel of Christ-killing Jews, but you'll have to admit they're brave," Lieutenant Glen remarked to John Savey, who, for some reason, appeared uncommonly thoughtful and absent-minded.

"Why?"

"Stands to reason most of these people are town-bred so, for them to come to this wilderness, required plenty of courage."

The shaggy, sunburned children of Savannah, however, weren't so tolerant; they couldn't resist teasing these shy, dark-visaged offspring with restless black eyes. David Cohen's children, Hannah, Abigail, and Grace, and Abraham Minis's daughters, Leah and Esther, at first were taunted to the point of tears because they couldn't understand what was being said, but, after a bit, the young first arrivals' curiosity overcame latent hostility and the little Hebrews, who soon became cruelly sunburned, were included in games and, incidentally, helping their young hosts with such chores as weeding gardens, herding geese, drawing water, and lugging firewood.

A few days later Dr. Nunis observed to Benjamin Sheftall as, after supper, they and their wives sat on a log before their tent, "Surely, since Jehovah has put an end to our sufferings and wanderings we should erect a synagogue; perhaps we will call it Mickya Israel."

"That would be fitting," Rabbi Sheftall murmured. "Tell me, Daniel, how do you fare among the *Goyim* doctors of medicine?"

Dr. Nunis shrugged, parted his thin hands, "There are only two of them and they lack so many drugs and medicines that were I an evil wizard"—he chuckled—"as Drs. Cox and Tailfer sometimes appear to suspect, they could not welcome me more heartily."

The rabbi removed and carefully wiped a pair of steel-rimmed spectacles with square lenses. "Are they well instructed?"

"Let us only say that I *have* encountered more knowledgeable healers, but they mean well, especially Dr. Cox. Poor man! I fear the dropsy soon will carry him off."

Abigail Cohen, plump and energetic, drew near the fire, then timidly inquired whether Dr. Nunis could find something to alleviate fever and pain resulting from sunburn? Her children wouldn't stop crying.

Watched from a distance by another group of settlers who had arrived in the *James*, the two Jews conversed in Portuguese as, from a battered, brassbound wooden traveling medicine chest, Dr. Nunis selected a squat stone jar. He then employed a horn spoon to extract a dab of yellow-green ointment which he wrapped in a twist of paper. Abigail Cohen grabbed the saturnine physician's hand, bent and kissed it, then disappeared among a miscellany of patched and threadbare tents pitched in regular rows.

A stoop-shouldered Englishwoman with "overworked servant" written all over her, advanced to the perimeter of firelight. "Kind sir, can ye spare a mite more of that stuff? My Benny's scorched to a cinder."

Dr. Nunis took the jar of ointment over to her. "Your little one, he also has been burned by the sun?"

"Oh yes, sir. Dreadful bad. Poor Benny can't go to sleep and yells all the while. I took him to Dr. Tailfer and he said to rub him with pig's fat. I did, but it don't seem to help at all."

"I would not recommend pig's fat"—a fleeting smile curled the Sephardic Jew's mobile, thin-lipped mouth—"at least for my own family. Here." He scooped out another smear of ointment, wrapped it as before, and placed it in the big woman's hand.

"But, sir, I can't pay. Harry and me are on the Charity. We haven't a groat to our name."

"No matter," Nunis said quietly. "Rub your child lightly and make him drink plenty of water. Then in the morning brew some tea and—"

"But, sir, I don't own even a smidgen of tea."

"I got enough, ma'am," a big, bearded man announced from the background. "I can spare ye sufficient to brew you a mess."

"You are a good man, a real Christian," observed the dark-eyed physician. "*Madame*"—he used the French pronunciation—"steep the tea strong and black, then pat it onto the burned areas using the softest cloth you can find. Bind a compress of tea leaves over the worst areas."

"Why, why, God bless ye, sir!" burst out the woman. "I declare I never suspected there could be so much goodness in—in a benighted Jew."

Benjamin Sheftall smiled wryly. "Well, you do now, *madame*."

Chapter 21

"—AS A THIEF IN THE NIGHT"

Two afternoons after the arrival of the *Two Brothers*, a gaunt Ranger, thorn-raked and burned by the sun to a dark red-brown, rode up to the garrison's headquarters and tied his sweat-grayed mount to a hitching post.

Militia Lieutenant John Savey heard him through the Commissary Office window and, on tiptoe, hurried over to see who had arrived; but he couldn't recognize him. He was back behind his desk long before the buckskin, sweating and smelling like a tanning yard, sauntered through the doorway.

"Heyo, mister," the Ranger greeted with that tolerant contempt native Carolinians reserved for newcomers. "You play-soljers better shake the lead out'n yer asses and smarten up!"

At his tone Savey reddened, but was at pains to remain courteous. "Thank you for your sage advice, my good man, but why do you offer it?"

"'Cause His Excellency ain't but a day's ride off."

Carefully, Lieutenant Savey put down the quill with which he'd been preparing returns of certain supplies supposedly issued gratis to the *James's* people in the company's name—but largely paid for by them.

Airily, he indicated a bucket of spring water recently fetched in. "Help yourself; sorry I can't offer a thirsty man something more worth drinking —but you know how 'tis."

"Yep. I know how 'tis in this here pious-talkin' Rascals' Heaven. Come sundown, I'll git paddled over to the Caroliny shore. Hear tell Tim Sully keeps some tolerable rotgut at his place."

Having, during the past few weeks, smuggled in a keg or two of Mr. Sully's Jamaica rum, John Savey could but didn't confirm this buckskin's opinion.

Said Savey, cooling himself with a turkey-wing fan, "So. His Excellency is only a day away?"

The Ranger sighed, sluiced the last of the water down the front of his hunting shirt. "Yep. He'd have come in tonight only his expedition ain't travelin' so fast; what with this heat everybody feels kind o' whipped down. Reckon he'll be pleased to find these new folks around here."

"No doubt of it," Savey said. "About what time of day would you say the garrison should be ready to receive His Excellency?"

For all that this smelly fellow almost surely could neither read nor write, John Savey folded over the sheet of foolscap he'd been working on.

"If 'twas me, I'd not get yer boys spruced up 'fore late tomorrow— mebbe even not till early the next day, provided ye're lucky."

Savey's slender black brows merged. "My good man, just what d'you mean by 'lucky'?"

"That'll give ye more time to mend discipline. Whoever's been commanding the garrison has got pretty goddam slack." He stared in open contempt at Savey's neatly uniformed figure. "Just now I rode in between two o' yer outposts; neither of yer brave boys even saw, let alone challenged me."

The young militia officer stared angrily a moment, then said stiffly,

"Thank you for the information. Immediate action will be taken." Savey then offered his most winning smile. "Will you be good enough to find Lieutenant Glen and repeat what you have just told me? I'd go myself, but I daren't leave the supply office unattended."

Once the Ranger, with powder horn and tomahawk swaying at his belt, had drifted out into the sunlight, John Savey remained motionless, staring at the raw pine boards opposite. Damn such luck! Why couldn't Jamie Oglethorpe have stayed away another few days?

Arising, the young fellow blew down the front of a sweat-soaked linen shirt. He was thinking, 'Tis a great thing to know when to stop. No point in being greedy and risk what's been won. Um. Two hundred seventy-five pounds ought to get me away from here and anywhere I decide to go. Too bad Micah Oxford isn't back. He's a useful sort; maybe I'll leave word for him to join me in Charles Town. One way or another, we should make a real packet of money.

Shortly after darkness settled over the river, Lieutenant John Savey quietly quitted his cramped quarters and departed with a small chest balanced on one shoulder. Among other valuables it contained a heavy canvas sack bulging with heavy gold and silver coins. When he thought of what his successor might think and say, once he began to tally the slender stock of supplies remaining in the company's Supply House, he almost laughed.

With any kind of luck, Savey figured he ought to reach Charles Town just about the time James Edward Oglethorpe returned to Savannah.

Chapter 22

OLD BATTLE

As a result of proven worth as a military engineer, Oglethorpe, a few days earlier, had commissioned Petre Ballou a major in the militia, an honor which had pleased the Swiss inordinately. Right now, he was rejoicing that the reconnaissance party's van had commenced to jog toward some deep woods; in there it should be cooler and the flies not so insufferable.

Savannah, he suspected, couldn't lie more than a couple of leagues to the south, but he wished the distance was shorter. *Mon Dieu!* What a relief it will be to leave the saddle, bathe, and change clothes.

No one can guess how awful I feel; my throat burns like a lime kiln and that old craving has begun to gnaw at my belly. This time I won't give in. *Mais non!* Too much at stake; besides, Petre Ballou isn't young enough any longer. Too old for hard campaigning. Come, *mon vieux*, let us ignore that thirst and think of something else!

For instance, everyone, from the governor down, is prepared to admit that I have not lied too much about my past—and that I am really a first-class engineer.

Not the least of the good things which have occurred during the last few weeks is my new friendship with *le bon capitaine* MacPherson. He must have thought me a bigger liar than I am when I described my service in the Low Countries with certain Jacobite friends who turned out to be relatives of his. Is it not curious to reflect that most of our governor's close family, at this moment, are living in France and devoted to the cause of that pretty carpet knight, Charles Stuart, called by some "Bonnie Prince Charlie? *Ma foie!* Never will *he* make a good soldier.

C'est presque incroyable that our governor's own father once was forced to flee across the Channel and only returned to his homeland in 1696 after swearing allegiance to that unattractive pair, William and Mary. Perhaps, by way of a bribe for continued loyalty, the new *régime* appointed Oglethorpe's *père* Lieutenant Governor of Surrey. Despite this honor, the governor's mother has remained a Jacobite while the big man who now rides at the head of this column while attending Oxford has participated in pro-Stuart riots.

The old Swiss spurred his horse and, despite himself, began to estimate how much time must elapse before he could down a great beaker of brandy and cool spring water. Not that he actually was going to drink much liquor; *mais non!* But where lay the harm in imagining such a pleasure? Probably his suave and good-looking young friend, John Savey, the supply officer, would have a little rum or brandy on hand.

To have this intolerable thirst recur was infinitely discouraging; what a fool he'd been to delude himself into thinking he'd shaken off his weakness forever! Bitterly, Major Ballou unslung his water bottle but only spat out the lukewarm stuff. And to recall that one of the principal reasons he'd embarked on the Georgia Company's charity was because, in the brochure they'd given him in the debtor's prison, it was stated that "the possession, use or sale of spirituous liquors in Georgia will be stringently interdicted."

For all Petre Ballou despaired at the thought of getting drunk again, he knew that, as surely as he was sitting this hot saddle, the passage of a few hours' time would reduce him to a noisy, belligerent, and possibly dangerous drunkard.

Non, Petre, non! You will not! You must not forfeit the good governor's confidence!

Sweating hard, Ballou watched patches of yellow sunlight pass over the men and horses plodding ahead. Although he kept repeating *non, non, non!* he could tell the old battle was about to be joined once more; the battle he never had been able to win. This was really too bad, because, during the last thirty years, his brain had escaped serious damage from alcohol—but would he be so lucky this time?

Frantically, Major Ballou made another attempt to direct his thoughts into other channels. Considered as a whole, this long and tiresome reconnaissance must be counted a great success—provided that the recommendations made by me and Vincent Palmer, that droll but capable engineer from Charles Town, are carried into effect. Yes, if forts and "strong villages" are built at the points we indicated this miserable colony may survive until sufficient reinforcements arrive—but if the Spanish attack soon, *en masse,* or if any great Indian force strikes, why then, *au revoir!*

The sun-seared and travel-worn expedition rode out of the woods and onto a wide field where felled trees lay dying to either side of a rough road. Fine red dust arose in billows which swiftly coated the already dusty horses and riders. Although Ballou tied a handkerchief over his mouth the dust penetrated the covering and augmented his already raging thirst, which he tried to ignore by drawing a mental contour map of the country he'd been over.

There was Fort Argyle, a regular fortification mounting guns, built on a high bluff dominating a principal crossing of the upper Ogeechee; to the southwest, a big blockhouse would be erected on Cornhouse Creek. These fortifications, along with Fort Moore, long since established by Carolinians on the Upper Savannah, *should* provide a series of rallying places, as would the enforted villages scheduled to rise at Thunderbolt, Cape Bluff, Ebenezer, and Abercorn.

Despite anguished efforts to ignore those white-hot pincers nipping at his stomach Petre Ballou failed and began, nervously, to bat eyes swollen and reddened by too much dust and sunlight. How much longer had he to suffer? Ugh! At least another hour.

A horse's length behind James MacPherson and the acting governor, Wallace Challenger followed across a series of clearings in which crops, hopefully planted last spring, had shriveled and died. They surely must be hungry in Savannah if the company's second ship had failed to make port.

What if the malcontents, led by Dr. Tailfer, Stonehewer, and O'Brien, had capitalized upon Oglethorpe's long absence to translate discontent into overt rebellion? Long before he'd left the place, he knew that a lot of settlers wanted to abandon exposed and struggling Savannah for the security and comfort of Charles Town and not a few were eager to return to lonely little Beaufort. Not that he blamed them; he didn't much like Rascals' Heaven either; it was growing too crowded, too noisy.

While his mount plodded along with head held low and almost too weary to switch flies, he fell once more to conjecturing about what part Thad Burton had played in the murder of Brodbelt and his companions. This time, he came to a definite conclusion: the surveyors *had* been slain by Sakwari-cra and his crew of strays and outlaws. Burton, cleverer and much more farsighted than a real redskin, had taken this means of discouraging further southerly expansion by Oglethorpe's people.

At long last, the sun-lashed column sighted the town as an orderly pattern of yellow, brown, or white structures; now there were even a few three-story buildings standing among them.

On the outskirts of Savannah the big Ranger captain recalled, to the least detail, Micah Oxford's account of his chance meeting with that Yankee skipper in Charles Town. Not to question the Yorker more closely, and so rouse his curiosity, had called for a deal of resolution, but, since he figured he already had heard about all that Oxford could tell him, he'd kept grimly quiet.

More often, lately, he'd congratulated himself that his first impressions of Winsome Brooks hadn't been far wrong. Under that cool, reserved exterior her blood must course, full and hot. It must be so, or why had she been forced to flee from Boston? Why had he exercised so much restraint? That wasn't his usual way with a female. Yes. He'd sure made a great, lop-eared jackass of himself! All along, she must have been fairly itching for a tumble in the underbrush. He ought to have caught on on that night of the indignation meeting; even a callow youth could have sensed her true emotions.

Then another disturbing thought struck: What was between the Brooks girl and that damned white Tuscarora? If there wasn't some bond, why had Sakwari-cra asked to be remembered, of all the people he'd once known in the settlement, to Winsome Brooks? Damn the impudent rogue! It could only mean that he'd managed to tumble her sometime, without anybody's getting the wiser. Ha! *That* must explain why she acted so stiffly toward him.

Challenger's gaze drifted over toward those four pines shading the town square, then flickered left and came to rest upon that rough dwelling which sheltered the O'Briens and Dr. Brooks's handsome daughter.

Chapter 23

THE MAGNOLIA TREE

Thanks to a cool breeze blowing strongly upriver, only a few mosquitoes whined about them as they sat, close together, under a shiny-leafed magnolia which grew, like a giant parasol, on a small rise near the river's edge. The night was so still that the occasional *plop!* of fish jumping and rustling noises made by alligators among the reeds carried distinctly to the silent couple. From their position facing the water, they could enjoy the effect of the August full moon upon Savannah.

The moonlight was so strong that Winsome Brooks's straight profile showed in cameo-like sharpness. Her eyes narrowed themselves as she sat with legs curled up under her studying Wallace Challenger and attempting to fathom the change in his manner. While the big man hadn't been anything but polite and soft-spoken since his return, there seemed to be an indefinable air of underlying insolence about his courtesy which hadn't been there before. It seemed as if the Ranger captain had been wrestling with some problem which, finally, he'd solved to his satisfaction.

In his fresh linen shirt, new knee breeches, and white stockings, Wallace certainly looked handsome, she decided, especially because he'd persuaded someone to shorten his tawny mane to collar length.

On the way to this spot Wallace had said very little, which rather surprised her; she'd expected he'd be eager to talk about the expedition. Now he sat with massive arms hooked about knees as, frowning a bit, he stared out over the river. For several minutes his silence continued while night peepers shrilled, whippoorwills complained, and bullfrogs grunted in the marsh below.

Finally, Winsome said, "I've heard about your finding those murdered surveyors. It must have been a terrible experience."

She watched his wide-set eyes swing almost reluctantly in her direction.

Said he in a low, tense voice. "Yep. It was particularly unpleasant to think that a dear old friend of yers most likely did them in."

The graceful arc of her back stiffened. "Who might you mean by 'dear old friend' of mine?"

"Who but that damned renegade, Thad Burton?"

She was so astonished she blurted, "You saw Thad! How—how was he?"

"Yes. To quote him exactly, he sent you his 'fond respects.' He's doing pretty well, by all accounts," he told her in a voice so strained that she should have taken warning. "His band's grown considerable; seemed like he was livin' pretty high on the hog. By the way, he's married that red-headed girl he was keeping."

"*Married?*" Winsome looked startled, but added quickly, "Oh, I'm so glad. I—I suppose her baby must have been born by now?"

"Yes. 'Twas a boy. They named him James after His Excellency. More often they call their woods colt Little Buck, which I reckon is a sight more suitable."

"Oh, I'm so happy for him—for both of them."

Hell! Why hadn't she taken offense over his suggestion that Sakwari-cra had been responsible for the murders? He felt his throat gradually tighten and a rushing noise commenced to sound in his ears. "Did ye hear me say that yer dear friend Burton knows plenty about the Brodbelt massacre?"

"Of course," came her cool admission. "But the idea was so absurd that I didn't grant it second consideration."

Lord! How beautiful she looked with wavy brown hair dressed high, crown-like, in an unusually attractive way. Fighting for control, he noticed that she had arranged some gauzy material as a ruche which only inadequately disguised the rich upper contours of breasts revealed by a new, rather daringly low-cut gown.

To her further inquiries concerning the grand reconnaissance, he replied absently, because once more he was debating the truth of what Micah Oxford had said. It was proving hard work to keep his breathing anywhere near even. When, in a fluid movement, Winsome tilted back her head to contemplate the moon she again presented her profile high-lighted in silvery tones. Wallace felt his neck swell and his limbs quiver like Claymore's when surging against his leash, eager to chase a fleeing deer.

He heardly recognized his own voice when he said, "While we were scouting south'ard I—well, I noticed a place by the Ogeechee's mouth which the redskins call Chaugee Landing. 'Twould be a good place to take up land and settle."

He watched her eyes, luminous now as those of a night-hunting cat, flicker in his direction. "Tell me about it, please."

"Chaugee's got everything—plenty of rich bottom land, deep water right close to shore, plenty of fish and game all around." He drew a stuttering breath. "What d'ye say—would ye—will ye go there with me?"

Disconcerted, Winsome glanced aside, unfortunately gave the impression of having shaken her head.

"So, you won't?" he rasped, bearded jaw working. "Well, by God, ye're wrong! You *are* coming to Chaugee!"

Eyes grown enormous, she drew back. "Please, please, Wallace, don't look at me so! I—I don't want—"

"I don't give a damn what you want! It's what *I* want that's going to count from now on."

She tried to get up, but he grabbed her skirt to pull her down and gave it such a powerful tug that there followed the snarl of rent cloth. While she swayed, throat closing in terror, his hand shot up and gripped the front of her gown.

"Sit down, damn it!" Then he pulled so hard that the fabric parted, exposing her breasts all the way.

He expected her to start screaming, but, curiously enough, Winsome didn't make a sound, not even when she found herself bared to the waist and imprisoned within the unyielding arc of his arms. All she did was to roll her eyes, gasping, "Oh-h, oh-h, no, don't!"

"From the start I deemed you no virgin," he choked, breath heating her face, "and now I aim to prove I'm right. If ye *are* one, then, when I've done, by God, ye'll *have* to marry me, so quit strugglin'. This will be real fun an you let it be."

So overwhelming was his assault that he never realized that she was offering no real resistance when he pushed her back onto the dry, moon-mottled ground beneath the magnolia. In a frenzy, he ripped open his breeches—so much less convenient on such occasions than an Indian breechcloth—shoved apron, skirt, and petticoats above her waist and, gasping, flung himself upon her.

Soft, anxious, moaning sounds escaped her. "Oh-h, Wallace—dear Wallace! Oh-h, please—gentle."

When he was truly into her, Wallace knew that someone had been this way before. Dr. Brooks—or someone else? She uttered only rapturous sounds as, fluttering her eyelids, she rolled her head slowly from side to side and drew him tight, tighter to her with fingers that dug hard into his shoulder blades, while her long legs flashed in the silvery moonlight.

Wallace Challenger enjoyed Winsome Brooks as he'd never enjoyed a young squaw, a compliant backwoods filly, or any of the experienced trulls who plied their trade around Charles Town. Deaf, blind, and in-articulate, the two of them seemed to float through space delicious be-yond expression. The universe whirled crazily about them; even the force of gravity became a myth.

Later, as they lay, side by side and utterly spent, beneath the magnolia she murmured, "When you finally get around to it, you've a most con-vincing way with you, Captain Challenger. But you really needn't have been so forceful."

"For God's sake, why not?"

"I've wanted to be with you like this, and someday to marry you, ever since that day we watched Mr. Oglethorpe come ashore."

He raised his head and, grinning a little, looked sidewise into her serene, warmed features. "Well, I'm damned if you didn't keep such notions a mighty close secret."

He sat up, brushed grass from her clothing, then rubbed dirt from his knees. "Now listen to me, Winsome Brooks, and listen carefully because I'll speak of this no more." He peered steadily into the swimming yet somehow languorous eyes. "Whatever happened up in Boston—or didn't happen—will make no difference between Wallace Challenger and his wife. Understand?"

She nodded. "Now may I say something which I'll never repeat?"

"Go ahead."

"No matter what you may have heard, there were never any unnatural relations between my beloved father—no matter how dearly we loved one another." Her voice dropped. "No. It was not he who took my maidenhead, but someone who was lost at sea."

BOOK IV

Chaugee Landing 1736–39

Chapter 1

THE SMUGGLERS I

As he'd always been able to do, Micah Oxford roused himself at approximately the time he wanted to wake up—roughly an hour before dawn. For a moment, he lay still on the sour-smelling cornhusk, listened to night noises in the forest enclosing that clearing in which he'd put up his log-and-chink truck house.

He heard also the monotonous, muted snores of Tchimi, his Tuscarora-speaking "woods wife." Slender, with luxuriant sable hair and skin like buff-hued silk, she was also industrious, obedient, and concerned for his comfort. Further, she claimed to be distantly related to Mary Musgrove.

Grinning in the darkness, Mike reached out, patted Tchimi's distended abdomen. What shade of color would their offspring's skin turn out to be? Ought to be light-colored, for, although Tchimi was a little darker of complexion than her celebrated cousin, she still was considerably paler-skinned than the average Creek woman.

What an extra-fine bargain he'd made in accepting Tchimi from her rum-sodden father in lieu of debts—which he couldn't possibly have settled, anyhow. Tchimi, moreover, through her ability to speak Tuscarora, could translate his Mohawk Iroquois into Muskogean and so made an ideal business assistant.

Yep. She was real smart, too, about quickly determining the true worth of a fur for which she'd haggle until she'd cut its purchase price to the bone. Tchimi had proved equally clever about tactfully disposing of stray Indians who appeared at the truck house broke, and mad for rum. But for her, he'd have to have thrown out a lot of potential customers who might come back later, sober and better heeled, and with some fine pelts.

The Yorker sat up, stretched, and yawned until his jaws cracked, then swung legs from under a greasy, dufil blanket and slipped moccasins onto dirty, bare feet.

God! Wasn't it fine to have done with those stinking-hot summer nights! Perhaps this would prove to be a hard winter? Still too early to tell, but, all the same, October 1736 had commenced with a spell of such uncommon sharp weather that many turtles, snakes, alligators and crocodiles, and other reptiles already had gone into hibernation. However, there were still enough sluggish rattlers around the woods and moccasins along the creeks to make a fellow mindful of where he reached or planted his foot.

After momentary hesitation, Micah decided to leave his palmetto hat on its peg and, for the first time that season, pulled on the new, gray fox fur cap Tchimi had sewn for her master. After slinging on his powder horn and war ax, he paused to cast the sleeping girl an almost affectionate glance before he stooped to prod her.

She sighed, turned onto her back, and smiled sleepily up at him through gloom relieved only by coals winking dully in the fireplace.

"Bar the door after me," he directed, "and don't unbar for *anyone* till I get back. Understand?"

Tchimi stretched prettily, then yawned. "Yes, my master. When will you return?"

"Dunno. Maybe not till round noon." Ignoring a blunderbuss which stood beside the bed, ready for instant use, he lifted down from its pegs a long-barreled Deckert which was one of the few rifles in the vicinity of Chaugee Landing. He knew he wasn't really expert with the Deckert yet; so delicate and precise a weapon needed a lot of knowing, but he was improving so, pretty soon, he ought to become a crack shot.

The long-haired black dog—as big and savage as it was ugly—which he kept chained and kenneled close by his front door roused up bristling and snarling, but quickly subsided; the mongrel was smart enough not to raise an alarm over nothing.

Trailed by breath vapors, Oxford in wraith-like silence set out over frost-crisped weeds carpeting that well-traveled trade trace which wound past his truck house. After covering a couple of hundred yards, he disappeared effortlessly into a tangle of frosted myrtle, honeysuckle and dense underbrush: only the eye of an experienced frontiersman could have identified that point where the Yorker had entered the woods.

About a quarter of a mile from the trace the air became tinctured by a faint, sour order. Micah paused on the edge of a small clearing and

looked carefully in all directions before heading for a tumble-down shack
and a wall-less shed which stood a little to one side.

Damn' if that drunken furriner ain't let the fire die down again. Cursing under his breath, the Yorker strode over to the shed, which sheltered
that small copper still which was yielding him such a tidy income. From
beneath a weathered tarpaulin, the bandy-legged trader pulled out some
chunks of well-dried oak which he fed into the firebox. Burned at night,
such fuel would not raise betraying smoke columns to reveal how astutely
he was breaking the colony's laws—even a fool one.

All the same, Micah was sufficiently smart to foresee that, despite all
precautions, he'd get caught eventually. However, by that time he figured
on having made sufficient money to pay even a stiff fine and still come out
well ahead of the game.

His new and growing trade in illegal firearms and munitions was
another matter. If things went wrong in that direction, he'd likely get
his neck stretched on Savannah's brand-new gallows.

The Yorker's anger mounted while he arranged logs that would bring
his still back to a boil, yet burn out before broad daylight and leave
enough big hot stones to carry on the good work.

Selecting a thick faggot, Micah then tramped over to the shack, where
he brought his stick down with a vicious *whack!* across the backside of the
disheveled figure who lay, sprawled and snoring loudly, on a filthy pine-
tip couch.

"*Aie! Qu'est que—*"

"Rouse up, ye stupid son-of-a-bitch!" Oxford rained blows on the
struggling figure. "Let that fire die down just once more, and I'll surely
kick yer ass clear out o' this country!"

"*Pitié! Pitié! Pour l'amour de Dieu,*" gabbled the wild-haired wretch,
scrabbling backward. "Oh-h. Please do not hurt me more!" Wailing, Petre
Ballou tried to clasp Oxford's knees but missed, and so continued to
writhe under the beating.

Breathing hard, Oxford tossed away the stick. "I won't call ye a pig, ye
goddam furriner, 'cause that'd be insultin' a useful animal. Now get up
and fer God's sake quit that damn' sniveling!" He planted a kick on the
old man's rump—but not a very hard one, for Petre Ballou was growing
frail of late.

"Never again will I fail you! On that, *monsieur*, you have my word of
honor," he added with a pathetic attempt at dignity.

Ignoring the red-nosed old fellow, whose lank gray locks were writhing
about his head like Medusa's snakes, Oxford went over to the still. Employing a long-handled wooden paddle, for a short while, he stirred the
thick, slowly steaming mash. He was trying to decide whether or not the
brew was ready for "running off" tonight; it might, provided those big

stones beneath the boiler retained heat long enough to complete the cooking process.

The Yorker rasped, "Now if this here wood don't burn down clean inside of a hour ye're to rake out the coals and drown 'em. There ain't even a hatful of wind this morning."

"Yes, *monsieur*. That I will do." The Swiss scuttled about with such frantic eagerness to please that he overturned a half gourd of that colorless and terrible-tasting liquid which, last night, had lent a blessed, if temporary, surcease to his sorrow and shame. When the spilled liquor melted some hoarfrost Petre's dazed, red-rimmed eyes filled. Mouth quivering, he watched the Yorker's chunky figure lose itself in the underbrush.

When he regained the trade trace, Mike judged by the stars that he was running behind time, so he took up an easy trot in the direction he'd come from, but, before he sighted his truck house, he turned onto that rough cart track which led to Chaugee Landing, a mile and a quarter distant.

He was too wise to risk running past the village. Some dog or chance early riser might hear or see him, so, when he sighted the frosted cypress shingles on Tom Trippe's millhouse roof, he slowed to a quick and silent walk. A smart man, Trippe, he'd built his current-operated sawmill slowly, with great skill and care.

By the first streaks of dawn Mike glimpsed high piles of fine, straight logs waiting to be cut into planks. Closemouthed and often surly, Tom Trippe sure was a hard worker; had to be, what with a wife and three children to feed who, worse luck, all were girls.

The paling sky next revealed Archibald Glen's factory, the only two-story structure in Chaugee Landing. Criminently! Didn't some people have all the luck? The ex-lieutenant of militia unexpectedly had inherited a bequest just large enough to set him up as a factor to Indian traders beginning to operate to the east and south of Savannah.

Not long ago, Micah had decided that this good-natured young fellow wasn't likely to make a go of his venture; there weren't anywhere near enough trading posts in this region to yield a working profit, even if Glen were a smart merchant—which he wasn't.

Already, he was figuring on buying out the ex-Guardee—provided the Georgia Company would countenance such a deal; the trustees had written so damn' many fanciful laws back in London that a man really couldn't tell what he might, or might not, be allowed to do.

Just as well that Archibald Glen was absent, and even luckier for his activities that the district's Indian agent, Captain Wallace Challenger, also was away, off on a scout somewhere south of the Satilla River.

It didn't bother the Yorker at all that a big-boned new settler called Will Woodroofe had gone along to find out whether some of his bride's relatives might be among a parcel of Scottish ex-paupers which the company recently had settled as an outpost on the Altamaha River.

While ghosting by a vineyard planted close by John Stonehewer's big, enforted log house and a smaller cabin jointly occupied by James Papot, Oglethorpe's former servant and an acid-tongued widower called George Buncle, Oxford reviewed recent events.

Two days ago, a big expedition from Savannah had halted and camped around his trading post. Captain James MacPherson had been in command, with black-visaged and leather-tough Captain Lachlan MacIntosh for his lieutenant. Numbering just over a hundred men—Rangers, surveyors, road builders, and laborers, they'd stayed only one night, not really long enough to permit Challenger and Will Woodroofe to get their affairs in order, so they would have to follow as soon as they could.

During their brief stay, the Yorker had found no trouble in ascertaining that this column had been ordered to select, survey, and partially clear a road designed to serve as a land link between Savannah and New Inverness, the Scottish outpost on the Altamaha.

The only thing which had bothered Micah Oxford was that accompanying the expedition was a young Scotch-Irish trader named James Adair, who, by all accounts, had been very successful in dealing among the Cherokees and Over-the-Mountains Creeks. His presence gave the Yorker to think a bit. Why was this smart young feller headed south? Hum. Since he knew that sometime he'd be forced to clear out of Chaugee he was figuring on going west or maybe south. The more he'd heard about western Indians the less he liked the prospect of living and trading among them. He guessed that Jimmie Adair had got himself a license and was on his way to establish trade among the Yuchis and the Abecas, if not with the Appalachis, whose lands were reported to extend all the way down to the Gulf of Mexico. Nor was it lost upon the Yorker that Adair had brought along a number of heavily laden pack horses guarded by a half-dozen surly-looking Cherokees.

Maybe, he asked himself, he'd made a mistake in not getting licensed to trade farther south? Hell no. He'd been doing all right where he was; he could always move on—when he had to.

Micah hurried his pace, for dawn was breaking; bobwhites, rain crows, and turkeys were beginning to call; deer began browsing closer to the forest; jays bickered, myriad songbirds trilled, warbled, or uttered drowsy tentative notes.

A mongrel belonging to Antoine Duché sighted the soft-footed figure and raised a halfhearted alarm, but Micah knew that no one would pay any attention; the dog was a fool and would bark at anything. For over a year, the dark-complexioned Savoyard and his family, with European patience and skill, had been cultivating native wild mulberry trees, which flourished hereabouts, and had set out, successfully too, some European varieties.

An ebullient but substantial fellow, the French-Italian—nobody could make sure which he claimed to be—had built a "strong" house; what with the help of two half-grown sons the swarthy silkworm cultivator ought to be able to defend himself—provided he didn't get jumped without warning.

Oxford's admiration for James Oglethorpe's common sense and readiness to learn attained new heights. In Georgia, there'd be few, if any, lonely and therefore vulnerable homesteads such as dotted the rest of the Atlantic seaboard.

While jogging along, the Yorker wondered why people had taken to calling the acting governor "General" for all he'd refused a commission making him captain general over all militia in Georgia and South Carolina, saying he declined to accept such responsibility without the backing of at least one regiment of infantry from the Regular Establishment.

What a pity Oglethorpe hadn't been able to persuade the Home Government to oblige him during the summer of 1734, when he'd made a brief visit to England, taking along Tomo-chichi, his wife Senauki, Toonahowie and Umpychi a great speech maker.

Once past Duché's, Oxford resumed a ground-eating lope through cypress and live-oak woods crowding darkly down to the marshes. The sun was ready to peer over the dark line of pines on Ossabaw Island when he sighted the entrance to the creek he was looking for; narrow, but very deep, the stream, now stained brown by fallen leaves, drained into the marshes, then writhed seaward, created a series of confusing meanders.

A pilot would have to be mighty 'cute to work his way into high ground—especially after dark; but it really wasn't necessary to approach by night; the chances of a vessel's being sighted by anyone were almost nil, the country around here was so very sparsely settled.

Although he couldn't spy a masthead the Yorker expected to find Don Miguel's lugger lying where she should be because gulls, terns, and gannets were wheeling about and delivering raucous protests. Flocks of migrating ducks kept flaring away from the entrance to what he and his fellow smugglers had come to call Wall's Creek.

By force of habit, the Yorker stopped and checked the Deckert's priming. How many more times would he be able to visit this place? He'd been here three times before now.

Everything appeared to be well, but Micah slowed his pace and, dodging from tree to tree, circled upstream until he could part a curtain of dark green myrtles and pendulous beards of Spanish moss. Peering downstream, he was reassured to glimpse the lugger, a fair-sized, single-masted vessel lying moored, bow and stern, to a couple of huge, knobby-kneed cypresses.

Not by accident had this lugger of Mediterranean design been painted an inconspicuous shade of marsh green, while her leg-of-mutton sail, loosely snugged along the main boom, was striped in alternating bands of green and brown. Señor Miguel Wall deplored nothing so much as betraying flashes given off by even dirty white canvas.

Oxford continued to study the landing place until he was sure that only two whites and four Negroes were aboard the smuggler. The blacks were cooking breakfast over a sandbox hearth set up just forward of the cockpit.

He also noted that two mulattoes were ashore and were watching the path upon which he was expected to appear. Both guards were armed with brass-barreled blunderbusses and wicked-looking, yard-long machetes slung over ragged hips. One wore a blue bandanna knotted about his bullet-shaped head, the other, less wisely, favored bright red.

Satisfied that he now knew what was what, Micah Oxford stealthily returned to the path, then whistled five notes in a rising scale. The mulattoes on the trail whirled, snarling curses that this nock-bearded figure should have come so close, unnoticed.

On the lugger's stern a slight but well-proportioned figure got to its feet and called in perfect English, "Ah, there you are, Mike! Come aboard, I'm delighted to see you."

Chapter 2

THE SMUGGLERS II

The last tendrils of mist engendered by the night's cold air were dispersing above reed beds where bobolinks and red-winged blackbirds whistled and swayed perkily on stalks of wild rice when Micah Oxford swung up a plank shoved from the lugger's rail to the shore. At its inboard end, Señor Miguel waited with slim brown hand extended. At first, Micah didn't recognize the former lieutenant of militia; since they'd last met three months earlier, John Savey had grown a pair of black mustachios which he'd trained into rapier-thin points; these seemed to balance upon a goatee of the same hue and proportions.

The renegade's regular white teeth flashed amid features burned much darker since he'd deserted Savannah.

Once they'd shaken hands, Savey beckoned his companion, a tall, muscular fellow who might have been Savey's senior by a year or two. "Friend Oxford, I have the honor to present Capitán Don Pedro Lamberto from St. Augustine."

Like Savey, Captain Lamberto wore loose white linen pantaloons and a sweat-marked shirt that sagged, unbuttoned, halfway down to his belt. The butts of two short-barreled pistols protruded from his waistband.

"Captain Lamberto serves on the staff of His Excellency, the Governor of St. Augustine."

The Spaniard offered a hand which Oxford took only warily, thinking, By damn! This here's the first honest-to-God Spaniard I've ever met up with. Funny, he's got no horns, nor split feet, either.

In heavily accented English, Captain Lamberto declared himself enchanted to make the acquaintance of Señor Oxford, about whom he had heard so much.

Savey indicated the sandbox hearth. "How about something to eat? I presume you haven't breakfasted?"

"Fact is, I ain't."

The breakfast of ripe *piños*—later to be known as pineapples, incredibly mellow and sweet, toasted white bread, and a fried chicken leg went down fine; a dandy change from bacon, samp, and yaupon tea.

This float-an-iron-wedge-strong coffee, laced with fiery Spanish brandy, went down better. The Negro sailors, sinewy, tough-looking characters, squatted about on the bow and consumed their rations in silence, but their yellow-and-black eyes kept flicking aft, watching the three white men confer.

Employing a splinter to ignite a *cigarro* nearly a foot long, Savey queried casually, "Well, and what have you to offer this time?"

"Not too much. Ye see, Injuns despise traveling during hot weather but I've managed to lay hands on quite a few bundles of assorted furs, most of 'em prime; a few kags of clear bear's oil, some skins of wild honey and plenty of beeswax cakes."

Under his wide-brimmed gray felt hat the renegade's expression darkened. "What? You've no deerskins?"

"Uh-huh. Only fifty t' sixty, but all of 'em are Number Ones."

This wasn't exactly true. The best Mike had been able to scrape together during the hot weather were hard old skins or damaged culls no English trader in his right mind would even have considered—except, perhaps, to retain the good-will of some valued customer.

"That's good. Can you fetch them aboard tonight?"

"Reckon so. Now what did you bring me?"

"Before we speak of that, here's a small present." Smiling, Savey held out a fat bundle of brown-black *cigarros*. "If you find you fancy such *puros*, next trip I'll gladly fetch you plenty more."

Furrows deepened on the trader's saddle-hued forehead as, perplexedly, he tugged at his cropped ear. "This is mighty handsome of you, but I ain't never smoked such contraption so, in order not to make a fool of meself before yer friend, I'll enjoy this tobacco my way."

The Yorker selected a *cigarro*, sniffed it, then broke it in half and stuffed an end into his bearded mouth. Once he'd chewed a few times he nodded. "Say, this's a sight milder and sweeter'n any of that stuff they grow in Virginny."

Don Pedro, who'd been considering the Indian trader through half-closed eyes, suddenly clapped bronze-yellow hands and called out something in Spanish. One of the Negroes disappeared into the lugger's forecastle, then returned on deck bearing a round bottle of red earthenware neatly caged in wickerwork.

Don Pedro smilingly decanted fragrant-smelling sherry into half-coconut-shell cups, then said in hesitant English, "To toast the new sun is a worthy act. *¿No es verdad?*"

"*Bien sûr.*" Mike grinned, they being about the only foreign words he knew aside from fearful obscenities acquired through dealings with assorted *voyageurs* and *coureurs de bois*. "Always helps a man out o' bed, I claim."

The Spaniard's restless black eyes widened. "'*Bien sûr?*' Then you are Frenchmans?"

Savey broke into low-pitched laughter. "By no means, *amigo mío*, Mike is a true buckskin. He comes from upper New York where he was a most successful er—merchant and dealer in firearms."

After a certain amount of verbal fencing, it turned out that Señor Miguel Wall had imported several pipes of Malaga, kegs of rum, and, best of all, some bolts of scarlet silk. At the mention of silk, Mike's jaws worked more rapidly on his chew; Creek nobles and micos were mad to own some of this gaudy, terribly expensive material. It made them feel superior.

"Also, I've brought along pepper, bars of salt, cane sugar, spices and two half casks of brandy smooth enough to suit your most finicky white customer."

A bandit-masked raccoon carrying a fish struggling between its needle-sharp teeth had trotted along the far bank, clouds of ducks had continued to veer away from the creek's entrance, and the sun was casting shorter shadows before the smugglers were ready to discuss the most important aspect of their business.

Oxford lifted a brow as he spat over the cockpit's splintered coaming. "Presume ye've imported some—er, hardware?"

"'Hardware'?" John Savey's expression was a masterpiece of innocent curiosity. "And just what do you mean by 'hardware,' my friend? Axes, kettles, nails—"

Oxford abandoned his relaxed, good-humored manner and spoke sharply. "Quit funnin' me. You know what I mean. Question is, how much have ye brought and what do ye want for it?"

John Savey's smile was mechanical. "Much depends on how much you are prepared to offer—trade goods aside."

"Don't worry. You got what I need, I'll pay hard money. Now ye'd better show me yer stock, and this time ye'd better not trot out any more o' them worn-out relics like you unloaded on me last time." Calmly, he spat the remains of the half *cigarro* over the rail and at the same time shot a quick glance at Captain Lamberto, who had settled comfortably against a thwart and was puffing on a *puro*. If this army officer had any financial interest in the present negotiations, he gave no indication of it.

"'Worn-out relics?' My dear friend, you pain me."

"I ought to. A lot of those trigger springs was rusted so bad they broke and plenty of locks fell off them muskets 'fore the Injuns got halfway home. They raised holy hell and it cost me a lot of good rum to get 'em friendly again."

"How deplorable," Savey commented casually. "No doubt it was the fault of the factor who supplied me. However, I fancy you'll approve this lot, which are from a different dealer."

"Seein's believin', John."

"Wish I could buy something like that for myself." The renegade nodded toward the Deckert resting within easy reach of its owner. How handsomely the long rifle's richly red-brown stock of curly maple with its bright brass mountings shone in the sunlight.

"An we get along successful," Oxford grunted, "I'll try to find ye one, but down this way rifles are scarcer'n white deer."

The Negroes fetched up twenty-odd muskets and musketoons which the Yorker examined with great care. He had to admit that what Savey had claimed was true; while these weapons were sadly blemished by rust and far from new, their locks appeared to be sound.

Oxford began to wonder why Don Pedro should be so much readier than John Savey to dispense liquid hospitality. Why? Apparently, Don Pedro had no interest in this bit of smuggling and, besides, he had an air of dignity about him that was no part of John Savey's character, that slippery rascal who'd fled Charles Town just a jump ahead of constables spurred into action by the wrath of James Edward Oglethorpe.

Mike had heard that the former lieutenant had bought passage aboard a slaver out of Norfolk, Virginia. Her captain had been ready to gamble on sailing for Havana, where he hoped to pick up a cargo of African slaves which could be resold at a fabulous profit to labor-starved planters along the southern coast of North America.

Savey, half Spanish to begin with, evidently had found it wise to remain in Havana, where he had assumed the name of his contact in Charles Town and had called himself Miguel Wall.

The handful of English merchants licensed to trade in that island capital reported that this personable young rascal soon had won access to the Governor's Palace.

While black seamen began to rewrap the contraband firearms, Savey inquired, "And how do things progress in Savannah?"

"Folks up there ain't oversatisfied over that fool male-tail law, and no liquor nor slavery bein' allowed, but they ain't hungry nowadays. Town's grown so ye'd scarcely recognize it."

Oxford kept scanning the creek's greasy-looking mudbanks because he didn't think much of Savey's outposts. Now that the tide had begun to drop, numbers of tall gray-blue cranes, dainty white egrets, and roseate ibises began to feed along freshly exposed mud flats.

"How many are these people?" Captain Lamberto flicked away his *cigarro's* butt; it hissed briefly in the tawny current. A fish surfaced to examine it then turned away, disgusted. High in the sky, an osprey screamed when a bald eagle dived and forced it to drop a fish it just had taken. The eagle caught the fish long before it struck the water, flapped heavily over to a dead oak, there to enjoy the fruits of his piracy.

"Nigh on four hundred men and grown boys; 'bout half as many women and children."

The Spanish officer nodded, blinked owlishly, as if the increasingly hot sunlight hurt his eyes. "All English peoples?"

"No. Worse luck," Oxford grunted with such force that little brown threads of tobacco juice ran from his mouth's corner and meandered down his unshaven jaw. "By God, the company's sent over 'bout everything but papists. Up in Savannah they've got Moravians, Jews, French-Italians, Salzburgers and other Germans along with Switzers and a sprinkling of Highlanders; most of the Scots, though, have left, gone south."

"Where?" demanded Captain Lamberto.

"To a new settlement they're buildin' on the Altamaha."

"You mean New Inverness?" Savey prompted.

"Aye. Only sometimes they call it the District of Darien."

Don Pedro sighed. "Darien is unlucky name among my peoples. Tell me, Señor Oxfor', now that so many peoples are at Savannah, they have put up many new—how you say it—*fortificaciones*? No?"

A belch escaped Oxford as he shook his head. "Naw. Settlers're too damn' busy growin' enough to eat and get their silk industry started."

Idly revolving a measure of brandy and water in his coconut cup, Savey suggested, "So you're doing a thriving business with the garrison of Fort Argyle?"

Complacently, Micah stroked his little forked beard and permitted himself to grow expansive as the sherry "spread out" in his stomach. "Reckon so. You'd be surprised how much tangle-foot twenty Buckskins can down at one time and, since they ain't quartered but a few miles away, they drop in at my truck house right regular." He nodded to himself. "Believe it or not, some Rangers will ride all the way down from Fort Moore—nigh sixty miles upcountry—to lay in a stock of rum."

The Yorker scratched inside his homespun shirt and winked at Savey. "I know ye'll not credit this, my friend, but quite a few pious citizens of Savannah ride down to tank up. Sometimes they stay a while, if they can figger out a sensible excuse, so ye'd better bring more rum on yer next trip, Mr. Savey."

The dark-haired young man flushed. "How many times must I remind you that my name is Miguel Wall!"

Oxford started to get mad, but ended by snickering, "Keep yer shirt on. Savey or Wall, 'tis all one with me. But, as I was sayin', on yer next trip ye'd better fetch in a double cargo o' rum which, by the way, the savages fancy over brandy, since it's not so costly and gets 'em drunk quicker.

"Also, I want three times as many muskets, guns, lead bars, molds and gunpowder. Oh yes, and a few swords, too; dunno why, but the savages have taken a sudden fancy to 'em."

"Why is this so?" demanded Pedro Lamberto. "The English, do they plan some expedition?" He smiled faintly. "Or do they expect trouble?"

"Why, no. 'Tain't English settlers want guns so bad, 'tis the Injuns. What with all that raiding the Yamasees did against their towns last year, the Lower Creek tribes are fair itchin' to raid 'crost the St. Mary and get their own back."

Captain Lamberto sat up, listened carefully. "You are sure of this?"

"Yep. Ouechachumpa would have sent out the red sticks long ago only General Oglethorpe wouldn't have it; so far, he's just been able to hold the Atalis in check."

The visitors exchanged fleeting glances. Don Pedro queried, "Why should the English governor restrain his allies?"

"Maybe I'm crazy, but I figure Oglethorpe don't want trouble till he finds himself a damn' sight stronger'n the field than he is right now, him havin' no more reg'lar troops on hand than a tomcat has morals."

In increasing good humor, the Yorker settled back against the cockpit's coaming with jaws working on a fresh *cigarro's* end. "Come to think on it, I somewheres heard that yer governor in St. Augustine—say, how's the old billy goat called?"

"Capitán General Don Francisco del Moral y Sanchez," Captain Lamberto informed him a trifle stiffly.

"Je-sus! Must be a powerful feller to lug around all them names. Haw! Haw!"

Smoothly Savey interjected, "What was it you heard?"

"Somebody let drop that yer governor and ours are dickerin' to keep their Injuns from raidin' across the St. John. That so?"

"It could well be," Lamberto admitted. "British officers, one Major Richards and a fellow named 'Dempsey,' appear' in our capital not long before Señor Wall and I left Havana." He diverted his attention to a pair of beady-eyed muskrats which, quite unconcerned, came swimming by the lugger.

For some reason, John Savey chose to elaborate in precise, clipped English: "Before I left St. Augustine I was informed that His Excellency, Don Francisco, is ready to authorize an armistice, provided the English dismantle Fort St. George and allow no settlers to cross the St. John River."

Oxford turned to Captain Lamberto. "Will Governor Sanchez *really* call off the Yamasees if Fort St. George is pulled down?"

The Spanish officer's smooth, well-chiseled features displayed disgust. "*Sí*. That is the intention of His Excellency."

The Yorker passed a hand over his shiny, berry-brown scalp and remaining hair and looked incredulous. "But, but, what about all them little forts and fortified villages that was built last year, places like Carr's, Caroline, Mount Venture, St. Andrew's and the rest? Heard yer people was hoppin' mad about it."

Captain Lamberto's olive features assumed a bland expression. "Perhaps, because they are so small we not fear them; Don Francisco can finish such silly little outposts—like that!" He smacked an incautious mosquito into a tiny red spot.

The Yorker turned again to John Savey. "Well, fer the sake of future business, let's hope this here truce takes place."

"There is an excellent chance that it will." Savey's teeth flashed. "But, between you and me, I'm not at all convinced that the royal government in Madrid will respect such lenient terms. But, for a while, we should be able to continue our traffic."

The sun had climbed high above the vine- and moss-festooned forest when Mike, feeling only jingled, shook hands and, promising to return that night, went ashore.

Carrying the Deckert butt-first, he struck off along the same route by which he'd arrived, carefully avoided that broad deer run which he'd follow in leading his pack horses down to Wall's Landing.

Fervently he prayed that, by nightfall, a strong enough wind would rise to disguise the trampling of hoofs. He certainly didn't want to be seen, least of all on his return trip; James Oglethorpe and his fellow trustees felt very strongly about the importation of illegal arms.

For a full half hour after the trader had disappeared, Don Miguel Wall and his companion lingered in animated conversation, then, proceeding with experienced caution, went ashore and, guided by one of the mulattoes, followed the Yorker's tracks toward Chaugee Landing.

Careful as they were, the smugglers almost got sighted by Antoine Duché's fifteen-year-old daughter, Lucie, who, with a younger sister and brother, were cleaning underbrush from beneath a clump of wild mulberry trees.

"Think you those children saw us?" breathed Don Pedro.

"No, assuredly not. They would have called a greeting."

When Savey judged they'd come as close as was safe to Chaugee Landing he and the mulatto mounted guard at the base of a massive black gum. Well concealed near its top, Captain Lamberto hooked legs under a strong limb then produced a pocket telescope through which he studied the hamlet.

Next, he drew out a notebook and roughed in the position of the various dwellings, the wharf, and the sawmill. This accomplished, Governor Sanchez's aide stuffed the notebook inside his sweat-soaked shirt and started to descend, well pleased until a pair of jays and a squirrel spied him and began to scold so insistently that any real woodsman in the vicinity couldn't have helped become curious.

Seguro! Chaugee would make an admirable landing place for his purpose. That little backwater behind the sand bar had a sand beach which should render it easy for cavalry and artillery to disembark. Only one thing troubled Captain Lamberto; something resembling a small earthwork or battery had been thrown up on a sandy point which jutted into the Ogeechee's tawny current. From his perch he'd been unable to see into it, so he couldn't tell whether or not this work mounted cannon, let alone how many pieces defended it, if, indeed, there were any guns there at all.

Once they were well on their way back to Wall's Creek the Spaniard observed, "*Seguro!* This place will serve admirably for the landing of troops of all descriptions."

"Why so?"

"Quite a large bark lies tied up to the bank," came the crisp reply. "The water, therefore, must run deep close inshore. Also, I observed an earthwork, but I could not see into it. What armament does it contain? Do you know?"

Savey's grin was bland. "Of a certainty, *Señor Capitán*. But to me such information should be worth a few trifling doubloons."

Don Pedros' fine dark brows merged as, in Castilian, he rasped, "What a greedy pig you are! Can you not understand that this trafficking for information, piece by piece, is ignoble! Surely, His Excellency pays you well enough to excuse such base maneuvers."

Quite unruffled, the renegade drawled, "I don't deny, *amigo mío*, it is a base maneuver, as you put it. Nevertheless, I have never overlooked money which can find its way into my *bolsa*. You understand my position?"

"Perfectly!" snapped the Spaniard. "You are more completely devoid of honor than the worst gypsy in Andalusia!"

Chapter 3

THE ROAD BUILDERS

Among those included in this the greatest concentration of white men ever to assemble in Georgia were civilian carpenters, stonemasons, horse handlers, blacksmiths, and common laborers handy with ax, spade, and crowbar. Many of them had been lured down from South Carolina by the promise of high wages. Together with the detachment of Rangers to guide and guard them, the road builders numbered roughly one hundred men—or had on leaving Savannah. Several had died from snakebite, through sickness, alligators or by drowning while crossing creeks and rivers swollen by unusually heavy autumn rains.

At the head of the winding, slowly moving column, Captain James MacPherson, lounging in his saddle, considered a succession of hardwood crowned ridges rising almost due north of the settlement called New Inverness.

The veteran Ranger was happy, first of all, that he'd escaped for a while the tedium of duty at Fort Argyle, and second, over the prospect of greeting fellow Scots so fresh from the Highlands that the smell of peat and heather still would cling to their tartans.

At his elbow was jogging restless-eyed Wallace Challenger, whom

MacPherson considered a Scot, for all he'd never even seen the Old Country.

Close on the heels of these two was riding shrewd, long-faced Will Woodroofe, one of the most recent householders to settle at Chaugee Landing. He, too, considered himself Scottish, but true Highlanders mocked this claim and called him "Sassenach" because once, in an unguarded moment, he'd admitted to having been born in the free town of Berwick-on-Tweed. Sassenach or not, Will Woodroofe was as fierce, tough, and quick-tempered as the darkest-complexioned Gael ever to descend from the mountains.

Right now, Will was feeling moody over having left at Chaugee Landing his lively, pink-cheeked bride, who'd been Jeanie Baillie till, on the passage to America, he'd met and persuaded her to marry him.

Rain had drizzled down all of yesterday and had continued into the night, so now no dust clouds arose above the plodding stream of men bent under spades, axes, shovels, and mattocks. Neither did mud impede their progress, the soil hereabouts being so sandy.

Commanding the rear guard was former Lieutenant of Militia Archibald Glen, now a civilian and proprietor of the modest traders' factory at Chaugee Landing. One of Savannah's original settlers would have found it difficult to identify this easy-riding, buckskin- and homespun-clad horseman with that ex-cornet of The Blues who'd ridden about Savannah stiff as if he had had an iron ramrod jammed up his touchhole.

Once the road builders started down one of the last pine-dotted hillsides short of the Altamaha, Challenger cast MacPherson a quick glance. "Tell me true, Jamie. How do the Musgroves make out at Mount Venture?"

"Weel enough," grunted MacPherson, bloodily crushing a deer fly on his horse's neck. "They're on the edge o' wild Indian country; Captain Matthews and his men are there to protect their post, not to mention the puir families that went along."

Will Woodroofe overheard. "Is Musgrove's truck house far from here?"

"Aye. All of seventy miles up yon river. Comes trouble, they'll be too far off to help."

The sandy-haired Lowlander appeared puzzled. "But why are they so far away? Thought His Excellency wanted all outposts able to reinforce each other."

"True enough. Johnny Musgrove has set up a post at Mount Venture only because the general wants him to—trusts his wit and courage. Besides, Mount Venture controls the best trade routes to the west. Like Fort Augusta, it makes a verra useful lookout."

The hurried *thwack-thwack!* of unseen axes at work in the rear rang sullenly through the still-soaking woods. Now and then would come the washing noise made by a felled tree crashing earthward. Presently the leaders came upon an advance party of surveyors and chainmen guided by Captain Lachlan MacIntosh and that wiry, youngish Scotch-Irishman named James Adair. Together, they had been determining the route to be followed.

Since the terrain hereabouts was rolling, only thinly wooded, and contained no considerable streams, the road builders were having an easy time clearing a rough wagon-wide road.

After a while, MacPherson wiped a spatter of rain from bristling brows and turned to Challenger. "Weel, Wallace, and what d'ye think the Dons will think when they learn of this road cutting?"

"They'll like it no better than the tribes whose country it crosses," drawled the Ranger captain. "The savages will claim, and rightly, too, that such a road will forever spoil their hunting grounds. They'll have no choice but to move west or starve. Mark my words, Jamie, a heap of trouble will come over this road. An ye doubt me, ask Jimmie Adair."

Around noon, a sullen-looking sun appeared just as a rider from the advance party trotted back to report that, at long last, the Altamaha had been sighted. Encouraged, the road builders quickened their advance, pausing only to hack down and pull aside small trees and obstructing branches; the tedious business of building culverts, bridges and of doing some rough grading was postponed for the return journey.

Dark-visaged Captain Lachlan MacIntosh, who in many ways suggested a younger James MacPherson, wiped sweat from his forehead with the end of a ragged tartan scarf. "Ye'll sight the town, sir-r, from the summit of yon rise. I'm thinkin' ye'll agree 'tis a fine, strong spot His Excellency has selected."

Although woods along the river had not yet been cut back very far, the road builders were able to see, from the summit of a low, pine-crested ridge that New Inverness, like Savannah, had been sited on a bluff, but a lower one, for it rose a scant thirty feet above the debris-strewn and rain-swollen Altamaha.

What Will Woodroofe saw, along with his shaggy and roughly dressed companions, was an orderly village built of freshly sawed and barked logs surrounding what appeared to be a chapel. It stood within a high palisade of pointed logs. Protecting it further was a small blockhouse, the cannon of which were trained downriver.

Would Jeanie's uncle, brother, or other members of Clan Baillie be among the settlers? His gaze then shifted east of the palisade where a disorderly collection of Indian huts and lean-tos was giving off streamers of dreary gray smoke.

Two narrow and well-guarded gates pierced the palisade; one fronted the Altamaha and an uncompleted wharf. The other faced inland and even now was being swung open to permit the passage of about a dozen armed men wearing kilts of various tartans which were too far off to be recognizable.

When a pair of tall men wearing Highland bonnets and looking gawky on wiry little Spanish horses cantered through the gate, MacPherson ordered a Ranger to sound a series of eerie, mooing notes on the battered conch-shell trumpet he carried slung to a rawhide thong.

Leaving the rest of the column to descend toward the river at their leisure, MacPherson, Challenger, and Lachlan MacIntosh trotted down the slope to meet the two mounted Scots. The closer they came together, the wider grew James MacPherson's grin. It had been years since he'd seen men so fresh from those Highlands he'd quitted so long ago.

Quickly, he identified half-forgotten tartans: those of Brodie, MacKay, MacQueen, Baillie, and many more. Just for the hell of it, he suddenly cupped hands and raised his clan's war cry, "*Creagh Dhu!*"

Instantly, a deep voice yelled back the rallying cry of Clan MacKay, "*Bratach bhan calann aoidh!*"

Soon, Challenger, intensely curious, formed detailed impressions of the newcomers; for the most part, these hairy, lean, and hardy strangers still wore native dress: bonnets topped with rakish, golden eagle's plumes, short jackets, and scarves and kilts of ragged tartan. Many wore coarse, knee-length woolen stockings knitted in their clans' colors in which were tucked skean dhus. Some were armed with dirks, others with heavy, basket-hilted claymores. Some carried, strapped to their left arms, round shields or targets identical with those their ancestors had carried against the legions of Rome.

Although Jamie MacPherson never before had beheld him, he recognized, by hearsay, one of the horsemen as George Dunbar, a short, thick-bodied individual whose complexion was the hue of rare roast beef. By his tartan, the chief Ranger recognized a young officer riding at Captain Dunbar's elbow as the redoubtable Captain Hugh MacKay.

To a squealing of bagpipes there ensued a deal of handshaking and ribald congratulations; everyone knew what the new road would mean to this settlement situated so perilously close to Spanish power.

Chapter 4

NEW INVERNESS

Once the united group had swung their horses' heads toward New Inverness, Challenger noted that these Highlanders seemed to be sharing some private joke so rich that they could hardly keep straight faces.

When they neared a gaping, wild-looking crowd of all ages milling about in the mud before the landward gate, George Dunbar chuckled. "Captain MacPhairson, we've a wee surprise in store."

"Aye? And what might that be?"

"Ye'll learn in a wee bit."

MacPherson looked wistful. "Ye'd no be offering me a wee drappie whusky?"

Dunbar's smile vanished. "Na, na! The damned English trustees took ours awa'."

Inside the palisade a dense throng was waiting; they set up a cheer, waved cloaks and scarves of plaid or tartan cloth while calling greetings in broad Scotch; some even hailed the visitors in Gaelic. Also hopping about and screeching a welcome were a good many Indians. Among them both Rangers recognized some Yamacraws—Tomo-chichi's nephew and Umpychi among them.

Despite alligators, snakes, insects, and the torrid sun, these people in a short while had accomplished much and had built their homes as if they intended to stay here forever. There was not a single slipshod or jerry-built structure among dwellings which must have sheltered close on one hundred fifty immigrants.

Although Wallace Challenger never had seen Scotland he reckoned that these folk dressed and acted very much as they would at home. Most of them were dark complexioned, sparely built, and short of stature; there wasn't a fleshy figure to be seen. The children, too, were thin, mostly dark-eyed and as alert as squirrels. The women, almost without exception, were plain, gaunt, and tired-looking.

Captain MacPherson searched his memory and, with some difficulty, identified some of the tartans although often they were badly faded. There was his own, of course, which had broad, dark and light gray crossbands interspersed with narrow orange and blue lines; MacKay, dark green background, narrow black lines crisscrossed by slender lines of dark blue and black; the tartan of Clan MacIntosh was easy to identify because of its bold, bright red background and stripes of black and dark green. Here and there, the hawk-faced captain of Rangers glimpsed the colors of Clans MacQueen, MacLachlan, and others.

"And noo, friends MacPhairson and Challenger, I'll gi'e yer sur-rprise. Come along." So saying, Dunbar lifted his sodden cloak clear of the mud and drove a path through the crowd to a tent pitched beside the chapel. Just before they arrived before it, its flaps parted and out stepped James Edward Oglethorpe, cloaked and kilted in the dark green, light green, and white tartan of the Royal Scots Fusiliers! On his brown hair he had set a Highland bonnet to which a single, sharp eagle feather had been pinned with a cairngorm and silver brooch.

Immediately, the visitors noted that the general's Highlander garb was well worn and had been patched and mended in several places. In his usual warm but always dignified fashion, Oglethorpe made the road builders welcome. To Challenger, at least, he appeared thinner and there were lines in his long, thin face which had not been there a year ago, but the light in his somber and close-set eyes shone as vital as ever.

Once greetings had been exchanged, Oglethorpe disappeared into his tent to reappear, a moment later, with an arm linked through Tomochichi's. For all that the ancient mico thlucco now was well into his nineties he was freshly painted, walked firmly, and stood almost as straight as he must have when a lusty young Raven.

When the rest of the expedition, footsore and very glad to have reached the end of their journey, struggled down to New Inverness, they were forced, through lack of space, to camp outside the palisade near the Indian encampment.

The Scots, however, did their best to feed and otherwise provide for their more-than-welcome guests. Dunbar and his officers insisted on offering a modest banquet in celebration of this epic event in their settlement's brief history.

During the repast, consumed to the music of bagpipes, the visitors learned that Oglethorpe, variously referred to as "General" or "Governor," was on his way back to Savannah after having intercepted his armistice negotiators, Captain Charles Dempsey and Major Richards from South Carolina at the St. John River. These gentlemen, explained the guest of honor, had been visiting St. Augustine to conduct important negotiations with the Governor of Spanish Florida.

On hearing that terms, almost incredibly favorable to Georgia, had been agreed upon, Oglethorpe then had retreated northward to inspect Fort St. Andrew, a small sand and palmetto-log fortification being thrown up on Cumberland Island under the supervision of Captain MacKay.

"Gentlemen, I was both astonished and pleased," Oglethorpe announced, "to observe the excellent design and clever emplacement of this fort. It is all the more to the credit of Captain MacKay, here"—he bowed in that bronzed young officer's direction— "that neither he, nor any of those who were with him, had had previous engineering experience."

He glanced down the table strewn with wooden plates and bowls and addressed Major Richards, a swarthy, jug-eared individual with fat and ruddy cheeks. "I imagine, sir, that these gentlemen would appreciate a description of your dealings with Spanish authorities."

The negotiator gulped down a half-chewed chunk of beefsteak as he struggled to his feet. "Well, friends, while a lot was said, not too much was accomplished. All the same, I'm pleased to tell you that we have been promised compensation for damage inflicted on our Indian allies during the raids inspired by that rascally trader Ben Drake."

"Exactly what, sir, did this Drake fellow do?"

"Why, he sold illegal weapons to a party of Frog Clan Yuchis, then he got their leaders drunk and incited them to attack a nearby Yamasee village.

"Well, sirs, this unprovoked assault touched off a whole series of fierce raids and counterraids which went on all last fall and into the winter. The Spanish, of course, backed and supplied their allies, the Yamasees, while Drake and certain other unlicensed British traders equipped the Yuchis and Alibamus.

"This border fighting soon involved Creek bands who are allied to Georgia. But for His Excellency's patience, we'd have had a full-fledged war with Spain on our hands last spring."

Without difficulty Wallace Challenger recalled Ben Drake, a dirty, shifty-eyed fellow whose pack train had camped for a time near Micah Oxford's truck house. That was when he'd become certain that the Yorker was back at his old trade—selling contraband arms to the savages.

Silently, Challenger decided that, as Indian agent for the Chaugee District, he'd better make sure about what was going on around Oxford's place, which was far from a pleasant prospect, since he and Mike had been among the first to settle Chaugee Landing and always had admired one another's wisdom in the woods.

Challenger no longer listened to what Major Richards was saying, but conjectured about the source of Mike's munitions. Almost certainly, he wasn't getting them from Charles Town. From Philadelphia, possibly? No, most likely they were coming down from Boston; didn't everyone say that a Yankee would sell his mother to a Turk if the price were right.

He returned his attention to the present when Archibald Glen spoke up. "Can you tell us, sir, where our frontier with Florida is to run now?"

The Carolinian hesitated, then replied, "Although our friend Tomo-chichi swears that the land ceded to us under your treaty with the Atali Creeks extends down to the St. John River, we deemed it politic to yield to the Spaniards and agree that the frontier should follow the St. Mary's course which, I might add, is a damned sight farther south than we'd dared to expect. In fact, to start out with, the Dons insisted that the Ogeechee River must be considered as the southern boundary of this colony."

Absently, Major Richards picked at a hirsute nostril. "Well, my friends, we bickered, threatened and argued until they accepted the St. Mary as the frontier until a formal treaty can be drawn up and ratified by the crowns of England and Spain."

Captain MacPherson snorted, wagged his dark and narrow head, mut-tering, "The royal government in Madrid will ne'er tolerate so great a comedown in their claims."

Oglethorpe made no comment, but looked grave, for privately he too felt convinced that the Spanish Crown, as a matter of pride, would never peacefully relinquish its claim to so vast a territory.

He felt encouraged, however, to read relief on so many hard Highland faces, and the Lord knew these Scots stood in need of encouragement if even half of the reports concerning Spanish preparations for war were founded in fact.

"In return," concluded Major Richards, "we have only to dismantle Fort St. George which is small, a sand and palmetto battery which the Spaniards could wipe off the map the moment they take a notion to."

By force of habit the commissioner's hand groped for a nonexistent wineglass; he smiled wryly. "Finally, 'twas agreed that a system of passes and certificates will be set up by which trade across the border can be resumed."

After the dinner party broke up most of the settlers retired to their cabins for bedtime prayers and well-earned slumber, but Challenger lin-gered and led Major Richards aside. "Sir, what is your private opinion? Do the Dons really intend to raise the Yamasees and go to war before long?"

For almost a minute, the Carolinian stared hard at the tall, weather-beaten figure before muttering, "Yes. That's as sure as we stand here. Can you keep your mouth shut?"

"Always have when it's important."

"Very well. While we were in St. Augustine, Captain Dempsey and I learned that the Captain General of Cuba is preparing to aid Don Francisco in every possible way; why, sir, at this very moment he is col-lecting ships, drilling militia and soliciting troops from home. Moreover" —Major Richards glanced about, made sure the room was almost deserted, before continuing—"like the Captain General of Cuba, Don Francisco is begging the royal government to send out a division of regulars and a squadron of men-of-war."

Deep lines formed about the Carolinian's mouth. "Make no mistake, Captain, the Dons are preparing to exterminate every Englishman they find south of Virginia. Why, they've gone so far as to offer to settle their quarrels with their fellow Catholics in Louisiana!" He smiled faintly. "We learned that a French emissary, the Chevalier d'Erneville, was most appreciative of this offer of friendship and left St. Augustine only a few days ago with the express intention of inciting certain micos on his way back to Louisiana. You can imagine what he's going to say to them?"

"I can," Challenger said slowly. "Tell me, did the Frog Eaters promise to join in an attack upon us?"

"No. But D'Erneville hinted that Governor le Moyne would send arms and persuade his Indians to take up the hatchet against us."

Challenger's broad brown hand crept up, tugged thoughtfully at his chin. "How much militia does the Spanish governor command?"

"Around a thousand, plus about three hundred mulattoes and blacks who are free Spanish subjects and rule themselves at Negrito, a settlement not far from St. Augustine. It is sort of a dependant kingdom. They are ruled over by a savage black giant who calls himself the Kumassee King. His subjects are all Negroes, mustees or mulattoes. No whites or Indians are allowed to live there."

Challenger caught his breath. "He isn't named Quobah?"

It was Major Richard's turn to look surprised. "Yes. How did you know?"

"'Twas just a wild guess."

"Odd thing. While this black king speaks fairly good English, he hates everything British with ferocious intensity."

"I can tell you why, Major, if this Kumassee King is the rascal I'm thinkin' of."

"Who is he?"

"Used to call himself Quobah Tutu and claimed to have been an Ashanti prince before he got enslaved. Maybe so, maybe not; anyway, he tried to start a slave uprising on a Carolina plantation a few years back. I took some Rangers up from Savannah and we whipped the hell out of him and his crew. Killed most of 'em."

Richards jerked a nod. "He's the blue-black African with little scars all over his face?"

"Yep."

"Did you know he's lost the use of his left arm?"

"No, but I guess maybe he got crippled in that fight I just spoke of. What else can you tell me about this Kumassee King?"

"They say he once was a sub-mico in a mongrel tribe called Sakwaris. Heard of 'em?"

The Ranger captain nodded. "Plenty. More than I enjoy."

The fat-faced Carolinian yawned and stretched. "Reckon that crippled arm explains why he hates us English. Nowadays he always keeps a left-handed warrior on his left; calls him the King's Left Arm.

"Anyway, this Quobah is a force to be reckoned with. I hear he commands Fort Moosa, which is near Negrito, and can lead near a hundred men against our settlements."

Challenger listened a while to a renewed drumming of rain on the roof of cypress shakes. "Wonder why Quobah went back to Florida? Fellow named Thad Burton told me Quobah once had been held there in slavery. Why would he want to go back there?"

Major Richards yawned once more, then peered doubtfully out into the streaming darkness. "Now that's a real good question which may be answered in blood sooner than we think."

"What's your meaning?"

"Just this. Of late the Spanish have been sending secret messengers along the Guale Coast promising freedom to any Negro who will run away or kill an Englishman. Of course these blacks first have to turn Catholic, but they're free once they get across the St. John."

"The hell you say! Now ain't *that* a cute idea. These spies gettin' any-where?"

"Don't know, but I heard in Florida that a couple of English renegades already are at work. One of these rascals goes by the name of Tom Bacon; a well-set-up fellow of around forty-five years old. He's got thick gray hair and ought to be easy to spot because he's shy his left ear."

"Hum. Who's the other?"

"Calls himself Miguel Wall but his true name is known to be John Savey. He works out of Havana."

"John Savey! So *that's* where that smooth bastard got to."

"Yes. That's where he went. Bacon and Savey should be arrested on sight"—Major Richards' lips flattened themselves—"and hanged after—er —persuasive questioning."

Chapter 5

REVIEW BY FIRELIGHT

Although he'd been riding, sailing, and marching the length of the Guale Coast for over a month James Edward Oglethorpe felt only reasonably weary after quitting the banquet. With characteristic courtesy the accompanying trustee insisted on escorting Tomo-chichi to his encampment outside the palisade.

As they splashed through cold, invisible rain they reviewed their memorable trip to England, back in 1734, when the mico thlucco and his wife Senauki, together with Toonahowie and Umpychi had created a deep, and eventually useful, impression upon the Court of St. James's. Arriving before the Yamacraw chieftain's cedar bark wigwam, they shook hands, Indian fashion, then gravely bade one another good night.

Under the fly of Oglethorpe's patched and mildewed tent a pair of sodden Rangers, standing huddled under brief capes of oiled deerskin, presented arms. Even as the acting governor moved in out of the downpour, he decided for once to yield to impulse and sent one of the sentries in search of James MacPherson, whom he'd liked and respected since his first shipload of ex-paupers had come ashore at Savannah. Since then, he had grown to admire that tough old Scot's rare gift of compressing a deal of straight thinking into few words.

After dismissing his servant for the night, Oglethorpe knelt and fumbled in his traveling chest until he located a dented silver flask containing whisky; Jamie MacPherson, he knew, disdained even the finest French and Spanish brandies as "foreign belly wash."

The Ranger entered the sour-smelling command tent, silent as a hunting owl. To Oglethorpe's surprise, he was wearing, pinned to his Highland bonnet, a new cockade made of Clan MacPherson's gray, orange, and blue tartan.

"My thanks, Captain, for coming out on so foul a night. This may serve as a partial recompense." Smiling, he uncapped and held out the pocket flask.

MacPherson's deeply lined features lit as he lifted the offering and sniffed. "*Creagh dhu!* Is't whusky I smell, sir-r?"

"Best judge for yourself, Jamie." He indicated a pair of pewter noggins. "Pour yourself a good tot."

Aware of the Oglethorpe family's strong Jacobite connections, MacPherson barely fought down an impulse to toast "the King o'er the Water," said instead, "To Yer Excellency's continued gude health and wise leadership!"

"Seat yourself, Jamie, and, for the time being, let us forget the matter of rank and talk like the old friends we are." Settling onto a camp chair, Oglethorpe smoothed his kilt before setting straight the skean-dhu knives tucked into the top of a muddied stocking. "I sorely need to consult someone who can keep his mouth shut."

Savoring the whisky, MacPherson's cavernous dark eyes narrowed. Losh! The general neither looked nor acted as if he'd donned Highland dress merely to create a favorable impression around New Inverness. He was wearing the Royal Scots tartan—even if it was only military—as if he'd never worn anything else.

Oglethorpe unwound a damp neckcloth and slowly began to massage the back of his neck. "Well, Captain, and what is your opinion of this colony's present state?"

MacPherson rolled a quarter-mouthful of whisky over his tongue, then drew a long, long breath that he might fully enjoy the liquor's peaty aroma.

"Weel, sir, taken, all in all, since coming to America ye've accomplished little short o' a meeracle."

" 'A miracle?' " Stiffly Oglethorpe extended long, muddied legs before him. "So? Then I'm a magician of sorts?"

"Aye. Only a wizard could ha' fetched nigh on a thousand hopeless souls across a great ocean, bend them to his will and settle them safe among savages in an unknown wilderness."

By the feeble light given off by a hog-fat dip, Oglethorpe held up mosquito- and chigger-nipped hands in protest. "Now! Now! I fear you make too much of too little, friend Jamie; all the same, I'll confess your praise comes as music to these sometimes discouraged ears." He laughed, then demanded in genuine curiosity, "Tell me something: why is it that our Scottish paupers as a rule don't display the hangdog and spiritless bearing worn by too many English ex-debtors?"

Using a gnarled brown forefinger, MacPherson combed from his forehead a lank lock of sable hair, then emitted a brief cackle of amusement. "Why, sir-r, no doubt 'tis because we Highlanders ha' always been poverty-poor and so are well accustomed to being dragged off to a debtor's prison for want of a few sixpences. Since we hold an honest man's poverty is no disgrace, why, we go to jail and think little of it; for all too many Scots 'tis the common way o' life."

The general sighed, then nodded and was mimicked by his shadow cast against the tent's reeking wall. "So *that's* it!" He poured out a little more whisky and passed it over. "Here's a bribe to encourage you to puff my battered ego a little more. What other of my alleged accomplishments merit your approval?"

The Scot's bony features lit. "Why, sir-r, think o' the way ye've ringed Savannah with forts and outposts." He raised his cup. "Someday, Yer Excellency will be best remembered for having, through gude faith and fair dealings, won the love and trust of the Creeks—and all the savages around us, for that matter."

Smiling, Oglethorpe shook his head, but was inordinately pleased all the same. "You still give me too much credit, Jamie. What success I've met with—so far—in a great measure is due to guidance given by the Musgroves, Colonel Bull, yourself and certain others."

"Nay! Nay! 'Twas the wise application of our advice that has turned the trick as you say—'so far.'"

A brief silence ensued in which the Ranger guards could be heard bragging about what they'd do when they got back to Charles Town.

Oglethorpe stared at the few drops of whisky remaining in his pewter cup. "And I owe a great debt of gratitude to Tomo-chichi. May the old gentleman live another ninety years! Here's to him!"

They sipped sparingly, listened to still another flurry of rain drum upon the canvas while Oglethorpe rearranged his kilt to cover badly scratched knees. "'Tis a shamelessly flattering picture you've painted of me, Jamie, but, for all that, I know I've made many mistakes—some grave, still, I've done the best I could."

"'Tis a gude best, sir. Yer colony's growing stronger day by day."

"But not fast enough. If the Spaniards and French don't hold back, they can annihilate us in a few days' time."

Oglethorpe leaned forward, broad bronzed chest exposed half the length of his linen shirt's stained front. "*They* know how *very* few Englishmen live south of Virginia. D'you imagine I could raise a force of even fifteen hundred whites without robbing the cradle and the grave, leaving hundreds of homes unguarded?"

"I fear 'twouldna be possible." Feeling his whisky at last, MacPherson nodded owlishly. "Ye've a grand lieutenant in Wallie Challenger. I ha'e guessed 'tis largely his doing that's kept the Lower Creeks, Yuchis and the rest from raiding across the St. John."

Relieved to be able for once to think aloud, the acting governor said, "I'll confide in you, Jamie; *if* the Georgia Company keeps their word, given in London last year, nearly a thousand immigrants will reach Savannah within the next few weeks."

The Scot's tangled black brows rose. "What sort of immigrants, sir-r? That's most important."

"'Twill be a mixed bag, I fear, but first and best of all, they've promised me near two hundred Scottish debtors; then a parcel of Salzburgers— Protestants persecuted and expelled from central Austria; and Moravians —another German-speaking people. These last, worse luck, have forsworn war so they can't be counted on to fight. On the brighter side, there are also supposed to come over a few Swiss, who usually make first-class soldiers; I truly don't know about the martial qualities of the rest who are Piedmontese and French Huguenots."

MacPherson's hand flew to the pistol in his belt when an Indian dog suddenly thrust its head through the tent's flap. It looked quickly about then pulled back, *kiyi-ing*, when booted by a guard. Both men burst out laughing and when MacPherson elaborately drained the last amber drops in his cup, Oglethorpe emptied the dented silver flask into their cups. "Is there anything better than good whisky?"

"If there is," sighed the Ranger, "I dinna want to hear aboot it."

"Jamie." Oglethorpe sharpened his speech. "What is your true opinion of the armistice arranged by Major Richards and Captain Dempsey?"

"Why, sir-r, 'tis a stopgap, but a good one. Such a truce may delay invasion a year, perhaps longer, which time you can use to gude advantage." He paused, cocked a sable brow at the accompanying trustee's kilted figure.

"And how do you recommend that this respite had best be utilized?"

"Sir-r, I'm thinking the fir-rst move is to outfox the Dons by placing a buffer o' friendly tribes 'twixt them and their fellow Papists in Louisiana."

Frowning, Oglethorpe selected a couple of *cigarros* from an earthenware jar and tossed one to his companion.

"Say, by establishing a line of trading posts along the Tallapoosa?"

"Naught else, sir-r. 'Tis a shining wonder Don Francisco didna stipulate that Fort Okfuskee be destroyed at once; for our protection 'tis worth a dozen Fort St. Georges."

Oglethorpe lit his own and his guest's *cigarros* from the smelly candle's end. "You always have taken the long view, Jamie, and once more you are entirely right."

"Och aye, but there's another advantage to planting outposts on the Okfuskee and Tallapoosa—a new, and still-neutral, tribe are settled nearby. Their mico is someone we both know."

Oglethorpe's dark and close-set eyes widened. "You mean Sakwari-cra?"

"None other. Around a year ago he moved his people inland from the Ogeechee and settled, so they say, 'mongst the ruins of an old Spanish mission called Capola."

Interest eased Oglethorpe's weary expression. "'Capola'? Where is Capola?"

"Near the headwaters o' the Suwannee and the Satilla, Yer Excellency. Capola must lie almost astride our new frontier wi' Florida, an I understand aright."

"What decided Burton to settle there?"

Moodily, MacPherson reached inside his shirt and scratched at a flea. "'Tis my guess, sir-r, he wanted to occupy hunting grounds he could control after a strong band of outlawed Yuchis joined him."

"What would be his effective strength nowadays?"

"Over a hundred seasoned warriors which, as Yer Excellency kens, is no' a force to be ignored wi' war in the offing."

Ignoring the monotonous *plop-plop* caused by a leak along the tent's ridgepole, Oglethorpe settled back on his camp chair, somber eyes fixed on his *cigarro's* glowing end. "What you tell me is most interesting, but not surprising. I never deemed Sakwari-cra an ordinary leader. What was his stand during last year's border troubles?"

"Neutral. I'm told Burton is verra fierce aboot keeping strangers out o' his bailiwick. So far, he's refused to let any trader do business among his people."

"Then he's not been trafficking with the French?"

"Not that I've heard of, sir-r, but if ye wish, I can soon make sure."

"You better had, and quickly. It seems to me"—Oglethorpe spoke more slowly now—"that this renegade's territory divides the French from the Spaniards. Were he to be won over to the French, his warriors could strike along our frailest line of defense."

Oglethorpe drained the last drops from his little pewter cup before saying, "Jamie, I'll confess something; this fellow Burton is one of the most completely baffling persons I have ever encountered. While he may talk and sometimes act like a savage, he doesn't think like one, so we will have to act accordingly. Is there a licensed trader who might work for us in Capola, somebody Burton might accept?"

"Only one, James Adair, because he's new to this country."

"Where has he traded before?"

"Among the Chickasaws and Cherokees. Adair's a shrewd, sound mon for a' he's Scotch-Irish and youngish. I'm thinking he might be able to persuade the Panther King, as this upstart so grandly terms himself because the Chickasaws have their Squirrel King and the Yamasees their Dog King."

Following a short silence, Oglethorpe said over the continued beat of rain upon canvas, "Very well, try to get Adair permission to do business in Capola. I will send gifts lavish enough to win even Sakwari-cra to His Majesty's service.

"Oh, by the bye, don't forget that Major Richards has reported that Monsieur d'Erneville is on his return voyage to Biloxi and, no doubt will attempt to win him for a friend."

Deliberately, MacPherson relighted his half-consumed *cigarro*. "Then, sir-r, ye'll be wanting a deputation to accompany Adair to Capola?"

"Aye, and the sooner the better, Jamie. Who should head it?"

MacPherson hesitated not an instant. "Wallace Challenger, sir-r, wi' Jamie Adair as second-in-command and, perchance, 'twouldna be a bad idea to send along Tomo-chichi's nephew and Umpychi, who's a powerful orator, which counts for a lot 'mongst the Muskogeans."

Chapter 6

CAPOLA

Seated under a palm-thatch porch he'd built across the front of an ancient Spanish house, Thad Burton prepared to check his firearms. Already he had fetched out a box of tools required to keep his firearms in prime condition. Seated on a low bench, the white Tuscarora selected a hard brush to cleanse pans and frizzens, a thin steel picker to free the touchholes of any obstruction from among spare flints, copper flasks of priming powder, and a worm screw which could be affixed on the end of a rod and used to draw out an unfired bullet.

There was also a new *éprouvette*, or powder tester, which looked very much like a barrelless pistol mounting a circular brass gauge which registered the exact strength of the powder to be used. Without one there could be no telling some unknown powder's force.

He set to work on his most prized possession, a practically new long rifle fashioned up in Lancaster, Pennsylvania, by Martin Meylan. He'd bought the piece from Ben Drake, a fast-talking, unlicensed trader who had passed through Capola last spring.

Although at the time he'd felt that the Meylan was dreadfully dear, by now he knew it was worth every buck he'd given for it. It was a truly beautiful piece of work, what with its four-foot ten-inch octagonal barrel of well-forged iron, grooved to one turn in three feet, and its lovely stock of bird's-eye maple hand-rubbed until it almost glowed in the dark.

Further, the rifle's stock had been decorated with inlays of Spanish coin silver cut into moons, stars, and comets. Best of all, on the side opposite the weapon's brass patch pocket, a gunsmith in Drake's party had affixed to the stock his initials, "T.B." Yes, mused Sakwari-cra, here was a weapon fit for use by the Panther King; its half-ounce spherical bullet could drop a walking deer at two hundred paces.

After sliding the long rifle back into its case of well-greased deerskin, he turned his attention to those silver-mounted Highlander pistols James Oglethorpe had given him. He oiled, then tried the locks on both Alisons, made sure that both pans and frizzens were bright and clean and that the neat, French-made flint clamped between each cock's jaws were screwed firmly into place.

"Has the rain stopped? After five days I'm tired of it." Laure Burton appeared carrying a wriggling baby over one arm. She paused in the doorway to untie the front of her blouse for the benefit of John Musgrove Burton—close on a year old, and growing fast.

Thad had named his second son after Musgrove because, unlike most Indian traders, he always gave the red man a fair shake. Lord! What a lot of water had reached the sea since that long-gone day when he, Taqua, and Quobah had reconnoitered Goggle-Eyes's village.

"Hi, youngster! Where do you think you're bound?" He grabbed little Jeems by the wrist as, stark naked, the infant started to follow his round little stomach into the downpour.

"Better let him go, Thad, he needs washing off," Taqua pointed out while the little redheaded creature she held in her arms began to suck and to knead her breast with tiny pink hands.

"I suppose, by now, almost all the fords and most of the trails are impassable." Laure spoke in precise, carefully enunciated English because, on Brother Barnaby's advice, for over a year she and Thad used only that language when by themselves.

"You are right. Nobody will be able to travel very far for another two days," Thad predicted.

"That will mean that you must delay your departure for the Alibamu country?"

"That is about the size of it. I am not eager to drown."

When Laure Burton's slanting gray-green eyes came to rest upon her husband she discovered that she still wasn't accustomed to his changed appearance. Bent over his weapons, the Panther King, in his red woolen shirt, kilt of bleached buckskins and fringed leggings, was almost indistinguishable from a Ranger, for, some time ago, but not without many misgivings, he'd at last cut off his Tuscarora crest and had allowed his hair to come in naturally. Thick and light brown, it now dangled low enough to brush his massive shoulders.

Although Sakwari-cra still clung to his precious silver-and-turquoise earbobs he painted his face only for feasts, ceremonial occasions, or war. To

Laure it remained difficult to understand why he'd made these changes, because if anyone even hinted that he might, someday, decide to live as a white man, he would flare up into a rage that was terrible to witness. This was strange because Thad obviously enjoyed talking with men of his own race—even downright thieves, rascals, and dangerous plotters like Ben Drake and Tom Bacon. Most of all, he anticipated the irregular and increasingly infrequent visits of Brother Barnaby. At such times the two men would talk for hours on end.

Mechanically, Laure shifted the baby to her other breast. It was cheering to note that, recently, the Wanderer seemed to be enjoying longer and more frequent intervals of lucidity; but, even so, the Reverend Edward Nicholson remained unable to recall anything from his past beyond the certainty that somewhere, sometime, he had been ordained a priest of the Anglican Church.

It had been he who, a week or so ago, had reported of the impending armistice and, more vital still, news of the road being built between New Inverness and Savannah.

Johnnie, having slaked his appetite, started to nod, so Taqua heaved him, naked save for his swaddling clout, onto her shoulder and patted his fat little back.

"Thad, what is this armistice worth?"

"Not much."

"Which side will you support if war comes?"

He tossed his cleaning rag onto the bench and peered steadily out into the silver-gray drizzle. "I will keep my people neutral as long as possible."

With unseeing eyes, Thad continued to look across a puddled, mud-covered area which, nearly a century earlier, the inhabitants had termed "la plaza mayor de Capola."

When, on a hunting expedition, he had chanced upon the remains of this ancient mission there hadn't been much left of it except for a crumbling chapel, the iron bells of which lay half buried at the base of a vine-shrouded tower; the smoke-scorched walls of what probably had been a granary and the forlorn, roofless shells of nearly two dozen dwellings of durable tabby stone.

Upon a rise that commanded the village Thad had come upon traces of a lunette battery containing four small, but still serviceable, four-pound bronze cannon. At a glance, he had recognized that this fortification had been astutely emplaced, dominating as it did the road and a ford below Capola which still were well used because the trace ran parallel to the Gulf of Mexico.

Nor had it escaped Thad's attention that Fort Capola—as he had named his crudely restored battery—would again become important; it must lie pretty close to that line the Georgians were claiming as their southern frontier.

Then and there, he'd conceived the notion of occupying and restoring Capola to be the third and final capital of the Sakwaris. To his angry surprise he had met with considerable opposition to this decision because his followers feared that the ghosts of massacred Spaniards still might haunt the ruins.

A small band of Abecas, living nearby, always avoided the site, believing it to be an abode of Chitokaka, the Supreme Devil. Sakwari-cra's will had prevailed when, solemnly, he announced that, in a dream, Sotolycaté, had directed that the wanderings of the Sakwari people must end in Capola. If they settled here, Sotolycaté promised that the tribe would prosper and increase until it became a mighty nation, equal in strength with the Creeks, Cherokees, and Chickasaws.

He was recalled to the present by Laure's persisting, "If this armistice fails, whose side will you take?"

"Why do you wish to know?"

Thad certainly had changed! That the Panther King actually should invite the opinion of a mere squaw was astounding. To lend the impression that she was thinking hard, she delayed her reply.

"The French, the English and the Spanish soon will come to bid for an alliance with you." With pride, the full-breasted young woman added, "Now that you have become the Panther King whose power increases from moon to moon." She knew she should have said, "from month to month," but she couldn't help, now and then, from slipping back into the old phraseology.

"I do not know. I will decide when the time comes," he announced stiffly, then, to put her in her place, he added, "Go fetch my pipe."

When Laure picked up Johnnie and disappeared into their dark and moldy-smelling home he considered a group of warriors squatting under a rude shelter across the plaza.

Some, like himself, were attending to their weapons; others gambled, but another group was busy tattooing a young gunman using a razor-sharp shark's tooth and paste made of mixed bear's grease and gunpowder.

None of the old Spanish houses, saving his own, had been repaired beyond the construction of wooden doors and window shutters; roofs, originally of red clay tile, had been replaced with palm thatch. Most of Capola's windows gaped, freely admitted multitudinous flies, gnats, mosquitoes, and an occasional bat or even an incautious owl. Nevertheless, his followers appeared quite contented.

Some, in the Muskogean fashion, had painted a wide red band around their dwelling to let everyone know that a fighting man dwelt within. Such families as could find no shelter among the yellow-brown tabby-stone ruins had built solid log houses or circular cedar-bark lodges upon meadows near the river where rich pasturage for their pigs and horses was readily accessible. Recently, a few rack-ribbed cows had appeared; contemptuously treated as "the white man's buffalo."

Listening to the endless drip and piddle of rain trickling off the porch roof, Thad recalled what Laure had just said about the tribe's growing importance, began to feel full of himself. Why shouldn't the white powers try to curry favor with the Panther King? Granted more time, there wasn't any reason why he shouldn't become an emperor as mighty as Mary Musgrove's famous uncle.

Nowadays he could field a force of over a hundred hardy and well-equipped warriors. This increase in strength only recently had become possible through his having absorbed a leaderless band of wandering Abecas—a minor Creek tribe speaking the Stinkard dialect.

Laure, having changed Johnnie and deposited him in his woven-willow crib, came back onto the porch and settled down to wiping mud off Jeems, who seemed no more affected by the cold rain than a papoose. Turning her red head, she said, carefully, because she knew she was being persistent over something Thad didn't want to talk about, "If war should break out you will favor the English, won't you?"

Thad's jaw closed with a *click!* and it looked for a moment as if he might be working himself up to one of his rages, but he ended by snapping, "Never! I distrust them. They are more stubborn and pushing in their hunger for new territory than the French or the Spaniards. English settlements spring up like toadstools. Just wait! Any day, some Georgian will come here asking leave to establish a trading post on Sakwari land, but he will ask in vain! I do not need such a post. Always, when a trader becomes established he marries some young squaw or sends for his family. Other families follow and soon there is only an English village where an Indian town once stood."

Laure stuffed Jeems, grinning and wriggling like a speared eel, into a warm flannel shirt before pushing him indoors. "There is a kettle of samp on the coals," she told him. "Eat some." Then she turned to her huge husband, angrily fingering a pistol as he went to occupy a rush-bottomed chair—a recent acquisition.

"I think a long time must pass before the English will venture this far from the Guale Coast," Taqua predicted. "But when they do appear, they will come in such strength that they cannot be denied anything and then you will have to accept a trading post."

Sakwari-cra whirled, gray-blue eyes flashing. "The Panther King will not be forced to act against his will by anyone, now or ever! Soon, he will become so mighty no one will dare to enter into his kingdom unsummoned!"

The young woman whose skin had remained the color of buckwheat honey knew that, all last fall and winter, Thad had sent out men to blaze trees and erect stone cairns to mark the perimeter of a rough circle some sixty miles across and centered on Capola.

But for this abnormally long rainy spell Thad would have been away on a mission aimed at recruiting an Alibamu band dwelling on the Chattahoochee's eastern tributaries. Recently these people had been so ravaged by chicken pox that Shatara, who'd been there on a spying-hunting trip, reported that many Alibamu fields had been abandoned; everywhere he had come upon deserted huts and lodges; even whole villages stood empty. Therefore, did it not stand to reason that these people should be ready to sell or to cede to the Panther King a tract of hunting land so vast that it would double the Sakwaris' present territory?

Toward noon the rain diminished and, here and there, the lead-hued sky began to show patches of sickly yellow. Suwannee Creek, however, continued to rise ominously, choked as it was by many days' accumulation of broken branches, uprooted trees, and other debris. The water had only to rise a little higher before Thad must give the order to leave Capola and head for higher ground.

Hum. How would Shatara's boundary-marking party be faring? Farther down the Suwannee lay wide, low bottom lands on which men might all too easily get trapped and drowned. He was beginning to regret having sent away so large a group, twenty-five fighting men, but, at the time, such a move had appeared advisable; a lesser force might have invited a fight with the fierce Moviles, whose lands lay to the westward.

Hachey, his newest sub-mico—a Tala Yuchi—was leading a similar detachment to the upper Satilla and another sizable group was away hunting wild horses, so only a handful of fighting men remained in Capola to grump and curse the weather.

Among the huts farthest downriver sounded a sudden, furious barking which could only mean the presence of strangers.

It was characteristic of Sakwari-cra's discipline that somnolent warriors immediately caught up weapons and splashed out onto the quagmire covering the *plaza mayor*.

The stranger turned out to be a pox-scarred Tala Yuchi who, when he staggered into sight, had an arrow stuck in his left shoulder. The missile, a heavy-shafted war arrow, must have been loosed at long range for it had only slightly penetrated the runner's shoulder muscle.

Sakwari Slave Catchers seized the apparition, then led him, unresisting and trailing blood drops, up to the Panther King.

Sakwari-cra growled, "Why have you dared to come to Capola?"

"Two sleeps ago, O mighty Tostenuggo-Hlako," panted the Yuchi, "a war party of the Dog King's people, with the cunning of the Rabbit Trickster, took Katsagli, my village, and slew many of us."

"How can you be sure they were Yamasee?"

Thin chest heaving, the runner swayed between the Slave Catchers gripping his rain-brightened arms. "They were Yamasee, I saw them close by."

Eyes narrowing, Thad demanded in rapid Creek. "How long ago did this take place?"

"Two sleeps ago."

"Yet your wound looks fresh. How is that?"

"It was made when, running toward Capola, I was attacked. I do not know who sped the arrow as I ran by." Although obviously suffering, the Yuchi did not wince when Thad strode over and yanked out the arrow. It was a Yamasee shaft all right.

"How many warriors are in the second party?"

"I cannot be sure, O Tostenuggo-Hlako. So many, perhaps." The Yuchi shoved forward both hands and three times extended quivering, rain-wrinkled fingers.

"What direction did they travel?"

"They followed the Suwannee."

A tall young Raven spoke up. "Ho! So these dog-delivered Yamasees mean to strike us!"

"It could be so," wheezed the runner. "But perhaps they mean to fall upon Creek villages across the Satilla. The Dog King is hot to avenge those Abecas raids made during the Deer Rutting Moon."

Chapter 7

THE STRANGERS

Ever since Oglethorpe's mission to the Panther King had quitted New Inverness a week ago rain had fallen almost incessantly—sometimes softly, sometimes hard-driven. In all that time the sun shone on only a few occasions, and then not long enough to do any good.

The generally flat and often thinly wooded country over which Tsi-Skwa, a silent and somber-eyed Alibamu, guided Wallace Challenger and his small party appeared to be drowning; there were so many wide pools and lakes formed by accumulated rain water. Leafless hardwoods looked ugly, bare, and unfriendly. Tiny rivulets swelled into rushing creeks full of creaming, boiling eddies; creeks had become transformed into furious rivers which, overflowing their banks onto low ground, created treacherous and often impassable swamps.

Snakes and alligators, fortunately dazed and sluggish, were forced out of their hibernation holes to keep from drowning. Here and there coons, possums, rabbits, squirrels, and other small quadrupeds, their fur muddied and bedraggled, crouched morosely on logs or stood marooned on bits of high ground.

After a few days the downpour seeped into every bit of a man's clothing and equipment. When the party made camp for the night and attempted to dry out after a fashion, the men's feet, when they pulled off mud-filled moccasins, were found to be deeply wrinkled and as dead-white as those of corpses.

Even Umpychi, usually a cheerful soul, snarled that Sotolycaté must be mightily annoyed over something. Had some rite or sacrifice been omitted during the Great Corn Festival celebrated during the Turn-Yellow-Leaf Moon?

Despite every precaution, the pack loads of gifts intended for the Panther King became soaked; many items, such as the bolts of scarlet cloth, were ruined beyond recovery.

James Adair grunted, "Hope to God our powder's still fit for use."

Everybody wondered, although the powder casks had been calked with tar and further waterproofed by heavy coatings of red lead.

"E'en in Scotland we seldom see it rain like this," snuffled Hamish Baillie, Jeanie Woodroofe's cousin. He managed a short laugh. "Wull, there's one thing to the good. Most o' my fleas ha'e drowned and dropped off."

Challenger swallowed the last of a raccoon stew, then glanced across the sputtering campfire at Tsi-Skwa, the taciturn Alibamu guide who always carried his head tilted somewhat to the right. "How many more walks to Capola?"

"One sleep, maybe two; depends on how big streams have grown."

Next morning, it was raining harder than ever; icy drops fell with such bullet-like force they soon knocked off the hardwoods their few remaining dead leaves. Some of them they plastered upon the riders following a track which resembled more a brook than a trail.

Time and again, Challenger's short column was forced by flooded bottom land to leave the track and detour, sometimes for a long way.

Around noon something happened which abruptly took the riders' minds off their misery. They had come upon a point where, not long before, a considerable body of horsemen had ridden onto this same trail and then had headed in the direction of Capola!

After making a careful examination of these hoofprints Tsi-Skwa and Challenger told Umpychi and the four Yamacraws sent along by Tomo-chichi to dismount and learn what they could through following the party's back trail for a while.

Leaving the pack animals and the rest of his men under Woodroofe's command, Challenger took Adair to scout along the route to the Sakwari capital.

At length, the young Scotch-Irishman queried, "How far ahead of us are they?"

The Ranger captain used the heel of his hand to wipe rain from his eyes. "Not more than two or three hours at most. Damn' good thing we know they're here 'stead of the other way round. What d'ye make of 'em?"

Briefly, Adair's small, pale-blue eyes surveyed the trampled earth. "For a guess, I'd say they're Yamasee raiders."

"Why?"

"Because they cut this trail from the southeast and are riding Spanish-bred horses. See how small and round most of the hoofprints are?"

"Yep, I do. Well, we better turn back. It'll get dark extra early tonight."

After reining about his mud-marked mount, Challenger said over his shoulder, "Think ye're likely right about them bein' Yamasees, but they just *might* be a bunch of Sakwaris headed for home. Don't know what sort of horses Burton's people ride."

When the men who'd scouted the back trail came in everyone had pretty well decided that the strangers numbered between fifteen and eighteen men and that their mounts must be very tired—their average stride was so very short.

The Ranger captain beckoned forward Tsi-Skwa. "How well d'ye know the country 'tween here and Capola?"

Following a series of smothered coughs, the Alibamu declared, "Often, I have hunted this country. Capola lies across the Suwannee, on the north bank."

"How near to the Suwannee are we?"

"The roaring noise to our right is made by the Suwannee."

"Good." Challenger swung off his horse and pointed to the soaked carpet of red-brown pine needles at his feet. "Speak me a map before it gets too dark to see."

The Ranger broke off a dead stick, sank onto his heels, and began to draw while Tsi-Skwa talked.

"Half a sun travel upriver two great swamps lie to the right. How far toward rising sun they extend Tsi-Skwa not know. A high wooded ridge divides these swamps for long long way. It may be that sometime they join."

Bent over, the party listened so intently that they failed to notice that at long last the rain appeared to be letting up for good.

"At lower edge of these swamps is pond made by old beaver dam. It is shaped like war club. Near head of this pond is ford across Suwannee." Tsi-Skwa took Challenger's stick. "Second crossing lies here."

Challenger's bright blue eyes probed the guide's black ones. "Is there any crossing *below* War Club Pond?"

"Here," the Alibamu stated. "Not much far from this place."

"Everything depends," the Ranger captain said as if to himself, "on whether the strangers will try to use this ford *below* the pond."

"Doubt if they can," Adair grunted, and shook out fringes dripping along his sleeves. "Sounds like there's too much water in the river."

It turned out that the trader was wrong, for when, just before dark, Oglethorpe's men reconnoitered the ford south of War Club Pond the tracks they were following went right down to the ford and disappeared. Whoever the strangers were, they must have been either very brave or foolhardy to urge tired horses into such a raging white torrent. Whether they had gained the opposite bank was another matter.

Now it was growing dark, so to attempt a crossing at this hour would have been suicidal folly. Challenger therefore ordered the party to bivouac in a sheltered hollow where they were able to stretch their only shelter— a well-worn tarpaulin—among four trees.

After a miserable and tasteless supper, Challenger ordered all firearms fetched in to be dried before a small, carefully screened fire kindled beneath the tarpaulin.

"I want you all," he instructed his malodorous followers, "to refill your powder flasks and horns, but only from keg Number Two. God alone knows why it's stayed dry."

Snuffling, coughing, and spitting, white men and Indians alike by the uncertain firelight used worm screws to extract bullets and buckshot. Then they drew damp and therefore useless charges from pistols and muskets. Finally, priming pans and frizzens were heated just enough to remove traces of moisture without damaging the lock's mechanism.

Wallace Challenger, lying with head pillowed on his saddle, tried to ignore the chill beginning to bite through soggy, slimy-feeling buckskins and seeping under the soaking saddle blanket which was his only covering. Although far wearier than he ever would have admitted, he found himself unable to go to sleep, so he watched James Adair, standing guard with one of the Yamacraws, and envied Woodroofe and Baillie, who were snoring like drunkards.

The Ranger captain sat up, yawned, and knuckled sunken eyes when, with teeth chattering, the young Scotch-Irishman ducked under the tarpaulin and kicked together sufficient embers to kindle a small flame over which he could warm his stiffening limbs. He'd been cold and miserable before, plenty of times, but never quite like this. He got so close to the fire that soon his leggings commenced to steam.

"Well, Wallace, no doubt you've plans for the morrow?"

"Aye, but I'm not too sure how good they are."

"They'll work out all right."

"Thanks, but tell me this. Do you think we're following a war party, or some Sakwaris on their way home?"

"It's a war party."

"Why so?"

"Because they're careful to light no fires and leave no sign behind. They're hurrying, too, as men on home ground aren't apt to."

"True enough. Then what is a war party doing so deep into Creek and Sakwari territory?"

Adair crouched over the flames, his smooth but powerful features glowing bronze-red. "Reckon it's about as Tsi-Skwa said, they're either getting set to surprise Capola or mean to by-pass the place and hit the Abeca Creek villages along the Satilla. God knows which they'll try."

"That's the big question."

Whenever he lifted his face the young trader's eyes looked preternaturally large—like some gigantic owl's. "And how d'you figure to find an answer?"

Drops of water leaking through the sagging tarpaulin caused an occasional hiss among the embers and raised brief cloudlets of steam. Off in the gloom, the swollen Suwannee roared on and on.

"Comes first light I want you to take Umpychi and his Yamacraws across the ford yonder; if the hostiles *did* get across, trail them takin' damn' good care ye don't get jumped.

"Meanwhile, I aim to lead the two Creeks, Baillie, Woodroofe and Tsi-Skwa and the pack animals. I'll circle round War Club Pond till I reach the first of the two fords above it"; softly, the big Ranger added, "Pray God that Alibamu rascal knows this country like he claims to."

"That means you aim to split this party six and six?"

Challenger's tangled yellow hair glinted faintly to his nod. "Sure. I want to watch the upper crossing so, if by any chance, this party *is* Sakwaris I'll know it in plenty of time to make the peace sign and parley till you can come up.

"If they're Yamasees, we'll wait till they're halfway across the ford then cut loose. Caught in midstream like that, they won't be able to fight back too well."

Challenger drew a slow breath and grinned. "We ought to raise such hell with them that these hostiles will be glad to turn back. If they do, it'll be your turn to give 'em a licking."

Enveloped by a sudden swirl of wood smoke, Adair coughed softly. "Sounds like a reasonable plan, only remember I'll have just five men with me and two of them have no guns—just bows."

"True. But if the hostiles do retreat, remember they'll be fleeing with empty guns—no Indian I've ever heard of would think to stop to reload under such conditions. Besides, they won't be expecting you. Handle matters well, and you ought to make a real killing. The Panther King won't be displeased. His enemies will have been beaten and at no cost to him."

Chapter 8

THE FIGHT AT WAR CLUB POND

Long before sunup, Challenger, having followed another and more direct trail, with sure skill had disposed his handful of followers among a jumble of water-smoothed rocks and in a windfall lying opposite the exit to the ford above War Club Pond. Riders emerging from the Suwannee's surging yellow current would be forced to come within easy musket and arrow range—an essential advantage, since neither Creek carried firearms and the reliability of Tsi-Skwa's ancient musket was doubtful.

At the same time, the Ranger captain remained anxious over a new and unforeseeable aspect of the situation; during the night that same cold west wind which had made the bivouac so miserable died out and left behind a blanket of mist so dense that a man couldn't see for more than a few yards in any direction.

Once mounts and pack animals had been tethered in a dense thicket of alders, Challenger posted Will Woodroofe on the right of his skirmish line behind a mossy log.

"Remember now, don't anyone shoot till I fire. Understand?"

Hamish Baillie, remarkably cool for his first Indian fight, he also placed on his right, next to himself. The young Scot lay well concealed behind a jumble of boulders.

The Creek bowmen crouched, well hidden, but close in, on the left of the semicircle he'd drawn about the landing point. Tsi-Skwa, he posted next left to his own position, on a willow-crowned hummock.

The ugly Alibamu was warned that the moment he obtained a good look at the strangers, he was to raise his right hand if they proved to be

Sakwaris; such a gesture could only be interpreted as a peace sign. Should the strangers prove to be hostiles he was to fling up his left arm. Was this clearly understood? Grunting an affirmative, Tsi-Skwa wriggled, snake-like, into his hiding place and then pulled his rusty old gun in after him.

Challenger then returned to the center of his line, checked the flint and priming not only of his musket but also of two boarding pistols he'd placed ready to hand on a flat stone.

Although the sky continued slowly to brighten, the ground mist seemed reluctant to lift; if anything the vapors grew denser.

A flock of parakeets settled on high branches, began to whistle and chatter. Challenger lay so completely motionless that a scarlet tanager settled onto a branch not three feet away and commenced to preen the damp from its plumage.

Then a possibly significant occurrence took place; from *behind* him quite a few deer could be heard crashing through the mist-veiled woods; from the racket they made they must be in full flight. Could the strangers possibly have crossed the ford already? No. There certainly were no recent hoofmarks visible on the bank. What could have scared those deer so? A panther perhaps? Maybe a bear or . . . ?

Although definitely uneasy, Challenger returned his attention to the ford and strained eyes through the eddying vapors, since it was almost impossible to detect untoward sounds over the Suwannee's rush and roar.

Nevertheless, after a space, the giant captain felt certain he could hear unusual splashing noises, so he turned onto his side in order to watch Tsi-Skwa. Judging by the Alibamu's tensed attitude, he too must have heard some abnormal sound. With the intensity of a bird dog who suspects, but isn't quite sure, that a covey of quail is somewhere near, he was peering hard into the slowly shifting wall of mist.

When a capricious puff of wind momentarily twitched up the silvery curtain Challenger's heart gave a spasmodic leap, like a buck shot in its vitals. With their horses chest-deep in the surging current five, six—no, seven Indians were beating forward their mounts. Hell! The foremost already was halfway across the ford!

Then Challenger got the biggest surprise of his life. The rider third in line was a bearded white man who was wearing a Spanish officer's soiled red and yellow tunic!

From a corner of his eye he watched Tsi-Skwa's left arm shoot up to full length. Spanish-led Yamasees! Yamasees! A vast sigh of relief escaped the Ranger captain. Now his party couldn't help win the Panther King's gratitude and at the same time do James Oglethorpe a great good turn.

He eased his musket barrel over a water-polished boulder and aimed not at the spade-bearded Spaniard or at the leading Yamasee, a tall warrior wearing an egret headdress and the streaked remains of red and black war paint, but at the fourth rider in line. He knew better than to waste his musket's longer range on the nearest enemy; pistols should suffice to dispose of at least two men if they tried to close in.

While, amid a welter of flying spray, the hostiles were splashing and plunging nearer, six more Yamasees rode down the Suwannee's far bank and into the water. How long dared he to delay firing that shot which would precipitate the action? Challenger darted a look to his right at the Scots and was amazed to see how wonderfully well their faded tartans blended with their surroundings. They had leveled their weapons and quietly were awaiting his order to open fire. At that moment he loved them like brothers; men who would obey orders, no matter what, were mighty hard to come by.

He delayed until the nearest Yamasee wasn't over forty feet off, then drew a deep breath which he half expelled before squeezing with his whole trigger hand till the hammer snapped its flint against the steel frizzen and drove a pencil of sparks into the gunlock's pan which touched off the priming charge.

Automatically, the Ranger captain closed his eyes a split second before a spurt of orange flame sprang vertically from the vent, then the weapon kicked him like a bad-tempered mule. Subconsciously, he heard three other reports boom in rapid succession. Peering through a veil of mist and gunpowder, he was elated to see that two horses were down and struggling, their riders carried off by rushing water, and two other mounts were plunging about, riderless and panic-stricken.

Living up to their reputation as uncommonly tough and courageous warriors, the Yamasees howled war cries and urged their horses forward. Not one of them got off a shot; too long they had postponed drying out and recharging their weapons. Besides, from their rearing, plunging horses they couldn't see anything to shoot at.

Yelling, "Viva el Rey!" the Spaniard spurred on until a yellow-fletched Creek arrow sank deep into his thigh; although almost across he in the red and yellow tunic then wheeled his mount and went plunging back over the ford. Challenger lost track of him, for now the Yamasee leader, who wore a huge red eagle painted across his chest, had reached water shallow enough to permit his charging Hamish Baillie. Challenger glimpsed the young Scot rising to point a pistol, but he must have been careless about repriming it, for the weapon misfired. The Yamasee dropped his own gun and, abandoning his mount, raced forward, toma-hawk raised and flashing. Terribly lithe and swift, the savage cut down Jeanie Woodroofe's cousin before Challenger had time to snatch up one of his pistols and send a heavy ball smashing into the Yamasee's naked back.

At the same moment Woodroofe raised his clan war cry, "Calann *aoidh!*" and pistoled another Yamasee as he splashed ashore with water squirting out of leggings and hunting shirt. Screeching, the rest of the Yamasees, to the number of seven or eight, kept on so determinedly that Challenger sensed that his skirmish line was about to be broken.

Five dark-complexioned Yamasees scrambled up onto the riverbank and succeeded in killing Tsi-Skwa, but not before the Alibamu had slain one just as another hostile uttered a bubbling scream and toppled off his mount while clawing at the Creek arrow which had lodged in his throat.

A warrior wearing a clump of scraggly turkey feathers twisted into his scalp lock yelled something from the middle of the ford, then wrenched his horse about as another Yamasee went down under a Creek arrow.

Then it happened, and so suddenly that, for once in his life, Wallace Challenger was completely surprised and didn't know what to think or do. A volley of musket fire roared along the edge of the woods *behind* his skirmish line. The two Yamasees who were busy taking Tsi-Skwa's scalp clapped hands to their bodies, spun about, and fell, kicking, among the willows. Bullets raised miniature waterspouts about the four or five hostiles who were trying to escape across the river. Bent flat over their horses' necks, they galloped back along that trail upon which Adair and his companions should be awaiting them.

To Challenger the fight became grim confusion when a line of dismounted Indians ran, whooping, out of the woods; his bewilderment increased when he realized these newcomers were shooting indiscriminately not only at the retreating Yamasees but also at Woodroofe and himself! Apparently, they hadn't yet noticed the two Creek bowmen posted on his far left.

With the suddenness of an exploding rocket, an explanation offered itself. Somehow, the Panther King had been warned that Yamasees had penetrated his territory and were advancing on Capola! Challenger left off reloading a pistol and jumped up, waving empty hands, shouting, "*Tchipanat!* Peace! We come as friends!" but a huge figure wearing a yellow and red turban kept running toward him and brandishing a pistol in either hand.

In desperation, the Ranger captain yelled, "Burton! Sakwari-cra! Stop! Stop your men! I'm Wallace Challenger, your friend!"

The Panther King did halt a few yards away, but only to level one of his weapons. Quick as a stooping hawk, Challenger could only bend, catch up his second pistol, and fire, all in the same motion. Its report sounded at precisely the same instant that Sakwari-cra discharged his weapon. It seemed as if someone had hit the Ranger such a vicious blow that he was spun half around. He felt as if a red-hot iron ramrod had been placed along his side. Although swaying like a drunken man, Challenger jerked free his war hatchet and peered dazedly through mingled mist and gun smoke in time to see Thad Burton's huge body sway before, convulsively, he tossed arms high in the air and, falling, disappeared amid the dripping underbrush.

Once the Panther King's followers saw Sakwari-cra collapse they stopped whatever they were doing and, raising ear-piercing cries, converged upon his body.

Despite searing pain in his side, Challenger, still clutching his smoking pistol, yelled to Woodroofe, "Get across—river. Quick!" Nauseated, reeling in his stride, he splashed out into the turgid Suwannee and was swept down to the carcasses of horses which had become entangled with a barrier of broken boughs and storm trash.

Woodroofe plunged in too, bent well over, for the Sakwaris, having recovered from the shock of their mico's fall, were rushing forward howling bloody murder. The Scot threw an arm about the Ranger's waist and heaved him erect. Arrows were falling short, but bullets hissed by the floundering fugitives but didn't prevent them from getting across.

Only a few rods down the back track the fugitives came onto a horse whose reins were imprisoned in the clutch of a fallen Yamasee.

Although blood continued to pour hotly down Challenger's side he managed, with a heave from Woodroofe, somehow to straddle the beast. The Scot immediately swung up behind him and kicked the scrawny mount into a trot which quickly concealed them amid the slowly lifting mist.

Chapter 9

NIGHTMARE RETREAT

The captured horse, though small, proved strong beyond expectation, but, supporting Wallace Challenger's huge frame and Will Woodroofe's not inconsiderable weight, it was either unwilling or unable to proceed at more than a slow jog. As if to compound their difficulties yet another storm broke and drenched the fugitives with ice-cold rain.

All the same, Wallace Challenger dimly rejoiced; such a lashing downpour soon would obscure hoofprints and the betraying line of blood drops dripping down his leg soon would become washed away.

Growing steadily dizzier, Challenger, to keep his seat, wound fingers in the pony's tangled mane. God a' mighty! He'd been wounded before, plenty of times, but never like this.

Fuzzily, he reckoned he had taken such a hard wound on his left side that Burton's ball must have either cracked or broken several ribs, for the horse's every stride seem to drive a volley of heated arrows into his side. Although he ground his teeth he soon grew so weak that he'd have slumped onto the ground but for Woodroofe's arm clamped around him.

Although his head swam through shock and loss of blood, Challenger knew that if they were to stand any chance of getting away something would have to be done in a hurry. Before long, the Sakwaris would recover their wits and start in pursuit, misinterpreting no sign no matter how insignificant. What Thad Burton's warriors would do if ever they caught up with him wouldn't bear thinking about.

Somehow, Challenger managed to raise his head and look ahead until, through lancing rain, he glimpsed a flat stone just high enough to force the trail to swing around it.

"That rock. We get on—"

Woodroofe grasped his intention at once, snapped, "Brace yersel'."

The horse proved more than willing to halt beside the rock upon which hard-driven raindrops were shattering themselves. Woodroofe scrambled onto the great stone, then gripped Challenger's hands, grown slippery through futile attempts to compress the wound so it would leave behind fewer telltale splotches.

The Ranger barely was able to suppress a yell of anguish when Woodroofe heaved him upward onto the bare, flat surface; the streaming woods spun crazily about him as, gasping, he was forced to sink onto all fours.

Relieved of the men's weight, their mount moved off, slowly at first, but soon vanished down the trail at a brisk trot. Hazily, Challenger thought, Hope the brute's too worn out to gallop; if it does, the Sakwaris will wonder why, rain or no rain. Steadied by Woodroofe, he struggled across the rock toward a row of dripping cedars. Dully, he noticed that the young Scot still had a pistol jammed into his belt. He was glad of that. He'd lost his own while struggling over the ford.

Once they were concealed by a green tangle of wild grape and supplejack he pointed backward. "Go back—wash blood off rock." By hooking his arm over the limb of a tree Challenger managed to remain erect. To think sensibly was becoming almost impossible—it was as if he were waking from a profound sleep—or a real big drunk.

He couldn't tell how much time passed before he thought he heard something like gunshots somewhere in the distance. But he was too far gone to be sure; the noise had been too faint and muffled by the drumming downpour.

After an indeterminable interval, Will Woodroofe came crawling back, unshaven features speckled by bits of bark and small leaves. His eyes widened at the size and deep color of the blood-and-rain puddle in which stood the Ranger captain.

Painfully, the wounded man raised questioning eyes. "Wha' happen'?"

"I'd just cleaned off the rock when a lot of savages rode by."

"Fast or slow?"

"Slow. They were studying our horse's hoofprints."

"They notice where—stopped?"

"I think not."

"How many trackers?"

"Above a dozen—"

"You heard shots?"

"Aye. 'Twas something of a bicker."

The broad-faced young Scot hitched forward a small haversack and pulled out the remains of a dirty old neckerchief which he folded into a clumsy rectangle. After cutting away gory buckskin framing the wound, he used a length of rawhide lacing to lash, effectively enough, his compress into position and partially slowed the hemorrhage.

Growing ghastly pale under his beard, despite grime and tan, Challenger whispered, "Did I hear two fire fights?"

"That ye did. One, I figure, took place when the Spaniard and his men ran into Adair's detachment. The other when the Sakwaris chased our horse into the first fight; no telling what's happened or who won."

"Not Adair—too few men—God help him." Feebly, Challenger propped himself up on his good arm. "Must get farther off trail; when they don't find us with Adair, Sakwaris—come looking for us."

The rain stopped again—this time as if it really meant to—and presently the sun came out, hot and bright. An arm loosely hooked around Woodroofe's sinewy red neck, Challenger, sweating in agony, swayed and stumbled along an old deer run. Progress wasn't easy; fallen branches, blown-down trees, and slippery stones lay everywhere. Often there hardly was room for a single man to proceed, let alone two abreast. After they'd struggled several hundred yards along a ridge with the glimmer of swamp water showing on both sides Wallace Challenger collapsed without warning; unconscious, he sprawled on the mucky ground breathing stertorously.

Will Woodroofe, although a fairly recent immigrant, had acquired considerable woods lore since his arrival in North America; besides, having lived for a while in the Highlands, he felt at home in rough country. Sweating and panting, he managed to drag his huge companion off the deer run and conceal him in the heart of a dense clump of moss-hung red cypresses. Here, years of deposits of fallen leaves had created a soft carpet which, lying on high ground, promised to dry out quickly. But his hopes sank when he backtracked a way and saw what a plain trail they'd left. Even a half-blind man would find no trouble in following it.

After rearranging and retightening the compress's bindings, Woodroofe deliberated and became torn by indecision. To light even a tiny fire he knew would be risky, yet it would render their chances no worse if Burton's warriors discovered the trail; besides, he knew that his companion must drink something hot; Challenger's face and hands were growing icy. The Scot unslung his haversack and dumped out a cow's-horn tip filled with gunpowder and three bullets, then reloaded his pistol before he took up a battered copper cup, a deer's bladder stuffed with foul-smelling pemmican, and the pair of coarse woolen stockings which completed the war bag's contents.

A good thing he had hung onto his skinning knife and war hatchet, but it was too bad his MacKenzie musket was lying in the ford above War Club Pond unless, of course, some sharp-eyed Sakwari had spotted it.

After he'd folded the spare socks into a pillow he pulled off his hunting shirt of homespun, wrung it out and draped it over the unconscious giant. Then shivering and with every scar, scratch, and cut above his belt showing livid purple against his dead-white and cringing skin, Woodroofe explored the surroundings till he came on a lightning-killed pine and dug splinters from the underside of a thick bough until he'd collected sufficient material for a tiny fire.

When his big copper cup began to give off rank but not unsavory-smelling steam he stamped on the coals. Then, after swallowing a couple of mouthfuls, he made his way, as quietly as possible, through the dripping but now sun-dappled woods.

He was nearing the cypress copse when a small sound from behind caused him to spin about so fast that he spilled some of the precious stew and realized that an Indian with bow drawn and arrow nocked had arisen from behind a bush. A wave of despair engulfed him but subsided when he recognized the savage as Umpychi, Tomo-chichi's orator.

There was no friendliness in Umpychi's eyes as he hissed in the almost perfect English he'd acquired in London. "You were a great fool to light a fire! Do you want us *all* to lose our hair?"

"Of course not, ye great ninny, but Captain Challenger lies yonder verra close to death; this hot drink I hope may save him."

Umpychi lowered his bow, spoke in guttural undertones. "Even so, to light a fire was a crazy thing to do; I smelled it a long way off. Sakwari warriors range this country like hungry wolves. We must move on."

During Woodroofe's absence Challenger, being tough as a hickory ax handle, had regained a measure of consciousness and so was able to swallow what remained of the pemmican broth. Even to Umpychi it was astonishing to witness how quickly traces of color appeared in the Ranger's yellow-bristled cheeks and he became able to focus his eyes.

"Umpychi," he whispered, "what 'ap'?"

Although the Yamacraw sank onto his heels his bright black eyes continued to flit about as he spoke in hurried undertones. "I bring evil news, Captain. When Adair and the rest of us heard shooting at the upper ford we started to close in, but a Spanish officer and five Yamasees came galloping back along the trail so fast that they broke right by us. We were able only to kill two!"

"Spaniard was one?"

"No."

"What happened next?" Woodroofe couldn't help asking.

"We were busy lifting the Yamasee scalps when, suddenly, a swarm of Sakwaris fell upon us. Chula, the Chickasaw who used to camp with Thad Burton outside of Savannah, was leading them."

"What about Adair?"

"With one other, he was taken prisoner," grunted Umpychi. "Only I escaped. The rest of us were killed."

"Adair a prisoner?" wheezed Challenger. "God help him now that Sakwari-cra is dead."

As if struck by a cottonmouth the Yamacraw started; his coppery features grew taut. "The Panther King dead! How did he die?"

"He took aim at me—we fired together."

Poor Adair! Recently Woodroofe had heard gruesome accounts of what could take place around a Muskogean torture frame.

Somewhere, back along the ridge, a bluejay began to scream raucous alarm.

"You two clear out," whispered the big Ranger. "Don't argue! I can't travel so why—all three die?"

Umpychi jerked a nod. "There is no sense in that. I will backtrack and try draw off the Sakwaris. When the right time comes, I will shake them off and then come back. If I am successful we can look for an Abeca village Tsi-Skwa spoke of. If he wasn't lying, it cannot be very far off."

"And if you don't shake off the Sakwaris?" Woodroofe whispered.

Umpychi shrugged. "If the Sakwaris find you, you had better shoot the captain and then kill yourself with your knife. Now I go. Perhaps I shall return, perhaps not."

Chapter 10

LONG VIGIL

Since sunset a ring of pitch-pine knots had flared redly, smokily around that hut in which reposed the fallen mico's body. It lay on the same litter of pine branches fashioned by Chula and his men to fetch in the Panther King's body. Among the palm-thatched, old stone houses of Capola sounded the unbroken wails of grieving females.

With eyes closed, Thad Burton's remains lay supine with that scarlet groove which had brought him down, plainly visible on the right side of his head. His great hands, loosely clenched, barely showed under a beautifully woven reed mat which covered him from the neck downward. For all his muscle-corded chest remained motionless, he did not suggest a newly dead man, but rather a heroic bronze figure plunged into profound slumber.

Following Muskogean custom, the litter had been placed overnight in a hurriedly evacuated house—no corpse could rest properly among the living. Meanwhile, a circular pit six feet deep by four in diameter was dug in the earthen floor of the fallen mico thlucco's residence.

Toward nightfall of the day of the fight at War Club Pond the former Chickasaw, Shatara, and the men he'd led on the boundary-fixing expedition rode into Capola hungry, soaked, and bedraggled. One and all they were stricken, dumfounded by the evil news.

When Shatara learned that he who had slain Sakwari-cra thus far had escaped, he raged so fearfully that, for a time, none dared to approach him.

Finally, he snarled, "With daylight I, Shatara, the most famed tracker in all the land, will take up the search and run down Captain Challenger. I will bring him back that he may suffer properly for his great crime!"

Grimly, Chula snorted. "To accomplish that, Shatara must first become half a bird and half an alligator. We followed his trail along that ridge which divides the swamps until, in his fear, he ran off into the deepest swamp of all where it is impossible to track him. But the villian has not escaped—without doubt, the snakes which abound there will have killed him."

"Chula, you have the eyes of a bat. Tomorrow, I will pursue until I find him or his body."

Laure Burton, tearless but numbed, had blackened her face, but she'd not yet cut off her flaming hair; this could only properly be done once her husband, shrouded in fine cedar-cloth matting and bound into a sitting position, had been buried in the pit with his dearest possessions arranged about him. Hour after hour, the young woman crouched silent and with head bowed.

For some time she retraced her life with Sakwari-cra, starting with that unforgettable day when the Iroquois had descended upon Tosneoc. Then there was their long run—that incredible, ever-glorious long run. The meeting with Quobah; the long, hard winter spent in Goggle-Eyes's village; the rescue of Shatara and Chula from the French traders and the running fight that followed. It had been in Guaxule that, for the first time, she'd begun to think of Thad and herself as other than Indians.

A slant of orange torchlight beating through a glassless window danced across the bier and lent an illusion of life to those beloved features.

And what of the strange life they'd led in the village outside of Savannah? Laure stared blankly at the ground, decided it was about then that a still-unresolved question had arisen; could they, should they try to think, and live, like persons of their own race or had their characters too long hardened in the Indian mold?

She heard someone replace one of the pine knots sputtering and flaring outside, roused, and fixed anguished eyes upon the matting almost concealing Thad's body; it had slipped a little to one side. She righted it, then, yielding to a sudden wild hope, tested his wrist. But it was ice cold and there was not the slightest trace of pulse, either.

Mournfully, Taqua again sank onto her heels and rocked slowly back and forth, wondering whether Chula's squaws were taking proper care of Jeems and Johnnie. They'd behave of course; children brought up among the Indians weren't given to whining, tantrums, or deliberate disobedience more than once. Still, Johnnie was so very young he just might start squalling for her.

Somehow, she couldn't feel too outraged that Wallace Challenger should have gotten away. But Shatara would catch him—nothing could escape that Chickasaw's tracking. Thanks to the Wanderer, she foresaw that she wouldn't enjoy watching Challenger perish on the torture frame; only a short while ago she would have. On the other hand she wished that Winsome Challenger might witness her husband's ordeal.

Bitterly, Taqua then admitted to herself something she'd always known but never had mentioned. Thad had desired Winsome, had loved her, even though he likely wasn't aware of how much. Slowly, Laure's charcoal-blackened features contracted. Why should Thad have yearned for such a cold creature even though she never had treated him with anything better than contemptuous courtesy?

Too bad James Adair and that poor Yamacraw must suffer in the Ranger's stead.

She coughed and tears gathered after a puff of acrid torch smoke drifted through the open door. Drearily, her imagination wandered off on another tack. What's to become of me and Thad's children? Since I'm a sort of queen, I suppose I won't be able to marry anybody lower than a mico and because the Sakwaris are an upstart tribe of mongrels, no Creek, Cherokee, or Chickasaw noble would even consider taking me to wife, especially because I'm a full white. At best I'll end up as some Long Warrior's concubine—unless, unless I could get the boys back to the Guale Coast. But should I? How would I and they live among the whites? Too bad I'm no Mary Musgrove, with a Creek emperor for an uncle.

Through smarting eyes, she stared hopelessly on that massive form lying so rigid and still under the matting. With the realization that, never again in this life, would she see Sakwari-cra move with all his unconscious power and grace, she shuddered. She ended with the hope that one of his sons might grow to approach Thad Burton in character, if not in physique.

Next, she meditated on how far he and she had progressed since that night they'd bivouacked beneath an overhanging rock and possessing not a thing in the world beyond a skinning knife and the scanty garments they'd stood in. How far Sakwari-cra's courage, foresight, and ambition had brought them! Out of a collection of strays, runaways, and the remnants of broken tribes he had forged a strong and growing nation. Were he still alive, he could lead to war so many well-armed and experienced warriors. Granted only a few more years, Sakwari-cra would have been qualified to treat on equal terms with such rulers as Ko-Mingo-in-Cush, Squirrel King of the Chickasaws; Ouechachumpa, *tostenuggo-hlako* of the Lower Creek tribes, or Hachey, Dog King of the dreaded Yamasees.

A draft stirred a lock of the fallen king's light-brown hair because, with loving tenderness, she had cleansed it of matted blood, it shone in the torchlight. And now, just because of Wallace Challenger's bullet, all his lofty ambitions had come to naught! How high might Thad Burton not have climbed? Conceivably, he could have become a second Moy-Toy and rule as an emperor over all the peoples of the southeast.

Far more astutely than his red associates, Thad had foreseen an inexorable expansion of English influence into the southwest, for, unlike the French and Spanish, the British were fixed in their eagerness to *own* land. Once they acquired or were admitted to a territory, they stayed and soon began to farm as well as to trade. Quite as clearly, Thad had sensed that a bloody clash of interests among the three European nations must soon take place.

A pretty, fawn-colored mouse with big ears and a snow-white belly squeezed through a crack in the tabby wall beyond the litter. Laure remained so motionless that soon the dainty little creature began to range about; finally, it climbed onto the mat-shrouded figure and sat there, its protuberant jet eyes bright and questioning, until the widow shifted to ease a cramp forming in her thigh. Instantly, the mouse disappeared through the crack, leaving her to wait for daylight and a final parting with Sakwari-cra.

Once the two captives had been tortured to death before the slain king's bier, the Outacitys, Ravens, Slave Catchers, and sub-micos would drink deep of *foskey*—the magical "black drink"; then, howling like demented wolves, they would start the ghost dance, which would continue until the sun went down.

Then, in semidarkness, the Panther King's body would be bound into the usual sitting position and lowered into its burial pit. As this was done Laure would cut short her hair and toss it into the grave.

Once the pit had been filled, the house in which they had lived would be set afire. Being of tabby-stone construction, it wouldn't burn flat, any more than it had when the Spaniards had been wiped out nearly a century earlier. Not for generations would any Indian dare to reoccupy the blackened, roofless ruin for fear of incurring the wrath of Sakwari-cra's ghost.

Chapter 11

TORTURE FRAMES

Across the ancient *plaza mayor* torches blinked and sputtered around another tabby-stone structure, in which James Adair and the Yamacraw named Taklet, or He-Who-Stands-on-One Leg, sat shivering on a dirt floor. Their limbs ached and had swelled from the tightness of thongs which had bitten so deeply into wrists and ankles that these bindings were now nearly invisible. Miserable as he was, Adair was thankful that the Sakwaris hadn't stripped them naked, although there was little warmth to be derived from their moist and malodorous garments.

Infinitely menacing, with features painted white in mourning, Chula and Shatara stood over the prisoners, war clubs in hand. Across the crumbling dwelling's dirt floor two guards squatted on their heels hopeful that the prisoners might do something to afford them an excuse for adding to the many cuts, weals, and bruises already sustained by the captives.

His one eye glaring, Chula rasped, "Once more, English dog, why did your general send you to make war on the Panther King?"

The young Scotch-Irishman made a gurgling sound as he swallowed blood and spittle—someone's club had hit him across the throat and had so bruised his larynx he could barely croak. "Again I swear, and I speak with a straight heart, we came to Capola not in war but seeking only peace and friendship with the Panther King and seeking permission for me to build a trading post among you. We were bringing Sakwari-cra many rich gifts." He blinked. "Did not your warriors find two pack horses laden with presents?"

The Outacity Shatara spat into Adair's face. "You speak with a twisted tongue! Those gifts were not for Sakwari-cra but intended to win favor with the *Francani* to keep them away from the *Ispani.*"

Thinking hard, Adair wheezed, "Our general never attempted any such a thing. If you doubt me, ask Taklet."

The Yamacraw, whose front teeth had been broken off just short of their gums, spat blood. "We came bearing gifts only for Sakwari-cra."

Chula whirled up his casse-tête and made as if to brain the speaker. "You are liars and the sons of liars! You speak with the crooked tongue of Chitokaka!"

"We are *not* lying!" Adair persisted. "If Captain Challenger were here he would tell you I have spoken only truth."

"Challenger!" Shatara's features contorted themselves into a demonic mask and Chula bent forward, hands on knees, so that his single eye, aglow with hatred, was level with the prisoner's face. "*Hushoni!* Skunk! When we find the Ranger, your death will seem short and easy as to what his end will be. Think of this when you writhe on the torture frame, when flaming splinters skewer your man-parts."

In his rage the former Chickasaw chattered his teeth like an angry monkey. "Yes, *Englasi*, before darkness fills your eyes you will squeal and cry out like a young squaw pinned beneath her first warrior. You will beg to die. Ho! Death will come, but not soon, not until after glowing-hot iron ramrods have burned their way through your belly and up your backside. You will see everything that happens because your eyelids will have been cut off."

To all the torments predicted by the sub-micos, Adair remained outwardly unshaken, and insisted, "We came here in peace, not to make war. Were we not slaying his Yamasee enemies when—"

Deaf to Adair's logic, Shatara used the handle of his casse-tête to deal the young trader a silencing blow which started a torrent of blood gushing from his nose. By torchlight, his gore looked purple rather than crimson.

Throughout their visit both sub-micos had ignored Taklet as being of little or no importance; besides, they found much more satisfaction in abusing a white man.

At last, the Sakwari sub-micos departed into the darkness, leaving behind the two guards. Head aching like a huge bad tooth, James Adair racked his memory in hopes of recalling some subterfuge, some clever ruse which might enable him and Taklet to get away. But he was forced reluctantly to admit that, although he'd heard tell of countless escape dodges, he couldn't think of a single one which offered any hope of success.

Cold as it was, the Scotch-Irishman began to sweat as he attempted to reassure himself that he would not cry out or beg for mercy, no matter what they did to him. But he was scared all the same; terribly apprehensive that this fine strong body of his—he'd always been secretly proud of it—soon would be reduced to a mangled and mutilated lump of flesh.

Then his apprehension gave way to an overpowering rage. By God! It wasn't right that he should die before realizing at least some of those projects he'd been nursing for years. Most infuriating of all was the knowledge that he was about to perish through no stupidity or miscalculation on his part; hadn't he been shrewd and farsighted in his dealings with the Choctaws and Cherokees, whom he had understood so well that, often, he could predict what they were going to say before they said it.

In sudden, insensate revolt, Adair strained at his rawhide lashings until his head spun, but he accomplished nothing beyond suffering fresh pangs in his wrists and ankles.

The worst fact he had to face was that, unlike Northern tribes, who simply bound a victim to a tree or a stake, these Southeastern Indians had devised a strong wooden frame which, erected vertically, permitted executioners to spread-eagle the doomed wretch and thus expose his supersensitive crotch and underarms to whatever torments they might select.

The women's discordant wailing continued without a break, hour after hour; probably they'd keep up their screeching until the time came for his execution. Manfully, James Adair struggled to ignore his terrible thirst, the griping of a long-empty stomach, and the savage bite of the thongs upon his wrists and ankles.

The sun already was shining brightly when white-painted wizards came to drag the captives out to die. Already the entire population of Capola had arranged themselves in a wide, silent, and irregular circle enclosing two torture frames raised in the center of the *plaza mayor's* muddy yellow-red expanse.

The bier supporting the Panther King's body had been placed slightly in front of the frames, his remains were concealed under a magnificent albino buffalo robe which even Ouechachumpa might have coveted.

By the body's head squatted the red-haired queen, her freshly blackened face half-concealed under a length of dark cloth. Taqua was wearing a handsome blue gown which, as evidence of her grief, she had ripped and torn in many places.

In semistupor, James Adair felt his rawhide bonds loosened and then removed; he couldn't help gasping when searing pangs shot through his limbs as blood commenced to flow freely again through his veins and arteries, and he would have fallen but for the pair of red-painted executioners who supported and half-dragged him to a frame. There, amid a rising mutter from the onlookers, he was stripped of his garments and quickly lifted to stand, stark naked, on the bottom spreader.

Taklet also was unbound and similarly spread-eagled by the lashing of his extremities to the frame of raw pine. Bitter acids began to flow in Adair's mouth while his body went alternately hot and cold when he saw some wrinkled hags rake apart a hardwood fire. Kindled close to the bier's foot, it had been burning long enough to furnish a heap of glowing coals.

James Adair fixed sunken eyes on that forlorn figure crouching beside Thad Burton's body, then was astonished to hear his own voice calling hoarsely, "Mrs. Burton! Mrs. Burton! You are white! For God's sake, make them stop! This is all a horrible mistake. Before the Almighty, we *weren't* coming here to attack!" He sensed, rather than saw, hundreds of hostile dark eyes swing in his direction. "Listen well, all of you! If you murder us, the *Englasi* will never rest till your tribe is beaten, broken and scattered!"

The widow's slightly oblique greenish eyes rose to meet his and, for a moment, he hoped she was going to speak, but, instead, she pursed blackened lips and spat in his direction.

"Peace, friend. To plead is useless," called Taklet, then tilted back his head to fix his gaze on a buzzard planing high about the clean blue sky, a dread omen; the buzzard ever had been a precursor of death.

At a signal from Shatara, a hideous old woman bent and filled a wrought iron skillet with rose-white coals. Then, while the spectators raised savage cries, she advanced upon Taklet, stretched, rigid and silent, upon his frame.

Evidently, the sub-micos had doomed Adair to suffer in an anticipation of his own torments. Inch by inch, the crone raised the skillet between Taklet's legs until a puff of bluish smoke arose when his pubic hair took fire, but, beyond an involuntary shudder, the Yamacraw's copper-brown body remained motionless.

Adair watched Taklet's eyes close, saw his teeth clamp down so hard upon his lower lip that blood began to dribble over his chin. Not even when the coals touched his scrotum did the least sound escape him. Meanwhile the crowd clamored insults, calling him a woman, a skunk, a lover of sows, a cowardly cur, and, lowest of all, an eater of frogs and snakes.

While the fierce heat continued to be applied to Taklet's testicles, Adair felt sweat begin to stream down his face, chest, and legs. For all he hadn't tasted water in many hours he felt an urgency to urinate, but, of course, he couldn't.

Once more the young trader yelled, "Taqua! Mrs. Burton, for God's love—make them stop! He's innocent!"

His appeal died incomplete when he realized that Thad Burton's wife was not watching Taklet's torment, but was staring, wide-eyed, at a stirring beneath the buffalo robe's glossy folds. A hand, a living hand, had crept into sight, fingers slowly flexing. Laure Burton leaped forward and jerked back the covering far enough to expose the Panther King's head and open eyes.

In the Tuscarora tongue Sakwari-cra breathed, "Water. Water."

Following a sharp order from Taqua, the old squaw hesitated, then reluctantly lowered her skillet.

Laure Rivard Burton straightened and turned to face Shatara and Chula, her gray-green eyes grown simply huge. "Not yet has Sakwari-cra's spirit departed to lodge with Sotolycaté. He, and he alone, shall decide the fate of these captives."

BOOK V

St. Augustine

Chapter 1

FREDERICA

On the morning of August 3, 1739, a long line of hoary-brown pelicans flapped lazily across the passage separating St. Simon from equally low-lying Jekyll Island. Soon they were forced to veer aside to pass under the ornately carved and freshly gilded stern of H.B.M.S. *Hector*, fifty guns, Sir Yelverton Peyton commanding.

Shortly, this Fourth Rate of the Line would shape a course to the south-southeast in order to resume her blockade of the coast of Florida and, if she were lucky, to intercept certain Spanish men-of-war reported to have sailed from Havana for the relief of St. Augustine.

Low to the muddy brown water, the ungainly birds beat past little Fort St. Simon, recently constructed on a low strip of land forming the southernmost tip of an island known by the same name.

Later, these pelicans headed northward and, in doing so, drew abreast of the new and bustling settlement of Frederica, at present Oglethorpe's headquarters for the defense of Georgia. Had they flown to the left they soon would have entered the Ogeechee; had they continued up the river a little farther they would have sighted a village called Chaugee Landing.

Some twenty-five miles on up the coast, they would have entered the Savannah's delta; but the birds didn't keep on. Shortly after passing the roadstead and harbor of Frederica, they settled upon a sandspit, newly exposed by the tide, to mix with others of their species. Above them wheeled, shrieked, and laughed gulls, terns, and gannets, still busy at their fishing for all the sun was now high and growing very hot.

From the Cottage, as the commanding general called his headquarters at the end of a raw pine wharf piled high with all manner of munitions and supplies, James Edward Oglethorpe, High Commissioner for Indian Affairs, Captain General of His Majesty's Forces in Georgia and South Carolina, and also Colonel of the then Forty-second Foot of the Line, was certain that this was to be another exceedingly hot day.

Even though sweat was pouring down his neck into an already sodden shirt collar, Oglethorpe continued to wear a thick serge tunic, the emerald-green revers and cuffs of which already showed hard usage, but the scarlet cloth was spotless and gold buttons and lace decorating it glittered.

The general settled back in his chair and, while awaiting the arrival of Militia Lieutenant Archibald Glen, allowed his gaze to wander out of a specially constructed window designed to afford him an unrestricted view of the harbor.

In deep satisfaction he noted a Royal Jack floating over that new tabby-stone fort which guarded the harbor's entrance.

Now that the usual morning offshore wind had died out, the shipping lay, faithfully mirrored, as on a huge gold-white platter. Moored, or at anchor, were clusters of plantation boats and pirogues secure under the protection of the Georgia Colony's scout boats, *Hawk* and *Georgia*. A third, *Carolina*, was away on patrol duty in the vicinity of Beaufort, guarding approaches to the Savannah River; one never could tell from what direction the enemy might strike. Farther offshore, H.B.M.S. *Flamborough*, twenty guns, Captain Pearce, should be patrolling, patiently, watchfully.

The crews of both ships, as well as those of other more recently arrived vessels belonging to the Royal Navy and now on duty off the coast of the Carolinas and Georgia, should be on the *qui vive* in accordance with a secret directive authorizing and directing that His Britannic Majesty's ships should "Seek, take, burn or otherwise destroy" any and all vessels flying the Spanish flag.

The long-featured general's somber eyes sought a small boat pulling out to H.B.M.S. *Squirrel*, sloop of war, twenty guns, Captain Warren, and found her indeed a pleasant sight to behold, what with her sleek brown and white hull, tapering white-painted masts, and standing rigging bright with a fresh application of tar.

Although he couldn't see them, the general knew that detachments of the Forty-second—already becoming better known as "Oglethorpe's Regiment" or, more simply, "the Regiment"—had finished drill for the morning; the incessant, rasping bark of N.C.O.s was fading. He wondered how these two hundred fifty hard-bitten transfers from the Forty-fifth, garrisoning in Gibraltar, would turn out. Already two of their number had attempted to murder him—and had died by consequence. That was the trouble with transfers; for the most part such men were hard cases and troublemakers whose previous commanders must have been very glad to see depart.

He hoped he wasn't going to have more trouble with this Gibraltar draft, because all manner of reports and rumors kept cropping up that the men still were dissatisfied with their pay and food allowance.

If only these sunburned veterans were like either the draft of two hundred men he'd received from the Earl of Rothe's Irish Regiment, or the two hundred and fifty men he himself had recruited in England!

At the sound of boots ringing along a brief corridor leading to his staff room, Oglethorpe's bronzed head swung to face the doorway. A brisk rap sounded, then an orderly appeared, clicked heels, and saluted smartly. "Sir, there's a milishy officer here to see you. Leftenent Glen, 'e says 'e is, sir."

"Thank you. You may show him in."

Archibald Glen had retained enough of his training with The Blues to appear in probably the neatest and best-cut uniform in all that heterogeneous array known as the Militia of Georgia. Standing ramrod straight, the ex-cornet reported himself.

"At ease, Mr. Glen; you may seat yourself if weary."

"Thank you, no, sir. I've been sitting all the way down from Savannah."

The past six years had sobered and matured Archibald Glen considerably, decided the general. Of course, Glen would never make as clever or cunning frontier fighter as MacKay, MacPherson, or Challenger, but most certainly he was possessed of sufficient intelligence to win promotion.

"Well, Mr. Glen, and what do you have to report?"

"It is as you feared, sir. Captain MacPherson says that that Jesuit, Christian Priber, is beginning to wean the Atali Creeks away from our side. In fact, Priber seems to have quite won over Malatchi and has gained considerable influence of Chikilly who, as you very well know, sir, is the late Emperor Brims's own son. In my humble opinion, sir, we stand in grave danger of losing the Lower Creek nation's support."

Oglethorpe inclined his graying head. "If only John Musgrove were still living. What do you hear concerning her new husband?"

"Why, sir, Captain Jacob Matthews is a former redemptioner; a brave, robust fellow no doubt, but not too bright—at least that is what I heard said about him in Savannah."

"Will this Captain Matthews be able to handle matters cleverly at Mount Venture which, as a listening post, grows daily more important?"

"Sir, about that I don't know. But knowledgeable men I talked to are very worried over what may chance in Coweta unless something is done to keep the Creeks loyal."

A prolonged sigh escaped Oglethorpe as he reached out and picked up a turkey-wing fan. He employed it both to cool himself and to disperse clouds of stinging little sand flies that persisted in buzzing about his head. At length he said, "I suppose there's nothing else to be done."

"Sir?"

"After what you have told me I must visit Coweta. Yes." He stared, unseeing, at the piles of papers littering his desk. "There's no other course. God help us all if the Creeks desert us at this time."

"Yes, sir." The tall young man in the green tunic turned up in dark red hesitated. "Has no declaration of war yet arrived from Whitehall?"

"Not yet—which I cannot comprehend since, to my mind, war has been inevitable since the Spanish repudiated the armistice concluded by Governor Sanchez and my commissioners. Did you know that the poor Sanchez was recalled and executed for treason because of it?"

"Yes, sir. I've heard so. I wonder if this abrogation is not what the Parliament needs as a pretext for declaring war."

Oglethorpe tapped a paper recently forwarded from Charles Town by dispatch boat. A bleak smile curved his lips. "I wonder whether the 'pretext' you mention has not already been found."

"Sir?" Archibald Glen was too well disciplined openly to question a superior.

"As you no doubt are aware, for years the Spanish have forbidden British merchants to import into their American colonial possessions more merchandise—excepting Negro slaves—than two merchantmen can bring in each year."

"Yes, sir." Archibald Glen was streaming sweat, yet stood to rigid attention, his head brushing the staff room's ceiling of oyster-shell plaster.

"It follows, therefore, that our countrymen for a long time must have —er—indulged in smuggling. As a result, the Spanish *guardacostas* haven't been tender with such British subjects as they've caught more or less red-handed."

Through the open window sounded the ringing thud of hammers at work on a new scout boat, and the shouts of fish peddlers offering their catch to the men-of-war.

"Well, Mr. Glen, some time ago a smuggler, one Captain Robert Jenkins, was taken off the coast of Cuba. After his vessel had been plundered and stripped of sailing gear, the Dons, by way of discouragement, nailed him by an ear to the mainmast. Seems that to free him his crew had to cut it off." Oglethorpe stowed the report in a neat pile. "At least that is the story Jenkins is telling round London, whenever anyone will offer him drink enough. 'Tis said this gallant captain carries what he purports to

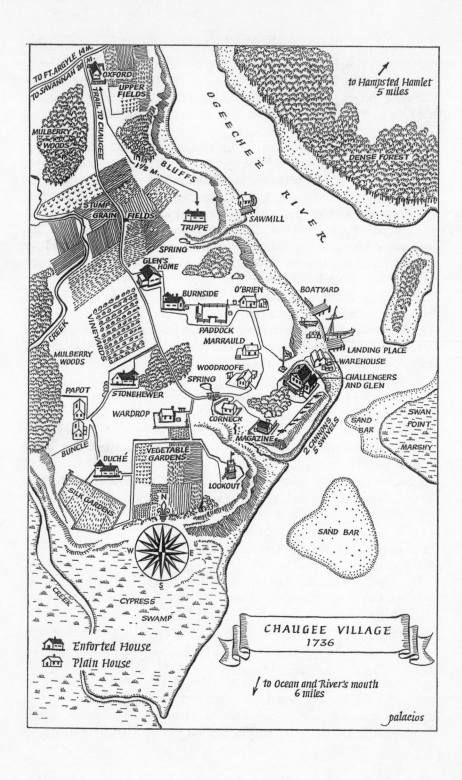

TO FT. ARGYLE 14 M.
TO SAVANNAH 20 M.

OXFORD
UPPER FIELDS

MULBERRY WOODS

TRAIL TO CHAUGEE

OGEECHEE RIVER

to Hampsted Hamlet 5 miles

DENSE FOREST

1½ M.

BLUFFS

STUMP GRAIN FIELDS

TRIPPE

SAWMILL

SPRING
GLEN'S HOME

BURNSIDE

O'BRIEN

BOATYARD

PADDOCK
MARRAULD

LANDING PLACE
WAREHOUSE

CREEK

VINEYARDS

WOODROOFE
SPRING

CHALLENGERS AND GLEN

MULBERRY WOODS

PAPOT

STONEHEWER

WARDROP

CORNECK

MAGAZINE

SAND BAR

SWAN POINT
MARSHY

BUNCLE

DUCHÉ

VEGETABLE GARDENS

2 CANNONS
5 SWIVELS

SAND BAR

N

SILK GARDENS

LOOKOUT

W   E

SAND BAR

S

CREEK

CYPRESS SWAMP

🏠 Enforted House
🏠 Plain House

CHAUGEE VILLAGE
1736

↓ to Ocean and River's mouth
6 miles

palacios

be his lost ear around in a box, well salted, no doubt, and wears a black silk bag over its stump."

"Sounds like a bit of a tall story, doesn't it, sir?"

Oglethorpe smiled. "That well may be the case; anyhow, his tale has so roused the public at home that we may expect a declaration of war at any time."

From a red earthenware *olla* sweating on its saucer, Oglethorpe poured cool water for his guest and himself. "Now, Mr. Glen, this is what I wish you to do; you will use my private pirogue and hasten to Chaugee Landing. Once there, you will please present my compliments to Major Challenger—"

Glen's slender eyebrows rose a trifle. " 'Major,' sir?"

"Yes. I have commissioned him as such in the Georgia Rangers."

"A deserved promotion, sir, an I may venture to say so."

"When you meet Major Challenger tell him I wish him to proceed to Savannah with all possible speed, where he is to await my arrival. Tell him to prepare for an extended journey. I wish him to accompany me to Coweta."

"Yes, sir."

"Because of this, Mr. Glen, I will appoint you to act in Major Challenger's stead as military commander and Indian agent for the Chaugee District." He looked the ex-cornet straight in the eye and spoke with quiet emphasis. "I shall expect you to take every precaution against surprise by the enemy and to keep this headquarters informed of any significant occurrence."

Chapter 2

REUNION

General Oglethorpe was in such a hurry to get started on his way to Coweta that he sent Lieutenant Glen to Chaugee Landing aboard his private dispatch boat, a speedy sloop used by him on his frequent inspection trips of forts already built or rising at strategic points along the Guale Coast. The *Lady Digby*—named after a fellow trustee's wife—was so trim and the breeze so favorable that the dainty little sloop sighted the scattering of houses composing the village called Chaugee Landing about sundown of that same day Archibald Glen had appeared in Ogle-thorpe's headquarters.

Beside the lieutenant stood a new settler, beetle-browed Peter Buncle, on his way to join his brother, George. Like the latter, he was a farmer from Hampshire. "We both be bachelors," Buncle remarked. "Used to farm together. George wrote that ye've plenty o' main good farm land hereabouts. That true?"

"Yes, that is so. Rich bottom land for the most part which will grow almost any kind of crop except tobacco."

An impassive, ox-slow fellow, Peter Buncle studied the settlement's un-pretentious structures, somewhat distorted by a bluish heat haze. He saw that the dwellings yonder stood fairly close together under a grove of great, moss-draped water oaks and cypresses. Beneath some of these a number of cattle lay chewing their cuds while waiting to be milked. "How many folks live yonder?"

"Forty-eight," Glen told him, then added, smiling, "Unless Jeanie Woodroofe and Bettie O'Brien have given birth."

When the *Lady Digby* skimmed around the last marshy bend below Chaugee Landing, Buncle queried, "And what, sir, is that tall building?"

Not without pride Glen explained, "Why, that's my warehouse. You see, I'm factor for Indian traders in this district." The ex-cornet rubbed his powder-burned cheek. "I had a hard time getting started, Mr. Buncle, but was lucky in having a wife who has a rare fine head for accounts. For a fact, I'm doing so well nowadays that I can't begin to import sufficient goods to satisfy my customers; especially since those damn' Spanish privateers have been snapping up our coasters."

He indicated a trio of battered and ungainly plantation boats slowly swinging to face the ebb. Aboard one, the heads of several horses were visible. "Those will be some animals Hendy O'Brien is readying for ship-ment to New Inverness."

Buncle nodded. "O'Brien? He'll be the horse breeder Brother's writ about?"

"Yes. He's the one. You'll like Hendy; everybody does."

"Who owns 'e sawmill?"

"One of the original settlers, name of Trippe. Tom saws most of the lumber used in this district." Glen's wide-set, pale blue eyes wandered and came to rest upon a low palmetto, log, and dirt earthwork. As a real defense, this battery wasn't much, but, nevertheless, its revetments pro-tected two eight-pound cannon and a half-dozen brass swivels which, properly served, could sweep the decks of any vessel attempting to ap-proach or pass through a narrow channel created by a fish hook-shaped sand bar which jutted boldly from the Ogeechee's north bank.

The fact that there weren't nearly enough men living in, or near, Chau-

gee to serve even half of these guns had worried both Archibald Glen
and Wallace Challenger for a long time. Somehow, they never seemed
able to assemble, at one time, even half of the Landing's able-bodied
householders. Always, they found some more or less valid excuse to
avoid drill.

It was with a surge of pleasure that Glen viewed his home's new
shingles gleaming golden in the sunlight. Placed near Wallace Challenger's
dwelling, it was of almost identical proportion and design—two-storied
and boasting a narrow porch along two sides. Their backhouses, three-
holers, stood so close together it was possible for occupants to chat while
answering the call of Nature.

Already children, shrieking in excitement, were pelting down to the
village wharf, an unpretentious but sturdy affair which covered the few
yards required to reach the edge of deep water.

To Glen's deep relief, he noted that the well-shaped green pirogue,
used by Wallace Challenger, lay drawn up on a sandy beach beyond the
boatyard started by James Wardrop almost a year ago. Thus far, Jim
hadn't attempted anything fancier than flatboats and a few fishing smacks,
but now the resinous yellow hull of a sizable pinky stood, half completed,
upon his stocks.

"Way enough!" called the *Lady Digby's* helmsman. "Leggo them halyards! Jackson, just you ready the bowline."

The *Lady Digby* was brought alongside the wharf so skillfully that, a
moment later, Archibald Glen was clambering onto the dock, where, as
usual, Helen was awaiting him with Jemima, a leggy six-year-old, and
Archie, Jr., aged five, clinging to her skirts. The ex-cornet hurried forward
with arms widespread, thinking, This is a mighty fine family I've got me—
for all their bare feet, touseled heads, and faded garments.

"I trust everything is well with the business, my pet?" he queried after
soundly bussing all three.

"Well enough," Helen reassured him, "but everybody wants duffel cloth,
and we're altogether out of it. You came across any in Frederica?"

"No, lovedy, never a stitch. But I've a vessel due from Philadelphia any
day now." He waved forward Peter Buncle. "Here's George's brother, at
last. Mr. Buncle, meet Mistress Glen."

"How d'ye do, ma'am." The farmer grinned and touched his lock. He
could recognize quality here as well as at home. "Where is George's
place?"

Glen told him, then watched the bandy-legged fellow swing a bundle
onto his shoulder and tramp off through the sunset.

"Where's Wallace?"

"Gone up to Fort Argyle where he's trying to talk a party of settlers
into coming here. Ought to be back tonight, sometime."

Together, they watched black-bearded George Buncle hurry out of his cabin to throw a thick brown arm about his brother's equally wide shoulders. "God send we see more such; we'll have sore need of 'em, the way things are going."

On going over to the Challengers' to await Wallace's return, the Glens found Winsome busy cooking supper at an outdoor fireplace, which the settlers had come to favor during the hot months. Little Robbie, of about the same age as Archie, Jr., was playing with ever-patient Claymore, now grown white about the muzzle and leisurely in his movements. The mastiff mongrel hadn't taken gracefully to growing old and always raised a rumpus, mourned for hours whenever the major departed on a trip and left him behind.

Winsome restrained her son just as he was about to tweak a tuft of hair from Claymore's already moth-eaten tail. "You wicked imp! Someday I hope the poor old fellow will turn and nip you!" She started to cuff her offspring, but heard voices and turned about instead, smoothed her apron.

Glen said, "Evening, Winnie. How soon d'you think Wallace will be back?"

"No telling," Winsome informed him. "He's so seldom at home nowadays. Why?"

"I've orders from the general for him."

Winsome's damp and reddened features clouded. "Don't tell me he's supposed to go away *again!*"

Glen blinked and looked out over the Ogeechee. "I fear so, and it's likely to prove for a good while."

Winsome bent, stirred her corn-meal mush with unnecessary vigor; meanwhile the children wandered off to watch Mrs. Marrauld milk her cow.

"D'you know, Archie, sometimes I find it difficult to credit that I really have a husband."

With a touch of asperity Helen said, "Oh, fiddle-faddle! I don't know of a woman in this place who wouldn't swap places with you, and gladly!" Her large sherry-brown eyes crinkled at their corners as she turned to Glen. "And that, sir, includes me."

When Challenger's big form materialized amid the twilight he was accompanied by someone Glen recognized at first glance; it was James Adair! What errand could have fetched the Scotch-Irishman across near four hundred miles of perilous wilderness?

Glad of a new face, Winsome Challenger persuaded Adair to stay the night for all that he protested he should continue his journey by moonlight. With the hurried assistance from Helen Glen and Belinda Trippe, quite a respectable repast was set before the traveler: sea-turtle stew,

Indian potatoes, corn bread, and roasted pork washed down with Indian beer and yaupon-leaf tea.

"I ain't surprised," Adair announced, easing his belt, "that the general feels he ought to get to Coweta in a hurry. Heard tell there's serious unrest among the Creeks; even in Capola I heard that the French and Spanish are making Chikilly and Malatchi some pretty fancy presents. Seems that that Jesuit fellow, Christian Priber, really is beginning to sway the Atalis. That's why I'm going to Savannah for a talk with the general."

Challenger nodded and tossed Claymore a chicken bone. Deftly, the mastiff caught it in mid-air. "I'm off in the morning to meet the general in Frederica."

"Frederica, where's that?"

"On St. Simon Island."

"Where's this island?"

"'Bout thirty miles south o' here; that's where the gen'ral's headquarters are these days."

"Then Frederica must lie about opposite New Inverness?" Adair suggested while swilling the last of the turtle-meat broth.

"Yes. Just about. It's a well-chosen site."

Winsome asked softly, "How do things progress in Capola? I suppose Thad Burton still rules as the so-called Panther King?"

"He does, and his Sakwaris are growing steadily in number. In fact, he has almost doubled their strength since"—he grimaced at his towering host—"since a certain little bicker took place by War Club Pond."

"I ain't likely to forget it." The major touched his side. "In damp weather this still reminds me."

"Unless something happens to Burton, he's bound to become a power to be reckoned with."

From the doorway in which he was standing to cool himself, Glen demanded, "How does Burton feel about this war that's coming on?"

"Damned if I can be sure, and I know Sakwari-cra about as well as anybody, except maybe Brother Barnaby. Burton comes to my truck house whenever he can find an excuse, but I honestly can't tell how he'll line up."

"You're making a good thing of your trade with the Sakwaris?" Helen Glen suggested from the shadows.

"I've made out fine," the trader admitted, fishing for his pipe. "All the same, I'm figgerin' on moving up north and west to trade among the Chickasaws. They bring in finer quality skins and furs—and more of 'em." He grinned at Glen. "Besides, you goddam factors are getting choosier every day, while game grows scarcer. Fact is, I'm getting ready to sell out."

"The hell you preach!" Challenger looked his surprise. "Will Sakwari-cra let anybody take from you?"

"If I name the man," Adair said. "Burton's changed. Without saying it in so many words, he figures that, someday, the white man is going to run the whole of this country—be he English, Spanish or French."

After getting a pipe well aglow, Adair settled back, listening to bull alligators booming. "By the bye, Wallace, Burton sent you a message; says he'll never forget the fight you put up at War Club Pond, nor the neat way you escaped from Shatara, half dead though you were."

"That's a lot of balls! I'd never have made it without Umpychi and Will Woodroofe."

"All the same, I figger he's grateful for your jumping those Yamasees." He jerked his deeply sunburned head in Winsome's direction, "Oh, I near forgot. Burton also sends his respectful service to you, ma'am."

A grim smile crossed Challenger's features when he recalled that other occasion on which Thad Burton had forwarded regards to his wife, only then she'd been Winsome Brooks.

They talked on and, among other things, discussed the rumored activities of such British renegades as Bacon, Savey, and Ben Drake.

"There ain't a doubt," Challenger said seriously, "that such scoundrels *are* trying to stir up the Negroes in Carolina. D'you know whether Burton's old sub-mico, Quobah Tutu, is among 'em?"

"If he is, I ain't heard of it," Adair said while stooping to pat Claymore's scarred head. "He could be, though. That's one smart black, by all accounts."

The old dog sighed, thumped his frayed-looking tail a few times, then snuffled and went back to sleep.

At length, Challenger heaved his huge body erect. "By your leave, Jim, I'll let you and Glen entertain the ladies. Reckon I'd best be getting my possibles together."

In a cool voice Winsome suggested, "You'll be off first thing in the morning?"

"I've no choice, my dear, have I? Orders are orders."

"But really, Wallace, Robbie is beginning to run about like a little savage! You're needed here at Chaugee Landing too. Archie does all he can, but even I can see that our people need to drill and learn a lot more about protecting this place."

The last items of Major Challenger's gear had been selected when Claymore lifted his head and growled a little, then padded over to peer through the door, opened to encourage a cool breeze off the river.

Winsome, who had departed upstairs after a subdued "good night," heard her husband call out, "Who's out there?" All the same, she knew it couldn't be a stranger or Claymore would have raised the roof; most likely, Archie Glen had come back, having forgotten to mention some detail of Wallace's orders.

She was mistaken; it was Micah Oxford who stepped inside after having taken a good look among the nearby houses now showing up sharply and casting jet shadows under a full moon.

Although the evening still was young, hardly a light was to be seen around Chaugee Landing except for one in Antoine Duché's place. This wasn't surprising; the Savoyard and his family often sat up late selecting tender young mulberry leaves to feed their silkworms or to laboriously unwind onto curious little machines threads lifted from the day's harvest of well-boiled cocoons.

Challenger was a bit surprised to recognize the Yorker, since he'd halted at Oxford's trading post only that afternoon.

From upstairs Winsome called down, "Who is it, Wallace?"

"Mike Oxford." He turned to the trader and motioned him toward a barrel chair. "What's up?"

"Come sundown, Jack Murray, a Ranger I know, rode in from Charles Town bringin' a bit o' news I reckon we'd better chew on."

The big man continued to decant 4F priming powder into a dented copper flask. "What did Murray have to say?"

"Well, seems that last week he was up close by Stono in Carolina—"

"Well-l?"

"Said he came on something which could lead to trouble—big trouble for us."

"What kind o' trouble?" Challenger demanded, glancing up from under brows glowing golden in the candlelight.

"He chanced on a clearing in the woods where a big crowd of slaves was gathered listening to that same big nigra you've spoken of—the one with the crippled arm."

"You mean Quobah?"

"Yep. Must have been, because, like you said, he was blue-black and had little scars all over his face. There was a Spaniard with him, could have been Captain Pedro Lamberto—who, like you know, I've done business with. Murray didn't get a good look at him, so I can't be sure who it really was."

"What was said?"

Oxford paused long enough to bite off a chew of tobacco. "Those varmints promised that, if the slaves would turn on their masters, Governor Montiano would send arms from St. Augustine and furnish leaders for 'em; also, they were reminded that they'd become free the minute they cross the boundary line into Florida—as if anyone knows where such a line runs, now that the armistice is over."

"I've heard all that before," Challenger said, "provided, of course, they accept Roman baptism."

The trader's balding head inclined, emphasizing his mangled ear. "Murray says there're other outfits like Quobah's at work so, sure as shootin', there'll likely be a revolt break out 'fore long."

Challenger picked up a leather bullet bag, poured into it a handful of freshly run silver-gray leaden balls, then drew tight and knotted its pucker string. "D'you figger your pal Savey is party to all this?"

"More'n likely."

"Why?"

"He's failed by a month of fetchin' in some weepons I ordered. I figger maybe Señor Wall got cold feet when he learned that my arms, accordin' to our understandin', are bein' sold only to new settlers or to sure-fire friendly Injuns."

A soft creaking of floor boards above suggested that Winsome was moving about, getting ready for bed, while Challenger, for the hundredth time, wondered what Oglethorpe might say or do if ever he discovered that, far from suppressing Micah Oxford's illegal traffic he'd actually encouraged it on the sensible thesis that, with a major war brewing in Europe, the local inhabitants must arm themselves however possible.

Too bad it had proved well nigh impossible to import weapons either from New England or from the mother country. Despite various misgivings, he'd learned that the Yorker really *had* abided by their tacit understanding.

Quite as faithfully, for a long time now—probably because he was a smart, rather than a law-abiding, man—he had distilled just enough whisky to keep selected Indian customers satisfied; Oxford also had proved mighty discerning about which white men would get hold of his corn liquor.

Common sense warned that, long ago, James Oglethorpe *must* have become aware that his Chaugee District commander was countenancing these illegal practices; it would appear, however, that that farsighted individual had been turning a blind eye, else why would he have promoted Wallace Challenger to the rank of major? Undoubtedly, this was another case of, "See everything, turn a blind eye to much of it, correct a little."

Both men turned to view the ladder steps upon which Winsome had appeared wearing an old boat cloak over her nightrail. She was shielding a candle whose dancing flame illumined the sun-darkened oval of her features and emphasized the natural curliness of her waist-long, dark-brown hair.

Micah Oxford stared unashamedly when the cloak parted to her stride and partially revealed long legs molded by the cambric nightgown's folds. By God, there *was* a tasty-looking piece of woman flesh!

"It's much too hot upstairs for sleep." She set down her candle beside the one on the kitchen table. Lightly, she said, "I trust, gentlemen, you won't mind if I join you for a while?"

To his surprise, Challenger experienced a curious, uneasy sensation, but couldn't identify its origin. Of course, Winsome was angry over the prospect of still another separation, but, somehow, this didn't seem a sound explanation.

Amid a swirl of cambric, Winsome settled onto a rush-bottomed chair woven last winter by James Wardrop, the settlement's only carpenter, stavemaker, and wheelwright. "Pray continue talking," she invited, "unless you are discussing something not for feminine ears." Her dimples appeared momentarily; she looked really beautiful when Challenger smiled at her.

"Of course not, my pet. You know very well most of what takes place around here." He then returned his attention to Oxford, who hurriedly shifted his gaze from the major's wife. "How many muskets you got on hand?"

"Round a dozen, I guess, but half of 'em is old and ain't too sound. I'm hopin' to get better ones on a schooner I'm expectin' from up north.

"Say, Wallace, when you get to see the general I want you to ask him a favor."

Challenger stifled a yawn. "What kind of a favor?"

"Has to do with that old rascal, Petre Ballou. You won't believe it, but, for nine months now, the old coot's been sober as a judge—soberer than a heap of judges I've met up with," he added with a grin that lifted his little, forked beard.

"Ballou sober? By God, the Age of Miracles ain't over yet!"

"Ask yer wife if 'tain't so. She's seen him around my place, plenty of times, and he ain't had even the trace of 'breath.'"

"Yes, dear, that's quite so," Winsome laughed. "Colonel Ballou is quite the reformed drunkard." Then, as she became aware of the sudden intensity in her husband's gaze, she flushed in the candlelight. "You, you will help him, won't you, Wallace?"

"I promise nothing, but I'll see what can be done. There's no denying Ballou's a first-rate military engineer and, God knows, we've none to spare here in Georgia."

While slapping a mosquito bloating on his neck, Micah Oxford got to his feet and said, "Say, Wallace, wouldn't it be a smart idee to start patrollin' the New Inverness road by night?"

"Sure it'd be a fine idea," Challenger agreed acidly, "only just where in this damn' sparse-settled country am I going to find the men to go do the patrolling? The commander at Fort Argyle is scared to let a man of his out o' his sight; not that I blame him, what with the Creeks acting so damn' chancy."

The Yorker spat pensively. "Aye. There just ain't enough white men in Georgia yet. Why, there ain't above two hundred fellows fit for field duty in the whole o' the Savannah District—which I guess you know better'n I. 'Thout the Creeks we're helpless as a nest o' naked young jay birds."

Frowning over this observation, Winsome arose to a faint rustle of garments and crossed to a food safe from which she lifted a wooden platter of bread and cold meat. She wished she could have brewed proper tea, but she couldn't; she'd have to stick to yaupon leaves till a coaster discharged some bohea at Glen's factory.

Munching, Oxford poised a slab of cold pork before his mouth. "Heard tell ye're going away again, Wallace."

"That's correct. General's ordered me to go along with him to Coweta."

The trader's hard gray eyes grew speculative. "How long you figger to be away?"

"How can I tell? Such a damn' serious powwow can drag on for weeks. You know how Indians love to talk!"

"Yep. They're champion speechifiers."

Challenger secured the ties of his saddlebags, then said quietly, "You and Glen will have to keep things in order round here. Anything happens, you'll see to Winsome and the boy first of all?"

"I'll sure 'nough look after yer family."

Chapter 3

NEWS FROM AMELIA ISLAND

Although a week had elapsed since the arrival of George Buncle's brother, neither Jeanie Woodroofe nor Bettie O'Brien as yet had seen fit to increase the population of Chaugee Landing. This surprised everyone, for the O'Brien woman's belly had grown so enormous that her closest friends, Winsome Challenger and Helen Glen, agreed with Mrs. Marrauld, the Savoyard silk grower's slender, brown-faced wife, that something would have to be done pretty soon to induce labor; otherwise, she might die.

Winsome was all for sending up to Savannah for Dr. Tailfer, who probably would be forced to deliver the baby in the same unnatural fashion as Julius Caesar. Jeanie Woodroofe was even less comfortable with this, her first child.

As if to add to the O'Brien family's troubles, their son, Toby, born shortly after the first dwellings had gone up at Chaugee Landing, became stricken with a low fever which rendered the little fellow delirious at intervals.

To top the sum of Hendy's misfortunes, two of his horses escaped from a big paddock he'd constructed on the edge of town. One, a colt, strayed into a nearby marsh where it was promptly run down and devoured by the enormous crocodiles which infested the place; the other animal simply wandered off into the wilderness, never to be seen again.

This was the first real setback suffered by the diminutive Irishman, who, recently, had imported from Charles Town blooded stallions and some well-bred brood mares. Over the past four years, through shrewd purchases and swapping deals, Hendy gradually had been able to improve the quality of his animals, so much so that his reputation as a breeder already had spread along the Guale Coast and he could have sold twice the number of beasts he was raising.

Noontime found Hendy in the midst of a disagreeable situation which arose when four stray Indians, headed by an ugly and arrogant Catawba Raven, appeared at the stable and insisted upon viewing such horses as O'Brien had for sale. Only one of these visitors was mounted and he bestrode a ribby, undersized animal which appeared barely able to carry a boy. Hendy didn't like these raffish-looking Indians any more than the Stonehewer twins, Tim and Tom, fifteen now, and standing almost as tall as their bushy-bearded father.

Despite Hendy's sharp "Don't go in there!" the Catawba vaulted the paddock rails and strode across the manure-speckled ground, his headdress feathers flashing in the sun. The Indian indicated a light bay gelding. "Me take. Me pay good."

"No, you don't! All these beasts are spoken for," Hendy lied. "Besides, I don't sell to strange Indians." At the same time he cast Tim Stonehewer a meaningful glance. While the dispute swelled, the youth sidled away and ran for Archibald Glen's house but discovered the acting district commander down by the waterside where some settlers were unloading a pirogue come down from Fort Argyle.

The Catawba, his green- and yellow-streaked features contracting into a ferocious scowl, snarled, "Me take him. Two more. Me pay plenty. See?"

Hendy's round eyes widened when the nearly naked savage—he was wearing only moccasins and a scarlet breechcloth—reached into a war bag and fetched out a fistful of coins; they were mostly silver, but there were also a few small gold pieces among them.

That money was Spanish-minted the Irishman realized, but it didn't worry him; most hard money current along the Guale Coast was of the same origin. Hendy grew madder with the knowledge that he was being offered almost double the going price, but all the same he strode over to the paddock's gate, shaking his head under the wide-brimmed palmetto hat that shaded his flat red-brown features.

In an undertone, he warned Tom Stonehewer, "Stand close and pass that gate bar."

Smoothly as copper-hued snakes, the dismounted Indians slipped between the paddock's rails carrying coiled lariats.

"Get the hell out o' here, you stinking savages!" Hendy roared. "Keep your damn' money and clear out!"

When, from the inside, the Catawba raised the gate's wooden latch, Hendy brought the bar down sharply on the Raven's wrist. He uttered such a startled yelp that the impounded horses began to snort, plunge, and rush about, raising clouds of dust.

The Catawba lurched backward, jerking his war hatchet out of its sling. Easily, he vaulted over the top rail and, grimacing, made for Hendy O'Brien; undoubtedly he would have cut the horse breeder down had not young Tom tossed a whiffletree so dextrously between the savage's legs that the Catawba dropped his tomahawk, went sprawling onto the dust. He sprang up at once, only to be clipped on the jaw by Hendy's hard little fist. The Raven fell for a second time while his money rolled and scattered about him.

The other Indians snatched out skinning knives and, yowling, started forward. They stayed where they were, however, when Archie Glen's deep voice rang through the still, hot air. "Halt! Halt where you are!" With three others, the lieutenant came running up, muskets held at the ready. He halted beside the Catawba's dust-splashed figure and stirred him with a toe, then stooped to take away his war hatchet.

Under the menace of those muskets the other savages froze in midstride, then wheeled and made for the woods with their mounted fellow in the lead.

Hendy walked over to the horse trough and filled a bucket which he emptied upon the prostrate Catawba. When he stirred, opened his eyes, and swayed to his feet, Hendy snapped, "Take your dirty money and git! Mind you ain't seen near these parts ever again!"

Furious with humiliation, the Catawba glowered and hissed like an angry wildcat at the white men ringing him in. Nobody said anything while he scrabbled about in the dust to retrieve such coins as were visible.

In an effort to regain dignity he stalked over to Hendy O'Brien, snarling, "You be sorry! Me come back—take all horses—no pay!"

Quite unabashed, O'Brien snapped, "Try that and ye'll earn yerself such a sore head ye'll never get over it."

Meanwhile, the O'Brien family was experiencing trouble of a different sort. Tom Trippe's ten-year-old daughter, Ann, went pelting over to Winsome's house with her eyes large as saucers.

"Quick! Come quick!" she pleaded in scared fashion. "Missus O'Brien's water has broke and I can't get her to answer me."

Having long since decided upon her course of action in this inevitable situation, Winsome sent Ann running to fetch Mrs. Marrauld, who was something of a midwife, then she sped over to Hendy's place with skirts flying like laundry in a high breeze. She found Helen Glen already there and busy in the O'Brien's dark little bedroom, which occupied the whole second floor.

Only semiconscious, Bettie was moaning and breathing heavily.

"Wouldn't it just have to happen this way?" Winsome sighed as she fell to tearing an old nightgown into strips; fortunately, a caldron of what appeared to be fresh water was steaming in a corner of the kitchen hearth.

When Helen Glen turned back the bedclothes she had to stifle a gasp; the undersheet was drenched with a yellowish fluid streaked by threads of blood. Winsome, too, was shaken; that Bettie's slightly formed body could support so huge an abdomen seemed impossible. An eternity appeared to pass before Mrs. Marrauld hurried in, breathless, sweat-soaked, and carrying a heavy basket. Her arrival soon was followed by those of Agnes Burnside and Ruth Wardrop.

After a bit Hendy ran in and promptly was sent downstairs, where he roamed the living-dining-cooking room like a distracted terrier until Archibald Glen took him by an arm and led him outdoors.

"Come with me, Hendy, and while you're waiting we'll sample a bit of Mike Oxford's best panther milk." He grinned, " 'Tis good stuff—all of a month old. Come on, man, there's nothing to be gained by listening to what's going on upstairs."

"Thank ye, kindly. I—I reckon I'd better clear out." And they did, for Bettie had begun to utter shrieks so eloquent of agony that they made hairs squirm on the back of a listener's head.

To everyone's surprise and relief, Bettie O'Brien's ordeal proved to be short-lived. Just after the sun had set over the forest, Winsome appeared at Glen's door to announce, "I believe I need a dram of whatever that is you men are drinking."

Without hesitation, the ex-cornet measured out a stiff tot which, to his astonishment, Winsome did not dilute, but downed in a single gulp which caused her eyes to water and the men's to widen.

"Well, Hendy, I've brought you great news," she choked.

Hendy burst out, "And what is it, ma'am? A son or a daughter?"

"You've both!" Winsome laughed, and, after wiping her eyes, set down her cup. "And a fine, lusty pair they are, judging by their yells."

"Why then, Bettie's made a 'bracket in salvo,' as the artillerists say," chortled Archibald Glen. "How'd you manage it?"

The horse breeder gulped another drink, grinned, "Why, man dear, 'twas easy. If me foot hadn't slipped I'd have got us a basketful."

Winsome flapped her apron several times to cool heated features before saying sharply, "You might at least ask how Bettie's doing, you unfeeling little rascal! She's just had a terribly hard time."

"Och! 'Tis a thoughtless bugger that I am!" Hendy burst out. "Pray God, the dear girl's restin' easy. She is, ain't she?"

"For the moment. But you'd better pray that her hemorrhages let up. She's been bleeding like a pig with its throat cut."

As if enough excitement for one day had not already taken place at Chaugee Landing, more was added. Winsome had just started home to get supper for Robbie and herself when a little sloop appeared, scudded around the long marshy point lying just below the settlement. One of its crew fired a musket, the report of which brought everybody hurrying down to the wharf.

She proved to be the *Swallow*, a dispatch boat from Frederica, bearing a highly excited subaltern of Oglethorpe's Regiment. Through cupped hands he shouted, "Spaniards landed on Amelia Island yesterday and murdered some people!"

"How many?" bellowed Glen.

"We don't know yet, but you'd better get ready for trouble. They may head this way!"

Chapter 4

TWO COURIERS

It no longer proved trouble for Lieutenant Archibald Glen to convince the men and older boys that they should attend drill, but, unfortunately, they numbered only nineteen, excluding Major Wallace Challenger and Micah Oxford, both of whom were absent. As on previous occasions, the latter, without warning or explanation, had vanished into that limitless wilderness which stretched westward from the seacoast. To Glen, the Yorker's pale-skinned Creek "wife" insisted that the fork-bearded trader hadn't granted her even a clue as to where he might be headed, or when she might expect his return.

"I'll warrant that slippery rogue is up to no good," growled John Stonehewer at gun drill that afternoon. "Seems there's always some shifty character, white or red, hanging round his place."

"Wish to God the major would come back," Tom Trippe grunted while sloshing a sponge staff's end about a tub of water.

The settlement's defenders, for the most part, had stripped to the waist, including frail James Corneck, the silk weaver who with his brother kept bachelor quarters with Papot, Oglethorpe's former servant. Now they stood grouped about the battery's Number Two gun—an ancient eight-pounder.

They were mopping faces and necks while trying to comprehend Lieutenant Glen's earnest instructions. So far, these amateur artillerists had fired none of the ordnance gleaming dully behind a double-thick breastwork of palmetto logs.

Under the hot sun the purple-faced men in wide palmetto hats continued to strain and sweat in running out and then withdrawing the carriage guns from their embrasures. Long since, the group of freckled, towheaded children who had been watching the drill had lost interest and wandered away.

In weary patience, Glen barked at deliberate and heavy-footed James Burnside, "Number Four, stand two paces farther back else you'll get knocked silly by the recoil. You, Buncle, when you pick up those cannon balls do it straight-backed or you'll likely rupture yourself"—which warning was slightly ridiculous because the balls weighed only eight pounds apiece and everybody knew that George Buncle could easily lift a yearling heifer clear of the ground; but nobody laughed, only doggedly continued at this unfamiliar form of labor.

At the end of an hour Glen perceived that his amateur gun crews had had enough. "That will do for now, men. Put away your gear as you've been told, then form up in two ranks. Corporal Papot, you'll make note of who's in attendance and who isn't." He summoned a tired half-smile. "Someday, maybe, there'll be a bit of pay for those who drill regularly."

He removed his hat, fanned himself, then glanced up into the brazen sky about which the inevitable buzzards wheeled in endless patience. "Oh, by the bye, I believe it would be better if, in the future, we were to exercise the guns earlier in the day."

"The earlier the better, sir," remarked Hendy O'Brien, who was so proud of his twins that, nowadays, he strutted about wearing a perpetual grin.

As Steve Marrauld laughed, "Little bugger acts like he did it all by himself."

The men had fallen out of ranks and were dispersing when a lookout, stationed on a tall observation mast erected beside the battery, reported a horseman tearing along that cart road leading to Oxford's place and on to Fort Argyle. The rider pulled up beside Glen, who was doing up his shirt, and announced that he'd been sent by the authorities in Savannah.

"You Mr. Glen?"

"Yes, I am."

"Then I've got news for your ears alone."

Once they'd sought the water's edge, the dispatch rider reported, "Sir, the truth's out about that Spanish raid on Amelia Island but there's no need for the rest of your people to hear it."

Glen asked evenly, "Is it as bad as all that?"

"No. It's so much better than first reported that the Colonial Council don't want the truth spread for fear that some folks will slack off on their drilling for defense."

"Well?"

"After I've had a drink of water, sir, I'll tell you. Swear to God I'm drier than a Wesleyan sermon."

"Then come to my house."

Leading his lathered horse, the dispatch rider went over, tethered his mount to a post planted on the shady side of a water oak. Once he had drunk, the rider spilled the rest of the water inside his shirt, asked, "What have ye heard 'bout what happened on Amelia last week?"

"Only that it was a bloody business; suppose you go on talking."

"Well, like you know, Amelia Island is our southernmost lookout station, so the general has been keepin' a dispatch boat based there. Manned by a crew of sixteen—mostly Scotsmen—they take turns sailing on patrol; them's as if off-duty work their allotments because some of 'em have brought down their families.

"Just lately, the gen'ral sent down a corporal's guard o' his regiment to put up a palisade and mount a couple of cannons.

"Well, last week a parcel of Spaniards landed on Amelia by night and hid in the woods till a couple of poor Highlanders came out looking for a stray calf. They weren't armed, but, all the same, those goddam Papists killed 'em and whacked off their heads. When the scout boat heard the firing it came tearing back, but the scoundrels had got away in boats hid on the island's east side."

The dispatch rider took another long swig of cool spring water. "And that, sir, is what really happened *this* time. O' course, everybody figgers this won't be the last such a raid the enemy is fixin' to make."

The messenger had started to lead his horse over to O'Brien's paddock for a drink and a bait of food when he checked himself, "Oh, I near forgot, sir. 'Tis reported that the general's been took awful sick in Coweta."

A shiver descended Glen's back. "What ails him?"

"Don't know, sir. They say he took a fever sometime back and came *that* close to dyin'."

"How is the general now?"

"He's supposed to be gettin' better, but reports say 'twill be a good while 'fore he's fit to travel."

Lord God! thought the acting commandant of the Chaugee District. That means Wallace must be away longer and just when we need him the most.

Glen decided to accompany the rider over to O'Brien's stable yard and so learned, among other things, that Oglethorpe's power of persuasion with the Indians again had triumphed; he'd not only coaxed Chikilly and Malatchi, the Creek mico thlucco, to quit flirting with the French, but also had got them to promise him a thousand warriors for the King's service whenever he called for them—which allowed Archibald Glen wholeheartedly to enjoy a belated supper.

Three nights later, Winsome Challenger was awakened by the sound of a shot. Skin pebbling with fright, she roused and, hair streaming free, pulled on her boat cloak because, when Wallace was away, she generally slept in the nude during such stifling hot weather, although she knew very well she'd be terribly criticized if anyone found out about her indulging in so shameless a comfort.

Following her husband's oft-repeated instructions, she lifted a light musketoon from its pegs, double-barred the door, and locked all the ground floor shutters save the one facing the Glens' house. Meanwhile, Claymore's excited whines grew more piercing as, everywhere, sounded the *bang!-bang!* of closing shutters and the sound of sleepy voices calling out to know what was amiss.

Winsome peered out and, by the light of a waning moon, watched a horseman pull up before the Glen dwelling, yelling, "Wake up! Wake up! The nigras in Carolina are rebelling! They've slaughtered a lot of people in Stono and other places round Charles Town. They're headed south, killing and burning."

Despite Glen and Woodroofe's persistent questioning, this proved the sum of the courier's knowledge. He demanded the loan of a fast horse, saying that he must alert all trading posts and hamlets down to New Inverness. This alarm, he stated, also was being spread by sea, but what with so many Spanish *guardacostas* and privateers hugging the Guale

Coast it wasn't by any means certain that a dispatch boat could get through.

On this occasion the bad news proved not to have been exaggerated. During the next few days a few travelers reached Chaugee Landing and reported atrocities so horrible that some squeamish persons vomited on learning the details.

Out of this spate of rumors only a few firm facts appeared: first, the rebellion had been engineered by Spaniards and English renegades who, even now, were occupied in arming and directing the revolted slaves; second, General Oglethorpe had issued orders for the Georgia Rangers and militia units to block escape routes to Florida. But, in many sections of South Carolina, the militia—not unnaturally—thought first of their own families and had failed to report for duty.

Finally, extraordinary funds had been voted to defend both struggling little Savannah and wealthier Charles Town, and appeals had been dispatched to the colonies lying farther north imploring ships and men to aid in the suppression of this terrifying rebellion.

Winsome held forth in Helen Glen's kitchen. "Why did this awful thing *have* to happen with Wallace away?"

Sharply, Helen reminded her, as she picked up her youngest offspring to change its swaddling cloth, "Don't forget, my dear, Wallace was *ordered* to join the general."

Glancing sidewise at the young New Englander, she wondered at the change which seemed to have come over her. Why did she so often appear critical and discontented? She occupied the most comfortable house in the settlement and Wallace Challenger was the most influential man in the Chaugee District and trusted, if not admired, by everyone, no matter what the hue of their skin.

Strange, mused Helen, that lately she'd found herself spending more and more time in the company of Bettie O'Brien and olive-skinned Joanna Marrauld, for all that the latter was a French-Italian who spoke only halting English. Probably Joanna Marrauld worked harder than anyone else in the settlement, but she never complained; somehow, Joanna made a body feel better whenever they were with her.

Winsome sighed and bent to retrieve a cornhusk doll baby from the floor, said, "A pity that this revolt should happen at a time when our crops need extra attention; a lot of them will be lost."

"Perhaps so," Helen murmured while tickling her baby under its plump double chin, "but at least *we* don't have to fear what a lot of black slaves may do to us."

Winsome looked up quickly. "Why so sure? Really, Helen, who can tell whether those black fiends can be kept from crossing the Savannah? How awful it would be if some of them pass this way.

"Have you ever stopped to think how much good our silly little battery would be if we're attacked from inland? You know as well as I, hardly one in five of our brave defenders can hit the broad side of a barn with his musket."

"That may very well be so," Helen said deliberately, "but Archie believes the blacks will pass us by if they hear that we're ready for 'em. Besides, Mike Oxford may return anytime."

Helen replaced her toddler on the floor and gave him a pat on the bottom to start him out gravely to survey a hen busily scratching for her chicks. She passed over a kettle of peasecods. "Know what I think, Winsome? I think Mike must have got some sort of a warning before the news of Stono reached us. I think he's gone to bring in some Indians to help us."

An expression of surprise crossed the Boston girl's face. "Why, Helen, I shouldn't wonder but maybe you're right! But if that's what Mike's doing I wonder why he didn't tell me so?"

"Tell *you*? Why should he?"

A brief laugh escaped Winsome Challenger as she began to shell peas. "Why—why, I suppose it's because we've always been good friends. You see, like me, he comes from the Northern colonies."

"What's that got to do with it?"

"Oh, silly, don't you see? You English and the Scots stick together tighter than burrs, and so do the Carolinians, so, somehow, it's good to talk with someone who remembers the same things I do. Oh, drat!" A series of shrill wails from the direction of her home argued that Robbie must have gotten into trouble. "Really, Helen, I declare that child is a real limb of Satan. I can't leave him alone for ten minutes but he's into mischief of some sort."

Winsome stood up, shook pea shells off her apron, and hurried past the bole of a great, moss-draped water oak that was doing its best to shade the Glens' home.

Chapter 5

ONSLAUGHT I

Some ten days passed after they'd heard the news of the slave uprising before the inhabitants of Chaugee Landing felt able to resume, more or less, their daily routine, despite terrifying and conflicting rumors which kept coming in from Charles Town, Beaufort, Savannah, Thunderbolt, Frederica, and Fort Argyle.

Among these were reports that parties of armed Negroes had been seen crossing the Savannah north of New Ebenizer while, from the south, emanated warnings that bands of Spanish-led Yamasees had crossed the St. John River and were marching northward. Therefore, everyone was delighted when Micah Oxford brought to his truck house a Georgia Ranger sergeant named Bob Slack and five tough-looking Creek warriors whom he armed with good muskets.

The trader, however, privately continued to worry over the nonarrival of that coaster from Philadelphia which was supposed to bring him arms and ammunition.

Even while at work, the people of Chaugee Landing kept an eye on the signal mast, which now boasted a lookout platform on its cross-trees. It had been added right after the news of the killings on Amelia Island had come in. Night and day, someone remained on watch; always a loaded pistol was kept there which the lookout was to fire the instant a sail was sighted or any untoward situation arose.

The moment the whole population had been dreading occurred on a Wednesday afternoon; James Burnside's wife, Agnes, using both hands, lifted the signal pistol high above her head and, closing both eyes, pulled the trigger. Sullenly the explosion reverberated across the village and into the woods, rolled up the river, for far down the Ogeechee's delta, Agnes had glimpsed the flash of a sail. The distant craft of course might be only a plantation boat or a dispatch vessel; but Glen's orders had been dinned into her ears for a long while.

Men came pelting in from the fields, from the mulberry groves, from the sawmill, and from Trippe's boatyard. Women dashed about, shooing children indoors and slamming shutters. It was too bad, thought Will Woodroofe, that Oxford's place lay too far upriver to hear a single shot unless the wind was right—which it wasn't at present, blowing as it was out of the northeast and strongly enough to raise white-crested waves on the clay-hued channel.

Glen rushed out of his house carrying his uniform's coat and a musket balanced across his left arm; a pair of powder horns and a bag of bullets swung from his right hand. He felt encouraged to see how promptly the men turned out and made for the battery. They were tense, alert, and breathless, especially those who had had to run a long way.

The two cannon were manned first of all, then, as more men appeared from among the houses and live oaks, powder and matches were fetched from a small underground magazine and the swivels otherwise made ready for action.

Lieutenant Glen, his English crisp and precise, shouted, "Remember to swab the tubes out clean after every shot; leave a spark in the bore and you'll surely lose a hand or maybe an arm. Now listen, all of you! Nobody is to fire till I sound this whistle."

While slow matches were being ignited, the ex-cornet sent Tom Trippe up the lookout mast, the boatbuilder being familiar with craft customarily plying the Guale Coast.

The amateur gunners settled down to wait, spat, dug at the sand with bare feet, spoke of anything except what might happen in just a little while.

Meanwhile, Lieutenant Glen seized this lull to order Stephen Marrauld's long-legged son, Philippe, to run to Oxford's place and alert the people there. The barefooted and shock-haired youth nodded, then raced away at such speed that he overtook Winsome Challenger trudging along that sandy cart road which led to the truck house.

When Philippe had panted out his message she remarked, "I thought I heard a shot. Is this strange vessel definitely a hostile one?"

"No, ma'am, most everybody figgers likely it's that brig due in from Philadelphy. Got to get on now." He ducked his wheat-colored head, then sped on with legs working like pistons until he became lost to sight among the red-brown trunks of pines crowding in on the road from either side.

For a moment Winsome debated turning back to the Landing, but there had been so many false alarms of late that to retrace her steps didn't seem sensible; besides, Robbie would be in good hands while playing with Helen Glen's children.

What really decided her to keep on was her desire to exchange gossip with Mike Oxford; the Yorker had an amazing knack for amassing bits of significant news and, quite often, he was able to pass on something of what was going on up in New England. Once, he'd even given her a tattered copy of *The Boston Gazette*, the sight of which had started tears in her eyes.

Tom Trippe, perched on the lookout's platform, reported the strange vessel to be a sizable brig which was coming upriver at a smart clip, thanks to a wind steadily blowing from astern.

Balanced on the parapet, Archibald Glen steadied a heavy brass spyglass over Hendy O'Brien's shoulder and discovered that now he could make out the approaching vessel in greater detail.

Tom Trippe bellowed down, "Stand easy, boys. I reco'nize her: she's the *Wolverine* out o' Charles Town. I c'n even make out the Union Flag on her real plain."

Glen called back, "Do I see some people in scarlet coats standing about her quarter-deck?"

"Yep. That's right. Reckon the council must be sendin' some Lobster-backs to reinforce us."

When about half a mile distant, the brig dipped her colors in salute, then her master sent seamen scrambling aloft to take in her forecourse. Others clewed up her mainsail, but even under topsails and royals she kept bowling right along.

Stonehewer grunted, "Be that so, where's the use in us standing round here with our thumbs in our mouths? I'm going back, else my cows will stray into the woods."

Hendy then threw Glen an awkward salute, said, "Beggin' yer pardon, sir, I've got a mare standin' only half shod so, by yer leave—"

Glen hesitated, then called crisply, "All right, you fellows can fall out and go about your occasions—except for the crew of Number One gun. I want them to help dock the brig."

"Ain't we going to fire a salute?" demanded Acting Sergeant Buncle—he loved to hear a cannon roar. "The King's troops out there will be expectin' one."

Glen shook his head. "Sorry, George, but we've no powder to spare on courtesies."

The men slouched off under the early autumn heat and scattered through the settlement. Only Archibald Glen and Will Woodroofe lingered on the battery's parapet to watch the brig's crew take in her topsails. She was less than a quarter-mile away from the wharf when the furling of her main topsail rendered her Union Flag to become more visible.

Even while Glen studied the flag he sensed, rather than knew, that something was amiss, the onshore breeze was conveying a faint, fetid odor.

All at once Trippe shouted down from the lookout station. "Hey! Mr. Glen, look at her Union Flag! It's flyin' from a bridle, foreign-style, not straight up and down on halyards, like us!"

The crew of Number One gun halted halfway to the wharf.

Over his shoulder, Woodroofe yelled, "My God, Glen, d'you recognize that stink? 'Tis the same as a slave ship's!"

Without hesitation, Glen clapped his whistle to his lips and sounded a series of four ear-piercing blasts before, cursing his gullibility, he jumped down into the embrasure of Number One gun and frantically tried to train the piece.

Settlers wheeled and started running back to the battery, but at that moment the brig yawed and half-a-dozen gun ports on her larboard side banged up just before her gunners let fly a broadside. One cannon ball moaned harmlessly past Tom Trippe's head as, in frantic haste, he scrambled down the signal mast's ratlines, but another shot struck the battery and dismounted a pair of swivels.

Although Will Woodroofe also began to heave on a handspike, Archibald Glen knew it was no use. The embrasure just wasn't wide enough to permit their bringing the eight-pounder to bear. In a futile rage, the ex-cornet of The Blues nevertheless grabbed up a slow match and ground it into Number One's touchhole. The cannon spouted fire and smoke, then kicked at its breechings like a curried horse with a ticklish belly, but the shot only raised a harmless waterspout fifty yards aft of the brig's stern.

Glen now realized that there wouldn't possibly be time to reassemble his gun crews; the men had become too widely dispersed and, worse still, the stranger's broadside so had dismayed the crew of Number One gun that they kept on pelting away from the river's bank to seek shelter behind trees and houses. The defenders' disorganization became complete when the brig let fly a second broadside, which crashed into Glen's warehouse and blew the Challengers' fine backhouse into smithereens.

Aghast, the settlers glimpsed a column of sable-skinned figures appear on the *Wolverine's* deck. They were screeching outlandish cries and wildly brandishing cutlasses and pikes. A few white men lined the brig's rail and opened fire with muskets and other small arms.

A heavy musket ball caught Will Woodroofe in the back, dead center, which tumbled him into an inert, dust-covered huddle, half a rod short of his front door. Ignoring the hiss and whine of bullets, Glen ran to the Lowlander, but as quickly realized that nothing could be done for him. Blood was pumping too freely from the hole in Woodroofe's back.

Straightening, Glen shouted, "Get to—strong houses, everybody! Shutter up, quick!"

Next, he barked to Hendy, who hadn't run but seemed uncertain what to do, "Ride! Warn Oxford, then get on to Fort Argyle. An we get quick help we just may hold out."

The former jockey didn't delay long enough to answer, only sprinted for his stable yard. Not wanting to lose his stock if the raiders took over, he pulled down the paddock's gate bars, then yelled and waved his hat until the beasts rushed out and made for the woods. He began bridling Ardnagashel, his prized thoroughbred stallion, at the same moment as the *Wolverine* ground alongside the wharf and a tide of screaming, sable figures surged over her rail. While securing the bridle's throat latch, Hendy, glancing toward the river, saw the brig's Union Flag flutter downward; quickly, it became replaced by a gaudy yellow and red Spanish ensign.

That there were some fine runners among the raiders Hendy soon appreciated; already a party of blacks were racing along the road to Oxford's, apparently headed for Trippe's boatyard. Accordingly, the ex-jockey guided his stallion, half-crazed by the continued musketry, onto a cow-path, then booted him into a tearing gallop. Branches lashed his face like hot wires and, because he was riding bareback, several boughs almost swept him from his seat.

At the thought of Bettie, the twins, and Toby, the little Irishman almost pulled up; by rights, he should have stayed at the Landing to protect them, but, at the same time, he realized that they'd stand a better chance if even a small reinforcement appeared unexpectedly.

Once the cowpath widened on joining the direct road to Oxford's, he let the stallion run flat-out while praying that this magnificent beast wouldn't slip on some rounded stone or trip over a fallen branch; Ardnagashel was much too fine a piece of horseflesh to be lost in so futile a fashion. Despite everything, Hendy felt his heart lift; not since Newmarket had he sensed such a wonderful surge of power between his knees.

On nearing Oxford's truck house he guessed the trader must have heard the cannon, if not the musketry, for when he pulled up at the clearing he saw that there was nobody in sight; the log structure's mas-sive front door and shutters were fast. He'd barely recognized the gleam of musket muzzles at various loopholes when the door opened and Ox-ford came running out with a strange Ranger.

Chapter 6

ONSLAUGHT II

Quobah Tutu, bullet head swathed in a splendid red and gold turban, was the first to strike the wharf at Chaugee Landing. Roaring a war cry, the Kumassee King sped shoreward so fast that his useless arm began to sway like a pendulum and a powerful young Sengalese he'd trained to protect him from the left was hard put to keep abreast.

Just before slamming the door to his house, Militia Lieutenant Archi-bald Glen whirled to take a snap shot at that towering sable figure in the van, but he missed, killed instead the giant Ashanti's Left Arm. More shots were fired from the Burnside and Marrauld dwellings, with the result that two more revolted slaves sagged to the ground, kicking and screaming.

"Take that!" Quobah roared at a passing black. Using his assegai, he indicated a loaded musket dropped by Woodroofe as he died.

Yammering, the ex-slaves rushed forward and scattered among the houses although Captain Pedro Lamberto furiously attempted to direct them to the village's west side, where, as he well knew, lay most of the Landing's unfortified dwellings; arms found in these should prove useful in assaulting the enforted homes later on.

Although Lamberto employed the flat of his sword again and again, the frenzied blacks ignored him. Eyes white and rolling, teeth gnashing, the Africans scattered to spear stray shoats, chickens, geese, and even puppies. Fervently, the Spaniard cursed his volatile followers. How differently this attack would be going if he were commanding a few white men, or even Yamasees! So many escaped slaves were armed only with a cutlass, a hatchet, or a pike that to destroy Chaugee Landing was going to prove unexpectedly difficult.

He led a party of mustee sailors from the *Wolverine*—she had been captured off Beaufort nearly a month ago—in a charge on Wallace Challenger's big house because for some reason its front door remained blackly, invitingly open. In the district commander's home plenty of arms should be discovered!

Unfortunately for Robbie Challenger, who'd been romping with the Glen children when the brig opened fire, he'd run to hide himself in a henhouse instead of following them to real shelter. Jabbering Africans discovered him cowering in a corner. Chickens squawked and scattered when one of the blacks hurled a spear which so effectively pinned Robbie's slight body to a whitewashed wall that the child had time to scream only once before his brief life came to an end.

As shooting from the enforted homes slowed because the settlers had to reload, Archibald Glen tried to estimate the situation—and found it desperate. The whole settlement was being overrun by knots of dark-skinned figures who were breaking into unoccupied or unfortified dwellings. As usual when shots were fired, buzzards and vultures appeared and began to circle about the sky.

At this time died most of the settlers who perished in the attack. The raiders burst in the door and hacked to pieces pregnant Jeanie Woodroofe and her four-year-old daughter. The killers pranced wildly about the bodies, then rushed on, leaving the murdered pair lying in the dust amid glistening, widening pools of blood.

Quobah Tutu personally pistoled James Corneck who, with the Buncles, had attempted a dash for Duché's enforted home.

Although wounded and cursing the day he had immigrated to America, Peter Buncle managed to reach the woods where he discovered the Stonehewer twins, ghastly pale under their freckles, hiding in a tangle of myrtle and honeysuckle. They had been wise beyond their years in not attempting to gain their father's house; certainly they would have been killed had they tried to get there. The three crouched, shaking and wide-eyed, listening to dreadful cries raised by Mrs. Burnside and her two small children before they died.

Another casualty was Claymore, who'd been asleep under the house when the attack began. Roaring, the old mastiff had rushed at and torn out the throat of a black before a club crushed in his ugly gray head.

James Wardrop figured he could hold out even in the absence of his sons, Chauncey and Luke. He was mistaken. It didn't take the revolted slaves long to batter down his door for all that Duché and other neighbors kept on shooting at long range and even caused a few casualties.

Soon smoke and flames began to whirl up from Glen's warehouse, from the O'Brien place, then from Woodroofe's, Wardrop's, and Corneck's. By this time Challenger's empty home had begun to spout fire through its roof so violently that Glen, who had been shooting as fast as Henri Marrauld could reload a spare gun, began to fear that his own house might take fire.

Fortunately for Glen and others who'd taken refuge with him—the Hendy O'Brien family, the Marraulds, and James Papot—the wind shifted and began to blow strongly out of the northwest and so carried brands and sparks toward the wrecked battery and out over the peaceful, sunlit marshes.

Peering through a loophole let into a shutter on the second floor, Glen, through the drifting smoke, could see a throng of Africans looting houses to which they had senselessly, prematurely set afire. Drunk with excitement, the savages whooped and capered about, flourishing a weird miscellany of plunder.

Glen watched the Spanish officer, still in his deceptive scarlet tunic, start to direct the removal of swivels from the battery. What he could not see was that short enemy column which started toward Oxford's truck house. Leading it was someone Glen would have had no trouble in identifying. While on duty at the guardhouse in Savannah he'd frequently had to do with John Savey.

He missed seeing the detachment because Marrauld and Papot were yelling from the ground floor, "Shift to the other side, Glen! They're attacking the Trippes'." Again the house reverberated to the roaring boom of muskets interspersed with squealing whimpers of children as they clutched their mothers' skirts. Abruptly, Helen Glen discovered that Robbie Challenger was not present. To make matters worse, her offspring were so terrified that they could tell her nothing about Robbie's whereabouts.

People were coughing because of drifting burned-powder fumes while ramrods hastily driven home caused a harsh, slithering sound. Throat tightening, Archibald Glen watched a detachment of Negroes armed with axes collect before his front door. "Get those men in front!" he shouted, then poked his musket out of a loophole in the front window's shutter.

Unfortunately, Quobah's red turban was nowhere to be seen, so he drew his sights on a tall Negro who seemed to be a leader. Fire flashed in the pan and Glen's gun kicked hard. While he was fumbling for a fresh ball the burned-powder smoke cleared away sufficiently to reveal his target writhing in the dust.

The African's followers hesitated, then when shots from the lower floor dropped others of their number they scattered among the houses. Some ran over to the already mangled bodies of settlers and, in childish fury, further hacked and battered the fallen. Their own dead and wounded they ignored. The shooting died out almost completely except for firing from the direction of Antoine Duché's big house—but Archibald Glen was sufficient of a soldier to foresee that, when darkness fell, even the enforted houses easily could be set afire.

He had, of course, no idea that, at that moment, the brigantine *Susan Peabody*, an armed merchantman out of Philadelphia, had begun to pick a course among that cluster of marshy islands masking the Ogeechee's delta.

Winsome Challenger reached Oxford's truck house only a moment after the *Wolverine* had fired her first broadside, and the report came rumbling over the pine tops like distant heat thunder. Flushed and breathless, she saw Micah, a Ranger sergeant named Bob Slack, and five Creek warriors grouped in front of the store, obviously trying to decide the meaning of this cannonade. One and all, they held their weapons ready and looked set for action.

When the Yorker sighted Winsome, running toward him with long legs flashing and revealed, garter-high, by skirts caught up before her, he sang out, "What the devil's going on down to the Landing?"

"Don't know!" she gasped while the Indians stared at her from blank, obsidian eyes. "Oh dear, what am I to do?"

"Do about what?"

"I left Robbie at the Landing—he was playing with Helen Glen's children."

"He'll be looked after, all right," rasped the trader. "Archie Glen is—" His next words were forgotten because the *Wolverine* had fired her second broadside.

When the solitary *boom!* made by the one gun the battery had managed to fire came rumbling inland, Bob Slack gaped, "Now, by Jesus, what does *that* mean?"

"Quiet! Winnie, you get in the house," hissed the Yorker, then, like the Creeks, he spun about to face the truck house, for, from behind it was sounding the snapping of twigs.

The noise was caused by Petre Ballou, who, as soon as he recognized the distant grumble of cannon fire, left off stirring a mess of mash and ran to fetch an ancient flintlock Oxford had lent him since the news of Stono had come in.

Eager to justify restoration of his commission, the old Swiss started along the most direct path leading to Oxford's in much too much of a hurry to pick his footing. There sounded a sudden *whir-r-r!*, then it seemed that a pair of hot needles had pierced the skinny calf of his left leg.

Ballou was tempted to stop long enough to blow the rattlesnake in halves, but figured that a shot coming from this direction might give Oxford a wrong idea, so paused only long enough to sit down and hurriedly slash the fang holes. Next, he used the thong securing his shirt's neck opening as a tourniquet placed above the bleeding punctures.

He didn't notice when the knot, too hastily tied, slipped, so, by the time he reached the clearing's edge, burning spears of pain were shooting up his leg and the blazing sky seemed miraculously to be darkening.

When he saw Oxford and a couple of Indians pointing guns in his direction, Ballou retained just enough sense to call out, "Not shoot! *Ne tirez pas!* I—friend."

Oxford unshouldered his musket. "What the hell ails you? You drunk?"

The old man reeled forward. "*Non*, the serpent he bite me!"

"Oh, for Christ's sake! You *would* pick a time like this to get bit!" Turning, he sang out, "Winnie! Come out and help this old fool indoors. Do what you can for him. You, Paksee!" he instructed the senior Creek warrior in fluent Muskogean. "You and Slack make a scout around the Landing, learn what's happening, but don't stay too long." His steely, little eyes glittered. "I think big trouble's headed this way."

Since she'd dressed many a snakebite since coming south, Winsome didn't take long in deciding that Colonel Petre Ballou had fought his last campaign. The white-haired old man's features, due to long sobriety, had become refined and his manner was almost courtly when he whispered, "Thank you, *madame*. I am finish', no?"

"I fear so, Mr. Ballou. You see, you kept on running after your ligature slipped; the venom has spread beyond control."

The old man's breathing was growing more labored, "*Hélas!* And I had wished once more to bear a brave part. Believe—I was—the good soldier —victory or—defeat. Water. *Pour l'amour de Dieu*—a little water—"

For a little while the dying veteran babbled in French, then in German, and, toward the end, in Polish and Turkish as well. He mentioned outlandish places such as Cracow, Stettin, Levadia, and Jassy.

At the sudden clatter caused by Hendy O'Brien's horse, Petre Ballou's faded blue eyes widened and he gasped, "No, Marcovitch! The embrasures must be constructed deeper and much wider!" The death rattle then began to sound deep in the Swiss's throat, but Winsome didn't notice it; she was listening to Hendy O'Brien's panted, "A lot of Spanish and nigras are ashore, killing and burning!"

"Dammit, who leads 'em?" snapped Oxford.

"Don't know."

Winsome left the bedside and dashed out into the sun-drenched clearing. "Robbie! What's happened to Robbie? Tell me, Hendy! Tell me."

"Can't say," Hendy gasped. "Everything's all mixed up, things are bad, back there. Bad."

"How many raiders are there? Speak up, ye fool, how many?" snapped Oxford; the Indians, expressionless, watched him rather than the gasping, wild-eyed rider.

"Fifty at least—maybe sixty—no tellin' for sure."

"How'd they get there?"

"In a ship wearing British colors."

"Sixty's too many for us to tackle so you'd better git on to Fort Argyle. Warn 'em to shake the lead out o' their arses else they'll likely find Chaugee wiped off the map!"

Once the ex-jockey had galloped off through the hot afternoon sunlight, Oxford started for the truck house. "Come along, you fellers. Winnie, how's Ballou?"

"He's dead!" Winsome told him woodenly. "A fang struck an artery and the venom got into his blood stream."

The Yorker, obviously perplexed, tugged at his torn ear an instant. "The poor, old bastard. Wisht I rightly knew what to do. Too bad Wallace ain't round. He'd know."

Winsome's lips tightened into a flat, colorless parallelogram and her voice grew shrill. "Aye. *Why* isn't Wallace here looking after his family and friends? Just tell me that! Why must he go traipsing off all the time? If anything's happened to Robbie—I—I'll never forgive him!"

Oxford shook her by the shoulders. "Just you cut out that kind o' talk and get busy! Fill every damn' crock and bucket you can find at the spring. Lest I'm mistook, we're goin' to have stand siege. Hope to hell Paksee and Slack show up in a hurry."

Chapter 7

JOHN SAVEY

At a smart trot John Savey, alias Señor Miguel Wall, led his detachment of about fifteen Negroes along the familiar cart track to Micah Oxford's trading post. Thus far, he was feeling less than pleased with results of the attack; also, he felt uneasy that so few of the ragged, skinny Africans jogging at his heels carried firearms.

At any rate, it was pleasant to have this excuse for getting away from Chaugee Landing, where the settlers were putting up such an unexpectedly stubborn fight. After all, but a single bullet was required to let the life out of a man!

Mike Oxford, of course, would be overjoyed to get paid for his guns in gold which was tugging and clinking at his belt. By now, the Yorker must be ready, if not eager, to join what would prove to be the winning side; what possible chance would these weak, sparsely settled colonies stand against the might of His Most Catholic Majesty's empire? They were doomed because, as he well knew, the English could expect to receive little or no help from Home. Furthermore, Savey reasoned, the Yorker recently had complained over his inability to secure those mirrors, scissors, burning glasses, cloth, hatchets, and, above all the firearms upon which his trade depended.

As the truck house, standing sun-drenched in the midst of its clearing, came into sight, the renegade was disturbed to find no one about. Mike must be away, Savey reassured himself, but, as quickly, realized that a thin strand of smoke was curling from the truck house's mud and stick chimney.

A wide gesture from Savey waved forward his followers. "Fan out! Let the trader see how many we are." Then he strode confidently, his captured British officer's jacket blazing scarlet.

It took time to explain to the ex-slaves what he wanted; hardly a man of them could understand more than a few English words, but he could tell by the way they gripped blunderbusses, hatchets, and spears that they were eager to get ahead with the business in hand.

Savey advanced toward the front door, teeth agleam in his swarthy

features. "Hi, there, Mike! Come out, friend! Want to talk!" Silence.
"You are in there, aren't you?"

"Yep. I'm right here." The trader's voice boomed through a loophole, the heavy wooden shield of which had been lifted and secured by
a latchstring on the inside.

"You hear me, Mike? I want to buy every damn' gun you've got."

Again Savey boldly advanced a few paces, but his followers looked apprehensive as they started across the expanse of trampled hot sand. The
few Africans holding guns kept their eyes fixed on that row of loopholes
let into the long side of the truck house.

"Hey, Mike!" called he in the scarlet tunic. "Come out and let's talk."

Muffled sounds came from within the log structure. "Go ahead, talk.
What's on yer mind?"

"We've been doing good business for a long while, Mike, so I'm sorry
it can't continue, but I propose that we make a deal which will do well
by us both."

"Well?" invited the trader's distorted voice. "Spit it out!"

"I'll pay you *in gold* for such guns as you have in there, three times
the going price. After that, I invite you to come and join the winning
side and make lots of money out of this war."

"You'll pay gold? Hold on, I'll come out." Oxford's voice faded when
he stepped back from the loophole.

Relief flooded Savey as he motioned his semicircle of followers to close
in.

Breath bated, Winsome watched the store's interior brighten when the
Yorker unbarred, pushed open the door, and went out. Oxford had left
his musket behind, but she knew Micah wasn't unarmed; he was carrying a brace of pistols in the pockets of his grimy buckskin jacket. The
Creeks and Bob Slack didn't even turn their heads to watch him depart;
they remained behind their loopholes with flintlocks cocked and poised.

Walking lightly on the balls of his feet, the Yorker emerged from the
narrow porch shading the front of his store and, tight-faced, stalked right
up to John Savey.

Micah's Indian "wife," Tchimi, holding ready a spare musket, watched
him narrowly; she knew her owner well enough to guess what was about
to happen.

Smiling broadly, Savey eased his flintlock into the crook of his arm,
then stepped forward with hand outstretched. "How are you, old friend?"

"Fine. What's new?"

"Sorry to disappoint you over that last shipment; guess you know now
why I couldn't make delivery." He noted a metallic glint in Oxford's
narrowed, cold gray eyes, said hastily, "Hope you're not angry over it?"

"Hell, no, but it's a surprise yer showin' up here like this."

As the two men drew closer to each other a few Africans stirred and shuffled forward another few feet, but the most of them stayed where they stood; from the truck house came no sound whatsoever.

"Glad you're not angry, Mike!" Savey's even white teeth flashed, "because, as I've just said, I've brought plenty of coin money. What have you got for me?"

Oxford said almost pleasantly, "This, you treacherous bastard!" He jerked out a pistol and shot John Savey through the center of his chest.

Stark disbelief in his large dark eyes, John Savey doubled over, then, clutching his breast, tottered a step forward before crumpling to the ground so heavily that puffs of dust spurted from under his body.

Without a moment's delay the Yorker then used his other pistol on a little Negro who was attempting to shoulder a blunderbuss. From the loopholes muskets blazed, killed several blacks, and set others reeling about, screaming in pain and terror.

Yipping war cries, the five Creeks and the Ranger raced out of doors, whereupon the remaining ex-slaves fled and went crashing off into the woods. In lithe and deadly pursuit the Creeks followed.

Chapter 8

EMBERS

The Creeks, as they stood above the sable bodies sprawled around the truck house, were complaining. Negro scalps, because of their crinkly short hair, made miserably unsatisfactory trophies. Only Paksee, who had thought to take Savey's hair, had nothing to say.

Suddenly, they all quit talking, listened to the thudding of a horse's hoofs on along the Landing road.

"Who's that!" Mike sang out from behind a tree.

"Only me!" called the rider, who proved to be young Chauncey Wardrop, wild-eyed and ghastly pale under his tan. The youth, who was tall and nearing twenty, broke into a torrent of words as he tumbled off one of O'Brien's strayed horses.

Winsome, who just had finished washing Petre Ballou's wrinkled features and combing his scant white locks, dropped a blanket over the corpse and ran out into the deepening sunset, crying, "Robbie? Is my Robbie safe?"

The Yorker then went over to her and, with a surprising tenderness, urged, "Now, just you hush for a minute. Young Wardrop's so excited he can't hardly make sense."

He turned to the youth and put a series of questions which Chauncey, gradually calming, commenced to answer intelligibly.

Presently, Micah went back to Winsome. "Seems something queer has happened down at the Landing. Maybe the folks there ain't been hurt too bad, after all."

"Then, then Robbie's safe?"

"Don't yet know fer sure," he told her. "Young Wardrop and his brother was hidin' in the woods so they didn't get to see too much before they caught this horse."

"Oh dear! Then, please, tell me what you *do* know." Her hazel eyes were rounded, had become dark-rimmed by anxiety. The voices of the Indians and the Ranger questioning young Wardrop continued to rise and fall in the background.

"Well, Chauncey says that, 'bout an hour ago, a second ship was sighted standing in toward the Landing, so that bastard, Lamberto, figgered he'd better get away in a hurry. He and a big black called Quobah rallied as many as they could, piled back into their ship and cast off. Must have left quite a few of their people behind which we'll have no trouble in runnin' down, 'cause these black fellers don't seem no ways woods-wise."

"Whose was the other ship?" drawled Bob Slack, leisurely wiping his skinning knife on a tuft of dried weeds.

"Can't say, Son, but Wardrop thinks she's a armed British merchant-man. Anyhow, her skipper tried to close with the raiders, but the wind blew wrong for the best he could do was to loose a few shots at long range." He glanced at Winsome, standing stiff and drawn-faced to one side. "They'd be the shots we heard a little while back."

"Didn't they halt those villains?"

"Reckon not. Wardrop says the Spanish and their blacks sailed off down the coast, scot-free."

"Why didn't the second ship chase her?"

"Reckon her skipper figgered he'd maybe accomplish more by setting his crew ashore to fight fires and drive off skulkers."

"What fires?" whimpered Wallace Challenger's wife. "*Whose* homes were burned?"

"We don't know yet," Oxford told her. "So take it easy, will you?"

He turned to Tchimi. "You shutter up and I'll leave a Creek to help. Winnie, expect ye want to go see what's happened."

"Just anybody try to stop me!"

"Then take this along, if it ain't too heavy fer ye." He passed over Ballou's rusty musket.

When the party from Oxford's silently set out through gathering darkness Winsome couldn't refrain a long glance at Savey's body and found it almost impossible to recognize the remains of that handsome, suave young fellow who'd courted her back in Savannah. Right now, John didn't look very pretty with his scalp lifted and his face gone loose and shapeless because muscles supporting his features had been severed by Paksee's knife.

The musket's weight dug into Winsome's shoulder, but, all the same, she took up a trot when the brief column set off, eyes smarting in waves of the acrid-smelling smoke which came drifting lazily between the trees.

To Winsome it seemed that they would never cover the mile and a half to Tom Trippe's sawmill, the most northerly building in Chaugee Landing. The afterglow having lasted unusually long, the runners were able to see their way without difficulty.

All at once, the Yorker halted so abruptly that the Creek immediately behind collided with him, caused their musket barrels to clang.

Immediately, Tom Trippe's deep voice yelled, "Halt! Stand where you are!"

Oxford sang out, "Fer God's sake, don't shoot, Tom!"

"That you, Mike?"

"Ain't nobody else!"

Winsome pushed by, ran forward, sobbing, "Oh, Tom! Tom! Is Robbie safe?"

"Don't know. We've just begun to count noses."

Flames from the O'Brien home leaped high, bathed Trippe's sawmill and the Burnside strong house in garish, red-gold light. Farther on, other columns of flame whirled and danced high above the water oaks. Oxford quickly identified the places on fire: those of Wardrop, Corneck, Woodroofe and O'Brien—and Glen's warehouse; there might be some homes aflame farther away, but he couldn't be sure.

Winsome uttered a stifled cry on realizing that her dwelling had become reduced to a flaming pile of embers. Sobbing, she burst through a bucket line forming to save Stephen Marrauld's house, which had had its cypress-shake roof set afire by flying brands.

A man's arm was flung about her, then Glen, in a strained voice, ordered, "Come with me!"

"But Robbie! Is Robbie all right?"

"I fear not. We haven't seen him since the attack began." Glen halfpushed, half-hauled the distraught young woman toward his home, where Helen stood waiting with tears drawing clean channels down her smoke-smudged cheeks.

"Oh, you poor dear! I fear poor, little Robbie has been killed." Then Helen Glen said exactly the wrong thing. "If *only* Wallace had been here, all this mightn't have happened!"

"You're right!" railed Winsome Challenger. "If he'd been where he belonged my son wouldn't be dead!" Features working convulsively, she cried in a cold, intense voice, "God forgive him for having failed us for I cannot! I hope never to see him again!"

At that, Helen's overtired nerves flared. "You stop such wicked talk this instant! He was only obeying orders, just like a good officer must."

Mike Oxford thrust his head inside Glen's house just in time to overhear Winsome's outburst. A hard smile creased his bearded lips before he called, "Heyo, Archie. Ye'd better know that the fires are mostly under control and ye're needed down by the battery to get some swivels remounted."

Winsome sped over to the Yorker and grabbed his arm. "Tell me, Mike, how did Robbie die?"

When she learned the truth she moaned, dropped onto a chest, and for a long while sat rigid as a figure of stone, staring blankly before her.

Two mornings later, Tchimi appeared, wooden-faced, at the Glen house. She was leading her two buff-skinned children by the hand and carrying a large pack. After easing her burden from her shoulders she remained silent, stood staring fixedly at the floor.

Glen looked up from a report he was preparing to forward to Frederica. "What are you doing here, Tchimi? What do you want?"

"Work. Last night my man take trade goods, ride away with Mrs. Challenger."

"Mrs. Challenger! Good God! Where have they gone?"

"Only the winds know," Tchimi admitted acidly. "Always, he go where he please."

Chapter 9

INDEPENDENT HIGHLAND COMPANY OF FOOT

On the morning of May 7, 1740, H.B.M.S. *Flamborough*, 20 guns, Captain Vincent Pearce, with Union Flags flying from both her masts, dropped anchor in the river off New Inverness, a maneuver repeated by her convoy, which consisted of four bluff-bowed merchantmen serving, for the time being, as troop transports.

People collecting along the Altamaha's north bank chattered excitedly to spy so many redcoats thronging the decks. In many a Scot poignant memories were aroused by the sight of the King's scarlet—such uniforms usually had meant only grief and trouble.

Out there there were also as many more men wearing a miscellany of civilian clothing, which argued the presence of militia and volunteers from South Carolina. This encouraged Major Hugh MacKay who, with his immediate subordinates, Captains Hodbury and John MacIntosh, stood waiting at the end of a newly constructed pier reaching well out in the river below New Inverness's original wharf. How taut and neat the dark-blue-hulled man-of-war appeared among those dun-colored merchantmen!

Behind the Highland Company's officers lounged sixty rawboned and hairy Scots, very proud over having enlisted in this newly formed Independent Highland Company of Foot. For the most part, these volunteers were old settlers who, long ago, had left off wearing kilts and tartans to adopt the more practical, if less colorful, garb common on the frontiers. Nevertheless, every man jack of them was wearing a bonnet, a scarf, stockings—something to indentify the clan to which he belonged.

The company, on command, commenced soberly to shuffle out onto the wharf toward barges sent in from the transports. A few grinned and turned to wave to family and friends, but the majority only stumped stolidly along, managing their weapons and gear with conscious care.

From H.B.M.S. *Flamborough's* quarter-deck, Brigadier General James Edward Oglethorpe kept a wary eye on gulls wheeling overhead and, at the same time, considered the village of New Inverness, which now extended well beyond the original palisade. To Major Wallace Challenger, who had aboard some twenty leathery, semidisciplined, and profane but entirely capable Georgia Rangers, he observed, "Wouldn't you say that New Inverness has about doubled in size since we last were here?"

Challenger, uncomfortably hot in his thick, dark green tunic, snapped shut the lens cover to a small brass pocket glass. "Aye, sir. These Scots have cleared a deal of land. Just look about."

On both sides of the river, wide stump lots were visible and veils of pale blue smoke given off by burning trees, girdled the year before, came drifting over the Altamaha.

Presently, Captain Pearce's gig, sent to bring on board the Independent Highland Company's officers, bumped and thumped alongside.

"Welcome aboard, Major MacKay!" called down Oglethorpe. "Sincere congratulations on having raised so large a company. You can't have left many able men in New Inverness."

"Not too many, sir," replied Major MacKay, lifting his hat and revealing a broad, red-brown face.

As soon as the officers came clumping up to the quarter-deck, a round of introductions followed. Personally, the general presented various officers of his regiment and a number of Charles Town gentlemen who had been inspired to form a corps of mounted volunteers which largely consisted of well-to-do merchants, planters, and their sons.

So expeditiously was the Highland Foot Company's embarkation accomplished that the convoy was enabled to take advantage of the ebb and set sail shortly after noon. By midafternoon, the transports and their guard were scudding down the Guale Coast toward the mouth of the St. John, where the British Army's vanguard already had encamped around Fort St. George, a new, but not powerful, fortification thrown up on the site of that defense which had been demolished during the short-lived armistice of three years ago.

When the low-lying coast of Georgia, smoky as usual, began to turn yellow under the sinking sun, Oglethorpe summoned his staff to the sloop of war's stuffy little wardroom. Only a few officers could find seats, so most had to stand, swaying with the man-of-war's gentle motion, with heads bent to avoid bumping beams supporting the deck above.

Among those present were Captain Richard Norbury and Lieutenant Primrose Maxwell of the Forty-second, Lieutenant Colonel Pierre Lejeau of the South Carolina Militia Regiment, Colonel Stevens of the South Carolina Volunteers, and the Independent Highland Company's senior officers, Major Hugh MacKay, and Captain John MacIntosh.

From the background, Wallace Challenger considered these officers upon whom the success of this venture would largely depend. It would have been difficult, he decided, to assemble men more dissimilar in speech, manner, and dress; consider the patronizing, stiff-backed regulars—most of whom he couldn't get to like—and the informal, easygoing manner of his fellow colonials and the even less disciplined Gentlemen Volunteers. What annoyed the Ranger most of all was the thinly disguised contempt in which Captain Pearce, R.N., held army men—no matter what their organization or origin. And then there was the general, who, now that the invasion was actually under way, had become more reserved and formal, yet at the same time, younger in appearance and more vital in manner.

"I have invited you gentlemen to assemble," Oglethorpe began, "that you may better understand the nature of some of the problems which soon will confront us." Over the slow *creak-creak!* of *Flamborough's* fabric and the dull tramping of feet aloft, he continued, "It is my conviction, gentlemen, that we are about to play a part—a small, but, nevertheless, an important part—in a conflict which may well encompass the globe!"

His voice deepened. "It is very likely that once the French enter this contest, we British will be fighting among the cold forests of Canada, along the Mississippi and on the Gulf. Aye. This war will extend to both coasts of Central and South America, to Europe, to India, to the Mediterranean and even to lands of which none of us yet has heard."

"The French are bound to come in, sir; that is obvious," acidly observed Captain Pearce. "In fact, we may even be at war with the Frog Eaters this very moment."

Ignoring the naval officer's comment, Oglethorpe continued, "In support of my contention, I may inform you gentlemen"—he glanced to the two Scots—"that His Majesty's Government already has equipped and dispatched two powerful expeditions against our Spanish enemies.

"One, under Admiral Vernon, I believe, is due to arrive in Jamaica shortly with the mission of capturing and harrying Spanish possessions in the West Indies and their colonies in Central America.

"At the same time, Commodore Anson, in command of a strong squadron, has been ordered to sail round Cape Horn, enter the Pacific and attack Spanish possessions upon the western coast of South America."

All eyes clung to the commanding general's long, deeply bronzed face.

"It is contemplated that the expeditions led by Anson and Vernon will unite at some mutually convenient point on the Isthmus of Panama and thus divide Spanish colonies in North America from those in the southern hemisphere.

"Since to equip these, and other forces, has strained the Establishment's resources to the utmost"—Oglethorpe spread his hands in a gesture of eloquent resignation—"it stands to reason, gentlemen, that we cannot hope for appreciable reinforcements from Home. However, I am pleased to inform you that a squadron of His Majesty's warships will shortly join those vessels already engaged in blockading the port of St. Augustine."

"Then, sir, they surely will have aboard marines, troops of some sort, who can assist us in this campaign?" suggested Lieutenant Colonel Lejeau.

Oglethorpe shook his head. "That is a reasonable assumption, sir, but unfortunately incorrect. I have been told, and in no uncertain terms, that we are expected to stand upon our own feet and attack the Spaniards so violently that they will weaken their garrisons in Cuba, in Mexico and in Central America."

Burly, sandy-haired Major MacKay spoke up. "Sir, the day before you arrived off New Inverness a coaster brought word that Governor Horcasitas of Cuba has ordered a powerful expedition to sail for the relief of St. Augustine. Do you know, sir, if this is so, or only a rumor?"

"As yet we have received no reliable intelligence to that effect," Oglethorpe evaded while staunching sweat from his forehead.

"May I inquire, sir," Major MacKay asked, "what force have we in these transports?"

At a nod from the general, his aide-de-camp, Major Colleton, spoke up.

"We have aboard this convoy two hundred twenty officers and men of the regiment, one hundred twenty-five Carolina Volunteers, thirty-three gentlemen Volunteers from the same colony and twenty Georgia Rangers which, in addition to your sixty Highlanders, makes a total of around four hundred sixty effectives." He glanced at a notebook. "Already encamped around Fort St. George there are around three hundred Indians and various troops."

Grunted Lieutenant Colonel Lejeau, "To my mind these are hardly enough men to storm a fortress like the castle at St. Augustine—if what we hear about its strength is anywhere near correct."

Oglethorpe quickly raised a hand. "Lest you become discouraged, sir, you should know that the South Carolina Regiment, which numbers around four hundred men and is commanded by Colonel Alexander Vanderdussen, is expected to arrive at Fort St. George within a few days. Also expected is an armed brig from Carolina and a strong squadron of His Majesty's men-of-war. As yet another encouragement you should know that a force of above one thousand Creeks and Cherokees already is on its way to join us."

He raised a brow in Challenger's direction. "Has any word been received concerning the attitude of the Yuchi and Sakwari tribes?"

"Not yet, sir, but I expect to hear something on reaching Fort St. George. Over a month ago, I dispatched two of my smartest Rangers to try to find out what the Panther King aims to do."

Colonel Stevens, staring at fingers steepled before him, drawled, "One thing that bothers me quite a lot, sir, what have we by way of siege artillery? I hear that the walls of Fort St. Mary—also called the Castle—are of stone and *nine* feet thick."

Oglethorpe's expression grew solemn. "Alas, sir, there you have touched upon our greatest weakness. Since we have with us only a few coehorns and middle-sized mortars, we shall be forced to call upon the Navy to furnish the required heavy bombardment."

Captain Pearce uttered a barking laugh. "You may count upon it, sir, *provided* our ships are able to cross a dangerous shoal which bars the entrance to St. Augustine harbor. I trust, therefore, that you will be sent more siege guns."

"We have the promise of some heavy cannon," Oglethorpe said quickly, "but they will be of small advantage unless Colonel Vanderdussen has some trained artillerists in his force."

The spare, red-jacketed figure seated at the mess table's head straightened. "One matter I forgot to mention is that the balance of my regiment, numbering about three hundred men, should reach Fort St. George at about the same time as Colonel Vanderdussen. So, counting sailors and marines, we shall, at a rough estimate, have a force of about twenty-five hundred white troops and at least fifteen hundred Indians with which to reduce the castle and town of St. Augustine."

Chapter 10

FORT ST. GEORGE

The British and their Indian allies lay encamped on the sandy, palmetto- and pine-dotted plain which surrounded Fort St. George on three sides. Advance elements of Oglethorpe's Regiment had pitched their tents in precise rows on flat ground behind the feeble little fort—it mounted but two cannon, one of which was useless because of a plugged touchhole.

More troops, mostly colonial, were encamped on the Florida shore of the St. John. Smoke raised by their campfires went drifting off toward St. Augustine, lying a scant forty miles to the south.

The St. John's estuary was almost clogged by a swarm of anchored pirogues, flatboats, sloops, schooners, and rakish-looking dispatch boats.

Well offshore glinted the snowy topsails and royals of those men-of-war which had established a blockade of the Guale Coast from St. Simon Island to Cape Canaveral.

Following a prolonged search, Major Wallace Challenger finally located his advance party, bivouacked along the western perimeter of the British camp. Until now, this platoon had been under the command of Captain Dempsey, an ex-Indian trader who had survived a deal of frontier fighting. Among his followers were several men from Chaugee Landing: the Wardrop boys, Chauncey and Luke, who'd enlisted in the Rangers hoping to get even for the murder of their parents and small sister. Present also, was Philippe Marrauld, a lithe, darkly handsome stripling, who had deemed the business of "going for soldier" more exciting than the culture of his father's silkworms.

Hendy O'Brien approached with hand outstretched. "God's love, Major! Ye've sure taken yer time joinin' us, but we're *that* glad ye're here at last!"

When Challenger gripped his fist the ex-jockey's wide mouth expanded in a grin, but all the same he was worried to see the major looking so careworn and grave. He little resembled that genial blond giant who'd always been eager for a fight, a frolic, or a horse race.

"Came as fast as I was able. Y'see, Hendy, there's more to waging a war than blazing away at somebody you think you might not like. How are the horses?"

"The best in camp." Hendy chuckled. "And that's not braggin'. Most o' them billy goats the Carolina dandies have brought down with 'em are the sorriest lot of crow baits I've seen in a long time."

Challenger turned to Captain Dempsey, a spare, sharp-featured man of about forty, who claimed that, under torture by the Catawbas, his hair had turned snow-white during his early twenties. "Say, Charley, either Felton or Bartow come in yet?"

"Reckon not. Why?"

"Just wondered. While back, I sent 'em among the Yuchis and Sakwaris."

Hendy noticed that as the major pronounced the word "Sakwari" his sweat-shiny, red-brown features contracted momentarily. Of course, everybody at Chaugee Landing had known for some time that Micah Oxford and Winsome Challenger had settled down in Capola, where the Yorker had taken over James Adair's trading post. Privately, the little Irishman wondered just what had taken place when the major's runaway wife had come face to face with the Panther King and his red-haired wife. Studying the big man's deeply lined face, he decided that he'd rather not occupy the eloped couple's shoes when, and if, Wallace Challenger caught up with them.

As Dempsey and his superior inspected a picket line along which the troop's horses snuffled and switched flies, the latter reported, "Along with Toonahowie's Yamacraws and Captain Tom Jones's warriors we've been scouting 'crost the river."

"Captain Tom Jones? Who in hell's he?"

"A half-breed Creek mico you'll hear plenty about before long."

"What else you been doing, Charley?"

"We've been tryin' to keep the Lobsterbacks the general sent here ahead of him out of trouble. Honest to God, they ain't got squirrel-sense about gettin' along in this country."

"What do you make of the Forty-second? They likely to prove dependable?"

"Guess so. For the most part they're young and strong, but not too smart. Once they've learned our kind of fighting I allow they'll likely render themselves useful." The white-haired Ranger smiled. "I saw that when, 'bout a fortni't ago, we rode point when they marched to take a couple of little forts the Spaniards built back of St. Augustine on either side of the St. John to protect their line of supply from the Gulf."

"How are these forts named?"

"Picolata and San Francisco de Pupa. Right now, a bunch of fellers from Carolina are garrisoning 'em." Dempsey then treated his towering commanding officer to a brief glance. "Tell me, Wallace, are them Carolina fellers *really* going to give us all the support they promised us last spring?"

"If you mean eight hundred men and some siege guns, we'll be lucky if we see even the half of it. Howsomever, Charley, I've heard that Colonel Vanderdussen *will* be coming in with around four hundred South Carolina militia any day now."

The two officers wheeled to watch the approach of a runner who came trotting over from the main Indian encampment.

The message was from Toonahowie. He said that his men had brought in a Negro prisoner who claimed to have deserted from Fort Diego, lying about halfway between the St. John and St. Augustine.

This fort, in fact, was a private fortification, owned and maintained by a wealthy mulatto named Don Diego Spinola. The African stated that, for some reason, about half of the Spanish regulars had been recalled to St. Augustine and those who had been left behind were hungry and greatly dispirited by the presence of so many Creek and Cherokee scouting parties.

Toonahowie, after making his old friend welcome, produced a jug of captured Spanish brandy and served his guests a generous measure. Unsmiling, the late Tomo-chichi's nephew raised a wooden cup. "Now that you, Major, and General Oglethorpe have arrived we will cut the enemy as meat for pemmican."

A bit flattered, Challenger couldn't help laughing. "You rank me with too fine company! How d'you know whether I'll be of any use in fightin' a siege?"

The young Yamacraw mico thlucco, who appeared to have adopted something of Tomo-chichi's sedate manner, said quietly, "I doubt if you will be called to fight against walls. There is too much scouting, raiding and patrolling to be done. I am sure our general will not misuse your skills or mine, nor do I think he will neglect this fine opportunity to take Fort Diego."

As usual, Challenger was secretly amused to hear English so well spoken by a full-blooded Indian.

Darkness had fallen before the African deserter was brought into Oglethorpe's presence in that little log and sand fort around which scarlet-jacketed sentries walked their posts as stolidly as ever they had in Gibraltar or in Ireland.

When he had heard the Negro's story and had caused him to repeat it several times to determine whether the fellow was lying, Oglethorpe at once made up his mind and called a council of war. As a result, a hundred of Oglethorpe's Regiment, one hundred Carolina Volunteers, a sprinkling of Carolina militia, and a few officers and men of the Independent Highland, who'd begged to go along, were ordered to prepare to move out with first daylight.

As for Wallace Challenger, he received instructions of a different nature; he and his Georgia Rangers, together with a body of Indians largely composed of Cherokees—the Creek main force under Malatachi and a Raven named Caesar had not yet arrived—were to cross the river shortly before dawn and make for Fort Diego at their best speed.

Once on the scene, they were ordered to engage the garrison's attention, cut off reinforcements, and create such a racket that the Spaniards would assume that they were being attacked by strong forces.

The British main body, meantime, would advance over the sixteen miles that separated Fort Diego from Fort St. George as rapidly as possible. That his march promised to be an ordeal Oglethorpe foresaw; the terrain to be traversed reported to be of loose sand most of the way, treeless, and devoid of water.

Challenger found it a real luxury to shed his hot and uncomfortable regimentals and don the Rangers' loose and comfortable campaign garments—Indian leggings, buckskin breeches, and hunting shirt of homespun. That he'd enjoyed only a couple of hours of sleep since quitting H.B.M.S. *Flamborough* didn't bother him in the least.

He strode among men inspecting their equipment and seeing to it that they washed and curried their mounts' saddle places. It was a relief to note how well Philippe Marrauld and the Wardrop boys were catching on. As a final gesture toward the home folks, Challenger made Hendy O'Brien a corporal and detailed him to be his personal orderly. When he learned of this, the little Irishman beamed from ear to ear and strutted about camp, pleased as a happy dog with two tails.

A little before midnight, chunkily-built, florid and laconic Captain Dunbar of the regiment rode into the Rangers' camp bearing additional instructions and an order that he be allowed to accompany the scouting force as an observer. Challenger didn't mind. George Dunbar didn't much resemble the rest of the Forty-second's hardheaded and harder-drinking line officers; that he was of Scottish origin might account for the fact that he seemed eager to learn how war was waged in America, whereas most of his fellows clung tenaciously to tactics and concepts laboriously drilled into them since first they'd entered the King's Service.

Captain Dunbar had brought along a pair of dispatch riders fortunately mounted on good animals. After reporting himself, the regular stood to one side silently studying the Rangers as, smoking and talking, they waited beside their drowsing horses. Dunbar made a swift count of this scouting force and figured that, including Major Challenger and Captain Charles Dempsey, the Georgia Rangers numbered thirty-five men in all.

Captain Dempsey Dunbar considered with special attention, knowing, as he did, that this striking individual had been one of the commissioners sent by Oglethorpe to St. Augustine to negotiate the armistice of 1736—which had been so quickly repudiated by Spain.

For all his white hair Charles Dempsey could not have seen more than his fortieth birthday and his face was distinctive because, at some time in the past, a vicious blow had broken his long, thin nose and had slewed it to the right at almost a thirty-degree angle. Somewhere, Dunbar had heard it said that this shrewd former Indian trader entertained by no means modest political ambitions.

The Rangers and their horses swung heads at the shadowy approach of a body of Indians commanded by the unpredictable Creek half-breed known as Captain Tom Jones. He too was remarkable because when he strode into the ring of firelight it was noticeable that his left eyelid drooped, which lent him a peculiarly sinister expression.

Most of his feathered and soft-treading warriors were dismounted Cherokees, all painted for war. Immediately afterward, appeared a small reinforcement consisting of nine dismounted Creek warriors led by the redoubtable Toonahowie.

After conferring briefly with the Indian leaders, Wallace Challenger gave the order to move. So, in a loose column, the expedition set out under starlight so brilliant it proved easy to pick a route down to the St. John where enough flatboats to ferry over the entire detachment lay waiting.

Chapter 11

FORT DIEGO I

Standing beside his horse on a low bluff rising on the St. John's southern bank, Quobah Tutu, the self-styled Kumassee King, strained eyes across the river's black and star-dotted surface. While he made a quick estimate of the number of enemy campfires redly winking and blinking on either side of the river's mouth, the old hatred commenced to stir within him; his wide but thin lips contracted and exposed his pointed teeth while the cicatrices on his forehead rippled into a ferocious scowl.

Yonder lay the accursed English, a nation whose people had never caused him and his race other than grief and pain, sorrow and death!

Long since, he'd seen that this was the nation to fear if he and his people were to remain free—not the French or the Spanish.

Slowly, but inexorably, the British had kept on pushing their way southward, avowedly prepared to enslave or re-enslave every Negro or part Negro they came across.

Possibly, he conjectured, the English wouldn't or couldn't accomplish their object immediately, but surely they would, the moment they grew strong enough, for there weren't nearly enough slave laborers in North America to make the white men rich or to spare the humbler sort bitter toil under a pitiless sun.

With the night breeze from the ocean stirring the gold fringe on his scarlet turban's end and tickling his scarred cheek, the giant Ashanti allowed his mind to run back to that memorable day when he'd approached Sakwari-cra about raiding that plantation in Carolina and decided that the white Tuscarora's blunt refusal had been the deepest disappointment of his life. That his old friend and blood brother should have led the Ranger detachment which had thwarted his project still remained incomprehensible. It was then that, for the first time, he'd begun to wonder just how much of an Indian Thad Burton really was. And to think that Sakwari-cra was largely to blame for the useless state of his arm!

Could the Panther King possibly be among those slaveholders across the river? If only he were! But this appeared unlikely. Every report reaching St. Augustine agreed that Sakwari-cra intended to remain neutral.

The big Ashanti scowled again when he reflected how that great slave uprising he had helped to plan had proved such a dismal failure; less than two hundred escaped Negroes had survived to cross the St. John to be baptized into the Roman faith and so earn their freedom.

When a horse snuffled in a hollow behind him, the Ashanti snarled a command to keep the beast quiet. Bitterly, he regretted that Captain Diego Spinola, commanding at Fort Diego, had allowed him so few men to conduct this patrol. As it was, he'd with him only four fellow Africans and half-a-dozen Yamasees who were acting insolent and surly over finding themselves commanded by a Negro.

A little wearily, Quobah listened to familiar night noises: the roaring of alligators, the querulous hooting of owls, the grumbling of bullfrogs, and, now and then, the croak of a heron, but the Ashanti's round, little eyes continued to probe the far bank at that point where some flatboats had been assembled for some yet undetermined project.

All at once he started, then peered intently through starlight and made out a dark rivulet of men descending the bank toward the scows! So the English were on the move! The Ashanti's anger returned and swelled as, sharply, he beckoned the Left Arm who'd replaced the one killed at Chaugee Landing.

The starlight was so strong that the Kumassee King could recognize an occasional flash of steel and the breeze had become so feeble that, distinctly, he could hear low-pitched voices and the splash of horses being unsaddled for being swum across.

Pretty quickly, Quobah estimated that over yonder must be around ten-times-ten fighting men—therefore this could not be the main British force on the move; only a powerful detachment whose mission he needed to grasp without delay.

Again his resentment flared against Captain Diego Spinola. *Kwee!* Had he been given twice-ten more men it would have been possible to exact a very heavy crossing fee from the British!

He called his principal Yamasee, told him in guttural undertones, "Ride back to the fort. Tell Señor Spinola a strong enemy party is crossing."

The savage jerked a nod that sent lank, shoulder-long hair to rippling below the cloth band he wore twisted about his head.

"Tell him I watch, will see where they go."

The Yamasee at once swung onto a pony and trotted off across a lush savannah bordered with turkey pines and coontie plants. Soon he merged with the shadowy background.

Quobah gathered his men below the skyline. Several looked apprehensive about the enemy's numbers, so Quobah abandoned his first impulse to wait in ambush and shoot up the leading flatboat when it was about to discharge its passengers. Almost necessarily, this craft would be conveying the detachment's officers.

As it was, the Ashanti and his followers rode upriver to a low knoll from which they could make an accurate count of the enemy's strength as they clambered onto the riverbank. It was discouraging to note how quick the invaders were about resaddling their still-dripping mounts; nor was it reassuring to see so many scalp-hungry Indians accompanying this force.

Since his bridle-holding hand was useless, Quobah, never a first-class horseman, met with some difficulty in leading his little column through tangles of dahoons, scrub oaks, and saw palmettoes on a route which paralleled this column of swift and silent enemies. It wasn't long before the African prince decided two things: first, that these invaders undoubtedly were making for Fort Diego; second, that, judging by the speed at which they were traveling, they'd attain their objective well before daylight.

For some reason the enemy's point unexpectedly reined toward that cedar copse in which the Ashanti and his followers stood concealed, gripping their mounts' ears and forcing down their heads—a horse cannot whicker with its head lowered. The enemy rode by so close that Quobah found no difficulty in recognizing Toonahowie and that huge blond Ranger who, with Sakwari-cra, had shattered his hopes before Major Smollett's plantation.

Quobah's good hand closed over the cool, brassbound butt of a pistol. At such a range he could not possibly have missed, but, just in time, the Ashanti remembered his mission. Besides, it would be foolish to warn these enemies that their presence had been observed. Grinding his teeth in futile rage, the African watched the Rangers ride by, made note of the presence of an officer and two other riders wearing British regimentals among the colonials who, as usual, looked hard and capable in their shapeless garb. He recognized the Indians, padding softly along, like gray-brown ghosts, as Cherokees and didn't like it—next to the Chickasaws the Cherokees were the best fighters in all the Southeast.

Minutes after the enemy became lost to sight and sound, Quobah gave the signal to mount, then, crossing the invaders' trail, he set out for Fort Diego at a brisk canter. His scouting party ought to arrive in time to prepare an unexpectedly hot reception when the British attempted to rush the fort at daybreak.

"The fort must have been warned," grunted Toonahowie, crouched among trees near the edge of that wide clearing in which stood the fort and its palisade.

"Why so?" whispered Captain Dunbar.

"I see no horses or cattle standing around, no pigs, no fowls. Nobody is getting breakfast in any of those houses." He pointed to a cluster of white-painted huts standing on low brick stilts just west of Fort Diego, which was square-shaped and built of tabby stone. Its second floor was studded with loopholes and its flat roof crenelated as if to accommodate swivel guns and lightweight cannon.

A short flagpole, flying a ragged ensign of some sort, sprouted from the top of the fort, which stood alone in the center of an area enclosed by a tall palisade of pointed cedar logs.

"I don't like the looks of this either; still, when it gets lighter we'll get on with our business," Challenger grunted. "Toonahowie, I want you to lead half the Indians through the woods to the left, till you're opposite the south wall. Captain Jones"—he treated the half-breed to a hard look—"you and the rest of the warriors will circle around to face the north wall. Me and my men will charge the main gate. Don't make a move till you hear the conch bugle sound."

That the garrison of Fort Diego had been forewarned became only too evident, for when the conch shell sounded its eerie, mooing notes to send the raiders, yipping and yelling, out of the woods, the attackers were only halfway across the five-hundred-yard-wide clearing when swivel guns banged and all along the fort's parapets—forty feet on a side—blazed flashes and the rattle and bang of musketry.

Major Wallace Challenger instantly ordered his bugler to sound the retreat; not for a moment was he overlooking the fact that this mission was not to try to take, but to demonstrate around, the fort until the main body under Oglethorpe could reach the scene.

Perhaps because they retained the red man's ingrained fear of artillery, Toonahowie's and Tom Jones's Indians for once did as they were ordered and bolted back to the woods. The Rangers, too, were glad enough to pull foot, the prospect of charging nearly a hundred yards across open ground in the face of fire delivered from behind thick stone walls was not attractive to such practical fighting men.

Thanks to the swiftness of Challenger's decision, not a man of his command had been hurt by the time they regained the shelter of the trees.

Panting, Dunbar reined in his horse beside the commanding officer. "Well, sir, and what do we do now?"

Bright blue eyes hard and piercing, Challenger snapped, "Mr. Dunbar, we ain't going to *do* a damn' thing. I only want you, Captain Dempsey, and the Indian leaders to throw a loose skirmish line about the fort. From time to time your men will run or ride out into the open, fire a few shots and then get to hell back into the woods. Tell 'em to yell and make all the noise they can. The enemy's got to think they've got a powerful force to deal with."

Drawled Captain Dempsey, "Say, Wallace, about when c'n we expect the general and the Lobsterbacks to show up for the party?"

Captain Dunbar flushed, snapped, "Captain, sir, I'll thank you not to refer to His Majesty's troops as Lobsterbacks."

Dempsey grinned like a friendly wolf. "All right, mister, then when are the regulars and the rest likely to appear?"

"On that score I can make no prediction, sir," the lieutenant said stiffly. "I only know that the general expected to bivouac his troops last night at a place called Lacanela. With any luck, he should appear by midday."

"Well, I'll sure be surprised if he does," drawled Captain Dempsey.

"Why so?"

"Well, yesterday it was powerful hot and those foot soldiers in their fancy dress parade uniforms must ha' suffered aplenty before they reached Lacanela—if they got there at all."

Challenger spoke sharply. "Be that as it may, I want you fellows to go and— Oh, goddamit to hell!"

Some Cherokees had run out from the trees and could be seen swarming about the house farthest from the fort. Some of them were pursuing a few hard-running black-skinned figures which quickly were overtaken. The Indians leaped onto the fugitives' backs and rode them, struggling, to the ground; tomahawks and knives flashed and screeching scalp yells arose. Moments later, tendrils of smoke began to rise from the building.

"I protest, sir!" Dunbar burst out. "This is *contra* the general's order that there shall be no pillaging or destruction!"

Half amused, Wallace Challenger treated this young fellow in the scarlet tunic to a taut smile. "I know that just as well as you, Mr. Dunbar; suppose you go tell them to stop."

Twenty minutes later, Fort Diego lay encircled by a loose, barely visible cordon of besiegers. At intervals the attackers would dash out in the open, fire a few shots at the parapets and then retreat as soon as the defenders opened fire.

About half-past one a sweat-soaked galloper brought information that General Oglethorpe and the main body were only a mile away.

At two of the afternoon a screen of Carolina Rangers made their appearance, shortly before the general and his staff, all cruelly sunburned, rode up to Wallace Challenger's command post, established in the shade of a grove of sycamores. Before long appeared the advance guard of what once had been an orderly column of regulars. Most of the soldiers long since had stripped off crossbelts and scarlet tunics.

They looked half dead from thirst after their tortured advance among those broiling sand dunes which lined the seacoast. Dispiritedly, they shambled into the cool of the woods grumbling and carrying their equipment any which way.

To even the most inexperienced officer present it was abundantly evident that these troops and the equally exhausted South Carolina Volunteers who straggled in shortly afterward were dead-beat, weren't fit to accomplish anything this day.

Chapter 12

FORT DIEGO II

On the night of his arrival, the commanding general thickened the cordon about Fort Diego, sent out parties of Rangers and Indians to scout for enemy reinforcements, which persistent rumors had on their way from St. Augustine. There was cause for vigilance; the relieving troops could arrive at any time, since the capital of Florida lay only twelve miles to the south-southeast.

After the searing temperatures of the preceding day—the heat had been so intolerable that over a hundred soldiers had fainted on the march and two of them had died—the cool winds that began to blow up the St. John after nightfall came at first as a blessed relief to regulars and colonials alike, but soon they began to shiver as, endlessly, they cursed mosquitoes and midges which, by the million, pounced upon their ill-smelling victims.

The garrison of Fort Diego, however, continued on the alert. Whenever anyone appeared on that great clearing which encircled Fort Diego muskets blazed and spent bullets thudded into the parched and sandy ground.

While the besiegers might have to subsist on meager rations—already it was rumored that nowhere near enough provisions had been brought along—there was no need for anyone to go thirsty; any number of clear, fresh-water ponds dotted this rich country, so greatly at variance with the scorching sand dunes and scrub-covered plains near the seacoast.

The sun had yet to appear over the treetops when Oglethorpe sent for his senior officers, who included snappish Major Colleton, his personal aide-de-camp, Lieutenant de Saussure, frosty-haired Captain Dempsey—Challenger was absent on duty—and Captain Richard Wingst of the Gentlemen Volunteers from South Carolina. Also present were Captain Horton of the Regiment and Major MacKay of the Highland Company. His Indian allies were represented by Captain Tom Jones and Toonahowie; the latter obviously resented the Creek half-breed's presence.

"I have summoned you gentlemen," the general announced briskly, "to hear the terms I presently shall offer the enemy commander."

Expectantly, the officers moved closer.

"First: Señor Diego Spinola shall have a guarantee that he and his garrison will be accorded all the rights required by the laws of war. Second: the enemy, with the exception of weapons, shall retain their personal possessions."

Captain Tom Jones, his sagging eyelid drooping lower than ever, growled, "Then we are not to be allowed to strip those dogs naked and take their goods?"

"Certainly not!"

"But, General," Jones protested hotly, "that is the way we always treat enemies too cowardly to surrender without a fight."

Coldly Oglethorpe's close-set, dark eyes fixed the arrogant half-Creek. "Such may be the custom among *your* people, but it is not the way of the British Army.

"Third: Señor Spinola will be allowed to retain possession of all his property, including slaves."

"My God, sir!" burst out Captain Wingst. "You mean we ain't allowed to replace slaves stolen by these same Spanish villains?"

Oglethorpe was at pains to appear sympathetic. "I quite understand your point of view, sir, but at this moment I do not deem it wise to make the enemy fear that they will lose everything through capitulation."

"Hell! Why traffic with a greasy mulatto?" exploded Captain Hodbury, red-whiskered and slab-sided face turning redder still under his sunburn. "Why don't we just take this damn' little fort and have done with it? What we need, sir, is to blood our troops, and at the same time throw the fear of God into the Dons in St. Augustine! Think how such a victory will enhance your military reputation!"

Paint-streaked features expressionless, Toonahowie spoke up. "Yes. An attack should be made; the general should know that many warriors are impatient to win the scalps and booty which they were led to believe would be theirs."

A dull red tinge spread out over Oglethorpe's high and prominent cheek bones. "Toonahowie, old friend, I will answer you as best I can. Suppose I order a general assault on the fort; how many of our men will be killed or wounded? The fort yonder mounts sufficient swivel guns and cannon which, if they are well served, easily can destroy fifty or sixty of our number.

"If you think that, at this time, we can afford such a loss"—he drew a quick breath—"I most emphatically do not!"

He now addressed the other Indian. "As regards fighting, your warriors soon will have more than enough of it; concerning the plunder which you may discover in this fort, you will do well to recall that you already have received valuable presents and stand to receive more, in addition to your regular pay as allies of His Majesty's forces."

The commanding general's gaze successively came to rest upon all the officers standing about in fresh morning sunlight now beginning to sift through the treetops. "When, as and if St. Augustine falls, will be time to reopen the matter of plunder, but not until then.

"Finally"—this time he directed his attention to Captain Wingst—"if any fugitive slaves are found in the fort, sir, rest assured that they will be returned to their owners. In the meantime, I will thank you to remember, sir, that we have not embarked upon this campaign for the sole purpose of reimbursing or supplying slaveholders in South Carolina."

His manner changed as he slipped a plain, heavy-bladed sword into its sling. "Captain Dunbar, pray fetch me an intelligent-appearing fellow from among our prisoners."

A few moments later, a pair of redcoats tramped up with a Spaniard slouching between them. Crumpling a battered palmetto hat, the prisoner stood before Oglethorpe with head bowed; beneath his dirty white shirt and pantaloons he was shaking with fright.

Through an interpreter the general began, "Pray present my compliments to the commander of the valiant garrison of Fort Diego." He broke off. "I say, tell this fellow to look up and that he has nothing to fear."

When the prisoner raised fear-haunted brown eyes, Oglethorpe restated his terms and added but a single point. "Lastly, runaway slaves from Carolina or deserters from the British services cannot expect to be treated as honorable prisoners of war. They must be surrendered at discretion. Do you understand?"

The brown-faced prisoner emitted a sigh of relief, then, smiling, jerked a series of nods. "Sí, Illustríssimo General. To Señor Spinola I will repeat exactly what you have said."

It came about, therefore, that at about ten o'clock of the morning a drummer from the regulars commenced to beat a parley. Then, in company with the prisoner and a tall sergeant who kept waving a white neckerchief secured to his espantoon, he set out from the shelter of the woods.

Rangers, regulars, colonial militia, and Indians appeared on the clearing's rim and, displaying a rare mixture of emotions, watched the space between the white flag and the palisade decrease. How thin and lonely that drumbeat sounded! Although many soldiers cursed, there were more onlookers who vented sighs of satisfaction when the fort's gate creaked open just far enough to admit the white-clad emissary. Once the Spaniard had disappeared, both regulars about-faced and, grinning broadly, started back over the broad, sun-lashed clearing.

About an hour passed before a ragged shout arose because Fort Diego's weather-beaten red and yellow flag had commenced, jerkily, to descend.

Chapter 13

REINFORCEMENTS

At about the same time that the formalities of surrender were being observed at Fort Diego, Major Wallace Challenger and a detachment of Rangers had started back to camp, following a sweep of the countryside which had yielded fifty horses badly needed by the Army. Since, for some time, no shots had been heard in the distance, Challenger guessed that Don Diego Spinola must have given up; to further this suspicion, he noticed that carrion birds, which always hung around when guns were going off, had commenced to disperse.

The Rangers, herding the captured horses through clouds of choking dust, were still some miles short of Fort St. George when Hendy O'Brien, who'd been riding on the party's extreme left flank, came galloping up to Challenger. "Sor! Sor! There's a damn' lot of horsemen ridin' in from the north."

"You're sure they're comin' from the *north?*"

"Aye, sor! And by the noise they make, sounds like they're maybe a hundred strong!"

That no friendly cavalry could be advancing from a northly direction Challenger was well aware, so, gathering the reins, he snapped, "Ride for the general's field headquarters and give the alarm. Let's see how fast that nag ye're always braggin' about c'n travel."

The ex-jockey didn't even bother to salute, only put Ardnagashel to a surging gallop which, in a few minutes, nearly got him shot by a nervous sentinel posted outside Fort Diego.

The clearing, Hendy saw, now was dotted with scarlet-coated regulars and militia, a few of whom wore dirty green or blue uniform jackets but, generally, they were clad in drab-hued civilian clothes. The former garrison, consisting of some sixty dark-faced men, mostly dressed in dingy white shifts and pantaloons, was sitting or standing dispiritedly in the midst of a hollow square formed by the Regiment.

When the commanding general received Hendy's report he unhurriedly, and in a calm voice, issued orders that all mounted men in the vicinity should form in a column of fours prepared to move out at once.

While spurring to the column's head, Oglethorpe told Colonel Palmer of the South Carolina Volunteers, "I feel there is every reason to believe that the force detected by the Rangers is that reinforcement Don Diego has been expecting."

Even as the ragtag cavalry column moved out, Captain Wingst commenced to divide captured arms among the Indian allies—a step Oglethorpe calculated, correctly enough, that would go a long way toward smoothing their ruffled feelings.

At the head of about forty alert and keyed-up horsemen, Oglethorpe followed O'Brien into woods which appeared steadily to grow denser until almost any space could have concealed an ambush. The general, therefore, was both surprised and pleased to note that, trotting behind the riders was a pack of painted Cherokees. Superb runners, they had small trouble in keeping up with horses through such difficult terrain.

At length, Hendy reined in so sharply that his great stallion reared. "If the enemy's kept on the way they was headed, sor, you ought to find 'em on the far side of yonder ridge."

At the prospect of coming under fire for the first time since the siege of Belgrade, James Oglethorpe recaptured a once-familiar sense of exhilaration when, drawing his campaign sword, he bent to avoid low branches and spurred his charger up the slope. Without being told, his followers trotted out on each flank and formed a line of skirmishers.

On gaining the ridge's crest, Oglethorpe's heart gave a great surge, for, on the counterslope was milling a body of dark-complexioned riders in broad hats, yellow jackets, and white pantaloons. The instant they sighted them, the Cherokees howled blood-chilling war cries and bounded forward; the white men raised a deep shout and the whole force swept down upon the larger enemy array.

Soon, British muskets began to boom, but did little damage because the enemy didn't linger to meet the onslaught; they fired only a few random shots before wheeling their horses and racing wildly off in a northerly direction, toward the St. John.

After the chase had covered but a few hundred yards it appeared that not a few Spaniards must be astride inferior animals; the better mounted among the British began to overhaul them. Oglethorpe, among the foremost, shouted like any subaltern as he swung his heavy-bladed sword and cut down a bearded Spaniard who went rolling over and over among the trees like a shot hare.

For a brief moment, tumult reigned: Indian screechings, white men's yelling blended with a clatter of pistol shots; shrieks and cries of pain arose as more saddles were emptied.

The enemy retreat degenerated into a headlong rout when Challenger's Rangers poured down a low hill onto the Spanish flank, killed a couple of men, and took several prisoners before the Spaniards, abandoning their most cumbersome weapons, scattered through the woods and became lost to sight.

The Creeks and Rangers found it easy to track the main enemy body, but the going became so difficult that, by the time the first British closed in on what must be the landing place for Fort Diego, they found it deserted save for a pair of twenty-oar half galleys and a number of riderless horses. Three other, well-crowded half galleys could be seen pulling furiously for the St. John's northern bank.

The commanding general was jubilant to learn that, although his men had slain, wounded, or taken prisoner over two dozen of the enemy, they had not suffered a single casualty themselves.

A terror-stricken Spanish subaltern called out in anguish when a group of Cherokee warriors started to close in, wearing evil expressions and jerking out long-bladed knives. "*Por el amor de Dios!*" screamed the thin-faced cavalryman. "Remember, we are prisoners of war! Do not let your savages kill us."

Oglethorpe, waving in his officers, rode his horse between the snarling Indians and their prey. "Be assured, *señores*, you have nothing to fear!"

Curtly, he then ordered the Rangers to surround the prisoners so that the Cherokees, yammering in thwarted rage, were forced to fall back and content themselves by grabbing abandoned equipment.

Leaving Captain Dunbar, and Lieutenants Hogan and De Saussure and fifty men to garrison Fort Diego, General James Oglethorpe, first thing next morning, started back to the camps near the St. John's mouth.

The victors departed in two contingents; one, largely composed of infantry, guarded the prisoners—black, brown, and white—and felt themselves lucky that they hadn't been left behind to throw up various earthworks Oglethorpe had laid out in order to strengthen the fort—he intended using it as a northern base. The place should prove invaluable when it came time to besiege and attack the capital of Spanish Florida.

The other contingent was smaller, being composed of the commanding general, his staff, and nearly all of the mounted officers. They proceeded at the best speed possible under a searing, murderous sun.

Riding point were Major Challenger and Captain Dempsey, together with that hot-blooded Carolinian Captain Wingst. A bright trickle of sweat escaped the sodden handkerchief Challenger had bound around his head like a skullcap and upon which his palmetto straw perched at a ludicrous angle.

Before long, the estuary of the St. John, with its dark flotilla of transports, supply ships, and guardian cruisers, should be sighted through the shimmering heat. Glancing sidewise at Charley Dempsey, Wallace saw that he was riding loose in the saddle, just the way Jamie MacPherson had used to. How much he missed that dour, capable, and dependable veteran! Too bad Jamie'd been ordered to stay near Coweta and make certain that neither Chikilly nor Malatchi wavered in their loyalty to His Majesty, King George II.

Luke Wardrop, who was blessed with unusually keen vision, suddenly called out, "Say, Major, I spy a Lobsterback ridin' this way!"

He spoke only an instant before the distant horseman disappeared into a fold in the hot, desolate, and sandy terrain. The rider presently turned out to be a lieutenant of the Regiment who excitedly wanted to know where the commanding general might be found. When told, he spurred his lathered mount onward at such a furious pace that Hendy O'Brien shook his head.

"That fellow keeps up such a pace much longer, he's goin' to find himself afoot and goddam thirsty."

News brought by the dispatch rider was fine as could be. He reported that another contingent of Oglethorpe's Regiment already had landed under command of Lieutenant Colonel William Cook. Also come ashore was a company of mounted Highlanders and important elements of the

South Carolina Militia. Best of all, nearly five hundred Indians, Creeks for the most part, had made their appearance and were encamped on the Florida shore of the St. John. Malatchi and a Raven named Caesar were supposed to be leading them.

The reinforcements raised to an apex the spirits of those troops who, short of food and water and tormented by a variety of insects, had been broiling among dunes and on sand beaches around Fort St. George and across the river. So many small transports and supply ships now lay in the estuary that navigation was getting to be a problem. Swiftly, elation ebbed; nobody knew for sure how many supplies, or of what sort, had been brought along. Only one thing was certain; no heavy cannon or siege guns were aboard the new arrivals.

Following the commanding general's orders, most of the reinforcements were landed on the Florida shore to join the Regiment, which already had been concentrated there in anticipation of a general advance upon St. Augustine. Perhaps, intentionally, the bulk of the colonial forces and the Indian allies remained, sweltering, on the Georgia side.

Wallace Challenger, stripped to the waist, washed dust and sweat from his face before a stained little tent Hendy had found, then went in to snatch a bit of sleep. He'd had less than an hour's rest before Hendy began tugging at his bare foot.

"Sor, there's a couple o' yer Rangers outside. They need to speak to you, immediate-like."

Yawning, muscles rippling over his deeply tanned torso, Challenger stepped out into the blazing sunlight to find Sergeant Felton and Corporal Bartow awaiting him.

Grinning through short, sun-bleached beards, the Rangers vigorously pumped hands with their half-naked commander.

Challenger burst out, "Well, and how did you bastards make out in Capola?"

Felton summoned an almost impudent, snaggle-toothed grin. "Why, Cap'n"—he'd never grown accustomed to his superior's promotion— "reckon there's somebody over there can tell you better'n we can. Eh, Sam?"

"Reckon so."

The sergeant pointed to a very tall man who stood waiting in the shade of a clump of saw pines. Recognition did not come immediately, but when it did, Wallace Challenger could only gape.

The big man was wearing a headdress of delicate egret plumes bound into place by a strip of scarlet cloth; streaks of red and black war paint descended his cheeks and neck all the way down to the opening of a homespun hunting shirt. Otherwise, he was dressed like a frontiersman in buckskin breeches, leggings, and ankle-high moccasins such as commonly were favored by Rangers.

It seemed hard to credit that yonder was standing Sakwari-cra, the Panther King.

Chapter 14

A LIEUTENANT OF MILITIA

For several in the small group assembled at the edge of the Ranger's encampment, this moment became memorable. For several moments, the two massive figures remained separated by a good twenty feet of sandy ground and stared fixedly, shrewdly at one another—expressionless.

Felton and Bartow were recalling that tricky visit they'd made to Sakwari-cra's village following the murder of Brodbelt's party. Thad Burton, as they'd already learned, was greatly changed since then. Except for his egret headdress, silver-and-turquoise earrings, and war paint, the mico thlucco of the Sakwaris resembled most of the Rangers now hurrying up from all directions, anxious to witness what was about to happen.

Umpychi who, with mixed emotions, had watched the Sakwaris' arrival with Malatchi's Creeks, thought back to that brief but bloody fight above War Club Pond. The Yamacraw Raven was interested to notice that, since he'd last seen him, the Panther King's hair had been cut as short, or shorter, than that of most white men in Oglethorpe's force. Fleetingly, he recalled that flight from the scene of battle, then, in deep satisfaction, how, with consummate skill, he'd lured Shatara and his raging Sakwaris away from Challenger until he'd been ready to shake them off and return to the stricken captain.

Thad thought, How can he look at me so boldly? Every grownup in Chaugee Landing and Savannah knows that he's a cuckold whose wife ran away with an ignorant timber beast. Long ago I could have had Oxford killed and, certainly, I could have taken Winsome anytime I wanted after they'd come to live near Capola. How sad are the depths of this big fellow's eyes. Perhaps, because he so nearly killed me. Yes. I'll take his wife for a concubine when I return from this war. It will be a fine revenge against this proud man.

The one-eyed Chickasaw sub-mico, Chula, was wondering what Sakwari-cra was likely to do; after all, this yellow-headed Ranger had come within a finger's breadth of sending him to live forever in the Happy Hunting Ground. Yes. Sooner or later a fight must take place; especially if the mico thlucco taunted the white man about his faithless wife.

Wallace Challenger, at the same time, strove to conquer seething and conflicting emotions. Desperately as he resented Winsome's conduct, he intended to find out what had become of her. Was she happy with Mike Oxford? Did she now appreciate the extent of harm she'd done? Did she fear the retribution he expected someday to exact?

While his bright blue eyes bored unwaveringly into Burton's cold gray ones, he quivered inwardly. What if Helen Glen had been right when she'd cried, "Don't judge Winsome too severely because she went rushing off. Remember, she was half out of her mind over Robbie's murder and that you weren't there to have prevented it." Hastily, she'd added, "You've no idea how lonely Winsome was and how she grieved whenever you went away."

He remembered demanding harshly, "D'you mean to say that Oxford didn't have to persuade her or take her by force?"

Helen's smooth features had crumpled. "I wish I could say so, Wallace, but, being in the state of mind she was, she went almost eagerly."

The furious cawing of crows battling with buzzards over some choice bit of garbage sounded in the near distance—that and the rhythmic *thunk-thunk!* of hand drums in the Creek encampment seemed to intensify the taut silence.

Wallace Challenger caught his breath, but then decided to wait for Sakwari-cra to speak first. Thad Burton remained silent, standing straight as any British grenadier, with his long rifle canted over the bend of his left elbow.

For once Thad hardly knew his own mind: yonder stood the man who had done so much toward shaping his life, in fact, ever since that time they'd ridden off together to thwart Quobah's raid. There was something impressive about this former Carolinian who had so nearly terminated his dreams of an empire. It was, perhaps, fortunate that James Adair, long ago, had convinced him of that expedition's real purpose, so now he had no real excuse for killing the Ranger major—or trying to.

Thad ended the hiatus by slowly passing his hand over a thin whitish streak in his hair which marked the bullet's course. "Greetings, Major Challenger," said he evenly. "I have this, among other things, to remember you by."

Challenger's teeth glimmered. "Greetings, Sakwari-cra. And I remember you for this." He touched a wide, dull red scar running across his naked left side; it still throbbed and hurt like hell whenever rain clouds darkened the sky.

Watched in absorbed interest by a tense and growing crowd of Rangers and Indians, the two advanced stiffly and shook hands Indian fashion; but they still looked wary of each other.

Deliberately, Challenger folded arms across his naked chest as he queried, "You've come to serve with General Oglethorpe?"

"Yes," came the sedate reply. "I have brought with me forty strong warriors; if the general needs them I can send for thirty-five more who are still in Capola."

"To guard your family?"

Challenger got a big surprise when Burton said, "No. They are over there." He tilted his head toward a scrub-pine thicket in which a group of Sakwaris were throwing together a number of palmetto-thatched lean-tos.

"The general will be pleased to have such fine fighters along with him. What do you expect as a reward?"

"Seven pounds and ten shillings every month for each of my men."

"The standard pay is seven; you must know that."

"Yes, but my men are worth more because they are very strong and disciplined to obey my commands without question."

Challenger began to relax, scratched at his tawny pate. "That might be so, but I doubt if he'd pay more than the going rate."

Stiffly, Burton demanded, "Why not?"

"It might cause trouble among the other allies. However, it just might be done, if you'll guarantee to keep the matter a secret. Anything else you want?"

Thad's silver earrings glittered as his head went back and he said a surprising thing. "I must have the commission of a lieutenant in his militia and a seat in all councils of war where Indians are present."

For all Wallace Challenger was taken aback at such brazen effrontery, his expression betrayed no reaction. "Personally," he said, "I see no reason why yer ambition shouldn't be satisfied. Perhaps you'll come over to my tent where we can talk a while?"

"Gladly." The other big man turned to Chula and issued orders that sent the Sakwaris present loping back to that pine patch where smoke already was commencing to climb and fires to gleam in the fading light.

For a good while after drumbeats had sent weary, dehydrated regulars stumbling to their tents, even after the last drumming and caterwauling from Indian camps had died out, Thad Burton and Wallace Challenger squatted on a log and, staring into a dying cook fire, continued to talk in undertones punctuated by strident snores from Hendy O'Brien, who lay near the brief picket line to which he'd secured his and the major's horses.

"So you and yer band have covered near three hundred miles in ten days?" Challenger stretched and yawned. He was sleepy and very tired.

Thad nodded. Some time ago he'd removed his headdress, so, saving for his earrings and black- and red-painted cheeks, he might readily have been taken for a militiaman or Ranger.

"Why not? Your Rangers knew the way and the weather was fine."

Challenger picked up a splinter, then started to sketch aimless designs in the sandy soil between his moccasins. He raised his eyes to the broad and powerfully sculptured features beside him. "Tell me, Mr. Burton, what happened to Brodbelt's party? *Did* yer people kill them?"

"No, we did not," Thad said, slapping a mosquito from his forehead. "What happened was this: at the time there was a party of leaderless Yuchis roaming in the vicinity. These I wished to take into my band and almost had persuaded them when Brodbelt came along."

The Sakwari leader's eyes swung and fixed themselves on the yellow-headed giant beside him. "It was they who surprised and murdered the surveyor and his men. When, in my camp, I heard shooting in the distance, I led some men to the scene, but got there too late; the Yuchis had already done killing. Wishing to win them for recruits, I made no effort to punish them, only told them to go away; which they did. I had only just returned to camp when you came along with Brother Barnaby and Jim Bartow.

"You can understand why, needing those Yuchis, I could not very well denounce them to you," explained the Panther King. "So I allowed you to draw your own conclusions—which were wrong."

A brief yawn escaped the major. "Yer strategy paid off?"

"Yes. Ten of those same Yuchis now are encamped in yonder pine patch."

To Challenger it remained amazing how almost perfectly the former white Tuscarora managed his English. "You spoke just now of that loon called Brother Barnaby—do you see him often these days?"

Burton extended a massive leg to shove a brand end into the fire. "We never know when he will appear, but the good man seems to grow sensible as time goes on."

While fresh flames gleamed on his face paint, Burton hesitated a moment, then said, "Would you like to have news of your wife—or is the subject too painful?"

Slowly, Challenger's shaggy, tawny head inclined and his lips tightened. "Tell me what's become of her."

Behind the seated pair one of the picketed horses lay down, sighing softly. "As, undoubtedly, you have heard, that fellow Oxford and Mrs. Challenger made straight for Capola after leaving the coast. I could not have been more astonished to see your wife riding in his pack train."

A faint smile flitted across his face. "The trader swore that you were dead and that they were married. I made inquiries and found that they were not, which puzzled and annoyed me, for, as you know, at one time I thought very highly of Winsome Brooks."

"She fooled me, too," Challenger muttered. "Someday I'll—well, no matter. Go on."

"Oxford gave me a recommendation from James Adair so, being aware that my people had to have certain trade goods, I permitted him to build a truck house near, but not in, Capola. I accepted Oxford for two reasons: first, he is a clever man and, second, he is fairly honest in his dealings."

Lowering his voice, Challenger asked, "They live together?"

"Yes."

"Do they seem contented?"

"They did at first, but soon the differences in their natures began to tell and now they quarrel all the time, especially when they drink. I think Oxford will, one way or another, get rid of her or move on by himself."

"Shouldn't wonder but what he will."

Chapter 15

HENDY O'BRIEN

Encouragement lent by the arrival of further small but welcome reinforcements from Carolina, and the appearance of half-a-dozen more fighting ships of the Royal Navy, became nullified when a Spanish squadron from Cuba reached St. Augustine in safety. It consisted of six half galleys carrying two hundred men and two sloops full of provisions and munitions.

To augment the commanding general's problems, scouting parties reported that large bands of Yamasees and other Spanish-controlled tribes had been seen massing south of the town as if preparing to flank in any troops attempting to attack St. Augustine from the landward side.

Nevertheless, Oglethorpe's main force, now based on Fort Diego, commenced a slow advance to the southeast, carefully feeling their way behind a screen of scouting parties. It seemed to the Georgia and Carolina Rangers and the troop of mounted Highlanders that they were never out of the saddle, or had enough time even to eat and drink.

Almost every day they had inconclusive brushes with Spanish cavalry patrols operating out of the port, but hardly anything came of these skirmishes beyond the capture of a good many horses and a few Spaniards and Negroes.

The invaders were surprised to find so many Africans serving as *volunteer* soldiers! An unusual Spanish unit was a corps of *forsados*—transported criminals who, having been pardoned, were given arms and ordered to labor on earthworks designed to strengthen the defenses of the provincial capital.

At length the British knew that but a single obstacle remained between them and the sturdy stone ramparts of St. Augustine. This was a strong stone fort variously known as Fort Moosa or the Black Fort. Here, and in nearby Negrito, lived the Kumassee King and his savage band of mulattoes, mustees, and pure African ex-slaves.

Nor was it encouraging to the invaders that this fort, according to spies and prisoners, was far stronger and better defended than Fort Diego, being protected by tabby-stone walls, a deep fosse, or ditch, and plenty of strong abatis. Further, this defense was reported to mount no less than four carriage guns on each curtain wall.

Oglethorpe felt that, if this were true he'd better make a reconnaissance in person, so, early one morning around the middle of June, he summoned a party of mounted Highlanders and set out through sparse, piny woods.

To Wallace Challenger it came as a surprise and vast relief that, for once, he and his bone-weary men hadn't been ordered to accompany the ever more drawn-looking commanding general. He suspected that this consideration was not due to any particular regard for the Rangers, but because serious discontent was arising among the Indian allies. In fact, the mico named Caesar, who was acting as a sort of field commander for all the Creeks, had complained—and in most undiplomatic language—when the English general refused to let his allies butcher captured cattle whenever they wanted fresh meat.

What really had brought matters to a head was Captain Tom Jones's fury over the refusal of British quartermasters to pay for horses captured by his warriors. Squalling like a gut-shot panther, the Creek half-breed had vowed that, on the morrow, he and all his following would depart for home. For another thing, he roared, not enough scalps were being taken to keep his warriors content. Stay-at-homes would mock them and say that they hadn't been fighting a war, only getting drunk all the time and lying with foreign women who very probably were diseased, poor, and ugly.

What fighting had occurred that could be boasted about in the council lodges? Thus far, nothing! Only a few skirmishes. They could find better fights nearer home. So it wasn't by chance that Rangers and Highlanders had been ordered to camp between the red allies and the balance of the white troops.

Challenger was cleaning his gear while Hendy O'Brien, stripped to the waist, whistled cheerily as he curried the four fine mounts drowsing at a picket line, tautly strung between trees, when a Scottish rider appeared; the Scot was red-faced and sweat trickled in rivulets down his half-exposed, hairy chest.

The messenger swung off and touched a sable forelock. "Sir-r, the gen'ral sends ye his compliments."

"Good of him. What's he want?"

"Why, sir-r, his horse has got bit by a serpent so he wants the loan o' one o' yer-r animals."

"In that case, I'm not surprised. Hendy, get yourself a horse, then saddle Ardnagashel and lead him to the general."

A few minutes later the wiry black stallion, wearing Challenger's best saddle, was led off by Hendy O'Brien and escorted by the red-faced Scot.

It was still early enough in the day for a degree of freshness to remain in the air and render travel pleasant. While jogging along, Hendy and the Scot discussed the near impossibility of obtaining decent fodder, the terrible supply system, and the hidebound arrogance of the regulars.

Hendy had begun to brag about his twins when they skirted a pine-framed savannah, but interrupted himself to say, "Friend, I've been this way before; we c'n save a deal of distance by cutting right across this flat ground." He indicated a little grassy plain dotted with scrub pines and dwarf palmettoes.

With Ardnagashel following on a lead rein, the ex-jockey took up a brisk trot which soon left the Scot a dozen yards behind.

Disaster struck so suddenly that Hendy could only gape when, seemingly, right from under his horse's belly sprang a pair of painted Indians. While one of them grabbed his reins close by the bit, the other shoved Hendy's foot out of his stirrup, then, snarling, dragged him off the horse's back. The little Irishman became aware that more Yamasees and some Negroes were leaping out of the long grass, but had time only to utter an outraged curse before a white-hot line was drawn across his throat. A torrent of choking blood flooded his windpipe and silenced him for all time.

The stallion reared and, lashing out with his forehoofs, removed the face of a yelling African who was attempting to grab his lead line. Ardnagashel then killed a Yamasee with a kick in the belly before tearing off after the Highlander, who just had had time to wheel, bend low, and then gallop away with bullets humming and hissing about him.

The Rangers' camp began to buzz like a disturbed wasps' nest when

Ardnagashel trotted riderless into camp; the Highlander soon appeared to gasp out news which set Challenger's eyes to blazing like blue fire.

"They killed Hendy?"

"They must ha', sir-r. Knives and axes flashed the minute he got pulled out o' the saddle."

The furious buckskins, half-naked because of the heat, found Hendy's small, bloodstained body huddled amid a clump of knee-high bunch grass and scrub palmettoes, but no stranger could have identified it; the ex-jockey's head had been hacked off and carried away. Gouts of bright arterial blood, spattering the sandy gray ground, indicated the line of the killers' retreat.

Sergeant Felton had come to the point where the enemy had mounted up when a party of horsemen appeared at the far edge of the savannah and yelled. They were friendly; among them showed the red jackets of regulars and the blue or green tunics of Carolinians.

The moment he recognized Oglethorpe's reconnaissance group, Captain Dempsey spurred to meet it, but Challenger remained bent over his friend's headless corpse. It was if he were paralyzed by grief. He was thinking, What, in God's name, is going to become of Bettie now; four children and no man? Poor, poor Bettie.

Many agreed later that never had anyone beheld a more outraged expression on the face of James Edward Oglethorpe than when he heard the details.

"Kill every horse if need be!" he shouted, glaring about. "But don't let the murderers escape!"

Hendy's severed head continued to bleed surprisingly long, so it was no trick for the tight-jawed Rangers to follow the winding trail left by the ambushers in fleeing through the woods. Oglethorpe and Captain Dempsey took the lead and set a stiff pace. Jumping fallen logs as if riding a steeplechase, they sped among the trees and raced, flat-out, across open spaces until Major Heron, a devoted fox hunter, raised the view halloo—"Harkaway! Yoicks!"

A few half-clad riders became visible. Some were black-skinned, others brown, and for the most part rode bareback. White-haired Captain Dempsey, astride Ardnagashel, soon outdistanced the commander-in-chief, who now was riding an aide's tall but cold-bred charger and overtook the hindermost fugitive, a Yamasee, whom he pistoled at arm's length between the shoulders. Screeching, the ambushers scattered. Oglethorpe whirled up his sword to cut down a powerful African rider, but, characteristically, took the fellow prisoner instead.

Not so Dempsey and the other Rangers; they kept pressing after what seemed to be the main body of the enemy and, yelling war cries of their choice, killed a couple more.

All at once Dempsey reined in sharply, for, in a little clear space, lay a dusty human head whose small pale blue eyes stared blankly, reproachfully into the brazen sky. Dismounting, the Ranger captain jerked off his shirt and bagged Hendy's head in it. Then he tied his bulging shirt to the pommel and rode on.

The pursuit would have continued had not some extensive clearings gleamed ahead. Someone called, "Hold hard! Yonder's 'e Black Fort!"

Anticipating a sally, Oglethorpe ordered the winded pursuers to rein in while still under shelter of the woods and, for a good ten minutes, studied the big stone fort and a village of African round huts which rose beyond a series of ill-tended maize fields.

Finally, the general turned his horse about, commenting, "Gentlemen, since the enemy's capital lies only three miles farther on, we shall have to take this place—but not now."

Chapter 16

THE BLACK FORT

In his cool and well-shaded private quarters in the Black Fort, otherwise Fort Moosa, Quobah Tutu, the Kumassee King, sat moodily tearing at a chicken leg. He glanced up when one of his personal servants, another blue-black Ashanti, pattered in on broad bare feet, fell onto his knees, and salaamed, just as he would have back in Kukuma.

Before signaling the servant to arise, Quobah tossed the leg he'd been gnawing to one of several hopeful dogs. "Well, Kabak, what is it?"

"O Magnificent Lord, a Spanish officer has just arrived from the Castle and demands to address Your Highness."

Something about the fellow's manner caused the Ashanti prince to scowl and query sharply, "What does this *buckra* want?"

"Your Highness, I do not know, but he insists he speak with you at once."

"Show him into my audience room." Unhurriedly, Quobah wiped grease from his chin and wide, thin lips, then stalked into a large, whitewashed chamber in the center of which stood an elaborately carved ebony chair lavishly inlaid with designs done in bits of ivory and mother-of-pearl. Upon it lay draped the magnificent jaguar skin which he'd

bought in St. Augustine because it was spotted, like a leopard's, and reminded him of home.

He took time to set a fresh turban on his head, then seated himself,
big, bare feet crossed before him. "Send the man in," he called, and picked
up a short, ivory-handled assegai, the broad blade of which gleamed with
gold leaf. This he customarily used for a scepter, but, occasionally, he
favored a huge knobkerrie.

Already irritated by so much barbaric pretentiousness, the messenger,
Lieutenant Juan de Molino, tramped in, his sandals slap-slapping softly.

In sudden anger Quobah noted that the Spaniard had not bothered to
secure the buttons of his sweat-stained yellow and red tunic, and that he
offered only the briefest bow imaginable.

"Colonel Quobah," began the messenger, "I bear greetings from His
Excellency, Don Francisco de Montiano."

"Always we are glad to hear from our cousin. What has he to say?"

Without permission, De Molino plunked himself down on a chair with
an alligator-hide-covered seat, removed a floppy Panamá hat, and commenced to fan himself. "First, you must know that the accursed British
have begun siege operations."

Quobah leaned forward, scarred features intent. "And how?"

"Some of their troops have occupied a deserted battery of ours on Cape
Quartell which lies across the harbor from the Castle of Santa María.
More of their bigger ships-of-war have anchored within extreme range of
the city."

Quobah listened, small, yellowish eyes intent, but he said nothing—
only picked up a fly whisk and used it.

"Our spies have reported," the messenger continued, "that the English
are preparing to capture this place. Large numbers of their troops have
been observed drawing ammunition and food."

Crooking a forefinger, De Molino flicked a beading of sweat onto the
stone flooring, created a pattern of dark dots that reached almost to the
jaguar skin's edge.

The Ashanti's doglike teeth glinted briefly. "Let them try! They will
fail, but first I will kill many of them."

A contemptuous smile flitted across the lieutenant's sallow face. "You
are ridiculously confident."

"No, I am not!" growled the huge Kumassee King. "My followers can
fire the great guns. We have much food, aside from those crops out
there—" He flung his good hand toward a shaded window. Beyond it
could be seen patches of corn, wheat, and other grains, as well as plots of
vegetables.

"Nevertheless," De Molino said acidly as he jerked a folded paper from
under his belt, "here are His Excellency's orders. They direct you to re-

move all supplies, wagons, weapons and other munitions from this place. He orders that you, with all your people, shall retire immediately within the fortifications of San Augustín."

For a long minute Quobah remained rigid on his throne, then he leaped up, features contorted with fury. He waved his ceremonial assegai so menacingly that the Spaniard involuntarily recoiled on his seat.

"But why?" raged the Kumassee King, broad, scar-seamed chest heaving. "Why am I told to run like a jackal when the lion roars? My men are many and brave. We do not fear the slavers!"

Lieutenant de Molino, resuming his dignity, stood up. "Who are you, you boastful black fellow, to question His Excellency's decisions? If Don Francisco believes that the enemy will take your fort, then they will take it! If he calls upon you to retire within the wall of St. Augustín it is because your men are needed."

The Spaniard's dark-blue eyes—no doubt inherited from some remote Vandal ancestor—hardened. "Disobey at your peril, Colonel Quobah! For, as surely as the sun shines above us, the British will be defeated and driven away. Then the disobedient and treacherous will suffer—and terribly!"

Quobah Tutu's breathing quickened, he began visibly to shake, and his teeth clamped down so hard on his lower lip that blood drops dribbled over his chin.

Speaking in hard, crisp tones, De Molino continued, "What if you disobey and the British capture you in this place? What then will be your fate and that of your people? All of you will be chained and shipped north to work out your miserable lives in slavery!"

That this argument was a telling one with the Kumassee King De Molino saw immediately, for the magnificent African dropped rather than sat back on his throne and, pulling his useless arm onto his lap, glared at the stone floor.

Chapter 17

"TO OVERAWE THE ENEMY"

On the last day of May 1740, almost everyone among the British forces felt convinced that, at long last, the general advance and grand assault they'd been waiting for so impatiently was about to take place.

For two days now innumerable gigs and dispatch boats had been seen passing and repassing between General Oglethorpe's headquarters at Lacanela and the stately squadron of men-of-war anchored off the yellow sands of Anastasia—that long, low island which formed the eastern side of the harbor of St. Augustine.

Although considerably affected by the sudden desertion of the half-breed, Captain Tom Jones, and most of the Cherokees, the rest of the Indian allies took renewed interest in this campaign; all night long they howled, sang, and danced around their fires, boasted extravagantly about the terrible things they were going to do to the *Ispani.*

The Scots prayed, then danced wild Highland reels to bagpipe music. The more sober-minded among them honed dirks, claymores, and bayonets to razor keenness. They wanted to get this business done with and get back to their homes as fast as they could. No less eager to win this campaign in a hurry were the South Carolinians. The English regulars drank, gambled, and wholeheartedly cursed the climate, but went about their preparations with professional thoroughness.

Security being all but nonexistent, even the least drummer boy knew that Oglethorpe's plan was for the army to march down the coast, swing inland short of Fort Moosa, and then deliver the all-out assault from St. Augustine's inland side. Meanwhile, the men-of-war were solidly, methodically, to bombard the town before dispatching strong landing parties against the port. As for the Indians, Rangers, and mounted Highlanders, they were supposed to make a wide sweep, deep into the country behind St. Augustine, and then to advance swiftly from the south.

By midafternoon of May 31, it became inescapable that a change in this clear, hot weather was imminent. Eying the sky, Commodore Pearce grew apprehensive; it wasn't cheering or sensible to find his ships anchored so close to a lee shore. A gale sweeping in from any direction, saving the west, would render his position untenable. The humidity intensified—if that were possible—and the wind died out completely, leaving the Atlantic a vast, bright-blue mirror, but the sun kept on lashing the earth and tortured almost beyond endurance the troops preparing to march.

Guided by a Negro deserter calling himself Captain Jack, the main column set out along the coast, cursing the soft sand that kept giving under their feet, and dragging by hand a single four-pound gun—not much by way of siege artillery. After the troops had struggled over a few miles they commenced to collapse from sunstroke, so Colonel Alexander Vanderdussen, his bony, horse-like face gone scarlet, protested continuance of the march. So did several other colonial officers. But to no avail.

Grimly, Oglethorpe insisted. "Gentlemen, we shall continue our march. On arriving before the walls we will draw ourselves up in battle order.

When the enemy realizes that British regulars are present and thinks of what the fleet's heavy guns can accomplish against them"—he summoned a confident smile—"why, then I feel assured that they will surrender at once.

"In my experience, it is customary and profitable to overawe the enemy with a show of force and then, if that fails to impress, to make a feint."

Lieutenant Colonel William Cook of Oglethorpe's Regiment, straight as a ramrod for all his nearly sixty years, nodded gravely, but Colonel William Palmer, commanding the South Carolina Volunteers, looked most unhappy.

"I'm sure ye're mistaken about this, sir," he said loudly enough so that all could hear. "The Dons are mostly colonials, like ourselves, so they ain't to be scared by noise and parades."

Elegant Captain Wingst demanded, "And, sir, what if those sailor fellows don't do their part?"

For the first time General Oglethorpe appeared a trifle disconcerted. "I am positive that when the ships recognize our signal they will do their duty."

The march was resumed, proved to be an exhausting horror because the route was difficult on account of traversing a succession of little creeks populated by a multitude of snakes and alligators and scrub-palmetto roots had a nasty way of tripping a heavily laden soldier and sending him sprawling on the burning sand. Long ago, all but a few veterans had drained their water bottles and now lurched along with glazing eyes and thickened tongues.

Then, as if to cap their miseries, the expected storm broke toward sundown. Livid clouds quickly blotted the sky. The wind rose steadily, drove sand into the soldiers' eyes until rain fell with the force of bullets fired from the sky.

So dense became the downpour that men could see only a few feet around them. The tearing wind ripped off their hats and filled their eyes with tears. Units lost contact and strayed off into the blinding gloom. Many men just sat down where they were, buried their heads in their arms, and wished they'd never heard of either St. Augustine or General James Oglethorpe.

Nothing could be done save face the inevitable and abandon the advance; even the commanding general had to admit that.

All night long the most vicious thunderstorm many could recall raged in spectacular, terrifying vividness. Fortunately, it ended around sunup.

By ten of the morning the British van had arrived within two miles of the objective and everyone could see the short, squat tower on the Castle Santa María, glowing golden-brown upon the skyline and flying an enormous Spanish flag.

In order to give stragglers an opportunity to close up, the troops were
ordered to halt and to sort themselves out—which they did, gladly enough.

In the late afternoon, Oglethorpe's staff and all the commanding officers
appeared before him, turned out as well as they could manage, and stood
about, talking in undertones. Color guards were improvised to escort the
ensigns of various organizations, a band of field music—fifes and drums of
various sizes—was directed to form up before a "demonstrating detachment" composed of two hundred of the tallest and best turned-out
grenadiers of Oglethorpe's Regiment.

Meanwhile, the rest of the Army, grumbling and disgusted, was deployed into a continuous line abreast, usually three ranks in depth. The
officers had orders to keep their men marching short distances back and
forth to confuse the enemy into thinking that the invaders were far more
numerous than they actually were.

The general and his staff, looming tall above the infantry, rode near
the center of the demonstrating detachment's front. The music struck up
a march, then, with the lowering sun drawing brief and dazzling flashes
from burnished bayonets, the regulars advanced in precisely dressed ranks
behind their colors.

To European eyes the developing demonstration looked satisfactory,
if not impressive, but wizened little Colonel Vanderdussen and lanky Colonel William Palmer—the latter had greatly distinguished himself during
the ghastly Yamasee War of 1727—were thoroughly, if not outspokenly,
disgusted.

As they rode behind the general's broad, scarlet-clad back, Vanderdussen growled, "Say, Bill, you know where that there fork in the road
leads to?"

"Fort Moosa. It's about a mile and a half from the sea. My scouts tell
me it's been bandoned."

"Then why the hell ain't the general ordered it occupied?"

Beneath his palmetto hat, Vanderdussen scowled. "Damned if I know.
I just don't understand him these days. Can't seem to act boldly—or
decide what's the right thing to do. Seems fearful of getting a few men
killed."

"That's no way to fight a war. Now will you look at all that showy,
time-wasting nonsense?"

"Hell! We ought to be attacking right now."

Some two hundred yards short of the city's high orange-brown walls,
which were swarming with defenders, General Oglethorpe reined in,
ordered the detachment to halt. At a signal from the general, the drum
major raised a tasseled, silver-knobbed staff, then lowered it sharply. At
once the music advanced, drums rattling and fifes squealing fit to wake
the dead. At the same time a light breeze sprang up which set a big Union

Flag and the regimental banners to fluttering and making a colorful show.

In the rear of the staff group, Lieutenant Colonel Lejeau grunted when the regulars commenced to march stiffly, and in step, back and forth before the ramparts. They made a smart showing, but, somehow, it didn't seem to impress the enemy for, suddenly, the battlements spouted fire and smoke. Fortunately, small arms only were employed; cannon certainly would have slaughtered some musicians and caused not a few casualties among the regulars, drawn up and sweating hard in their heavy red and green regimentals.

Once the defenders opened fire, a mass of Indians, swarming restlessly about on the British right, reacted in character and fired wildly back— for all they couldn't possibly have hoped to range the defenses.

The contagion, due, perhaps, to frustration, spread to some colonial troops deployed well behind the general's demonstrating detachment, so, for a few minutes, volley followed volley. The musketry grew deafening, but had not the least practical effect.

Rasped Colonel Vanderdussen, "Now I wonder what the Navy's making of all this fooferaw? Why the hell don't they fire a few salvos in answer?"

Exactly as if matters had turned out as he had planned, James Oglethorpe, expressionless, turned his horse, then ordered the musicians to play *The Grenadier March* as he and the staff led the demonstration party back to the angry, amazed, and chagrined troops.

Next morning, after the various elements comprising the British invasion force had arrived at preassigned positions, everyone waited expectantly for their four-pound signal guns—three more had been brought up—to let the fleet know that they should begin bombarding. The little battery fired four shots: two close together—pause—two more, in quick succession. Nothing was heard on the ocean side of the port so, after twenty minutes of continued silence, the signal was ordered repeated.

Still there came no answering of guns.

"That's just like those seagoing bastards!" growled Major Alex Heron, one of the general's aides-de-camp. "Trust the bloody Royal Navy to let the Army down in a pinch!"

During a miserable half hour the commanding general continued to sit his horse, head bent as in thought. But the squadron's guns remained obstinately silent.

At length Oglethorpe fetched a deep sigh, said, "I fear, gentlemen, that we shall have to postpone our assault. Lacking siege guns, there is nothing we can do for the present without suffering appalling losses. Order the troops to return to their camps."

This was too much for Billy Palmer. Long features crimson with anger, the colonel kicked forward a thorn-scarred buckskin. "Oh, for Christ's sake, Gen'ral! Ye ain't fixin' to go home now, are ye?" Weather-beaten features aquiver, the old frontier fighter yelled, "Just give me two hundred Caroliny boys and as many Injuns as will follow me, and I'll damn' well be into that town 'fore sunset!"

An awed silence descended; it wasn't every day a British general officer got told off like this, and by a mere colonial!

Oglethorpe's jaw clicked shut and his close-set, dark eyes flashed as, with an obvious effort, he succeeded in fighting down an order to arrest this insubordinate officer forthwith.

Instead, he snapped, "Sir! Such an attempt would prove too hazardous. We must wait for the artillery." He then put his horse to a trot and rode off, stiff as a poker in his saddle.

Not everyone was as disappointed as were the Indians, Rangers, and some of the Carolina Militia. By God, those walls looked almighty high, solid and well defended! Privately, the regulars and a great many thoughtful men among the colonials rejoiced that they had not been sent against such defenses—especially if the cannon visible on them were brought into play.

That evening, Colonel Palmer became somewhat mollified when a courier from headquarters found him eating supper with some Indian leaders and Ranger officers.

Sakwari-cra, for the first time since Challenger could remember, was wearing no war paint and had donned the usual, wide-brimmed hat which anyone with sense had taken to wearing. He had clung, however, to his turquoise-and-silver earrings.

"Sir," informed the courier, "you are directed to take a sufficient number of Rangers, Indians and proceed to Fort Moosa as soon as may be. Gen'ral said that some Scots will be sent to reinforce you."

A spurt of savage pleasure shot through Thad. At last! At last he would be able to show these white soldiers the kind of disciplined fighters he had made of his Sakwaris.

Chuckling, Challenger reached forward to dump the sand out of first one and then the other of his moccasins. "I'll bet we'll have a pretty bicker. The garlic-eaters *must* have reoccupied Moosa after our glorious parade, so I expect we'll meet with some real action at last. Eh, Burton? You should add to your tally of *coups*. Yer men, too."

"That is well," Thad said, nodding gravely. "Chula tells me many of my warriors are growing disgusted and want to go where some loot and scalps are to be won. I understand how they feel," he added significantly.

It turned out that Challenger and Lieutenant Thad Burton—he'd received his commission at last—were wrong, for when the Creeks and

Sakwaris, with eighteen Georgia Rangers, swooped on Fort Moosa they found the place silent and empty, save for a few hungry dogs.

Deeply curious, Thad ranged about the fort, which was the first formal European-designed fortificaton he had ever seen. *Wagh!* Like the ruins of Capola, these walls seemed built to stand forever.

The occupying force soon discovered that the departed garrison, after spiking their cannon, had carried off anything and everything of value.

Equally deserted were the round, whitewashed huts with pointed roofs of thatch which composed the village of Negrito; even the crops in surrounding fields had been spoiled.

"Well, boys," drawled Colonel Palmer, "reckon we'd better get busy fixin' a welcome for the Papists."

Major MacKay nodded—his detachment from the Independent Highland Company of Foot had only just arrived. "Too bad we can't always fight from behind walls thick as these."

In less than an hour the Rangers, Scots, Carolinians, and Indians—all in high good humor now—had been assigned posts and duties, had made every preparation to beat off an attack in force.

They enjoyed the cool shady barracks and gulped quantities of sweet, cool water drawn from a well in the barrack's square; unaccountably, it hadn't been fouled.

All in all, the occupying force was well pleased; especially the officers, who appreciated their luck in having won, at no cost at all, this fine, strong fort and well-constructed village lying a bare three miles outside the besieged capital. It seemed almost too good to be true! Why, this was a natural command post with plenty of shelter for sick and wounded men.

Palmer, Burton, and Challenger were amazed. "I just can't understand this," remarked Wallace, "because I'm told Quobah Tutu was commandin' here, and I know damn' well he's a fierce fighter. Why would a man like him pull out without loosing even one arrow against us?"

Thad reflected a long moment. "You are right; it is not like the Kumassee King to surrender his capital so willingly. If I understand him, Quobah has some trick in mind. After dark we had better double the pickets and patrols."

He glanced through a broken window at one-eyed Chula, who was assembling the Sakwaris, freshly painted and naked save for breechcloths. They, with a party of Chickasaws who recently and quite unexpectedly had appeared at Fort Diego, had been ordered by Colonel Palmer to occupy Negrito Village and hold it unless attacked by overwhelming numbers.

The redskins trotted off, intending to have a good time among the deserted huts. They did; there were plenty of stray chickens, guinea hens, and other fowl roaming about, even a few pigs and a cow or two. In the huts they found enough abandoned pots, platters, and other household gear to ensure a pleasant stay. Soon cook fires commenced to send up silver-blue spirals.

They didn't yet know it, but they were in for a considerable disappointment; that same afternoon, General Oglethorpe and an escort rode up to Fort Moosa. With brows merged and hands locked behind him, the commanding general tramped about, apparently absorbed in a mental struggle. When he'd done inspecting the defenses, he called Billy Palmer and the rest of the senior officers into that same room in which the Kumassee King had kept his throne.

In Wallace Challenger's opinion, Oglethorpe appeared very tired indeed; during the past two weeks he seemed to have aged by ten years and, for the first time, a frosty stubble stood out along his cheeks and chin.

"Gentlemen," he announced in measured tones. "I have reached a decision: I want this place first rendered defenseless, and then evacuated."

Overwhelming astonishment momentarily held the listeners silent as they stood about in this dim, relatively cool apartment. Only Challenger's long experience and profound admiration kept him silent, but Colonel Palmer and Major MacKay and Captain MacIntosh burst into a torrent of furious protests.

"My God, sir! You can't mean what you say!" bellowed Palmer. "We can hold this place against anything the Dons can send!"

"I advise you"—Oglethorpe's voice was as cold as the sound of breaking ice—"not to argue again, sir! I command here, and am not disposed to discuss the matter further. Do you understand?"

"But, but, sir-r," burst out MacKay. "We are in full possession, have plenty of men and ammunition!"

Oglethorpe treated the sunburned Scot to a withering glance. "So it may seem to you, sir. But, to an experienced soldier, it is perfectly obvious that, with St. Augustine so close, it would be a very simple matter for the enemy to hurl an overwhelming force against you and trap you inside these walls like"—he managed a bleak smile—"like so many mice in a trap!"

Barely in time, Thad Burton caught himself and didn't put in his penny's worth. What did he know about forts and the white man's way of waging war? Tread warily and listen; that was what he must do until—until when? Well, time might disclose that. All the same, he was burning to prove himself and his warriors, felt very sure that the general had enough friendly Indians in the vicinity of St. Augustine to risk an assault.

MacIntosh spread wide hands in appeal. "Sir-r! Sir-r! I beg ye to reconsider. Ye're mistook. Why, I'll gladly stake my life that we—"

A sharp gesture from Oglethorpe cut short the Scottish commander; he got stiffly to his feet, then slapped puffs of dust from the skirts of a long scarlet tunic. "I am confident, Captain MacIntosh, that you do not intend to appear insubordinate so I will forget what you've just said."

Hot and angry, his sunken eyes flickered from one face to the next. "Here are my orders, gentlemen. Immediately after my departure you will remove the valves of the main gate and burn them. The walls are to be well breached at the three points I will indicate. You will then return to your respective encampments and await further instructions. Good day, sirs."

Into the back of Challenger's mind popped a half-remembered quotation: "Whom the gods would destroy, they first make mad!"

Chapter 18

DESERTIONS

Seldom had Laure Rivard seen Thad appear so thoroughly disgusted and uneasy as when he rode into the Sakwari camp after the evacuation of the Black Fort. Turning over his horse to a warrior, he made for that hut in which Laure had remained to tend a few sick men and a brave who'd been so badly bitten by a rattler that his leg remained discolored and swollen to twice its normal size.

From the dejected way that the Rangers had split off from the returning party in the direction of their tents she guessed, readily enough, that a mighty unpleasant incident must have taken place at Fort Moosa. To get Jeems and John out of the way during what was sure to be a touchy moment, she sent them to help water the horses, then crossed to where Thad stood rubbing down his mount with short, angry strokes.

She noted, also, that Chula was wearing a very sour expression and his one eye sought the sandy ground when she passed by. In rising alarm, she realized that, almost without exception, the returned Sakwaris were silent and scowling as they dispersed to their various shelters. Nevertheless, Laure summoned a bright smile while holding out her arms for equipment to be carried in—to kiss in public was not to be thought of.

"Welcome back, Thad. I see you haven't lost any men."

In the rugged bronze expanse of his features his gray eyes narrowed. "Had no chance to. We've brought in no scalps, either."

"Then you got driven away from the Black Fort?"

Thad spat angrily. "Hell, no! The Spaniards abandoned it, left it wide open to us."

"But—but why? What happened?" Laure's faintly tilted eyes rounded themselves.

In brief, bitter sentences Thad explained what had happened, concluded, "I just can't understand what the general was thinking of when, right away, he gave up such a strong place. Any fool can see it's of great importance!"

"I wouldn't say your braves understand either." Laure hung up the equipment, then, with hair gleaming coppery in the sunlight, she went to put a kettle on a slowly smoldering cook fire.

"Aye, they're damned well disgusted—especially the young bucks; they grumbled all the way back."

"What were they saying?"

"Oh, the usual; said they hadn't followed me all this way just to wander around the countryside and win nothing in the way of scalps, loot or glory."

Thad sent his hat sailing into the spacious shack, then stood and stared with unseeing eyes at a watering party of stark-naked Sakwaris who were riding silently over to the nearest pool. They were fine specimens, all of them. Too bad they hadn't been allowed an opportunity to show what first-class fighters they were.

Thad remarked at length, "Chula especially is angry. If I didn't know him better, I'd think he might run off and join a bunch of Creeks who are reported ready to pull out and start raiding Spanish settlements along the west coast."

In the act of plopping a chunk of issue salt beef into her pot, Taqua peered up through drifting smoke. "Chula would never desert you, would he?"

"No. He's too well disciplined—"

—for an Indian, thought Laure.

"—besides, he is my Long Warrior. He has done much to build the band." Thad began to untie his leggings, soon exposed a peppering of half-healed stab wounds inflicted by yuccas, prickly pear, and other forms of cactus. "No. I count on him and Shatara to follow my orders to the end. They know I won't allow disobedience of any sort."

Next day, ill news spread through the English and allied camps. It seemed that a number of Carolina Volunteers, in utter disgust, had broken camp and had departed from Fort Diego for Fort St. George, there to await transportation for Charles Town.

Colonel Vanderdussen and Captain Wingst, however, had prevailed upon their men to hang around a little longer; pointed out that some siege mortars finally had arrived, so action might soon be expected. A few wavering Indian micos also decided to stay and see what happened, thanks only to their deep respect for the commanding general.

But still no preparations for an attack were made. Apparently, nothing could shake Oglethorpe's determination to delay an all-out assault until more siege artillery arrived and batteries had been constructed to receive them. Playing for time, he held a council of war in Fort Diego at which he showed plans for the batteries to be erected on Cape Quartell and on Anastasia Island. From both of these positions, he pointed out, it should be easy to bombard the Castle of Santa María into submission.

Once the enemy defenses had been reduced, St. Augustine would be assaulted from all sides and there would be sufficient fighting and plunder to please everybody.

Thad rode back from the staff meeting secretly but inordinately proud to be wearing a big copper gorget and Challenger's second-best militia tunic. The two men being almost of size, it fitted surprisingly well after Laure had repaired the garment to the best of her ability.

It was only when he had decided to wear a uniform that Thad had removed his long turquoise-and-silver earrings to substitute plain gold rings —there were plenty of white men in the British land forces and on shipboard, too, who affected such ornaments. Riding along, the two, to a casual observer, might have been mistaken for brothers.

At the council of war it had been decided that Colonel Vanderdussen and his South Carolina regiment would throw up the battery on Cape Quartell while the general's regiment would be barged over to Anastasia to do the same.

As the two big men turned onto a road paralleling the St. John, Challenger drawled, "That's a mighty pretty commission they've written. Don't lose it. It'll come in handy, plenty of times. Should grant you officer's treatment if you get taken."

"That will never happen."

"Nobody ever thinks it will—just like everyone figgers 'all the rest may get killed, but I won't.'" He swung a leg over his pommel in order to ease his backside. "Well, Burton, tell me, how d'you think the cat's fixin' to jump?"

"Our army's spirit is very low," Thad replied carefully.

"Dispirited, hell! They're plain disgusted. Wouldn't bet a farthing on what most of us Rangers and Indians may do in a few days' time.

"Still, discipline ought to keep the regulars on duty for a while and I don't think the Carolina boys are quite yet set to trot off home, for all they're talkin' mighty big about quittin'."

Once they reached the edge of the Rangers' camp, Challenger said, "Likely be some patrollin' tomorrow. If ye're needed, I'll ride over. Want to say howdy to Mrs. Burton, anyhow." He looked a bit sad as he added, "Expect yer youngsters are growin' fast?"

Poor Robbie had been about the same age as Jeems.

Thad nodded. "Looks like Jeems is going to grow into another hulk, like his pa—only redheaded. See you later, Major."

On gaining the summit of a low rise from which he could see his camp Thad realized that something must be wrong. On reaching the Sakwari camping place, he noticed only a few horses drowsing along the main picket line and ever fewer men were in sight.

His breath halted, half drawn. Where were all his lithe, greasy-brown followers? Could Chula have gone off to join the disaffected Creeks? Of course not; he was no ignorant black savage like Quobah. He was the new nation's senior mico under him.

Probably, orders came while he was away and Chula's only off making a scout for the general. He put his horse to a trot and only pulled in to dismount before his shack.

One look at Laure's stricken features and the frightened expressions worn by his sons warned the mico thlucco that the incredible had happened. Harshly, he demanded, "Well, and where are my warriors?"

"I don't know where they've gone," Laure told him in a taut voice. "Right after you left for the council, Chula talked to them, asked them if they wanted to go on playing at war like children—in the *Englasi* fashion—or did they want to go and kill enemies like real warriors?"

Noises like those of an avalanche thundered about Thad's mind.

Hushoni tchigi! Skunk spew! Everything he'd believed in and had worked for for so long seemed about to topple in ruins. "How many stayed?"

Laure found it difficult to reply; her heart was aching so over the stunned incredulity of Thad's expression. How ironical that, at this moment, he should be wearing the white man's uniform! She felt an impulse to rush over and fling her arms about him, but she knew he wouldn't like it.

"Only six men refused to go with Chula—including the man the snake bit."

Several times Thad mumbled, "Chula would never desert me. Not after I freed him, not after we have fought so many battles together. Chula will soon come back! *I know he will!*"

On the same day that Chula was leading the malcontents to join a big party of equally dissatisfied Creeks near San Francisco de Pupa, on the St. John's western bank, another band of Sakwaris was traveling in the opposite direction.

Riding in single file, they were traversing the flat pine- and palmetto-dotted country stretching northwest from Fort St. George.

Shatara really didn't know what to expect from Sakwari-cra when he came up with him. It stood to reason that the mico thlucco would be very angry over his having, without orders, left Capola practically unguarded. On the other hand, Sakwari-cra was certain to welcome the arrival of an additional thirty-five warriors. They would make him cast a longer shadow among the haughty Creeks and Cherokees. If Sakwari-cra got angry, he wouldn't stay so for long.

The former Chickasaw flattered himself that he'd been bringing his reinforcements along at a fine rate of travel—for all that they'd been accompanied by a pregnant white woman. During the last few days on the trail it hadn't bothered Shatara that, at the end of each day's riding, Winsome Challenger slipped from the saddle, heavy, shapeless, and ungainly as a trader's pack, to lie gasping and exhausted. Often she was too weary to get herself a bait from the party's common kettle, so Shatara sometimes was forced to order a young Bow Man, stiff with shame, to fetch the wretched female a drink of water and a few mouthfuls of food.

He looked back and saw that the white woman was riding near the middle of the column. She'd her hands crossed on the pommel to support her weight and her head sagged so far forward that long brown hair, dangling loose and disorderly, concealed her sun-blasted features. The Indian was only mildly interested that she'd lasted so long; surprisingly, she'd not complained or tried to slow the party down.

Why hadn't she, long since, pulled out of his column and quietly given birth under some bush? Squaws did so all the time and thought nothing of it. For all that the mico thlucco and his squaw were white, Shatara guessed that he never was going to understand the *Englasi* and their ways.

Laure guessed she'd never forget the hour when Shatara led his party, freshly painted and decked out in their best, out of the piny woods and among the deserted shacks and lean-tos of the camp.

When Thad first noticed him, he gaped as at a ghost. He was thinking, This can't be Shatara—just someone who looks very like him—but then he recognized familiar faces among the horsemen crowding in around his shack and knew the bitter truth. Swiftly, Sakwari-cra roused from the sullen black mood into which he had plunged deeper and deeper during the past forty-eight hours, for never a word had come from or about Chula.

Clean-shaven features gone dark with rage, Thad was about to hurl Shatara out of the saddle and squeeze his throat until he strangled, but as had happened ever more frequently of late, the cool hand of Common Sense checked him. Like it or not, at present he was a leader without a following. Shatara's arrival would change that! So he only glared and demanded harshly, "What do you here? I sent no messenger to summon the sub-mico called Shatara."

"O great and valorous Mico Thlucco who counts his scalps as leaves on a tree, Shatara came because he believed you needed him to make you stand among other mico thluccos tall as a mighty oak; now you will lead a big war party."

It never occurred to the sub-mico to note that the pregnant white woman wasn't present; in fact, he'd never noticed when, dazedly, she'd pulled out of column and into a yaupon thicket.

Chapter 19

THE YAUPON BUSH

Ranger Sergeant Bob Slack felt disgusted, dog-tired, and altogether sorry for himself. Why in hell had his horse got so poorly shod that it had gone lame? He'd be damned if he'd ever again go near a British Army farrier. He could cold-shoe better than that.

Leading his limping mount along by the reins, Slack trudged along a freshly made trail; for sure, a good many horses, maybe thirty or forty, must have passed this way and not very long ago, either. Familiar by now with this neck of the woods, he reckoned he had about three miles to tramp before he reached camp. By God, he was that thirsty he could drink bear piss! Hadn't had a swallow of water since midday.

The sergeant entered the cool of a patch of woods keeping a sharp lookout for rattlesnakes, which seemed to be particularly plentiful in this region. Sure enough, he soon saw a diamondback, a big, beautifully marked rattler tightly coiled under a shiny-leaved yaupon bush. When the snake set up a thin, dry rattling, his horse heard it, too, and reared back off the trail, crazy with fear. Slack, after quieting his animal, tied it to a tree, then broke off a thick branch and used it to club the reptile to death. This diamondback was so big and wellmarked he wished he'd time to skin it; it would make a dandy belt, like the ones most of the fellows had taken to wearing.

He stood a moment over the still-writhing snake and was about to go and untie his horse when a faint moaning sound caught his attention; it seemed to come from the heart of a clump of ilex bushes—which the Indians called *yaupon*. Slack stiffened. What the hell was this? Then he noticed that a horse had been turned off the trail he'd been following and into a thicket of yaupons from which those dolorous sounds were rising.

The sergeant slipped his war hatchet out of its sling, then, watched by his still-apprehensive horse, made a quick cast around the clump, his hard, lean face alternately sunlit and shadowed by the pines shooting at least forty-five feet high all around him.

Just as he glimpsed something white behind a big yaupon bush he heard someone call in English, "Oh-h! Oh-h! Help. Help me." The voice was so low that Slack hesitated in his tracks, trying to make sure that this wasn't some sort of a trick. Plenty of Yamasees spoke this much English.

The moaning soon stopped, so, with infinite care, the Ranger parted the yaupon's prickly branches, then, on getting a good look, he fetched up sharp. Sprawled loosely on the pine-needle-browned ground lay a tall white woman whose tangled brown hair fanned out from under her shoulders in a damp and sorry mess.

She was so pregnant as to appear grotesque. After peering in all directions, Slack went to stand over the pitiful creature whose face and arms and bare legs were a mass of insect bites and thorn scratches, many of which were infected.

Almost timidly, he bent, asking, "My God, ma'am. What's happened to you?"

Dazedly, the woman opened hazel-hued eyes. "I—sick. I—I—baby."

Bitterly, the sergeant regretted his empty water gourd. "God, ma'am, what can I do? I don't know nothin' about birthing."

"Any—women near?" Each syllable seemed to be pronounced only with the utmost pain.

Slack thought fast, then his anxious, dusty features lit. "Why, ma'am, there's a white lady livin' not a half hour's ride from here." He knelt and used a fairly clean gun rag to wipe some of the dust and sweat from her features. All at once it dawned on Bob Slack that, somewhere, some time, he might have seen this woman before; but he couldn't be sure, at least not right now. "You want I should stay with you—or go fetch?"

"Fetch." A terrible pang must have seized her, for a sharp cry burst from Winsome Challenger's writhing lips.

Miserably aware of his inadequacy, the Ranger could only clutch her hand until the pain eased. Then he said, "All right, ma'am, I'll go, but I may be slow. My nag's gone lame."

"Take mine!" panted the prostrate woman, convulsively turning on a thick mat of pine needles which must have rendered the ground not too uncomfortable, while the yaupons shielded her from most of the sun's heat.

Bob Slack made a quick scout, but, apparently, the horse this hauntingly familiar woman had ridden must have become frightened; its tracks went plunging off into the wilderness.

He returned to the yaupon clump. "Critter's cleared out, there ain't nothin' I c'n do but get the best speed out of my nag." In turning away he checked, then eased his skinning knife off his belt and put its leather sheath in her hand. "When the pains git too bad, try bitin' on this."

Winsome managed a grateful nod; soon the ground under her head conveyed the sound of a horse taking up a halting, irregular trot.

To force a lame animal to hurry was dead against Slack's experience, but he guessed maybe he was justified in running the risk of crippling this critter for good. A wailing cry from behind sealed his decision. That poor young female in the stained garments sure needed help in a hurry.

Now where in hell had he— Then the recollection came all of a heap. It was during that fight at Chaugee Landing. Yep. It was her, all right, who'd tried to doctor that old, snake-bit feller. Try as he would, Slack couldn't recall her name. Likely, he'd never heard it mentioned.

By sheer good luck he came across Laure Burton cooking in front of her shack. When he blurted out the main facts of his discovery she went into immediate action. Thad called two of his men and prepared to accompany her once she'd got together whatever she thought might be useful.

Thad said, "Shall we saddle a horse for her?"

Laure whirled on him in fury. "You *are* a simple fellow! From what the sergeant here says she probably won't be fit to ride even a litter for some time, whoever she is."

Less than half an hour after Sergeant Slack had arrived he was back in the saddle, astride a fresh horse. Thad rode beside him, then came Laure, skirts tucked above strong brown knees and steadying a pair of bulging saddlebags. Bringing up the rear were the two Sakwari braves. Nobody said anything, only maintained the usual sharp lookout; there were still plenty of hostiles ranging the countryside.

"She's in that there thicket," Slack told Thad, pointing. "Say, I just remembered somethin' to tell you. I once seen that female near Chaugee Landin'. Ever been there?"

"No. What's her name?"

"Don't know. She looked in pretty bad shape," he added.

"She must be. I don't hear her crying out," Laure said, and turned off the trail. "Thad, suppose you keep the men here? If I need help I'll call."

She slung her saddlebags over one shoulder and, lugging a large water bottle, disappeared among the yaupons.

"So that is where the squaw left us," remarked one of the warriors.

Thad stiffened in his saddle. "What do you mean? Speak up, you stupid *sulitatwa!* Did she ride with you?"

The Sakwari's gaze wavered aside. "The trader's squaw came with us from Capola."

Thad whirled. "*Yo-he-wa!* Why did not you speak of this before?"

"She was only a squaw."

Then the implication of the fellow's words struck home. There was only one white trader near Capola—Mike Oxford—and this brave had spoken of the trader's squaw! *Wagh!* She who lay in the yaupon thicket could be none other than Wallace Challenger's runaway wife! Now wasn't that something?

They heard Laure parting branches, then the gasp she emitted on entering a little clear space in which Winsome Challenger's contorted body, sprawled among pine needles, kicked and furrowed in her agony. She already had given birth. Even though inured to brutal sights, Taqua felt revolted; blood was everywhere, the soiled skirts and petticoat stained with bloody water.

Pulling herself together, she rushed over to the tiny, purple-pink creature lying between the mother's legs and across the slimy, purplish placenta. She snatched up the infant by its feet, ignoring the umbilical cord that trailed from it.

The tiny ankles were slippery, but she managed to hold firm, though she slapped the minute buttocks briskly a dozen times, there came no reaction whatever. The bloodied little thing just dangled limp from her hand—like a fresh-skinned raccoon.

Then Laure called for her husband. "Do you know who this is?"

"Yes. I have only just been told she comes from Capola."

Laure nodded. "She has lost so much blood I doubt she will live. Please build a fire. I must heat something for her to drink."

Sakwari-cra, studying those sweat-bathed and discolored features he'd once secretly admired, remembered Winsome Brooks moving about the market house in Savannah, straight, cool, and ever so sure of herself. Right now, she didn't much resemble that memory.

At length he said, "I must return to camp to receive tomorrow's orders, but I will leave one of my men to guard you. He will do what you tell him."

He had turned to go when Winsome's lips moved. "Wallace? Oh, my God—Wallace—you—near?"

Once Laure had passed a damp cloth over her face, Winsome stirred and began to babble. In muffled, disjointed mumblings she touched on all manner of subjects: her father, Robbie, Helen Glen. In hatred she mentioned someone called Starbuck. All through the distorted pattern of her mouthings Wallace Challenger's name appeared and reappeared. Only once did she mention Micah Oxford—complaining about something he'd promised to do and hadn't.

When Lieutenant Thad Burton rejoined the group waiting beside the horses, he said crisply, "Sergeant, she's still alive. All right, mount up." He repeated the order in Creek.

"We're headin' back to camp?"

"Yes. I must find that poor lady's husband and tell him what has happened."

Silently Thad wondered, What will Wallace Challenger do when he learns his wife is nearby and sick unto death?

Back in camp Thad was astonished to find that Shatara and Hushoni, the sub-mico's second-in-command, had assembled the Sakwari replacements and that they were stuffing themselves around a cook fire—like men who expected not to eat much for a while. While it was a temptation to curse out Shatara for having failed to mention the white woman's presence in his party, he restrained himself. This wasn't the right time.

Bowlegged, hawk-faced, and saturnine, Shatara lost no time in conveying news of importance.

"O Mighty Mico Thlucco, the Long Warrior of the Rangers would speak with you as soon as may be."

"Very well, but why are my warriors stuffing food? Why are they armed and their horses ready?"

"Because," said Shatara solemnly, "an *Englasi* Raven said we must go out tonight."

Thad, clad in Challenger's old green militia tunic, rode up to the Rangers' command tent and decided that, surely, some major move impended; not only was towering Major Challenger present, but also tough old Colonel Palmer, whose rough brown skin resembled the inner side of a badly dressed buckskin. Standing beside him was one of his sons, a captain in the Carolina Volunteers. By the fire stood Captain John MacIntosh of the Independent Highland Company, wearing a Scottish bonnet, tartan sash, and a faded kilt showing his clan colors.

Challenger greeted the new arrival with a curt nod. "Time you got here. Where the hell you been?" Without waiting for an answer he went on. "Now you fellers better listen close to what Colonel Palmer's goin' to say."

The veteran, who was standing to leeward so that the smoke would thin out some of the mosquitoes, squirted tobacco juice to sizzle among the coals at his feet. "Seems the general's come to his senses at last; says he wants the Black Fort took back, quick as possible." His eyes swept the circle of fire-bronzed faces. "And 'quick,' I take it, means right now! I want everybody to get their people down beside the river inside of a hour." He spat again. "Beats me why we've been quartered back here on the St. John all this time when, by rights, we should ha' been camped near Fort Diego."

As he turned away Palmer grunted, "That's all. Ye c'n get on your way, boys."

He noticed that a big young fellow wearing a well-used Georgia Militia uniform coat didn't break away with the rest. "Well, what's keepin' you, Son? Didn't you hear me say to get a move on?"

Thad managed an awkward salute; he'd not had time yet to practice much. "Yes, sir, but I've an urgent message for Major Challenger."

Wallace Challenger heard the news granite-faced, then demanded harshly, "Well, Burton, what d'you expect me to do? Burst into hosannas of joy?"

"No," came the quiet response. "But I thought you ought to know."

"All right, I know. Now get going."

Chapter 20

DISPUTES

Although it proved strangely thrilling, if unfamiliar, to wear European uniform and be addressed as "Mister" or "Lieutenant" or "Sir" by white troops, Thad Burton deemed it politic when among his Sakwaris—which he was most of the time—to dress as he always had and to draw broad bands of red and black paint across his face. To tell the truth, he felt a lot more comfortable and at ease in a breechcloth, leggings, and a simple headdress of turkey feathers, but whenever he thus shifted apparel he thought of Chula and bitter anger constricted his heart. Would Chula come back? His hurt pride kept insisting that he would.

During the past two days he had learned a lot about the whites' way of warfare largely because an English-born Scot, Major Hugh MacKay, who was acting adjutant of Oglethorpe's Regiment, had taken a strong and inexplicable liking to him.

Only a little older than himself, MacKay was patient about explaining, in simple terms, the organization of regular European troops. He took evident enjoyment in exploring the Black Fort with this strange young white man about whose fabulous career he had heard so much. On the second night of their return to Fort Moosa, after the daily demonstration made before the walls of St. Augustine in obedience to Oglethorpe's orders, he undertook to name the fort's components.

"This is called a 'curtain wall,'" he explained as, pipes in mouth, they wandered along the narrow battlements. "It's that stretch of battlement which connects the salients; they're these masonry points which project from the fort's corners and allow the garrison to take attackers in enfilade. Your colonial engineers call 'em 'flankers.' What we're walking on now is called a 'fire step' and I don't need to tell you that these stone-faced openings are embrasures; they're really just oversized loopholes through which a cannon can be fired. These are 'crenelations'"—he touched the nearest one—"which shelter musketmen. Now that ditch out there"—MacKay pointed to a dry trough dug some ten yards outside the walls—"is what our engineers term a '*fosse*,' which is French for '*ditch*.'

"Now, those felled trees lying beyond the fosse with their branches sharpened and pointing outward, are 'abatis.' Such are especially useful against cavalry, but"—in the deepening dusk he smiled wryly—"not much hindrance to Indians or you frontiersmen who can wriggle through a knothole if you need to."

It was a beautiful evening with pines on the edge of that clearing on which stood the fort etched sharp and black against the sunset. A Union Flag, which was kept flying day and night because it could be seen from the ships and by the troops occupying Cape Quartell, fluttered as if tired out.

"One thing I can't understand," MacKay remarked, sucking so hard on his pipe that its coal picked out his thin, straight nose in gold, "is why doesn't the general send us the reinforcements and supplies he's promised Colonel Palmer, or yield to my prayers and those of MacIntosh, that we be allowed to stop up the breaches and to replace the gates?"

To his own surprise, Thad heard himself say slowly and thoughtfully, "Captain, I think it's because, as Colonel Palmer keeps saying, we weren't sent here to occupy this place—only to deny its use to the enemy and to demonstrate before the town. We're so few, the general fears we may get trapped inside."

MacKay looked startled, then his easy mood vanished. "Bosh! Rubbish! The general's grown overtimid. Why, man, we've a hundred stout Highlanders in here and I, for one, agree with MacIntosh there's small sense camping about in the woods catching the rheumatiz and risking snakebite. We've enough sick as it is!"

Gruffly, the adjutant demanded, "Tell me, Mr. Burton, what is your opinion on the subject?"

For a long moment Thad surveyed the smoke-hazed courtyard and the windowless barracks lining its far side. Everywhere, Highlanders were taking their ease; some were cooking, some slept comfortably enough on piles of dried palm fronds, others gamed or listened to a piper practicing soft trills on a chanter.

"Well, sir, if you want an honest answer, I believe Colonel Palmer and Major Challenger are right. Without more white troops in garrison, or without those breaches being stopped up, a surprise attack might succeed and spell death for men caught inside."

The adjutant frowned but made no comment as they resumed their leisurely circuit of the walls. They were passing the officers' house when voices rang out in anger. Both officers recognized William Palmer's rather high-pitched but strong and carrying voice.

"I tell ye, Captain, ye'll go on disregardin' my advice and warnin's at yer peril! Yer men should turn out and stand to arms no later than four o'clock of the morning, if ye're determined to stay in this ruin."

So easy as to sound insolent came Captain John MacIntosh's faintly burred reply. "Noo, sir-r, ye ken we've been over all that before. I know ye mean for the best but I say again, yon Spaniards are naught but a pack of lazy, cowardly dogs who'll never dare to assault us."

"Ye're wrong, Cap'n, dead wrong, and I hope that it won't take death to prove me right! And what if I *order* yer men out into the woods— like the general commanded?"

"We won't go, because ye've no' the authority to order us tae do any- thing! Till ye show us a proper commission," snapped MacIntosh, "Major MacKay and I refuse to heed your commands."

MacKay sighed in the deepening purplish twilight. "What a stubborn old fool that Palmer is! No doubt a stout Indian fighter in his day, he's grown a bit long in the tooth; 'tis careless of the general to leave him in such a position."

Thad looked quickly at his companion.

"Of course you don't understand." MacKay was at pains to be patient. "MacIntosh and I are both only captains, but *we* hold royal commissions, while poor old Palmer could only show a colonial one—if he can pro- duce it—which I doubt."

Thad kept quiet because now Palmer, down in the officers' house, was flying into a rage, squalling like a hungry panther. "Then have it yer way, ye damned, blind ijit, but remember *I* value my life no less than you do yours. Don't stay in like kenneled dogs and get yer throats cut!"

"Now, now, Colonel. Dinna fash yerself. Ye're free to go on camping- out along wi' the Georgia buckskins and that queer duck called Lieuten- ant Burton."

It followed, therefore, that Major Challenger's twenty Georgia Rang- ers and a like number of Sakwari-cra's warriors continued to bivouac and move about in the woods, thereby observing Oglethorpe's injunction that they should shift camp each night.

To everyone's amazement, the half-breed deserter Captain Tom Jones abruptly appeared at Fort Moosa leading a small party of Creeks. Jones, peering from under his drooping eyelid, said he'd decided not to go home just yet, but failed to mention that Caesar had sent messengers threatening terrible punishments if Jones and his band did not return at once. But still there came no sign of Chula; Sakwari-cra's expression grew steadily grimmer. Shatara was going to need a talking-down pretty soon. Obviously, the sub-mico had heard about Chula's defiant—and thus far unpunished—defection.

Deeply disturbed by the implications of that dispute in the officers' house, Thad slept lightly and therefore awakened the minute he heard Colonel Palmer, softly cursing his stiffened joints, get up, relieve himself, and then pull on his Ranger's gear.

Judging by the stars, Thad guessed it must be around four of the morning and once again resolved to own a watch; he'd beg, borrow, or steal one somewhere. Most regular officers and a good many colonials carried them. Besides, rough guesses about the time weren't good enough for this strange, new kind of warfare.

Shivering a little, Thad slid out of his blanket, for, no matter how crushingly hot the days were, when darkness fell, it grew very cool, almost cold on occasion.

On his way over to Palmer's bivouac, Sakwari-cra, again in Indian regalia, took care to step on a twig. The colonel and his son left off stretching and yawning and whirled, hands on pistol butts.

"Who's there?" Rangers sleeping under nearby trees were instantly, completely awake.

"'Tis only 'that queer duck called Lieutenant Burton,'" Thad announced in an undertone. "Heard you rousing, sir. Can I be of use?"

The veteran Indian fighter's eyes bored through the semidarkness. "I doubt it, but ye may as well come along and bear witness to the folly o' those blasted, hardheaded Scotchmen!"

Never a sentinel challenged when the three soft-stepping figures left the dark of the trees and, silent as hunting owls, started across the clearing toward Fort Moosa. By brilliant starshine it was very easy to distinguish that black gap in the fort's south wall created by the missing gate; another sinister hole marked a wide breach made in the west wall.

Although the colonel continued to mutter angrily as he advanced, no one had challenged by the time the trio came right up to the empty portal.

"Listen to 'em snore! The stupid tug-muttons!"

On entering the gate, Thad could distinguish the outlines of two Highlanders seated just inside the portal sound asleep, with shaggy heads sagging far forward. They had propped their guns against the wall be-hind them and one of them was doing a fine job of snoring.

Unnoticed and unhindered, Palmer and his companions entered the court, saw knots of men asleep on pallets of palm fronds among clumps of stacked muskets. Some of these slumberers had wound tartan cloaks around them, but most must have been oblivious to the air's nip, so hadn't covered themselves at all.

Now and then a Highlander would turn over, mumbling and grumbling in his sleep; others would cough or sigh—they were tired men—while a chorus of variously pitched snores rose and fell in all directions.

The veteran made straight for the officers' house, strode inside, and grabbed MacKay by a shoulder.

The adjutant turned over sluggishly and, batting his eyes, sat up, a thick mat of blond hair visible on his naked chest. "What is it?"

"Had I been a Injun er a Don, ye'd not be askin' anythin'. For God's sake, Cap'n, *will* ye wake up and make yer men stand to? 'Tis the very hour for a attack."

Captain MacKay broke into a volley of curses. "God damn your ugly eyes! Get out of here, you timorous old fool, and let us rest while we can."

Captain MacIntosh also awoke with explosive Gaelic curses on his lips and joined in heaping abuse upon the interlopers standing, grim and contemptuous, in the doorway. A few Scots sleeping nearby roused briefly.

"*Will* you clear oot o' here!" roared the Independent Company's com-mander. "We've sore need for our rest."

"All right, yer God-damn' fools. Ye'll get yer throats cut or find yer scalps ain't where they ought to be!"

Men both within and without the Black Fort were consuming, to the last scrap, a meager breakfast when, one and all, they heard what sounded like distant thunder. Puzzled, they looked at one another, for the morn-ing sky was a clear, unrelieved whitish-blue. At once it was realized that this thunder was not thunder at all, but the grumble of distant artillery which, on this, the eleventh day of June 1740 had commenced to bom-bard St. Augustine.

Colonel Palmer at once sent a young and agile Ranger swarming up to a crow's-nest he'd caused to be built at the top of a very tall pine. From this precarious platform one could obtain a clear view—when the weather was right—not only of British batteries going up on Anastasia Island and Cape Quartell, but also of men-of-war such as *Hector, Phoenix, Tartar, Wolf,* and *Spence,* which had worked inshore as close as they dared to a sand bar shallowing the entrance to St. Augustine Harbor.

Through cupped hands, Challenger yelled up, "What d'you spy?"

"Not much," replied the now invisible lookout. "Only that our batteries and the ships are shootin' some."

"What's their castle doin'?"

"Firin' back so 'tis all blanketed wi' smoke. Hi! I spy a lot o' row galleys making toward the cape. Our people are shootin' at 'em. I kin see the shot splash ever so clear!"

While the Black Fort's garrison assembled and got stiff necks through peering up at the crow's-nest, a conviction spread that now the general would send strong reinforcements. Then, at long last, they'd get orders to attack the town along its landward side.

"Hi! What d'you know!" called out the young Ranger. "The Spanish galleys are turnin' and pullin' for home!"

"Any of 'em hit?" shouted up Captain Palmer.

"Not that I c'n see, and they're still shootin' at our people."

The bombardment didn't continue much longer; soon only familiar sounds prevailed in the vicinity of Negrito Village and Fort Moosa. Eager to obtain intelligence concerning the results of the bombardment —also to report the garrison's desperate need of food—MacKay and MacIntosh started a runner toward the seashore; commissary officers over there must be made to understand that, by now, the countryside had been swept bare of edibles, so, the Black Fort stood in urgent need of salt beef and flour.

Then, glumly, the garrison set about preparing for their usual "demonstration" before St. Augustine, which consisted of firing a few shots, waving flags, and generally making a show of themselves.

Next morning, bombardment by the men-of-war and the new batteries was resumed. This time their salvos sounded heavier and lasted longer, but, nevertheless, a lookout reported that no small-boat or infantry attack was being made. Nor did any staff officer arrive in Fort Moosa bringing instructions for its joint commanders.

On the third day, however, British gunnery improved; he on the crow's-nest called down jubilantly, "I just seen a great bomb bust square o'er the center o' their fort."

But the garrison was too damned hungry to react with enthusiasm, since the only supplies sent inland consisted of a few small sacks of rice and a half cask of very malodorous salted beef.

Colonel Palmer's anger deepened and Captain Tom Jones again began to mutter about going off—this time for keeps—and said so so loudly that Sakwari-cra overheard, and didn't enjoy the evident interest taken by Shatara in the half-breed's threat. Therefore, Thad took care to keep the sub-mico nearby most of the time, made frequent unannounced visits to Sakwari campfires.

After sunset Colonel Palmer sent for Thad; he found the veteran seated on a log and thoughtfully cutting himself a chew of tobacco. "Glad ye're in yer Injun outfit," said he, "'cause I've a special job for ye. Take a seat."

Sakwari-cra, however, only sank onto his heels as he had done for many years. You could get up and take action quicker that way.

Silver-bristled jaws beginning to work, the veteran queried, "Remember that big yeller two-story house stands 'bout a mile west o' the town?"

Thad nodded; he'd seen it several times.

"Well, for some reason them high-mucky-mucks over yonder"—he jerked his head toward the seacoast—"wants us to throw a scare into the Dons, so I want ye should take yer men and Tom Jones and his boys and set that house afire. Guess they figger a blaze might throw a scare into the enemy and cover up somethin' they're fixin' to do. Think ye c'n find yer way?"

Thad nodded.

"Well, ye'll have to look sharp. Like you c'n see, it's blacker'n the insides o' Satan's pockets tonight and that place lies a far piece from here."

"I'll do my best. When shall I start?"

"Not till around midnight—by then Spanish patrols will have gone home fer sure."

Colonel Palmer had not been exaggerating in the least when he'd said that this night was dark; an unbroken mass of high cloud was obscuring the stars almost without exception. The party proceeded on foot, since horses were apt to snort at the wrong time or trip over something and cause a racket. Half-a-dozen times Thad thought to glimpse the building he was to burn, but always it was only an optical illusion and nothing was there.

Following Palmer's instructions not to waste so much time that he couldn't, for sure, be back at the fort by four, Thad, angry clear through, reluctantly decided to turn back. He could tell by the taut way they walked that his followers also were disgusted; another fruitless sortie!

Sakwari-cra was leading his brief column across a sandy place where even soft footfalls were completely deadened, when he heard something like the thudding of a distant drum; that pulsing sound seemed to be coming from a big grove of slash pine.

Captain Tom hissed gently, like a small snake. "You smell smoke?"

"Yes," Thad breathed. "You and I will go and see what's going on. Shatara can lead the men back to camp."

Employing infinite skill and patience, Sakwari-cra and the half-breed Creek were able to crawl within earshot of an open space near the center of the pine grove. Easily four hundred Yamasee and other Spanish Indians were gathered in a ring and watching a number of wildly caparisoned warriors prance before a bright ceremonial fire.

Another blaze was flickering and flaring farther on. What chiefly alarmed the onlookers was the presence of some fifteen or twenty Spanish soldiers! Some were wearing yellow jackets, others were clad in the blue-and white-striped cotton uniforms worn by colonial forces.

Thad soon decided that most, if not all, of the many Negroes present were crouched about the farther fire. Some of their companions, too, were cavorting about, brandishing spears, hatchets, and long-bladed knives. Their gyrations, however, differed markedly from those of the Indians prancing around the larger blaze.

Somehow, it didn't astonish Sakwari-cra that a huge black man whose left arm swayed useless by his side suddenly leaped to his feet and broke into the wildest sort of dance; even though Quobah Tutu was a good distance off and was liberally smeared with weird designs done in white paint, Thad recognized him at once.

At a quick glance, he estimated that the Kumassee King was accompanied by no less than a hundred followers. Seen by firelight, the gigantic Ashanti created an unforgettable picture in his jaguar-skin cloak and a high headdress topped with a clump of glaring, bright blue and scarlet macaw feathers. As easily as if it were a band leader's baton, the Kumassee King twirled and spun a massive knobkerrie high above his head.

The African drums, deeper-toned and, in a way, much more pulse-quickening than those of the Indians, changed their beat, began to roar so loud that even some of the Yamasees turned in time to watch some burly Negroes drag forward a furiously protesting, large black billy goat.

An outlandish figure, probably a witch doctor, pranced out, howling and brandishing a broad-bladed curved knife. Once four huge blacks had heaved the struggling beast clear of the ground, the witch-doctor jerked back the goat's bearded head and cut its throat in such a fashion that Quobah and the nearest warriors were sprayed by blood bursting from the severed arteries.

Captain Tom suppressed a grin. *Wagh!* Here was something new! A rite worth copying, sometime.

Eyes glittering bright as those of a stalking fox, Thad returned his attention to the closer fire, watched a succession of warriors leap up and whirl around the fire, all the time brandishing tomahawks, knives, war clubs, and even an occasional firearm. Their chanting grew hysterical, savagely stirring, as they lashed themselves and the onlookers into a murderous frenzy.

Thad tapped the half-breed's bare back—they both went naked above the belt—and commenced to wriggle backward. They made no more noise than a pair of snakes.

When, finally it was safe to stand up, Captain Tom whispered, "I think, Sakwari-cra, we had better start running. The night is dark and it is a long way to the Black Fort."

Chapter 21

MASSACRE

Afterward, it was judged that Thad and Captain Tom must have returned to camp sometime between three and four of the morning—which continued "lightless as the inside of a large black cat," as Captain Charles Dempsey put it.

Wallace Challenger and the Palmers, father and son, already were awake and alert. They listened with care and in silence to all that the Indian leaders had to report, then took immediate action: a long while back, they'd agreed on what should be done if a surprise attack were indicated.

It didn't take long for Indians and Rangers to throw a loose circle of pickets in the shadowy woods surrounding Fort Moosa. The line was being drawn too close in, thought Challenger, but there was no help for it; the clearing's circumference had grown so great that to post lookouts farther away would have left such wide gaps between posts that the enemy easily might filter through unnoticed.

There was an explosive conversation in the officers' house when William Palmer, accompanied this time by Wallace Challenger, burst in to give the alarm. Incredibly, neither MacKay nor MacIntosh would credit the report of war dances going on.

"Bosh! The savages are always dancing, for one reason or another," said MacKay yawning, and turned his face to the wall. "If you're so sure those redskins are a great threat, go tackle 'em yourselves, but as for me, I refuse to turn out my men at this ungodly hour because of another crackpot report."

Although Palmer cursed, ranted, and raged and pointed out that the line of pickets around the Black Fort was perilously thin and liable to penetration, neither MacIntosh nor the adjutant would heed him.

"Oh, go awa', auld mon. Ye're just crying wolf again, 'twad seem," grunted MacIntosh, settling back on his pallet of palm fronds. "Ye'd best get some sleep yersel'."

As they were picking a route among the figures sleeping about the fort's courtyard Challenger growled, "I'd never have believed it! An you agree, I'll call in enough outposts to muster a force sufficient to launch a counterattack when the time comes."

Darkness, as opaque and enveloping as a thick woolen cloak, enveloped the earth. Under its cover, Captain Lamberto, Quobah Tutu, and Tolemato, a half-king of the Yamasees, signaled their followers to halt, suspecting a trap; their luck against a wary enemy simply could not continue so unbelievably good, for, thus far, not one of the four columns converging upon Fort Moosa had even been challenged!

Crouched at the edge of the woods, Quobah was just able to sense the outline of the fort's squat tower and that of a shadowy flag fluttering above it—the flag of the accursed English! He ground his teeth and his thigh muscles began to quiver; tonight, many an outrage would be paid for.

"Come," he whispered, and was reassured to feel his "Left Arm," invisible in the gloom, grip his useless hand.

The Kumassee King got almost halfway across the cleared ground before someone finally saw him and yelled, "Who's there? Halt, or I'll shoot!"

Quobah made no reply, only quickened his pace. Expecting a shot to blaze out, he heard only the harsh panting of his followers as he dashed for the main gate. He hoped that the other detachments were sweeping as fast toward their respective objectives—those wide breaches in the wall ordered by James Oglethorpe. Of course, the party ordered to penetrate the third hole in the walls had farther to go, so could not be expected to strike until after the fight had got well under way.

Since, with one arm crippled, he couldn't fire the blunderbuss he would have preferred to use, Quobah was armed with a heavy boarding pistol, but his "Left Arm" was carrying his heaviest knobkerrie. He heard, off to his left, a sudden yelping of Indian voices—whose he couldn't tell— then muskets crashed and flamed. Deadly cool, the Ashanti slowed to allow his men to come up with him, then ordered them to deploy into a broad column lest the enemy had a cannon mounted beneath the main gate.

The instant Wallace Challenger heard the sentry sing out and his challenge go unanswered he faced the fort and yelled at the top of his lungs, "Enemy's here! Stand to arms but, for God's sake, don't fire till ye're fired on!"

To shadowy Rangers grouping about him he snapped, "Take it easy, boys! And ye'd better keep yer heads, those fellers in the fort ain't likely to. They'll panic first."

At the same time Colonel Palmer, once more outside the walls, raged like a lion, roared for the Highlanders to look alive else they'd get their gullets slit.

A spattering of shots to the westward served to convince the garrison that here was no false alarm. Half or wholly naked sleepers arose and, still off equilibrium through sleep, blundered about, bumped into each other, tripped, and sometimes fell. "What's amiss? Whaurs m' piece?" "Who's took my fusil? Damn it, 'twas right here!"

The only answers they got were blood-chilling Yamasee war whoops rising from right and left.

A Spanish voice—Captain Pedro de Lamberto's—bellowed, "*Adelante! Aprisa! Aprisa!* Forward! Quick! Quick! Forward with bayonet!"

At a brisk trot Lamberto's platoon of regulars and colonials converged on the breach, looming black and inviting in the east wall.

After what seemed an age, some Highlanders appeared, silhouetted upon the parapets. Fearfully, Challenger wondered whether they'd obey his order not to fire until fired upon, because he'd decided to mass his Rangers in the fosse some twelve yards out from the walls and to the left of the main gate.

Sergeants Slack, Felton, Corporal Bartow, and most of the men, for that matter, acted just as cool as if they were only witnessing a battle royal at some county fair. The Georgia Rangers hit the ditch only an instant before muskets flared along the parapet as bewildered Highlanders opened a ragged, indiscriminate fire.

"God damn yer stupid souls!" roared Felton when a bullet creased his buttocks. "Just fer that I'll make ye kiss it!"

Colonel Palmer came scrooching along the ditch until he recognized Challenger's huge outline. "For Christ's sake, go in there—tell them Scotch bastards to quit killin' us. Tell 'em to run through the breaches or drop over the walls whilst they can! Tell 'em—" The old Indian fighter's voice was drowned out by a thunderous enemy volley that followed a sudden, sparkling sheet of fire.

By the light of it, Challenger glimpsed Quobah's towering, barbaric figure. The Kumassee King, a smoking pistol in his good hand, was waving on his followers who, yammering like maniacs, were charging the undefended gate.

Challenger barely was able to beat a swarm of Yamasees to the western breach. He began shouting, "MacKay! MacKay! MacIntosh! MacIntosh! Where are you?"

For a time he had no luck; the confusion was incredible; everywhere wild-eyed Scots were milling about in the dark yelling senselessly. Swearing, using his musket's barrel for a club, the Ranger tried to beat the Scots into a line facing the main gate—and partially succeeded; a few Highlanders presented their pieces and fired blindly into the arched area.

For a moment muskets flashed, illumined the scene in garish detail, then darkness closed in leaving eyes blinded for priceless instants. Howls and yells resulted, then gun smoke combined with darkness to create a confused inferno.

Thus the first enemy rush was halted, or so it seemed. After warning the men to stand fast and use their knives and claymores, Challenger fought his way onto the court, all the while calling for the co-commanders. MacIntosh he never did find, but he came across Hugh MacKay armed with a dress sword and clad only in half-done-up breeches.

"My God!" he cried. "Where're they coming from?"

"From all directions," panted the Ranger while dim figures bumped and blundered into him before vanishing into the murk. "Quick! Quick! Get your men out of this place any way you can," he shouted, but MacKay only shook his head, then ran aside and, waving his sword, attempted to rally some men to join in the fight raging around the main gate.

"You bloody fool!" Challenger roared. "Any you Scotch dumblocks want to save yer hair had better follow me!"

Figuring that it would be the last to be sealed, he fought his way toward the breach in the north wall, leading the dozen or so Scots who, though mostly unarmed, had retained enough sense to follow. They struggled out onto the sandy clearing just as a fresh tumult arose announcing an attack on the fort's east side, where the breach was guarded only by Captain Tom and a handful of Creeks.

Crouched low in the ditch, the half-breed snarled, "White men! Fire when they come close. Kill with clubs and tomahawks, then run like hell!"

Captain Tom waited while the cacophony of disaster behind him swelled and the night rang with hideous sound. Thanks to approaching daylight, he was able to make out a tall Spaniard wearing a gorget and a tricorne. Rising to his knees, Captain Tom pointed a musketoon and, at the range of ten feet, blew that officer half apart. Other Creeks carrying guns used them, then started forward, but they flinched aside and began to run; they could sense, rather than see, a rank of bayonets closing in upon them.

A scattering of shots and plenty of bullets hissing about his head convinced the half-breed that little was to be gained by lingering in the ditch, so, with his remaining warriors, he headed for the woods' somber shelter. Running, Captain Tom became aware that almost the entire clearing was occupied by indistinct, hurrying figures. Once among the trees, he hooted like an owl, calling for his warriors to join him.

Pursuant to Colonel Palmer's previous orders, Sakwari-cra, without difficulty, restrained Shatara and his disciplined Sakwaris, kept them in the ditch outside the west wall. He felt a glow of pride; any other Indians would have gone running off, indiscriminately, to loot or to take scalps. Thad knew that Palmer's intention to take enemies seeking to rush the gate in the flank and then driven them off. The old Indian fighter's reasoning was sound, but the enemy were too numerous, by far, for anything to be accomplished by the Sakwaris.

To his last hour Thad Burton—reloading and directing his men to remain in the fosse—would remember the confusion, as appalling as it was complete, but he would retain no clear memory as to the succession of events. The mico thlucco could recall ordering his Sakwaris to fire a volley into an indistinct dark mass of enemies surging into the western breach, the thudding of blows, the yells and screams that resulted.

Uttering a yelping war cry, Shatara started up, but Thad gripped his belt, pulled him back into the ditch. "*Holwaki!* Bad! Reload, *atasi!* Watch what happens."

The next few minutes were appalling, ultimately tragic for the trapped Highlanders. Shrieking, leveling assegais and Indian spears, Quobah's Africans at last won the main gate and, hurdling a barrier of writhing, threshing bodies, rushed onto the fort's crowded and confused drill square.

Again, firearms boomed, created brief bursts of jewel-bright flame. At about the same moment the Spaniards entered the east breach while Yamasees, ignoring the Rangers' fire for the time being, rushed, screeching, through the west breach and drove the bewildered, half-armed Scots in utter rout.

"Save yourselves! Save yourselves!" MacKay began to shout. "Drop over—walls!"

MacIntosh, who had attempted, courageously enough, to stem the enemy's rush through the main gate, had gone down, helpless, a bullet through his thigh. Luckily for him, he soon found himself buried underneath a swiftly increasing pile of gory dead and wounded.

Like berserk, painted demons Spanish Indians ranged about the drill square, pitilessly clubbing, hacking, and stabbing disarmed and wholly bemused Highlanders. Quobah, ululating Ashanti war cries, brained several whites with his massive knobkerrie. Every time he struck he grunted, "Die, slaver!"

In passing through the gateway he had become separated from his "Left Arm," but that didn't faze him. Chattering filed teeth like an enraged mandrill, he glared about until he saw some Scots on the fire step. Howling, the Black Panther King started after them, but when the defenders saw him coming they risked sprained ankles and broken legs to drop out of sight before the raving African could reach them.

Fearing that these white men might get away, Quobah yelled to his nearest followers and headed a charge toward that section of the fosse where the Sakwaris already desperately were defending themselves against a pack of Spanish Indians. Time and time again, Sakwari-cra rushed out and, towering above the melee, used his hatchet to kill or disable some leaders.

When Quobah recognized his former blood brother he bellowed, "Smollett's farm!"

Groups of warriors momentarily left off fighting to open a path for the gigantic sable figure who, with crippled arm flapping grotesquely at his side, rushed at Thad with all the power of a charging bull bison.

Thad, who had just tomahawked a Yamasee and, finding trouble in wrenching free his blade, was swaying off-balance when the African closed in, whirling upward his bloodied knobkerrie. Thad knew he wouldn't be able to dodge, let alone use his war hatchet to parry.

The Ashanti's staring eyes, double-ringed by white paint, seemed to fly toward him with the speed of arrows. Sakwari-cra gasped defiance and, frantically, lurched backward, only to trip on a body and fall onto his back. This was just as well for him because his fall caused the crushing sweep of Quobah's club to fall short.

Growling Tuscarora curses, Thad rolled aside but sensed that he couldn't possibly avoid the Kumassee King's next blow. While vainly attempting to hurl his tomahawk in time he watched the great club whirl skyward and braced to meet its impact, but, suddenly, the knobkerrie wavered and, as in a distorted reflection in a pool, he saw an arm flung about the Ashanti's waist. Quobah's second blow accomplished nothing because he was dragged sidewise, struggling, with a knife blade plunged deep between his heaving ribs.

Whooping like a Chickasaw, Wallace Challenger grappled, then, disregarding a half-seen tangle of fighting Sakwaris and Yamasees, pulled down the Kumassee King and stabbed him again and again.

Half-blinded by sweat, Thad leaped to his feet, only to become involved in a knot of struggling savages. By the time he'd fought free, the Ranger wasn't to be seen. Only a mass of twisting bodies marked the spot where last he'd seen him. He'd no opportunity to investigate because Shatara, spouting blood from a heavy wound in the shoulder, ran up, grabbed him by the arm, gurgled, "Must run. Enemy too many."

There could be no denying that this was so. Instantly, Thad bellowed an order to retreat, but Shatara wasn't able to obey, for his knees buckled and he fell onto all fours with blood pouring onto the ground in great splashes.

Several times the remaining Sakwaris—they numbered only six—had to fight their way through scattered, hostile groups hurrying through the early dawn toward the Black Fort, but finally they broke through and raced into the woods in which horses, cut loose from their picket lines, were rushing and plunging about in white-eyed fear.

Only by chance did Colonel Palmer, fighting coolly, tellingly, farther down the fosse, see Challenger dash out of the ditch to grapple with a Negro quite as big and tall as himself. He couldn't see what happened after that, being distracted long enough to fire at yet another party that was pouring through the main gate.

When he glanced back in Challenger's direction he was nowhere to be seen, but there were a lot of Negroes visible. He couldn't know that the Ranger major was lying, half stunned by a glancing blow, and pinned down by panting Africans, but, nevertheless, Palmer ordered a volley from the entrenched Rangers which mowed down most of the black men over there.

"Steady, boys!" called the old man. "They're mad to get into the fort."

When Colonel Palmer stood up to reload, his son heard a hollow *thock!* which sounded very like the thud a bullet makes when hitting a deer in the intestines. Captain Palmer heard his father utter a sharp gasp as if he'd had his wind knocked out, then saw him drop his musket to grab at his abdomen with both hands.

"You bad hurt, Pa?" he screamed over the tumult.

"Hell, no! Been wounded lots worser," wheezed the veteran, then bent and picked up his musket. When he continued to reload, Captain Palmer, naturally enough, figured he'd only taken a graze so, like the grimly silent men around him, he kept on reloading and firing. But the next time young Palmer found time to look at his father he saw that a dark stain was spreading down the front of the old man's shirt, had spotted his breeches and leggings; dark trickles were running from the corners of his mouth.

"Pa! Pa! You *are* bad hurt!"

"Hell, no!" The colonel pulled off his cap and called out, "Hurrah, my lads! Today's our own! I been in a lot o' battles and never yet lost one."

Dempsey yelled, "Make sense, Bill! We're sure 'nough licked. If you aim to get us out o' here alive, time's come to pull foot!"

It took young Palmer only one swift look round about to realize that the white-haired captain was right. Momentarily, the space separating the ditch from the woods seemed all but clear. The enemy appeared intent, at any cost, to get into that fort from which came hideous, squealing sounds, like something made by pigs about to be slaughtered.

Somehow, they got the old frontiersman onto his feet, then half-dragged, half-carried him toward the nearest trees.

Growled Captain Dempsey after drawing a deep, shuddering breath, "I claim us boys have just taken one hell of a beatin'."

Colonel William Palmer died shortly afterward, while unwounded Rangers—they weren't many—were out cautiously rounding up horses and Scotsmen who were straying through the woods like lost cattle.

Just before the end came, he gasped, "Where's Wally Challenger? Don't see him."

Nobody knew.

Chapter 22

AFTERMATHS

How long he remained half buried under dead and dying compatriots Captain John MacIntosh retained no clear impression; the night had become too hideous for rational thinking. From every direction, it seemed, appalling howls, screams, and groans were arising. Although the hole in his thigh was bleeding fast and he was losing strength by the minute, he dared not make the least move to stanch it for fear of being noticed. He felt that, surely, he was about to die, when some Spanish Indians began to tear apart the heap of bodies above him.

Through slitted eyes he watched hideously daubed Yamasees haul out a body-wounded, blond young fellow named Craigie whom he'd often seen around New Inverness.

"Mercy! Ha' mercy! God save me!" bubbled the wounded Highlander; evidently he'd been shot through the intestines. "I—I've caused ye nae grief. Oh-h-h—"

The painted warriors paid no heed, only pinned Craigie on the hard-packed earth of the drill court. MacIntosh bit his lips—wished he could close his eyes. But, somehow, he couldn't. First they tore off the brawny young Scot's kilt and then in barbaric deliberation amputated his penis while the Highlander raised unearthly cries. The Indian sprang up, waved his trophy, then tucked it above one ear.

Other savages were wearing virile members stuck into their headdresses. One even had a bleeding phallus clamped between his jaws—like a dog carrying a bone. Then, and only then, did they take Craigie's scalp and cut his throat.

Judging by the number of dreadful cries, such atrocities must be t₍
place all over the dim and blood-splattered courtyard.

When another body was dragged off MacIntosh, he guessed his tu.
would come next, but a Spanish sergeant, chancing by, noted the richness
of a sword hilt projecting from beneath the captain's shoulder.

"You—officer?"

"Yes! Yes! And I surrender to you! For God's sake, save my men."

"Get up!" the Spaniard cried while using his espantoon to beat off
ravening Yamasees.

Somehow, John MacIntosh managed to sway to his feet but staggered,
and would have collapsed had not the sergeant, a tall and muscular
fellow, supported him toward a corner where some dazed prisoners stood
under the guard of a few yellow-coated regulars.

In the woods a good mile clear of the fort, Sakwari-cra and the remnant
of his men—only six in number—joined forces with the surviving Rangers,
for, fortunately, the Spaniards had been unwilling, or unable, to mount
a pursuit. Their Indian allies must have been too occupied with plunder-
ing the dead and tormenting the living.

A bitterness, as of green persimmons, soured Sakwari-cra's mouth and
mind. With Chula deserted and Shatara dead, along with at least a dozen
warriors, there could be no blinking the grim fact that the military strength
of his tribe had evaporated—unless he started rebuilding; right now, he
had no time or inclination to arrive at a decision on the matter. His
chief concern must be the protection of the women, children, and disabled Sakwaris so blithely deserted in Capola by Shatara. Although Thad
didn't know it, he'd no need to worry on that score.

He asked Dempsey, "Where's Major Challenger? He saved me from
death at the hands of the Kumassee King. After that I didn't see him
again."

Dempsey stanched an arrow graze that still was weeping crimson drops
along his gray-stubbled cheek. "Most likely dead. Under the circumstances,
there ain't much chance them crazy blacks would take him prisoner."

The Rangers then carried old Colonel Palmer's body over to a sun-
dappled glade in which rain had dug a little gully, and laid the cadaver
in it. Lacking spades, the grieving buckskins did the best they could and,
with their hands, scooped sandy earth into the declivity until it was full.

Once they had smoothed over the grave, young Palmer planted a short
length of a dead branch which he'd been whittling smooth and flat on one
side. Using his knife's point he'd traced an inscription upon it: "Colo.
W. Pamer"—the Captain could spell no better than most of his contem-
poraries—"B. 1681 D. 1740"

"I'll make you a better one, Pa, firstest chance I get." He patted the sandy ground twice, then stood up. "All right, fellers, let's get a move on. Burton, reckon you'd best tag along with us and we'll all be better off."

Among the few unwounded survivors of the massacre Hugh MacKay probably was the most miserably unhappy. Leading a party of about twenty half, or wholly, naked and almost unarmed Scots, he fought his way through greenbrier tangles regardless of thorns that clawed at his unprotected body like the talons of a bird of prey. In a later day it would have been deemed that he was in a state of shock. Try as he would, he still couldn't get it through his head that the disaster old Colonel Palmer so often had foretold had come true—terribly so. God above! At this time yesterday he and John MacIntosh had been in command of a hundred stout Scots. Oh God, he thought, what will the general do to me? He can't do anything less than have me shot.

That he had Quobah to thank for being alive Wallace Challenger was well aware: only a moment before the Kumassee King had died he'd rallied, reared off the ground on one elbow and had gasped to his men, "Hear my command! Take this man prisoner."

The more he thought about it, the more Challenger doubted whether Quobah Tutu had intended to confer a great favor by saving him from immediate death—he would only die later, very slowly, under the most exquisite tortures the African mind could devise. Too bad someone hadn't slashed his throat and abruptly terminated the sorry business of living.

He wouldn't have minded too much, for, somehow, life for him hadn't been particularly rewarding since that day he'd ridden into half-destroyed Chaugee Landing to find his home burned to the ground and, worse still, to learn that his son had been murdered and that his wife had run off with Micah Oxford.

Still nauseated by the head blow he'd taken, he resisted not at all when chattering, grimacing Negroes lashed his hands behind him and then hauled him to his feet. They had started to lead him away when a mounted Spanish officer, no doubt attracted by the prisoner's great size, rode up with a squad of cavalry clattering at his heels.

Coldly, the Don peered down from his saddle at this disheveled giant with a mane of tawny-yellow hair.

"Who are you?" he demanded in unaccented English. "If you know what is best for you, you will speak up and be truthful."

"I'm Major Wallace Challenger of the Georgia Rangers—and to hell with you!"

Captain Pedro de Lamberto's yellow-clad figure stiffened in the saddle.

"Challenger!" Then, peering through the rapidly graying light, he snapped, "It was you who commanded the defense at Chaugee Landing?"

"No," growled Challenger. "I was away."

"How very unfortunate, because we might have met there, rather than under these circumstances when you are at—well, shall we say at a disadvantage."

"Then you'll be the bastard who murdered all those people—my son among them."

"During a raid people are expected to die," rasped Captain Lamberto, as so many nightmarishly painted blacks began closing in that he began to have trouble with his mount. Curtly, he ordered his lancers to drive them away, whereupon the Negroes retreated toward a group of Africans who stood staring, grief-stricken, on Quobah Tutu's body.

To Challenger the Spaniard said, "You must quickly surrender to me or, by nightfall, there will not be a bee's weight left of you in one piece."

It came hard to say, "Suppose I've no choice, sir, so I'll surrender to you as a prisoner of war." Anything! Anything just to keep on living long enough to exact vengeance from this sardonic murderer.

Probably thanks to his rank as a field officer, Wallace Challenger that afternoon found himself occupying a cramped, but relatively clean, cell high in the tower of the Castle Santa María. What cheered the new prisoner most was the fact that a narrow loophole-window was admitting fresh salt air.

John MacIntosh did not fare half so well. With other captive Highlanders the wounded officer was pushed into an already crowded, dark, damp, and stinking dungeon.

Chapter 23

THE VANQUISHED

A few days after the Rangers and Sakwaris had ridden off to reoccupy Fort Moosa, an order came for those left behind to make their way to Fort Diego, near which General Oglethorpe had established temporary field headquarters.

Laure hadn't thought that Winsome Challenger possibly could make the trip, she being so very weak, and, worse, so dispirited, but an advance was made under the protection of a pair of Rangers on their way to

join Palmer's command. It was they who, joshing all the time, contrived
a litter of sorts. They took turns carrying the disabled woman with the
fifteen hard-faced braves of Shatara's party who, to their chagrin, had
been left behind when their mico thlucco had set out for Fort Moosa.

The better part of three hot and windless days was required to cover
fifteen, seemingly endless, miles to Fort Diego. Winsome, tight-lipped and
silent most of the time, stood the ordeal surprisingly well; only once did
she begin to bleed when helped to stand erect and then was apologetic.

Thanks to the good offices of sun-scorched and peeling Lieutenant
Archibald Glen, who finally had appeared leading a half company of
Georgia Volunteers, the two white women—forever a matter of deep curiosity in this all-male world—were installed in a rickety, abandoned one-
room farmhouse which lacked its doors and windows; however, the adobe
boasted a blessedly cool stone floor, so, after pallets of dry palmetto fronds
had been arranged, the women and Laure's children, leggy and spirited
but silent, found themselves comfortable enough—all things considered.

Shatara's warriors proved to be skillful providers—even though the
countryside had been foraged over many times; inevitably, some copper-
hued warrior turned up by nightfall lugging a strayed chicken or even a
limp shoat or two. When these were added to the army rations Glen drew
for them, they didn't go hungry.

On the third night following the arrival at Fort Diego, Winsome Challenger seemed stronger than at any time since Bob Slack had reconnoitered
the yaupon thicket; she even insisted upon staying up to launder one
of her two torn and indelibly stained petticoats.

Laure, who had taken this opportunity to wash her flaming hair, peered
through a smear of dripping locks. "I think it's time you explained why,
in your condition, you ran away from Capola."

"Didn't any of the Sakwaris say anything?"

"No. All any of them would tell me was the *Englasi* trader suddenly
rode off and left you behind. Why would he do such a thing?"

"I suppose I grew so—so bloated and unattractive. Besides, I—well,
I wouldn't sleep with him—I hadn't, for a long time." A mirthless laugh.
"What really brought matters to a point was that I kept on having nightmares in which I'd beg Wallace to forgive what I'd done to him." She
commenced to wring out her petticoat. "I remember Micah said, 'God
damn ye fer a faithless, calculatin' slut! I've given ye an easy life, and yet
ye keep on hollerin' for the man ye were eager enough to run out on! I
won't stand fer it. Better I'd taken along Tchimi, the poor redskin bitch—
at least she was true!' "

Winsome raised brown-ringed, haunted eyes. "Micah defied me to
swear that I'd ceased to love Wallace, that I loved only him."

The New England girl's sloping shoulders rose in a small, infinitely pathetic shrug. "I couldn't. At least I—I'm honest enough for that. Every passing day had taught me to see what a miserable, selfish fool I've been. And now—" Suddenly, she hid her face between her hands. "I—I don't know what I'll do if Wallace won't at least listen to what I want to tell him. Oh-h dear, I—I can't—I couldn't bear it if—"

Winsome commenced to sob so violently that presently Laure wrung water out of her lank red strands, then, in no great hurry, went over to pat her shoulder, for, despite her better judgment, Laure was beginning to take to Winsome somewhat; the Northerner was so uncomplaining, so very appreciative of any kind word or deed.

"Don't worry your poor self. They'll come riding in any day."

"Why do you say that?"

"Mr. Glen's heard that the people in the Black Fort are soon to be relieved."

"Oh, I'll pray that that's true!"

"And so do I," Laure said, "even more than you." At the same time she wondered just what the gigantic Ranger might do, if ever he decided to confront his wife.

Next day, it became Winsome's turn to try to comfort an unhappy female. The copper-haired young woman left the boys in her charge while she investigated a sudden hubbub in the Sakwari bivouac; the cause of it proved shattering. She recognized Tonak, a well-made youth she'd often seen around Capola, standing, thorn-scarred and wild-eyed, beside a jaded pony. From the excited way a circle of Thad's warriors were talking and waving their hands, she went cold.

Tonak stopped talking when his mico thlucco's squaw forced her way to him.

"Why is Tonak here?" she demanded in ringing Muskogean. "Who ordered Tonak to leave Capola?"

"Tonak came, O Taqua, because he alone can say what evil things happened in Capola."

"Loosen your tongue and tell me what you mean."

The boy, shivering with exhaustion and malnutrition, looked aside. "Taqua must know that soon after Shatara left Capola, the *Francani* mico in Fort Toulouse heard about this. He called together a war party of *Francani* and dog-descended Moviles." He fell silent, stared dully at the ground.

"They surprised Capola?"

"Yes, O Taqua. The *Francani* and their allies struck us, quick and hard; they slew everyone save some strong young squaws and boys numbering my seasons." Tonak rolled sunken, lackluster black eyes. "They set a torch to everything that would burn. They carried off all the horses and the beautiful, big guns of brass in our fort."

"Why did Tonak escape?" Taqua demanded in lifeless tones; somehow, her mind refused to comprehend the implications of this catastrophe. Yo-he-wa! What of Sakwari-cra's ambitions?

"Tonak was hunting a stray horse when the hostiles swooped. Tonak hid and watched. Then, when they had taken all the scalps and went away, Tonak caught the stray horse and rode here." It was typically Indian that the youth should make nothing of the remarkable fact that, unarmed and unguided, he had made his way to the seacoast three hundred miles away.

Thought Laure, it can only be God's will that Thad allowed me and the children to go along with him and Chula. Why? Never before has he taken other than warriors on a warmaking expedition.

It wasn't in Laure to weep, but when she thought of Thad she wished that she could. First Chula had betrayed him and now the very heart of his young nation had ceased to beat! Why had Shatara, cunning and war-wise above all others, elected to ignore Sakwari-cra's command? Was remaining completely loyal—no matter what—too much to expect of any redskin? "Redskin!" Laure was startled to find herself even thinking the white man's term!

The dire news from Capola took immediate effect; the morning after Tonak's arrival only three Sakwaris, too sick to travel, remained in bivouac.

During the night, Thad's cherished warriors had drifted off into the woods and hadn't returned.

Around noon of that same day, a wild-eyed Ranger, riding bareback, galloped up to headquarters, flung himself onto the ground, and, ignoring sentries, ran headlong into the command tent. Within minutes the news spread with the rapidity of fire in a drouth-parched fir forest: the men guarding Fort Moosa had been surprised and wiped out, almost to a man!

When Jeems and little John heard, they ran in, eyes very round, "Is Papa dead?"

"No one knows," Laure said, staring blankly straight ahead. Then she said in Catawba, "If Sakwari-cra is dead he will have taken many enemies to serve his spirit."

Winsome's muffled voice queried, "What—what of the Rangers? Were they—"

"They formed a part of the garrison," Laure said, then drew herself up briskly. "Suppose you grind some of that corn. Later, I'll bake us a pone. Come what will, we have to eat. You boys go and see if you can't hear some more news. And maybe trade for a rabbit."

Winsome steeled herself to match her companion's self-control, but her mind kept on spinning like one of those toy windmills boys had liked to whittle up in Boston. *Could* it be that solid, vital Wallace Challenger was dead? No! Never in the world! And yet, and yet!

Sometime early during the night lit by a magnificent full moon, a deal of noisy challenging began among the outpickets and the interior guard cursed loudly on being turned out in a hurry, but the excitement soon subsided and both women, miserable to the bottom of their beings, resumed thus far futile attempts to obtain forgetfulness in sleep.

All of a sudden Jeems, who'd ears like a lynx and slept as lightly as the Indians among whom he lived, ran to the door, bare bottom shining in the moonlight. "Ma! There's some men comin' this way. They're armed. Oh!" He raced out the empty doorway, yelling, "Papa! Papa!" just like any white boy.

Papa? Laure sat up in a flash. She slipped feet into moccasins but never bothered to pull on a cloak and rushed outdoors clad in a thigh-long shirt that left her graceful long legs silvered by moonlight.

Ignoring the presence of the few warriors trudging at Sakwari-cra's heels, she flung wide her arms and bounded toward him. *"Taskaya! Hokludsh!* My Warrior! My Sweetheart! *Ye pun hutupeces!* My God in the likeness of man!"

Thad's huge, barbaric figure straightened from trying to loosen the boy's frantic clutch about his knees.

"Tuni, Taqua," was all he said, then groaned softly.

Taqua intently studied her husband's face. It was wearing a totally unfamiliar expression. "Defeat" written all over him. When she realized that only six Sakwaris were with him she caught her breath sharply.

Where could she find courage to break the terrible news from Capola? How to inform him about the disappearance of those warriors he'd left to guard the camp?

Winsome brushed by and, eyes grown enormous, cried, "Please, for God's love, tell me—is Wallace Challenger safe—and well?"

As if he'd never seen Winsome, Thad Burton stared on the young woman whose hair was cascading over her shoulders. "He is neither—and because of that, I still live."

"What do you mean?" she faltered.

"He is dead."

Clutching at her throat with both hands, Dr. Brooks's daughter swayed a long instant, then went limp and collapsed onto the sandy gray ground.

Chapter 24

PRISONER

By standing on a three-legged stool which, with a pallet bed and a wooden pail, constituted the furnishings of his cell, Wallace Challenger found that he could peer out of an arrowslit and obtain a fairly good view of St. Augustine's seaward side. Best of all he was able, whenever the British mortars emplaced on Anastasia Island and Cape Quartell opened up, to watch the high, graceful arch of their shells as, trailed by whitish smoke, they came flying across the harbor. He could also spot most of the bomb bursts and could see that they were too light to do much damage; here and there a few bricks would be dislodged from the masonry or a shallow, star-shaped scar dug into the tabby-stone facings. Several shells had dug holes in the hard-packed earth of the Castle Santa María's parade ground.

As a rule, these bombardments were of short duration but successfully they provoked retaliation from heavy cannon mounted on the parapets and a battery in a small isolated fort lying off to the right. After a while both sides would quit and relative silence return.

For several days, endless days to the restless prisoner, there appeared to be no remarkable activity in the British positions visible to him. All there was to do was to watch a continual stream of supply craft, transports, and dispatch sloops pass and repass in the channel separating the cape from the island.

Larger supply vessels sometimes sailed or pulled out to the British squadron anchored close in beyond Anastasia. The two most powerful men-of-war, H.B.M.S. *Colchester* and H.B.M.S. *Hector*, both Fourth Rate of the Line, towered impressively above their consorts, dainty little sloops of war: *Tartar, Phoenix, Squirrel, Wolf*, and *Falcon*. When a general bombardment began, these joined the liners in hurling their heaviest shot into the town and its guardian forts—generally without appreciable results. Still, to Challenger's frustrated eyes, they presented a brave sight, all wreathed in gun smoke and with their flags and ensigns boldly aflutter.

At length something of significance did take place: the prisoner could tell by the number of red coats to be seen aboard a line of barges that Oglethorpe's Regiment was being transferred from Anastasia to the cape and that South Carolina's less colorfully clothed troops were being sent to replace them. Whether this exchange of positions was intended to discourage desertions Challenger could only guess, but, recalling the discouraged talk among the colonials, he suspected that this could be the chief reason for the shift.

What bothered the prisoner most was that he was forced to remain completely ignorant of what was transpiring on St. Augustine's landward side—where, of course, the remainder of his men and the Georgia Volunteers were stationed—or had been.

Being ignorant of Spanish, he could learn nothing from voices clearly heard on the battlements not twenty feet below. No one ever came near his cell save a sullen mestizo who might have been a deaf-mute for all he said. Twice a day this turnkey shoved a wooden plate of food—usually fish and rice—and an olla of water into his cell, then emptied the malodorous slop bucket which was the only convenience.

For a man of Wallace Challenger's physique and disposition, confinement of any sort always had been intolerable. At times he wanted to howl like a wolf, to batter head and hands against the slimy stone walls; they seemed to close in so inexorably. Plot as long and hard as he would, he could arrive at no scheme for escape which stood even a slight chance of success. Soon the half-naked giant in bloodstained rags became so mentally disturbed that he lost count of days; when night fell he only sat on the stool, mumbling and staring at inscriptions scratched on the wall by generations of prisoners.

It was the devil not knowing how much of a licking his Rangers had absorbed. How many had been killed, wounded, or, like himself, taken prisoner at Fort Moosa? Had the place been retaken by the British?

Had Burton's Sakwaris fared any better? Probably not. The last he remembered, Thad and his warriors were being rushed from three directions by masses of screaming Indians and Negroes. Had Burton survived after his narrow escape from getting brained by the Kumassee King's knobkerrie?

Not even now did it occur to Challenger that Sakwari-cra undoubtedly owed him his life—although it was only by pure chance that he'd come up to grapple with Quobah at that critical moment.

Often the huge figure lay motionless on the pallet, fingers locked behind head. To occupy his mind, he set about recalling even unimportant details of events that had happened before James Oglethorpe had come ashore that gray winter's day seven long years ago.

Odd, how repeatedly the image of Thad Burton entered the pattern of his recollections: that night ride to Major Smollett's plantation—their confrontation after the massacre of Brodbelt's party—the fight above War Club Pond. What a strange, unpredictable character—if he still lived. What unfathomable working of his mind had prompted him to bring his wife and children along to this war? Certainly, never before would he so have encumbered himself on the warpath.

Most obstinately recurrent of all was Winsome's image, the devious intricacies of her character equaled, if they did not surpass, those of Thad Burton. Time and again her face returned, for all he was resolved to banish all thought of her. What fate had befallen her? All he had learned, for certain, was that she'd come east with one of Sakwaricra's sub-micos and that she'd been delivered of a stillborn child—Mike Oxford's brat! Or—or could it possibly have been of his getting—conceived just before the attack on Chaugee Landing? Yes. They *had* made love just before he'd set off on that expedition from which he'd returned too late. He attempted to count back the months but found that he couldn't.

Could she possibly have survived childbirth following such a long and grueling ride? Probably not; she was no squaw, nor was she anywhere as tough as Taqua. Everybody knew that riding horseback in advanced pregnancy was about the worst thing a woman could do.

He sighed, thankful at least that this cell was high enough above the ground to keep it free of mosquitoes. On the ramparts a sentry raised a melodious, long-drawn cry of "*Centinela alerta-a!* The man guarding the next post then made his report, "*Centinela alerta-a!*" By degrees the reports faded, died out.

How did he really feel about Winsome? At times he hated her, wanted to shout his loathing and contempt as he took a thick stick to her, before striding off for good. After all, if she'd been at home, Robbie wouldn't have been murdered. Then again—they'd been so very happy for so long. If only Robbie hadn't died! But he had.

When, next morning, the barefooted prisoner climbed up onto his stool he saw that, during the night, *Hector* and *Colchester* had moved in as close to the bar as they dared. His breath quickened when he realized that most of the smaller sloops of war had crossed the bar and now lay anchored bow and stern, broadside on, in the channel between Anastasia Island and Cape Quartell.

Surely, these dispositions argued that a general assault was imminent? Like gargantuan beetles, dozens of small boats kept crawling across the bright blue water conveying troops, supplies and munitions to the batteries on Anastasia Island. Only a little wind was blowing out of the east, just enough to unfold and flaunt the ensigns and jacks on His Britannic Majesty's ships.

Challenger hung to the single bar dividing the arrow slit and craned his neck this way and that until his arms ached.

Of course, these activities had not been ignored by the defenders. Row galleys and half galleys mounting at least one cannon each were being manned and armed against landing parties from the ships. Whole companies of infantry and artillerists appeared to man the parapets of the Castle Santa María.

Finally, Challenger's hands cramped so badly that he had to let go the bar and, cursing his uselessness with every obscenity he could lay tongue to, he raged about his tiny cell. He yearned to do so much, to lead, to make the fight of his life and so perhaps to drive some of the sickness from his soul.

Chapter 25

GRAND COUNCIL

At noon on the third day of June 1740, a flotilla of small boats commenced, from many directions, to converge on H.B.M.S. *Flamborough*, sloop of war presently serving as flagship in these waters. The boatswain's pipe twittered almost without stopping as gig after gig rounded up below the main Jacob's ladder and discharged Indian chiefs, officers in blue, scarlet, green, and ordinary homespun.

Captain Vincent Pearse, commodore of the squadron, waited at the break of his quarter-deck to receive visitors. Under an awning, rigged to cut off the worst of the sun's heat, chairs and stools had been ranged along the quarter-deck railing and a table placed to one side. At it a trio of secretaries, sweating heavily in their black coats, occupied themselves by sharpening quills and setting out all manner of papers.

They came aboard, navy officers first, wearing a wide variety of costumes—a naval uniform had yet to be devised—Captains Lance of *Colchester*, Sir Yelverton Peyton of *Hector*, Warren of *Squirrel*, Crawford of *Falcon*, Townsend of *Tartar*, and others. Next to appear was Lieutenant Colonel Cook of Oglethorpe's Regiment, green-faced scarlet jacket blazing bright as a bonfire; old Colonel Vanderdussen in faded blue. He was followed up the ladder by some gaily caparisoned but sedate Indians: Caesar, the Creek leader, Wolf of the Cherokees, and Toonahowie of the Yamacraws.

To Colonel Vanderdussen it came as a grim reminder of the tragedy at Fort Moosa that the Georgia Rangers should be represented not by Major Challenger but by white-haired Captain Dempsey. Nor was tough old Colonel Palmer in attendance.

To the number of around thirty, officers gathered along the port rail to witness the approach of a twelve-oared barge flying a large Royal Jack. Everyone recognized the tall, spare figure of James Oglethorpe sitting, bolt upright, in the stern sheets. Wearing the splendid uniform of a colonel of the Regular Establishment, Oglethorpe gained the main deck to a frantic shrilling of silver pipes.

Respectfully, the commanding general lifted his tricorne to the quarter-deck, then, hand on the pommel of a fine dress sword, he stalked between a double file of scarlet-clad marines standing under gleaming bayonets, towards the quarter-deck ladder.

A stillness descended upon the quarter-deck as Commodore Pearse, wearing a long-skirted tunic of bottle green, went down to meet the commander-in-chief. Lifting his hat, he bowed stiffly. "Welcome aboard, sir. The council stands ready to convene."

Everyone under the awning bowed and the Indians, with great dignity, made the peace sign while Oglethorpe marched briskly over to a large armchair placed behind a small table-desk.

That a critical moment for this campaign was at hand everyone appreciated. Even the Indians appeared preternaturally solemn.

"A very good day to you all, gentlemen," Oglethorpe began pleasantly. "I have summoned you because of certain advices forwarded to me last night by Commodore Pearse."

The navy officers, who had gathered in a close, varicolored group, held their breaths; they knew, well enough, the gist of that message, it having been discussed at length and drafted in Sir Yelverton Peyton's comfortable cabin on *Hector*.

"For your benefit I shall request Captain Pearse to repeat the burden of his communication." Oglethorpe's voice sounded flat, but his manner remained courteous.

Pearse cleared his throat, started to look uncomfortable but took refuge in a stiff, slightly defiant manner. "At a council held last night aboard the *Hector*, the captains of this squadron came to the unanimous conclusion that it will be extremely hazardous for His Majesty's ships to delay their departure from these shores by more than a day, or two at the most."

His hard black eyes swung to Oglethorpe, sitting as stern and expressionless as the bust of some early Roman general. "The hurricane season, sir, is at hand. We, who are charged with the safety of His Majesty's ships and men, are convinced that we must quit these waters for a safer place."

Oglethorpe's fingers caressed a large ruby set in the guard of his sword. "I quite understand. It would be folly to risk these valuable ships and more invaluable men to no purpose." His gaze shifted to the knot of naval officers. "In view of this admitted fact, gentlemen, I invite your opinion as to what should be done."

Captain Warren of *Squirrel* spoke up. "Why, sir, if you'll order an immediate general assault, delivered by *all* the forces at your command, we will facilitate it by bombarding the enemy to the limit of our capability."

The general's narrow, graying head inclined once, twice. "In other words, you deem a general attack today or tomorrow advisable?"

"No, sir!" Commodore Pearse broke in. "Not advisable, but essential, sir, if you mean to win this siege with naval assistance."

With halted breath, Lieutenant Glen, representing his captain, who'd come down with one of many fevers riddling the besieging army, watched Colonel Vanderdussen step forward. In a ringing voice the bittern-thin old man cried, "Sir, we *must* make this assault at once! There is every reason in its favor."

"And what are these reasons?" Oglethorpe's voice remained level but incisive.

"First off, sir, many of my men are sick—more every day; all but a few of the healthy have become discouraged through long inaction suffered under rigorous conditions. Desertions, sir"—he paused and knew that everyone was thinking the same thing—"desertions are mounting, but we have not lost so many poltroons that my regiment cannot acquit itself with honor. Believe me, sir, the men burn to fight. For God's sake, sir, give the word!"

Deliberately, Oglethorpe straightened the sword on his lap. "And what, sir, would you estimate to be the butcher's bill for an attack such as you advocate?"

Colonel Alexander Vanderdussen flushed under his wrinkled sunburn. "Why, sir, an attack of this sort shouldn't cost us over—say over five hundred men, killed wounded and missing. Then we'd have our victory and at a modest price."

"Thank you, sir." Oglethorpe then turned to Lieutenant Colonel Cook. "And what, sir, would be your estimate of losses?"

The regular took a deep breath, stroked his chin a moment, then said, "Why, sir, I venture that Colonel Vanderdussen ain't far wrong. But, having had some experience against assaults upon largely undamaged fortifications, I'd venture casualties of around seven hundred men might come considerably nearer the mark—and that estimate, sir, would not include men from the Naval Establishment."

Commodore Pearse spoke up in a hurry. "It has not been contemplated that these ships will send out landing parties."

The Raven, Caesar, who to a marked degree resembled his namesake sculptured in bronze, stalked out into the open space before Oglethorpe's chair, pink flamingo feather headdress asway. "My father, let the warriors tonight wet their knives and war hatchets. The young men become insolent, hard to restrain. No more than their elders, do they understand why, at this late day, the town still remains in hostile hands."

Although awed by such important company, Captain Dempsey spoke out, "My brother Caesar speaks from a true heart. Unless an assault is made quickly our red brothers will disappear like a little puddle under a hot sun."

One after another, members of the council, at Oglethorpe's invitation, had their say. Glen alone, perhaps, understood or could comprehend something of the general's dilemma. When it came his turn to speak, he tried to lend encouragement. "Sir, the Georgia Militia now stands at half strength—the poorer sort having deserted. However, sir, you can count upon the rest of us to do our part."

Before Glen could continue, mortars on Anastasia opened, sent flat, dry-sounding reports over the shimmering channel.

At the end of an hour's discussion it became evident that the progress of the siege turned upon a single point. Was General Oglethorpe prepared, come what might, to order a grand assault before the men-of-war departed?

Sweating heavily, Oglethorpe got up from his chair. "Gentlemen, I believe I have heard all opinions—pro and con. I understand your arguments and the reasons which have caused you to advance them.

"Believe me, nobody desires a swift and successful termination of our expedition more than do I. However"—the assembled officers began to exchange glances, as if they'd been expecting qualifications all along—"however, I must give a decision affecting so many people considered thought. I, therefore, direct that, this evening at the hour of eight, all commanding officers shall appear before my tent on Cape Quartell.

"At that time I will render a decision."

Chapter 26

GETHSEMANE ON A DUNE

"You lads are really lucky to have drawn this relief," observed Lieutenant Archibald Glen to the Wardrop youths. "It'll be almost cool in a little while."

The two, who sometime ago had outgrown garments they'd worn on leaving Chaugee Landing, beamed through their freckles like a rising sun. "Aye, sir, if our relief's tardy we won't mind it a bit out here."

The relieving detail of pickets was plowing over a high dune from which they could see the ocean and the dark clusters of ships concentrated about Anastasia Island. Although a sea breeze had commenced to move inland the sand, though, still was hot under the militiamen's calloused bare feet.

Glen had halted in order to relieve a sentinel of the old guard when tow-haired Luke Wardrop dropped his eyes and squirmed big toes into the sand. "Please, sir, kin I ask you somethin'?"

"Fire away."

"Are we goin' to fight tomorrow? Some of the fellows thought so."

The ex-cornet shook his head. "Maybe. But we won't know for sure till sometime tonight."

"Hi! Look, Mr. Glen!" Chauncey Wardrop shielded pale brown eyes against the setting sun. "Ain't that somebody ridin' this away?"

It didn't require Glen long to recognize that solitary horseman. His scarlet uniform jacket was giving off so many flashes they could only have been made by a very high-ranking officer's; in fact, the commander-in-chief was cantering up.

"Form up, you men! Form up in two ranks," barked Glen, "and try to look as if you haven't just escaped from the nearest cow pasture."

The guards, all furnished by the Georgia militia, set straight their floppy hats, did up what few buttons remained to them, and lined up the best way they knew how, but they remained a scruffy-looking lot in their worn-out civilian clothes.

Aware of the intended honor, James Oglethorpe reined off his course and pulled up while the militiamen presented arms and Archibald Glen saluted with his sword.

"Ah, Mr. Glen. I see you've here the makings of some very fine soldiers." Kindly, he frowned as he noticed the Wardrop boys. "I've seen you before. What are your names?"

Standing as stiff and straight as if under inspection before Whitehall Palace, Glen told him.

"Wardrop? Wardrop? I say, Glen, weren't these young fellows and their family aboard the *Anne* with you and me?"

How like the general, thought Glen, to phrase his question like that. "Aye, sir. We all were aboard the *Anne*."

"Is their father here?"

"No, sir. He was killed last year during that sorry business at Chaugee Landing."

"Oh, sorry."

While restraining his creamed and high-strung charger, Oglethorpe paused long enough to speak to each of the ten tatteredemalions drawn up before him; invited questions.

A tall, black-bearded fellow drawled, "D'you figger, sir, we can get this siege over with in time to get home and make the crops?"

The rider's lined features tightened. "I venture that I can promise you that. One way or another, you all should be with your families within a month's time."

After lifting his hat in acknowledgment to the flash of Glen's blade, he put his horse into an easy trot and continued riding along the beach with sand flying in measured spurts from beneath his charger's hoofs.

Glen, uneasy that the commander-in-chief should ride unattended, told off the Wardrop boys. "Just you follow after His Excellency"—he still thought of the general that way—"make sure that nothing goes wrong."

"Yes, sir." Chauncey, older of the two, said seriously, "Don't fret yourself, Mr. Glen. We'll look out fer him—like, well, like he's looked out fer us."

When they saw the distant horseman pull in and dismount on a high dune peppered with clumps of sand grass the militiamen were infinitely relieved—they weren't going to have to march halfway to kingdom come. When they got within a quarter mile of the solitary figure, Chauncey halted, said he figured they'd come close enough; nobody could get to the general before they did.

Feeling lonelier than ever in his life, James Oglethorpe seated himself on the warm sand and, staring out over the ocean, idly allowed particles to sift through his fingers while his imagination traveled back over the years to the day when first he'd heard of the Margravate of Azilia. Although plenty of people were laughing over the failure of poor Sir Robert Montgomery's idealistic, if impractical, scheme, he hadn't been one to join in.

In detail, he then recalled his shameless importuning of fellow members of Parliament, long hours spent patiently waiting in the lobby of some powerful lord and minister who possibly might be persuaded to lend aid to the humanitarian project which had become his life's ambition.

In even sharper perspective he recalled visits to those ghastly prisons of Marshalsea, the Fleet, King's Bench, and all too many other haunts of misery, depravity, and death. Then there were endless interviews with would-be supporters, most of whom were self-seeking, dishonest, or impractical zealots.

Absently, Oglethorpe's gaze watched a line of black cormorants flying by a short distance offshore, so low to the water that their wings seemed to touch the lazy rollers. Infinitely distressed, he listened to a soft obbligato played by waves upon the wide and shelving beach, then turned and looked over his shoulder to consider the piny lands, the endless miles of palmetto scrub. He then scooped up another handful of sand which, slowly, he poured from one palm onto the other.

Although the scenery here was barren and hostile he visualized countless miles of cool, dark forest, sparkling, lively streams, and serene blue-green mountains that he'd traveled. Then there was the incredible richness of great savannahs and wide bottom lands capable, it seemed, of growing every crop known to man. Also he thought upon the miles upon miles in which no sign of human life was visible until one came upon a lonely cabin or perhaps a little trading post and a few crude shacks peopled by dull, hard-working folk living in the shadow of the tomahawk and scalping knife.

How truly defenseless they were, especially at this moment. If one faced facts, the Colony of Georgia lay defenseless. If the Indians became alienated or were seduced by the French and Spanish, it would vanish as completely as a child's sand castle under a rising tide.

When a sand fly stung his neck he slapped it away, noticed the tiny speck of blood left on his palm. Well, there'd be a lot more blood lost than that if the colony were left defenseless for a year or two.

A small, sad smile quirked Oglethorpe's lips when he thought about Glen and the militiamen he'd just talked to. What could they accomplish toward Georgia's future if they choked out their lives under a Spanish rampart? How fortuitous that he should have chanced on Glen and his awkward squad. Even if one multiplied them by hundreds of new immigrants, they still would constitute the frailest kind of a barrier against merciless destruction, but were he to give the word, they'd go forward, full of fight, along with the regulars and the Carolinians.

He heard again Lieutenant Colonel Cook's gruff voice, "—nearer seven hundred casualties, I'd venture." Fourteen hundred strong, irreplaceable hands lost at this critical time! And who would be to blame if the colony vanished with the loss of so many fit and able men?

If only the troops weren't so pathetically willing to risk their lives! If only his senior officers would stop thinking of him as a timorous old woman, as a fainthearted politician, or, at best, an overcareful, semiprofessional general.

A slow, shuddering sigh escaped Oglethorpe as he remained sitting while the sunset sky flamed scarlet and gold. A gentle breeze sprang up off the ocean and commenced to cool his body but failed to relieve the burning anxiety of his mind.

Suppose he did order a general assault? To do so was a temptation, greater than he'd admit even to himself. As a normally ambitious leader of troops, he yearned to have his name listed in British history as

"James Oglethorpe, Conqueror of St. Augustine." Besides, he was experienced enough in siegecraft to know that the city and fort almost certainly could be stormed by the forces presently under his command; he could walk the streets of St. Augustine a victor! Years afterward, men would boast, "I was at the in-taking of St. Augustine with General Oglethorpe." He knew also that the cost probably would far surpass those estimates given on the *Flamborough*.

If he did not attack he foresaw that he'd run the risk of being called pusillanimous, if not an out-and-out coward by subordinates burning to enhance their military reputations, eager to improve their personal fortunes; plenty of valuable plunder should be found in a Spanish provincial capital! Then there would be others who'd complain that all the sacrifices they'd made and the discomforts they'd suffered were going for naught—and needlessly so.

While the sunset deepened to purple-red the lone figure locked hands about knees, didn't even look up when his horse shook itself to get rid of flies pricking at its mouth, nostrils, and eyes.

His inner turmoil increased when he foresaw that if the siege were won he'd undoubtedly be honored by the King. Very likely he'd be commissioned a lieutenant general and raised to the nobility. All manner of delightful possibilities rioted about his imagination. "Lieutenant General Sir James Edward Oglethorpe, Bart., K.C.B.," would look imposing engraved on a calling card and if he ever decided to marry, why, such a title ought to sit well with the future Lady Oglethorpe.

With doubts still assailing him he turned to consider the distant camps, then, for the first time, noticed that a pair of soldiers were sitting on a dune about a hundred yards behind him. When he recognized them as the Wardrop boys he sighed and slowly shook his head.

At length Oglethorpe arose, brushed sand from his clothes, and remounted, wondering if he possibly could find the right words to tell those officers who were due to appear before his tent at eight o'clock why he was going to do what he'd decided to do.

Chapter 27

RETIREMENT

When, early on the morning of July 4, Wallace Challenger again climbed onto his stool and peered out, he gasped and almost fell back into the room, so great was his surprise. Gone from behind Anastasia Island were the two line-of-battle ships and most of the sloops of war! All that remained to be seen of them was a line of tiny white dots of sails far out on the Atlantic. A disorderly flotilla of supply ships, plantation boats, coasters, and transports lay off Cape Quartell and was taking troops and baggage aboard.

Even while the Ranger looked on, one of the sloops—it looked like H.B.M.S. *Tartar*—began hoisting anchor, topmen swarmed on her yards, then gallants and royals commenced to flash in the morning sun. Presently, she pointed her bowsprit toward the open sea. After crossing the bar *Tartar* cracked on topsails and courses, then, making a picture of great beauty, the dainty little man-of-war started in pursuit of her consorts barely visible on the horizon.

Astounded and still unable to grasp the fact that the siege actually was being lifted, Challenger, consumed by burning rage, sank onto his pallet and, groaning, buried his face between filthy hands. How *could* James Oglethorpe, heretofore, so shrewd, fortunate, and farsighted, suddenly throw away a victory when, surely, it lay within his grasp? Had he gone mad under the weight of his responsibility? It wasn't like the man to betray those who'd trusted him so completely, who'd suffered by his side, who'd been prepared to die for him if called upon.

My God, what's happened to the general? Can't he understand what'll be said in Charles Town and London when the authorities learn he's played the poltroon, has flinched aside in the moment of victory. What will he have to show for this enormous waste of money, time, and energy?

The big man got up and on broad bare feet started pacing—three short strides up, then three back—his cell was that tiny.

He was still pacing when, in the afternoon, several very loud reports as of big explosions sounded in the direction of Anastasia. For a moment a wild hope flared; the fleet's departure had only been a ruse! Soon it would return.

As if provoked into action, some Spanish batteries began to roar, even dropped a few balls near the crowded merchantmen and transports. Since, after those few extra-loud reports, there came no more firing from across the harbor, it occurred to the prisoner that the departing troops had only been blowing up guns they could not carry away.

The big man's rage and resentment seethed all day and only commenced to dissipate toward evening. For the first time, dispassionately, he attempted to fathom Oglethorpe's reasoning and what had motivated this inexplicable decision. Despite everything, he retained a profound confidence in the man who, so skillfully, had handled the Indians, had kept Georgia's frontiers free from bloodshed—and with a mere handful of followers.

Four seemingly endless days dragged by before the last units of the departing forces either took ship or set off up the coast for Fort St. George. During that time the Ranger gradually had come to understand—or thought he did—what had been the general's real reason for refusing to order a grand assault. Oglethorpe had appreciated, as few others, Rangers excepted, how pitifully, how dangerously unpopulated and defenseless Georgia was. In all the new colony there weren't fifteen hundred whites fit to bear arms, even if the recruiting officers robbed outlying hamlets and those solitary farms which, despite Oglethorpe's policy, nevertheless had begun to appear on the western side of the grant.

Gradually, the conviction grew that Oglethorpe, ever a devout humanitarian, deliberately had spared his people a list of casualties they could not possibly have afforded. Come to think on it, aside from Hendy O'Brien and the men who'd been killed in the Black Fort, the British and colonial forces had suffered incredibly few battle casualties. Most of the men lost had perished through sunstroke, snakes, or disease. Hum. Perhaps, after all, the expedition hadn't been a total failure? Now, the Spaniards must have learned that the English colonists would unite and could field a formidable body of troops. Probably, they would think twice before they tried, once again, to harry the Guale Coast.

Challenger, however, found almost immediate reason to doubt this conclusion. A number of sandals came slap-slapping along the corridor, then fell silent as a key rattled in the lock. When the door swung open he saw that two armed guards were standing behind the mestizo turnkey. The soldiers, regulars by the look of them, acted both haughty and contemptuous.

"*Venga!*" The turnkey ordered, and crooked a gnarled forefinger.

Wallace Challenger, wondering, but not especially alarmed, over what was about to happen, found himself conducted down a narrow stone staircase. He was thankful to be out of that miserably small cell; accustomed to wide-open country, he'd suffered more than most men at being so cramped.

The guards led him from the ground floor down winding stairs to a level where the air was cool but dank and reeking of many evil things. Selecting a rusty iron key from the ring he wore at his belt, the turnkey inserted it and, the moment it *click-clucked*, from the far side of the door arose a dull, murmuring sound.

Once the door was pushed open, there escaped a rush of air so indescribably fetid that, for a wild moment, Challenger debated making a break for freedom. The guards must have read his mind, for they jumped back and leveled bayonets.

"*Vaya!*" the turnkey ordered, then, using the butts of their muskets, the guards jolted the prisoner into malodorous semidarkness.

Someone said, "B'God, if it ain't Wally Challenger come to visit us."

Just enough light was admitted by a small, heavily barred skylight to reveal a throng of half or wholly naked and incredibly shaggy apparitions.

After the door had grated shut and bolts were shot behind him, Challenger for a while could only stand gasping, trying to accustom himself to the gloom and stench of this place. The first man he recognized was John MacIntosh, although the Scot's once solid frame had wasted to skeletonic proportions.

The prisoners crowded about him, avid for news.

MacIntosh croaked, "Welcome tae the kirk, Major, and how does the siege progress?"

"The siege was lifted days ago. The ships and all our people all have gone home."

"Then God help us all," groaned MacIntosh, whose leg appeared to be suppurating badly. "What's tae become of us?"

Chapter 28

WARRIORS' RETURN

Since the raid last summer modest rebuilding and even some new construction had been undertaken at Chaugee Landing. Archie Glen's rebuilt warehouse was nearly completed, but where the Challengers' house had stood there were only a few charred beams nearly concealed under honeysuckle, morning-glory, and Virginia creepers.

On this quiet August afternoon life around the Landing was proceeding at its usual leisurely pace. Stonehewer and his sons worked slowly but diligently among his mulberry groves. So did Stephen Marrauld, Antoine Duché, and such of their offspring as were big enough to do a bit of work.

Tom Trippe was putting the finishing touches on a big plantation boat he was building for a merchant up in Purysburg. Bettie O'Brien, tagged after by Toby, her oldest child, was down by the paddock keeping an eye on a lanky, walleyed youth she'd hired and brought down from Savannah to look after Hendy's horses. He seemed to be doing all right; at least he was conscientious about feeding and watering Hendy's increasing herd.

Helen Glen occupied a rush-bottomed chair in the shade of that big water oak which stood just outside her front door, sewing and keeping an alert eye on Jemima and Archie, Jr., who had arrived at that stage when, as she described it, "they were all legs and no brains." They could vanish from sight in nothing flat.

Lord, she reflected, it's near four months since Archie Glen sailed off to the war along with the Marraulds, the Wardrop boys, and a new settler by the name of Marston. All this time and never a word. The chilling possibility occurred that some of them might be sick or dead. Archie, of course, would be all right—wasn't he a trained soldier?

Briefly, Helen debated whether she ought to go over to that cabin which James Papot, Oglethorpe's former servant, had occupied until he stepped on a water moccasin with fatal results. Now, Winsome Challenger lived in it; had ever since homeward-bound Carolina troops, out of the kindness of their hearts, had put her ashore at Chaugee a week ago.

Probably because life wasn't very easy for anyone these days, the inhabitants of Chaugee had been cool but not downright impolite to the major's runaway spouse when she had reappeared in their midst. Even John Stonehewer, who'd for a long time branded Winsome as a shameless wanton, had found nothing critical to say. In fact, it had been he who'd suggested that, so long as her own home had been burned, she'd better occupy Papot's empty cabin—for the time being, at least. Later, Susan Stonehewer had sent one of the children with a loaf of bread and a half side of bacon. The Marraulds, Trippes, and other old settlers sent food, but none of them, except Helen, came by to talk, and even she never stayed very long.

The villagers became accustomed to her wandering about the edge of the mulberry groves and along the forest. Sometimes they saw her sitting in the little graveyard where those who had died during the raid lay buried. At this time of the year wild flowers were hard to find, but always there was something green; even just a spray of shiny, dark-green magnolia leaves lay upon a short mound marked by a wooden headboard crudely inscribed, "R. Challenger—B. 1737—D. 1739."

The new settlers—who consisted of four families—curiously enough, were much less helpful to this handsome, straight-backed woman who hardly ever spoke, and appeared always to be looking for something in the far distance, than those who had come from Savannah along with Wallace and Winsome Challenger. Mrs. Marrauld shut up one woman pretty sharply when she ventured to refer to Winsome as "a loose woman," and Mrs. Trippe with another newcomer who'd attempted to classify Wallace's wife with Jezebel.

Although the returning South Carolinians reported that the siege had been abandoned, Sergeant Tom Trippe insisted that always someone remain on the lookout platform.

So when, one afternoon, the signal pistol banged and the lookout yelled that a small schooner was standing upriver, men and the bigger boys dropped whatever they were doing and, arming themselves, rushed to man the rebuilt battery.

Followed again the grim business of shuttering up, shooing children indoors, and hurriedly rounding up the most valuable livestock.

Once again, Tom Trippe climbed the signal mast carrying a battered brass spyglass.

The men grounded muskets, stood looking up anxiously at the boat-wright. A collective sigh of relief arose the moment Trippe called down, "All's well, boys! I've just made out Archie Glen. He's standing in the bow and waving a white cloth."

In no time at all the news spread to even the most outlying dwellings. Doors and windows clattered open as the glad tidings circulated that, almost certainly, the men of Chaugee were back from the wars.

Since Winsome Challenger had kept so much to herself and had said nothing about what had happened during the siege, nobody could guess who might be aboard the approaching schooner—and who would be missing. Numbed by her anguish, Dr. Brooks's daughter hadn't been able, couldn't bring herself, to speak about certain things that had happened in Florida. Certainly, she did not want to let Bettie O'Brien know that her Hendy would never return. Let her live in hope as long as she could— even for a few blessed days.

Everyone in Chaugee Landing able to walk went down to the water-front and out to that same pier onto which had jumped John Savey's murderous gang. The only able-bodied inhabitant who wasn't present was Winsome Challenger, for, once the news had spread that the inbound vessel undoubtedly was friendly, she'd gone to sit under a magnolia rising behind the late James Papot's residence.

Winsome didn't know, or care, what this vessel was, or her business

here, until the youngest Marrauld boy came streaking by, bare legs flashing. "Come on! Come on, ma'am! Mr. Glen's aboard!"

Winsome started up, but as quickly settled on her chair. Dully, she
listened to a series of cheers but, of course, she couldn't hear Bettie
O'Brien's wail of "Where's Hendy? I don't see Hendy!"

Helen Glen patted her shoulder. "Don't worry. He's probably below or
else he's coming home in another vessel."

Honeybees hummed by, heading for those conical straw hives Papot
had constructed. Winsome stared blankly at a little brown hen leading a
covey of fuzzy chicks over to drink from a puddle. She heard more cheers,
then the thump and rattle of running rigging, watched the schooner's
weather-beaten canvas sink jerkily out of sight—she'd learned to recognize
such sounds aboard the *Mystick*.

There was a tremendous commotion in the little crowd when Glen,
gaunt and brown, stepped ashore and, grinning, hugged and kissed his
wife and children.

"Well, we're back," said he.

The Wardrop boys, to demonstrate how strong and manly they'd grown,
strutted about doing the manual of arms with their muskets. Of course,
there was no one to meet them—pa and ma and baby sister had been
killed in the raid.

As for Helen Glen, she simply couldn't stop weeping joyful tears and
sobbing, "Thank God, thank God," until she saw Bettie O'Brien, suddenly pale and wide-eyed, draw near with her brood hanging onto her
skirts like young opossums clinging to their mother.

"Archie," she called. "Where's Hendy? I don't see him."

Glen had been pleased that he'd only one death to report here in
Chaugee Landing, but, because it was Hendy's, his gladness evaporated.
Leaving the children with Helen, he took Bettie aside, then, as gently
as possible, and skipping details, told her that Hendy would not be coming home, now or ever.

Bettie remained motionless as a stone figure, stared straight ahead of
her, then, walking stiffly like an old, old woman, went over to take Hendy's
twins by the hand. "It's getting late," said she tonelessly. "Time you were
fed."

Helen watched the usually brisk little woman stump away. Her first impulse was to hurry after Bettie and try to comfort her, but, on second
thought, decided to delay until the initial shock was over.

Turning, she peered intently into the ex-cornet's grave but still handsome face. "What about Wallace Challenger?"

"He's still on the schooner."

"But, but we heard he'd been killed."

"He wasn't. Just got taken prisoner. The general arranged for an exchange of prisoners so Wallace, MacIntosh, a parcel of Scots and some others were released just before Oglethorpe sailed for St. Simon."

"But why does Wallace linger aboard ship?"

"He wants to come ashore alone; I think you can understand why. No home, no Robbie, no wife. Isn't much to come back to."

His wife uttered a small cry, "Didn't you know? Winsome's here!"

Archibald Glen's pale blue eyes flew wide open and he batted them several times. "Well, I'm damned! Don't know whether this is good or bad news. When did she return?"

"Less than a week ago some Carolina volunteers dropped her off on their way home."

"Well, I reckon I'd better go back aboard ship and inform Wallace—God knows how he'll take it." He slipped an arm about Helen's no longer tiny waist. "Oh, by the bye, there's another couple aboard keeping Wallace company. You'd never guess who they are?"

"Well, I suppose I won't," Helen said with a touch of asperity. "So you may as well speak up because I've got to prepare the best dinner I've ever tried to cook."

"You remember that strange white Indian called Sakwari-cra who camped for a while outside Savannah with a redheaded white squaw?"

"Of course. Who could forget him? You don't mean to tell me!"

"Yes. He, his wife and children are aboard."

"But—but— But why?"

"Lieutenant Thad Burton—as he wants to be known since he got a commission in our militia—had a run of hard luck at the siege. Most of his warriors either got killed or deserted. Meantime, some French and Indians wiped out his town while it was unguarded, burned it flat and killed almost everyone. Burton's pretty low-spirited these days but I guess he's doing the right thing."

"What right thing?"

"He intends to live as a white man and bring up his family like us"—Glen smiled briefly—"if that's a commendable ambition. He may even settle in or around Chaugee Landing. D'you know, Helen, I shouldn't wonder but he'll go far as a white. Who else has a greater knowledge of Indian ways and woods fighting? Besides, he's as ambitious as Julius Caesar. No. I wouldn't be surprised if someday he doesn't become a big man in this colony—provided that he handles himself right."

"Well, when is he coming ashore?"

"Not for a while. He wants us valiant and victorious heroes"—this, bitterly—"to enjoy our homecoming without any strangers around."

"Victorious or not, it's wonderful that so many of you came back." Helen started to sniffle, wiped away her tears with the hem of her apron. "You have n-no idea how awful it was t-thinking of your f-fighting those

Papists and their Yamasees. My h-heart used to s-sink when I-I thought
of your charging that great stone fort of theirs!"

Glen stroked his wife's bent head, said soberly, "If we had assaulted it
we most likely wouldn't be here and there'd have been plenty of buzzard
bait down in Florida."

When Archibald Glen finally went aboard the schooner to seek out
Wallace Challenger he discovered the big man lying on his bunk, dripping
with sweat and staring through the gloom at deck beams above.

All Glen said was, "Welcome home, Wallace."

"Thanks, but to what home?"

"Aren't you coming ashore? It's almost dark and you can eat with us."

"Don't know that I'm ready yet. Besides, I'm not hungry."

"All the same, I think you'd better come with me, Wallace. There's
a special reason."

A faint stirring of interest animated Challenger's half-seen features.
"What reason?"

Softly, soberly, Archibald Glen said, "Winsome's here."

Slowly, the Ranger lifted his head, propped himself on an elbow, queried thickly, "She's *here*?"

"Yes. Seems some Carolina men dropped her off the other day on their
way to Charles Town." He paused, trying to read Challenger's reactions
by the half-light. "Thought you ought to know about that. She's living
in Papot's old cabin. They tell me he died of snakebite a while back."

When Challenger remained silent the ex-cornet started to back out of
the cabin. "Well, I'm going. Come along anytime you're ready. Helen
will keep some food hot."

"Thanks, Archie. Tell Helen I'll be with you directly. Sorry I've appeared such a—an ungrateful bastard."

The evening star was hanging bright as a small sun over the horizon
when Challenger finally went ashore. But he didn't head for Glen's familiar two-story house, only tramped by the ruins of his own home and,
ignoring yapping dogs and greetings from various dwellings, made straight
for that cabin which had belonged to James Papot.

Its door stood open, emitted a faint light. He shoved it farther open,
bent, and looked inside, his tawny head leonine and magnificently powerful. Winsome, who had been sewing by the light of a single tallow
dip, uttered a small, strangled noise when she saw him and got slowly to
her feet.

For an eternal instant they just looked at one another. Finally, he said,
"The schooner departs for Frederica in the morning. I think it might be a
fine idea if you and I go on her."

"Together?"

"Yes. Together."

ADDENDUM ON JAMES EDWARD OGLETHORPE

1740 *August*   Oglethorpe retreats to Frederica. Strengthens the coast and inland defenses of Georgia.

1741   When Vernon's and Anson's expeditions fail to rendezvous in Central America, Oglethorpe realizes that Spanish power will be free to proceed against him. The Spaniards in Cuba and Florida build many privateers.

1742 *May*   Fifty sail arrive in St. Augustine, bringing 5000–6000 Spanish troops. The British Royal Navy promises help but fails to appear in strength.

June 1   Oglethorpe evacuates Fort St. Andrew to strengthen Frederica. Calls in Indian allies.

July 5   The Spanish enter St. Simon's Harbor with thirty-six ships in line of battle. Land batteries and colonial ships stand off the invaders for four hours. When they withdraw Oglethorpe destroys the defenses at St. Simon and, to consolidate his forces, retires to Frederica—on the same island.

July 6   The Spaniards land 5000 on St. Simon under Governor Don Manuel de Montiano, commander-in-chief, and Major General Redondo of Cuba with orders to grant the English no quarter.

July 7   The Battle of Bloody Marsh. Oglethorpe's Regiment assaults Spanish camp. Many invaders are killed. Routed, the Spanish retire to the ruins of St. Simon.

July 14   The Spaniards sail away to harry the Guale Coast, but meet with little success.

1743 *January*   The Spanish viceroy plans new attack on Georgia.

March   Oglethorpe makes a second attack on St. Augustine. His forces penetrate to the city but withdraws when a formidable Spanish force arrives to relieve St. Augustine.

Oglethorpe returns to England for good.

1744 *Sept. 15* Oglethorpe marries Elizabeth Wright (no children).

1785 *June 30* Dies, aged 88.

F.

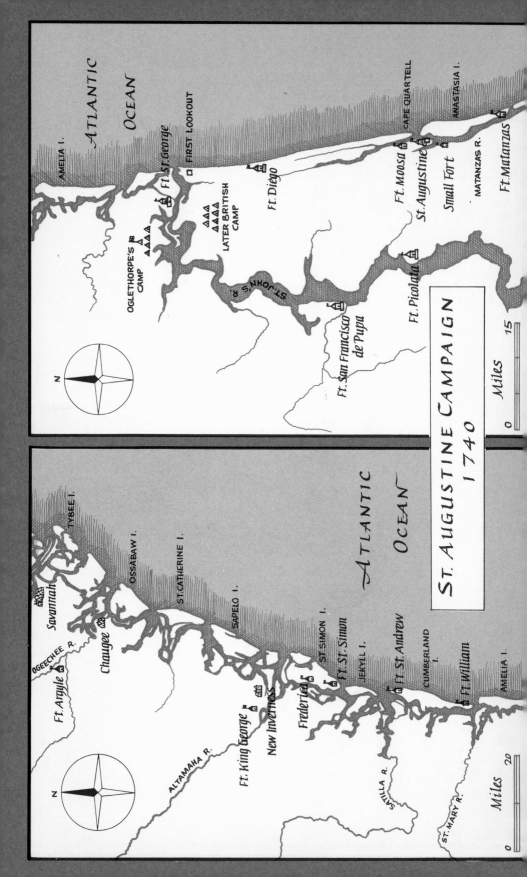

ATLANTIC OCEAN

AMELIA I.

Ft. St. George

FIRST LOOKOUT

OGLETHORPE'S CAMP

LATER BRITISH CAMP

Ft. Diego

ST. JOHNS R.

Ft. San Francisco de Pupa

Ft. Picolata

Ft. Moosa

St. Augustine

Small Fort

CAPE QUARTELL

ANASTASIA I.

MATANZAS R.

Ft. Matanzas

N

ST. AUGUSTINE CAMPAIGN 1740

Miles

0   15

ATLANTIC OCEAN

OGEECHEE R.

Ft. Argyle

Savannah

TYBEE I.

Chaugee

OSSABAW I.

ST. CATHERINE I.

SAPELO I.

ALTAMAHA R.

Ft. King George

New Inverness

Frederica

ST. SIMON I.

Ft. St. Simon

JEKYL I.

Ft. St. Andrew

CUMBERLAND I.

SATILLA R.

Ft. William

AMELIA I.

ST. MARY R.

N

Miles

0   20